ANNAPOLIS

Also by William Martin

Cape Cod

The Rising of the Moon

Nerve Endings

Back Bay

ANNAPOLIS

WILLIAM MARTIN

WARNER BOOKS

A Time Warner Company

Publisher's Note: This is a work of fiction. Names, characters, places, and incidents either are the product of the author's imagination or are used fictitiously, and any resemblance to actual persons, living or dead, events, or locales is entirely coincidental.

Warner Books, Inc., 1271 Avenue of the Americas, New York, NY 10020

Printed in the United States of America
First Printing: June 1996
10 9 8 7 6 5 4 3 2 1

Library of Congress Cataloging-in-Publication Data

Martin, William
Annapolis / William Martin.
p. cm.
ISBN 0-446-51511-6
1. United States Naval Academy—History—Fiction. 2. Family—Maryland—Annapolis—History—Fiction. 3. United States— History, Naval—Fiction. 4. United States. Navy—History—Fiction. 5. Annapolis (Md.)—History—Fiction. I. Title
PS3563.A7297A84 1996
813'.54—dc20 96-1021
CIP

Book design and composition by L&G McRee

for Chris
and three great kids
...always

ACKNOWLEDGMENTS

On a bitter cold Sunday afternoon sometime in January of 1960 (I know the year because I remember being in the fourth grade at the time), my father took me to visit the USS *Constitution*, at the Charlestown Navy Yard in Boston.

I don't recall my first impression of the spar deck. But I'll never forget the sense of awe that I felt when I descended to the gundeck and saw those great black cannon, sitting there silently, like sleeping beasts. Our guide, a young sailor, told the story of the ship and her battles, and when he was done, I went running from gun to gun, fighting an imaginary battle of my own, complete with the sound effects that every little boy seems genetically programmed to make.

My love of American naval history was born that day, so I should thank my father before anyone else.

One of the joys of writing a novel that requires a wide range of research is that I get to meet a wide range of people who offer me their insights and opinions, share their experiences and expertise, answer my questions and challenge my assumptions, all for the simple love of their work. Some will see their contributions here in black and white; others will find them buried between the lines. But my deepest thanks to all who helped.

In Annapolis: Linnell Bowen, formerly of the Historic Annapolis Foundation, and all the docents and staff at Historic Annapolis; Alfred A. Hopkins, mayor of Annapolis; three women whose writings and knowledge place them among the leading historians of the city—Phebe Jacobsen, Mame E. Warren, and Jane McWilliams; Christopher Nelson, president of Saint John's College. Greg Stiverson, former director of the Maryland State Archives; the archives staff; Pam Williams and Mary Lou Beatty of Three Centuries Tours; innkeeper Rob Zuchelli.

At the United States Naval Academy: Admiral Charles R. Larson, superintendent; Captain Tom Jurkowsky; the many junior officers and midshipmen who took time to talk with me. Also James Cheevers; the staff of the Academy archives; and especially Kenneth Hagan, professor emeritus and director emeritus of the Academy museum and archives, who helped me to think like a naval historian.

Also in Maryland: Patti and Dawson Farber; the staff and docents at Sotterley, in Saint Mary's County; the people who keep the past alive at Historic Saint Mary's City.

Aboard the USS America: Captain R. E. Suggs, commanding officer; Commander J. Michael Denkler, executive officer; Lt. Commander Steven Lowry, public affairs officer; and all the officers and crew of the giant aircraft carrier. They gave me the run of the ship, from the engine rooms to the flag bridge, and sent me off with what they call the E-ticket ride: a catapult shot in a C-2 Greyhound.

Aboard the USS Annapolis: Commander Steve Chapman, commanding officer; Lt. Commander Jeff Hughes, executive officer; and all the officers and crew of the attack sub. Again, they gave me the run of the ship, from torpedo room to sail. I took the helm at four hundred feet and got the submariner's version of an E-ticket ride: the emergency blow, when the submarine surfaces like a breaching whale.

Other active duty naval officers: Rear Admiral Richard Buchanan of Submarine Group Two; Commander Michael Beck of the USS *Constitution;* Lt. Commander Scott Harris; Lieutenant Jeff Dodge; Lieutenant William Fenick; and a special thanks to Commander Dave Morris, public affairs officer for New England, who opened doors, made contacts, and got quick answers to all my questions.

Retired officers and families: Captain Roger Deveau; Captain Basil "Buzz" Livas and his wife, Jan; Captain Daniel O'Connell and his wife, Sheila; Commander Richard B. Amirault; Lt. Commander Peter Bagley and his wife, Adrienne; Commander F. H. "Skip" Fumia; Commander Peter Kallin; Lieutenant (jg) Hank McQueeney, an intelligence officer aboard the carrier USS *Ticonderoga* in the Tonkin Gulf, August 1964; and Richard G. Wohlers.

And the people who preserve the ships: Across America, historic vessels have been saved from the scrap heap, sometimes with public funds, but usually by private groups who recognize that these vessels are more than naval artifacts; they are windows onto the times in which they were built and into the lives of those who served aboard them. So, starting from my home port of Boston: the frigate *Constitution* and the destroyer *Cassin Young*; in Fall River, Mass., the battleship *Massachusetts*, the destroyer *Joseph P. Kennedy*, the submarine *Lionfish*; in Groton, the first nuclear submarine, the *Nautilus*; in New York, the carrier *Intrepid*; in Philadelphia, the *Olympia*, Admiral Dewey's flagship, and the submarine *Becuna*; in Baltimore, the frigate *Constellation*; at the Washington Navy Yard museum, the destroyer *Barry*; at Pearl Harbor, the submarine *Bowfin*, and of course, the memorial at the battleship *Arizona*.

And to a few others: David Baker, at the Office of Naval Intelligence; Bart Davis; Ned Downing; Peter Drummey, of the Massachusetts Historical Society; Professor William Fowler; Robert Anthony Nolan; Ann Rauscher; Randy Wayne White; Anne Grimes Rand and the staff of the USS *Constitution* Museum; the staff of the Submarine Force Library and Museum in Groton, Connecticut.

And finally, to my editor, Jamie Raab; my agent, Robert Gottlieb; and of course, to my wife and children, who never complain.

WILLIAM MARTIN
December 1995

ANNAPOLIS

PROLOGUE

The Last Chapter

"Don't have your tongue between your teeth."

The line snapped through Steve Stafford's head before every cat shot.

It was what his flight instructor had said to him the first time he launched from an aircraft carrier, and he'd never forgotten it.

He throttled up. He flashed his lights, signaling that he was ready.

The catapult officer dropped to one knee, touched his illuminated green wand to the deck, then pointed it toward the bow, playing his part in the launch ballet, relaying his orders without words while the jet engines roared and the wind whipped over the bow at twenty-five knots.

Steve Stafford did not hear the plane. Instead, he felt it . . . at the base of his spine and the center of his chest. But inside his helmet, there was a strange quiet. He could listen to his own breathing . . . to the voice of Joe Digger, his bombardier-navigator . . . and to the calm voice inside his own head: Don't have your tongue between your teeth or you might bite it off. And be professional.

It had come at last. All the training—Naval Academy, flight school, carrier quals, replacement air group—would finally mean something.

The catapult—a steam-driven slingshot that could throw a pickup truck two miles—grabbed his A-6E Intruder by the nose gear and fired. The plane shot forward. The jolt slammed Steve against his seat and snapped his jaws. Then eighteen thousand pounds of Pratt and Whitney turbojet thrust kicked in, lifting him off the deck of the USS America *and out over the Red Sea.*

He formed with his wingman. They formed with their squadron. And the night blazed with the man-made stars of Operation Desert Storm—thirty A-6s and F-14 Tomcats, vectoring northwest, screaming low over the Arabian desert, rocketing toward an Iraqi airfield designated H-2. Their mission: to strike a blow for the New World Order. And be professional.

Steve had the controls. Joe Digger navigated from the AVA-1, which delivered flight data and a synthetic terrain/sea and sky image on the CRT screen.

In two hours, they were closing on H-2.

As long as the Stealth bombers had punched holes in Iraqi radar cover, the A-6s would be in and out before the Iraqis knew what hit them, and if any Iraqi MiGs came up, the F-14s would be waiting to send them right back down again.

This was not a pretty mission. No laser-guided bombs here. Just twelve thousand pounds of Rockeye, big cannister bombs that carried little bombs designed to tear up runway concrete like a plow tearing up dry ground. They shot in low, not much more than two hundred feet. Steve made a perfect approach at ninety degrees to the runway, and Joe Digger delivered the ordnance. "Bombs away."

Flash and flame stitched themselves across the ground and lit the desert all around.

"Bingo," said Joe Digger calmly.

"Uh, roger." Sound professional.

Alarm! Alarm! Buzzing in the headsets. Flashing on the CRT screens. Surface-to-air missiles locked on.

"We got SAMs," said Digger.

"Roger. Visual contact," said Steve, his eyes fixed on two tails of flame rising toward them through the darkness. "Release countermeasures."

The air beneath the plane was suddenly littered with aluminum chaff intended to confuse the missiles.

Whoosh! One SAM blew by just fifty feet to starboard, chasing the aluminum. And whoosh! The other shot under the plane, its exhaust burning so bright that it lit the two faces in the cockpit. American countermeasures worked. Iraqi proximity fuses did not.

But now, tracers began to rise in long, delicate strands all around H-2. That meant triple-A: antiaircraft artillery. Slow, primitive, altitude-fused explosives, the same thing they shot at B-17s over Europe fifty years ago. But if there's enough triple-A going up, someone's bound to come down. And tonight it was Steve Stafford.

Impact. *The A-6 was tough, but a lucky shot cut the hydraulics to the left wing.*

"Uh, we have a problem, Steve," said Joe Digger.

"Roger." One look told Steve there was no hope.

They were out over the desert again, and it was time for the unthinkable.

"Prepare to punch out," Steve said as calmly as he could.

"Roger. Sending our search coordinates."

"Let's hope the helos find us before the bad guys." Steve grabbed for the yellow ejection handles and pulled. In an instant he became a missile himself, rocketing straight up through his own Plexiglas canopy.

Even with the protective helmet shield in place, the force of ejection at five hundred miles an hour could break a man's nose, blacken his eyes, tear the skin clean off his face. But the explosion was so intense, the eruption so instantaneous, the dislocation so complete that Steve couldn't tell what was his face and what was his ass and what was in between.

As he rocketed upward, the jet rocketed away, first out, then down. Then it was nothing more than a shadow riding a dying orange arc of flame.

He felt the impact of the plane's death just as he felt the gallows-jerk pull of the parachute saving his life. For a moment, the desert floor burned bright with fuel and avionics and high-alloy metals. Then there was dark.

In the distance Steve could hear the rumble of war. In his gut he felt the vomit of despair. But in his head, the small Academy-trained voice was reminding him, Stay professional . . . and survive.

As soon as he hit, he unsnapped the Koch fittings and climbed out of his chute. Then he called to his partner. "Joe. You okay, Joe?"

"Shit hot, Steve. Shit hot."

"Good." Be professional. Even on the ground. Even in despair.

Preflight briefings had set three collection points where Apache helicopters, under the cover of A-10 Warthogs, would be waiting to pick up downed fliers. From his seat cushion, Steve took out a map, a compass, and six foil-wrapped packets of water. Then he unholstered the pearl-handled forty-five his grandfather had given him when he graduated from flight school. "We'll be out of here by dawn. Let's get moving."

Then three sets of high beams came bouncing toward them.

Bad guys . . .

That was where Jack Stafford stopped writing.

Always stop when you still have a little left in you. That way you'll have a place to start in the morning. Hemingway used to say that. Leave it to Hemingway to find a reason to stop writing and start drinking at five in the afternoon.

Jack was just cheating. He had worked for a year on the story of Annapolis and his family and the navy that had given them both meaning. But he couldn't write the chapter that had drawn him from the start. So he was writing the one after it, an easy one he would call "Pax Americana," about Ronald Reagan's six-hundred-ship navy and his own great-nephew's adventures in the Gulf War.

He lit a cigarette and looked out the window of his hillside bungalow. In Los Angeles, the Santa Ana winds were blowing. They swept down from the high desert, scrubbing the air clean and drying it through, so that everything stood out in speed-freak clarity—the names on the boxcars in the train yards on San Fernando Road, the silvery leaves on the chaparral bushes at Chavez Ravine, even the people moving about in the downtown skyscrapers.

L.A. was no place to be in Santa Ana season. More drive-bys. Uglier wife-beatings. Arson fires. Some said it was the heat that did it. Others said it was the dryness you could feel in your sinuses, way up inside your head. Jack blamed the clarity. With the smog blown out to sea, everything appeared in unrelenting relief. Nothing gray, nothing imprecise, nothing uncertain.

And people needed uncertainty. They needed to know that there was always a chance for good in the bad guys, or bad in the good guys. They needed to know that life was not simple and never had been, no matter how simple the past looked in the rearview mirror. People who thought otherwise, people who thought they could see beyond the curve of the earth, the way Angelenos thought when the Santa Anas blew—those people were dangerous.

So he was writing *The Stafford Story*. But when he came to the grayest area of them all—the things the Staffords had done, and failed to do, in the war that ended certainty for good—he couldn't finish. He sat on his alien hilltop, perched between the certainties of his upbringing and the Pacific horizon that so many Staffords had tried to see beyond, and he struggled with the truth of history.

And he was blocked . . . and hot . . . and feeling very old at seventy-eight. He had decided the only thing to revive him would be Annapolis. He was going back to buy the house that had been at the heart of his family's history for over two centuries. He wasn't sure why—maybe for a place to finish his book, or a place to die, or a place to feel something that was certain and deserved to be. But he had to have that house.

And in Annapolis, a young woman named Susan Browne would be waiting. She had written to him a few days before: "I am a distant cousin and an independent filmmaker working on a PBS project called *The American Family.* I'm researching the Staffords of Annapolis. Your perspective as a liberal journalist would be quite different from that of your military brother. Would you consent to meeting me?"

He had mailed her a note and the first chapter of *The Stafford Story,* which would take her to a time and place where no one could have imagined the USS *America.* But it was the time and place where Stafford history began in America. If she was a good reader, he might give her more, but nothing was certain.

The Stafford Story
Book One
Jedediah's Credo
July 1745

"One son for the soil and one son for the sea."

That was what Jedediah Stafford said to his wife on the bright summer morning that the Lord blessed them with their second boy.

And his wife understood, because she had labored with him to bring tobacco from the soil, and she knew what happened when pirates came from the sea.

Both sons would follow their father's credo, and so would the generations that came after. Sometimes more than two sons arrived in a generation, and sometimes there were daughters, who could be as independent as the Chesapeake tide. But each generation understood. Each fought its own pirates and fit Jedediah's credo to its own times.

One son for the soil and one son for the sea. One for family and one for nation. For plantation and privateer. For free soil and slave state. For the Big Stick and the democratic dream. For a polyglot nation forged finally to a single purpose. For unquestioned loyalty faced finally with a questioning conscience.

From that summer day in 1745, the Staffords lived by a credo of opposites, opposites linked by the imperfect logic of history.

But it all began with soil and sea . . . and pirates.

ii
Little Jed and the Pirates

Jedediah Stafford was six years old when he first went to Annapolis.

The year was 1712, and the English queen had given her name to both the capital of Maryland and the current war with France.

Queen Anne's War had brought French pirates and privateers into the Chesapeake. But in Queen Anne's capital, life continued apace. And when word went out that a ship had arrived from the Indies, carrying molasses, spices, and two dozen black Africans consigned to tidewater plantations, Jedediah's father decided it was high time for his son to see Annapolis.

Thomas Stafford was known as one of the best judges of black flesh in the Maryland colony. It was a skill he had learned from his father, who had learned from his before him. And Thomas meant to teach it to his son. That, he said, was the natural order of things.

And the Staffords had followed the natural order of things since they arrived in 1634, with thirteen other Catholic families and a charter from a Protestant king. They had settled between the rivers that the Indians called Patawomek and Patuxent. There they had built a capital called Saint Mary's City and the first Catholic church in English America. Then they had set about the business of cultivating the weed that the Indians had taught the first Europeans to smoke, a weed with the power to invigorate or relax, depending only upon the way a man smoked it.

Life, to be sure, had not been easy. Planters had faced the vagaries of weather and London markets and their own vexing inexperience, but by the grace of God, English ships had soon begun following rivers and creeks to every plantation on the tidewater, where docks sagged under the wondrous weight of tobacco hogsheads.

English ships had also brought Puritans, who wished to settle on the Severn River, some sixty miles up the Chesapeake. So the Catholics of Saint Mary's had proclaimed the Toleration Act, protecting Puritans, Anglicans, and anyone else who sought the grace of God on the great bay.

But by the time that little Jedediah was born, it was the Catholics who begged for toleration in a colony grown more Protestant with each generation; it was the Catholics who had attacked the Severn settlement when the Puritans took power and tried to stop them from practicing their faith; it was the Catholics who had seen Saint Mary's City wither while the Severn settlement became the new capital.

Through it all, the Staffords had worked their Patuxent plantation, practiced their faith quietly, and called themselves good Englishmen. And while they grew tobacco, the house they called Stafford Hall grew from four rooms to six and then to eight, their holdings grew, and the province grew as well, not only with free Englishmen, but with indentured servants contracted to labor seven years in return for passage, and black Africans chained to labor forever for nothing.

Thomas Stafford's sloop, the *Patuxent,* was crewed by four indentured servants and could make seven knots with a good breeze. In light summer airs, however, the trip to Annapolis took twelve hours, and it was dusk when they dropped anchor under the shore battery at the mouth of the Severn.

That evening father and son made a fine picture strolling the streets of Annapolis. Thomas Stafford was blessed with good height, a rugged lean body, and a forthright gaze that made men believe him, whether he was sealing an agreement or making a threat. And people said he would never need a will to guarantee his son's inheritance; all it would take was one look at the boy's face.

"This, lad, is a *city.* Granted, 'tisn't much of a one. But it'll grow. Be sure of that. And England'll see that a colony born of toleration can be a prosperous place—even when the toleration fades—prosperous enough to support a fine city."

Jedediah thought that if "city" meant crowded dwellings, piles of steaming horse dung in the streets, and the stink of the local leather tanneries choking everything, then a city was not worthy of his father's enthusiasm.

But when other memories of his father had faded, the boy needed only to think of Annapolis and he would feel his father's strong hand holding his once more, hear again the enthusiasm in his father's voice. "See how fine it's laid out, lad—straight streets, public circles for the public buildings, slanted streets joining the circles. Just like London after the Great Fire, except it sits on this fine prospect above the Severn."

They were climbing the hill at the back of the town, but Jedediah was not interested in the fine prospect, because the mosquitoes were biting his neck.

The father led his son around the circle atop the hill and admired the government house from every angle. "What finer place could there be for the royal proprietor to dispense the law of this new land?" he exulted.

Then he led the boy a short distance to a second, smaller circle on a second, smaller hill, to admire the golden finial on the spire of Saint Anne's Church. "And what better place for a bishop to dispense the law of God, even an Anglican bishop?"

"Ma's an Anglican."

And Thomas Stafford's enthusiasm waned. In a land where women were scarce, he had married one who was not a Catholic. She had reluctantly agreed to raise their son in her husband's faith, and her husband had suffered greatly for the pain this caused her. But in front of their son, they had showed only their love.

And next morning Thomas Stafford showed only a brave face when a rumor ran around the waterfront that a French schooner was loose in the lower Chesapeake.

"Pirate or privateer?" asked someone in the crowd gathering for the landing of the slaves.

"What does it matter?" demanded Thomas Stafford. "A privateer's no better than a pirate with a license. I'm Admiralty agent for the Patuxent, and I guarantee the Royal Navy don't let pirates or privateers into the Chesapeake. So us Staffords, we'll sail where we will."

Such confidence calmed both the crowd and the boy.

When the slaves came off the ship, the pirates were forgotten altogether.

But Jedediah would never forget the sight of those black bodies. His father had ordered five males on consignment, five fine young breeders, and he paid a top price of twenty-five pounds apiece. The slaves had been fed and exercised on their ship, then washed down and well-oiled, so that their skin would shine and their muscles ripple, and their buyer would not reject them. But no amount of cleaning could cover up the fear in their wide, white eyes or quiet the furious clanging of their manacles after they had been chained to the mast of the *Patuxent.*

They seemed much wilder than the slaves at Stafford Hall, and all the way down the bay, Jedediah watched them with a combination of fascination and fear.

"They smell funny, Pa."

"They're afraid. Once they see how we treat 'em, they'll be as docile as old mares."

Then one of them growled and pulled at his chains.

The little boy jumped back. "He's like an animal, Pa."

"Well, son, there's some would say that in some ways he is a poor dumb creature that the Lord gives us to care for. We'll do our best, just as we always have."

In the freshening breeze, they made the run back to the Patuxent in half the time it took to sail up the bay. They were just passing Hog Point, at the river's mouth, when a sixteen-year-old indentured servant named Nervous Duncan Parrish spied a sail.

"Big schooner, makin' fast." Thomas Stafford peered through his glass. "A good three miles away yet."

"Can you see a flag?" asked Nervous Duncan.

"No, but that means nothin'."

"It damn do." Nervous Duncan seldom held his tongue, and never when his nerves got the better of him. "It mean she got a reason for not showin'. I say she's a pirate."

"We'll keep an eye on her and keep the four-pounders ready."

"Four-pounders?" Nervous Duncan spun one of the little cannon mounted at the stern. "Fight a pirate ship with a pair of four-pound swivels? Pirates kill people who fight 'em. Except for slaves and little ones. Them they steal and sell."

Jedediah's father told Duncan to go below if he could not hold his tongue. He spoke calmly, but the boy saw the worry in his father's face, especially when that two-master rounded Hog Point and headed upstream after them.

"Is they really pirates, Pa?"

"No. 'Sides, the *Patuxent* is the fastest sloop on the river."

But over the next hour, the big schooner came on, riding a full spread of canvas like a black-hulled spirit.

Then the winds grew erratic. One moment, *Patuxent* had the air and widened the distance; then the wind faded upstream while it gusted below, and the schooner shot ahead, sometimes all the way into cannon range. But she didn't fire, and Jedediah's father said that was a good sign. The fluky airs, however, were not.

Soon the sky turned a strange yellowing black, and little Jedediah felt the hairs stand up on the back of his neck. Such a thing had never happened before, but he sensed that it meant something worse would happen soon. And the squall hit with a hammer blow that almost rolled the *Patuxent* on her beam end. Then the first thunderclap exploded in their face. Then ragged forks of lightning slashed down all around. Then the *Patuxent* was swallowed into a black belly of wind and rain.

But Thomas Stafford kept all sails set, letting the winds push the *Patuxent* far and fast upstream. And even little Jedediah realized the danger, for his father had never run through a squall before, saying it was a good way to blow a sloop to pieces, not to be done unless there was greater danger in taking in sail and letting the storm pass.

But it worked. When the rain blew off, the schooner was gone and the afternoon sun came cutting through the clouds in brilliant blades of gold.

"Was they really pirates, Pa?"

"Royal Navy don't let pirates in the Chesapeake. My bet is they were merchants, puttin' in downstream. Just means more work for me, of course. Admiralty agent has to make certain everyone pays their duties."

At Stafford Hall, Thomas told his wife that Nervous Duncan had gotten more nervous than usual and started everyone worrying with talk of pirates. Then he showed her his customs book to convince her that one of the downstream planters had been expecting a big schooner.

As his mother tucked Jedediah into bed that night, the boy

searched her eyes for signs of fear and saw none. If his father could convince his mother that there was no reason to worry, Jedediah knew it was safe to surrender to the exhaustion rolling over him.

Loud voices awakened him some time later. Loud voices and the pounding of the plantation bell and the strange flickering light on the ceiling of his room.

So he crawled out of bed and went stumbling to the front dormer. At first he could see nothing but the scrawny shadows of the sycamores that his father had planted between the road and the house. Then his eyes found light in the darkness, and he saw Nervous Duncan pounding the bell by the hitching post, and he heard above the bell the cry *"Pirates!"*

He scuttled to the window that looked toward the river and saw torches casting their strange, flickering light, bobbing up the rolling road from the river, as though carried by evening guests. But no evening guest had ever before thrown a torch into one of the slave huts or herded screaming slaves toward the river.

And then strong arms pulled Jedediah away from the window.

"Pa! What's—"

"Be still, boy."

Jedediah was swept up in his father's arms and rushed through the darkness to the top of the stairs, where his father stopped and gasped the Lord's name.

Through the stairwell window, Jedediah saw the torches crossing the back lawn, poking into the smokehouse, moving toward the servants' quarters, surrounding the main house, as calmly as wolves flanking a deer.

Then a gunshot silenced the alarm bell.

Then came another gunshot, closer by, and the sound of breaking glass. His father said the Lord's name again, and suddenly Jedediah was plunging through the darkness, riding his father down the stairs, across the hall, into the study.

He was set down before the fireplace and told again to be quiet. Someone was fumbling to unlock the closet beside the fireplace, and for a moment, in the light of the torches flickering past the windows, he did not know that it was his mother.

Then she said, "Don't worry, little Jed. You'll be safe in a second." Her voice was shaking, and she smelled of the same fear he had smelled on the slaves.

"Be quick, Elizabeth." Jedediah's father grabbed the brace of pistols he kept loaded on the mantelpiece.

And the voice of old Cicero, the house slave who slept off the kitchen, came screaming ahead of him. "Marse Tom! Marse Tom! They's in the house!"

"Jesus God!" cried his mother. "In the house."

In the house. Jedediah realized now what this was—a bad dream. *In the house.* But it was a long house, expanded over the years like an ever-lengthening row of boxes, one room deep, eight rooms long, with the study in the middle.

"Stay calm, Elizabeth." Jedediah's father put himself between his family and the dining room door. "Just press the third board down from the ceiling. And—"

Old Cicero's white hair appeared. "They's in the dinin' room." And a gun went off behind him, thundering like a cannon, splattering him into the room.

Jedediah was too shocked to scream, and shock became terror when a huge shadow appeared in the doorway, holding a blunderbuss. *"Ah, la petite famille."*

And Jedediah's father shot the Frenchman right in the forehead.

Jedediah screamed at the flash and the thunderous roar of the pistol.

"Quiet, boy." His father calmly shot the next pirate through the door, then sprang to the bodies, pulled their pistols, and peered across the dining room. "The rest are in the kitchen, breaking things. Hide the boy, Elizabeth, and hide yourself."

"You come, too."

"I defend my family or I'm no man."

"Then I'll defend it with you."

And there was no time to argue, because they were coming. Jedediah's father raised a pistol and fired at another pirate.

Jedediah's mother dragged him through the gunsmoke-choked darkness to the closet and shoved him into the tiny passageway that ran up along the chimney to the bedroom above. "Stay there, darlin'. Don't come out for anything. No matter what you hear."

"And be quiet," said his father.

"We love you," said his mother, and she closed the panel, sealing the boy into the wall, into complete blackness, where sound was the only sense.

He heard his father tell his mother to hide the tea service in the closet, where it would be easy to find. "That'll satisfy 'em when they open the door." And silver jangled in the space below him. Then the closet door was shut and sounds were muffled. And that was by the grace of God.

Because there were more gunshots, deep-throated growls and high-pitched cries, the sounds of scuffling feet and grappling bodies. Then a gunshot brought a scream that seemed to cut through the wall itself and right into Jedediah's belly.

It was his mother's voice, and the scream went on and on until Jedediah brought his hands to his ears in the blackness. They had killed his father. He knew.

Then the closet door opened below him. The pirate murderers were just feet away. He could see the torchlight through the cracks in the rough closet walls. Someone grabbed the silver, and he prayed they would not hear him whimpering.

Then his mother screamed, "Get off! *No.* Get off!"

Then she screamed as though pierced by a knife, and the pirates roared with laughter, until a gunshot caused screaming and laughter to stop suddenly, and the boy knew that his mother was dead too. He heard a body thump to the floor. He shivered, but he was too frightened to cry.

Then a man said something, though it was hard to understand because he spoke so strangely. "He no rape you with a bullet in him."

"He's raped enough," growled a woman's voice. "And killed."

She was still alive! Jed clapped a hand to his mouth to keep from crying out.

"We kill who kill us. Your man a fool."

"He had more honor than all of you."

The man laughed. "Still dead, and no need to fight. I tell my men, no rape now. No time. English ships in the bay . . . You 'ave money? Little boys?"

"You'll find no children, unless you search the fields and streambeds."

"I need cabin boy."

"If you have no time to rape, you have none for child-stealing either."

"*Oui.* And more plantations . . . We no rape you, we no steal children, but we burn your house. And you watch."

"Burn it," she answered, "and I'll watch. Then I'll build it again."

In the crushing darkness, Jedediah heard footsteps, people dragging things. Then silence. He wondered if he should try to get out. But he was a boy who did as he was told, so he stayed put. A short time later, he smelled smoke. And some time after that, he could feel the rising heat. And by the grace of God, that was all he remembered.

As the flames swallowed the ends of the house, the pirates left for better pickings. Only when they were away from the dock did Elizabeth try to save her son. But the flames set her nightgown afire, and a falling beam drove her back, and she screamed in despair, dropped to her knees and screamed her fury.

But Nervous Duncan Parrish was not only nervous. He was also resourceful enough to have played dead beneath his bell. Now he covered himself with a water-soaked blanket and braved the flames, finding the boy, hidden and half roasted in the walls, covering him with the blanket, and bringing him back to what remained of his world.

That night, before the burning house, Elizabeth Ryder Stafford gave Nervous Duncan his freedom.

And with the help of the servants who had hidden in the woods, she saved the four original rooms of Stafford Hall.

At dawn they stood beneath the new sycamores, watching smoke rise over the remains of the house, and Jedediah's mother said she would rebuild, to honor a brave husband and son.

"You . . . you the brave one, marm," said Nervous Duncan. "You watched 'em burn the house with little Jedediah inside, and you didn't say a word."

"If I said a thing, they would have hunted for him." She held the boy tight and stroked his hair. "Better dead than in their bloody hands."

Little Jedediah said nothing. He would say nothing for many days.

"He's a fine boy." His mother tousled his hair, then announced,

"We'll bury his father in the family plot. A priest will pray over him. After that, no papist is ever to set foot here again. The French are papists, and they did this. Papists deluded my husband. I'll not allow them to delude my son."

iii
Anglican Sons

The French were defeated soon enough, and the Royal Navy routed the pirates from their Caribbean hideouts. Tobacco and the hardheaded spirit of Elizabeth Ryder Stafford rebuilt Stafford Hall. And the sycamores grew taller.

Along the Chesapeake, men said that soil and sea were like lovers. The sea flowed up through the loins of the land, two hundred miles or more, and as it rose, it entered a hundred tidal rivers, and in each river it mingled its essence with the brown, silted waters of a hundred tiny tributaries. And along its banks, young families grew.

Jedediah was raised a good Anglican and married a good Anglican, and when his sons were born, they were baptized Anglicans. One would bring tobacco from the soil, while the other would make certain that pirates never again came from the sea.

The first son was named for his father, but people called him Black Jed, because he had inherited his mother's black hair and square jaw, which made the dark Stafford gaze even darker. He spent his summers in the fields, learning the science of tobacco cultivation, and when the time came, he went to the College of William and Mary, to prepare for life in the planters' society. And there he found that he preferred the mercantile life to one spent tilling the soil.

The second son was named for his grandfather, but people called him Big Tom, for reasons that were clear to any who looked at him or listened to him pour forth opinion and voluble spirit in a voice twice as loud as he needed. Through his father's influence, he earned a rare midshipman's warrant in the Royal Navy, but Big Tom had a big temper, and he never learned to brook the insults that the second sons of British gentry heaped on the second sons of Colonial tobacco planters, and he never earned a commission.

All of this was a great disappointment to Jedediah, for it seemed that his sons had forgotten their father's credo. Then, in the decade before England's American sons turned against their royal mother, Jedediah's sons went to Annapolis and made their fortune.

CHAPTER ONE

Sycamores and Submarines

October 7

So, thought Susan Browne, Stafford Hall should be her first stop.

If the story began on the Patuxent, that was where her work should begin, too. And if those sycamores were still growing, she might even start her film there.

She got to Washington National on the early flight from Boston, rented a Plymouth Neon, and headed south into Saint Mary's County. Some still called this triangle of land between the Potomac and the Patuxent the Confederacy of Maryland. Some called it the Tobacco Coast. Susan called it an hour of Divided Road, Anywhere, U.S.A., until she turned off the boring commercial strip called Route 235 and was embraced by the past.

Here the land seemed to stretch, like an animal in the warm October sun. Split-rail fences edged meadows and peanut fields. Stands of trees leapt from the long-fallow earth. And the well-tended houses and the ramshackle dumps all leaned east toward the river.

By the grace of God—to borrow a phrase from *The Stafford Story*—this little world had escaped the boom-and-bust burb-building of everywhere else. Or maybe it was by the grace of the Maryland taxpayers, who funded a park just upstream from Stafford Hall. Or maybe by the grace of Jedediah's father, who had planted the sycamores, because they were still growing.

She could see them swaying in the breeze long before she saw the house. They grew in a perfect double line almost a quarter-mile long.

And as she drove under them, she imagined a moving shot, with the sun dappling down and the narrator describing one family's impact upon nation, history, earth. . . .

Maybe . . . But maybe too pretentious. Maybe just wrong. Like the idea of her doing a film about a family of navy bulletheads and their loose-cannon relatives.

Susan Browne was an independent, which meant she made films for short money and small audiences. Sometimes they splashed at festivals. Sometimes not. But after she finished one, she always had to scrape together the money for another. It was a tough life for a divorced mother, and nothing helped more than an assignment like this.

A few years earlier, Susan's film on American Impressionist Mary Cassatt had caught the eye of a PBS producer in Boston. Over lunch they had talked about the hot topic that winter—the Gulf War. Susan had mentioned that a captured navy flier, whose battered face graced the cover of *Time* magazine, was a distant cousin. His name was Stephen Stafford.

Now she was on her way to interview his grandfather for *The American Family,* a series about the families who had really built America, from West Virginia coal miners to Boston educators to military families like the Staffords. Susan was getting eight thousand dollars to research the Staffords; if their story was worth telling, she'd get a quarter million more for two hours of prime time on PBS. A good deal, even if she'd rather have been making a film about the art of Georgia O'Keeffe.

Of course, Susan's film would be about more than battles. She wanted to show what made the Staffords tick, explore their secrets, know their women, find the glue that held them together. She had started by sending out letters to a few famous Staffords.

Her first response had come from Jack, L.A. loose cannon, newspaper columnist, author of books with titles like *Riding the Thousand-Dollar Toilet Seat and Other Pentagon Tales* and *Middle-Aged in the Revolution, 1965–1972.* Susan's mother had said three things about her distant uncle Jack: (1) he had spent most of his life with a reputation as a ladies' man and still worked at it; (2) he was not to be trusted (a year earlier, he had come to Boston, wined her and dined her, just to get any old diaries or letters she might have relating to the Staffords and the Brownes); and (3) he and his brother, Thomas, had barely spoken in years.

All of which piqued Susan's interest. But in addition to the first chapter of his new book, *The Stafford Story,* Jack had sent her a note: "Let's meet, October 8, in Annapolis. I'm hoping to buy the old family manse, called Stafford's Fine Folly, a name that could describe the family's whole history. But there's good news and bad news. The good news is that I've dug up all the research on the family. The bad news is I'm using it for *The Stafford Story*. If you want it, it'll cost you."

Screw him.

Then she'd heard from Jack's brother, Admiral Thomas Stafford, USN, retired. His note invited her to Stafford Hall on any Monday in October. "My wife and I will be glad to speak with you. If the project is worthy of our support, we'll help."

So the admiral did things because he considered them worthy, not because there was money in them. If that was what made a navy bullethead, Susan might prefer him to the loose cannon, after all.

Stafford Hall was not what she would have expected.

It did not sit on some high foundation and impose itself on its surroundings. No antebellum extravagance here. The house was built close to the ground and rambled, following the contours of the land and the instincts of those who had been adding new wings and dormers for three centuries. The style was called Tidewater Vernacular, which meant nothing too special, but it was. The first impression, to anyone driving toward the house through that time tunnel of sycamores, was one of confidence . . . simple and direct.

It was the roof that did it. The roof sloped down around the dormers and out over the veranda to enfold the entire house. And it was red. A proud color to proclaim the pride the Staffords must have taken in all that they had built beneath it.

"Good morning, Ms. Browne." The voice came from behind her as she reached for the doorbell.

She turned and looked up into the enormous nostrils of a chestnut horse that snorted right in her face.

"Dammit, Admiral," another voice came from behind her. "Dismount."

Susan turned again and looked into the face of an old woman. "The admiral spends too much time in the saddle, dear. I'm Betty Stafford."

"And I'm the admiral."

Susan turned again, feeling like a figure in some kind of clockwork. "I'm—"

"You're Cousin Susan," said Betty.

"Welcome," said the admiral. He looked the way a retired admiral should—tall, trim, full head of white hair, imposing but accessible—and he had her wondering already how his face would photograph. "I ride too much, and Betty complains too much."

"But we never sit still." Betty Stafford looked the way Susan would want to look at that age—a lined face that had known bright sunshine and probably a few dark nights, too. Another good face for film.

"And this is Wildair," said the admiral, introducing his horse. "Named after Thomas Jefferson's favorite mount."

"Jefferson was a family friend," said Betty.

"And Washington visited Stafford Hall several times—"

"That explains your red roof." Susan finally got a word in.

"It explains *Washington's.* He liked ours, so he put one on Mount Vernon."

"Come in, dear. Come in." Betty was already beginning her tour. "This is the sitting room. The latest addition, built off the front of the house in 1947."

The overstuffed sofas and chairs and chintz fabric *looked* like 1947. A thirty-five-inch television and a VCR were the only concessions to the nineties. And on the walls hung—what else?—ships. Old ships, new ships . . . photographs and paintings . . . and officers too—from stiff nineteenth-century figures done in oil to a boyish lieutenant aboard a patrol boat in Vietnam, with a framed Purple Heart beneath his picture.

Was that fresh-faced young guy the Staffords' son for the sea? She knew they'd had two sons. One was a Seattle lawyer, the other had been killed in Vietnam. But Susan wasn't ready to ask probing questions, and Betty was moving quickly through her tour.

"Here's what we call the drawing room, once called the Great Hall."

"Great indeed," said the admiral. "Two stories high, matching shell alcoves on either side of the grand fireplace, magnificent view of the river. . . ."

But Susan didn't have time to admire it because Betty was moving again, leading her into the hallway, pointing out the Chinese Chippendale staircase built by Duncan Parrish, an indentured servant who became a plantation owner and whose family's history had been entwined with that of the Staffords ever since.

"Staircase came after the fire," said Betty.

Susan looked up the stairs and imagined a little boy in his father's arms and the torches swirling outside. She felt the image tugging at her, pulling her back in time, but it was only Betty Stafford, taking Susan's sleeve to lead her into the study on the opposite side of the foyer.

"Pirates burned this house," said the admiral.

"Pirates were in this *room,*" answered Susan.

"You know about this room?" asked the admiral.

Susan could do no more than nod. "Why is everything painted red?"

"Because of blood, or so the legend goes," said Betty Stafford.

"After the pirates," explained the admiral, "this room was stained with blood. Elizabeth Ryder Stafford didn't want us to forget how it got there. So she painted it red to cover the real blood, red to remind us of the honor of sacrifice."

"And, Lord, have we been reminded," said Betty with sudden bitterness.

"Betty, perhaps our cousin would like a cup of coffee," said the admiral gently.

"Yes, I'm forgetting myself." Betty picked up a little silver bell and gave it a ring, as though it could drive away bad memories and summon coffee at the same time.

"How did you know about this room?" asked the admiral.

"Your brother wrote about it."

"You've read *The Stafford Story*?"

"Only the first chapter."

"This room is where it all began. But that—" The admiral pointed to a pair of submarine models on the mantel.

"—is how it's ended?" offered Susan.

"Not ended. *Evolved.* The smaller one is the *Nautilus*, my first

World War II boat. The other is the *Annapolis*, one of the 688-class nuclear attack subs."

To Susan's eye, the older one was more interesting. Its surface was studded with deck guns, railings, gratings, tubes, and it was shaped like a pregnant snake. The *Annapolis* had three times the girth and twenty percent more length—a giant black tube, a bridge, and a completely featureless surface. The truth was that neither of them was much to look at. Not like putting a model of a graceful old sailing ship on your mantel.

"I helped design 688s to hunt the Soviets," said the admiral. "Now we're trying to anticipate the next phase of warfare. It's called forward thinking."

"The admiral is consulting on the next generation of attack sub right now," said Betty, "out of his think tank."

"I'm an overseer at the Institute for Advanced Naval Planning. Old admirals never die," he chuckled, "they just become defense analysts."

"Oh," joked Susan, picking up on the admiral's mood, "so *you're* to blame."

"For what?" The admiral's smile froze.

"The deficit."

And the frozen smile dropped off. "Are you on my brother's side already?"

"No, sir," said Susan, realizing that she had put her foot right in her mouth.

Just then, the ancient Filipino houseboy brought the coffee. He was small and stooped, with little wisps of gray hair and wrinkled yellow skin, like parchment. Betty and Susan sat in the wing chairs flanking the fireplace and for a moment gave him their complete attention.

"Juan's been with us since before Pearl Harbor," said Betty. "A member of the family. Aren't you, Juan?"

"Oh yes. Been for all the good time and the goddamn bad."

"Just pour the coffee." The admiral stood in the middle of the room, letting his presence be felt. After Susan had sipped her coffee, he said, "I must warn you, if you're planning to use this so-called *Stafford Story* as the source for your film, I don't think I can help you. I know the sort of thing my brother writes."

"I'll use whatever sources I can. I might even put Juan on film—"

The old houseboy almost dropped the pot. "Oh, hell, I got nothin' to say."

The admiral dismissed Juan and picked up the pot, aimed the spout at his cup from two feet above it, and didn't spill a drop. He did it without show, as though no coffee would dare to spill while he was pouring it.

"Now then," he said, "this so-called *Stafford Story*—"

"Since he's expecting me to pay him for it, I—"

"Just like my brother, trying to squeeze a few bucks out of the family history."

"Well, he wants to buy the Stafford House in Annapolis," said Betty.

"*This* is Stafford House," he said angrily. "Besides, the Fine Folly in Annapolis should be put to better use than he has in mind. I'm going to see to it." Then the admiral sat and took a few sips of his coffee. "It's like this, Ms. Browne—"

"Call her Cousin Susan," said Betty.

"Cousin Susan. Using my brother's version of things will be like . . . well . . . like reading the *National Enquirer* when you should be studying a history book."

"Speak her language, Tom. Television terms." Betty looked at Susan. "If you're doing *Hard Copy* when we're expecting *The American Experience*—"

"It'll be a class act all the way," answered Susan.

"Just don't believe everything my brother writes," said the admiral.

What was between these two old men? Susan didn't have the courage to ask, not yet. She was no hard-hitting journalist plowing into a story. She came to the truth in gentler, more roundabout ways.

And the Staffords seemed to like her approach, because they promised to help. For starters, the admiral set up a lunch date with Susan and his grandson, Lieutenant Steve Stafford, who had survived Iraqi imprisonment and was now flying a desk at the Pentagon. By then, thought Susan, she might be ready to ask tougher questions . . . about two old men, about a mother's veiled bitterness, about the fresh-faced young guy in that boat in Vietnam, who had probably been Steve's father.

• • •

It was dark when she reached Annapolis.

She could get no sense of the town, except that it seemed an ancient place of red brick and narrow streets, trapped in a web of strip-mall feeder roads. She had seen towns like this in New England, small gems of historic preservation suspended in the plastic present. And she liked them because to her, they weren't relics of the past, but centers that held.

She checked into a bed-and-breakfast on Prince George Street, a block from the Naval Academy and a block from Saint John's, a liberal arts college with a Great Books curriculum. Nowhere in America could you find two more unlikely neighbors "linked by the imperfect logic" of geography. Susan was beginning to think that with the Staffords, she would encounter many pairs of opposites linked imperfectly yet inextricably. And that was what would make things interesting.

The innkeeper was a friendly young man of thirty or so who padded about the house in his stocking feet and took great pains to make her feel at home. He showed her to her room, told her about the good restaurants, and gave her an envelope, which contained manuscript pages and a note from Jack Stafford: "Twenty-four hours from meeting me. Bet you can't contain yourself. I enclose the second chapter of *The Stafford Story*. Read about Black Jed, his brother, Big Tom, their nemesis Rebecca Parrish, and the big house they built in Annapolis. See you tomorrow. Have intelligent questions."

Egotistical asshole.

At least the next chapter made good reading while she ate alone at Café Normandie.

The Stafford Story
Book Two
Staffords and Parrishes, Rebellion and Revenge
October 1774

Jedediah Stafford had made many a voyage to Annapolis, but few had been as joyous as the one he made on that crisp autumn day.

He had put sixty-eight summers behind him by then. The effort to haul his girth around grew greater by the month, and the loneliness of his widowhood never abated. But a grandson had been born to the old master of Stafford Hall. And that was enough to have him gazing hopefully toward a future he doubted he would see, in a world where the natural order of things could no longer be predicted.

For all his life, that order had been tobacco for tea, American raw material for English manufacture. And his sons had learned it well.

Black Jed took tobacco consignments, shipped them in Stafford vessels, and brought English goods back to sell. Big Tom built the vessels that did the carrying—topsail schooners with arrogantly raked masts and hulls that cut scythelike through the great fields of water between England and America.

After a decade of tax disputes and a century of British control over where Colonials could sell and what they could buy, Stafford Brothers still prospered. That was what made their challenge to the natural order of things so hard for their father to understand.

But Jedediah put his worries away because he was sailing to a christening, and Nervous Duncan Parrish was sailing with him. They stood together at the starboard rail of Big Tom's flagship, the *Hannah S.*, two old friends in tricornes and brown traveling coats, talking and feeling the timeless roll of the Chesapeake.

Success as a Patuxent planter had made Nervous Duncan less nervous, but even at seventy-eight, he twitched when he talked, tittered when he laughed, and spoke in a high-pitched whine that grew louder as his hearing grew weaker. None of this bothered Jedediah, however, nor did Duncan's daughter, who stood alone on the larboard side, where the shadow of the sail kept the sun from her pallid skin.

Rebecca Parrish was not unpleasing to the eye, but most tidewater bachelors said there was no dowry large enough to dull her sharp tongue. When the ship went on the tack, she followed the shade of the sail to the starboard side and said to Jedediah, "Did you know that my father breaks a vow by going to this christening?"

"How so?"

"He vowed he would not visit our Annapolis house till the Annapolis Resolves were lifted. Didn't you, Father?"

"It don't make much sense for us to withhold payment on honest debts to London creditors just because the British close the port of Boston," said Nervous Duncan.

"It serves Boston right for all the trouble they caused," agreed Jedediah, "yappin' like scalded dogs every time our taxes went up a few shillings."

"It seems that the world has gone crazy." Rebecca cast a glance toward the stern and Big Tom. "So have some of our friends."

Big Tom saw her glance as an invitation and came ambling forward. "Are we discussing politics, prosperity, or feminine beauty?"

"Politics determines prosperity," said Rebecca. "Beauty has no part in it."

"But beauty is its own prosperity," said Big Tom, "both to the beautiful and to those who look upon beauty to . . . to . . . find prosperity."

"Beauty," she answered dryly, "is also a well-organized thought."

Big Tom grinned. He was a hard one to insult. "I leave *organized* thinkin' to my brother. He writes things like the Annapolis Resolves: 'Stop exports, resist tea imports, withhold debt service till we get to do our taxin' ourselves.' . . . Strong thoughts to go with my strong arm."

"Impoverished thoughts, mindless brawn," she said.

But Big Tom kept grinning. "And they've built us a fine, strong business."

"And that's somethin' to consider, darlin'." Nervous Duncan gave his daughter a wink.

Jedediah elbowed Nervous Duncan. "Hitchin' Rebecca to a merchant shipper would be—"

"An arranged marriage." Rebecca drew from her purse a snuffbox, but instead of taking a pinch in each nostril, she carefully placed one in her mouth, between her cheek and gum. "Just what I always a hoped for."

ii
The Annapolis Tea Party

"The genteelest town in North America."

That was what the English rector at St. Anne's Church had called Annapolis.

And while a long-legged man could still circumnavigate it in half an hour, Annapolis was now inhabited by fifteen hundred souls and had grown to be all that Jedediah's father had envisioned so long ago.

It was a town built and enriched by purchase, by sale, and by shipment. This truth was proclaimed each day along Factor's Row, at the head of the dock, where agents and buyers arranged consignments and credit and kept the wheels of commerce turning between the new world and the old. A fine market house accommodated them at the place where Main Street reached the waterfront. And when matters were not complicated by politics, the warehouses burst with the fruits of their labor.

Annapolis was not merely waterfront, however. The new capitol building was the grandest in the Colonies, and the cupola rising on its roof would make it the tallest. And each autumn, when the Assembly convened there, planters from all across the tidewater came for the entertainments that accompanied the business of government.

America's first brick playhouse had recently opened on West Street. The new revenue house could accommodate hundreds of bowing, promenading, pirhouetting dancers. The annual races drew horsemen from across the Colonies. There were card parties and musicales every night. Women wore the freshest European fashions. And in the decade since the end of the French and Indian War, no less than a dozen magnificent mansions had risen, proclaiming the wealth of the town to the world and the wealth of the owners to their peers.

When Jedediah had first heard that his older son was building a twenty-room brick palace on Prince George Street, he had called it folly. But when he had finally stood before it, he had admitted that it was the finest folly he had ever seen. So he had named it Stafford's

Fine Folly. And in the perfect symmetry of its five-part design—main house balanced by service wings and connected by hallways called hyphens—he had come to see the perfect symbol for what men were calling the Age of Reason.

So why couldn't reasonable men reasonably settle their differences over taxation? And why, late that afternoon, did his approach to the genteelest town in North America make him so uneasy?

A month earlier, a hurricane had roared up the coast and blown the new cupola off the capitol. The market house had been destroyed. And the great walnut tree on Prince George Street, which Jedediah had always used as a landmark to find his son's house, no longer waved in the breeze.

But none of this bothered him so much as the quiet at the waterfront, the kind of quiet that came when yellowing black clouds closed overhead and a storm threatened to burst.

From the quarterdeck of the *Hannah S.,* he aimed his spyglass at the dock, where a group of men were lurching out of Middleton's tavern. Their staggerings and hoarse shouts suggested Dutch courage, and one of them was carrying a torch, though daylight lingered.

Then Jedediah turned his glass to the brig anchored off Windmill Point. "Is that the *Peggy Stewart?*"

"Aye," said Big Tom. "I passed her on my way down the bay."

"Still rides damn low in the water," said Jedediah.

"Must still be loaded," answered Big Tom. "Could be tea."

"High time," grunted Nervous Duncan Parrish.

"Annapolis Resolves prohibit the importation of tea," said Big Tom.

"Maybe someone's putting them to the test," said Rebecca.

"High time," repeated Nervous Duncan.

"High time to build more gallows," said Rebecca.

The torches bobbed in the approaching darkness, and the stink of hot tar fouled the air. Nothing good ever came of such things, thought old Jedediah, or from the kind of mob that was gathered at the Annapolis Liberty Tree, the big tulip poplar near the head of Prince George Street.

Standing before them, his white wig bowed over a sheet of paper, the torches crowding around him, was Anthony Stewart, owner of the

Peggy Stewart. And beside him stood Jedediah's own son Black Jed, who seemed to be supporting Stewart while keeping him to his task: reading an apology for paying the duty on his tea consignment.

"We do acknowledge that we have committed a most daring insult and act of the most pernicious tendency to the liberties of America. . . ."

"What?" Nervous Duncan asked Jedediah. "What damn foolery is this?"

"Lower your voice." Jedediah recognized some of the faces turning toward them at the edge of the crowd, but a week-long battle of handbills and broadsides had been waged over the fate of the *Peggy Stewart*, and rebellious strangers had come from as far away as Baltimore.

"A pernicious tendency, Pa," said Rebecca. "Pernicious to pay your duties."

"What's wrong with payin' your duties?"

"Maybe you'd like to find out," said a burly stranger with a boil on his nose.

Big Tom slipped himself in front of Duncan and told the stranger, "We're gettin' what we want, friend. Leave the old man alone."

Someone gave the stranger a nudge, as if to warn that Big Tom was not to be trifled with.

"Thank you," whispered Rebecca.

"No one bothers my friends," said Big Tom.

"We'll see that *you're* not hanged," she said.

". . . And thereby we incurred the displeasure of those now convened, and others interested in the preservation of constitutional rights and liberties. . . ."

"My liberties are clear!" Nervous Duncan's whine, directed only at his daughter, could be heard by half the crowd.

Someone growled that women and old men should stay by their hearth.

Rebecca spat a stream of tobacco at that, and Big Tom squared himself for trouble.

". . . Therefore, we will commit to flames the detestable article which has been the cause of this, our misconduct."

"By Christ, they're going to burn the—" Duncan's last word was muffled by a hand coming from behind and covering his face.

Jedediah and Big Tom grabbed the man, who wore a black hooded cape, and they struggled for a moment, until Rebecca threw off the hood and revealed her own brother. "Dunc!"

"Quiet!" hissed Duncan the Younger, of the Governor's Council, who usually paraded about town in a silk coat, a satin brocade waistcoat, and a white peruke.

"Why the monk's cowl?"

He ignored her and told his father, "Say nothing more."

Suddenly the crowd was roaring again. Charles Carroll the Barrister cried, "Mr. Stewart consents to burn the tea. The Anne Arundel County Committee of Safety says that's enough."

"And we say tar and feathers!" cried the stranger with the boil on his nose.

"And burn his brig!" shouted a country doctor named Warfield.

"Burn his house!" shouted someone else. "Burn *all* their damn houses!"

Duncan the Younger whispered, "*That* is why we must be quiet. We're silent partners with Stewart. If they find out, they'll burn *our* house, too."

And a new voice boomed out over the crowd. "You all know me. I'm Black Jed Stafford. And I say Stewart's an honorable man. He's made his apologies. Now let him burn his tea and be done with it."

"Well spoken, son," muttered Jedediah.

"Aye," said Big Tom. "He's a good talker."

"Another we won't hang," whispered Rebecca.

Big Tom had always liked her spirit, from the time they were kids, and the torchlight gave her a hard-edged beauty he had not noticed before.

But the crowd did not like Black Jed's appeal. The cries for tarring grew louder. Pillows were torn apart and the feathers tossed in the air, falling like snow into the hissing torches, giving the scene a strange and frightening festivity.

Black Jed shouted for a vote to accept destruction of the tea as restitution for its importation. Half cried yea, but the rest continued to call for something to burn, for someone to tar. It was mob rule, and it was abominable, thought old Jedediah.

As if Nervous Duncan could read his friend's mind, he cried, "Abominable!"

"Quiet, old man," growled the doctor.

Ale-angry faces turned toward them in the torchlight.

"I been on the Chesapeake since the days of the French pirates," cried Nervous Duncan, "and I say you're all worse than they ever—"

His voice cracked, as it had a million times before. Then he brought his right hand to his chest, and with his left, he reached out, grasping the space where his son had just been standing. But his son had disappeared, so Nervous Duncan fell against old Jedediah, and the mob closed around them.

"Shut that old bastard up!" screamed the one with the boil on his nose.

"Get back!" Rebecca swung her folded parasol like a cutlass to sweep the crowd away. Some of them hooted at her. Someone spat. From under the Liberty Tree, Black Jed Stafford called for calm. And the one with the boil on his nose pushed Big Tom out of the way to get at Rebecca.

That was a mistake. Big Tom delivered a fist that left the stranger with a burst boil and a broken nose. Then he pulled his flintlock from his belt, threw Nervous Duncan over his shoulder, and shouted, "Stand back, the lot of you!"

With men screaming and the torches bobbing after them, they hurried down the street to the safety of Stafford's Fine Folly.

Jedediah knew that the mob and their torches and their hoarse-throated shouts were not for him or Nervous Duncan. They were driving Anthony Stewart to the waterfront, to make him pay for transgressing their so-called resolves. Still Jedediah ordered the slaves to bar the doors while Big Tom laid Nervous Duncan on the couch in the library and Rebecca poured brandy down the old man's throat.

Black Jed's wife, Sara—doe-eyed, soft-spoken, and dead-calm in a crisis—ordered one slave to fetch the doctor and another to brew tea.

But when Black Jed appeared an hour later, Nervous Duncan was dead.

"Where were you?" demanded Sara, who now held their crying baby.

"The harbor." Black Jed's coat was gone, his stockings and waist-coat were covered with mud. He touched the baby and left a smudge of river muck on its forehead. Then he looked at the blue and lifeless face of Nervous Duncan. "He spoke his mind. It's a brave way to die."

An orange flame flickered in the sky to the east.

"That'll be the *Peggy Stewart,*" said Black Jed, his voice drained of energy.

"What did you do?" asked his father.

"We persuaded Stewart to ground her and burn her. I helped him do it."

"*Mobocracy.* We live in a mobocracy." Jedediah poured a shot of brandy down his own throat. "And my son's a mobocrat."

"They would've burned Stewart's house, the Williams house . . . the Parrish house, too. One leaky brig for three houses . . . a good trade." In the candlelight, the sharp angles of Black Jed's face trimmed any tissue of doubt from his face.

"I thank you," said Rebecca, "and my brother thanks you, wherever he hides."

"He was smart to disappear," said Big Tom. "Black Jed can argue the middle ground. Your brother can't."

Out over the harbor, the flames were rising higher into the air.

Jedediah thought of pirate torches on that long-ago night. "I hope you're ready to see our ships burned, and this house—"

Black Jed lifted the baby from Sara's arms and held it before his father. "Your grandson, christened tomorrow with water and holy oil. But look"—he pointed to the dirt on the baby's forehead—"tonight we christen him with good Maryland soil."

iii
A Snuffbox

The rising tide extinguished the hulk of the *Peggy Stewart,* and the rising sun fell upon a town that seemed unchanged. The high-peaked mansions still fought for the first rays of light. The red brick seemed even redder in the dawn. And the dew running in rivulets down the roofs turned to steam in the warming sun.

The Annapolis merchant princes had been blessed. So why would they risk all that they had built? Why would they align themselves with a mob that had so little to lose?

In the bed where he had spent a sleepless night, old Jedediah was confounded by these questions. The mob was powerful, and there were men of property and intelligence, like his sons, who would guide the mob, harness its furies, feed it a burning ship now and then, in order to . . . what?

On the *Hannah S.,* where he slept like a plank, Big Tom dreamed that he had been laid over a cannon and British midshipmen were lining up to cane this Colonial son. The dream woke him, as it always did, and offered an answer for any question concerning rebellion.

In the nursery, where he paced the floor with his son, Black Jed knew the answers too. He needed only to look into the child's eyes or to consider the words of his friend George Washington, when they talked at the last meeting of the Annapolis races.

"If we don't assert our rights," the Virginia horseman had said, "we'll become like our own slaves, denied the rewards of our labor, abased before the Crown."

That was something that Black Jed could never countenance. The dispute was not, as his father believed, a simple matter of money, or Black Jed would never have risked his reputation. It was a matter of conscience.

But friendship was still in season.

That afternoon, despite their bereavement, the Parrishes attended the christening of Charlton Thomas Stafford.

That evening the Staffords paid their respects to Nervous Duncan at the Parrish home on Duke of Gloucester Street. His coffin had been filled with the last ice in Annapolis, then set on sawhorses covered with black crepe. Melting ice dripped onto the floor, and Annapolitans from both sides of the political debate came to the door.

After an hour of condolences, Big Tom followed Rebecca out onto the piazza at the back of the house. He watched her dip a bit of tobacco, then drew closer and said how sorry he was that they could not have saved her father.

"He would not have liked what's coming," she answered.

After a moment, he said, "I've been thinking—"

"A most unusual development."

"We're both almost past marryin' age—"

"I won't marry you."

"You're a difficult woman, Rebecca Parrish."

"Bein' a woman has *made* me difficult."

He leaned against the stone balustrade. "Would you permit me to call on you . . . when a troupe of players come to town, or next September, durin' the races?"

And she laughed in his face. "*What* races?"

"There's always September races."

"There's going to be a rebellion, Tom."

"Then . . . you won't give me permission?"

"Do you ask permission of the girls you bed in London and Baltimore?"

Bedding her was what he had in mind . . . but later. "Not only are you sharp-tongued, Rebecca. You're also very forward."

"I hate wasting time. Do you wish me to be your Annapolis girl, like your London girl or your Baltimore girl or your whore in Martinique?"

"I'd wish to kiss you, if you'd stop dipping tobacco. Beyond that—"

"I like tobacco more than I like men. But I like the theater, too. So you may take me to the theater, or to the races, whenever you're in Annapolis."

"You mean, whenever *you're* in Annapolis."

"No. I've decided not to return to the plantation. This may be the most interesting season in many a year, as well as the last. And brother Duncan needs me here, especially now."

Big Tom looked at the curtainless windows. "Sara says this house needs a woman's touch."

"It's the handsomest house in Annapolis. Handsomer even than your Fine Folly." Rebecca's pale skin, set off by darkness and black dress, seemed to shimmer. "I'll decorate it to show you so-called patriots that some still respect the Crown and all the protections it has given us, no matter how big the mob."

"Does this mean you won't give up your tobacco?"

They went to the theater several times that autumn.

But Rebecca did not give up her tobacco . . . or her opinions.

And Big Tom did not give up his girls in Baltimore or Martinique.

He did, however, bid farewell to his girl in London. Ordinarily he wintered there, enjoying its pleasures despite his dislike of the English. But that January he sailed south to avoid the Atlantic storms, then crossed to the Caribbean and the tiny Dutch Island of

Saint Eustatius, where anything could be bought and no English middleman could take a profit nor British warship interfere.

There, on his brother's instructions, he bought every ounce of gunpowder, every musket, flint, and lead ball he could load. He also managed to buy eight six-pound cannons, all of which he deftly smuggled up the Chesapeake, up the Patuxent, right up the rolling road and into a drying shed at Stafford Hall.

Jedediah Stafford could not imagine what his own father, the Admiralty agent, would have thought of a smuggling grandson. But the old man, bewildered by all that was happening in the spring of 1775, clung to his love for his sons, no matter how misplaced their passions, and he allowed the munitions to remain.

Then Big Tom sailed up to Annapolis and was met at Rebecca's door by an armed man. The door opened, and Rebecca announced, with mock pleasantry, "We've hired guards, Tom. But I know you'll be a polite guest, so do come in."

The foyer of the Parrish house always reminded Tom of a chapel—two stories, Palladian window on the landing, like a window behind an altar—a shrine to the success of a former indentured servant and his children. The April sun poured in the window, gleaming off the harp and the spittoon at the foot of the stairs.

Rebecca gestured for Tom to take a chair, and she returned to the stool in front of the harp. "I often play here in the afternoon. It reminds me of the musicales we once had. Wonderful times, when Annapolis was a civil place."

"Are you the only family with guards?"

"The Dulanys have hired them. Some other Loyalists. The *Peggy Stewart* proves what a mob can do." She folded her hands in her lap. "I would offer you a cup of tea, but—"

"Tea's a poison. I'll take Boston rum, or a strum of the harp, if that's your pleasure."

She ran her fingers once along the strings, then sat back and folded her hands in her lap, a favorite pose when she was seeking to unnerve someone.

"I've missed you," he said, surprised at how true those words were. Then he withdrew from his pocket a small silver snuffbox with the chinless profile of King George on the cover.

She examined the gift, gave a glimmer of a smile, and asked, "Does this mean I will not have to give up my tobacco?"

To answer, Tom knelt beside her harp, in the bright rays of sun, and kissed her.

She did not taste like other women did. The tobacco made it a bitter kiss. And she did not respond like other women did. It was as if she did not know how. Or perhaps she did not feel enough. But she did not push him away until the kiss was over and he whispered, "Keep your tobacco. Surrender your opinions."

"Why should I surrender what matters to me, simply for a kiss from you?"

"Because"—he smiled—"you are getting a kiss from me."

To that, she gave a delicate shot into her spittoon.

And, as if to seal the moment, Duncan the Younger came through the door with news: rebels had fought a day-long battle with the king's soldiers west of Boston.

It had begun.

iv
Providence and Privateers

In June, Black Jed went to the Philadelphia State House to deliver instructions from the Maryland Convention to the Continental Congress.

He arrived at midmorning. The congressional custodian, who was balancing himself on the back legs of his chair and trying to sleep, said Congress was in the room to his left, and they would welcome an interruption.

At that moment, Black Jed heard a voice proclaiming the name George Washington. This was answered by the sound of walking sticks pounded on the floor and hands pounded on tables. A moment later, the doors swung open and Washington, wearing the blue-and-red uniform of the Virginia militia, stalked out.

"George," called Black Jed. "George Washington."

The big Virginian hurried across the foyer, head down, eyes fixed resolutely on the floor. He was naturally distant and grew more distant when lost in thought, so Black Jed shouted, "Is that the best horseman on the tidewater?"

Washington stopped, his small eyes brightening. "Black Jed Stafford?"

"Why the old soldier's coat?"

"I've been nominated commander in chief of the New England militia . . . and I don't even like New Englanders."

"A high honor, in any event." Black Jed did not offer a manly slap on the back. He was no backslapper, nor was Washington's a back that invited slapping.

"A high honor"—Washington gave him a thin smile—"or a high gallows. Walk with me while my fellow congressmen debate my future."

They crossed the street, avoiding carts and carriages and steaming horse buns, and went into the shade of the park.

"I put this on"—Washington fingered the red facing of his uniform—"to proclaim a willingness to fight. I did not ask to be general. I may not be up to it."

"No man is up to what we're doing, I don't think."

"Still, without experienced officers—southern officers—we can never have a truly Continental Army."

"Continental Army? Is that what we're calling the New England militia?"

"Call a mule a horse and he may try to mount the mare."

"At least you have a mule." Black Jed stopped and looked hard at his friend. Though Washington's red hair was graying, he was only forty-two, still vigorous, and his six feet and three made him one of the few men Black Jed had ever looked up to. "Where will you get ships to defeat the Royal Navy?"

Washington made a sound that was half grunt, half laugh. "My hope is to convince Fat George in London that we're serious. If I can, this may be over by fall."

"And if not?"

"Providence will have to provide. Providence and privateers." Washington glanced at the windows of the State House. "If they give me command, I'll charter a few fast Massachusetts schooners, arm them, set them on the king's transports, and supply my army from the king's cargo."

"For a man who didn't ask for the job, you've made a close study of it."

"We may all be offered jobs we haven't asked for."

"You can rely on the Staffords, George."

Just then a cheer came from the open window. The vote had been cast.

Washington said, " 'Tis done. Honor or the end of a rope by fall."

But by fall it was only beginning.

In London, Fat George was not in a conciliatory mood.

And along the Chesapeake, smuggling was growing more difficult because Virginia's royal governor, Lord Dunmore, had collected a small fleet with which to raid rebellious towns and shipping on the lower bay. But Big Tom was smarter than any royal governor. He could read the Chesapeake shoals and currents like a blue-clawed crab, and he knew every creek where the water was deep enough and the trees tall enough to hide a schooner in plain sight.

Small wonder, then, that Black Jed was furious when Big Tom announced, one November night, over a quiet dinner with their father, that he was joining the new navy.

"What navy?" said Black Jed.

"Continental Navy. Been near a month since Congress named a committee to build it, 'for the protection and defense of the United Colonies,' or so they said."

"I know what they said," answered Black Jed. "I know they're authorizing privateers, too, like the ones Washington's running off Boston."

"Privateers," said old Jedediah, as though speaking the name of Lucifer himself. "Licensed pirates. I'll put up with smugglin', but privateers—"

"Privateers make sense." Black Jed chewed on his pipe. "They help their country and make money for their investors, too."

"Listen here." Tom took a letter from his pocket. It was from his friend Nicholas Biddle, a Philadelphian who had resigned from the Royal Navy when rebellion came. "'Considering your fine vessels, privateering will no doubt be your course, just as commerce raiding will be a course for our fledgling Continental Navy. But your training in the Royal Navy would serve this new navy well, and you might extract some measure of satisfaction from the British officers who—'"

"Foolishness." Black Jed bit down on his pipestem.

"'—treated you so harshly.'" Tom read these last words slowly, ignoring his brother's interruption. Then he looked at his father.

"My son, a naval officer at last . . . even if it's the wrong navy."

Black Jed shook his head. "A handful of ships is not a navy. But privateers like the *Hannah S.* and her sisters can run down merchantmen and—"

"No, sir," said their father. "You've got Dunmore on the loose already, and the Royal Navy'll damn soon send bigger ships to bother the whole bay. And them who'd be happy for Royal Navy protection, they'll be lookin' to you."

Black Jed folded his arms; Big Tom scratched at the dried gravy on the tablecloth: two boys being dressed down.

The old man jabbed his finger at them. "You started this thing. You're honor-bound to see it through. You won't find honor linin' your pockets with prizes and runnin' the other way when there's fightin' to be done. Honor's bein' able to say I stood where the Lord put me. Like your grandpa the night the pirates came."

"Pa," said Black Jed, summoning all his authority, "fightin' the Royal Navy is suicide. Washington knows it. Congress knows it. Our best chance is to hit 'em where they ain't, and run when we see 'em."

"You ever been caned, brother?" asked Big Tom. "Been put over an eighteen-pounder and had your arse laid bare? I can think of a few British officers that I'd like to fight when I see 'em . . . especially if there's honor in it."

"Honor matters, by God." Old Jedediah banged his hand on the table.

And Big Tom banged his elbow on the table, then put up his hand.

"What's this?" demanded Black Jed.

"This is where the Lord puts my right arm. Like the old days."

"Like the old days." Their father chuckled. "Like brothers."

Black Jed rolled his eyes.

"Come on, lad," said Jedediah. "Family rule. No fistfights. No pistols at a dozen paces. But a good honest arm wrestle to settle things."

It could not be avoided. So Black Jed pulled off his coat and threw it on the back of the chair. He puffed several times on his pipe, then spit on his palm and took his position. "You win, you sign with Biddle and commit suicide. I win, we take letters of marque on the *Hannah S.* and the others, cut in gunports, and go privateerin'."

They clasped hands and looked into each other's eyes. Then they glanced at their father, who nodded, as he had done so many times before.

And they pulled. Big Tom's big hand and big shoulder flexed. Black Jed's biceps tightened. And for several minutes, their hands remained upright, quivering with tension at the apex of the half-circle arena. Then Big Tom began to win, as he had since he turned fourteen and outgrew his big brother.

But Black Jed was like most big brothers: he instinctively knew the little ways to annoy a little brother. So each time Big Tom pushed him down a bit more, he took another long puff on his pipe and blew smoke in Big Tom's face.

"Pa," said Tom, "he can't do that."

"He's just breathin', and if you can't beat a man suckin' on a pipe, you shouldn't be arm-wrestlin'."

This made Big Tom even angrier, and his big shoulder flexed again, driving the back of Black Jed's hand closer to the tabletop.

But Black Jed was not about to lose. The future of the family was riding on this. So he sucked in another puff of smoke. He always said a man did not absorb the essence of the earth until he had drawn good tobacco through his whole system. Most men were amazed that he could stand it in his lungs, shocked when he blew it out his nose. And his brother was infuriated when he blew it at him.

"Pa! Now, dammit, he's blowin' that dirty nose-smoke. That ain't fair."

But it was distraction enough. Black Jed was able to fight off defeat and force the action back to the apex of the half circle. Two or three more bursts of smoke caused the candles to gutter and destroyed his brother's concentration altogether, and one big burst of strength put the back of Big Tom's hand onto the table.

"So I'm goin' privateerin' after all," said Big Tom when his anger had cooled. "But you know, Jed, if you were more of a man, you'd go privateerin', too."

"I'm the son for the soil . . . and the counting house."

V
Of Unions, Grand and Otherwise

Big Tom took his first prize in December, off the Jersey shore. There was no struggle and barely a chase because the quarry was a mere lugger, a military supply ship that could never outsail the *Hannah S.* on any heading, in any wind.

He herded his prize proudly up the Delaware on a cold gray morning when most ships were going down, ahead of the ice that would soon close the river. At his side was Jake Mifflin of Solomons, a mate so skinny he could stand sideways in a hurricane and not get wet, so skilled he could sail a dory through a hurricane and stay dry. Near the Philadelphia docks, they heard the feeble trilling of a fife, saw a crowd collected by a big vessel with yellow topsides.

Big Tom wondered if he should fire a cannon salute. Then he saw the gunports in her side, the officers in their blue coats, and cried, "Jake! Come about."

"What fer?"

"That's a British warship, and every Loyalist in Philadelphia's cheerin' her."

On her quarterdeck, a lieutenant was running up a flag. In the raw wind, the colors snapped out straight, like wash frozen on a line—thirteen stripes, seven red and six white, with the Union Jack in the upper left quadrant.

Jake said, "That ain't no British flag I ever seen."

"And the officers got red facings on their coats. The British wear white."

"Aye. And how many colonies is it we got, anyway?"

"Thirteen . . . thirteen stripes for thirteen united colonies." Big Tom grinned at his first mate. "That's no British ship. It's part of our new navy. I guess we can anchor after all."

"The flag is called the Grand Union. I be the first man to raise it over an American deck."

"I'm proud to know you." Big Tom introduced himself to the lieutenant that night in the Tun Tavern. "Now, then, the thirteen stripes make sense, but why the Union Jack in the canton?"

"The United Colonies will rule themselves as part of the empire, but we'll squash Mother England into a corner, where she belongs."

"Well said." Big Tom gave the lieutenant's back a slap. "Allow me to buy you an ale, to toast the Grand Union, Lieutenant—"

"Jones. John Paul Jones, of the *Alfred.*"

"I'm Big Tom Stafford, master of the *Hannah S.,* also known as Master of the Chesapeake." He liked Rebecca's name for him, even if she meant it as a joke.

Jones was a smart-looking Scot with a thick burr in his speech and a thicker one under his hat, once he learned that Big Tom was a privateer. "Ye can be master of nothin' when ye're runnin' from the Royal Navy."

"I run from nothin' I can stand up to," said Big Tom, as quick to take offense as he was to pat a back. "Not ships . . . not lieutenants."

The anger flashed in Jones's eyes, but he touched his mug to Tom's, as if anger had no value at the moment. "I dinna mean to insult the Master of the Chesapeake. The navy can use men like ye, sailin' under a new flag of freedom."

"My flag be right in here." Big Tom tapped his chest and felt the letter he still carried, the letter burning a hole in his conscience. "But you might tell me, sir, does my old friend Nicholas Biddle sail under your flag?"

"He's captain of the *Andrew Doria,* that black-hulled brig anchored upstream. A fine man who believes as I do."

"How's that?"

"Give us fast ships, for we intend to go in harm's way." Jones took another drink. "Yer *Hannah S.,* she looks like she'd be a racehorse."

"She is. So are her sisters."

"Best get her downriver afore it freezes. But dinna worry"—Jones drained his mug—"Congress orders that when our squadron's ready, we're to take action in the Chesapeake and chase off Lord Dunmore's fleet. The navy'll protect yer home while ye take yer prizes and run from trouble. Good night, sir."

That remark stung so badly that Big Tom spent the rest of the night numbing himself with ale. After he had drunk all that he could and was oblivious to bitter wind and blowing snow, he walked along the waterfront to Biddle's ship. Lights were still burning in the stern gallery. It would be a simple thing to go aboard and sign on. . . .

Then he remembered the prize money in his pocket—crisp new Continental currency, an investment in the cause, as good as honor and better than specie. Besides, a privateer could do as he pleased, when he pleased, and consort with any woman he pleased, even one as loyal to the king as Rebecca Parrish.

"You'd like me to sew *what*?"

"A flag." Big Tom shifted in his chair, which sat in the Parrishes' parlor, in the space where Duncan the Elder's coffin had sat a year earlier.

Rebecca dug through the package of red and white fabric he had given her and found, at the center of the pile, the small Union Jack that he intended for the canton. She held it up and said, "You *have* a flag."

"Sew my new flag, and this is yours." He pulled another package from under the chair and gave it to her. "You said you would like some damask for draperies."

Slowly, so as to convey no excitement, Rebecca opened the package. "And you were listening . . . for a change."

Big Tom looked around the parlor—chairs covered in rose-colored fabric with wings so high that he feared he would fly away if he sat in one; a seraph of yellow with plum-colored stripes, on which Rebecca perched gracefully in a plum-colored dress; and on the wall behind her, a portrait of her father by Charles Willson Peale, the Annapolis saddlemaker who had gone to London to learn portraiture and now spent his time painting the troublemakers in Philadelphia.

"You've already gussied up these downstairs rooms." He lifted the fabric from her hands. It was a forest green, as she had requested. "Where will you use this?"

"In my bedchamber."

He held the fabric out at arm's length. "I'd love to see how it hangs there."

"Could you be any more transparent?"

"Could you be any more impenetrable?"

"Is that why you keep coming back? For the challenge?"

He laughed. "When I want a challenge, I'll join the Continental Navy."

Angrily she snatched the fabric from his hands and threw it at him. "There's to your Continental Navy. *And* to your smuggled fabric."

Big Tom pulled the fabric off his head. "I keep coming back because of the kisses you've given. And the way you insult me. No man would ever dare."

At that, she seemed to soften. Then she took him by the sleeve and led him up the staircase. But she did not take him to her bedchamber, as he hoped. Rather, she stopped at a room empty of everything but two trunks.

"This is what you've done to us," she said, the bitterness in her voice echoing through the room. "We helped build this colony, yet we're ready to flee at an instant. Some of the Loyalists have left already. More will go, us among them."

"Where?"

"My brother Duncan to London, I back to the plantation and my brother Samuel."

"Parrish Manor is but a short ride from Stafford Hall. May I visit you there?"

"If you promise me something."

"What?"

"That you'll not allow the Committee of Safety to confiscate our home after we leave, because of our political beliefs."

"That's—"

"*Promise!*" she said fiercely.

"I promise to do my best."

"You'll have to do more than your best."

He saw something in her eyes—a frankness, a willingness to barter—that emboldened him. "Is there a way that we can seal this promise?"

"Do you love me?"

"Love" was a word Big Tom seldom used. "I . . ."

"I didn't think so. I don't love you, either. But if you promise—"

"Yes."

"All right, then." She kicked shut the door and told Big Tom to sit on a trunk. He considered the bedchamber, but thought his suggestion might break the mood, such as it was. So he did as he was told.

Then she stood before him and hiked her dress up to her hips. She gathered up the underskirt, revealing a pair of strong legs swathed in black cotton hose, white thighs spilling over the garters, and a triangle of hair at the place where her thighs met.

Big Tom could not believe it was happening, or that this was the way she would have wanted it. He looked into her eyes, as if to ask, but her gaze was fixed upon the wall beyond him.

"Come on, then," she said. "Unbutton your breeches."

He obeyed again, but he did not tell her what he told other women—that the name Big Tom had many meanings. It was a lie, after all, and he was not sure it would matter to her anyway.

"Moisten your fingers," she said, "then yourself. I've heard it goes better if—"

Instead, he tenderly touched her. But she made no sound of pleasure. And the sound she made when he fitted her onto his lap—her legs astraddle him, her gaze still on the wall—was like the grunt a woman makes when she lifts a heavy load.

He whispered, "This posture is considered quite . . . unusual."

"I saw a painting of it in a foul book. It's sufficient. Now do your business."

So he cupped his hands around her bottom and rocked his hips, lifting her body up and down, faster and faster until he had . . . done his business.

"Now," she said before he slipped out of her, "the promise is sealed."

And suddenly he yearned for a clean horizon and an open sea.

vi
Hard-Hearted Times

The Continental Navy at Philadelphia did not fail in its attempt to drive Lord Dunmore from the Chesapeake. It did not even try. Instead, the commander chose to raid British supply depots in the Bahamas. So much for protecting American shores. So much for obeying the wishes of Congress.

Six months later, the nine-pounders of the Annapolis shore battery, hidden behind the earthworks called Fort Severn, were trained nervously on His Majesty's Ship *Fowey*, and Maryland's Governor Eden was leaving under a flag of truce.

In the foyer of his fine house, Governor's Councillor Duncan Parrish stood before a looking glass, put on his peruke, and prepared to leave with the governor.

Rebecca looked into the reflection of her brother's sad eyes and said, "I feel as if all the faces that have gazed into this glass over the years are gazing back. Perhaps we should take it with us."

"Our baggage train will take it to Parrish Manor."

"God's pity we can't take the whole house."

"Just take your harp to Parrish Manor and stay there quietly."

"And you wear your monk's cowl in London." She put on her sunbonnet. "If the rebels learn you're raising funds for Loyalist brigades—"

"I'll work, but quietly."

Rebecca looked at the sunlight pouring through the Palladian window. "I am loath to leave this house . . . loath to lose it."

"The seat of a rebel government is no place for a Loyalist."

"All right, then." She took out her snuffbox and tucked a pinch of tobacco into her cheek. "Let us go, heads high. We'll return when His Majesty ends this thing."

Black Jed and Sara were waiting at the Annapolis dock when the Parrishes came down Green Street, their two trunks and harp borne by slaves behind them.

"So it's come to this," said Black Jed.

"Is there anything we can do for you?" Sara rocked baby Charlton.

Rebecca angled her parasol so that it blocked the June sun from the child's eyes. "Keep your brother's promise."

"To what?" Black Jed knew that his brother had made many promises.

"Protect our Annapolis home from confiscation."

"An ambitious promise," said Black Jed.

"A solemn promise." Rebecca lowered her voice. "Big Tom would seal our love and guarantee that we would marry."

"Marry?" Black Jed did not think "marry" was a word his brother knew. "This is . . . uh . . . wonderful news. I'll remind him of his promise when he returns."

"*If* he returns," she said.

"For one in love, you seem hard-hearted about your beloved," said Sara.

Rebecca spit a stream of tobacco. "These are hard-hearted times."

Just then the British captain called through his speaking trumpet that the governor was ready and his council should join him or be left behind.

Duncan put a hand on Black Jed's arm. "Our father saved your father's life. Promise that you'll do what you can to save our house."

"I promise," said Black Jed solemnly.

Then came a flurry of kisses and embraces, some sincere, some not, but one thing was certain, as Sara said later: "Big Tom has promised to marry no one."

"That does not release me from a promise of my own," answered Black Jed.

vii
Harm's Way

Few who ventured onto the Chesapeake a year later could have had any hope that the Parrishes would be exiled much longer.

From north to south, the full hundred-twenty-mile length of the bay, there were sails—the mightiest armada ever gathered in America, two hundred and fifty towers of Royal Navy canvas, gliding north as serene as summer clouds.

Black Jed sailed his skipjack out past Greenbury Point to see the awesome sight. His crew consisted of his son, now almost three, and his father, visiting from the Patuxent and growing heavier by the month.

" . . . fiveteen . . . sixteen . . ." While little Charlton showed his counting skills, Jedediah said how grateful he was that the British had no interest in Annapolis or the Patuxent plantations.

"Jefferson's Declaration denounced the king," answered Black Jed. "'He has plundered our seas, ravaged our Coasts, burnt our towns.' So the British hold a mailed fist for Washington, a velvet glove for Annapolis. They know that men like me are lost to them. And they'll never lose the Parrishes. It's the uncommitted, like you—"

"I've committed both sons . . . one we've heard from just once in a year."

"Big Tom's doin' fine, bringin' prizes into open ports."

Just then little Charlton stopped his counting and shouted that something was coming toward them—*a sea monster!* "And there, another! And, Papa, there's another one! They're all over, Papa!"

Black Jed turned to larboard and ran slowly toward the monsters, for that was what they looked like—dozens of gray and brown bloated masses, each with four legs sticking straight out, a long neck . . .

"What are they, Papa?" The boy did not have the dark brow or steady gaze of his father. In looks, he favored his mother. No one yet knew if he had inherited their mutual hardheadedness. "What are they?"

"British defeat."

"They're dead horses," said Jedediah.

"That proves the British don't know how to fight us. They seize land, extract oaths of loyalty, and as soon as they leave, the land reverts to rebellion. Do they chase Washington? Split New England from the rest of the colonies? Or sail up the Chesapeake and march on Philadelphia?"

"You see all that in dead horses?"

"They've been on those ships for six weeks, while their generals dither and their horses die. If we can hang on until the British people tire of dead horses—"

"That horse ain't got no eyes!" cried Charlton. "What happened to his eyes?"

"Gulls, most likely."

"Grandpa, I bet you the next horse ain't got no eyes, either."

"How much?" Jedediah chuckled.

"One . . . one . . ." The little boy took a penny from his pocket. "One money."

Black Jed chuckled, too. "Pa, what are you teachin' my son?"

"To gamble. A gentlemanly wager is a sign of good breedin'." Jedediah gestured to the ships. "Look at the wager you and your brother have made."

Had Big Tom lost his bet?

Black Jed asked himself this question each day as he took his dutiful walk from the Fine Folly to the home of the Parrishes, which now quartered troops mustering from Annapolis. The house was a mess inside—walls defaced, moldings stripped for firewood, bedrolls spread everywhere, even in the grand foyer where Rebecca had once played her harp. But there had been no confiscation, and if the Continental dollar remained healthy, there would be none.

As a patriot with a mind for finance, Black Jed had been named paymaster for Maryland troops. Large sums of currency were put into his care, which he put to work for himself, in the finest paymaster's tradition. He purchased cargoes of salt smuggled into Maryland in Stafford vessels, sold the salt to the Continental army, took payment in Continental money. And his fortune grew.

But where was Big Tom?

At Christmas, a letter arrived at the Fine Folly to answer that question. Black Jed brought it to the upstairs sitting room, where his father was playing cards with little Charlton. "The news we've waited ten months for, Pa."

"Dead?"

"In the navy. He lost the *Hannah S.*," said Black Jed. "They were outrunning a blockade ship off Charleston when a squall struck. *Hannah* pitchpoled. Took everyone but Big Tom and Jake Mifflin with her."

"Jesus wept," said the old man.

"They're in Charleston"—Black Jed read from the letter—"'where Nicholas Biddle overhauls the frigate *Randolph.* My deliverance seems a sign from God, or maybe Pa, for Pa's right when he says honor means standing where the Lord puts you. I was put here to sign on with Biddle. The son for the soil can go privateerin' for himself. From here on, I wear a blue uniform and go in harm's way.'"

"In harm's way?" said Jedediah. "What does he mean?"

"That he'll be challengin' all those white sails."

Charlton told his grandfather to play a card. Jedediah threw down a king.

viii
Standing Where the Lord Puts You

The *Randolph,* named for the first president of the Continental Congress, was one of thirteen frigates built or bought for the

Continental Navy. And no less a shipbuilder than Big Tom Stafford was impressed by her. She was a hundred thirty-seven feet in length, armed with twenty-six twelve-pounders, and big enough for two hundred fifty officers and men.

Most sailors preferred privateering to serving in the Continental Navy. Privateers never picked on anything their own size, and the prize money was better. But Continental commanders were not averse to taking prizes, and Biddle was one of the best at it. His *Randolph* had made ninety thousand pounds on her last cruise. She was known as a lucky ship, and men scrambled to serve on her.

Big Tom dined with Biddle the night before the *Randolph* sailed, and he toasted, "To harm's way, Nicholas."

"To harm's way, Tom." Biddle's eyes were smart, his features well cut, but the fullness of his face softened his expression, conveying a mix of certainty and good humor, a fine combination in a twenty-eight-year-old commander.

"I run from nothin'," said Big Tom. "I owe it to you and the men I lost."

"You owe it to yourself," said Biddle, "and to our new navy."

On February 12, 1778, the *Randolph* came down Rebellion Road in consort with four small vessels of the North Carolina state navy, under orders to break the British blockade and open the port of Charleston. But when they reached the Atlantic, the British were already gone. So Biddle turned toward the West Indies to search for prizes of his own.

A month later, the *Randolph* and her small squadron were sailing north, some sixty leagues off Barbados, when a sail was sighted to windward, bearing down. She showed no colors. But cruising warships seldom showed colors before an action, often luring unsuspecting vessels into cannon range first.

"She's still hull-down." Biddle studied the sails through his glass. "Either a merchantman looking for protection or a British frigate looking for a fight."

Biddle's lieutenants clustered around him, and Big Tom asked, "Shall we change our headin', sir?"

Biddle glanced at the sun, which was not far from setting. "Haul to windward. This stranger seems so intent on catching us, we'll make it easy for him."

Two hours later, a quarter moon hung like a feeble lantern on the eastern horizon. The black shadow of the British ship had already passed the lead vessel in Biddle's squadron, arrogantly firing a warning shot and demanding that the little sloop identify itself. Now, she was bearing down on the *Randolph.*

Big Tom, commander of the bow guns—one, three, and five on the larboard side—stood at his station, as close to the enemy as he could get, right in harm's way. When the action began, he would begin it. He whispered to his gunners to blow up their matches, and the flames glowed like spirits in their hands.

"She's in for a surprise, lads," he whispered.

It was then that he heard a gasp from the number one gun.

"Quiet," he growled.

"She ain't no frigate." It was Jake Mifflin. "She's a goddamn two-decker."

A two-decker. Bloody Christ!

Now she was close enough that he could make out the whole black mass of her. A two-decker for certain. Sixty-four guns, half of them run out on the port side, ready to deliver three times the weight of iron the *Randolph* could throw.

"Who are you?" came a voice from the darkened Englishman. "Hoist your colors or we'll fire into you."

We should have run, thought Big Tom.

But there would be no running with Nicholas Biddle on the quarterdeck. He shouted, "This is the Continental frigate *Randolph*!"

And up went the Grand Union.

"*Fire!*" screamed Biddle.

And thirteen jets of flame shot out of the *Randolph.* Thirteen iron balls stunned the Englishman the way a small man stuns a big one with a surprise blow.

Then the Englishman let loose with a crushing explosion and a blinding burst of muzzle-flash light. Big Tom did not see all that happened, but he saw Jake Mifflin's midsection burst open by a cannonball as though he were a melon struck with a rock, and again he thought, We should have run.

Then he regained himself and cried, "Sponge your guns!"

But the crews were already doing it—sponging the barrels, loading linen bags of powder, then solid shot, running out the guns, pricking pins through their touchholes to break the powder bags, then—

"Fire!"

And stand where the Lord put you.

Before the Englishman could fire back, the well-drilled *Randolph* gunners drove three more broadsides into her, shattering planks, tearing up rigging, ripping off limbs. Meanwhile marines in the fighting tops were raining musket balls at British officers, at the gun captains, and, most importantly, at the powder monkeys—boys chosen for their small size and nimble feet, who could race through the smoke and blood, dodge recoiling guns and falling bodies, to fetch powder bags from the magazine in the bowels of the ship.

The Englishman lost her mizzen top and her bowsprit. Blood ran on her decks. But before long, it ran just as black on the decks of the *Randolph.*

For fifteen minutes, flurry after flurry, cannon flash after flash, the *Randolph* drove her iron fists into the Englishman and withstood every blow the Englishman landed. But neither could knock the other down, and finally they pulled apart.

Big Tom stayed at his station, encouraged his men, and called for his powder monkey.

Nicholas Biddle, crippled by a splinter wound in the thigh, sat on a stool and ordered his ship about for another go at the Englishman.

The men at the guns cheered.

Big Tom shouted that this time they would take her maintop and cripple her for certain. It was the last thing he said . . . or thought.

Because in the next instant the *Randolph* blew up . . . exploded into a million pieces . . . disappeared in a flash as bright as day . . . consumed by its own flames and swallowed in a great cloud of smoke that rained fittings and planks, cannon barrels and casks, and the vaporized essence of two hundred and fifty men onto the surface of the sea.

No one would ever know what had happened.

But Big Tom Stafford had stood where the Lord put him.

ix
A Woman's Fury

Black Jed brought the news of Tom's death to the Patuxent.

Old Jedediah stood on the dock, overlooking the broad river that Big Tom had navigated so many times, and he cried. Then he went up to the house and closed his door and spoke to no one . . . for three days.

Meanwhile Black Jed rode upstream to Parrish Manor.

The house was handsomer than Stafford Hall—a classic structure of two full stories, set on a hill above the river. But rebellion had been hard on Loyalists like the Parrishes, who could not trade tobacco and had been forced to turn instead to subsistence farming. The docks had fallen into disrepair. Chickens and hogs ran about shitting in front of the house. And the shit stuck to Black Jed's boots.

When she heard Black Jed's news, Rebecca said only that she hoped one brother would honor the commitments of another. It was hardly the reaction of a lover.

"I have no intention of marrying you," answered Black Jed sarcastically.

"Just save my family's Annapolis house."

"Had your brother not gone to the Loyalist enclaves of London—"

"But I've remained, and I own a third of the house."

"Why have you stayed?"

"I was born here. The Maryland earth is in my bones."

"Is it true that your brother raises money to support Loyalist brigades?"

"If he does, he does not do it well, considerin' how paltry the Loyalist efforts have been in the field."

Two hard questions, thought Black Jed, and two glib answers. He tried one more. "Did you love my brother?"

"No. And he did not love me."

"But you said he intended to marry you."

"Let us say we had an understanding that involved certain marital privileges."

And Black Jed almost laughed because, in this, he knew his brother well.

• • •

The French joined the fight that year, and colonial rebellion became global war. The Royal Navy was forced to loosen its grip on the Chesapeake, and for a time, Maryland ships sailed out with tobacco and back with European manufacture. The Staffords profited, and Black Jed invested in more blockade-runners, leaving others to privateer.

But something ugly was happening. It was called depreciation. To finance the war, the Continental Congress kept printing money with nothing backing it up. More and more of it was needed to buy less and less, and paper was never as good as French gold or a man's personal promise to pay at full value after the war.

At the end of 1778, a dollar in specie—gold or silver—was worth five Continental dollars. A year later, it was worth forty; a year after that, ninety. To a man who took payment in Continentals or Maryland currency, it was a long, hard slide. And Black Jed made it even harder on himself by speculating in paper money, buying it for five cents on the dollar, then one cent.

Someone, he said, had to show faith in the government. Someone had to keep faith with those who had died.

But things only grew worse.

The French were dilatory allies, and British ships were soon back in the Chesapeake, supporting armies attempting to cut off the southern colonies. The flow of goods to Annapolis was reduced, and a government in need of hard money finally turned to those deserted Loyalist houses.

The Confiscation Bill was passed in January of 1781. Properties were put up for auction across Maryland, but Continental money was not accepted. Personal credit or specie only.

Several Annapolis properties went quickly, like Lloyd Dulany's house, which fetched 2,745 pounds from an innkeeper. Most of the commissioners for the sale of confiscated British properties wanted to take the Parrish house outright, especially since an army of green-coated Loyalists, funded from London, had been raiding the lower Chesapeake with Benedict Arnold.

But Black Jed Stafford argued that Rebecca Parrish should not be made to pay for her brother's transgressions on the other side of the Atlantic. She should be treated like other Loyalists whose Annapolis homes were safe, those who had simply retreated to the country and stayed out of the fight.

He argued hard, as he had done when the mob burned the *Peggy Stewart,* and he forged a compromise. The Parrish house would be sold and one third of the profits given to one-third owner Rebecca Parrish. It was taken for 2,100 pounds by a Baltimore speculator who paid in gold. Out of this sum military creditor Black Jed Stafford received 300 pounds in specie, which greatly improved his own financial picture, despite his misgivings at accepting it.

A week later, Jedediah greeted his son in the blood-colored study at Stafford Hall. He had his arm over a basin of warm water, and leathery old Doc Nearling was crouched beside him.

"More bleeding, Pa?" said Black Jed.

"Best thing I know for dropsy," said Doc.

Jedediah grunted and tightened his heavy legs as Doc Nearling's lancet sliced into his radial vein. When the blood appeared, the old doctor untied the tourniquet, then massaged the vein, coaxing the blood to come. Then he slid the arm into the basin, and in a moment, the stream was fast and red.

"I know why you come down here," said old Jedediah, keeping his eyes on his son so as not to look into the basin.

"Rebecca Parrish—"

"She's called down vengeance on you. It's the talk of the river."

"That it is," said the old doctor. "Heard it myself when I went to tend her."

"Tend her?"

"Caught her hand in a well wheel. Lost two fingers. Took 'em off myself. Asked her why she was fetchin' water when one of the slaves could do it, and she just said she was thirsty. Makes sense, I reckon."

"Will she play the harp again?"

Doc Nearling grunted. "One-handed, maybe."

Black Jed told his father that he was going to Parrish Manor. "When I get back, I want you packed. I'm takin' you to Annapolis."

"I ain't leavin' Doc Nearling. He's the one keepin' me alive." Old Jedediah yawned as the blood drained out of him.

"We'll talk on that later." Black Jed believed a man who did not care for his father was no man, even if his father was as stubborn as an oak stump. And a man who would not face his accuser was no man, either. So Black Jed rode to Parrish Manor, which looked even worse than it had on his last visit.

Rebecca's sister-in-law, a frail yellow-haired woman, led Black Jed to the parlor, where Rebecca sat with the drapes pulled and her harp forlornly beside her.

"Who is it?" she growled.

"Black Jed Stafford." He could see nothing but a shadow.

She raised her head. "Bastard."

"How is your hand?"

"Do you know what it's like to make music in the most perfect shaft of sunlight on earth?" Her despair sounded as dark as the room. "And then to know that you will never play again, never sit in that sunlight again?"

He dropped the bag of gold guineas on the table in front of her. "Your share."

"You broke your promise."

"I did what I could. Had your brother not funded Loyalist brigades—"

"He's no better than you. A man of talk and money who pays others to fight for him. A coward. Big Tom was the only man among you."

"I did what I could."

Tobacco hit the spittoon. Then the shadow moved its arm, the hand dipped into the folds of the dress, and a flintlock appeared. "You didn't do enough."

The muzzle flash nearly blinded Black Jed. He was so close he could taste the saltpeter in the gunpowder, but he could not feel the wound, and he could not believe that Rebecca Parrish had missed from so close. Then he realized that the bullet had buried itself in the bag of hard money between them.

She spat a stream of tobacco and called him a coward again.

And that was the last he saw of Rebecca Parrish during the rebellion. But the word "coward" echoed in his head until March, when a skinny, sallow, redheaded Frenchman named the Marquis de Lafayette arrived with a thousand troops, bound for Virginia to battle Benedict Arnold's raiders.

X
Black Jed Makes a Stand

In Annapolis, Black Jed saw to the supply and comfort of Lafayette's troops, and when the French fleet could not get through to support them, Black Jed collected the barges to take them back up the bay. Then two British warships appeared off the Severn—the *Monk,* twenty guns, and the *Hope,* eighteen—and Lafayette was blockaded.

"General Washington, he is most grateful of all you have done," said Lafayette over a meal of smoked ham at Stafford's Fine Folly. He wore the blue-and-buff uniform of a Continental officer, and he ate with the mannered delicacy of a girl.

"I've used my money." Black Jed packed his pipe. "*You've* risked your life."

"My husband is too modest," said Sara from the other end of the long table. She wore a blue dress that plumped her breasts and made her look most enticing. "In truth, we've risked *everything.* We've even lost a brother."

Lafayette raised his glass to the portrait of Big Tom above the fireplace. "Your brother is an inspiration."

"We do not want to lose anything else." Sara leaned forward, giving Lafayette a better view of her charms. "If you stay here, sir, the British won't dare attack us."

Black Jed cleared his throat to let her know he saw through her coquetry.

"Many 'ave asked me to stay. But *mon général,* 'e orders that I return." Lafayette smiled coyly at Black Jed. "The British make this more difficult, unless someone with the blood of a 'ero, like your brother, chooses to help."

Black Jed blew smoke out his nose. He saw through Lafayette, too, but he said without hesitation, "I'll lead you out in the *Sara.* It's the last of my brother's ships. We'll hold off the British until you're away."

"*Mon général* will not forget you, *m'sieur.*"

Sara was furious, and when they went to bed, she let Black Jed know it. "You should not be risking your life. We should be keeping Lafayette here."

"Do I smell jasmine?"

"Why did you promise your help? You have nothing to prove. You stood for the idea of rebellion and backed up your beliefs with your fortune."

"Big Tom would have done it." He slipped his arms around her. She was thirty now. She had borne one child, lost two others, but still felt slim and girlish. He buried his face in the brown hair that cascaded down her back, and after a few moments he whispered, "Listen."

"To what?"

"How silent our house is . . . like a church."

In the darkness, she rolled toward him. Her breath was warm and sweet. He felt the press of her belly and breasts against him, and he responded like a boy, although he was thirty-nine.

He raised her nightgown. "One son for the soil and one for the sea."

"Or, if we're lucky, a daughter for me." Sara raised a leg and slipped herself onto him, and they went like that, on their sides, facing each other, and when they were done, she was crying.

"Sara—"

"I've always feared that if we lose, the British will do to us what we've done to the Loyalists . . . confiscate our home, leave us with nothing. . . . Now I fear—"

"All the more reason for me to stand where the Lord has put me."

The next day, a fair wind blew from the northwest, and Black Jed wanted to vomit. But he was more frightened of showing fear than he was of the British. So he kept his breakfast in his stomach and stuck to his plan.

His *Sara* was armed with six-pounders, no match for the twelve-pounders the British ships carried. But before dawn, he had manhandled two eighteen-pounders from the earthworks onto the *Sara* and her little consort, Colonel Nicholson's *Starling,* positioning the guns as bow chasers. Now his two ships came down the bay, trailed by the troop-laden barges of Lafayette.

Out beyond Greenbury Point, the British tacked back and forth like nervous dogs peeing on the edges of new turf.

At the maximum range for the eighteen-pounders, Black Jed gave the order to fire. The big guns roared, and a splash of water exploded just astern of the *Monk,* making her skitter away.

On the barges, the men cheered and guffawed.

Black Jed's guns barked again and again in the morning air. But the British answered with nothing more than a few ranging shots that fell far short, because while Black Jed bared his teeth, he also kept his distance.

Finally the British hounds hauled their wind and showed their tails.

Perhaps they feared the damage the eighteen-pounders could do. Or maybe they feared a fight with an enemy who had the wind, the tide, and the local knowledge. Or maybe, as the story was told later, they heard that Black Jed Stafford was in command of the American ships and out to avenge his brother.

That fall, the French fleet stopped the British from sailing *up* the Chesapeake. French and Continental troops marched through Annapolis on their way *down* the Chesapeake. And Washington bagged the British army at Yorktown.

Old Jedediah said the French papists had finally made amends to America. He had moved at last to Annapolis. His ankles had swollen so badly that they looked like sausages stuffed into his shoes. He had grown another chin. His big belly drooped toward his knees. His breathing was more work by the week. And no amount of bleeding seemed to help.

His last conversation with his son took place in the garden behind the Fine Folly one warm December day. "The Lord has given you a country. Build it right and protect it with a good navy, like the French used to help us stop the British, like we could have used to stop the French seventy years ago. Then hurry up and have that son for the sea."

"By the grace of God, Pa. By the grace of God."

xi
Christmas Visitors

Two years later, December laurels decorated the portraits of old Jedediah and Big Tom. The son for the sea hung over the dining room fireplace. His father's likeness hung between the windows. And their eyes were locked forever in a gaze that by turns seemed affectionate, challenging, angry, and conspiratorial, like the expressions that passed each day between Black Jed and his son Charlton.

It was finally, officially over. The treaties had been signed. The last British troops had left. And George Washington was coming to Stafford's Fine Folly for the grandest party that house would ever see.

Sara had invited a hundred of their closest friends and all the members of the new Congress, which was currently sitting at Annapolis. She had planned a buffet of cold pheasant, Chesapeake oysters, two huge hams, six kinds of cheese, exotic fruits from the West Indies, a hot Christmas punch that filled the house with the aroma of cloves, and champagne. There would be dancing in the great room, whist and loo in the upstairs parlor, candles illuminating every window. . . . A night to remember after so many to forget.

Governor Paca planned an even grander party for the next night, in the State House itself, when all of Annapolis would greet Washington. The following day, Washington would surrender his commission to Congress and head for Mount Vernon as a private citizen.

Sara looked in the mirror and straightened her French-made wig, which rose almost a foot above her head. Then she stood sideways to check her waist, which was held nicely by a jeweled stomacher.

"As slim as a girl, ma'am," said Henrietta, her slave.

Sara gave a sad little smile. "Would that it would swell again. . . . Oh, never mind. There's much yet to do." Sara took a pair of white gloves from the buffet and pulled them on. "Starting with my inspection."

And she went fingering her way about, examining mantels and picture frames for dust, looking for her reflection in silverware and brass door handles, searching for cobwebs behind doors, in corners.

"Shipshape and Bristol fashion" was the phrase Big Tom had always used. And in many ways, Stafford's Fine Folly was like a ship.

It was as tall as a mast—three full stories, with twelve-foot ceilings. The keel was the center hallway that divided the house from the front entrance to the French doors. Balanced around it, like cabins on a berthing deck, were the dining room opposite the front parlor, the double-sized great room opposite drawing room and library; and at the stern was the staircase, rising on either side of the French doors to the second-floor parlor and the canopied beds.

Little wallpaper had been used, and for all the fine mahogany furnishings the floors were rough and unwaxed, as was the custom. But the painted colors were as vibrant as those on the sides of some ships—Prussian blue offsetting white woodwork in the dining room and front parlor, glittering sunshine yellow in the great room, an earthy magenta for the second-floor woodwork.

Sara came into the bedroom just as Black Jed finished powdering his hair.

"Let other men wear wigs," she said. "You and General Washington will dominate the scene with no more than a little talc."

"He doesn't even need talc anymore. The war turned him gray."

"Oh, Jed"—she threw her arms around him—"the war took so much."

"But the new government will make good on that paper money. We'll build more ships, have more children. We owe it to them who died."

"We owe it to each other."

About an hour after the party had begun, an uninvited guest made her way through the streets of America's provisional capital.

She did not go past her old house. She had no stomach for that.

And when she stood before the Fine Folly, she tried not to think of the joy that Black Jed and Sara Stafford had known there on nights like this, with the snow falling gently and the music playing, or on summer evenings when they rocked in each other's arms. Such joys had not been ordained for Rebecca Parrish.

She'd had her life at Parrish Manor, assisting at the births of her brother's children, sucking bitter juice from the tobacco in her mouth, and planning this night.

She did not go up the front stairs. Instead, she walked around to the back and up to the French doors. She could see people milling about in the hallway—merchants, planters, their wives, members of Congress. The laughter was loud, the music well played. And she could almost feel the heat generated by the dancers.

She removed her cloak and left it on the railing. She spit her tobacco into the snow and straightened the feathered headdress that she hoped was still in style. Then she stepped into the house.

Two gentlemen in white wigs—Congressmen, perhaps—looked at her oddly.

"A breath of air, gentlemen, so that I may dance all the more." Before either of them could insinuate himself with her, she went into the great room, where the minuet was moving at its studied pace. Washington was dancing with Sara Stafford and looked surprisingly supple. Black Jed was dancing with the wife of Samuel Chase and looked surprisingly gay.

Rebecca snatched a glass of champagne from a tray and gulped half of it.

There was gentle applause when the music ended, polite conversation among the dancers, a small conference among the musicians as to their next piece. And Rebecca Parrish stalked through the gathering, straight for the spinet.

By the time she reached it, she had been recognized by half of the people in the room, including Black Jed and Sara. She leaned over the spinet player's shoulder and attacked the keyboard, pounding out what she could of a piece by Mozart, pouring herself into it, building her fury. And then she stopped abruptly.

Two people actually applauded.

"I do not play for your approval," she snapped. "Merely for your attention."

"It's been a long time, Rebecca." Black Jed worked his way toward her.

"Because I have no home in Annapolis, thanks to you and your confiscators."

Washington instinctively stepped into the controversy. "Is this Rebecca Parrish of the Loyalist Parrishes?"

"Rebecca Parrish who remained in the countryside, with her neutral brother, asking those who might have been her in-laws to save her house," she answered.

"I saw to it that you received a third of the proceeds," said Black Jed.

"And saw to it that you received a share yourself."

"As payment for credit extended to the state of Maryland."

By now all conversation in the house had ceased and the doorways to the great room were crowded with people.

"Black Jed Stafford did his country an invaluable service in the late war, madam," said Washington. "He deserved compensation."

"And what about me? My father died. My brother was driven to England. My hand was ruined. Then they took the Annapolis house where you yourself dined."

"You have our sympathies." Washington gave her a slight bow.

"I would prefer to have my Annapolis house back. But now it's a hotel."

"You may have your Annapolis *life* back," said Washington. "From what I know of your neighbors, they'll welcome you. And I'll welcome you to our grand ceremony the day after tomorrow."

This brought polite applause for the magnanimity of the general.

"As my Annapolis house is lost, how can I enjoy my Annapolis life?"

"We all lost in this war," Sara said angrily.

"We both lost the companionship of my brother," added Black Jed.

"Who promised that he would not allow my house to be confiscated," answered Rebecca.

"He had no power to fulfill that promise," said Black Jed.

"But *you* did," she said, "and you failed. You are not a man of your word."

This brought a gasp.

Washington strode toward her, extending his arm. "You speak too harshly, madam. A dance will dispose you more favorably toward—"

"You don't impress me, George Washington. You couldn't play a hand of whist if your life depended on it. It's an everlasting wonder to me that you could dupe the British for eight years."

Another gasp, and Washington's face reddened. He stood for a moment like a statue, his arm extended, as if still expecting her to take it.

Instead, she stalked toward the door, haughty and triumphant. There was only one more thing to say as she went past Sara. "Lay lightly on your Annapolis pillow, dear. Someday, I'll snatch it from under your head."

And she was gone.

After a moment Black Jed thought of something to rescue the moment. With a flourish, he pointed toward the door and announced, "There goes the woman who said we'd all be hanged for burning the *Peggy Stewart.*"

And even Washington laughed out loud.

CHAPTER TWO

Stafford's Fine Folly

October 8

Washington still looked terrific.

Every hair in place, uniform perfectly pressed, nice glow to his complexion, arm slightly raised, almost as if he were still expecting Rebecca Parrish to take it and dance. But he was only wax, standing forever in the Old Senate Chamber of the Maryland State House.

To learn about the Staffords' town, Susan was taking a tour, along with two grandmothers from Philadelphia and a family with their Academy-bound son.

The tour began at the waterfront, where Kunta Kinte, of *Roots* fame, first set foot in America, along with thousands of other slaves not immortalized in hardcover or miniseries. It moved on to the little house on Cornhill Street where portraitist Charles Willson Peale, who gave the eighteenth century a face, began his work as a saddlemaker. Then to the Old Senate Chamber.

Susan's guide was a thirty-five-year-old housewife with the bright-eyed enthusiasm of a true believer and the clothes of an eighteenth-century tavern wench. The costume made sense, she said, because the years between the French and Indian War and the Revolution were known as the Golden Age of Annapolis, and from what Susan had seen, the eighteenth century was still alive and well, despite the tourist trappings.

Black Jed Stafford would have had no trouble finding his way around. Annapolis boasted of more pre-Revolutionary brick buildings than any other city in America, and most of them had been restored. The original baroque layout of the streets still remained, and fortunately, the Naval Academy had been built on the northern edge of this red-brick world, along the riverbank and the landfill beyond.

"After two nights of partying," the guide explained, "Washington came before Congress. He could have made himself dictator. He had the army. He had the loyalty of the people. Instead, he surrendered his commission and passed power back to civil authority. It's one of the most important moments in American history."

Susan wondered if Rebecca Parrish was welcomed at the ceremony, as Washington had promised. Did she ever make good on her threat to Sara? In every big story, there were many small ones.

And from what Susan had so far read of *The Stafford Story,* she couldn't figure out what had the admiral so worried.

The tour went from State Circle to the neat little campus of Saint John's where the Annapolis Liberty Tree still stood, looking venerable and worried over, perhaps because it was the only Liberty Tree still alive in America. And a sequence took shape in Susan's mind—shot at dusk, steadicam swirling among the torches, tree backlit and looming . . . the night they burned the *Peggy Stewart.*

As the tour headed toward the waterfront again, the names of the fine houses came tripping off the guide's tongue: The Hammond-Harwood House, and across Maryland Avenue, the Chase-Lloyd House, and down Prince George Street, the house they still called Stafford's Fine Folly.

But what was behind it? Susan had expected a garden. Instead, there was a flat-roofed three-story building, almost as high as the house itself, looking about as out of place as an incinerator.

"Two nights before he handed in his commission," said the guide, "Washington danced here."

"Not in that thing in the back," said Susan.

"Oh, no. That came in 1907, a hotel. But by 1956, business had gone so bad that they turned it into an old-age home. Now it's on the market."

"Who owns it?" asked Susan.

"*Owned* it. Their names were the Shank sisters, from Brunswick, Maine, of all places. Somehow the house passed to them after moving back and forth between two old Annapolis families, the Staffords and the Parrishes, several times. The Shanks kept the nursing home running until they were ready for a home themselves. Their heirs are scattered all over, and none of them wants to pay to upgrade the old place, so—"

"It sure is nice," said one of the grandmothers. "I hope nobody tears it down."

"That can't happen," said the guide. "Our historic commission protects everything, and there's always Historic Annapolis."

"There certainly is," said someone else. "Everything you see is historic."

"Historic Annapolis has been on the case since the fifties, when an admiral's daughter named St. Clair Wright realized that her backwater hometown could be, as she called it, a museum without walls."

Susan tried to see the house through the eyes of Rebecca Parrish on the night she went there to spit on the Revolution—candles and lanterns glowing in every window, snow fluttering down. Now the October sunshine revealed paint peeling on window frames, gutters rotting, mortar crumbling between the bricks . . . and that *thing* behind the house.

"Can we go inside?" she asked.

"Oh, no. The place is a wreck. They never fixed it up . . . just let all those old people molder and—" The guide stopped, as though realizing she had gotten all downbeat. "Let's go down the street and see the Paca House. It'll show you what the Fine Folly looked like once."

At the Paca House, Historic Annapolis had revived the eighteenth century in a glory of mahogany furniture, Prussian blue woodwork, and well-tended gardens. It all proclaimed the wonder that the golden age must have been in Annapolis, a time of grace and beauty, of intellectual curiosity and . . . slavery.

A little cynicism always helped to bring Susan back to earth. The ones who had slaves could afford the time for intellectual curiosity.

And for a town that cherished its history, one part of it had disappeared rather early: the Parrish house, torn down in 1870, when Conduit Street was extended across Duke of Gloucester and run through to Spa Creek. So there would be no shots of Rebecca's grand foyer or its shaft of golden sunlight.

There would be plenty of shots of the last stop on the tour—the

Naval Academy, amidst the midshipmen. Bulletheads in training—that was how Susan had described midshipmen to her daughter. It was an attitude she was going to have to get rid of, along with her cynicism about military spending and the military in general.

She had never been on a college campus that was so damned . . . orderly. It was those blue uniforms and white officer's hats that did it. And the midshipmen seemed to move with an unerring sense of purpose that made them look far more mature than they probably were. No guys with earrings. No girls handing out pro-choice pamphlets. None of the messiness of life. And even though there were civilians everywhere, Susan felt distinctly out of place.

This was a world unto itself. How on earth could she get close to it? Or to the Staffords?

She started by trying to get into Stafford's Fine Folly.

She went there just after lunch time, climbed the front steps, rang the bell.

No answer.

She peered through the sidelights, but there was an inner door, so she couldn't see into the center hallway.

"What do you want?" The voice growled up behind her and nearly startled her off the steps. The caretaker was a balding black man in his early fifties, with football-pad shoulders and a blank expression that made the growling voice seem all the more disconcerting.

She flashed him a friendly smile and told him she was a PBS filmmaker planning to tell the story of the Staffords, and could she have a house tour?

"No tours. Place is fallin' apart inside. And I ain't got no use for Staffords."

"Oh." She wondered why. "Can I write to the owners?"

"They're dead."

"What about the trustee?"

"Don't know no trustee."

"So who signs your checks?"

"None of your damn business. Now, if you don't stop hangin' around here, I'll call the police."

Oliver Parrish, member of the bar of Maryland and Virginia,

pressed the button on his speakerphone and looked out the window. The Washington lunch crowd clogged the street—the army of lawyers, lobbyists, and paper-pushers spending the taxpayers into oblivion, and the tourists swarming between Ford's Theater, where they could see the pistol Booth used to shoot Lincoln, and the FBI, where they could see a tommy gun shoot up paper torsos. *What a country.*

"Someone making a film?" he asked.

"That's what she said." The voice of the caretaker, whose name was Simpson Church, echoed off the glass walls.

"Don't let her in. There's no reason to let anybody in." Oliver Parrish rubbed his hand over the bristles of his crew cut—blond running toward gray—and flexed his shoulders like a boxer before a match.

"Whatever you say."

"If it all works out, Simpson, I won't forget you."

"I don't want no Staffords to have that house, any more 'n you do."

Parrish clicked off, unconsciously flexed his shoulders again, and wrote "Susan Browne, PBS" on a pad, right beneath the name "Jack Stafford." Which was right beneath "Admiral Stafford & Institute for Advanced Naval Planning." Which was right beneath two names he had already crossed out: "Naval Academy Alumni Association" and "Historic Annapolis Foundation."

The Naval Academy Alumni had enough space at Ogle Hall on King George Street, and Historic Annapolis didn't have a prayer of raising the three million dollars the house was worth. He was glad they had dropped out, but not at all happy to hear about new competitors for the Fine Folly.

At the bed-and-breakfast, three messages were waiting for Susan: (1) Overnight mail delivery. (2) Daughter called from Boston. (3) Lieutenant Stephen Stafford can see you day after tomorrow; noon, south parking lot entrance, Pentagon.

She had hoped to meet the latest son for the sea a little sooner. After a visit to Stafford Hall and a taste of Jack's book, she was ready for a younger perspective on the Stafford history and the Stafford brothers. But that would have to wait.

So she called home. Her mother had moved in to take care of her daughter for the week, but Susan was never quite sure of who took care of whom.

People often commented on how much Susan's teenage daughter resembled her. The long, slender limbs, the serious, elongated face, the short haircut, a nineties update of the twenties bob, a haircut with a message: here was the kind of woman who could be as fun-loving as a girl in a beer commercial but was definitely nobody's fool.

A good day in school. A good day in the town where the Staffords had lived. A mysterious old house. Home on the weekend. Love you. Love you, too.

Then Susan opened the envelope. It was from Jack Stafford: "I'm busy trying to raise some L.A. money to buy the Stafford house. So instead of my smiling face, I enclose Book Three, which will introduce you to one of your own ancestors. Meet some real pirates, and another generation of Staffords and Parrishes. If you believe in foreshadowing, read closely. Those dead horses floating on the Chesapeake mean something. So does the birth of American subversive activity in the Tripolitan Desert. See you tomorrow. That's a promise."

The Stafford Story
Book Three
Boys and Honor
September 1786

On a late summer night, Black Jed and Sara made love, though Black Jed at first had no interest, as his mind was sunk in the failure of the latest Annapolis Convention.

He had helped plan it with Washington and like-minded men who believed that their squabbling confederation of states had to be bound more tightly. The nation was drowning in debt, local taxes were rising, and foreign pirates were circling. But the states could agree upon nothing. Only five sent delegates to Annapolis, and the host state was not among them.

So, on the night that the convention ended, Sara slipped into bed next to her husband and said that perhaps she could soothe his disappointment.

"I see no reason to bring another child into the world," he answered.

"After all our tryin', what makes you think we'll achieve the miracle tonight?" Then she added more playfully, "Let us try to perfect the union of man and woman, make it the first link in the great chain of national union."

"Phrased in that way, it would be unpatriotic of me to refuse."

That same night, at Parrish Manor, a yellow-haired infant named Samuel cried for his mother. But there was only a wet nurse to soothe him, because his mother had died to give him life.

In the morning, the infant's aunt Rebecca took perfumed soap and water to the room where her sister-in-law's body lay. With the help of an old slave woman, she undressed the body and washed it, starting with the feet and working carefully, even washing between the toes. She worked her way up the legs. She hesitated to wash the pudenda, torn as they were by the passage of the child, but she took another pinch of tobacco and went on.

As she washed across the belly to the sadly deflated breasts, she wondered at the forces that caused women to ignore the fevers, hemorrhages, and other horrors of childbirth, simply to couple with men, and she wondered why she had never felt these forces within herself. She had known no desire to be embraced by a man, no need to be filled ever again as Big Tom Stafford had filled her.

But now she would have to be mother to a baby, and to the two other yellow-haired children of her brother Samuel—studious Walter, troublesome little Robby. She resolved that she would do the job well.

In June of 1787, the states took a step closer to union when twelve of them finally, miraculously, convened in Philadelphia to discuss a constitutional union. That same month, the private union of Black Jed and Sara Stafford miraculously bore fruit—a baby girl with black hair and a fierce cry, christened Antonia, for Sara's mother.

In 1789, the still more miraculous year that Washington became president under a new constitution, another Stafford miracle occurred with the birth of another child, named Thomas Jason.

As the years passed, it became clear that the boy did not have the playful spirit or size of his namesake. Those had been the birthright of brother Charlton. Thomas Jason was of average height, like his mother, dark-haired and intense, like his father and sister, a boy who listened to what was said, absorbed, calculated, then acted. He was never called Tom. The name did not suit him. He was known to most as Jason, to his sister as Stubborn Little Jace, and to his father as the son for the sea.

At the age of six, Jason could name the six cities in which the six frigates of the new United States Navy were being built. At seven, he could sail a skipjack by himself. And at eight, he knew about the Barbary pirates of North Africa.

These brigands, as he explained it to his sister, demanded tribute from nations trading in the Mediterranean. Those who refused saw their ships seized, their crews enslaved, their cargoes sold in the bazaars of Casablanca, Algiers, Tunis, and Tripoli. "Father calls it a sorry president that we pay them."

"That's 'precedent,'" said his sister haughtily. "A sorry precedent."

At nine, he explained to her that the French, who had been our enemies and become our friends, were once more our enemies, having loosed their privateers on our shipping because we were trading with England. "Father says there's small difference twixt Barbary pirates and French privateers, and it's good that we're finally finishing the six frigates. Would you like me to name them for you?"

Antonia said no. She would name them herself. "*United States, Congress, President, Constitution, Constellation*, and *Chesapeake*."

Jason called it a sorry precedent that a girl should fill her head with such things, but secretly he was glad that she did. It gave him someone to talk to.

Meanwhile, brother Charlton had dreamed of becoming the son for the gaming table, but he had become the son for the soil instead.

Shortly after he finished his education at the College of William and Mary, Charlton married a plump and withdrawn young woman named Hannah Redgate, of Fairfax, Virginia, and took her to Stafford Hall.

Tidewater gossips could not understand his attraction to her. Despite what were called his manly flaws, Charlton was considered one of the most eligible young men on the Chesapeake, well bred, well off, shrewd in the ways of the tobacco business, possessed of a lion's mane of brown hair and a lion's lust for life as well.

It was not until people heard that Hannah Redgate's dowry included American Sultan, the magnificent breed stud that carried the blood of Selim, the first Arabian stallion in America, that the marriage made sense.

ii
Jason Meets the Parrish Boys

In the summer of 1799, Jason and Antonia went to Stafford Hall to visit their big brother. They were not close, Charlton being so much older. Jason would not have been interested in visiting at all but for a chance to test his sailing skills, and Antonia would not have been interested but for the presence of the famous horse and the possibility of a ride.

"American Sultan isn't exactly a *ridin'* horse," Charlton told his little sister the day after they arrived, "unless *he's* doin' the ridin' on some mare."

"Oh, let her ride the silly old horse," said Hannah.

And Antonia decided that Hannah would make a fine sister-in-law.

Jason decided otherwise, because in exchange for Antonia's ride on American Sultan, Hannah wanted to sail up the Patuxent.

"Can she haul a sheet?" asked Jason.

"We have slaves to make the beds," said Hannah.

"It's a sailin' term," said Charlton. "It's a line to work the sail."

"Well, I don't like boats. But it seems much the best way to see the neighboring plantations. My slave, Becky, can sheet the line."

"Haul the sheet," corrected Stubborn Little Jace. "My slave, Zeke, can do it."

"But Becky learns quick," Hannah said proudly.

"Too bad she's a slave, then," said Antonia, just twelve and already speaking her mind.

Hannah smiled, showing stubby little teeth. "Your brother warned me about your opinions, dear. But look out there. . . ."

From the veranda where they sat, the tobacco fields rolled a quarter mile to a line of trees, beyond which was the river, flowing slow and serene.

"What darkie wouldn't think that was heaven?"

Antonia thought she might have to change her opinion of Hannah Redgate Stafford.

The breeze the next day was southwest and steady. No threat of change, so they would run far and fast upstream, then beat hard all the way back.

Jason did not mind, so long as he was at the helm of the *Patuxent V*, a big skipjack the like of which no other boy on the Chesapeake commanded. Of course, the presence of his slave, Zeke, was a comfort he always welcomed.

Sailing was not a skill most slaves learned. But when Black Jed taught his son, he taught Zeke, too, because Zeke was smart and bull-strong, and could be trusted to keep the boy out of trouble in any weather.

Hannah had a fine time on the upstream journey, having brought a map of the area plantations, from which she read the names of the owners as they sailed past, and if she had a little gossip about someone, she added that, too, although Jason did not care and Zeke was not supposed to listen to such things.

It was not until she brought out fried chicken, peaches, and minted tea that Hannah stopped talking. This coincided with a rise in the wind and a sudden chop on the river. Jason and Zeke did not notice that Hannah was turning as green as her dress. Their eyes were fixed on another skipjack, a quarter mile upstream, sails set loosely, course angled toward the mouth of a creek.

"That's Parrish Creek, Miz Hannah," Zeke said.

"Oh, yes." Hannah smiled wanly. "The ones who don't like the Staffords."

Zeke chuckled. "We don't see much of 'em 'round 'Napolis way, but when they comes through, we always hears they been cussin' Staffords."

Jason took out his small spyglass and aimed it at the boat. "There's two aboard, Zeke. Kids. The tall one at the helm is watchin' the other one."

"Do what?"

"Can't tell. Head's goin' up and down kind of funny, but—"

"What's the name?"

Jason steadied his glass. "*Aunt Rebecca,* out of Parrish Manor."

"Well, they sure ain't much for sailormen."

Jason grinned. "We could take 'em, Zeke . . . take 'em to windward and beat 'em up their own creek."

"Make 'em think twice 'bout cussin' the Staffords."

Jason looked up at the sail. "Sheet 'er in, Zeke."

Hannah groaned. She was seasick . . . in a little river chop.

The *Patuxent* gained fast, but the helmsman of the *Aunt Rebecca* had turned his attention entirely to the activity in the bottom of his boat.

"We got him!" said Zeke. "Bring her in close and give him a salute."

Jason put the helm over carefully so as not to spill any of the wind. "Hey, the one just standin' up . . . does he have any breeches on?"

Hannah groaned again.

"No, Marse Jace, it don't seem he do."

"And now the other one's droppin' his."

"Must be gettin' ready to give a broadside of his own."

The tall one turned, revealing his own weapon, primed between his legs.

"Good God!" Hannah brought a hand to her eyes and clapped the other to her mouth.

On the *Aunt Rebecca*, a slave girl with coffee-colored skin looked over the gunwale. She was not much older than Jason himself, with budding breasts and a look of absolute terror on her face.

"Get out of here," shouted the tall, skinny one at the *Patuxent.*

"Yeah," shouted the other one. "Mind your own business."

But Jason's father had taught him that a man never let anyone hurt a woman . . . even a slave. So he brought the *Patuxent* close to the other boat and demanded, "What are you doin' to her?"

"*Fuckin'* her. Now be on your way."

Stubborn Little Jace knew what that was, having had some fatherly instruction. He glanced at Zeke, and Zeke glanced at Hannah, who was retching up dry heaves at the side.

And Zeke leaned over her, whispering, "I'd sure love a sandwich.

Bluefish and sliced rhubarb. Wash 'er down with a drink of buttermilk. Mmmm-mm."

That did it. Hannah fired a vomit broadside that carried right onto the deck of the *Aunt Rebecca*, bringing a riot of curses and shaking fists.

"Nobody think about fuckin' after somebody puke on his feets!" cried Zeke.

And the *Patuxent* shot ahead, showing her transom to the other boat.

"A Stafford!" cried the tall one. "A bloody Stafford!"

Jason put over the helm, turning sharply to starboard, cutting directly across the other boat's bow. "I've crossed your *t*, mister. I could blow you to bits if we was carryin' cannon, 'cause I'm the best sailor on the Chesapeake. Cuss my family again, I'll tell everyone what a little pecker you got."

And that was how Jason Stafford met the yellow-haired Samuel Parrish and his brother Robby, two motherless boys raised by their aunt Rebecca.

iii
Farewells

Four years later, Jason Stafford looked up at the great black hull of the *Philadelphia* and tried to swallow his homesickness.

He was almost fourteen now, older than most new midshipmen. But his father had refused to surrender his son to the discipline of the sea until the boy had studied history and the classics. And Jason was thankful, because it had delayed his leaving until now.

But the Barbary pirates were at it again, and Jason's warrant had come through, ordering him to Boston and the new Mediterranean squadron—seven ships, led by the *Constitution*, one of the original forty-fours; and the thirty-eight-gun *Philadelphia.*

This time, the bashaw of Tripoli was demanding a payment of $200,000 and a yearly tribute of $20,000 more. The new president, Thomas Jefferson, was sending Commodore Edward Preble instead. Preble said the Barbary potentates were "a deep-designing and artful treacherous set of villains, and nothing would keep them so quiet as a respectable naval force near them." Jefferson agreed.

It was a cold and miserable day, typical for springtime in Boston. The east wind blew in damp gusts. The sailors moved quickly about their tasks. Great casks, containing everything from bread to dried peas to water itself, rumbled along the cobblestone streets to the docks. Hammers rang. Officers shouted. Men sang as they worked in the rigging. And young boys bade good-bye to their families.

"Take care, Marse Jace," said Zeke.

Jason clasped the slave's hand, then his sister's.

"Stubborn Little Jace." The tip of Antonia's nose had turned bright red in the Boston cold. "Stay stubborn."

"Keep askin' hard questions," he answered.

"She asks too damn many." Black Jed laughed, then coughed.

For Jason, the voyage from Annapolis had been a tutorial in paternal advice, dispensed through a benevolent haze of pipe smoke. Now a few final words: "Remember, a man stands where God puts him, where his peers expect him to stand, and he does what's right. That's honor."

"A fine speech." The voice came from behind them, followed quickly by a shot of tobacco on the cobblestones. A woman with graying hair, a sun-browned face, and more wrinkles than a tobacco leaf stepped from behind a row of pork barrels. "I like the part about doin' what's right."

"Rebecca Parrish?" said Black Jed. "In Boston?"

"After a six-day coach ride."

"You could have traveled by boat."

"I'm given to seasickness. It's a marvel to me that two of my nephews chose the sea. We've put Robby aboard the *Constitution,* and"—she ushered forward the young man standing behind her—"I believe you know my Samuel."

He was taller and less scrawny now, his yellow hair slicked back, his blue jacket giving him a look of authority that Jason considered nothing but bad news. Samuel's eyes lingered with extra interest on Antonia's face. But his expression changed to something altogether malevolent when he said to Jason, "The best sailor on the Chesapeake . . . shippin' with *me?*"

"I . . . I have much to learn." Jason added the word "sir" for good measure.

"Samuel's the one to teach you." Rebecca spat another shot of tobacco.

"I'll rely on his honor," growled Black Jed.

"Parrishes are always reliable," answered Rebecca. "Unlike Staffords."

When the time came to leave, Jason wanted to throw his arms around his father but feared that he would seem unmanly. So he shook his father's hand, inhaled his father's tobacco scent, and went up the gangplank, his seabag on his shoulder and Samuel Parrish at his heels.

"Don't look so frightened, mister," said the tall and bony New Englander who met them, Surgeon's Mate Dr. Jonathan Cowdery. "There's no finer place to become a man than a frigate. Mr. Parrish will show you your berth."

Jason followed Parrish down three decks to the midshipman's berth, which smelled of many things, the most prominent being piss, and there Parrish ordered him to pull down his breeches.

"What?"

"What, *sir*? Pull 'em down or I'll have you caned for insubordination."

"But—"

A dirk appeared in Parrish's hand. "Drop 'em. Now."

And in the strange half-light of the orlop deck, Jason did as he was told.

Then he felt the cold metal blade lift his limp penis, as if this were part of some inspection. "A boy, with a boy's pecker." Parrish brought his face close to Jason's. "My pecker could split your mother in half, you hairless eunuch. Cross me on this voyage, and I'll cut that little thing off at the root. Understand?"

Jason nodded, and Parrish slapped him across the face. "Say '*Yes, sir*.'"

And Jason obeyed, his insides shriveling because already he had disappointed his father.

On the dock, they stared at the *Philadelphia* long after the boys had gone below.

"Strange, how the fates do throw us together," said Rebecca Parrish.

"The fates do strange things," said Black Jed. "That's why they're called fates."

"They gave me a family, though I never even wanted a husband."

"And that family now serves the nation you thought wronged you."

"The nation did wrong me. The nation might as well have taken what your brother took."

"My brother took nothing you did not wish to give." Black Jed sucked on his pipe, as he always did when vexed. He blew the smoke out his nose, as he always did when trying to vex someone else. "Besides, that was more than twenty years ago."

"So was this." Rebecca held up her left hand. The last two fingers were missing, the others grotesquely twisted. She seemed to know just how long to keep the hand visible for maximum impact, then she sweetly asked Antonia, "And where is your mother, dear?"

"She . . . she gets seasick, too, ma'am."

"Give her my regards. Tell her I have not forgotten my promise."

Black Jed coughed again, several loud and uncontrollable hacks.

"And smoke more," said Rebecca. "It'll soothe your lungs."

After Rebecca had gone, Antonia asked her father, "What promise?"

"A fool's promise, like the one your uncle made when he promised to protect her Annapolis house in the War for Independence."

Antonia did not think for too long on this. She had another farewell to make, to a midshipman sailing aboard the *Constitution.*

His name was Gideon Browne. She had met him two nights before, at a reception for midshipmen at Faneuil Hall, a slender young man whose reddish hair, high forehead, and beaklike nose might give his face character as he aged, but left him looking more gawkish than heroic among the other midshipmen that night.

It was not his face that had attracted her, however, but his honesty.

They had made a bit of small talk across the punch bowl. And she had asked the question that she asked all midshipmen she met: "Why did you join the navy?"

Most offered the usual answers: to serve their country, to command their own ships, to fulfill their families' expectations. But this one had given her a grin and admitted he had been thrown out of school for striking an instructor.

She had asked if the navy was then his only option.

He had answered that it was only the least boring.

So her father went grudgingly with her to the *Constitution* that day, but the famously bad-tempered Commodore Preble, angry at the pace of preparation, had closed the ship to visitors.

Antonia managed to pass a message to her young man, however, and a message came back, shouted to her through a gunport. "I'll write."

"Write soon," she said.

Then an officer's voice bellowed, "Mr. Browne!"

And that was all she saw of him.

iv
A Midshipman's First Voyage

That night, huddled in his berth, Jason told himself that things could only improve.

Samuel Parrish was more than willing to pull rank on the younger midshipmen, as if he already knew that in the navy, seniority mattered more than skill. He was obsequious to his superiors, supercilious to his underlings, and held his mouth in such a way that he could change a smile to a sneer in an instant, depending upon who was walking by. Midshipmen either aligned themselves with him or avoided him entirely. Fortunately, avoiding him was easy once the midshipmen had been divided into watches and the huge ship was under way.

It was also fortunate that the captain was William Bainbridge, a stern, distant man with a stern, deep cleft in his chin. He drove the midshipmen hard on deck and harder in wardroom classes, where they learned navigation, seamanship, history. Bainbridge permitted no rivalry to get out of hand. And no one referred to him by his nickname, not even behind his back.

Bad Luck Billy had been the first captain to strike his colors in the late troubles with France. And while commanding the armed schooner *George Washington*, he had been forced by the Dey of Algiers, one of the Barbary potentates, to carry tribute, passengers, and three dozen sheep to his overlord in Istanbul, all the while flying the Algerian flag over the American. But Jason was proud to sail with him. And even prouder that the *Philadelphia* was the first ship to take up blockade station off the city of Tripoli.

• • •

On the bright morning of October 31, 1803, Jason was on the foretop studying the bashaw's city when he spied a little Tripolitan boat to windward.

He sang out, and his voice cracked, then it dropped a full octave. Nothing could have gladdened him more, except the sight of hair sprouting between his legs. He already had the strong Stafford jaw, but he had developed slowly in his other parts and still conveyed a blue-eyed innocence when he spoke. Sailors showed no respect to beardless boys, but when a *man's* voice barked at them, by God, they'd pay heed.

He sang out again, *"Sail ho!"*

"Where away?" shouted Officer of the Deck David Porter, a wiry lieutenant with the workaday manner and iron will of a Yankee farmer plowing a field of rocks.

"Larboard bow, sir . . . uh . . . four points . . . uh, no . . . uh, six points—"

"Good enough." Porter by now had the little Tripolitan in his sights and was ordering the drummer to beat to quarters.

A moment later the captain was on deck, ordering a full spread of canvas, and the chase was on. As the mighty *Philadelphia* rose onto the waves, the Tripolitan ran hard for the shallows, but the leadsmen on the American frigate were calling a steady eight fathoms, so Bainbridge pounded on in the brilliant sunshine.

Then, from his perch in the foretop, Jason saw light green water where it should have been dark blue. He cried out, but Bad Luck Billy's luck was still bad.

The *Philadelphia* struck the shoal and stopped, stopped as suddenly as a saw striking a knot in a piece of wood. . . .

The next few hours were the worst agony Jason Stafford ever hoped to endure.

First, Bainbridge tried to pound the ship up and over the shoal, but all he did was bury the bow deeper in the sand. He ordered anchors, cannons, and fresh water thrown over to lighten the ship. He backed every sail, right to the t'gallants, in the hope of blowing her off by the stern. But none of it worked. And soon the Tripolitan gunboats came swarming like hounds to the wounded stag.

If the *Philadelphia* could have brought her remaining guns to bear, she would have flicked the Tripolitans off as though *she* were the hound and they no more than fleas, but the hull of Bad Luck Billy's ship met the shoal at the perfect angle to render his remaining guns useless, half of them pointing at the sky, half at the water.

To fight would be suicide. So Bad Luck Billy struck his colors.

The tide lifted the *Philadelphia* a few days later, and the Tripolitans brought her into the harbor under the Muslim triple crescent flag. From the windows of their prison in the former residence of the American consul, the officers who could bring themselves to watch cursed furiously.

When Commodore Preble heard the bashaw's demand—two million dollars for the new hostages, he said, "Would to God they had chosen death to slavery. Such determination might have saved them from either." Then he set about the business of getting them out.

V
The President's Mockingbird

Ten months later, Antonia Stafford watched Thomas Jefferson's big toe play peekaboo with the hole in his carpet slipper. She could not imagine stately Washington or priggish Adams shuffling about the half-finished presidential mansion in carpet slippers at midday, but her father had warned her that Jefferson was a man whose words and deeds were close-knit.

He had been elected as an antidote to his Federalist predecessors, who had believed that an almost royal presidency would symbolize the strong central government they championed. Jefferson believed in a broader-based democracy. He did not hold with ceremony, and he most certainly did not stand upon it.

He called for tea and asked Antonia her impressions of the capital city.

She allowed as how the fork of the Potomac was a nice place.

"Come, girl"—her father coughed—"say what you said on the walk over."

Jefferson cocked a bemused eyebrow at her and swung one leg over the other, so that his toe looked like a shrew popping its head out of a burrow. He was sixty, but seemed younger, with a broad face, a thin upper lip, calm blue eyes. His six feet and three did not make him look like a scarecrow, as his opponents suggested, but like one of the grand architects of the Republic, which he was.

In his presence, a seventeen-year-old girl should phrase herself carefully, so Antonia carefully considered what she had seen on her first trip to Washington.

The spine of the city was a muddy cart path grandiloquently called Pennsylvania Avenue. This connected the presidential mansion to the legislative building on what was called, with equally comic grandiloquence, Capitol Hill. A row of scrawny poplars lined the avenue, along with a few buildings on the north side. Nothing had yet been built on the south side because the ground was too marshy, and when the Potomac or the Tiber—another grandiloquence to describe another trickling little nuisance of a stream—overflowed their banks, Pennsylvania Avenue became a swamp.

There was a feeble cluster of boardinghouses around Capitol Hill for the legislators, another around the presidential mansion for the administrators, and for the traveler who came to this miserable backwater, there were only a few hotels, including one that had been built as a mansion—the prize in a failed lottery designed to lure people to the city.

Antonia thought it the most depressed and depressing place she had ever seen. But she could not say that to Jefferson. So she pointed out that she'd gotten more mosquito bites while walking between the boardinghouse and the presidential mansion than she'd suffered in a whole Annapolis summer. "This place is muddy, smelly, humid, and—"

"Rank," offered her father. "'Rank' is the best word you used, because it describes a lot of the *decisions* that have been made here, too."

While her father spoke, the president stared at Antonia with that bemused expression. The great prose poet of independence was widowed, and she could almost imagine herself captivating him. She had the utmost confidence in her bearing, and, thanks to a mother who had insisted that she receive an education, she was the equal of any male her age in her knowledge of the classics, the sciences, and the practice of Aristotelian logic.

Then Jefferson said, "The girl—"

And Antonia's little reverie ended. Jefferson's bemusement was simply that, bemusement that a mere *girl* could harbor opinions about anything.

"—has a fine vocabulary. This *is* a rank place . . . no place to be caught in August. I escape the bilious atmosphere for Monticello on Friday."

And her father gave her a little wink, as if to say that even the president spent as little time here as possible.

Black Jed was constantly watching for signs of stress in the delicate chain of states the Constitution had cobbled into a nation. The way they resolved their differences, he said, would tell much about the way Antonia's generation would confront the question that *his* had avoided—slavery. And the location of the capital had been a major difference, because in a nation so vast, those closest to the seat of power had the greatest influence.

After the Revolution, most southern states paid their war debts, but northern states wanted the national government to assume debts that they considered national in character. Solvent states like Virginia were not about to pay the bills of the debtor states like Massachusetts without receiving something in return. So Jefferson proposed to put the capital in the South.

His political enemies considered it poetic justice that he should now have to live there.

He unfolded himself from his chair and ambled over to the window. "Some say our new city reflects the poverty of the new nation. I prefer to consider the potential. No one knows what riches we've bought in this purchase of Louisiana—"

"Your mind is turned too much to the west, Tom." Black Jed stood in the window light beside the president. "Why have we heard no word of action in Tripoli since the burning of the *Philadelphia*?"

In February, America had thrilled to news that a raiding party from the *Constitution* had sneaked into Tripoli Harbor and set fire to the captured American frigate. England's Admiral Nelson had called it the "most daring act of the age." Tripoli's Bashaw Yusef had been so infuriated that he removed the *Philadelphia*'s officers from the American consulate to a castle dungeon.

"I would expect news of further action at any moment." Jefferson idly picked dead leaves from a plant on the sill.

"But you can't promise it. You have to build more ships, Tom. Forget campaign promises about reduced naval spending to reduce the public debt."

Jefferson kept his body turned toward his plants, but his eyes shifted to Black Jed. "Have you come to hear my plan or to lecture me?"

"Your secretary of the treasury calls the purchase of peace through tribute a matter of mere calculation. Purchasing peace is not a plan. It doesn't work."

Jefferson's complexion reddened, but he calmed himself by watering his philodendron. "I wrote this bashaw and warned him that we would rest our survival on our bravery at sea. But he chose to remember the dealings of Barbary with previous administrations."

"What do we know about this bashaw?" asked Black Jed.

"That he's as rapacious as Midas. That he killed one brother and exiled another to take his father's throne."

"A bully, Tom. Give him a blast of solid shot and be done with him."

Just then the president's mockingbird flew into the room and perched on his shoulder. Jefferson patted the bird and said, "These Barbary rulers live by the sword and die by it. The bashaw may resist simply because the only other choice is death."

This, Antonia knew, was her father's great fear: sacrificing his son for America's honor or a Muslim's pride.

The mockingbird flew up to a valance and squirted a long white dropping onto the drapery.

Jefferson said, "I'm sending Tobias Lear as political commissioner of the Mediterranean fleet, to negotiate a treaty to free the hostages, if need be. William Eaton goes as my naval agent for the Barbary Coast."

"Eaton? The diplomat?"

"He thinks he can remove this bashaw and replace him with his exiled brother. We are not in the business of interfering with other governments, but—" Jefferson picked up a teacup—"we will do all we can to free young Jason."

Antonia took the presidential teapot—fine Federalist silver emblazoned with a golden eagle—and freshened the presidential cup.

"An ocean protects us from Europe. A continent exists to satisfy our ambitions until the millennium. And yet, Miss Antonia, we must beggar our treasury building warships, dirty our hands with intrigue against foreign thrones . . ."

"I . . . I wish only to see my brother again. And with men like Gideon Browne—"

"Browne?"

"A midshipman," said Black Jed. "A boy with three hairs on his chin."

"We shall watch for his name," said Jefferson. "Boys have a way of becoming men."

vi
Solid Shot, Ancient Walls

Gideon Browne sharpened his dirk for the fourth time that morning.

A few hours earlier, he had been certain that heroism would come in this action. But . . . perhaps this was not the place for the son of a Harvard classics scholar. Perhaps he should not have volunteered.

But given a choice between the boredom of blockade and the exhilaration of fear, he preferred the stronger emotion. He clambered down the side of the *Constitution* and into Gunboat Number Four.

"Take the bow gun, Mr. Browne," said Lieutenant Stephen Decatur.

"Aye, sir." Gideon knew that if he performed well today, he would gain favor in many places, from the quarterdeck of the *Constitution* to the big house in Annapolis where Antonia Stafford made her home.

In the bashaw's dungeon, David Porter drew chalk constellations on the walls for his next lesson, while Surgeon's Mate Cowdery delivered a lecture to fifteen midshipmen, all of them wearing mended blue jackets and no-longer white waistcoats, in what they called University of the Prison.

"All right, lads." Cowdery stretched his index finger before the nose of Jason Stafford. "Consider the louse."

Jason squinted at the vermin on the tip of the doctor's finger. "Well, sir, I consider I got more 'n my share of louses."

"Lice."

"Aye, sir. Lice. And they itch like blazes." Several midshipmen snickered, but there was no contagion of mirth. The sound echoed through the dungeon, hurling itself against the walls like a trapped bird searching for an open window.

"Don't consider the itch of the louse, son." The surgeon's mate brought the creature close to his face. "Consider the *miracle.*"

When a superior conversed with him, Jason tried to offer an intelligent response. The midshipman who grafted a gentleman's manner to an iron will would rise high in the navy, or so his father said. Jason was not certain of his will, but imprisonment had given him time in which to work on the manner. "From what the sailors tell me, I *should* consider the lice . . . for my soup, I mean. Lice are like meat, if you have enough of them."

Captain Bainbridge looked up from the table, where he sat squeezing limes into a tin. "Don't be listening to common seamen."

The sound of the captain's voice snapped Jason so quickly from his stool that he kicked it over and sent it clattering across the floor. "Aye, sir."

"Be an officer." The captain's voice grew stronger. "Even in this foul place."

There was about Bainbridge a quiet gloom, not surprising in one who had run his career aground along with a thirty-six gun frigate. But Jason saw confidence, too, in the set of the captain's cleft chin and the steadiness of his gaze: he had done what he thought was right and his men were still alive.

Now Bad Luck Billy put on his officer's coat, as though preparing to stride a quarterdeck that no longer existed. He brushed the lint from his shoulders, a forlorn gesture, since the Tripolitans had taken his epaulettes when they took his ship. Then, with a small flourish, he flipped back his swallowtails, sat, dipped his quill in the lime juice, and began to write.

In each dispatch that he passed through the Dutch consul to Preble, he included a secret message, written in lime juice, invisible until held in front of a flame. In this way, he and Preble had planned the burning of the *Philadelphia,* but there had been no secret messages in over a week.

"Now, then," Dr. Cowdery went on, "the miracle of the louse is its insignificance. If the Lord's seen fit to give this creature a home in your scalp, what rapture does he hold for Christians who—"

"Guards coming," someone whispered.

Porter snatched one of the lime rinds from the captain's table, Parrish grabbed another, Bainbridge a third. Every man within reach stuffed one into his mouth, so that when the iron door swung open, the Tripolitan guard was greeted by a dozen men sucking limes and making strange faces.

The guard made a face of his own and said something to the small man behind him, who wore a white turban and a yellow silk robe. The man stepped forward smiling an inscrutable little smile at Dr. Cowdery. "Why is it that Americans suck limes to make their faces look like those of the tree monkey?"

"We are seamen, Sidi Mohammed. We suck limes to keep away scurvy."

"But so many? We eat not this many in Tripoli, but we have no scurvy."

Bainbridge took his lime out of his mouth. "Tell him we are jealous to protect the health of the bashaw's hostages."

Sidi Mohammed Dgheis was the bashaw's foreign minister, considered by the Americans the most sympathetic of all the bashaw's functionaries. He gave the captain a small bow, the delicacy of the gesture matched perfectly to the delicacy of his position, and asked Surgeon's Mate Cowdery to accompany him to the palace.

Cowdery lived there, a privilege gained when he cured the bashaw's daughter of an eye infection. Now he went about the city on his own parole, cared for important Tripolitan families, and was regularly admitted to the dungeon to attend officers and crew. Like a courtier, he bowed and feigned concern. "Is the bashaw ill?"

"No. The bashaw, he says"—Sidi Mohammed ran his tongue around the corners of his mouth and cast his eyes toward the window—"he says that there will be many more Americans to care for before the day is out."

In an instant, thirty officers were on their feet, some clambering for the window, others crushing in around Sidi Mohammed. Captain Bainbridge was demanding to know if any of his sailors had been hurt. Lieutenant Porter was promising retribution if they had. And Tripolitan guards were hurrying into the room to form a wall around the door.

Then Bainbridge shouted to his men, "Stand down! Thirty men

can't fight their way out of a city of twenty-five thousand! Stand down."

"Wisely spoken," said Sidi Mohammed from behind the guards. When the room was quiet, he added, "I ask once more for Dr. Cowdery. The rest of you watch the harbor through your window."

Cowdery grabbed his bag and looked at the midshipmen as though trying to remember something.

Samuel Parrish stepped forward. "I believe I'm on duty with you today, sir."

Jason hooked a leg around Parrish's and said, "No, sir. It's my duty."

Parrish tried to elbow him out of the way, but Jason held his ground.

Parrish tried to take every tour as assistant to the surgeon's mate. It meant a day of freedom in the sunlight and perhaps a visit to the sick of the bashaw's harem. Most midshipmen surrendered to Parrish. But Jason had grown taller in ten months and less intimidated. When it was his turn, he took it, no matter how hard Parrish scowled.

A moment later, Jason was scurrying along the stone corridor, straining to put on his coat, stumbling to keep pace with the doctor. Up one flight of stairs, then another, and a third . . . then Jason heard shouting, smelled the strong sweat of frightened men, and in the dim light, saw the sailors of the *Philadelphia*. They were running, scuffling, scrambling along the stone floors of the castle, each weighed down with cannon balls or bags of powder. And if any were seen to falter, a Tripolitan lash snapped.

"Something big's happenin', lad," whispered Dr. Cowdery.

"Big . . . yes," said Sidi Mohammed.

Up they went, into the sunshine on the rampart, where Tripolitan gun crews were running out their guns. Jason tried to peer over the embrasures and down into the harbor, but he could see no more than glimpses of the whitewashed city.

The Tripolitan flag—three stripes red, three stripes yellow—fluttered on buildings and battlements, reminding Jason of a clown's pantaloons, and he could hear sounds of laughter, as if a clown truly was coming, and people had climbed onto their rooftops to see him.

Bashaw Yusef Karamanli was watching from his balcony, peering through a brass telescope and joking at what he saw. His guests were laughing loudly, which was no surprise, as all were advised to laugh loudly when the bashaw was in the mood to joke.

Jason, who had seldom been out of his hole since the burning of the *Philadelphia,* stood now on a handsome tiled floor, on a balcony railed in gold, while servants offered him plates of dried fruit and cups of Tripolitan tea sweetened with hazelnut oil, and all around him were men who wore silk robes and jeweled earrings and carried their daggers in curved gold scabbards. Even the Mediterranean sun looked gold in the azure sky.

So Jason took a gold cup of tea, which was so strong that after a small sip, he could hear the blood rushing through his ears. Then the bashaw turned toward him, and Jason's knees went weak.

Yusef Karamanli seemed about the age of Captain Bainbridge, in his thirties, but where the captain had lost his presence, the bashaw seemed to absorb the presence of those around him. He was about as wide a man as Jason had ever seen, a mixture of muscle and fat and simple bulk, draped in a green silk robe, with a gold belt around his enormous waist, and a gold silk turban that made his head seem twice the size of a normal man's.

But for all his size, the bashaw seemed to know that the best way to disarm a man was warmly. He smiled at the doctor, then looked at Jason and let out a stream of words as Sidi Mohammed translated: "His Highness the bashaw, he welcomes Surgeon's Mate Cowdery and the midshipman who assists him. His Highness, he hopes they enjoy the hospitality of his palace. What is the bashaw's is theirs."

Dr. Cowdery gave the bashaw a slight bow of the head, then looked at Jason, as if prodding him to speak.

Jason said, "Uh, tell the bashaw . . . His Highness . . . I thank him for the tea."

As Sidi Mohammed turned to translate, the doctor whispered to Jason, "Don't be impressed by him, lad. He's a brigand. Consider the louse."

The bashaw gestured for the boy to drink down the rest of his tea. He even managed a few English words. " 'Sgood. 'Sgood, yes?"

So Jason finished it in a single swallow, gagged it down, gagged it back when it tried to come up, then nearly fell over from the pounding it brought to his head.

The bashaw laughed and led Jason toward the edge of the balcony.

The men near the railing parted like a silken curtain, and the harbor at last appeared before Jason Stafford.

The curve of the shoreline resembled the curve of a Muslim dagger. The southeast point was formed by Fort English. The walls of the city formed the blade. The handle was a breakwater running northeast, called the mole. And in truth, the city of Tripoli looked like a giant weapon. Cannon bristled everywhere—in the forts, along the walls, and out of every gunport in the circular three-story battery that formed the tip of the mole, like the finial on the dagger's handle.

There was the burned hulk of the *Philadelphia*. There were the rocks running northeast from the mole. And there was the Tripolitan fleet of nineteen gunboats pouring out through the channels between the rocks, a sight to strike fear in the belly of any merchant captain.

But beyond the rocks was a sight to strike fear in the belly of any Barbary pirate: the American Mediterranean Squadron, drawn close and cleared for action.

Jason could make out six gunboats, along with the brigs *Vixen* and *Siren*, the schooners *Enterprise, Argus*, and *Nautilus*. And standing off, under topsails and jibs, the *Constitution.*

Jason fixed his eyes on the battle ensign fluttering at the stern of the frigate. And one word filled his head: *freedom*.

But the bashaw was talking again, or sneering. And Sidi Mohammed was translating. "His Highness, he says it is too bad Jefferson will not pay his tribute. Instead, another American frigate will soon be his."

A mile and a half away, beyond the line of rocks, the sea was running at no more than a foot, and the tide had taken the flood. Conditions for the attack, thought Gideon Browne, were perfect.

He gauged the wind at a few knots out of the east. Even with a big lateen-rigged sail helping the oars, it would be ten minutes before they came into range of the Tripolitan gunboats. So he braced himself against his twenty-four-pounder and tried to ignore the roll of the deck beneath his feet and the roll of his lunch beneath his belt.

Gunboat Number Four, like its sisters, was an unwieldy twenty-five-ton scow with nothing to recommend it but a shallow draft. Preble had hired the gunboats and their oarsmen in Naples because he meant to engage the Tripolitans, not simply blockade them. But the shoals that had claimed the *Philadelphia* were still there, so a shallow draft meant as much as a full spread of canvas.

Up ahead, the Tripolitan gunboats were forming lines of battle in front of the main channel and around the molehead battery. They were not better sailers, but there were three times as many of them, they carried more men, and they added two brass howitzers to their bow guns. The Tripolitan gunners also held their fire, demonstrating more discipline than many Americans thought they possessed.

Except for the creak of the oars and the gentle push of the wind in the sails, an eerie silence fluttered across the sea, making the charge of the gunboats seem like the slow march of the clouds across the sky on a calm summer day. Gideon swallowed the metallic taste of fear in his mouth and watched the distance closing.

"Eyes on *Constitution,* Mr. Browne." Stephen Decatur came up beside him. "We'll hold our fire until she shows the signal pennant."

"Aye, sir." Gideon put his hand on his dirk, to keep from shaking.

No man in the American Navy had brought more glory onto himself than Stephen Decatur when he burned the *Philadelphia.*

Gideon had read the classics, and he could imagine Decatur as Odysseus, leading his men through terrible straits. Everything about Decatur reminded Gideon of a two-dollar word he had learned in school: "archetype." Beneath his officer's coat, Decatur's body was no more than muscle. And his face was not simply handsome, but arresting, with a nose like a dagger in its straight severity. Furious in battle yet beloved by his men, covered in glory yet committed to his duty—that was what they were saying about Decatur in the American newspapers—and he was only twenty-five.

If he feared to see twenty-six, he did not betray it. "We're nearing range. But there's no worse gunners than these Tripolines. After they fire, they'll try to board, for they think there's no better hand-to-hand fighters. But they haven't met us!"

That brought a cheer from the Americans, and the Neapolitan crewmen cheered, too, though they didn't know why; then the men on the other gunboats picked up the cheer as well.

Then the Tripolitans broke and came on under sail and oar. They were not so disciplined after all.

On the balcony, the bashaw was still boasting.

"His Highness, he says you Americans are afraid. You must be goaded into fighting. You are wise to be afraid but unwise to refuse to pay your ransom. The bashaw, he says you must tell your Captain Bainbridge to beg for the ransom, as it is the only way you will leave Tripoli . . . alive, that is." And Sidi Mohammed shrugged, as if to say he was only the messenger. "A thousand pardons."

Thanks to Porter's classes in naval tactics, Jason knew exactly what was happening: American gunboats would engage the Tripolitan defenders, while two bomb ketches moved in to deliver exploding shells and terror onto the populace. Then the marines might land and demand the hostages. And . . . *freedom.*

Now two Tripolitan boats were bearing down on the lead American. But when the American changed course to engage them, they fell off, taking themselves out of the fight before it began.

On Gunboat Number Four, the men were jeering at the Tripolitans while Gideon Browne tried to decide if he was relieved that they had fallen off, frustrated that the fight had not yet started, or frightened to the edge of incontinence. In truth, he was all three.

Then the attack flag fluttered up the *Constitution*'s mizzenmast. Gideon held his bladder and shouted, "The commodore shows his signal!"

From somewhere to the west came the first shot, the crumping thump of a thirteen-inch mortar on one of the bomb ketches. And Tripoli Harbor erupted with smoke and thunder and exploding splashes of water.

But Decatur was right. The Tripolitans were terrible gunners. He aimed Number Four at the nearest enemy boat and called for fire.

Gideon Browne lowered the match. There was a flash of fine powder in the touchhole, a blast of the muzzle. The gun jumped against its tackles like a furious bull. And the Tripolitan bow gunner was shredded. Half a dozen oars went limp in their holes, like the legs of a wounded beast, while the rest clawed frantically at the water, trying to pull the gunboat out of the path of the attacking American.

Then Decatur turned toward the gunboats anchored under the molehead battery, which looked like some kind of Romanist censer spouting smoke, and the Neapolitan oarsmen began to pray. So did Gideon.

• • •

The bashaw was still smiling, but it was the frozen smile of a host whose lamb had burned, whose dancing girls had fled. Several guests had already slipped from his presence, as shells from the bomb ketches came whistling down near the castle. And across the city, rooftops and balconies had emptied, too. But the bashaw was still offering a commentary.

"His Highness the bashaw, he says the Americans prove very good at chasing our gunboats, but what will they do if they catch them?"

"Sink them, Your Highness," said Jason Stafford.

"Watch yourself," whispered Dr. Cowdery.

"Watch closely," whispered Sidi Mohammed, refusing to translate.

And Dr. Cowdery looked out at the squadron. "Watch old Preble, too."

At first, the *Constitution* had remained beyond the rocks, cruising above the sulfurous clouds like some great bird of prey. Now she was closing. And the bashaw was watching, transfixed, through his telescope.

Jason imagined her gunports opening, her long twenty-fours running out, Preble calling for the gunners to blow up their matches. And then . . . He saw the broadside before he heard it. A great cloud burst from the black-and-gold starboard side of the *Constitution*. Then came a flash of fire from the muzzles, then a rolling rumble that Jason felt as much as heard. And for a moment, he swore, absolutely *swore*, that he could see the blurred black line created by fifteen cannonballs screaming toward the walls of Tripoli. An instant later, a tremendous cloud of masonry burst into the air along the north wall and the work of some ancient Roman architect came crumbling down.

The bashaw slammed his glass shut, and as he turned to the loyalists still left on his balcony, his breath was sucked out of him by a shell exploding at the base of his wall. Before the debris stopped falling, he was scurrying inside, his guards and his guests at his royal heels.

Only Jason and Dr. Cowdery were left watching from the balcony. But as there was little now to see through the smoke, Jason asked if they should go.

"Where to?"

"With your permission, sir, there's a little felucca tied up right at the base of the castle wall. In all the confusion, we could make it out to the fleet."

"I'm here on parole. My word of honor."

Then Jason saw Sidi Mohammed and the guards coming back to collect them. In an instant he made his decision. None would call it insubordination if he ran. So he saluted the doctor and slipped down a staircase just inside the balcony door.

Gunboat Number Four was grappled to a boatload of screaming Tripolitans, and Decatur called, "Boarders away!"

And Gideon Browne lost his nerve. He pretended to fumble with his dirk, while two dozen men went screaming over the side and waded into the pirates, leaving him alone with the prayer-spewing Neapolitan oarsmen and his own shame.

Then he saw Gunboat Number Two, commanded by Decatur's brother James. It was bearing down on them with a midshipman at the helm.

"Bloody pirates!" shouted the midshipman. "They surrendered, and when we boarded, the pirate captain pulled a pistol and shot . . . shot Lieutenant Decatur."

Stephen Decatur cried, "My brother?"

"Aye, sir. I'm taking him back to the *Constitution*."

"How bad?"

The midshipman looked at the body. "In the head, sir. Mortal, I'm afraid."

"What boat?" screamed Decatur from the deck of his captured Tripolitan.

"Sir?"

"What boat did this? What bloody *boat*?"

The midshipman pointed to a Tripolitan sweeping back through the rocks.

"She's damned!" cried Decatur.

In the darkness of the castle, Jason Stafford ran. And wherever he could, he ran *down*—down a long deserted corridor, down a stairwell, past a guard post at a narrow window, past a guard who did not see him because he was watching the battle and did not hear him because of the battle's roar, down and around a corner—at every turn expecting guards to grab him.

He avoided the corridor that led to the rampart. He knew that if he was caught, it would be the bastinado . . . or worse. So he found another dark stairwell and kept going. At a narrow window where the staircase turned, he stopped and peered out.

The *Constitution* had just unleashed a broadside that collapsed a minaret. In the inner harbor, one of the American gunboats had overtaken a Tripolitan and wild fighting had begun. *That* was the boat he would aim for.

As for the felucca in which he would make his escape, it was still two stories below him, and though he craned his neck, he could see no door in the base of the castle wall. But if he could find a rope and squeeze through this window . . .

Suddenly he sensed movement behind him . . . a whistling sound . . . a scimitar sweeping at his head. He ducked, and the blade struck the wall, splattering sparks.

One guard was coming up, the other down, so Jason dodged and double-stepped, slipped out of one guard's grasp, and went stumbling down the stairwell.

Gideon Browne fired a blast of close-range grape that raked the Tripolitan deck and killed half a dozen men. Then he joined his mates—eleven screaming Americans leaping onto the Tripolitan . . . eleven against twice as many . . . and a chance for Gideon to redeem himself.

In his goriest dreams, he had never imagined how ferocious he would become or the horror he would find in hand-to-hand fighting.

The gunpowder smoke and flowing sweat that all but blinded him . . . the stink of shit and fear . . . the smell of garlic and spit in the mouths of men close enough to be lovers . . . the blast of pistols . . . the clash of dirks and pikes and cutlasses . . . the sound of raw meat sliced and melons splattered, of flesh and skullbone struck by iron . . . the animal cries of agony and fury all mingled together . . .

In the middle of the deck, he saw Decatur fling himself at the Tripolitan captain, like a mad dog attacking a bear.

Another Tripolitan drew his cutlass and raised it to strike Decatur.

Seaman Daniel Frazier threw himself toward the Tripolitan, and without thinking, Gideon stepped between his captain and the cutlass.

The blade struck the seaman and glanced off Gideon just as he shot the Tripolitan dead.

Meanwhile, the mad dog and the bear went growling and gouging to the deck, and the battle suspended itself around them, for the winner of this single fight would win all.

A dagger slashed at Decatur.

Decatur bored his pistol into the Tripolitan's robe.

Gideon barely heard the pistol pop. But Decatur's fury ebbed as surely as the Tripolitan's life, and the spirit of the Tripolitan crew ebbed with it.

Gideon Browne looked at the man he had killed, his blood clotting on the deck. He had rescued his manhood, but he felt no bright light of glory washing down. He felt only nausea. Even boredom was better than hell.

They did not drag Jason Stafford to some dark chamber in the depths of the castle. They took him instead into the bright sun of the courtyard, where they removed his shoes and locked his feet into the stocks.

Now the bashaw stood defiantly on a pile of fresh-bombed rubble at the castle gate. Behind him a slave held a parasol over his head, while around him clustered guards, loyal guests, and the townspeople who had fled to the castle when the bombing began. "Bastinado!" he demanded, as though calling for a performance.

"You can't!" shouted Dr. Cowdery. Then he whispered to Jason, "You shouldn't have run, lad. Listen to me now, and maybe I can save your feet and your arse."

"Abase yourself," whispered Sidi Mohammed to Jason. "Beg the bashaw's mercy, and your suffering will be less."

But Jason had no room for more words in his head. He was too full of sensations: the heat of the sun on his neck, the pain around his wrists where they had tied him, the cotton-spitting thirst born of heat and fear, and the pride in what he and his navy had done. Even if it had led to this.

"The lad's off his head. He sees the master of the torture holdin' a club to beat on the soles of his feet and his arse, and—"

"I can take it, sir," said Jason.

Cowdery grabbed the boy by the chin. "Once they're done with you, you'll limp for the rest of your life. Say you're sorry."

"But the marines . . . they may be comin' through the gates any minute."

"The fleet's withdrawn, son. They came in to give the bashaw a scare. That's all."

Jason had hoped it would be otherwise, but he knew enough about warfare that he was not surprised. "Well, they scared him good, from what I could see."

"Scared indeed," said Sidi Mohammed, "but his anger they have not softened."

"Bastinado!" The bashaw now marched through the crowd to the stocks, which were mounted on a platform in the middle of the courtyard. The sweat dripped from the tip of his nose and soaked into his beard. Wet stains of fury and humiliation spread at his armpits. And his thick fingers played constantly at the dagger in his belt.

His closeness somehow intensified Jason's courage, like a magnifying glass focusing the rays of the sun. The boy sat up as straight as he could, though the movement rubbed the skin from his ankles. He clenched his teeth and set his square jaw so that the muscles flexed at the hinges, and he bore the stream of angry words that poured from the bashaw's mouth.

With a ministerial mixture of subtlety and deftness, Sidi Mohammed placed himself between the boy and the bashaw. "His Majesty the bashaw, he says to tell him why you ran away."

Jason tried to moisten his cracked lips, but his tongue was so dry it felt like holystone. "I did it because it's an officer's duty to try to escape. And a man who doesn't do his duty, he's a man who has no honor. And honor matters. His Majesty, he knows that. I'll bet he's even taught his sons that."

The bashaw listened to the translation and nodded. The mention of his sons seemed to soften him.

So Sidi Mohammed said something more, in a conciliating voice, to which the bashaw folded his arms and shook his head. "Bastinado."

Now the master of the torture came close, weighing his club. The crowd grew silent. Jason closed his eyes and thought about the Chesapeake. Then the first blow fell, and he heard the crowd roar. But for some reason, he barely felt the club strike the soles of his feet.

He opened his eyes and saw, instead of the master of the torture, the bashaw himself.

"Bastinado!" shouted the bashaw again, playing to the crowd. Then he pulled back the club and brought it whistling toward Jason's feet. And, a second time, he held the blow.

"Pretend it's hurtin', lad," whispered Dr. Cowdery.

Jason let out a loud yelp of pain, which drew a shout from the crowd and seemed to satisfy the bashaw, who turned once more to his people and spoke.

Sidi Mohammed translated: "His Majesty the bashaw, he says he lets no one escape punishment for his crimes, especially one who serves a criminal fleet, but he is a river of mercy. And his admiration for any who show bravery in the . . . holding up of honor . . . is great. The punishment is at an end."

Jason Stafford thanked his Christian God. When the bashaw looked at him and winked, Jason almost thanked Allah.

vii
Gideon Browne Meets the Bashaw's Boy

Rumors were flying like pennants in the American fleet.

The frigate *John Adams* had brought news that Commodore Samuel Barron would soon arrive with four more frigates and supersede Preble. The question now was whether Preble would remain on station as second-in-command.

"Preble deserves the glory of rescuing those men," said Decatur, as he and Gideon Browne took the captain's gig from the *Enterprise*, Decatur's new command, to the *Constitution*.

The gunboat action had changed Gideon's opinion about glory, to be sure, but glory still had its rewards, such as an invitation to dine at the commodore's table.

Up ahead, the *Constitution* rode at anchor, a deceptively peaceful silhouette against the red Mediterranean sky.

Decatur contemplated it for a time, then said, "It is also Preble's *duty* to rescue those men. Jefferson sends more ships, but he also sends Tobias Lear, a conciliator, and William Eaton, a conspirator."

"Eaton?" Gideon had heard the stories: the frontier soldier who masqueraded as an Indian and spied on a tribe in their own village; the diplomat whose diplomacy nearly got an American naval officer arrested in Tunis.

"Most officers speak badly of him," Decatur said. "But I like a man with spirit. You may like him, too. It was he who requested to dine with you this evening."

Gideon heard Eaton before he saw him. As they were rowed past the open windows of *Constitution*'s quarter gallery, a booming laugh shot forth like a cannon salute. Preble never laughed like that, and no officer laughed loudly in Preble's presence. It could only be Preble's guest, and he was still laughing when Decatur and Browne were ushered into the captain's dayroom.

Eaton and Preble. Fire and cold iron, thought Gideon. Or was it *ice* and iron? After all, Eaton was no more than forty, but his hair was already turning white. And he did not look like a warrior but like a bulky snowman with a broad red face, broad shoulders, broader belly, and beneath the swallowtail coat, a barrel of broad big ass.

He seemed a man of erudition, or at the very least, one skilled in the art of saying the right thing, delivering the requisite compliments and condolences to Decatur, then taking Gideon's hand to congratulate him on his bravery in the battle. "A pleasure to meet the son of the famous linguist, McCauley Browne. Commodore Preble tells me your papers indicate a command of French, Greek, and Arabic."

Gideon glanced at Preble, who nodded for the midshipman to speak. "I've studied Arabic, sir, though not mastered it."

"In the land of the blind," said Eaton, "a man with one eye is king. You may be of use to the president's naval agent for the Mediterranean."

The meal was as splendid as any Gideon had eaten since leaving America. One of the last of the ship's hogs was butchered for pork chops, then trimmed with dried peas and beans, along with pomegranates and dates from the countryside. They enjoyed the captain's port, and for dessert, a delicious seaman's concoction called duff—pork fat scrapings mixed with flour, raisins, and a little rum.

As they ate, Gideon heard Eaton's plan: find the bashaw's exiled brother in Egypt, raise around him an Arab army with American money and military advisers, cross the desert, and strike Tripoli from the land while the navy pounded away from the sea.

"A fine plan." Preble smoothed his thinning reddish hair, which was combed toward his forehead, in the fashion of a Roman warrior. "Were I remaining on station, I would help you to carry it through."

"In this navy, seniority sometimes outranks skill," said Eaton. "Had the president known of your recent attacks, he would never have superseded you."

"I will not remain as second-in-command." Preble strode to the stern gallery and stared out at the lights of Tripoli. "I have three weeks. No time to help you organize your lightning strike across the desert, Mr. Eaton. But as you're a diplomat, perhaps you would take my last offer to the bashaw."

"We'll see if your cannons have put a stripe in the skunk's beard. He might even tell me where his brother is hiding." Eaton then asked Decatur to detach his Arabic-speaking midshipman for the day.

"May he help you as much as he has helped me," said Decatur.

Eaton refilled Gideon's glass and raised his own. "To meeting the bashaw."

Gideon now felt as confident as a young man could in the presence of his superiors. He raised his glass and said sloppily, "To bashing the bashaw!"

When Eaton and the bashaw faced each other in the throne room the next day, each had a young American midshipman at his side.

In perfect Arabic, Eaton introduced his assistant, Mr. Browne.

Gideon nodded curtly to the bashaw, who did not even look at him. Instead, the bashaw raised his ring-studded left hand for Gideon's obeisance.

"Kiss the hand of the bashaw," said Sidi Mohammed Dgheis.

In English, Eaton whispered, "A distasteful thing to do, lad, but diplomats do distasteful things."

Still, Gideon hesitated. Every man had his pride. And kissing a brigand's hand was not a proud thing to do.

Then Gideon glanced at the midshipman seated next to the bashaw. Clearly this one had not suffered for swallowing what pride he might have. Compared to the sailors slaving on the walls of the castle, he looked downright healthy—glowing skin, shiny black hair, square jaw—someone without pride but comfortable . . . and someone quite familiar to Gideon.

Then Sidi Mohammed's voice hissed into Gideon's ear. "If the bashaw withdraws his hand, the interview will be at an end."

To give example, Eaton leaned forward and kissed the big ruby ring on the bashaw's third finger. "Go ahead, lad. Let's be done with the pleasantries."

So Gideon drew close, looked into the bearded frog face, and without breaking eye contact, bent down and touched his lips to one of the rings.

The bashaw withdrew his hand and grunted, "'Sgood. 'Sgood." Then he introduced *his* midshipman, Jason Stafford, whom he called his new teacher in things American, his one beacon of American honor.

Sidi Mohammed translated this, but Jason had been studying their language assiduously, so that he could follow even their private conversations.

He had also been studying Mr. Browne and saw the resentment in his eyes. There were many who resented the green sash Jason wore as a symbol of the bashaw's favor, many who thought he was a Turn-Turk. But when the name *Stafford* was spoken, Jason saw a new storm blow across Browne's face, from shock to anger to pained disappointment.

Jason said, "Would your first name be Gideon?"

"Would your sister's be Antonia?"

"I miss her," said Jason.

"What would she say if she saw the green sash?"

Jason could not answer that he had his captain's blessing to sit in the bashaw's palace, that he had been ordered to keep his eyes and ears open to everything while in the bashaw's favor. So he slipped his thumbs into the sash and said simply, "My sister would understand."

"I neither understand nor care why an American midshipman should be wearing your sash," announced Eaton in Arabic. "I have come for other reasons."

"Are you not him who told my brother he could steal my throne?" The bashaw popped a date into his mouth, chewed, and spit the seed at Eaton's feet.

"It is your brother's throne. He is older."

"He is a coward who ran away"—the bashaw's face brightened into a smile that promised a joke—"when I turned my face to the east and sneezed." And a great gust of laughter burst out of the bashaw.

Sidi Mohammed laughed as well.

What surprised Jason was that Eaton joined in, letting out a guffaw that lasted longer than the bashaw's.

And Jason felt the bashaw's eyes on him. The bashaw even made a small gesture, encouraging Jason. But Jason was no courtier, a fact he would make clear to Gideon Browne, so he barely cracked a smile.

Eaton, however, kept laughing. "Imagine, a single sneeze blowing a man across the desert. If our fleet could borrow some of the bashaw's snuff, we could sail 'round the world on the sneezes of the crewmen." He elbowed Gideon in the ribs and coaxed a laugh out of him, and that got Jason to laughing. Then Eaton looked again at the bashaw, made a mock sneeze of his own, and pretended to be knocked backward by the recoil.

The bashaw reacted with a great, silent intake of air. Rising to his role, Eaton sneezed again and staggered about like a harlequin clown in some Italian farce. The bashaw held his gut while tears of hilarity streamed down his cheeks.

And between laughs, Eaton took his advantage. "Tell me, Your Majesty, how far did your sneeze blow your brother?"

"All the way . . ." The bashaw gasped for breath. "All the way to Alexandria . . . where the Turkish viceroy—" Suddenly he stopped laughing.

"The Turkish viceroy? Yes?" Eaton coaxed.

The bashaw pulled himself up straight and turned to Jason. "Do you see why I have contempt for Americans? There is no honor in a man who steals a truth while pretending to offer good cheer. Do you not agree?"

Jason shifted his gaze from the bashaw to the Americans. His loyalty was being tested. No answer would be the right one.

"Do you not agree?" repeated the bashaw.

And Eaton interceded, speaking now in a cold and mirthless voice. "I have not come here to watch you taunt a midshipman, or to trick you. I am here to negotiate."

At this word, the bashaw's anger faded. He settled back and focused on Eaton. "Then no more tricks. *Negotiate.*"

"Commodore Preble offers forty thousand dollars for the hostages."

The bashaw studied Eaton in the motionless, sleepy way that a frog studies a fly before pouncing. But instead of flicking his tongue, he raised his left buttock from the chair and emitted a fart so loud that it echoed.

"Unh . . . His Majesty is not pleased," whispered Sidi Mohammed after a moment. "But he is a man of mercy, and has lowered his demand."

"To what?" Eaton kept his eyes on the bashaw.

And Jason cringed as the bashaw reached out and stroked his head. The look that crossed Gideon Browne's face made Jason feel even lower.

"This boy sees dishonor in his own country but misses his father," said the bashaw. "To send him and the others back, I will accept $200,000, with annual tribute of $20,000."

For a moment, there was silence. Then Eaton did the unthinkable: he walked up the three steps to the bashaw's throne.

Immediately, the bashaw's guards crossed their scimitars. Eaton ignored them and dug his eyes into the bashaw like two grappling irons.

Jason would never forget the tone of Eaton's voice, or his words, spoken in cold, clear Arabic. "The honor of my country will be redeemed by steel, not gold."

Sidi Mohammed gasped.

And Yusef Karamanli leaped to his feet. "Do you threaten the bashaw? Do you dare to threaten the bashaw?"

And a dozen more members of the guard raced into the room.

Karamanli shoved his face close to Eaton's. "You *do not* threaten the bashaw!"

Jason knew what a transgression Eaton had committed. He was certain that Eaton knew as well.

And the bashaw raged on. "I have American prisoners in my dungeon. You will pay me in *gold*, or I will use *my* steel"—he snapped his dagger from his belt—"to execute every one of them!"

Eaton did not even look at the dagger. "If one prisoner dies, I will see to it that Commodore Preble hangs you from the yardarm of the *Constitution.*"

Jason expected that the bashaw would drive his dagger into Eaton's breast, but the bashaw was so shocked by Eaton's boldness that he simply sputtered while his blade quivered in his hand.

Sidi Mohammed said, "These words are . . . are not diplomatic.

The bashaw is a merciful man, for Allah smiles upon the merciful, but you test his mercy."

Eaton, however, stood as calm as a rock in a thunderstorm and looked around the room. "I call on every man here to witness my oath, and I will remind them of it when this brigand swings from the yardarm."

The bashaw took a step backward, as though he had been struck in the face. Then he bellowed, "His head!"

And the guards descended on Eaton and Gideon Browne.

"*Both* of their heads," bellowed the bashaw, "before the sun sets!"

"But Your Majesty," said Jason, wrestling with his Arabic, "they come with a flag of truce!"

"No one insults the bashaw. Not even those he likes."

"Thank you, lad," Eaton said to Jason in English, "but before the bashaw takes my head, let him chew on this: if I don't return, the most powerful naval force ever assembled by the United States will batter this city to dust. *President, Congress, Essex*, and *Constellation* are joining the *Constitution*. If the bashaw takes our heads, he should cover his own and pray that Allah protects damn fools."

While Sidi Mohammed translated, the bashaw's expression evolved from contempt to concern and finally to fury. "You do not call the bashaw a fool! It is not permitted."

Sidi Mohammed drew close to his sovereign. "He must speak the truth to speak with such arrogance."

"Your Majesty," said Jason, reverting to English, "if it is my job to teach you of things American, remember . . . Americans will negotiate to free sailors, but they will not stand for killing a diplomat. Only *one* frigate has fired at you so far. When five broadsides hit at once, Tripoli will collapse."

The bashaw listened to the translation, his eyes narrowing, so that his brows drew into a single line across his face.

"Two American heads in exchange for a city," said Jason. "A good bargain."

And after a moment, the bashaw agreed. He curtly reiterated his demands, reduced but still exorbitant, then waved his hands for the Americans to be gone.

Before the bashaw changed his mind, Sidi Mohammed ordered the household guard to escort the Americans straight back to their gig.

Eaton shouted, "Well spoken, Mr. Midshipman! You'd make a fine diplomat."

"I'd prefer to be a naval officer, sir," said Jason.

That night, Gideon wrote a letter that would be posted to Annapolis: "I have seen your brother, and he seems in excellent health. For some reason he has been taken into the favor of the bashaw and sits at the bashaw's left hand. I am sure it is with the approval of Captain Bainbridge. He has my approval also, in that his wise counsel saved my head during negotiation between the bashaw and our naval agent, William Eaton. Weather is hot, duty mostly dull. I find that I think of you often."

viii
The Bashaw's Favor

A few nights later, as Gideon Browne studied celestial navigation in his billet, he was visited by Robby Parrish, a midshipman of solid physique and yellow hair who chafed enviously at the tales of glory he had heard of the gunboat raid. He had missed that action, and he yearned to do something heroic. After all, his brother was a prisoner, and who would not wish to free a brother from captivity, if only for the bragging rights?

Gideon kept his eyes on his book. "Did you know that man first learned to travel by the stars right here in the Mediterranean? We sail in the mother pool of civilization."

"The mother pool of cutthroats—"

"One and the same."

"And we're going to cleanse it. Preble has authorized another attack, and I've volunteered. Dicky Somers commands. Glory lies ahead."

This was news to get Gideon's attention. "How is this glory to be won?"

"We're loading a sloop to the rails with powder and shells. A giant floating bomb we'll make of her, then sail her up to the molehead battery, set the fuse, jump into our cutter, and pull for our lives."

Gideon slammed his book shut. "A single hot cannonball will blow you into a fine mist. A bomb ship is nothing but suicide."

"You've won your glory. Now you urge your friends to cowardice."

Gideon stood up so quickly that he bumped his head on the beam above him. "I urge you to do your *duty*. Sailing a bomb ship into Tripoli harbor is not your duty."

"Mr. Browne." The voice was as soft and intense as a flame. Decatur appeared from behind the mast footing. He wore only breeches, blouse, and white waistcoat, and his fingertips were ink-stained from writing in his log. "Confine yourself to quarters. I'll not have you questioning the valor of your mates."

"But, sir—"

Decatur stalked toward his cabin. "In fact, I'm transferring you to the *Argus* and Lieutenant Hull. You'll be hauling passengers to Egypt, well out of trouble."

And Parrish said to Gideon, "I'm sorry for you."

Gideon was even sorrier for Parrish, but he only wished him luck.

It was an hour later that Gideon heard another knock.

Decatur stood before him. "It may be suicide, the bomb-ship raid, but the volunteers are brave men. As for the *Argus*—let Parrish believe your transfer is a punishment. It will serve to stiffen his spine. In truth, your language skills put you once more in demand. Eaton wants you to sail with him to Egypt. He puts his plan in motion."

Jason Stafford now slept high in the castle, in a chamber of his own.

Such luxury caused him guilt, and many still resented it, especially Samuel Parrish. But Dr. Cowdery told Jason to enjoy his comfortable bed and his seclusion from thirty officers, their snores, sleep-farts, and imprisoned dreams of freedom, so long as he reported every conversation to Captain Bainbridge. He did this dutifully, and he slept soundly.

But one night, he was awakened by a cannon shot that drew him to the window.

The city slept. A layer of sea fog sat upon the water. On the ramparts, torches blazed, as they did each night. In the air above them floated the smoke of a signal cannon, fired on the approach of a little boat that had evaded the blockade and was now running into the harbor. The cannoneers were pointing at the boat and chattering, while a man on its deck could be seen running aft with a lantern.

It seemed of no great consequence, so Jason climbed back into bed.

A moment later the castle shook with the force of an explosion that lit Tripoli like the morning sun.

He knew in an instant what had happened. No blockade-runner would explode like that. It had been an American bomb ship. And her voyage had been a waste. She had exploded before doing any damage to the Tripolitan fleet, her mast spinning like a penny whirligig a hundred feet above the flames and smoke.

When Jason went to the officers' dungeon the next morning, Samuel Parrish met him first. "Midshipman Turn-Turk has arrived."

"I've come for Captain Bainbridge."

Parrish leaned close, so that none of the others could hear. "Does the bashaw think he can bugger Bad Luck Billy just because he buggers one of Billy's midshipmen?"

It was a moment for a man to make a stand. But this was no morning for personal fights. "I've come to fetch the captain."

Parrish slipped a finger into the green sash around Jason's waist. "Say *'sir.'* You've come for the captain, *sir,* Mr. Midshipman Turn-Turk."

"Take your hand off me . . . sir."

Parrish closed his hand on the sash, as if to rip it off. But the captain's cold voice came up behind him. "Leave him alone, Mr. Parrish. He is about my business. Now what is it, Stafford?"

It was a strange procession that moved that morning along the rocky strip at the base of the castle wall. Tripolitan guards led the way and brought up the rear, surrounding Jason, Captain Bainbridge, Dr. Cowdery, his assistant Samuel Parrish, and Sidi Mohammed.

Waiting on the beach was the bashaw, in a blood-red robe, surrounded by courtiers and lickspittles the like of which Jason had not seen since the day of the first attack. And all of them were taking great interest in what looked like twelve burned logs, lined up at the water's edge.

At some distance, Sidi Mohammed stopped and said the midshipmen could come no closer. "War makes awful sights of the dead and awful savages of the living. Be thankful that the bashaw spares your eyes."

Jason saw the gulls circling like vultures and realized that those logs on the beach were the bodies of the bomb-ship crew, and he was glad he had been ordered to remain where he was.

Bainbridge grew as grim as a twelve-pound shot. He straightened his waistcoat and clambered down the rocks.

The bashaw stood at the head of each charred corpse and made Bainbridge stand at the feet. He waved his arms, he shouted, he struck the dead men with the flat of his scimitar, and where a corpse still had hair, he grabbed it and lifted the head so that the dead face looked at the captain. Then he demanded that the captain identify the body. Each time, Bainbridge simply shook his head.

When the bashaw came to the corpse with yellow hair, Jason heard a gasp from Samuel Parrish.

The bashaw continued to shout, even as he turned abruptly and climbed the rocks. The rest scrambled after him while Sidi Mohammed scrambled to keep up the translation: "This is what will happen to every American who tries to sneak into Tripoli to strike terror or steal the bashaw's hostages. And this—I'm sorry—is what will happen to you if Preble does not pay the bashaw's tax."

"It's no tax," said Bainbridge. "It's tribute, and my country is done with tribute."

The bashaw climbed toward Jason, smiling as he came. The smiles of the bashaw expressed many moods. This one bespoke the cutthroat's pleasure at inflicting pain. And Jason hated him. So, it would seem, did Parrish, who whispered the words "bloody bastard" in Jason's ear.

"He is that," said Jason.

"I don't mean him," said Parrish. "I mean you, for consorting with him."

"I do as I am ordered," said Jason.

"And I do what honor commands." With that, Parrish sprang at the bashaw.

But Jason stuck out his foot and sent Parrish sprawling. In an instant, two guards were between their master and the midshipmen, but some futile fury had grasped Parrish and he tried to rise.

The penalty for a Christian striking a Muslim was death, and for striking the bashaw, worse than death. So Jason sat on Parrish and told him to stay where he was. "Or I'll order one of these guards to take off your head."

"Tell them to do it beside my brother."

And Jason understood: the yellow hair—two yellow-haired boys and a young slave on the *Aunt Rebecca*.

"Both of you, on your feet!" Doc Cowdery was hurrying to intervene.

Jason knew that the bashaw was about as full of himself as he could get, which made him the most dangerous. And Parrish was angry enough to think he could assault the bashaw, gain a bit of revenge and the admiration of the captain, and escape with no more than a little torture to enhance his reputation.

So Jason said to Sidi Mohammed, "Tell the bashaw it is a . . . a matter of honor. We were fighting over a matter of honor."

"We were fighting because—" Parrish tried to speak, but Jason stopped him by stomping on his foot.

"Hon-or." The bashaw said the word before Sidi Mohammed translated. Then he said it in his own language to the men around him, adding something that caused them all to laugh, and then they swept on toward the castle.

Parrish shot a glance at the captain, then turned to Jason. "We did not fight over honor. You struck me to stop me. I demand satisfaction."

"Stop you from what?" said the captain.

"Thrashing that bashaw. He defiled my brother's . . . my brother's corpse."

Bainbridge looked back at the towheaded body. "My sympathies. But if you were planning to thrash the bashaw, you owe Stafford your life. Now come along."

As he went by, Parrish said, "Someday I'll demand satisfaction."

ix
The Annapolis Races

It could take six weeks for news to reach America from the Mediterranean. So, when Rebecca Parrish went to Annapolis in September, she did not know that her nephew Robby was dead.

Of course, she seldom went to Annapolis. She found it difficult to see the once glorious capital fade. Most of her friends had gone to greener pastures or to their graves. Most business had gone to the deep harbor at Baltimore, the fastest-growing city in America. Most streets grew weeds along the edges.

Annapolis supplied surrounding plantations and provisioned an occasional warship. Otherwise, men raked oysters from small boats in months spelled with the letter *r*. Or they raked each other in political fights in months when the state legislature was in session. But sometimes in the fall, when the politicians came to town, the Annapolis Jockey Club put up a purse and the races were run once more.

So Rebecca came, not because she liked racing, but because she had a plan, inspired by the gentleman who walked with her that crisp September morning, a gentleman who had not been in Annapolis since the day he boarded the *Fowey.*

Few people recognized Rebecca or her brother Duncan. Age had withered him and wizened her. But passersby looked twice, because Duncan still wore a white peruke, a style that had gone out of fashion decades before.

"I've made provisions in my will to have all my horses shipped here after my death," Duncan said. "You and Samuel's children are my only blood."

"'Tis a pity you and dear Siobhan could have no children." Rebecca lied. The only thing luckier than his late wife's infertility was her inheritance, which had made Duncan wealthy a decade after he lost everything in the rebellion.

"The Lord deemed that I would father no children," said Duncan. "So I've bred horses instead. A few good horses can pay for themselves many times over."

Their walk had brought them to the front of their old house—red brick, slate gambrel roof, three steps above Duke of Gloucester Street, as handsome as ever. Then the door swung open and two men swaggered out, talking loudly about some bill before the Assembly.

"Would you like to go in?" Duncan asked. "They say the innkeeper turned the foyer into a handsome tavern with high ceilings and much light."

"No." Rebecca knew that even now she could not bear to see the house filled with drummers, horsemen, and politicians. "This place matters less to me now than the Stafford house."

"I think your hatred has outlived its use."

"Men can take satisfaction on the field of honor. Women need other ways."

"Black Jed and Sara will hold on to what's theirs."

"I'll outlive them, and I'll outsmart their elder son." She worked the tobacco in her cheek. "Beginning today."

The races were run about a mile outside the old town gate, on a course laid out before the rebellion. In the morning, the gentlemen—and a few ladies—gathered at the Three Mile Oak, beneath the fluttering pennants of the various tidewater stables, to inspect the horses and begin the betting.

As usual, Charlton Stafford could be found in a knot of bettors, bragging that his horse, Wild Rye, was unbeatable. Someone reminded him that he said that before every race, but today it seemed likely because he was running against Tory Dick, a skittish mount from the Patuxent plantation of Solomon Sherlock. In the midst of the betting, however, Sherlock received word from one of his slaves that his horse had come up lame. It was a ruse for which Sherlock, a Parrish neighbor, would receive the use of a Parrish tobacco field.

"I would happily offer my horse, sir," said the unfamiliar old man in the white peruke, "even up, for a match bet of two hundred and fifty dollars."

"Two hundred and fifty?" said Charlton.

Bettors all around stopped in the middle of their transactions.

"A large sum, sir," said Charlton.

"Do you accept?" asked the old man.

"Proudly." Charlton bowed. "Now, the name of the horse and his owner?"

"The horse is Duke of the Nile."

The name of one of the most famous horses in England brought a gasp of shock, which drew the attention of Black Jed Stafford away from a horse he was inspecting. At the sight of the white peruke, he cried, "Duncan Parrish!"

"My old friend." Duncan extended his hand.

Black Jed shook warily. "I've heard of the fame of your horses in England."

"So have I," said Charlton, who had lost most of his color.

"Have you accepted his wager?" Black Jed asked his son.

"I have, and—"

"Your word is good," said Black Jed firmly.

"My word is my bond," said Charlton, "though a horseman who conceals his identity—"

"I conceal nothing, sir," answered Duncan. "You accepted impulsively. . . . If you prefer to withdraw . . ."

Charlton set his chin at an elevated angle. It was followed—quite unusually for a Stafford—by a young and liquid roll of fat. "I withdraw from nothing."

And it was a race that Annapolis would always remember.

Wild Rye, ridden by a Baltimore jockey, bolted to an early lead, but Duke of the Nile never let the Stafford horse, or the Stafford bettors, feel comfortable.

Down the back stretch they pounded, around the first turn, and past the bubbling spring where Duke of the Nile made his move. In three powerful leaps, the big horse bounded ahead of Wild Rye and stretched his lead to three lengths.

Now the bettors began to shout for the English favorite.

Charlton watched through a spyglass. Black Jed sucked on his pipe. Antonia, who had come running when she heard about the race, whispered the name Wild Rye again and again.

And Wild Rye must have heard, because at the next turn the big chestnut horse seemed to find speed he had never shown before. To those with the best view, Duke of the Nile all but stopped in his shoes and Wild Rye streaked past the Three Mile Oak the winner.

The cheer that went up could have been heard on the eastern shore.

Antonia threw her arms around her brother's neck. Black Jed pounded Duncan Parrish on the back. And Charlton cried that all drinks were on him—or, more specifically, on Duncan Parrish—at Middleton's.

"I shall see you there presently." Duncan saluted the crowd with his cane, then offered his arm to his sister.

Rebecca whispered, "He now believes his horses are the equal of yours."

"It's a dishonorable thing we've done."

Just then an apprentice typesetter from the Maryland *Gazette* came hurrying down West Street toward the crowd, with a stack of fresh-printed newssheets under his arm. "Bad news from Tripoli!" he shouted. "Bad news!"

And the crowd clamored toward him. After all, in addition to

Jason Stafford and Samuel Parrish, Annapolis could claim one of the medical officers aboard the *Philadelphia* as well as Midshipmen William Mann and Robert Parrish of the *Constitution*.

Antonia prayed that the news did not concern her brother or Gideon Browne.

Rebecca prayed for her nephews.

It was Rebecca's prayer that was not answered, and in the fevered logic of grief, she blamed the Staffords for this, too.

A few months later, Antonia received a letter from Gideon.

His first letter had described a meeting with Jason in the bashaw's throne room. This had caused her father great worry. What, he had wondered, had his son done to deserve such favor? It was said that some Barbary rulers took more than a fatherly interest in young boys. Had his son been one of them?

The second letter described William Eaton's plan for crossing the Libyan desert to free the hostages. Gideon wrote that after they took the cities of Derna and Benghazi, he would personally lead the attack on Tripoli's walls to save her brother from the evil bashaw. This caused Antonia great hope and even greater worry.

X
Americans in the Desert

The vultures watched everything that moved on the desert plateau of North Africa. They soared on the currents of air rising from the hot sand. They glided in the breeze that blew off the Mediterranean. And they waited for things to die. That spring, they followed a great dust cloud traveling from Egypt into the Libyan desert.

It marked one of the strangest armies that ever marched. And while the desert was no place for a naval midshipman, marching was better than the boredom of blockade duty, or so Gideon Browne told himself.

Commodore Barron had offered Eaton little support—three small ships, commanded by Lieutenant Isaac Hull, eight American marines, and three midshipmen—to augment the forty thousand dollars authorized by the president.

So Eaton had hired a hundred European soldiers of fortune—Macedonians, Bulgarians, Greek cannoneers, Alexandrian Greek cavalrymen, deserters from the British army, deserters from the French—who fought for American pay and for the simple fun of fighting.

Two hundred Bedouin tribesmen, who considered a chance for booty reason enough to cross any desert, had also taken American coin.

And two hundred exiled Tripolitans had joined for no reason but to return the rightful bashaw to his throne.

And there was the problem.

When Hamet Karamanli, the bashaw's brother, came out of the Egyptian desert to meet Eaton, his first comment was that it was very hot, so he would need a cool tent in which to talk and a cool drink to soothe his throat. After tent and drink were provided, he announced that he was no warrior but would march if others fought and America paid the bill. With his sparrowlike gestures, sparrowlike voice, and corresponding powers of concentration, he was no leader of men, and surely no match for the brother who had taken his throne and imprisoned his family.

But Eaton said Hamet was America's best hope for an honorable settlement of the Tripolitan business, especially given the Muslim motto: "Never trust a Christian."

And the Christians showed the Muslims no greater trust than they were given. They camped separately at night, marched separately by day, and more than once stood off over some insult, real or imagined.

Only the force of Eaton's will had kept them together.

On the first day, he had ridden to the head of the column in his American officer's uniform. "The better to impress them," he told Gideon. But by the end of the week, he was dressed like an Arab, speaking Arabic, sitting on the ground cross-legged, and eating with his left hand, like an Arab, all but becoming Arab, as if to understand them so that he could better lead them.

Each day the dust rose like dense, choking smoke, the Bedouins shouted at the Tripolitans, the Christians at the Muslims, and Lieutenant Presley Neville O'Bannon of the U.S. Marines shouted at everyone. So Gideon was happy to scout ahead into a canyon that the Arabs said would bring good riding.

He sucked on three smooth pebbles to keep his mind off his thirst.

He did his best to ignore the sand flies buzzing about his head. He wore a kaffiyeh across his face to keep the sun off his nose. And he let his guide do the talking.

"Eaton Pasha is wise," said Idi, a small man with very bad teeth and a very long musket.

"How so?" Gideon asked.

"Each day you study your compass and look at the sun and say, 'No, Eaton Pasha, ride this way. Yes, Eaton Pasha, ride that.' Eaton Pasha thinks you have too many opinions, I think. He sends you ahead, so that you will not bother him."

"Eaton Pasha is wise." Gideon looked up at the rocks and decided to mark the place. So he took out his compass, the cover inscribed: "To Gideon, for finding his way, from McCauley Browne, his father, January 1, 1803." As he snapped it open, a musket shot cracked and a shower of Idi's blood struck Gideon in the face.

The shot had come from the rocks to the south. Then another came from the north, missing everything. A third struck his horse square in the face, and Gideon was down, pinned beneath the dying animal.

Then the bandits descended like hyenas ahead of the vultures. There were seven or eight, sheathed in dark robes, with black kaffiyehs covering their faces. One grabbed Idi's horse while another stripped his body of valuables and a third took his rifle. Two others came scuttling for Gideon.

He could kill only one, perhaps two if he fought while pinned beneath his horse, so he chose the route of common sense and put up his hands.

One snatched the compass glittering in the sand beside him. The other pulled Gideon's pistol and dirk from his belt.

And in Arabic, Gideon said, "Friend."

The eyes above the kaffiyeh opened wide in surprise. This one, who was the headman, growled, "Are you with that column of dogs crossing our desert?"

"No dogs. A great army. And they will be very angry if I do not return."

The headman examined the blue coat and polished brass buttons of Gideon's midshipman's jacket. "Are you the one they call Eaton, who is seen sometimes in soldiers' clothes, sometimes in the robes of a tribesman?"

"No. Eaton Pasha is far greater than I."

"Then you are of no use," said the headman casually, as though rejecting a melon in the bazaar, and he raised his scimitar above Gideon's head.

In the flash of the blade, Gideon thought how foolish it was to die here.

And someone shouted, "Stop!"

The headman turned to a man in black robes, who rode down into the ancient riverbed that formed the canyon.

One of the bandits laughed at such a fool. Another said it was a trick.

The headman told them both to be quiet and listen for their lookouts above. Then he called to the rider, "Who are you?"

"I am Ali Gurgheis, loyal to the rightful bashaw of Tripoli."

"Are *you* with that column of dogs crossing my desert?"

"I am your friend, and this red-haired Christian is *my* friend. Who are you?"

"I am"—the headman brought his blade to Gideon's throat—"I am he who plans to kill this trespassing Christian."

"He does not trespass. He blunders. He even needs a compass to find his way."

One of the bandits held up Gideon's compass and grinned.

"You do not need that, my friend," said Ali. "In the desert we live by our wits. We honor our fathers and find our way by the stars. We also offer our hospitality to those who are lost . . . even Christians."

"If you are our friend," said the headman, "prove it and throw us your musket."

To Gideon's amazement, Ali did as he was asked. Greedily the headman dropped his scimitar to catch the musket, and after inspecting it, he aimed it, first at Gideon, then at Ali.

And Gideon saw that the headman's scimitar was no more than a few feet from his hand.

"So," said Ali, "about my friend."

"We will trade him to you for your horse."

"But I have already given you my musket."

"Which proves you are our friend, as well as a lover of Christians."

So Ali slipped from the horse. Had he come alone? Gideon wondered. Had he ridden ahead and stumbled upon this scene? Or was this part of a larger plan?

The headman looked about, eyes shifting from one side of the canyon to the other, as if wondering the same thing. But all was quiet in the rocks above.

Now Ali offered the reins of his horse.

And after a moment, the headman lowered the musket.

And a shot struck him in the back of the neck, dropping him like a sack of oats.

At the same time, Ali pulled a pistol from his belt and fired at another one.

Gideon grabbed the scimitar and slashed upward, gutting the one who was closest to him.

And William Eaton burst out from among the rocks at the other end of the canyon, galloping fast, whistling his scimitar through the air, and sending the head of another bandit thumping onto the sand.

The rest went fleeing for the rocks, and Eaton's voice went echoing after them: "Tell your people that we are furious in our rage, but if they join our march, they will know our friendship and gain independence."

"They will not join us, Eaton Pasha," said Ali in English. "They are cutthroats, dog brothers to the bashaw."

Eaton dismounted and jammed his scimitar into the sand, wiping away the blood. For all his size, he was quick and graceful, on horseback or on foot. "A loyal populace is like the tide, Ali. Respect them and they will take flood beneath your boat. Ignore them and they will leave you stranded."

"I will remember, Eaton Pasha." Ali slipped the kaffiyeh from his face and crouched next to Gideon. He was about twenty-three, with eyes so black that it seemed as if the sun had burned two holes into his face. He was a cousin of Hamet and Yusef Karamanli, but loyal first to Tripoli. "The nose of you, Red-Haired Christian, how feels it this day?"

Gideon touched the dead skin at the bridge, where it had blistered twice already. "Better than yesterday. Like your English."

"English is a thing I must know. After this, our countries will have many talks." Ali put his hands under Gideon's arms to pull him free. "But if you keep losing your horses, Red-Haired Christian, we may never reach Tripoli."

"Be thankful that Ali remembered the name of this place," said Eaton, "the Brigands' Wadi. Otherwise you would be gazing at the face of God this very moment, and God would consider you very stupid for arriving so early."

"I thank all of you, but only one man could have fired the first shot."

Lieutenant O'Bannon, a rangy piece of Kentucky leather, rode down out of the rocks, his rifle across his shoulder and another Arab, bound and blindfolded, stumbling along behind him. "They had this one trussed up, hangin' from a rock. Can't quite tell what he's sayin'."

"He is Bedu," said Ali. "He says his people are loyal to Lord Hamet. He was bringing news when the brigands took him. He says Bashaw Yusef has put an army of eight hundred on the road to Derna." Ali's dark eyes widened as he spoke. "They have already reached Benghazi. We must tell my Lord Hamet right away."

"We must tell him gently," said Eaton.

"Benghazi! My brother's army in Benghazi?" Hamet sat in his princely pavilion, furnished by the Americans with hassocks and fine carpets, surrounded by his dozen or so most loyal and trusted supporters, and he trembled. "If my brother's army reaches Derna from the west, we can never take it from the east. We must stop."

"If this story is true, my lord," said Eaton, "*we* must reach Derna first."

"Yes, Lord," said Ali. "Eaton Pasha speaks the truth. We must march on."

Outside, the desert wind blew and the tent poles creaked. Hamet wrung his hands. "I . . . I do not know."

"What if American ships do not meet us before Derna, as they have promised?" asked one who filled Hamet's ear with distrust for the Americans.

"Yes," said another. "Without ships, we can never attack Derna or take Benghazi or move against Tripoli."

"Perhaps we should wait until we know for certain," said Hamet.

"I have given my word on this," said Eaton coldly. "Who questions my word?"

"None . . . None questions you," said Hamet in his high-pitched voice. "It is just that we live in a time to make the stones cry, and no nation can be trusted."

Eaton stepped closer to him. "My Lord, I have pledged my personal honor and that of my country. We will not desert you. It is as simple as that."

Gideon could see that Ali Gurgheis, at least, believed Eaton completely.

Hamet's hands fluttered at his belt. His eyes twitched from one face to another, met none so resolute as Eaton's, and so he said they would march on, because Eaton Pasha had given his word.

"And we will win the race to Derna," said Eaton.

xi
Jefferson Visits the Fine Folly

Antonia feared that her father was dying.

He had lost twenty pounds since autumn. His color grew grayer, his cough deeper. Consumption was taking him, and no matter how much he smoked, he could not soothe his lungs. Antonia was beginning to wonder if tobacco was the curative it was said to be.

So she wrote to Jefferson and urged him to rescue her brother, so that her father could die knowing that his son had not been enslaved to this bashaw.

Jefferson wrote back, inviting himself and Commodore Preble to Annapolis: "As Preble used gunboats so well in Tripoli, I have asked him to direct construction of my gunboat fleet. As Annapolis is a prime site for a flotilla, a visit is in order, and I'm certain that Preble will be a comfort to your father."

It was appropriate, Black Jed told Antonia, that they were coming on April Fools' Day. Jefferson knew he'd been a fool to replace Preble, who had done more damage to the bashaw with one frigate than Barron was doing with six.

Antonia had seen no famous warriors in the flesh before, and she was disappointed. Preble was simply another naval captain the color and texture of granite. It was said he suffered from stomach ulcers, which may have explained the color, and he spent the evening twitching painfully in his seat, though Antonia suspected that any sailor's bottom, granite or not, would have twitched after a day on horseback between Washington and Annapolis.

"To Commodore Preble," Black Jed toasted between the terrapin soup and the duck, "who redeemed American honor with solid shot."

Preble raised his glass. "To the men of *Philadelphia*, including the son of our most gracious host. May God grant that every man come home safely."

Antonia waited for another toast, but mention of Jason had momentarily robbed her family of their usual dinner-table eloquence. So she raised her glass. "To President Jefferson, may he free our brother from the bonds of Tripolitan slavery—"

Black Jed cut her off. "'Slavery' is not a word we use in this context. Jason may sit at the bashaw's left hand, but he's no slave."

"I'll attest to that," said Preble. "He delivered us valuable intelligence."

"Thank you, sir. He's no slave, and surely no"—Black Jed almost gagged on the words and began to cough—"no body slave."

"Jedediah," whispered Sara, as if her calming voice and gaze alone could stop her husband's fear and remind him of his guests.

Charlton quickly offered a toast. "To our brother, serving his country."

And Antonia apologized for using the word "slavery." Then she glanced at the slave in the white jacket who, with almost surreptitious grace, was removing the soup bowls. "But slavery is so entwined in our lives that one cannot help but use it as an analogy for many things."

Jefferson ignored the long black fingers removing the bowl in front of him. "Slavery wraps itself like a vine around the pillars of our nation. It is a thing we must consider carefully."

She knew that in the first draft of his Declaration, Jefferson had called for abolition. But then, to keep the slave states committed, he had surrendered to politics. Now, while he wrote and spoke privately of his opposition to slavery, he kept slaves, traded slaves, and envisioned a society of farmers drawing daily bread and riches from topsoil tilled, in many states, by slaves.

Did he now accept slavery? Or was it only a political decision? And what, beyond skin color, was the difference between a slave clearing the Stafford table and American Christians enslaved by Muslim potentates?

It was neither the time nor place for this argument, but Jefferson was a man who liked to wrestle with philosophical questions, and Antonia fancied herself a woman who liked to do the same thing, so she looked into that broad, calm face and said, "I see a time when the vine must be uprooted."

"Antonia," her mother interrupted, "what uprooting is needed? In Annapolis, our slaves pass naturally into the world of the freedman. There are more freedmen here than in any other city in America."

Antonia heard the tone of calm and threatening logic in her mother's voice, and she knew she had pursued the subject far enough. "I wish only to see the future through our president's eyes."

"I wish only to see my son again," said Black Jed.

Jefferson leaned across the table. "You shall have your wish—soon, I think."

"What has happened?" asked Black Jed.

"I've ordered Tobias Lear to negotiate the cheapest settlement he can."

"But what of Eaton?" asked Antonia. "What of Gideon Browne?"

"The young lady is very outspoken." Preble seemed to brighten. "Like Midshipman Browne, if I recollect."

She said, "His last letter described a plan to cross the desert—"

"A quixotic thing, I've come to conclude," said Jefferson. "If Commodore Preble could not batter this bashaw to his senses, I'm convinced we will not resolve this thing without negotiation."

"But if they're fighting in the desert," asked Antonia, "aren't you . . . betraying them?"

Sara gasped at her daughter's words to the president.

"I like a young lady whose beliefs are strongly held." Jefferson sipped his wine. "Strongly held beliefs mean a strong nation."

Black Jed tried to speak, but he was gripped by a fit of coughing that changed his color from paste white to arterial purple. When it was over, Sara asked if he would like to go to his bed.

"No. I want to hear good conversation from people I love."

And for a moment, no one in Black Jed's family could swallow their emotion.

So Jefferson kept up the talk for them. "You know, we and this Hamet Karamanli have a common enemy, but I've no intention of linking the fate of your son and our diplomacy to Hamet. Besides, we don't even know if Eaton found him."

Antonia noticed Preble look down at his plate, as if restraining himself from speaking. She said, "They might also be attacking Derna at this very moment."

"Then I'll welcome their success," answered Jefferson, "so long as it contributes to our own."

xii
Miracles and Betrayals

There were times when it seemed that they might starve, or dry up and blow away for want of water. There were times when it seemed that the whole expedition might disintegrate in a sandstorm of distrust.

But Eaton drove them on, over five hundred miles of desert, a desert no army had crossed since the Romans, and when it seemed that they could go no farther, the American ships met them, with cannons and food and cool casks of water. This, Eaton said, proved the friendship of the United States.

Truly, Ali Gurgheis told Gideon, it was a miracle. But the need for miracles had only begun. Ahead lay Derna, Benghazi, and five hundred desert miles more to Tripoli. But the Americans, said Ali, had shown that they knew how to make miracles.

So on they marched to the Wadi Derna and the whitewashed city in the valley by the sea. At Derna, the fortress turned its guns toward the Mediterranean. But no enemy had come out of the desert in centuries, so nothing more than a breastwork of rocks and rubble faced the heights to the southeast.

After a day of scouting, Ali Gurgheis came to Hamet's pavilion to report another miracle: they had arrived ahead of the bashaw's relief column.

And Hamet lost his nerve once more. He said he feared that his people were being used to frighten his brother, and after the men of the *Philadelphia* had been released, America would no longer care about his fate.

Gideon saw it as a weak man's final moment of doubt.

But Eaton calmed Hamet's fears, and the fears of his followers, once more staking his personal honor on the honor of his country. "We will take you to the throne of Tripoli, my lord Karamanli. You have my word."

"Then"—Hamet's birdlike hands fluttered—"We will fight."

"Honor," thought Gideon as he strolled the camp with Ali on that starry night, was a powerful word, and Eaton used it well.

The next morning, the desert light was like limestone, hard and bright.

On the hills to the southeast, the Arab cavalry had assembled. Out on the water, Isaac Hull was maneuvering his three ships into position. And on the flat ground before the breastwork, Presley Neville O'Bannon ordered his marines into position.

Gideon Browne, armed for the day with a musket, quickstepped forward with the other Americans, and there they were, stretched in a single thin line across the plain—three midshipmen in their blues and soiled whites; eight marines in blue coats, red breeches, leather collars, small-brimmed hats perched smartly—eleven men looking as stalwart and as foolish as any group of warriors ever had.

"Now, then," shouted O'Bannon to the Americans and the mixed brigade of fifty mercenaries and Arab foot soldiers behind them, "there's eight hundred men on that breastwork, but they ain't fighters. And they ain't come out of the desert."

"And none of them have us!" shouted one of the Greek cannoneers.

"Yes!" shouted another, shaking the sponge rammer. "We will—"

Suddenly the thunderous roar of eight cannon erupted from the fortress of Derna, and eight jets of smoke went shooting out toward the ships.

They were answered by a single shot from the twenty-four-pounder that Isaac Hull had mounted on his schooner, the *Argus.* A half second later, the iron ball sent a huge gout of masonry bursting from the fortress.

A gentle breeze blew the smoke across the field in front of the breastwork, and there was awestruck silence on the plain and heights southeast of the city. Many of Eaton's Arabs had never heard the sound of an artillery piece before, let alone seen the effects of one.

On Hull's second shot, a cheer rose from the marines, and the mercenaries picked it up, and now the Arabs seemed to find their voices, and the cheer rolled up the hill to where the tribal flags of green and red fluttered.

Another volley came splattering out of the fortress. Then the air was crushed by an invisible wave, a full broadside of nine guns jolting from the *Argus,* seven from the *Enterprise*, and four from the *Hornet*.

All across Derna, the rocks flew and the dust rose like smoke, and the three vessels were consumed by a gray cloud of their own making. The fortress fired another blast, weaker, more ragged, poorly aimed, and it was answered by twenty tongues of flame licking through the clouds around the American ships.

Then came the piercing sound of a bugle from the top of the hill, and Eaton cried to the Arabs, "Did I not promise that our navy would silence their guns?"

The Arabs roared, their blood rising. They could barely keep their horses and camels under control.

And Eaton whipped them higher, shouting, "We ride in the name of Hamet Karamanli, the rightful bashaw!"

"For our lord Karamanli and for Eaton Pasha!" cried Ali Gurgheis.

Hamet was bobbing about on his white stallion, waving his scimitar, completely transformed by the excitement and sound. He raised the scimitar above his head and shouted, "Let God be your agent!"

Eaton swept his scimitar toward the south side of the city.

And with a wild cry, the Arabs went thundering down the hill and swarming across the plains, playing their part in Eaton's plan—a flanking maneuver to cut off escape and reinforcement.

Then Eaton swung his scimitar toward the breastworks, and O'Bannon shouted, "Fix *bayonets!*"

Gideon fixed his with a shout, just like the marines.

"That's it, Gid," said Private John Whitten, a gangling New Yorker whose best feature was his Adam's apple. "Shout loud. And move quick. But don't run!"

Gideon's world was beginning to close down to the few things he could comprehend—the men close by, the goal, the voice of his commanding officer. And then a cannon shot came from behind and nearly blew off his hat. The Greek cannoneers had opened up on the breastwork.

And then the breastwork opened up on the attackers. A wall of musket fire—all of it aimed right at Gideon's chest. He dropped to the ground and half of the Arabs did the same.

"Get up!" screamed O'Bannon. "No musket can hit anything at two hundred and fifty yards. Get up and keep movin'."

The defenders were untrained. Fast loading and volley fire were alien to them. And the Greek cannoneers were as good as any American gun crew Gideon had ever seen. Every sixty seconds, they sent another ball screaming at the breastwork. So the advance became a kind of minuet with a sixty-second beat—cannon blast, run, drop, cover, and blast.

But as the attackers drew closer, the firing grew hotter. An Arab was struck down on the flank. A marine was shot in the foot but managed to hobble on. O'Bannon urged them toward a little gully two hundred yards from the breastwork, where they dropped and waited for another Greek cannon blast.

Gideon tried to hear what was happening with Hamet's cavalry. There was firing to the south, maybe some to the west, but above the thunder of the naval bombardment, it was impossible to know for certain. Without the Arab flanking attack, however, Gideon knew the Americans would never get over that wall. And then something else was going over it—a cannonball followed by what looked like a long, weighted spear.

"Up and run!" cried O'Bannon.

"Let's make the most of this," said Whitten. "Them damn fool Greeks forgot to pull the rammer out of the gun. They just shot it into Derna."

This advance brought them to within a hundred and fifty yards, the outer edge of accurate range for the muskets.

"Gettin' hot now, Gid," shouted Whitten.

"Make for those trees!" cried O'Bannon. And they went scrabbling and rolling for a stand of peach trees about thirty yards to their left.

They stayed there for what seemed an hour, though it could only have been a few minutes. All around them, peach blossoms were fluttering down through the streams of lead and exploding splinters of wood.

"Where the hell is Eaton?" Gideon wiped the sweat from his face and looked over his shoulder, toward the hill and the now-silent gun emplacement. And there sat Eaton, his white robes fluttering, two or three messengers around him.

Just then one of the mercenaries got up and started to fall back. Another followed him, then two Arabs. It took all the willpower Gideon had not to join men who were showing so little honor but such good sense.

Then Eaton was galloping across the plain, straight toward the retreating men. And the first one he came to, he decapitated with his scimitar. The body stood for a few seconds, a gushing fountain of blood, a warning to any who would run. Then it collapsed as the other men went scrambling back to the peach trees.

Eaton pounded his huge black horse into the knot of frightened men. "Mr. O'Bannon! We can't stay here all day."

"Then we can advance under volley fire, sir."

"Damn the volley fire! A charge. Now."

O'Bannon hesitated for only an instant before a mad, maniacal grin came to his face, as if he could see the brilliance of such audacity. "A charge, then!"

"Up! Up now!" Eaton wheeled his horse in the crowded little grove of trees.

"This is madness," said Gideon to Whitten.

Eaton whirled on him, like a superman who could hear whispered remarks in the din of battle. "You'll *charge*, damn your blood, or I'll have your head, too."

"There's *hundreds* behind that breastwork, sir."

And Eaton shook his scimitar at Gideon. "Show them the fury of the few, and the fearful many will run, Mr. Browne."

And that crazy proposition—as crazy as the notion that an American could march a thousand Arabs across five hundred miles of desert he had never seen, rendezvous with the U.S. Navy, and attack the second largest city in Tripoli—proved to be the final miracle.

When the defenders saw sixty madmen rushing toward them, most broke and ran, and the rest were routed. Then marines and Arabs charged through the city from two directions and fought all the way to the courtyard of the waterfront fortress.

It was said that when O'Bannon sent the American colors up the flagpole, the men on the ships let out a wild cheer. But inside the fortress, Gideon saw the anger in the eyes of Ali Gurgheis, who carried a Tripolitan flag he had planned to raise himself over his country.

"And they *took* Derna?" asked the bashaw.

"Yes, Lord," said the messenger.

The bashaw grew as gray as any Arab Jason Stafford had ever seen. "My brother's own children are hostages under my roof, but never did I believe he had the balls to father them."

"It would seem he is no gelding." Sidi Mohammed rubbed his eyes.

The bashaw looked at Jason. "Not one word of this. I want no panic."

Jason shook his head. He knew well when to keep his mouth shut.

Sidi Mohammed asked the messenger, "How many were the defenders of Derna?"

"Eight hundred . . . eight hundred brave souls, Lord."

"And with my brother?" asked the bashaw.

The messenger stretched his neck, as if he could feel the blade that might behead him for the news he brought. "Many thousands . . . many, *many* thousands."

"Many thousands?" The bashaw's anger faded to simple, expressionless shock. "In addition to the ships?"

"Many thousands, led by fanatical Americans and the madman Eaton."

Sidi Mohammed smiled. "In defeat, men sometimes enlarge the number of their enemy so that even in defeat, they, too, are enlarged."

"No, Lord." The messenger shook his head so vigorously that desert dust puffed up all around him. "I speak the truth."

The bashaw stalked to the balcony and stared out at the sea. "*Americans*. They cross my desert. They blockade my shore. They would rather fight than pay the piddling tribute that even mighty England pays. What kind of men *are* they?"

His son Muhammed, a scowling seventeen-year-old hulk who seemed always to be lurking in the shadows, said, "Show them what kind of man you are. Execute *your* Americans."

And the bashaw nodded, as though pleased that his son was learning the art of treachery. Some good was coming of this after all.

"Majesty"—Sidi Mohammed cleared his throat—"if you execute

them, you cannot trade them . . . not for money, not for your throne—"

"If the Americans would go away and take my brother with them," said the bashaw gloomily, "I would give up the hostages now."

"Do that, and your people will lose respect for you," said Sidi Mohammed. "Kill them, and the Americans will pound our city to dust."

This remark renewed the bashaw's bluster. In the best of times, he was a man of unpredictable mood, but nothing in Jason's memory had produced a more madly swinging pendulum than this morning's news. "I am not a man to threaten!"

"But you are a man of wisdom," said Sidi Mohammed in a soothing voice. "The man of wisdom will negotiate."

Jason cleared his throat. "Captain Rodgers is now in command, Highness. He is a fighter, but he answers to Tobias Lear, who is a negotiator—"

"And from what we read in all their lime juice letters," said Sidi Mohammed, "Lear considers Eaton as much a madman as we do."

Jason was not surprised that they had been reading the secret letters, but he was pleased that the bashaw's pendulum was swinging back to negotiation.

"Before I'd give you $200,000 for the hostages," said Captain John Rodgers, "I'd give you $200,000 to blow Tripoli off the face of the earth."

Sidi Mohammed sat at the mahogany table in the day cabin of the *Constitution*, his hands folded neatly in his lap.

Rodgers, a beefy man with a high forehead and fiery complexion, strode back and forth between the carriages of two twenty-four-pounders.

Tobias Lear, as tall as Rodgers, but far bonier and altogether white—white skin, white-powdered hair, white linen coat over white waistcoat—sat and studied the bashaw's earlier offer. "In addition to the money, you demand a promise of peace, the return of all Tripolitan prisoners, and full restitution of all property taken from them?"

"This is so."

"This is asinine," said Rodgers.

Sidi Mohammed shifted his eyes to Jason. "Asinine?"

"Something only an ass would do." Jason had come as the foreign minister's translator of difficult phrases. He stood at attention, his hat tucked under his arm, his buttons polished, his mind set on acting the model midshipman.

"You know their language well," said Rodgers to Jason. "How well do you know the spirit of your mates? Can they take more bombardment?"

"They're . . . *we're* navy men, sir. We'll do our duty."

"Bravely spoken," said Sidi Mohammed. Then he shifted his gaze. "Warriors must speak bravely, must they not, Colonel Lear?"

"And I must speak frankly," answered Lear. "There can be no accord until you bring us a proposal less asinine than this."

"And," added Rodgers, "do not insult us by dressing up midshipmen and bringing them out for show. If you wish us to see how well you treat our officers, bring out Captain Bainbridge or Lieutenant Porter."

Sidi Mohammed stood. "Any accord must include an agreement to stop those who have taken Derna from marching farther."

Lear stood in response. "Your worry should not be with a group of renegades in the desert, but with the guns of our fleet."

"Since the leaving of Preble, we have not once heard those guns. I think you are more judicious men than Preble . . . or Eaton."

"Preble is a fine officer," said Rodgers.

"And Eaton is a loose cannon," said Lear.

"Loose cannon?" Sidi looked at Jason.

"A gun broken free from its tackles on a rolling deck," explained Jason. "An unpredictable man."

"Ah, yes. Loose cannon."

Lear said,"My country does not rely on loose cannons to make policy."

"We rely on *loaded* cannons," said Rodgers.

"We rely on *right*," corrected Lear.

They were pawns, thought Jason on the return trip, pawns in a struggle between nations, nations represented by men. And men, he had found, were not perfect creatures. Not the bashaw, who blustered while he shook in his boots; not Bainbridge, who had struck his colors and lost his honor to save lives.

Eaton and Hamet could not have been perfect either, but theirs were the names the American seamen were chanting from their dungeon that afternoon. All the city seemed now to know of the events in Derna.

The chanting could even be heard in the bashaw's throne room, a muffled sound, like the rumbling of a stomach. It caused the bashaw to pace in wide circles while his stubby, jewel-encrusted fingers kneaded the air, as though itching to wrap themselves around a throat. When Jason and Sidi Mohammed entered, the bashaw stopped moving, fingers held before him in midair. "Have they accepted?"

"They wish us to make a more . . . reasonable . . . demand."

"What of my brother?"

"They do not worry about him, Majesty."

"I do. I—" The bashaw stopped, unable to ignore the chanting of the Americans. "'Eaton and Hamet. Eaton and Hamet.' For two turns of the hourglass."

"It is disrespect, Father," said the son Muhammed, perching on his father's cushions, "disrespect to the bashaw."

"So let us be rid of them," urged Sidi Mohammed. "Send Lear a better offer."

"Perhaps I should send Lear their *heads*."

"This," said Sidi Mohammed, "is not a constructive thought."

"Their heads," repeated the bashaw, warming to the idea. "No ruler should take disrespect from prisoners."

"Executing the prisoners will not stop Eaton and Hamet," said Sidi Mohammed.

"They are five hundred miles from here," answered the bashaw.

"But Commodore Rodgers is right outside your window," said Jason.

"Without reason to stay, he will leave." The bashaw pulled his dagger from his belt. "So I will send him their *heads.* All but yours, Jay-soon."

And Jason gave his answer before he thought it. "No, Majesty."

"No? No to what?"

"No to you." Jason's mouth went dry. He was only fifteen, but he had just made the most important decision of his life . . . perhaps the last.

The bashaw's pendulum might swing once more, when the good sense spoken by Sidi Mohammed sank through his turban . . . or he just might do what he was threatening. And Jason would do what he must.

"You are saying no to my mercy?"

"I am saying yes . . . to my honor. If you kill my mates and spare me, my honor will die and . . . and I might as well be dead." He said it as though it had all been rehearsed, and somewhere in his head, he knew that it had.

For a moment, the bashaw's blade quivered in the air. Then he sheathed it and grinned at his son. "A lesson is here. A man lives by his honor and dies by it. Today the American crew lives by the honor of our friend Jay-soon."

The son grunted. "So what about our money?"

"*My* honor will be served by a counteroffer."

Sidi Mohammed smiled a small smile of thanks at Jason and said to the bashaw, "I would counter at one hundred and thirty thousand."

"That will please me," said the bashaw, "and save Jay-soon's honor, which he values like his life, as any man should. Because honor matters."

A week later, the *Constellation* dropped anchor off Derna.

There was joy among Hamet's Arabs, who had driven off the attacks of the bashaw's relief column and now expected the American reinforcements that Eaton had promised for the final march on Tripoli.

But the captain's gig brought only a single grim-faced lieutenant.

Eaton received him at his headquarters in the fortress now called Fort Enterprise. He sat at a desk with a single candle guttering before him, Lieutenant O'Bannon and Midshipman Browne beside him.

"I carry two letters, sir." The lieutenant placed them on the desk in front of Eaton. "One from Tobias Lear, the other from Commodore Rodgers."

Eaton folded his hands and looked at the letters as though one carried his death warrant, the other his directions to the wrong side of the afterlife. The seals were broken, both were read. Then Eaton said, as calmly as if he were giving orders for the day's drill, "Lear is exchanging sixty thousand dollars and one hundred captured Tripolitans for three hundred and seven Americans. The bashaw promises amnesty to all who swear fealty. We are ordered to go aboard *Constellation* tomorrow."

"Are we to obey?" asked Gideon.

"How can we not?" said Eaton, the bitterness rising in his voice. "The navy has brought each of us our own personal cot to sleep in aboard the ship."

"I'd have preferred a coffin," said Gideon.

"Let this news out among the Arabs," said O'Bannon, "and we won't be needin' no coffin. They'll cut us into pieces and feed us to their camels."

The next morning, Eaton gave Hamet the news. Eaton described it later as the most painful thing he had ever done: "I told him his fears of American desertion were justified. I offered to continue the fight, as I had pledged my honor. But Hamet knows we cannot win without American ships, and he has no interest in a noble death. He agreed that if his followers learned that they were to be deserted, they would kill us all."

And for that reason, their great march ended in ignominious play-acting. It sickened Gideon Browne even as he participated in it.

On the afternoon of June 11, Eaton drew up the Arab troops to inspect them. He sat on his horse, the gentle breeze ruffling his robes and the bright sun glinting off his scimitar, and he told them how proud he was of them. He walked the ranks, checking weapons, testing the sharpness of blades, building morale for a battle he let them believe was imminent. Then he sent out the scouts.

One of them was Ali Gurgheis.

"Be back before three bells," called Gideon. "Nine-thirty."

"Arabs do not need compasses, nor do we carry hourglasses, Red-Haired Christian. We honor our fathers and live by our wits and find our way by the stars."

Shortly after sundown, when the light was purple in the sky above and shimmering silver on the western horizon, Eaton ordered all of the Greek cannoneers and European mercenaries to come to Fort Enterprise.

On the parapets, marines patrolled. In the fort, watchfires burned. At the wharf, the quarter boats from the *Constellation* waited, though only Eaton and his officers knew why.

When night had drawn itself across the moonless sky, Eaton ordered the Europeans to move the artillery into the boats. Then he ordered them to go aboard with the guns. Though puzzled, all did as they were told. And, as if all understood the sudden need for silence, barely a word was uttered.

As soon as the first boats were away, Gideon mounted his horse and rode along the waterfront, past the inner wall, to the bey's palace. Hamet was seated in the audience room, along with the dozen or so supporters who had gone into Egyptian exile with him. These men had been told of the plan, and they rose as soon as they saw Gideon. But one was missing.

"Majesty, where is Ali?" Gideon whispered.

"He has not returned."

"We must wait."

"Wait and die." Hamet hurried out with the others behind him.

Gideon went onto the balcony and looked out at the city they had taken. He waited five minutes. He might have waited ten, standing in the darkness, listening. . . .

Then he heard the sound he had feared, a single voice crying through the streets, "They are leaving! The Christians are deserting us!"

And that was the end of his waiting. Gideon reached the wharf just a few minutes ahead of the Arab soldiers now rushing toward the waterfront from the camps along the southern edge of the city.

"Hurry," shouted Eaton. "Hurry!"

Eaton pushed Gideon onto the boat and climbed aboard himself, the last American to leave, and the little vessel, overloaded with marines and midshipmen and shame, lurched from the wharf.

Then Gideon saw the figure of Ali Gurgheis galloping onto the wharf. He stood and waved his arm, as if to draw Ali toward him. "Hurry!"

"To what? Where do you go?"

Gideon told the boatswain to backwater.

"I'm afraid not, sir. We have all we can hold."

Now hundreds of Arabs were appearing beneath angry torches.

"Ali!" Gideon cried. "We live in a time to make the stones cry!"

"Truly," came the answer, as Ali realized what was happening. "Truly we do . . . in a time when our friends betray us!"

And those were the last words Gideon could hear. The rest were washed away by cries of anger, sporadic gunshots, and the screaming of men and horses. Soon fires of fury were budding all across the waterfront, and the American headquarters burst into flames.

And the stones, it seemed, were not the only things that cried that night. Gideon slumped onto his seat and looked into the face of William Eaton, who sat motionless in the stern sheets, eyes fixed forward and brimming with tears.

"Ali would never have come with us," he said to Gideon. "He has ideals, and idealism burns with a pure flame."

"He has honor," answered Gideon. But later that night, watching from the deck of the *Constellation* as Fort Enterprise burned, Gideon pulled out his journal and wrote only this: "So much for honor. It is a slippery thing after all."

xiii
Homeward Bound

William Bainbridge requested an immediate court-martial to investigate the loss of the *Philadelphia.* It was held aboard the *Constitution*, in Syracuse Harbor, and he would be acquitted in an afternoon.

But there were some who whispered that another court-martial should be held, and Midshipman Stafford should be the subject.

Gideon overheard these whispers in the wardroom, where midshipmen had gathered to await the Bainbridge verdict. He knew the one doing the whispering: the brother of Robby Parrish. Gideon had no siblings, but in the presence of this one, he saw what could compel brothers onto bomb ships in the eternal fraternal competition.

"For near ten months," Parrish was saying, "Stafford lived in the bashaw's own castle like some kind of Muslim prince. And I'd bet all the grog on this ship that he screwed his way through the bashaw's harem."

"Screwed 'em?" said some awestruck midshipman from the *Constitution.*

"Aye," answered Parrish, and his eyes met Gideon's. "While my brother was dyin' a hero's death and Mr. Browne here was crossin' a desert, Stafford was suckin' Muslim titties, and strike me dead if he wasn't suckin' Muslim pricks, too."

"You have firsthand knowledge of this, mister?" asked Gideon.

"*Common* knowledge. Ask any of the lads."

"Aye," said Midshipman Cutbush, a Parrish acolyte. "He went about wearin' a green sash like a regular Turn-Turk."

"And like Mr. Parrish says," added Midshipman Henry, another of Parrish's boys, "what was he doin' to get such special favor?"

"You're saying he gave aid and comfort to the enemy?" Gideon prodded.

"I'm sayin' he wore the sash and sucked the pricks, and on the day I saw my dead brother desecrated, he kept me from seekin' vengeance. It's what everyone in the squadron'll be sayin' before long."

"Not if you accept my challenge." Jason appeared in the lone shaft of sunlight that reached down the aft companionway. "You won't dirty my name."

"You've dirtied it enough yourself," said Parrish.

"I'll face you, Cutbush, Henry . . . *any* of you."

The ship rose on the harbor swell. The lanterns that lit the wardroom, even by day, shifted slightly, so that the shadows shifted as well.

"I accept." Parrish's grin looked like a saber slowly drawn from its scabbard. "Challenged chooses the weapons, so pistols it'll be. I'll kill you with one shot."

Then Cutbush and Henry accepted. All of them had been taught that dueling was as natural to an officer as fighting on the deck of a ship. And what better way to defend one's honor than to accept the challenge of one who would not live to fight?

"Now, will anyone second the bashaw's cocksucker?" said Parrish.

"I will."

"Browne?" Parrish's smile faded.

"Stafford saved my neck in the bashaw's throne room. If he's foolish enough to fight a duel, I'll do my best for him."

"Thank you," said Jason. "But defending one's honor isn't foolish."

"Honor is a slippery thing," said Gideon Browne.

Parrish stepped closer to Gideon. "They *said* you were different. Just the sort to second a Turn-Turk. But . . . Mr. Allworthy will second me. We'll meet at the earliest convenience. The heights above Syracuse Harbor are said to be good grounds."

"There will be no duels." Lieutenant David Porter appeared in the shaft of sunlight. "I'll not have my midshipmen engaging in anything so foolish."

"But, sir," said Parrish, "a naval officer must—"

"A naval officer must obey orders. Yours are to return to the *President* with Captain Bainbridge and go home. Mr. Stafford joins me aboard the *Enterprise*."

"You mean, I'm staying, sir?" said Jason.

"I want the best midshipman I can find. Now dismissed. *All* of you."

In a day, the friendship of Gideon and Jason was bound, and in six weeks of efficient service with Porter's new command, Jason's reputation was made sound. Only then did Porter send him home.

"You've served well," Porter said, "but the *Franklin* is sailing for Hampton Roads. She's taking Eaton back, and she has room for one more midshipman."

Jason had never voiced disappointment at his assignment to the *Enterprise*. If he hoped to rise in the navy, he knew that he must value discipline as highly as honor. Never complain to superiors, never explain to subordinates. Now he simply offered his thanks.

"You can be a fine officer, Stafford. Just remember your shrouds."

"Sir?"

"Think of yourself as a mast. And the shrouds are your good sense. It's all right to work a bit when the wind blows, for the shrouds will hold you upright."

"Thank you, sir." Jason decided that Porter was a man of some wisdom.

"In short, stay away from Parrish."

It was mania for a sick man to travel the eighty miles from Annapolis to Fredericksburg, Virginia. Antonia said it, and her mother agreed, as did Charlton, but Black Jed Stafford insisted. He could not wait to see his son.

When the *President* arrived at Hampton, word traveled quickly north, and now the men of the *Philadelphia* were being greeted as heroes all along the route to Washington.

"Hard to figure," said Black Jed between coughs and inhalations of his pipe. "Bainbridge grounded his ship. His men ended up as hostages—"

"But they bore imprisonment nobly, Father. They deserve to be welcomed," said Antonia, "especially Jason."

The mayor of Fredericksburg invited Black Jed and Sara to sit on the reviewing stand, beneath a pecan tree shimmering with autumnal orange. But when Antonia saw the familiar white peruke of Duncan Parrish and the wizened countenance of Rebecca, she decided to watch the parade from below.

Never before had she seen such enthusiasm. The cheering of the men resounded in her chest, while women waved their handkerchiefs and children cried out. A fife and drum brigade led the march, followed by a team of six horses hauling a wagon upon which had been built a grand model of the *Philadelphia*, correct in every detail, right down to the deadeyes.

William Bainbridge led his men, marching resolutely, never looking down, yet carefully avoiding the droppings in the road. Behind him came his officers, then the midshipmen, but . . . no Jason. With growing panic, Antonia ran to the front of the group, thinking that perhaps Jason had been promoted and she had missed him. But . . . no Jason.

So she pushed her way up to a tall gray-haired officer with a kindly face. "Excuse me, Lieutenant—"

"I'm the surgeon's mate, Doc Cowdery," said the old man as he marched along.

From him Antonia learned that her brother was still in the Mediterranean. Then he stopped and clasped her hand in both of his. "No matter what else you may hear, your brother rendered us a great service."

This remark struck Antonia as strange, but she could learn no more, because he was hurrying to regain his place in the parade, and the midshipmen were coming along. There were fourteen of them, and Antonia searched their ranks, half hoping she might still see Jason.

Instead, a handsome yellow-haired midshipman grinned at her, swept his hat from his head, and made a deep, almost mocking bow. "The Stafford sister . . . a pleasure to meet a *real* Stafford woman."

Antonia smiled, tried to seem friendly, but Samuel Parrish was turning his attention toward the reviewing stand, toward his aunt and the man in the white peruke.

Now Antonia saw the look of bewilderment cross her father's face as he realized that Jason was not part of the parade. She thought she saw him cry. She thought she saw Samuel Parrish laugh.

But the next morning, as their coach clattered back to Annapolis, Black Jed was full of praise for Captain Bainbridge. "A fine man, and a fine judge of character to speak so highly of our boy."

"Imagine our Jason a spy under the bashaw's nose," said Sara. "And so valuable to the navy that they kept him on station after all the other boys were sent home."

Antonia gazed out at the autumn colors creeping into the green countryside, and she wondered again what Samuel Parrish meant by "a *real* Stafford woman." With a little thought, she could find in those words something to turn her father's tears to acid, something to make his worst fears come to life.

In another coach, clattering back to Parrish Manor, Rebecca heard the story of Jason's challenge and the deferred duel.

"Someday I'll kill him," said Samuel, "no matter how pretty his sister is."

"I forbid you to duel with a Stafford," answered Rebecca.

"I like the Staffords," said Duncan, "but your aunt dreams of taking all they have. Killing one of them would only harden them against a greater assault."

"I can't refuse a challenge," said Samuel.

"That's the weakness of men." Rebecca sucked on her tobacco. "Far better employed on a weak man who will soon hold his family's reins than on some powerless midshipman."

The *Franklin* arrived at Hampton Roads in November, bearing

Jason Stafford, Gideon Browne, and the increasingly bitter William Eaton.

America now resounded with praise for Eaton, because in a letter to a dozen American newspapers, Commodore Preble had said what decorum had not permitted him to say at the Stafford table, before the president: If he and Eaton had been allowed to operate together, they would have saved the hostages and finished the bashaw without paying a cent of ransom.

Eaton appreciated the praise, but he said he had returned to a country which had sacrificed honor for an expedient, and before he was finished, everyone would know it. Receptions were planned for him in Richmond, Fredericksburg, and Washington. And no one, thought Gideon, could imagine what was coming.

"Be there for the Washington reception," Gideon told Jason on the dock at Hampton. "And bring your sister."

"I'll tell her what a good friend you've been."

"Tell her how handsome I am."

"I can't lie to my sister."

"What's a lie in the interests of love?" said Eaton, his voice strong, but the rest of him fading into shades of brown and gray—sparrow-brown waistcoat and trousers, dirt-brown cape and tricorne, a face the color of the winter woods.

"Aye," said Gideon. "All's fair in love and war."

"I can't speak of the love," said Eaton, "but we're living proof that war has no rules."

Jason had dreamed a hundred times of his journey up the Chesapeake. And always he had dreamed of a brilliant October day, when the blues of bay and sky flowed together, when fires of color consumed the trees on either shore, when the southwest winds were still strong enough to push a skipjack before them. He had never dreamed of the slate-gray gloom of late November.

It filled him with an inexplicable melancholy on what should have been the most joyous journey of his life. The gray made the world seem smaller. It left him wondering if anything in his life could ever again rival the excitement of living at the seat of an enemy's power. And what of the man who had walked his homesick dreams? Would his father remain a giant in his eyes, or would he too have been diminished by time and the approach of winter?

The mail boat on which Jason took passage made its leisurely way up the Chesapeake and, late on the second day, crossed the bay to the triangle of land between Spa Creek and the Severn River.

Jason's melancholy faded before the buildings that formed his home and the trinity of his youth: the earthworks of Fort Severn, in whose shadow he had first dreamed of military glory; the spire of Saint Anne's, where his father had taught him that he would meet God; and the massive layer-cake cupola of the capitol.

He stopped at Middleton's, hoping he might surprise his father over a pint and a pipe. But his father was not there, so he hurried on, greeting familiar faces, loping past handsome houses and wide lawns and fields of browning grass that rolled down to the river. Some things lasted. Some endured. Some might never change.

That was his prayer, and it seemed fulfilled when he saw golden light pouring from the house. That light had beckoned him home a thousand times from his boyhood adventures. It beckoned him now from adventures that few could imagine.

As a boy, he had always gone in by the kitchen. But that would cause a great commotion among the house slaves and spoil the surprise of his return. Besides, he was a man now. He had passed his sixteenth birthday. He had upheld his honor with Barbary potentates and Samuel Parrish both. So he went in by the front door.

He stood for a moment in the darkness, enjoying the delicious anticipation of the joy that would greet him, a smile spreading involuntarily across his face. He did not notice the black crepe draping the doorframe but went straight down the hallway toward the doors of his father's library. And there was Black Jed Stafford . . . staring down at him from the Peale portrait above the mantelpiece.

"Father," he whispered to the back of a chair that was turned to the portrait.

And the chair pivoted, revealing a beautiful young woman, a woman who had remained in his memory as a girl.

"Antonia!"

"Jason? My God." She came toward him, her eyes brimming.

He had expected the tears. Now he noticed that she wore black.

Joy flowed with grief that evening. Then grief and joy swirled together in the presence of mother and sister, brother and sister-in-law. And like colors which, when mixed, render a color entirely new, joy and grief became acceptance.

His mother, who had shown only stoicism when he sailed away, seemed now like Porter's mast, worked hard but still strong. "His pain is over," she said. "Consumption shredded his lungs. Not even a pipe could soothe him. But you gave him joy." From the folds of her skirt, she produced a letter and pressed it into his hands.

> By the time you read this, I will be gone. But always remember that your service in Tripoli filled me with the greatest pride in my final days.
>
> It is a marvelous time to be young and to be an American. Few men ever have the chance to build a nation or a navy. God has given you that chance and enough inheritance that you may live well, no matter how poorly Congress chooses to pay the protectors of the Constitution.
>
> Do not worry about management of our Stafford interests. Your brother will see to them. I expect you to see to our *national* interests, because those, after all, are the Stafford interests too.
>
> Remember your faith, remember your father, remember your honor.

That night, Jason felt his father's spirit still in the house. He heard it in the creakings, like footfalls in the hallway. He felt it in the wind, like the rhythm of a man's breathing in the next room. He knew it without rereading the letter, which echoed through his head as he drifted to sleep.

When he awoke, he felt no motion and heard no bells, so he knew he was not aboard ship, and for just a moment, he thought that he was back in Tripoli. Then he smelled coffee, and Antonia came toward him in a red silk dressing gown, bearing two mugs. He sat up so that the cold air stung his nose. But that simply heightened the pleasure of home, for the rest of him was covered with one of his mother's comforters, and the coffee was steaming, heavily sugared, half hot milk.

"It's been a long time since I've had coffee like this." He took a sip.

"This used to be our time," she said. "The early morning, when we talked about what we'd do when we grew up—about the navy, about planters and slaves—"

"I liked talk about sailing," said Jason.

She laughed, and then there was silence, as if both were remembering the children they had been. Antonia had always been serious and a trifle solemn, but never so sad. Her squarish face had filled out handsomely, but this morning, it seemed drawn, and the night before, she had left the others to say the comforting things, as if she had no comfort to give.

Jason looked out toward the river. "I dreamed of this view, even when I slept on silk sheets in the bashaw's castle."

She sipped her coffee and asked, "What happened there?"

"In Tripoli?"

"In the bashaw's castle. What happened to you there?"

Jason lowered his coffee cup. "What are you asking?"

"Samuel Parrish—"

"He lied. Whatever he said, he lied."

"He said he was glad to meet a *real* Stafford woman."

The taste of the coffee, the warmth of the bed, the comforting presence of his sister, all faded. "What else did he say?"

"Nothing. But Dr. Cowdery said you rendered them a great service, no . . . no matter what *else* I might hear."

Jason got up and went to the window. The air had finally cleared. The day seemed crisp and fair. "Parrish will not slander me for long."

That morning, Jason posted a letter to the Washington Navy Yard: "Dear Gideon, Parrish now spreads his venom among my family. So I practice my aim and stand ready to face him. Antonia sends her good wishes."

Gideon was staying in Washington until the reception in December. He had decided he could not desert Eaton, who was now taking Washington the way he had taken Derna: taking it only to lose it.

At first, newspapers praised Eaton and condemned the Lear negotiations, which he said had cost America a victory. Congressmen called for towns to be named after him. The president dined privately with him and heard his complaints. But soon Eaton's bitterness began to sting, and opinions began to change. Just as he had grown intemperate in his drinking, he grew intemperate in his words. Even his supporters found "treason" too strong a term for one of Jefferson's diplomats.

Nevertheless, senators, congressmen, Supreme Court justices, and the people of Washington gathered to honor Eaton with champagne toasts and music in the Capitol rotunda. No matter his opinions, he was still the hero of Derna.

A light snow fell that night. It melted where the marshy ground had not yet frozen and piled a few inches in the higher places. It frosted over the roofs of the buildings around the president's mansion and the Capitol, and it made the sorriest whorehouse look like a cousin to the two white symbols of power that dominated the Potomac marshland.

"In the snow, this mudhole actually looks like a city," Eaton told Gideon as they got out of their carriage before the Capitol. "But we could use a proper dome on the seat of government. It looks like a Greek temple topped by a wooden pudding bowl." Then, dressed in his officer's uniform, Eaton went up the steps and into the rotunda.

Gideon had decided that if Eaton chose to embarrass himself with spirits, either distilled or embittered, there was nothing to be done. So he would enjoy as much champagne and newfound fame as he could.

He had just ended a conversation with Chief Justice John Marshall and was alone in the swirl of handshaking and backslapping and noise echoing off the great dome. He was waiting for a tray of glasses to glide past, or for someone else to congratulate him, when he heard a voice behind him.

"Why, Gideon Browne, you look like a lieutenant already."

He turned and saw the face he had seen in a hundred shipboard fantasies and desert dreams. She wore a high-throated dress of royal blue silk, with blue satin at the wrists and the neckline. Her hair was fashioned into a neat swirl on the top of her head. And all of it served to emphasize the forthright line of her jaw.

Gideon sputtered a greeting more nervous than the one he had offered the chief justice. Then he executed a deep bow.

She curtsied and invited him to join the dance just starting.

Gideon did not come from a family, or a place, where dancing was valued highly. He moved in the wrong direction, led her too roughly, and sensed the annoyance of her feet, which seemed to know the proper way to go, in spite of her desire to do what a lady should and follow his lead.

Finally they found a rhythm that suited them both, and she looked into his eyes. "Your letters were most informative . . . when you bothered to send them."

He stumbled a bit, missing a change in the rhythm, and her remark caused a stumble inside his head. Then he recovered both his footing and his wit. "I could not be expected to describe the ugliness of war for such beautiful eyes as yours."

Antonia gave him a smile too broad to be sincere and batted her eyes. "Beauty is both the blessing and the curse of my sex."

Sex. This was not a word for polite company, and Gideon felt his heart rise to his throat at the mere sound of it upon the lips of Antonia Stafford.

"I . . . I beg to differ," he said, unable to think of another way to keep this unusual conversation going.

"Have you heard of the current fashion in Europe, Lieutenant?"

"I'm afraid I've been out of touch."

"To make themselves more beautiful, women soak their dresses in water before putting them on, so that the fabric clings to their curves and reveals all of their most . . . intimate . . . charms."

The best that Gideon could offer to that, through a tightening throat, was something about how chilly a wet dress must be.

"Indeed," answered Antonia with mock seriousness. "I've heard that some ladies have caught their death wearing wet dresses in January. Beauty is a curse."

"But a happy curse."

"You should know what women will put themselves through for beauty, so that you may defend against it."

"I've been too busy defending against Tripolitan bullets and sand flies," said Gideon. "Defending against flirting women is—"

"Truth-telling is *not* flirting," she snapped. "It is a way for people to know one another without resorting to wet dresses and"—she looked at his Tripolitan medal—"decorations. Wouldn't you agree?"

"Of course."

"Then perhaps you'll tell me a truth."

"I'll try."

"My brother has written to you. Has he written of a duel?"

He stopped dancing, then led her off the floor. "I'm not at liberty."

"You must stop the duel, Gideon," she said fiercely. "Parrish is a dead shot. Jason only began practicing with our father's pistols a week ago."

"Jason takes his honor seriously."

"Like Alexander Hamilton? Look at what the nation lost when he met Aaron Burr. And my brother proposes to fight a *gang* duel, three men in succession. Foolishness times three."

After a moment, Gideon said, "I agree."

"You do?" She brought her hands to his arms. "Then you'll do something?"

"I'll do what I can. But if there's to be a duel, I've promised to second Jason."

And there *would* be a duel, for at that moment, two midshipmen, late of the *Philadelphia*, were moving through the crowd. They were reaching for glasses from the same tray when their hands touched. Angry looks led to angry words. And the seconds were summoned.

xiv
Code Duello

Jason Stafford slipped from a guest room in the president's mansion before dawn. Somewhere in the house, a clock was chiming, though he had needed no bells to waken him from his fitful sleep. He tiptoed past the room where his mother and sister were sleeping, then past Jefferson's door.

In the foyer, he bent down to pull on his boots and almost retched. He felt as if a clutch of rats were chasing around in his gut. So he hurried outside, to keep the sound of his retching from wakening the household. He summoned the stableboy to bring him his horse, and he galloped off down Pennsylvania Avenue in a sporadic and miserable rain.

Gideon met him at the bridge over the Anacostia River. "Parrish went across a while ago, along with Cutbush and Henry and Mr. Allworthy."

Jason simply nodded. He feared that if he spoke, the rats would jump out.

"We can stop this thing now."

Jason shook his head.

"Don't throw up." Gideon spurred his horse. He knew the story of Jason's imprisonment, from the bastinado to the moment when Jason chose death with his mates to life with the bashaw. He knew that Jason had proven himself to the one who mattered most—himself. But this was not enough, nor would it ever be enough if he hoped to last in the navy.

And yet, if Jason was killed, no words would ever be enough for Antonia.

So Gideon had gone to Eaton the night before and asked him how to end this thing before it began.

Eaton, filled with champagne and bitterness, had said that men fighting for honor did not deserve meddling seconds. "Do what a second should. Demand the Irish code duello, and then let honorable men do their business."

So it would be for Gideon to save Jason by his own wit, if he could and, if Jason was wounded, by a willingness to fight in his place.

A short distance beyond the bridge, they came to a fallow cornfield on the riverbank. In the gray dawn, the water seemed like slate, and all the figures at its edge looked like shadows. The three who would fight were clustered with their seconds around their carriage. Two others stood at some distance, beside another carriage. Gideon had expected one of them—Dr. Cowdery, hired to attend the wounded. The other, shrouded in a wool cape and old-style tricorn hat, he had not.

It was Eaton.

Jason dismounted first and shook hands with Eaton. Then he turned to Dr. Cowdery. "Thank you for coming, sir."

"Watching young men shoot one another is not a happy task."

"Now, Doctor"—Eaton shouldered himself between them and wrapped an arm around Jason—"young men must look to their honor."

The solidity of Eaton's body helped Jason to calm his nerves. He felt at last that he was in the presence of someone who understood.

Gideon was hoping that Eaton might still use the solidity of his reputation to bring this to a peaceful end.

Eaton asked him if he had specified the Irish code duello of 1777.

"Yes," said Gideon.

"Good." Then Eaton slipped a small book into Gideon's pocket and whispered into his ear. Eaton's eyes were bloodshot, his breath smelled of rum, but his advice was sound.

"Do you know where the dueling grounds are?" said Antonia to the coachman outside the president's mansion.

"I don't think so, Miz Stafford."

"'Scuse me, ma'am." The stableboy was working nearby. "There's three different places—across the river near Alexandria, up at Bladensburg, and down the Anacostia bank."

"Did you see my brother this morning?" asked Antonia.

"He took to his horse and headed down Pennsylvania Avenue."

"Toward the Anacostia bank, then?"

"I reckon."

A short time later, her coach was pounding through the ruts, and Antonia was certain that the springs would be broken before they reached the little Anacostia River, but whenever she felt the horses slowing, she banged the handle of her umbrella on the ceiling and urged the driver along.

Gideon walked out to meet John Allworthy, a small-featured and precise midshipman with no great love for Parrish but a passion for doing things naval—like dressing ship or dueling—strictly by the book.

"Irish code duello of 1777?" asked Gideon.

"As agreed upon, sir," said Allworthy.

"Challenged chooses the ground, challenger chooses the distance."

"Aye." Allworthy flipped open the mahogany box he carried under his arm. In it were two polished pistols, lead balls, and small vials of powder. "Challenged also chooses the weapons."

"Fine pistols," said Gideon, without touching them.

"Call forth your man, and I'll call mine."

Jason put a hand on his stomach to quiet the rats; then he walked to the middle of the field. He thought an expressionless eye might unnerve Parrish. So he dug his gaze into Parrish's breast and tried not to let go.

"It is our duty to ask, a final time, Mr. Parrish, if you will satisfy the offense to Mr. Stafford with an apology," said Gideon.

Parrish did not respond, but made a great show of reconnoitering the field. "I choose the higher ground, to the left."

Allworthy looked at Gideon. "That would seem to be the final word on the matter of apologies, sir. Challenger chooses the distance."

Without turning to Jason for approval, Gideon said what Eaton had whispered in his ear: "Challenger chooses . . . three paces."

Parrish's face froze. Jason gasped. The other duelists drew closer.

"Three paces?" said Allworthy. "This is most unusual."

"It's not allowed," said Parrish.

"Please be quiet," snapped Allworthy at his man.

Gideon kept his voice calm, his eyes on Allworthy. "The code duello does not specify distance between the duelists."

"But tradition assumes a distance of ten or twelve paces," said Allworthy.

"Tradition is unwritten, sir. You're a man who likes things in black-and-white." Gideon pulled from his pocket a small book and held it up. "The Irish code, adopted at the Clonmel Summer Assizes, 1777, for the government of duelists, et cetera, et cetera. . . . You'll find no stipulation as to distance here."

"This is a trick," growled Parrish. "A coward's trick."

"But who is the coward?" William Eaton now approached, his hat pulled low, his figure still shrouded.

"And who is this meddler?" demanded Parrish.

"See to your tongue, mister, or I'll challenge you myself." Eaton now threw off his hat, revealing the shock of white hair.

Parrish could not conceal his surprise. "I . . . I did not recognize you, sir."

"However, you recognize that at twelve paces, you'll kill Mr. Stafford and go home. At three paces, he'll kill you, too. You want that?"

Parrish thrust out his chin. "I've been called onto the field of honor."

"You can clear the field with a simple apology."

"Excuse me, sir," said Allworthy, "but you are not supposed to converse with the duelists."

"Thank you, Mr. Allworthy," said Eaton. "Your name fits you. But it's in the book." Eaton took the book from Gideon. "Do you care to read Article Nine, on the mediation of disinterested parties?"

Allworthy shook his head and stepped back. "I accept your word."

Eaton stood in front of Parrish. "Now, then, do you want to die?"

"I do not intend to, sir."

"Spoken like an officer." Eaton's eyes bored into Parrish. "A very . . . dumb officer."

"Say that again, and I shall be forced to challenge you, sir."

And Eaton gave Parrish one of those grins that had disarmed Arab tribesmen a dozen times. "Come on, son. You've proved your bravery by standing here. You'll prove your magnanimity if you apologize."

"I meant what I said."

"He won't call me the bashaw's cocksucker," said Jason.

"Those *are* insulting words, Mr. Parrish," said Eaton. "And in using them, you also insult Dr. Cowdery and Captain Bainbridge, who speak highly of Jason's work in Tripoli."

"Insulting them was not my intention."

"Neither is dying, but Mr. Browne has seen to it that you will. So take the word of the hero of Derna when he tells you that he owes his life to Mr. Stafford."

"*Your* word?"

"Without him, the bashaw would have taken my head. He would have taken *all* your heads. You owe your life to Mr. Stafford as much as to me or Lear or Thomas Jefferson. So which will it be? Death or apology?"

A cold wind rolled up from the river, and rattled over the dried cornstalks. And Parrish chose an apology. "Because I take the word of a hero," he added.

Eaton looked at Jason. "Do you accept?"

"If Mr. Parrish accepts the truth, I accept his apology."

"He must agree not to speak of this matter again," said Gideon.

Parrish hesitated a moment, looked down at the tops of his shoes, and said grudgingly, "On the strength of Mr. Eaton's word, then."

"And, if you must," said Eaton, "you will take his part . . . in courtesy to me."

Just then a coach roared into the clearing, horses screaming, harnesses jangling, a young woman shouting from the window, "Stop! Don't fight."

Jason shivered with embarrassment.

Gideon took Jason's arm and pushed him forward, at the same time, saying, "Mr. Allworthy, your man's hand, if you please."

Let us finish this, he was thinking, before Parrish can make a mean-spirited remark on a man's sister coming to save him.

But Antonia was out of the coach and running toward them in an instant, and Gideon knew that if Parrish said something insulting, it could start all over again.

"Your hand, Mr. Parrish," urged Gideon.

But Parrish was watching Antonia, and his lip was curling into a smile.

Make it respectful, Gideon was thinking, or I may have to duel with you myself.

"I will gladly shake the hand of a man whose sister is so faithful and so beautiful." Parrish offered his hand all around, settling finally on Antonia.

"I'm sorry," said Antonia after Parrish and his mates had ridden off. "But I had to do *something*."

"You could have made me look like a fool," said Jason.

"Better a live fool than a dead hero . . . or a dead *fool*," she said angrily.

"She stood by you, son," said Eaton. "Be glad for that."

"And," added Gideon, "any time you can restore your honor without firing a shot, be glad for a bloodless victory."

"A bloodless victory. An excellent feeling," said Eaton. Another cold wind puffed up from the river, billowing his black cape.

"Let us leave these young people to plan their Sabbath," said Dr. Cowdery.

"Let us leave them to plan their lives," said Eaton, "now that they can live them."

"Thank you both," said Gideon.

Eaton placed a foot on the step of his carriage. "Mr. Browne, I'll trouble you for my handbook."

As Gideon passed the book, it dropped and flopped open, and Gideon saw that it was not a handbook at all, but a small journal, all of its pages blank.

"I thought you said this was the Irish code."

"I said there *was* an Irish code. I'm not sure of its fine points."

"Allworthy would have believed anything we said, so long as—"

"That's the general idea." Eaton slammed the door of the carriage.

"But . . ." Jason came closer to the carriage, "where's the honor in that?"

Eaton tapped the roof of the carriage and it lurched forward. "As Gideon has been heard to say, 'Honor is a slippery thing.' Defend it however you can. But hold tight to life!"

They stood and watched as the carriage clattered back through a stand of trees. They stood close and said nothing. And after a time, the carriage appeared out on the bridge, rolling back to the city.

"Defend your honor," mused Antonia, "'but hold tight to life.' I like it."

"So do I," admitted Jason. "So do I."

Antonia slipped a hand into her brother's. Then she slipped the other into Gideon's.

The day was brightening. They could see all the way to Capitol Hill and the great squat building with the pudding-bowl dome.

That morning, at Parrish Manor, Rebecca washed another body for burial. In preparing the bodies of her sister-in-law, her brother Samuel, and now her brother Duncan, she had come to see herself as the angel of the family tomb, the defender of the family birthright. She had two nephews left—Samuel and Walter. And she would give back to them what had been taken from her.

She set the white peruke on Duncan's head and thanked him for the means by which to do it, whenever it was done.

CHAPTER THREE

Talk of Ghosts

October 9

By morning, Susan had decided that the most sensible character in the book was Gideon Browne, her own ancestor.

And she had found nothing that would cause Admiral Tom to worry about this book, unless Gideon Browne was a forerunner of later characters who questioned the conventional wisdom . . . like Jack Stafford himself, maybe? That seemed to be where all this was heading.

Over a cup of coffee in the bed-and-breakfast dining room, Susan was reading the dueling scene again, hoping there might be a way to dramatize it. She could quote from the letters, follow Jason's journey from the White House over Capitol Hill to the place where it happened. Probably a gas station today. From manly honor to self-serve pumps in five generations.

She was so occupied that she didn't notice the man standing over her until he pulled out a chair and sat down.

Without a word of introduction, he said, "Did you know that between the War of 1812 and the Civil War, more American naval officers were killed in duels than in the line of duty?"

That fact was not nearly as surprising as the sight of Jack Stafford himself. But then, this was how she expected a reporter would reveal himself. You're in your own little world, hair still wet from the shower, brain still screaming for a second jolt of caffeine, and . . .

He offered his hand. "Got into BWI on the red-eye."

She gave him a once-over: denim shirt, tweed jacket, and blue paisley tie; good teeth, good tan, white hair swept back so it curled slightly at the neck, but none of those stray wisps that most old men showed at their collars; bigger than his brother, a broader face, a more subtle version of the Stafford jaw.

"If there weren't any wars"—she tried to play along—"I suppose duels *would* cause more deaths."

"No wars?" Jack shook his head. "You're going to need a crash course in naval history. You're forgetting David Porter's campaign against the Caribbean pirates in 1820, the antislavery patrols of the 1830s and 1840s, the exploring expeditions, the Mexican War . . . and more navy men *still* died over insults."

She shrugged, although she was a little annoyed at how stupid he was trying to make her feel. "I guess I just have to read more of your book."

"That'll cost you," said Jack. "But here's some free info: Eaton's own stepson was killed in a duel that finally broke Eaton's heart. That dashing Greek god Stephen Decatur was killed in a duel with James Barron in 1820. And that great navy lieutenant Richard Nixon said he wouldn't leave Vietnam until he had peace with honor."

"As my own ancestor is reported to have said, 'Honor is a slippery thing.'"

"It sure is. . . . Tell me, are you going to be the navy's worst PBS nightmare?"

"What's that?"

"A whining feminist who says the term 'military intelligence' is an oxymoron and thinks military spending is the work of *real* morons."

"Mother *said* you were a ladies' man." Susan rested her chin on her hands and batted her eyelashes. "But like you said, no easy answers."

"Very good." Jack settled back. "All of the above was a test. People who hang with me sometimes catch what gets thrown my way. You didn't even flinch."

"So, you actually *like* whining feminists who think—"

"No easy answers. None in the Tripolitan desert, none today."

"All right . . . so, when do I get to see more of your book?"

"I meant it when I said it'll cost you."

"There's no money at PBS for buying books. Unless, of course, we can convince the government to fund more films and fewer submarines . . ."

"Don't say that too loud. My brother has spies everywhere." Jack brought a finger to his lips. "Maybe we can work out a deal. You want to get me on tape, don't you?"

"After meeting you in the flesh, I think it's inevitable."

"Well, I'd like some footage of Stafford's Fine Folly to show potential investors back in Hollywood. Did you bring a video camera?"

"Of course, but the caretaker—"

"I'll work on him. Now, do you happen to have a laptop?"

"IBM compatible?"

"Good." He took a diskette from his pocket. "This is Book Four. You've earned it, just by being so pretty."

What a ham. Get him on camera, she thought, and the show was a cinch.

One of the hardest lessons for a warrior, usually not learned until a war ended, was that you'd never live anything quite so intensely again. This didn't mean you wouldn't enjoy life. Looking death in the face meant you'd enjoy *everything* a little more. But the biggest moment of your life, when you were the most frightened, the most focused, and the most alive, would have passed.

This thought usually crossed Lieutenant Steve Stafford's mind as he drove into the hardtop desert called the South Parking Lot at the Pentagon. He had been one of the youngest A-6 pilots in the navy. Now he was punching a clock in the famous five-sided building with the five rings, the five stories, and the ten connecting corridors of money and military power.

Steve and Joe Digger had tried to run that night in the desert, but the Iraqis had fired a flare that lit them up like two raccoons sneaking through somebody's back yard. The flare also gave away the Iraqi position, but no F-14s came streaking over, which was all for the best, because everyone within the light of that flare—good guys and bad—would have been toast.

The Iraqis were pretty pissed off, of course, considering that the sky had just fallen on them. So Steve wasn't too surprised when one of the guards whacked him off the side of the head with a rifle butt.

The next day, when Saddam Hussein dragged the captured pilots before the CNN cameras, Steve had a shiner the size of an eggplant—a badge of courage that made him the *Time* magazine Gulf War poster boy and also concealed a detached retina.

Five years later, Steve could see with a little blur and didn't even need a patch, though he wore one sometimes just to look intriguing. But he was no better than one-eyed in a cockpit. And there wasn't much call for one-eyed pilots.

He had gone from CNN subject to CNN watcher, from Unrestricted Warfare Specialty to Restricted Staff Corps, in a single night. After the Gulf, he could have chosen law, oceanography, medicine. Like most flyers who flared out, he had also considered the Office of Naval Intelligence. Or he could have left the navy altogether, which he considered seriously.

But his experience in the Gulf had taught him this: in a world where mass communication made it all but impossible to keep a secret, telling your story the way you wanted it told was as important as shooting straight. That was why Saddam Hussein had put him on CNN. That was why his grandfather spent his retirement writing about submarine warfare. That was why the navy had its own PR branch.

So Steve had decided to serve his country by telling the navy's story. Pentagon, south parking entrance, second deck, E Ring, home of CHINFO—one of the navy's ten thousand acronyms, this one standing for chief of information.

The E Ring was the outer ring of the Pentagon. But young lieutenants didn't get a view of the Potomac. They got televisions tuned to CNN, and the navy's standard-issue light green paint on everything, and the same kind of steel desks and filing cabinets that could be found everywhere in the navy, from recruiting centers to aircraft carriers.

Steve decorated his little CHINFO cubicle with pictures: his mother, Beck, his stepfather and his half-brother, sitting in front of their house in Santa Monica; his father, Lieutenant James Stafford, smiling out at the camera from under the T-top of a PBR (Patrol Boat, River) in Vietnam; and a blank space where the picture of his last girlfriend had been. Everything else was business.

He was currently working the Submarine Warfare Specialty

account. This meant that if a news organization or media outlet wanted to know something about subs, from the disposal of reactor waste to the monthly menu, Steve would field the call and give the answer that the navy wanted to give.

Before he settled in that morning, his grandfather was calling.

"This better be a question about submarines," he joked.

"I've forgotten more about submarines than you'll ever know," said the admiral. "Although . . . I may have some questions next week. I'm writing an article for our institute journal on NSSN swimmer delivery vehicles . . ."

Steve imagined him, sitting on his veranda, looking east across the river into the warm morning sunshine.

"I called to hear how your lunch with that PBS woman went."

"It's tomorrow."

"Oh. I must be slowing down."

Like hell, thought Steve. Something was on the old man's mind.

"Well, listen, be careful with her."

"Yes, sir."

"She may be a cousin, and she may want to tell our story. But—"

"I went to Defense Info School, remember? I deal with the media all day."

"I know . . . but Jack has his hooks into her, too."

Steve glanced up at the cubicle wall, at a Jack Stafford column pinned above his desk, about funding for the first *Seawolf* submarine. The headline was "Run Silent, Run Deep, Run Dead Broke." When people asked him why he kept it on his wall, he told them that it was good to know your enemy. He never told them what he now told his grandfather. "I've always liked Uncle Jack."

"Your mother's influence. She has the same politics as Jack. It's a wonder she ever let you go to the Academy."

"Don't sell her short, Grandpa. She told me that my father would be proud and told me to go."

"Well, your father *was* proud. He *is* proud. He looks down on you every day." There was a pause at the other end of the line, then the old man went on, his voice a little weaker. "Now, when you talk with this PBS gal, try to find out what she's going to focus on, what her political agenda is . . . And ask her how much of Jack's book she's read."

"Jack's book? It's finished?"

"Not yet, but he's passing out pieces, and I don't think we can rely on him to do anything for the Stafford image."

"The Stafford image": a phrase Steve had heard often. The admiral's older son, William, a sixties radical turned Seattle lawyer, did his best to live up to the image, working as house counsel for Boeing, one of the biggest of America's defense contractors. But Steve's father had been the one who was going to burnish that image where it mattered most to the admiral—in the eyes of the navy.

Steve glanced at the picture of his father again. He knew Lieutenant Jimmy Stafford only through family stories, official documents, and a letter from his father's Academy buddy Oliver Parrish, delivered to Steve on the day that he graduated from the Academy. "A good man," was the last line of that letter.

Steve had spent a lot of nights wondering about that guy and what really happened on a muddy little stream called the Tien Doc, one dark night in 1968.

Nothing he had been able to glean, from pictures, reminiscences, or the official documents, had ever answered his questions completely.

And maybe that was why he had become one of the navy's storytellers—because the central naval story of his own life was still a mystery.

Jack called Susan's bed-and-breakfast at three o'clock: "We're all squared with the caretaker. Five o'clock. Bring your video camera."

Susan wondered what kind of magic he had worked with that sullen old black man. "I'll be there. Just don't forget it gets dark early."

"Yeah," he cracked, "I want to be out of there before the ghosts wake up."

"Ghosts?"

"Sure. Ghosts scare the hell out of me." Suddenly the wiseacre voice was gone. "Every generation has its ghosts, you know, and some of them are kind of scary."

"Do you have a few of your own?" That sounded a little bald, she knew, but she was no investigative reporter.

"Don't play games when I'm showing my weakness, or I won't

show it. Now, have you been reading what I gave you this morning?"

"It's long."

"Well, the generation that built the navy is growing in stature now. My ancestors and yours are helping that to happen."

"Why would you write a novel instead of a straight history?"

"No sex scenes in a history book." He chuckled.

"That's it?"

"Not really. But in a novel I can write about things that go on in the dark, see what it was like at eye level, feel as well as analyze. . . . One boy makes an honorable decision and saves his whole crew; the other one finds out that honor is a slippery thing. There's a lot of the story in there."

"But no easy answers," she said.

"You're learning."

The Stafford Story
Book Four
Men and Glory
June 1807

Preble was dead of consumption. Eaton was dying from drink. And the officers who had served under Preble, who now called themselves Preble's boys, were languishing in a navy that the president and his partisans meant to shrink.

Midshipman Gideon Browne had left the navy and gone to Harvard, to see if honor was any less slippery there. Two other Tripoli veterans—Jason Stafford and Samuel Parrish—had been assigned to the frigate *Chesapeake*, which had just been ordered to the Mediterranean after years laid up in the Washington Navy Yard.

And for once, Stafford and Parrish agreed: the *Chesapeake* was barely ready to sail down the Potomac, let alone across the Atlantic. She did not even have a gun ready to deliver a salute as she passed George Washington's Mount Vernon grave. Since she was scheduled to be on station for a year, her decks were piled with supplies, from salt pork to furnishings for an American embassy. Small matters like clearing guns and exercising her inexperienced crew could wait.

Jason considered unpreparedness a bad idea under any circumstances, and especially in that summer, with Great Britain and France at war. The British were trying to stop trade with France, the French were trying to stop trade with the British, and neutral America was caught squarely in the middle.

Heightening the tension for American seafarers was the matter of British impressment. The Royal Navy was a vast machine of a thousand ships and a hundred fifty thousand men that every year consumed ten percent of its own manpower, as though sailors were no more than lubrication that needed regular replenishment. If a British warship needed sailors, she stopped whatever merchantman was sailing by and took a few sailors off. By 1807, the British had impressed close to six thousand Americans. But there was little that the United States and its tiny navy could do to stop them.

At least, thought Jason, no British warship had ever dared stop a vessel of the American navy, even one as ill-prepared as the *Chesapeake*.

That changed on June 22, off the Virginia capes. The *Chesapeake* was just leaving American territorial waters when the fifty-gun British warship *Leopard* came alongside and requested that she heave to for a message. Naturally, it was done. A British lieutenant was received aboard and ushered to Commodore James Barron's cabin.

In the meantime, Midshipman Stafford studied the *Leopard,* an old ship, past her prime. He was puzzled by the open gunports, amazed when she ran out her guns.

He turned to Lieutenant Parrish, who was standing nearby. "There are no tompions in those guns, sir. I think this may be more serious than it appears."

"You are not paid to think," said Parrish, "but I think you may be right."

At about this time, the British lieutenant stomped up the gangway and, without so much as a doffing of his hat, went back to his ship. He had just presented a demand that the crew be mustered so they could be searched for British deserters.

Barron knew a British search would sully the honor of his ship. But he had not prepared her to defend her honor. In truth, when he came on deck and ordered the crew to go quietly to battle stations, there were none to go *to*. So he hauled sheets and braced yards to the wind.

Now Humphries, the British captain, shouted through his horn, "Heave to or I shall fire!"

Barron played the seagoing possum, cupping his hand to his ear. "I cannot understand you, sir."

So Humphries sent a shot across her bow, as though this American frigate were no more than a square-hulled lugger loaded to the scantlings with salt cod and rice.

Samuel Parrish was the first to recover from the shock of this insult. He called for powder monkeys and hurried to the gundeck. Jason Stafford turned to go to his forward station. The *Chesapeake* heeled a bit and began to run. And the side of the *Leopard* erupted.

Huge splinters of wood exploded wherever the balls struck and flew like daggers in every direction. Then the balls careened about the deck, striking and smashing as if thrown by a madman in a game of ninepins.

Jason was hit by a splinter that went clean through the fleshy part of his calf, but he did not even notice the pain.

Barron staggered about, a splinter stuck in his buttock, crying, "Return the fire! Return the fire! My God, will no one do his duty?"

A second broadside, then a third, and Barron dived for cover with a cry for his men to save themselves. The deck by this time was a river of blood, the ship was holed in a dozen places, and the air was rent with moans and curses. Jason Stafford's crew managed to bring up powder bags and load one of the bow chasers. But there was not a single powder horn filled for priming, nor a single slow match lit for firing the gun.

But Jason Stafford was always resourceful in the defense of his honor, and he would defend it now, for everyone aboard the ship. . . .

What Jason did next was better described by Samuel Parrish in a letter sent a week later to Antonia Stafford:

> I once said I would take your brother's part and speak well of him if ever he did well. Herewith, I keep my word.
>
> You are by now familiar with the events which befell the *Chesapeake* on June 22. Americans are justifiably

> furious. And the officers of the ship, which endured seven broadsides and a British search, are justifiably humiliated.
>
> Only your brother can hold his head high. In the midst of the beating—it cannot be called battle—I had come down to my station on the gundeck to work my guns, but was uncertain as to how it could be done, since no matches were burning in the tubs.
>
> Suddenly your brother came tumbling down the companionway, blood seeping through his stockings and breeches from several splinter wounds.
>
> He rushed headlong to the galley stove and likewise back, cupping something in his hands like a thief who had stolen a biscuit and feared to be caught. What he carried was a burning hot coal.
>
> Running topside, he laid the coal to the touchhole of his gun, which went off in defiance of the British and, more importantly, in defense of our honor. Only then could we strike our colors like men and submit to the search.
>
> I have never liked your brother, but on that day he saved us from the ignominy of surrendering without firing a single shot. He proved that courage runs in his family and he deserves my admiration. And may I say that I have admired your courage for a year and a half, since the day you rode onto a dueling field to save him. If I may be so bold, I have also admired your rare beauty.

Antonia wrote Parrish a polite note of thanks for his kind words, and Samuel Parrish wrote back the first of many letters.

ii
Three Lieutenants

It took five more years, but British impressment and the rising truculence of a young nation led finally to war. In that time, the letter-writing persistence of Samuel Parrish drew him closer to

Antonia; Gideon Browne found his way back to the navy; and three lieutenants—Parrish, Browne, and Stafford—were all assigned to the USS *Constitution*.

On the night of July 4, 1812, with war just declared and the *Constitution* taking on supplies at Annapolis, the young officers gathered at Stafford's Fine Folly for a meal of pickled oysters, crab cakes, fresh peas, and thick ham steaks cured in the smokehouse.

The talk was of their upcoming cruise, but every time that Gideon looked across the table at Antonia, he asked himself why he had ever let her hand slip from his that day on the Anacostia bank. By the end of the meal, this frustrating mental exercise had all but worn him out.

So he turned his attention to the concoction of frozen cream, sugar, and strawberries that Antonia's mother was ceremoniously spooning out. If he could not enjoy the sight of Antonia and look forward to a kiss, he could at least admire the dessert and look forward to a taste.

"Ice cream is one of Tom Jefferson's favorite desserts," Sara Stafford was telling them.

"I'd bet it didn't taste too good to him the day we declared war," said Charlton.

"Nor the codfish to the New England Federalists," said Parrish.

"A great puzzlement, that"—Charlton looked at Gideon—"New England resists war, saying it will hurt trade, but New Englanders like you rejoin the navy."

"I've rejoined"—Gideon dipped his spoon into the ice cream—"in response to a national crisis."

"A noble reason, sir," said Miss Mary Maynard, the dark-haired young woman sitting between Gideon and Jason.

"His true reason is cussedness." Parrish smiled, and the polite line of perspiration on his upper lip glistened in the candlelight. "When Gideon learned that his father's New England friends opposed the war, he decided a little war might be a good idea."

Jason leaned close to Miss Mary and whispered, "In truth, he was bored."

Gideon looked at Antonia. "I'll admit to the cussedness, the boredom, the patriotism. But reading the law can never offer the sense of . . . purpose I knew while crossing a desert to rescue your brother and Mr. Parrish."

Antonia took a mouthful of ice cream and thanked him for his bravery.

Parrish gave Gideon a look that a second lieutenant could give to a fifth, a warning not to sail farther on this tack, because Tripoli and its aftermath were not things that Parrish wished to recall at the Stafford table.

Jason did not like such looks. Parrish had courted his sister as a gentleman, but no matter how much Jason had come to respect Parrish's adherence to the code of honor, it was a small matter to revive ugly memories.

And Jason wanted no ugliness to mar this dinner, his last with his fiancée, Miss Mary, for some time. So he raised his glass. "To the *Constitution.* May she be covered in glory in the coming struggle."

"Here, here." Charlton toasted to making the sea safe for Stafford tobacco.

And Parrish toasted, "To the cussedness, patriotism, and *boredom* of one of the few New Englanders who support his Republic."

"That is not a gentleman's toast, Samuel," said Antonia.

Jason felt, if not ugliness, a distinct unpleasantness around the table. "I'm sure Miss Mary hears no such discussions at her family table in Alexandria."

Mary Maynard gave a little giggle, which immediately she tried to stifle by bringing her napkin to her mouth.

Jason saw this as a mark of good upbringing. She did not show her teeth when she laughed, never came to the table without her hair done in fresh little hot-iron curls, and seemed never to have let the rays of the sun touch her porcelain-white skin.

Gideon saw Miss Mary as all but otherworldly in her genteel naïveté and the heart-shaped perfection of her face.

Antonia saw her as all that she had sought to avoid, starting with the genteel naïveté. Perhaps that explained why Miss Mary, at nineteen, had set her wedding date, while Antonia, at twenty-five, was sitting next to Samuel Parrish, wondering what kind of husband he might make.

"An Alexandria dinner has never been as lively as this," said Miss Mary.

"Lively table talk never hurt anyone," said Sara, the family's force of gravity, grown so proud of her own matriarchy that she encouraged all to call her *Mother* Sara. "No reason for women to be excluded from important matters."

"Indeed not, for their opinions will be heard sooner or later, intelligent or not." Charlton glanced at his wife.

Hannah smiled, though without much mirth. She was a force of gravity in her own right, a woman grown heavier with the demands of running the Stafford plantation, a childless woman with honey-colored hair and an ineffable air of sadness, despite the huge mound of ice cream before her.

Charlton, on the other hand, was all high spirits. A fine belly had expanded beneath his waistcoat, and a fine filigree of red veins had appeared upon his nose. Badges of prosperity and good management, he called them, though his gambling debts had lately become a source of rumor. But his cheerful demeanor hid that damage well. "I must say, New England's war resistance is a bothersome thing."

"Is it true," asked Mother Sara, "that New England might secede if the British strangle New England trade?"

"New Englanders are practical men," answered Gideon. "They know that the British have a thousand ships to blockade us. And we have only sixteen to stop them."

"Sixteen?" Charlton sounded shocked.

Antonia looked at her older brother. "Nine frigates, three brigs, two sloops, a schooner, a cutter. You should know these things."

Charlton scowled. "Women can know a little about everything, sister. A man must know one thing well before splashing in little puddles of knowledge. These men know ships. I know tobacco."

"It's for certain you don't know horses," said Antonia.

That remark caused Charlton to sit back as though he had been slapped.

Moving again to deflect any ugliness, Jason offered a toast. "To a nation united, where New England is bound like a brother to the South."

"Pray that the nation *remain* united"—Antonia cast her eyes at Mother Sara—"whenever one section confronts another over anything, from free trade and sailors' rights . . . to the end of slavery."

"Oh, not that again," said Samuel Parrish.

"She has even been teaching her little slave, Iris, to read," said

Mother Sara, as though announcing that her daughter had been selling the family silver.

"I'm planning to give her freedom when she's twenty-one," said Antonia.

"In which case"—Mother Sara folded her hands on the table—"she'll be the only slave you'll ever own."

Gideon looked across the table and winked at Antonia.

"In that wink, sir," said Charlton, "I see more Massachusetts conspiracy."

"What you see," said Antonia, "is a conscience. Familiarize yourself."

Antonia could not sleep that night.

It was oppressively hot. But it was not the heat that vexed her.

It was a new dilemma: Samuel Parrish or Gideon Browne?

Parrish had grown greatly since Tripoli. Youthful failings had faded as he rose in rank. He had kept promises made on the dueling field, had corresponded faithfully, and had never taken a liberty with her that she did not encourage.

But he believed in the righteousness of slavery. He did not believe her opinions could ever matter as much as his own—though in that he was like most men. And he accepted a stiff-spined definition of honor, which she sometimes found a blessing but often a curse.

Her mother said that despite his shortcomings, he would make a fine husband in a field growing fallow. But Antonia simply did not love him.

And now, after years of fitful correspondence, Gideon was back, full of formal learning but lusting once more for adventure . . . and what else?

She stared out the north window and considered the matter of lust.

Ladies were not supposed to allow such thoughts to linger. But at twenty-five, most women were married. They could do more than imagine the physical pleasures of marriage. A few claimed these pleasures did not exist, that the act of love was simply one more fulfillment of the male appetite for possession. But . . .

Something rattled against the north windows.

Pebbles. Someone was throwing pebbles.

Then a familiar voice whispered in the thick, humid night. "Antonia?"

"Gideon?" She jumped to the window.

A wisteria blossom beside her window began to vibrate. A voice called up through the rustling leaves, "I must speak to you."

"In the morning, and . . . Gideon, you can't climb that old vine!"

Beside her window appeared a face covered with perspiration, grinning like a fool. "If I can climb a mast, I can for certain climb a wisteria."

"You're drunk."

"It's the glorious Fourth, but I'm intoxicated by your beauty."

She pretended to be unmoved. But suddenly he was leaning into the window, slipping an arm around her waist, pressing his lips to hers. And she could no longer pretend. She opened her lips and tasted the sweetness of ale.

And something rattled against the *other* windows, on the east side of her room.

"What was that?" asked Gideon, still clinging to the wisteria.

"More pebbles." Antonia pulled away so quickly that Gideon lost his balance.

"Antonia!" whispered someone from below the east windows.

"Antonia!" whispered Gideon as he started to fall.

"What!" she whispered in two directions at once.

"Come to the window," came the voice from below.

"Come back," came the voice from the window. This was followed by the sound of grunting, tumbling, falling.

Antonia looked down from the east windows and Samuel Parrish looked up from below. "Antonia, what was that sound?"

"I was . . ." She picked up her chamber pot. "I was emptying my—"

Parrish smiled at her ladylike embarrassment. "Just say you were fertilizing the wisteria."

"All right . . . I was fertilizing the wisteria."

"Lucky wisteria . . . I need to speak to you."

"Just a moment." Antonia scurried to the north window and peered down. Gideon was in the bushes. Sitting up or lying unconscious? She couldn't tell.

Then Samuel announced, "I'll climb up."

"No! No, Samuel." She scurried back to the east window. "You can't."

"But I must talk to you."

"Tomorrow. Before you sail."

"Tonight." Parrish began to climb the tin drainpipe beside the east window.

Meanwhile, Gideon was picking wisteria blossoms out of his jacket and trying to shake some sense back into his head. He could not let Parrish see him here, out of respect for Antonia, if she truly loved him . . . but how could she love Samuel after the kiss she had just given? So he grabbed for the wisteria and began to climb again to the north window.

At the east window, Antonia was watching the drainpipe bend under the weight of Samuel Parrish. It went down slowly at first, and Samuel grabbed, almost casually, for a windowsill, a lilac branch, anything. . . . Then the pipe gave up all at once and Samuel landed in a yew shrub.

"Samuel! Are you all right?"

She heard grunts, muffled by the humidity, someone brushing off his clothes, a few muttered curses. Yes, he was all right.

"Samuel," she whispered, "in the morning."

"I can't sleep." Samuel sounded as though he too had been drinking.

"You can't wake my whole family because you can't sleep."

Downstairs, the clock chimed. One-thirty.

"Antonia," said Samuel, "I would ask your brother Charlton . . . I would ask him for your hand."

And a voice whispered from below, "I would ask him for your *foot*."

"Foot?" She looked down at Gideon, now crouched on the carpet, grinning.

"I said *hand*!" whispered Samuel. "I would like to ask for your *hand*!"

"My hand," she said. Then she felt Gideon's fingers on her instep. She kicked him away. "Unh . . . Samuel, this is . . . this is very sudden."

"*Sudden*? I've been writing to you for five years."

"I've been writing to you for *eight*," whispered Gideon.

Antonia could not believe what she felt. Gideon was actually kissing her foot.

Gideon could not believe the intoxication of his senses. It was only her foot, and kissing it was no more than a continuation of the joke, but the foot brought him close to the leg, and the leg led upward, and his hands followed their lead.

"I will ask your brother for permission," said Samuel Parrish.

"I . . . I . . ." Antonia stuttered, gasped at Gideon's intimate touch on the backs of her calves, then on her thighs, then whispered, "Stop."

"Stop what?" asked Parrish from below.

"Stop thinking my brother must give permission for me to marry."

"Then you'll marry me?"

"I haven't made that decision."

"I have," said Samuel with sudden firmness. "So make yours."

Gideon decided he could not let this challenge go without one of his own. He made it directly, letting his fingers advance again, like soldiers creeping through the forest to attack her resolve.

"Gideon," she whispered.

"What?" said Samuel from the darkness below. "What did you say?"

Antonia put her hand on the hands under her nightgown and pushed them away. "I said Gid . . . Gid going before your own third lieutenant finds you lurking beneath his sister's window."

"I hadn't thought of that. . . . Will you marry me?"

"I'll tell you when you return from your cruise."

Without even a profession of love, Samuel Parrish retreated into the shadows.

Without another word, Antonia slid to the floor.

"Gid . . . Gid . . . Gideon," she whispered.

"Gid going," he said. "You are a clever girl."

And they laughed. And that made Gideon unique, she thought. They could laugh together. Even here . . . even now.

But there was no more laughter between them, and no more talk, and no more thought, because they agreed without words to give themselves, at least for the moment, to sensation . . . and its sounds. . . .

The wet caress of lips . . . the rush of breathing . . . the rustle of a nightgown rising over shoulders . . . her sudden gasps of pleasure at the touch of his mouth . . . the thump of a jacket on a chair . . . a sharp intake of breath and a feminine "yes" . . . then again, "yes, there" . . . then another "yes," of decision rather than pleasure . . . "yes, now. . . ."

Then a dual-octave cry of surprise and pleasure and perhaps a little pain, one voice a soft soprano, the other a deep, vibrating groan. . . . To this duet was added a rhythm, not percussive but fluid, of movement begun slowly and steadily increasing . . . then the thump of bodies on a Turkish carpet . . . and then—

"I assume this means you're going to marry my sister."

All sound stopped.

Gideon looked toward the door. Candlelight fell across Antonia's face.

She tried to roll out from under Gideon. "Jason! What—"

"My fiancée sleeps under this roof," said Jason, "but I respect her honor enough not to invade her room."

"Maybe she's disappointed about that." Gideon rolled off of Antonia and pulled up his breeches. "Why don't you go and find out?"

Antonia sat up, holding her nightgown up against herself. "Get out, Jason."

"Will there be a marriage . . . or a duel?"

"Not another silly duel, Jason." Antonia stood. "And I'll decide on no marriage until after your ship is back. Now leave us alone, and don't tell mother, or I'll duel you myself."

The next day, Antonia's three lieutenants sailed on the *Constitution*.

She was an awesome thing, thought Antonia, half again as heavy as a British frigate, with stronger timbers, thicker planking, an acre of canvas, masts as tall as the State House. But for all of that, she was as nimble as a skipjack.

Under backed topgallants and reefed topsails, with her jib set for steering, she moved away from her mooring and made her turn into the channel. Then she shook out her courses, like a great butterfly emerging from a cocoon. The southwesterly breeze filled the sails, and she took flight in the glittering sun.

For as long as Antonia could see her, she watched the sailors on the yardarms, and for long after she could listen to their words, she heard their shouts. She envied them the freedom to sail away from their land-bound troubles and lose themselves in the simple business of fighting for their country.

"Miz Antonia?" Iris, Zeke's fourteen-year-old daughter, stood close to her mistress, in the midst of the crowd now leaving the dock.

"Yes?"

"I read what I could in the newspapers 'bout this war, and I can't figure it out."

"Free trade and sailors' rights. And more land in Canada, if we can get it."

"Is that good? More land for slaves to work?"

"It isn't good for a little slave girl to be worryin' her head about," said Mother Sara, who was standing with Miss Mary, staring out at the place where the *Constitution* had rounded into the bay, "not even a little slave girl learnin' to read."

"Yes'm," said Iris.

"She's *my* slave, Mother," Antonia said. "I'll teach her what I want."

"She's your *plaything*." Mother Sara gathered her skirts and started up the street. "A plaything for a grown woman who should get married and have little babies instead of little playthings. Imagine . . . teachin' a slave to read."

"Apple don't fall far from the tree." Rebecca Parrish, like Mother Sara, had been watching the ship take her young man off to war. "Teachin' slaves to read is a good way to start another rebellion."

"Mornin', Rebecca." Mother Sara did not make eye contact.

"'Cept, in a slave rebellion, we'll lose a lot more than our Annapolis houses."

"I haven't lost *my* Annapolis house," said Mother Sara. "And I offered its hospitality to you last evening."

"I told Samuel to beg my indisposition." Rebecca worked her tobacco around in her mouth, producing a strange effect in one who wore an expensive walking suit and a handsome bonnet. "I once promised you I would take your pillow, after all."

"I still sleep well." Mother Sara smiled a serene smile.

"That's what indisposes me." Rebecca smiled back, showing teeth that were all but brown from tobacco.

"And the matriarchs meet." Charlton came ambling into the conversation, with his wife in tow. "What will the matriarchs say if Samuel marries my sister?"

"I'd be too surprised for words." Rebecca spit tobacco.

"I hope no one is forgetting that I may have some opinion about this," said Antonia, "or that Samuel once wanted to kill Jason."

"A gentlemen's duel," said Charlton, "that ended honorably."

"Even if Samuel is a Parrish, I consider him more trustworthy than any Boston man," said Mother Sara.

Rebecca nodded. "Even a Stafford's more trustworthy than a Boston man."

"So you agree on something," said Charlton. "This calls for tea."

"My favorite beverage," said Rebecca. "Even when I'm indisposed."

"Then join us." Mother Sara could always be gracious.

Antonia told them to go on. She went back to the waterfront and sat on a cask in front of the victualing warehouse, determined to take no further part in the public or private discussion of her future.

A schooner was loading tobacco, and she stayed all through the midday heat, listening to the chatter of the seamen and the singing of the slaves. The seamen spent their time insulting one another and demonstrating their equality. The slaves sang spirituals about all they would enjoy in the *next* life.

Antonia sat and watched the gulls gabbling about the skipjacks. She smelled fresh tobacco and salt air. And every so often, she moved, just so she could feel the tenderness, not altogether unpleasant, in the intimate places where Gideon had gone the night before.

Around two o'clock, her dockside reverie was interrupted by a female voice.

"Tea has ended without incident." Miss Mary perched daintily on the edge of another cask. She wore a wide straw sunbonnet while her slave, a young girl named Rowena, followed her face around with a parasol.

"No fight between Mother and Rebecca?" asked Antonia.

"Brother Charlton saw to it."

"He seems more intent on my marrying Samuel than I do."

"You prefer Gideon."

Antonia looked at her. "I do?"

"I heard what went on last night."

Antonia searched the face of her future sister-in-law for some hint of the condemnation. "What was it that you heard, Mary?"

"The sound of suitors comin' to your windows, the sound of . . . of—" Mary took the parasol from Rowena and told her to go down the wharf. Then she drew close to Antonia. "I heard the sound of copulatin'."

"Copulatin'?" Antonia determined that she would not blush.

"What some folks call the act of love, which maybe it was. Others call it"—here she lowered her voice—"*fuckin'*, which sounds a trifle crude."

"Fuckin'." Antonia said the word as if to deprive it of its power to make her blush. "What do you propose to do with this knowledge?"

"Keep it secret and earn your friendship."

"Promise not to cover your mouth like a ninny when you laugh, and I'll be your friend for life."

"We women sometimes play small roles to please men."

Antonia looked at the water. "I play no roles."

"Perhaps you should."

"I don't need your advice on how to act."

"Nor do I need yours on how to laugh."

Antonia liked Mary's sudden firmness. "I'll not argue with you on that."

Miss Mary now moved her parasol so that it shielded Antonia's face from the sun. "Of course, my silence has a price."

If Antonia had not been shocked by Mary's knowledge, she was surely shocked that Mary was devious enough for blackmail. "What is it that you want?"

"Well . . . the copulatin' . . . I want you . . . I want you to tell me what it felt like."

"What it *felt* like?"

"Your brother will make no attempt to show me until our wedding night."

"And you would like something to look forward to?"

Miss Mary brought her hand to her mouth to cover a nervous giggle.

And Antonia began to laugh, softly at first, then a full blown laugh that she could not control. Miss Mary took her hand away from her mouth and laughed, too.

iii
Letters from the Constitution

They would call it the great sea chase. It was more like a race of turtles.

Sailing north off the New Jersey coast, Captain Isaac Hull of the

Constitution was searching for a squadron of American frigates. He thought he had found them, ran up the recognition signal, and was running toward them when he realized that the ships were British. So, with a quick sail change, he turned and ran the other way.

And then the wind died.

For two days, over a flat, calm sea, with sails as limp as an old man's nightshirt, the British wallowed after the big American frigate. But Hull kept his ship in the lead, wetting down sails to catch what breeze there was, hauling the anchors out in the ship's boats and cranking the ship up to them, and finally escaping in a squall.

Otherwise, Gideon would not have been able to write to Antonia from Boston:

> So we are heroes simply because we had the wit to sail faster than the British. What will happen if we win a victory? Hull hopes to slip out before British sails appear off Boston light so that we may do a little commerce raiding.
>
> Your brother, in tones of sarcasm, asked what I will do with any prize money I might make. I told him I will take my bride on the grand tour.
>
> "And who might your bride be?" he asked.
>
> I told him I hoped it would be you, and for the first time in three weeks, he treated me like something more than a cask of fouled water. He said he would not inform Samuel, in the interest of shipboard harmony. In the same interest, I did not tell him that my bride might also decide not to be my bride.
>
> That decision remains yours, but I have offered my hand.
>
> We seem to be of like mind. In a world where too many seem certain of things, we ask why.
>
> We may have been fated to walk the world together, arms linked when possible, spirits aligned when not. The tingling I felt for days after our Independence Night may have been a thing purely physical, or it may have been a sign of our alignment. Make no decision until our cruise has ended, but know my heart and my mind.

And now she had two proposals, but only the most roundabout professions of love. She was glad that the two of them stayed at sea, while she tried to decide what a woman should have for herself.

A month later, on her daily walk with Iris, Antonia saw a knot of people gathered around the office of the *Maryland Gazette*. Men were whooping and patting one another on the back. Women were laughing and applauding at what they read posted in the window:

A Great Victory!
Constitution Defeats British Frigate!
Casualties light:
five seamen, two lieutenants killed, seven others wounded.

Two lieutenants! Antonia went sick at her stomach, but she elbowed her way to the front of the crowd and began to read for the names of her lieutenants, to see which of them had died.

> On August 19, in the first frigate engagement of the present war, the American forty-four *Constitution* sank the thirty-eight gun *Guerrière* off Halifax. The fight lasting some forty-five minutes. . . .

Antonia read quickly, stumbling over facts and phrases while little Iris read aloud beside her . . .

> . . . *Constitution* sustained heavy British fire while moving into position, but given the weight of her timbers, British shot bounced off her hull . . . "Her sides are made of iron!" . . . At 6:05, *Constitution* finally maneuvered to within fifty yards of the enemy and unleashed a terrific broadside. . . .

Where were the names? Only the names mattered. Read faster . . .

> . . . seven hundred and thirty-six pounds of iron smashed into *Guerrière,* shattering her hull and dropping her mizzenmast. . . . Hull cried, "By God, we've made a brig of her! Next time we'll make her a sloop!"

The names! The details meant nothing to the woman looking for lost loved ones. Read faster!

> . . . Amidst clouds of smoke and thundering guns, the ships closed and boarding parties were mustered while marines fired from the fighting tops on each vessel. The valiant Lieutenant Morris leapt to the gunwales and was struck by a British musket ball. . . .

Here Antonia slowed down.

> He subsequently died of his wounds. Lieutenant of Marines William Bush died of a shot to the head. . . .

And Antonia began to cry, right there in the middle of the crowd. She cried for joy that her three men were safe. She cried for the lieutenants who would never see another day. She cried, whether she knew it or not, for herself, that she would never live life with the intensity that men must live it when sailing into battle.

One of the men in the crowd—Samuel Parrish's older brother, Walter, on business from Parrish Manor—asked her if she was all right.

Someone else said, "She's just touched in the head. Teaches her niggers to read . . . cries in the street . . . touched in the head . . ."

Little Iris stepped back as though she had been struck.

Teaches her niggers to read . . . Antonia wiped her eyes and straightened herself before Anson Duganey, a skinny, sour young barrister, and his skinny, sour old mother. Anson had once courted Antonia, but had entered the pantheon of rejected suitors, and simple sourness had grown to outright venom.

"She is touched only in her emotions," Walter Parrish said.

Antonia thanked Walter, a big, slow-moving, and surprisingly gentle character, for a Parrish.

Then she and her slave finished reading. And, in reading, there on the Annapolis street, with Iris reading aloud beside her, Antonia found her purpose: *teaching her niggers to read.*

She would teach all of them. And they would teach others. So that they could know what went on in the world beyond them, just as a crowd of Annapolitans could know of a battle hundreds of miles away and rejoice at the rising power of their young nation.

iv
Dreams of Glories

The church bells rang, from Georgia to Maine.

Constitution had beaten *Guerrière.*

In the same week, David Porter's frigate *Essex* masqueraded as a merchantman and lured a British sloop into range. The sloop was called *Alert*; its captain was anything but.

Then Decatur's *United States* met the British frigate *Macedonian,* and his men worked their guns so well that the British thought the side of *United States* was in flames, but it was *Macedonian* that felt the heat.

As Charlton Stafford remarked to his sister, "Three down, nine hundred and ninety-seven to go."

There was joy in America, disbelief in England, and no leave for American lieutenants. Getting to sea was imperative, not that ship-to-ship victories would ever tip the balance between America and Britain, but because a young nation out to prove itself needed every victory it could get, and a weak navy could damage a strong nation simply by sitting in the shipping lanes and pouncing on enemy merchantmen as they went by.

All of this meant that Antonia still did not have to confront her lieutenants and the question of marriage.

At least they were no longer on the same ship. Jason's mentor, David Porter, had asked *his* mentor, and new captain of the *Constitution*, William Bainbridge, to release Jason for duty aboard the *Essex*. Bainbridge had sent Gideon Browne, too, because he did not like the jealousy he sensed between Gideon and Mr. Parrish.

So, with two new lieutenants, the *Essex* cleared the Delaware Capes in early October. She was to meet the *Constitution* and the sloop *Hornet* in the South Atlantic and hunt in squadron for British merchantmen. But the Atlantic was a fickle beast, and it had a wide back. For most of a month, Porter cruised the Brazilian coast, taking British prizes and searching for his consorts.

Then, in late January, a passing Portuguese merchantman brought momentous news: the *Constitution* had crushed the British frigate *Java* off Rio, but she had been so badly mauled that she had turned back to Boston for repairs. And *Hornet* was far to the north, blockading a ship in British Guiana.

"We're alone, gentlemen," Porter told his officers that night. "We can stay where we are and wait for the British to find us in force. We can run for home with what little prize money and glory we have. Or we can do something daring."

No officer would have dared to suggest anything but something daring.

The next day, Porter posted a notice on the masthead:

> **Sailors and Marines!**
>
> An increase of the enemy's force compels us to abandon a coast that will neither afford us security nor supplies. We will, therefore, proceed to annoy the enemy where we are least expected. What was never performed by a single ship, we will attempt. The Pacific Ocean affords us many friendly ports. The unprotected British commerce on the coast of Chile, Peru, and Mexico will give you an abundant supply of wealth; and the girls of the Sandwich Islands shall reward you for your sufferings during your passage around Cape Horn.

Cape Horn: the last cold and miserable archipelago in the last cold and miserable place where any seafaring man would willingly go, where the wind whipped without cease from the west and a vessel going into it made a mile of leeway for every mile ahead, where the sky was a grim gray and the sea was the color of a bruise, where the waters could rise from a flat plane to a range of mountains in less time than it took to reef topsails.

Cape Horn had long ago replaced the edge of the flat earth as the place that mariners feared the most, and the men of the *Essex* had spoken of it with awe from the moment that Porter first posted his announcement.

Gideon Browne took hope from the writings of Captain James Cook, who had weathered the Horn twice. Jason Stafford read an account of Lord George Anson's 1741 cruise. Anson had sailed with six ships. After rounding the Horn, he had one seaworthy vessel left, but with it he plundered the unsuspecting Spanish in the Pacific and won glory at home.

Porter had said he would do to the British what Anson had done to the Spanish, and there were few aboard who disbelieved him.

The *Essex* was a good sea boat, as the sailors said, built by the shipwrights of Essex County, Massachusetts. But she was fourteen years old and had not been refitted since her last hard cruise. Her bottom needed recoppering; her waterways had opened; a leak in her bow could not be found; her masts worked and heaved in their seats; and the more canvas she carried, the more the masts worked. So the pumps were manned day and night from the time the passage began, while the carpenters spent every watch pounding oakum into leaky seams.

It was late summer in the high latitudes, and the temperature sometimes reached all the way to the forties, small comfort on a ship where spare woolen socks ran low and leather shoes had run out. Here frostbite stung fingers and toes. Rain and sleet struck the skin like needles. And no oilskin, no battened hatch, no boarded deadlight could keep the water from finding its way under every collar and into every seabag and onto every surface where men might sit or stand or sway.

With boarded deadlights and closed gunports, there was constant darkness belowdecks, constant dampness, too. And with three hundred and nineteen aboard, there was a constant crowd, because Porter had taken seventy-five extra crewmen to sail the prizes that he intended to seize.

It was the crowding that bothered Gideon Browne the most, not the belowdecks stink, which stunk even more, now that they had run low on vinegar and no longer sprinkled it on hot cannonballs for fumigation, not the diet of salt beef and weeviled bread, and not the constant worry at when the next storm of rain and sleet and shroud-ripping wind would strip them down to bare poles. It was the crowding.

The *Essex* was a hundred and forty feet from taffrail to billethead, thirty-six feet at the beam, and no matter where Gideon went, from wardroom to sick bay, from gundeck to orlop, there were men, and when the wind died down and the waves quieted, there was the din of men.

And when he went to his stateroom, there was a man there, too. Sometimes he and Jason passed in the companionway when the watch changed and one dropped onto the bunk the other had just left.

Sometimes they returned to their eight-by-four-foot space at the same time, and they would toss a coin to see who would sleep slung in a hammock above the bunk. And sometimes, during the worst of it, they would not sleep at all.

More than once, Gideon recalled what the Englishman Samuel Johnson had written: that going to sea was like going to jail, with the added danger of drowning.

And in a crowded jail, there was conflict. For some, this meant smoldering resentments, fights that went on in the darkness of the berthing deck, unwitnessed by marines, unreported to the officers. For Jason and Gideon, it meant friendly disputes, whenever the rotation of the watch brought them to the cabin at the same time.

They argued naval strategy, the politics of Federalist secession versus Republican warmongering and, one night, the merits of a magnetic leader like Eaton versus those of the more systematic Captain Porter.

"The hunger for glory binds them, no matter their differences," said Jason.

"But Eaton was big, all bulk and bluster." Gideon rocked in his hammock. "Porter's lean and hard. A prize-hunting glory-seeker with the face of a poet. When you do something wrong, he always looks more disappointed than angry."

"I've known ministers who looked like that." Jason yawned.

"But no minister would promise what Porter has."

"The Sandwich Islands?"

"Aye." And Gideon felt the rocking of the ship. Even during this miserable passage, there was a moment each day when he knew why men went to sea, when the rocking of his hammock in the enveloping darkness reminded him of something he could not remember but still knew. He felt it now, the almost liquid motion, and said dreamily, "The girls of the Sandwich Islands."

"What will you do when we see them?" Jason's voice was thick with sleep.

Gideon's mind was somewhere green and sunstruck. "Fuck every one."

An instant later, Gideon's canvas womb was spun over and he was tumbling through the darkness, landing so that his face was wedged against the door and his legs were splayed over Jason's berth. Then he heard Jason's angry wide-awake voice: "We're promised to good women. We owe them our faith. Is that understood?"

Gideon was too dazed to do more than mutter, "Yes, sir," and too sleepy to do more than climb back into the hammock.

The following night, Gideon wrote in his journal: "I must not forget how seriously Jason takes the roles life presents him—second lieutenant, future husband, brother. I trust him with my life in battle or heavy blow, but in matters of mind and heart he does no more than spin hammocks. To keep the peace, I will say no more about the girls of the Sandwich Islands, unless and until we see them."

But the men of the *Essex* could be heard on every corner of the ship, through every watch and meal, speaking of the glories of the Sandwich Islands.

In the officers' wardroom, they told tales of islander hospitality—of women who offered themselves as blithely as they offered a cup of water, of natives who believed white men were gods.

In the midshipmen's berth, boys talked of what it took to become men, and Porter's twelve-year-old foster son, David Farragut, listened wide-eyed to the older boys bragging of what they would do with their manhood.

On the sailors' berthing deck, it was no different, though coarser. One of the coarsest sailors—a hard-won distinction on a frigate—was Benjamin Hazen, or Badmouth Ben to his mates, and he spoke not of the glory to be won, but of the glory *holes*, waiting for his glory *pole*. His mates admired his foul-mouthed eloquence, but Chaplain Adams did not, and not on the morning of February 18, 1813.

For four days, the *Essex* had been running southwest, trying to escape the powerful winds and hard currents pounding off Tierra del Fuego, the land at the tip of the earth. But the farther they sailed, the harder the wind blew and the faster the current ran.

Porter had avoided exhausting his crew or his ship. He required the men to be topside only during their watch. He had sent most of his guns and lighter spars below, to lessen the load on the vessel. But he had resolved to make every mile he could, and he left orders each night that the ship run under close-reefed fore and main topsails and reefed foresail.

During his watch, from 4:00 A.M. to 8:00 A.M., Jason stood on the quarterdeck, close by the stern lantern on the weather side. He had come to be known as Lieutenant Discipline, not because he favored physical punishment but because of the discipline he imposed upon himself, standing the watch in the most exposed part of the quarterdeck, so the crew could see that he would face whatever weather he ordered them to face.

The wind squalled and softened and squalled again during the night. Three sailors were nearly snapped from the mainmast like bugs from a stick when one wave caused the ship to roll so violently the tips of her spars touched the water. But when the watch ended, all hands were accounted for, and Jason could report that he had made six hard miles every hour, which brought them that much closer to good sailing.

He was always thankful for a safe watch, and as it was the Sabbath, he ushered his men forward to give thanks under the direction of Chaplain Adams, a sad-faced New Yorker who left the impression that he would have been much happier ministering to the ladies of Wall Street than to the forecastle dregs of an American frigate.

There was some grumbling among the cold and hungry sailors, but if the preacher's words did not warm them, the galley stove most certainly would. So they crowded forward, beneath the swinging lanterns, for a simple service, a few readings from Scripture and an explication by Reverend Adams, who made the mistake of beginning his talk with a title: "The Glories of God and His Creation."

This brought a grunt from Badmouth Ben, and a raft of snickering.

"Glory is what awaits you all, all you who follow his path," said the chaplain.

"Glory awaits them what knows the way to the right hole," said Ben, and now there was audible laughter at the edge of the crowd.

Jason cleared his throat to gain the attention of the sailors. Then he turned his eyes front, giving them a silent order to shut up and listen.

"Yes," the chaplain went on, "we sail a wooden boat upon an angry rock-rimmed sea. We know the frailty of existence, but we see in those rocks the steadfastness of Christ and his church." He pointed toward the north, toward the rocks of the Horn. "That way lies glory!"

Badmouth Ben pointed at his crotch. "That way lies all the glory we need."

Reverend Adams glared at Hazen. "I condemn your disrespect, sailor."

And Lieutenant Discipline knew it was time for some discipline.

On the quarterdeck, gray sleet was whipping through gray sky, and the sea was running in an endless line of thumping five-foot waves.

Gideon Browne stood beside Captain Porter, in good position to hear and relay his orders. Gideon noted they were nearing seventy-seven degrees west, where Captain Cook made his turn north. "He knew he was far enough west to weather Tierra Del Fuego without being blown onto the Patagonian coast, sir."

Porter jammed his hands into his sea cape. "You know your history, Browne."

"History can be a comfort, sir."

"Take comfort where you can."

Gideon wondered where Porter found comfort. The captain had decided to run for the Pacific without orders. His ship was now a lone renegade, thousands of miles from friendly ports, in the midst of a raging passage, engaged in something that might satisfy his hunger for glory or end in disaster.

"Give us a change of wind, Browne, and we'll take Cook's turn."

Now four men were hurrying aft—Chaplain Adams, Lieutenant Stafford, Seaman Hazen, and a marine guard.

Marine and sailor stopped forward of the mizzenmast, as they were not allowed onto the quarterdeck without invitation. Stafford and Adams approached the captain and Lieutenant Browne.

"Stripes for him, sir!" said Adams, gesturing to Hazen.

"Reason?" said Porter.

"Disrespect to the chaplain," said Jason. "He was gesturing to his crotch and talking about . . ."

"About what?" demanded Porter, growing impatient.

"Blasphemy," sputtered Adams, "about glory being in his balls, not with God."

Gideon raised a hand to his mouth to cover his laugh. There had been little mirth on the *Essex* in recent weeks, and annoying Chaplain

Adams, who possessed no apparent sense of humor, seemed like good sport.

Porter summoned the sailor forward.

Hazen was about thirty, scrawny and leathered, a small man except in the hands, which were like grappling hooks, and the feet, which had worn through the toes of his last pair of shoes. Some sailors fawned before officers. Others looked at the deck and made no eye contact. Hazen pulled at his forelock, then looked an officer in the eye, offering respect to rank and demanding respect for service.

"Anything to say for yourself, sailor?" asked Porter.

"It was a long night, sir. We be hungry. I was pointin' to my belly and sayin' *that* was where the glory was."

A smile crossed Porter's face. "Belly and balls are close by, Reverend."

"My belly was rumblin', Captain, and disturbin' the men. I'm a hungry man."

Porter looked at Jason. "He's your watch. Recommend punishment." Then Porter turned to check the binnacle.

"Stripes," said Adams to Jason. "Men must be made to respect the Lord."

"They must be made to respect their officers first," said Gideon. "Leniency."

Jason fixed his eyes on Hazen. Here was a test of a man's ability to command. As always, Jason settled on a matter of honor to see him through. "You lied to the captain, Hazen. It was your balls you were pointing to. But for that, I'd consider leniency."

"Then stripes it is," said the chaplain.

"No," said Jason. "A flogged sailor is no good to his mates. He'll wear the yoke instead, like a berthing deck thief."

The yoke was a nagging misery, a heavy wooden collar that the sailor wore whenever he was not on watch. A misery, but better than having no back skin.

"Next time, Hazen, we'll yoke your balls." Jason dismissed the sailor to the custody of the marine guard. Then he looked at the chaplain and Gideon Browne. "Not an offense that calls for stripes, nor one that deserves leniency."

The chaplain stalked off.

Gideon restrained himself from muttering a few words of compliment on his friend's growing wisdom.

But Captain Porter looked up from the binnacle and said, "Mr. Stafford, it seems that you are learning to remember your shrouds."

And on they sailed.

Day after day, the wind whipped, and the sea struck the bow with a steady and simple rhythm, the misery of it made all the worse by the monotony. Water pounded up and over the bows, up and over and across the spar deck, up and over the hatch coamings and down the companionways, down to the gundeck and the berthing deck, down to where men sought escape by the warmth of the galley stove or in the tight-wrapped dampness of their hammocks.

Porter had planned for the worst—a month to round the Horn, a month to run up the coast to Valparaiso. His purser's report for February 1 had shown 184 barrels of beef, 114 barrels of pork, 21,763 pounds of bread, 1,741 gallons of spirits, 201 gallons of vinegar, 108 gallons of molasses. On that day he had ordered half rations on beef, two-thirds on everything else, so that he would be certain to feed his sailors all the way to the next stop.

By February 20 the reduced rations and the pounding miseries had drained the men of spirit. Some sailors had even begun to augment their diet with the only fresh meat left aboard: their pet monkeys and the ship rats. So Porter ordered a barrel of peas opened. The cold weather had tamped down the men's thirst, leaving fresh water for boiling, and the sweet taste of boiled peas might bring some cheer.

Gideon went below with a quartermaster and Midshipman Farragut, who seemed curious, serious, more than willing to assume any task, even command, if it was offered.

Gideon offered him a pinchbar and told him to open the barrel.

A dozen sailors drew closer. The crew was divided into eight-man messes, and each mess elected a man who saw to the rations for his mates. These twelve had come with pots and buckets to take their share of peas for their messmates.

"Peas is what we wants, lads," said Seaman Reuben Marshall, a brawny brute with a sloping brow and a penchant for philosophical pronouncements that were hard to understand because he had lost his upper teeth in a Boston bar fight. "Peas'll make us fart sweet parfum the whole night through. Green peas to remind us of the green fields of home. Sweet farts and sweet thoughts, eh, lads?"

"You wants peas 'cause they make good mush," said Crab Louse Tom Brannock, oldest seaman on the ship, whose nickname derived from his filthy clothes and scrofulous beard, his crabbed gait, and his ability to anger his mates over anything. "A toothless sailor needs baby's mush more 'n meat."

"I'm more man than you—" Marshall raised his pot at the Crab Louse.

"Stand down," snapped Gideon, "and look on a treat for a hungry crew."

The lid of the barrel squeaked open. The sailors leaned forward. And Gideon almost retched.

Instead of dried green peas, awaiting water to boil them back to life, the barrel was alive already . . . with worms. No more of the peas remained than hulls and chaff. The rest of the barrel was squirming with inch-long black-tipped white worms, worms grown fat on food that would have filled many bellies.

"Sweet farts and sweet dreams, is it?" growled the Crab Louse. "Maggots is what it is."

Reuben Marshall plunged his pot into the seething mess. "Maggot soup, lads."

"Maggot soup?" said young Farragut, eyes widening.

"Aye." Marshall laughed. "A little salt, a little pepper—"

"Over the side with it," ordered Gideon Browne.

Marshall looked down at the worms in his pot. "Even these?"

"Even those," said Gideon.

And the big, brawny seaman began to cry. His eyes filled with tears, and he said, in a soft voice that made his desperation all the more convincing, "I ain't sure how long I can handle it, lads."

"We'll weather it." The Crab Louse spat into the barrel. "We don't, we dies. And I'm for livin' and prizin' and wettin' me pecker in them Sandwich doxies."

"I ain't sure." Reuben Marshall pressed a finger to one nostril and blew out the contents of the other. "I ain't sure about any of it."

"None of us is," said Seaman Will Whitney, a slender and delicate young man who struck Gideon as altogether too gentle for the berthing deck.

Just then the ship lurched and a voice from above cried for all hands.

Reuben Marshall shuddered as mightily as the ship itself. "All hands" meant the captain sensed an emergency, and men would be sent aloft, into danger that a landlubber would find inconceivable.

From Gideon Browne's Journal, February 22:

> Brawny sailors cry at the sight of worms. The skin peels from my feet, which are constantly wet. And the ship rides like a cork in the Kennebec. After four days of beating to westward, clearing skies enabled us to to take a lunar sighting and showed that for all our suffering, the easterly set of the current left us a full degree *worse* than we were on the eighteenth.
>
> The captain took pains to hide his disappointment from the crew. He told the officers that no information about our position should be given, as it is now established fact that depressed spirits can bring on the scurvy.

Two days later, they had battled their way back to eighty degrees, and the wind shifted at last to the southwest.

So Porter mustered the crew and told them that their ordeal had come to an end. They had weathered the Horn and were turning north. In celebration, he said, he was increasing the water ration to allow them tea twice a day.

Gideon and Jason stood behind Porter, who stood ramrod straight in his best blue uniform. Beyond him were nearly three hundred faces—haggard, surly, hungry, but every hard eye fixed on the man who had brought them this far.

"I commend you for your conduct during our boisterous passage." Porter squared himself on the rolling deck. "And I promise you more than tea as reward in the Pacific."

The girls. This was the dream that had kept many of them going. The mere mention of it brought a loud cheer.

Gideon glanced at Jason, who kept his eyes fixed on Porter's back, as if he would not acknowledge the possibility of temptation.

"Now, then." Porter's voice rose above the wind. "As an indulgence in promise of future reward, I declare a general pardon on men wearing the yoke for petty offenses."

The crewmen cheered again.

"On one condition!" Porter threw up his hands. "The first offender brought to the gangway from below will receive two dozen lashes, as an example."

Jason looked down at his shoe tops.

The boatswain went to the gangway and called for the yoked sailors. The odds were good that Badmouth Ben would not appear first, but he did, and the captain ordered that he be grappled to the grate for flogging.

Two dozen lashes stripped the back of Badmouth Ben almost completely. The crew watched in silence, all knowing that it might as easily have been them. Chaplain Adams folded his arms and looked up at the heavens, as though God had delivered his opinion after all. Jason wished that he had been more lenient.

And Gideon wrote in his journal: "After punishment, I took Hazen to sick bay to have his wounds salted. He did not scream, as men often do when salt touches the pulpy flesh left after a flogging. Instead, he cursed. He cursed the surgeon's mate, who salted him. He cursed Lieutenant Stafford, who yoked him in the first place. He cursed David Porter, once he knew why he had been flogged. And when I warned him against cursing the captain, he cursed me. The man can curse."

Four days later, the *Essex* reached a latitude of 50 degrees, several hundred miles up the Patagonian coast. To celebrate, Porter brought together the surgeon, the chaplain, and five of his lieutenants—Downes, Wilmer, Cowell, Stafford, and Browne—for a meal of salt beef, a few peas that had escaped the worms, a glass of port, and a round of cheese.

"We're fairly out of danger, gentlemen. Tomorrow we bring up light spars and guns and become a warship again. We make for Valparaiso, then the Galápagos."

"Then the Sandwich Islands," said Lieutenant Downes.

Chaplain Adams made an irritated snort, like a sleeping dog whose tail had been stepped on.

"We won't see them for some time," said Porter.

Jason trimmed a small piece of cheese, a pungent cheddar that tingled on his tongue. "We could be six months in the Galápagos, sir."

"It will take that long for word of us to reach the admiralty and for a squadron to come after us." Porter leaned back and sipped his port, at ease with himself and the feat of seamanship he had accomplished. "That's when we run for paradise."

"May I say that you disciplined the right man the other day," offered the chaplain. "I prayed that the Lord would send Hazen first. Justice was served."

"*Command* was served." Porter filled the chaplain's glass. "Were I serving simple justice, I would have flogged them all. Flog a sailor and he'll hate you. But he'll respect you. When you order him aloft in a gale, he'll go because he fears your discipline more than he fears the storm."

"And the sailors you spare?" asked Gideon.

"They'll remember their mate's bloody back *and* your mercy. They'll take to the masts like they'll take to the Sandwich Islands."

"To the Sandwich Islands," said Lieutenant Downes.

Porter smiled indulgently at his second-in-command.

"Hear, hear!" Reverend Adams surprised them by raising his glass and forcing a smile up into his cheeks. "To bringing God's faith to the heathens."

Jason raised his glass, for a man of God deserved respect. "To God's faith."

"Thank you, Lieutenant," said the chaplain. "I shall count upon your example when we reach the islands."

"And I shall count upon all of you," said Porter. "In doubling the Horn, we've shown that there is nothing too daring for men who are resolute yet flexible, aggressive yet wise. Now we'll make history together."

There was no bombast in his voice, no grasping for drama in his delivery. The captain's calmness, thought Gideon, made his words all the more potent.

V
Into Hell

But Porter's words were premature, for that afternoon, the southwest wind freshened, then swung around to the west, and the *Essex* entered what Gideon Browne described in his journal as "a hell of wind and water."

There was no man aboard who could remember anything as terrifying, no man aboard who ever felt more insignificant beneath the ranges of ocean that slammed again and again onto the *Essex*.

The earlier storms were like July days by comparison. It blew so hard they thought it might blow itself out on the second day, but it blew harder instead, blew so hard that the ship would have been torn apart if she'd carried too much canvas.

But she had to carry some, or she would lose headway and the wind would pound her onto the Patagonian coast, which lay to the east, where the scudding clouds stopped and boiled against the great wall of the Andes. So the *Essex* went with storm staysails and close-reefed maintops and steady prayers from Chaplain Adams.

Jason was slammed against the rail on the second day and bruised his hip. His eyes burned constantly from the unceasing salt spray. He shivered from the water that found its way down his neck. But he stood every watch with his men.

Gideon was miserable, but he was not bored. Ugly boils sprouted at his cuffs and in a ring around his neck, where the skin had been rubbed by the collar of his sea cape. And he came to dread his watch only a bit more than the strange hours of soaked sleep, when he dreamed he saw the ship from afar, as God might see it, a collection of nailed-together trees, string, and canvas, a tiny vessel lost and alone, orbiting the continents in the immensity of the sea, a vessel that each night diminished to no more than a dot, then disappeared forever into the endless waves.

On the third night, his dream took life.

By then the pumps could barely keep up. And neither could the men. Contused legs and skulls, sprained wrists and ankles, joined the usual diarrheas and venereal diseases of sick bay. Porter himself had been thrown to the deck, wrenching his knee so badly that he was forced to his cabin, where he made plans for throwing over his guns, a last resort if the ship should founder. Jason's hip pained him like a knife. But by some miracle of training, skill, and instinct, not a single man had been lost.

Around six bells—two-thirty—Gideon was awakened by the pitching of the ship, or maybe by the throbbing pain of his boils. So he thought about Antonia. He tried to remember the perfumes of her body, tried to recall the feel of her smooth, warm skin. But for all his conjuring, she did not appear, clothed or unclothed, to take him back to sleep.

So he rolled to the deck and pulled on the pair of socks he had dried at the galley stove during the last watch. Then he slipped his feet back into his wet boots and left his tiny stateroom, feeling his way past the swinging hammocks until he reached the sick bay. He found the surgeon and his mates asleep, a state that he would have paid handsomely to enter, so he left them to their dreams and went staggering up to the gundeck.

There, Reuben Marshall, philosopher seaman, was tending the big Brodie stove, which was kept lit through every watch so that the men could have someplace in this horror of wind and sea to find a bit of warmth.

A dozen sailors and a few prisoners from prizes taken in the Atlantic were clustered around the stove. The prisoners were not confined, as some helped to sail the ship, and all knew that escape or rebellion were impossible. Many, in fact, rebelled only when Porter tried to put them ashore, because they preferred life in the American navy to their own.

All of them stiffened at the approach of an officer.

"At ease," grumbled Gideon.

"So damn tired you can't sleep, eh, Lieutenant?" Reuben pointed to the sailors, hollow-eyed skeletons in the swinging lanternlight. "Join the crew."

Gideon held out his left wrist and pointed to the throbbing red mound beside the knucklebone. "I've heard that you're good with a knife."

"That I am, sir. That I am." Reuben pulled a splicing knife from his belt. "It does a man good to bring another man relief from the pain we're in."

"Well said." Gideon rolled up his sleeve. "Now lance the boil."

• • •

On the quarterdeck, not even Jason Stafford could stand watch near the stern lights, for anyone near the rail might be swept away in an instant. So he tied a lifeline around his waist and stood by the helm, where he could shout orders to the two sailors steering the ship.

Normally, one man could handle the helm, but it was a double wheel for a reason: in dirty weather, when wind pulled one way and water pulled the other, two strong seamen were needed to hold the ship on point, two strong seamen like Jasper Reed, freed slave from Annapolis, and Badmouth Ben.

It had been a hard watch. The wind was no longer consistent in direction or intensity. The storm was entering what Jason hoped would be a final phase, and he meant to outlast it, just as he meant to follow orders and hold his course.

"You're falling off!" he cried at Hazen for the fourth time that night.

Hazen gritted his teeth. "I'll give up the wheel in a second, if you want. Go below and stand by the Brodie, 'stead of weatherin' this shitfuck night!"

Jasper Reed's eyes widened. "Better say 'sir,' Badmouth Ben."

"Aye, Lieutenant, *sir*. It's a shitfuck night, Lieutenant, *sir*."

"Just stay on point." Jason turned away, stood by the mizzenmast pinrail. He would give no embittered seaman a chance to vent his anger.

Then he noticed a strange smoothing of the waves. Later he would recall it as the sea taking a breath, sucking in all its power for a single blast.

He looked down the length of the ship, marked by dots of light where lanterns hung amidships and at the bow, and by shafts of light that rose feebly from the gangways. He never considered the insignificance of the lights in the consuming blackness around them. His job was simply to keep those lights moving steadily and smoothly, illuminating the blackness as they sailed through it.

And so he was utterly shocked when the blackness consumed the lights all at once.

At the same moment, the tip of Reuben's knife touched Gideon's boil—a little blood, a little fluid, and then the tallow-colored core popped out.

An instant later, the larboard gunports were burst in.

A broadside of water all but crushed the *Essex* from close range.

It exploded into the gundeck, slammed Gideon Browne against a timber, then lifted the deck and tilted it in a sickening roll.

Jason Stafford was consumed in the blackness. He was floating, spinning, tumbling. Then his lifeline pulled taut and what air was left in his lungs was squeezed out of him.

A massive rogue wave had shattered both quarter boats, tearing off the headrails, bursting all the hammock stanchions on the spar deck, and for a few moments, consuming the *Essex* herself.

Belowdecks, water was still shooting through the gunports while a cataract of green water poured down the gangway and doused the only lantern still burning.

Within the blackness, Gideon and Jason both had the sensation of struggle, of feet and hands, of arms and legs, of grabbing and grasping, of men trying to right themselves in the midst of the torrent.

Above decks and below, it seemed for certain that the *Essex* was going over.

She heeled so far to starboard and filled so fast with water that it seemed she could never right herself. But the sailors called her a good sea boat, and she was. When the wave finally thundered past, she rolled back to port like a stunned boxer trying to stand after a blow.

She found her keel, then settled from the weight of all the water in her belly. Then the wind took her by the bow as though taking her by the nose, and she followed groggily toward a heading where wind and waves together would cross her beam and pound her to pieces.

The men belowdecks did not need to feel the wind to know what was happening. They lived by the sea and could sense its rising malevolence like landlubbers smelling rain in the wind.

One-Eyed Mudge was the first to stagger to his feet in the knee-deep water and total darkness. "She's swingin' broadside, lads!"

"And this water ain't runnin' off!" screamed Reuben Marshall.

Gideon was stunned and soaked. He heard the sloshing of water in places where it shouldn't be. He heard the high-pitched shouts of sailors awakened by water pouring down to the orlop deck. And he heard the deeper bass shouts of those already awake and terrified in the darkness.

"Goin' over, we is! Abandon ship!"

Gideon recognized Mudge's voice and felt the crush of bodies fighting their way through the lurching darkness to the gangway.

He tried to stand and someone knocked him down. He fell face first into the water and thought that he was going to die . . . die in the blackness.

Then the ship shuddered and began to lurch in the other direction.

"Feel 'er shift!" cried One-Eyed Mudge.

Marshall screamed, "She's stove in!"

Gideon got to his knees, then to his feet. He fought his panic and grasped for command. All he could cry was "Steady, men." And no one heard him.

There was another lurch. The ship swung back again.

"She's founderin'!" screamed Mudge.

Foundering. Gideon could feel it. They were going down in the total darkness. Panic took command of him, and he heard himself cry, "Abandon ship!"

And Reuben Marshall shouted, "You heard it, lads. Abandon ship! Don't let yourself die in the dark."

And from behind Gideon came the hard, cold voice of Crab Louse Tom. "You won't die in no dark if you light a damn lantern."

The ship lurched again, and Gideon fell against the hot Brodie stove.

The burning on his leg and the voice of the Crab Louse drove the panic out of him. "Belay that order!" he shouted. Then he pulled open the door of the stove and reached for a firebrand to light a lantern.

But the men were already scrambling up the gangway.

On the spar deck, Jason Stafford grabbed his lifeline and hauled himself to his feet. The deck lanterns had been shattered, and the ship was enveloped in darkness. To his left, the great double helm was unmanned and spinning like a chronometer gone crazy. To his right, one of the helmsmen was leaning over the starboard side.

"Hazen! Reed!" cried Jason. "Man the helm."

"Help, Lieutenant!" cried Jasper Reed.

"Where's Badmouth Ben?" cried Jason.

"Gone over!" The big black freedman was holding a broken lifeline that held Hazen somewhere over the side.

"Help me secure the helm!" screamed Jason.

"I can't let go, Lieutenant. He'll be gone."

The wheel whipped about so fast that it made a *whirring* sound of its own.

"Help, Lieutenant!" cried Reed.

"Abandon ship, lads!" cried some sailor from the forward gangway.

"Who said that?" demanded Jason.

"Lieutenant Browne's order!" answered One-Eyed Mudge.

"Belay it!" screamed Jason. "All hands aft!"

The ship settled a bit more, and from somewhere deep inside her came the groan of wood straining under hundreds of tons of water.

"She's founderin'," cried Reuben Marshall.

"Help me and she won't!" Jason went for the helm but was stopped by the scream of Jasper Reed for help.

The darkness on the spar deck was almost total. And the ship was settling. And the crew emerging from below looked like frightened rats.

The wheel spun again, the ship lurching with it.

Jasper Reed cried again for help.

Sailors fell to their knees and began to pray.

Save the ship and its paralyzed crew, or save a single sailor? For a moment, Jason was paralyzed himself.

Then a light appeared at the forward gangway, and Jason heard the voice of Gideon Browne, bellowing, "All hands to their stations."

"But you said abandon!" cried Mudge. "She's stove in."

"You was hearin' things." That was the voice of Crab Louse Tom.

And the boatswain's mate, Big Will Kingsbury, who had been taken down by the wave, leaped onto a gun carriage and roared, "Damn your eyes and put your best foot forward! There's one side of her left yet!"

It could have been the words of Kingsbury or the Crab Louse, or the sight of Gideon's lantern, or another wave, much smaller, that broke over her and reminded them that abandonment was suicide, but suddenly the *Essex* came to life. Sailors leaped to the rigging. Others went below to man the pumps.

Little David Farragut appeared from nowhere to grab the wheel, which was spinning so hard that it almost threw him over, but he held it until Gideon grabbed hold beside him. At the same time, Jason pivoted to the rail and grabbed the lifeline with Jasper Reed.

And the *Essex* headed into the wind, gathering way as she went.

The Andes appeared late the next day, pristine and sparkling beneath their mantle of snow, as if they had been created from the clouds in the agony of the storm. And though they were thirty or forty miles away, every man on the ship felt that he might reach out and touch them.

At the dogwatch, when port and starboard alternated two-hour shifts for supper, Gideon stood at the rail, staring out at the mountains, and penciled a few words in his journal: "Our port side is sound. Repairs have begun. We survived not only the storm but our own failing. Porter commended those who had kept their heads and said, with great generosity, that any panic could be laid to the intensity of the wave breaking upon sleeping men. This . . ."

"Recording the storm?" Jason leaned against the rail.

"Had we not found our backbone when we did, we would have gone down."

And for a time they watched the rose-colored light descending on the mountains. One resisted criticizing, the other resisted explaining. In the pellucid air, it seemed almost immoral to discuss the murky events of the night before.

But for Jason, it would have been immoral to say nothing. "Did you order an abandon ship?"

"The sailors heard me give the order. Fewer heard me belay it. Men hear what they want to." Gideon kept his voice and annoyance low. "Porter said that for all my blundering, I helped save the ship."

"I'm simply protecting your honor, Gideon. Your children will carry Stafford blood."

"The sooner the better."

Jason laughed. He hated conversations like this, no matter how necessary he thought they were. "The sooner the better for all of us."

Gideon hated them, too. "When I came on deck, you were paralyzed between the helm and Hazen."

"I was never paralyzed. Officer of the deck can't lose his nerve."

"We are not perfect mechanisms, Jason."

But Jason knew that. He had learned it in Tripoli many years before.

vi
The Promise

Shot through the lung, and somehow he survived.

On the afternoon that the *Constitution* shattered the *Java*, the surgeon could easily have left Samuel Parrish to die. But he did not. He picked pieces of broken rib from the bullet holes, front and back, made incisions, front and back, through which he stitched the gray spongelike lung tissue. Then he stitched Parrish shut. *Then* he left him to die.

And it nearly happened. Parrish's lung filled with blood. He felt as though he were drowning. But aboard the *Constitution*, sailors said Lieutenant Parrish was too mean to die. And they were right.

By early March, he was back on the Patuxent, where Aunt Rebecca pampered him with crab cakes and cookies. But the woman he hoped would pamper him did not. She wrote him a letter and sent him a copy of Cook's *Voyages* instead.

The only Stafford he saw was Charlton, who came often to talk with Aunt Rebecca. Through all the years that Stafford horses had been losing, they had been able to defeat Parrish mounts often enough for Charlton to believe he was a good judge of horseflesh. After all, Parrish horses carried the best blood in Maryland and seldom lost to anyone else. As his other losses mounted, Charlton's desire to breed his stock to the Parrish line brought him more regularly to Parrish Manor.

But the answer from Rebecca was always the same: "Build your own stable." And he always left a bit more disappointed.

One late March day, Rebecca and her wounded nephew watched from the veranda as Charlton rode off.

"He tells me that his sister is now at Stafford Hall," said Samuel.

"Do you love this Stafford girl with all her wild notions?"

"The best mount's the one that's most spirited before she's broken."

"Why must men talk like that?" Rebecca took a pinch of tobacco and pursed her tobacco-stained lips.

"Well, she comes from a horse-loving family, Aunt Rebecca."

"I might by now have made a proposal to Charlton about his horses, if not for your interest in her."

"I don't understand."

"You don't need to."

"I do need to understand Antonia."

"I for one can't understand why she's tryin' to teach plantation darkies to read." Rebecca picked up the little Royal Doulton gravy boat that she carried around the house and deposited a brown string of saliva in it. "I don't think she knows the trouble she's likely to cause."

Antonia knew. It was no crime in Maryland to teach a slave to read, perhaps because the number of freedmen grew every year. But it was not seen as a way to win friends, and certainly not the way for a woman to win a husband, especially when she was ignoring her best marital prospect.

She had begun by teaching the house slaves at the Fine Folly just after New Year's. She had gathered Zeke, Iris, and half a dozen others, had distributed writing slates and readers, and had gone to work. Her mother was furious, the slaves confused, but Antonia remained adamant. And all through the winter, she had continued her work like a missionary.

Finally Mother Sara decided to end what she called her daughter's "cold-weather pickaninny pastime." She told Antonia that unless she stopped the lessons, she would inherit no Stafford slaves, and if she never owned any, she could not employ, free, or sell them when she had grown older and wiser.

Antonia saw the logic in this, but missionaries had to be zealous, so she headed south to Stafford Hall, to teach the slaves there, out of her mother's sight.

Brother Charlton was infuriated at her arrival. He told her there was nothing in books that niggers needed to know, especially when the tiny tobacco sprouts needed thinning. But when he ordered her to leave, she threatened to tell their mother how much he had lost at racecourses and gaming tables in the previous year. And brother Charlton retreated from his fury.

That spring, she set up her classroom in the little gatehouse.

There were six slaves in her first class: two young men, three children, and an old man too weak to work. They dutifully recited the alphabet as Antonia pointed from one letter to the next. And while it was clear that they understood what she was trying to do, it was also clear that they did not know *why* she was doing it.

But she kept trying. "A . . . B . . . C . . ."

"You know"—the door behind her opened on a cold March afternoon, and there stood Samuel Parrish, looking pale but still beautiful with his long yellow hair—"the darkie is mentally inferior. Teach him something complicated and it'll flow right out his shoes, if he's wearing any."

"Our slaves are always shod."

"They should be shod and cared for. But we should expect no more of them than we do of our beasts—service without question in exchange for kindness."

"They're human beings."

"Inferior beings." Samuel spoke as though the slaves could not understand him. "Now, I've been expecting you for three weeks."

"Expecting?"

"Common courtesy. To one who would marry you."

"I can make no decision until the *Essex* returns."

"But you have not even visited me." Samuel took her by the arm and led her out the door. In the cold air, he demanded, "Do you love me?"

"You have been constant, Samuel. And I did promise you an answer."

"I'll not hold you to it." He took her around the waist, winced with pain as he moved, coughed a bit. "By fall, I will be called back to duty. If we have not heard from the *Essex* by then, we will assume what any sane navy man would—that she's lost. Then I will ask you to marry me again."

"Do you love me now?"

"When I thought I would die, it was you that I thought of."

And that was almost enough, because it was the closest he had ever come to saying he loved her. Now she made a promise to Samuel. She would have an answer when he asked again. Then he kissed her, and it was in no way unpleasant.

But where was the *Essex*?

vii
A Perfect Bedlam

Riding the broad and sun-silvered Pacific, that was where the *Essex* was, riding among the magical Galápagos, riding down British whalers, and building a prize fleet that by late September numbered a dozen ships.

The biggest prize, the whaler *Atlantic*, had been refitted with twenty guns and renamed the *Essex Jr.*, under the command of Lieutenant Downes. The sixteen-gun *Greenwich* had gone to Jason Stafford.

Gideon Browne remained aboard the *Essex* as Porter's first lieutenant and filled his journal with the descriptions of the wonders of the Galápagos. He wrote of the giant tortoises that the sailors found easy to capture, easy to store belowdecks, and delicious. He described strange land iguanas, equally easy to catch, equally delicious. He sketched beautiful flamingos, also easy to catch, not very delicious at all.

In his journal on September 9, he wrote:

> The men hunger, but not merely for meat. These islands inspire many hungers, but satisfaction seems as ethereal as light. They hunger for prize money, and Porter tells them we have amassed two and a half million. (So long as we can bring our prizes to a legitimate court.) They hunger for glory, and Porter tells them they will have it before we are done. (We have swept the British whalers from the sea, but Porter does not think that is glory enough.) They hunger for the women Porter promised, and he promises again. (Though some of us have women waiting for us at home.)

A week later, after the capture of another British whaler, Gideon wrote:

> September 16. Took *Sir Andrew Hammond* just as she finished flensing a sperm whale. This noble creature was now no more than a mass of blood and fiber, floating like a sore on the face of the sea. It struck me that in satisfy-

ing their hungers, men sometimes make great messes, sometimes in pursuit of profit, sometimes in the name of glory, sometimes for no reason at all. Sometimes it helps to know this.

Two weeks later the *Essex Jr.* returned from Valparaiso with intelligence brought overland: three British ships, the frigate *Phoebe* and the sloops-of-war *Cherub* and *Raccoon*, were heading for the Horn. Porter told his officers that it was time now to rest and get ready. Some toasted to the girls of the Sandwich Islands. Jason toasted to glory. And Gideon silently toasted to the making of no more messes.

On the morning of October 24, 1813, a chain of majestic green mountains rose before the *Essex* from out of an amethyst sea.

The first European to see these islands, a Spanish explorer named Álvaro de Mendaña y Castro, found them so beautiful that he named them for his marquesa in 1595. But they were so remote that no white men had ever bothered to claim them, which Porter believed made them a far better place to hide than the Sandwich Islands, called Hawaii, some twenty-five hundred miles northwest.

The largest of the Marquesas was called "Nuku Hiva." The chart showed it to be about fifteen miles across, thirty miles long, with a fine bay cut into the south coast. What the chart did not show was its beauty.

Gideon was reminded of Genesis.

Porter was reminded that an explorer could name a body of water that a chart did not identify. So he named the bay for the state where the *Essex* had been built. Then he pointed her into it, well ahead of the other ships in his fleet. Massachusetts Bay was wide and deep, with water so clear that a sharp-eyed sailor could see crabs scuttling across the sandy bottom, and it was protected by mountains so tall that no gale could ever blow over them.

The trumpeting of conch shells flew ahead of the ship, from one tall peak to the next, so that when the *Essex* at last came to the upper reaches of this bay—so Edenic that Gideon Browne thought it deserved a better name—a thousand feathered and tattooed warriors had gathered to greet her.

More than one sailor groused that there was not a woman to be seen. More than one officer thought the same thing while barking at a sailor to keep his eyes on his task. And Gideon decided it was good that the heavens had opened up and soaked the ship the night before. Otherwise she might have burst into flames from the simple heat of anticipation.

The heat only grew hotter when Porter called the men together and announced, "You don't see 'em, lads, but the women are there."

That brought a few cheers, a few nervous glances at the warriors on shore.

"Be assured, I am intent upon establishing friendly intercourse with these natives, and they see the friendliest form of intercourse as no more than recreation for themselves, hospitality for their guests."

That brought huzzahs and shouts.

Porter raised his hands, and the men immediately, obediently fell silent. "But *guests* conduct themselves with respect for their hosts. So enjoy their company, give the women what they call *tie-ties*—such gifts as will make them pliant—but never insult them . . . and never trust them."

On the beach, drums were beating, conchs were still blowing, and on the ridges above more warriors were appearing.

Porter's eyes were on his men, his voice hardening as he spoke. "Let the fate of Captain Cook and others who have been cut off by the savages of the South Seas be your warning. And heed mine as well: if any man does anything to endanger our purpose here, I will make that man wish he had been born a woman, because it's a woman he'll look like when I'm done with him."

That afternoon, before the rest of his fleet had arrived, Porter went ashore with a detachment of marines and a few *tie-ties.* Gideon remained in command of the ship, and through his spyglass, he watched Porter wade into the crowd of warriors as though they were no more than children.

And that was how he treated them.

First he gave them presents—a knife for the old Chief Gattanewa, bits of iron hoop and fishhooks for the warriors. Then he gave them a show—his marines performed close order drill and musketry. Then he parlayed through Gattanewa's interpreter, an English shipwreck named Wilson.

And an agreement was reached: for as long as the Americans

remained, they would enjoy the hospitality of the Taeeh tribe and take the Taeeh side in their wars with their neighbors. Then the women began to appear. And Taeeh hospitality was offered right there on the beach.

Before long, all but his marines had disappeared into native huts, seeing an opportunity, as Porter later wrote, "which had not for a long time presented itself, and all were determined to take advantage of it, at all hazards, even at the risk of violating every principle of subordination and obedience to orders."

Porter sent marines to collect his wandering crew, and he waited, hands clasped behind his back, barely glancing at the bosoms and bottoms until "My attention was drawn to a handsome young woman, of about eighteen, her carriage majestic, her hair glossy black, her skin anointed with coconut oil, her whole person neat, sleek, and comely. She was Piteenee, granddaughter of the chief Gattanewa, and I felt that it would be necessary, from motives of policy, to pay some attentions to her."

Even the captain, thought Gideon, watching from the quarterdeck.

She received Porter's advances, as he later wrote, "with a coldness and hauteur that suited a princess. Yet this lady, like the rest of the women of the island, soon followed the dictates of her own interest and formed a connection with one of the officers."

However, Porter betrayed no annoyance when he returned to the ship. Annoyance over a woman would have been unseemly, and there was still sea work to be done.

By the time the *Essex* was snug at her moorings, native canoes surrounded her, and native women were singing and dancing on the shore. One group of five was moving in unison, pretending to be rowing a boat, inviting the sailors in. A few had even swum naked to the side. Gideon tried not to look at the ones who rolled over and swam on their backs, exposing their dark nipples and other charms.

But the crewmen were looking. They were all leaning over the starboard side and calling out like thirsty men calling for water. A few were even crying.

Porter said, "The loss of discipline is a frightening thing, Mr. Browne. All rules in force tomorrow morning at eight bells."

• • •

"A perfect bedlam." That was how Porter would describe that night in his journal.

Gideon never wrote about it, because he did not want to commit his actions to paper. He did not need to write about it, because he knew he would never forget a detail.

When the first boats went ashore, he remained aboard, a latter-day Ulysses resisting the siren song. But he did not lash himself to the mast. He went below, took out his copy of Cook's *Voyages,* and tried to lash himself to the book. And for a time, it worked. When he felt his resolve faltering, he tried to think of Antonia. When that did not work, he tried to think of Jason and his disapproval.

But when he heard the sound of female laughter on the deck above him, he could not stay in his cabin another seven minutes, let alone another seven weeks.

As he climbed to the gundeck, he saw the shafts of sunlight slanting through the open ports, and there—dancing about like dust motes in the light, filling the ship with the alien sound of their laughter, cavorting where men had so many times faced death—were *women.* . . .

Some were old, others mere girls. Some wore paper cloth dresses; others nothing but a necklace or a garland of flowers. Some were speaking their own language; others were mouthing the dirtiest of English words as though saying no more than hello. Some had missing teeth, broken noses, pendulous breasts; others were as perfect of feature as Aphrodite herself. And not one of them wanted for the company of a sailor.

Over by the galley stove, Will Whitney had mounted a *vahiena* from behind, and Gideon wondered if this was the only position he knew. There was, after all, a rumor among the officers that Whitney assumed the female position himself when there were no females to be had.

Between two cannons, Big Will Kingsbury, naked but for his lacquered top hat, pointed his personal cannon at two giggling girls. When he noticed Gideon, every part of him not already at attention stood up straight, and he gave an absurd little salute. "Bosun's mate on duty, sir."

Gideon managed to mutter, "Carry on."

"Thank you, sir," said Kingsbury.

As ventilation was better on the gundeck than below, sailors hung their hammocks here. Now the hammocks were swinging back and forth like the fluttering wings of great white birds in some seagoing rookery. The wings did not enfold birds, however, but bare white asses, slender brown legs . . . beasts with two backs.

A girl came up to Gideon, wearing no more than a string of flowers. "*Tie-tie?* Kissy for *tie-tie?*"

The bulwarks and planks, painted red so that the blood of battle would be less visible against them, flooded Gideon's vision. Beyond the color, he saw only her smile and her breasts. Clearly, he needed air. He hurried up to the spar deck and saw what no one would have believed could ever be seen on an American ship of war.

It was the bright sun that made it seem so unfettered and yet so innocent. There were no shadows to hide the coupling bodies, no hammocks to wrap them. There were sailors and women everywhere—at the forecastle, by the anchor capstans, even moving in rhythm high up in the fighting tops.

Naked girls wore sailors' hats. Naked sailors wore garlands of flowers. One girl paraded in a marine's jacket, calling and waving to her friends and chanting the word "tie-tie."

If a marine was giving up his jacket for it, thought Gideon, he might just as well give up the skin on his back, because the captain would be taking it.

The captain. Gideon did not see him. Nor did he see the lieutenant of marines. The only figure of authority was a marine private, still in full uniform, standing by the mizzenmast. His name was Wallis, and it was rumored that he preferred Will Whitney in the female position to any female.

A sweet voice said, "Fucky fuck nice cunny?"

Gideon turned.

Reuben Marshall stood there with two girls, grinning his toothless grin.

The first girl was naked, almost childish. The other was in her twenties and wore a long white dress that exposed one of her breasts.

"Crimson cocks," she said to Gideon.

"That's *quims* and cocks, sir," offered Reuben. "It's her way of sayin' hello."

"Can't she just say *hello?*"

"They're taught dirty words by the sailors who come through here."

"Dirty words?"

"It's scandalish, Lieutenant, but"—Reuben Marshall slid a hand down the naked girl's back—"marvelous scandal it is. Even the captain is . . . scandallin'."

Even the captain . . .

And Gideon, too. He looked at the girl in the white dress and surrendered. He led her down, past the sailors and *vahienas* copulating on the gangway steps, through the red-painted gundeck, to the berthing deck and his dark little stateroom. . . .

It took Lieutenant Jason Stafford until dawn to work the lumbering old *Greenwich* to an anchorage some two hundred yards from the *Essex*.

Then, through his glass, he scanned the villages and hilltops where the natives were stirring. All seemed green and peaceful.

"Bet they had fun around here last night," said Badmouth Ben, his first mate.

"That's not my concern," said Jason.

Badmouth laughed. "It's mine, sir. I do my job and ask nothin' from no man. I take my punishments and I 'spect my rewards. I want a crack at them *vahienas*."

"For now, take note that it's six o'clock. Do your job and ring up four bells."

"Aye, sir." The sound rolled across the anchorage and came echoing back from the *Essex Jr.*, but strangely, it was not answered by the flagship.

Jason shifted his glass to the *Essex* and saw a native wearing a marine's shako. His first thought was that the *Essex* had been overwhelmed.

"Mr. Hazen," he said calmly, "break out the muskets."

Then he saw that it was a native *woman* wearing the shako. And another woman, completely naked, strolled to the ship's bell and rang it, not four times, but a dozen. And the sound brought no more than laughter from the sailors strolling about. Sailors . . . but no officers.

"Are you sure you want muskets, sir?" asked Badmouth Ben. "That ain't fightin' they're doin' in the fightin' tops."

High above the deck of the *Essex*, a sailor and a woman were going at it.

"It may be a mutiny, Mr. Hazen. Muskets and cutlasses."

"I don't think so, Lieutenant."

"Do as you're told. I didn't save your life to argue with you." Jason knew mutiny was unlikely on a ship commanded by David Porter, but he believed in preparing for the worst.

The worst that faced his boarding party when they stepped onto the *Essex,* however, was more naked women. And he had even prepared for that by reminding himself that nakedness was the common state of the barnyard animal.

He ordered his men to stand fast at the gangway. One of them grumbled that his dick was standin' fast already, but Jason's attention was on Private Wallis, standing guard by the mizzenmast. "Who's the officer of the deck?"

"On this watch? Lieutenant Browne, sir."

"Where is he?"

"In his cabin." Wallis smiled a bit.

Jason glanced at the sailors and naked women. "And the captain?"

"In *his* cabin." The smile grew a bit wider.

Even the captain, thought Jason . . . and goddamned Gideon Browne.

The Crab Louse, who was sitting on a cannon, calmly sipping a cup of tea, spoke up. "The captain give us till eight bells . . . then it's back to work."

Jason looked at the naked girl lounging between the legs of the Crab Louse, her neck looped many times with necklaces of new glass beads. She smiled and said, "*Tie-tie*? Kissy for *tie-tie*?"

"Under the circumstances, sir," said Badmouth Ben, "could me and the lads stand down . . . till eight bells, at least?"

"Stand down . . . lie down . . . I'm going below." Jason went straight to the cabin he had shared with Gideon. Through the blinds in the door panel, he could see the bare back and black hair of a girl who seemed to be riding Gideon's bunk, though Jason knew that Gideon was her mount.

Jason could control his anger at Gideon for betraying his sister. What he could not control was his anger at himself, for the frustration and envy he felt in the presence of all this happy lust. The door nearly flew off its hinges when Jason's boot struck it. Gideon pushed the girl off, grabbed for his dirk.

"Plannin' to fuck every one?" demanded Jason.

"I'm . . . I'm sorry, Jace."

Jason looked at the girl cowering in the corner of the bunk, then stepped back. "I'm sorry, too. It's not my business."

viii
Chesapeake Miseries

By late summer, Antonia knew that the *Essex* was still afloat, that she had made it into the Pacific and had caused the British fits. It had been the only good news all summer.

In the spring, a British fleet had entered Chesapeake Bay and blockaded the frigate *Constellation* in the Elizabeth River. In June, the bad-luck frigate named for the Chesapeake had been defeated by HMS *Shannon* despite the exhortations of her dying captain, "Don't give up the ship." Near the end of June, the British had tried to capture the *Constellation*, but were driven back by American militia, so they turned their anger on the village of Hampton, burning, looting, and, it was said, raping their way through the Chesapeake town.

The elation of the early victories had given way to gloom. And nowhere was the gloom deeper, or more personal, than at Stafford's Fine Folly.

"There's no reason these things happen," old Doc Dunham told Charlton, Antonia, and Miss Mary Maynard one fall afternoon. "You shouldn't look to fix blame."

"But Mother's had many worries lately." Charlton looked at Antonia.

"She's worried about the *Essex*, if that's what you mean," said Antonia.

"We're all worried about the *Essex*," said Miss Mary in her softest voice.

Charlton kept his baggy eyes on his sister. "You know how hard it was for her to disinherit you of your slaves. Be thankful she didn't cut you out altogether."

Antonia turned to the doctor. "Tell us about our mother."

Doc Dunham made an annoyed clacking of his hippopotamus-ivory dentures. "These lumps on her breast . . . they're a cancer."

"What can we do?" asked Charlton.

"We can see what happens. In some cases, women live for years . . . or we can wait and see if—" the doctor twitched his mouth as his teeth slipped—"if she gets the cancer in the other one, then cut."

"Cut?" said Antonia.

Miss Mary seemed shocked. "Do you mean—"

"Take off my breast while I bite down on a leather strap." Mother Sara appeared in the doorway dressed in a blue cotton dress, her graying hair piled neatly atop her head. She glided into the room as smoothly as ice on a March river.

"Mother Sara . . ." Miss Mary reached out her hand.

But Mother Sara did not take it. She made it clear she wanted no sympathy. "We have a family decision to make. I want to see our fortune secure. See Jason marry. See my daughter come to her senses . . ."

Old Doc Dunham clacked his teeth. "If we cut now, it might not spread."

"You're certain of that?" asked Mother Sara.

"Waitin' and prayin' will buy you time. But—"

"Doc," asked Charlton, "do many women survive the . . . the . . ."

"The cutting," said Mother Sara with the coolness of that river ice.

"Enough . . . enough to play the odds." The old doctor looked at Sara. "Staffords have always played the odds."

Mother Sara nodded. "And we'll play them now."

"And win," said Charlton, forcing the joviality into his voice. "Doc, let me see you to your carriage, and . . . about the odds . . ."

Mother Sara smiled as Charlton's voice trailed down the hallway. She turned to the young women. "Your brother soothes himself with talk of the odds. I soothe myself with a walk in the garden. You may soothe yourselves with a sisterly chat. Perhaps my future daughter-in-law can convince my daughter that a Patuxent man, even a Parrish, is more desirable than a Bostonian who comes and goes through the years like a slow tide."

Then Antonia and Miss Mary watched Mother Sara go regally into the garden, down the path, along the hedgerow that Zeke kept so carefully trimmed.

"Your mother has a great heart," said Miss Mary, "no matter how angry she may be at you."

"She's angry that I learned the lesson she taught—to think for myself."

Miss Mary took Antonia by the hand and led her back to the settee. In most people, Antonia hated expressions of earnest concern—the furrowed brow, the sympathetic set of the mouth, the almost theatrical sincerity. But Miss Mary's streak of mischief made her concern palatable.

"So," said Miss Mary, fluffing her skirt, "Samuel Parrish is recovered?"

"He's bound for New York next week, second lieutenant aboard Decatur's new command, the *President*. He's expecting the answer I promised."

"Well, he's quite dashing and much more direct than Gideon. And your mother *did* say she would give you back your slaves if you married him."

"What would you do?"

"Tell Samuel that while a man's honor calls him to make a stand over this old thing and that, a woman's honor requires that she be true to her heart, and—"

"You can't be serious, Mary."

"I'm just helpin' you buy the time you want." Mary stood. "Personally, I think that while Samuel's somethin' of a bastard, he's an honorable bastard, and he worships you. But if you're willin' to swap your slaves and Samuel's worship because of what it felt like on your bedroom floor, why, go ahead."

Antonia looked up at the picture of her father above the fireplace. "Maybe I'll go back to my first decision—no answer until the *Essex* gets back."

"Oh, piss or get off the pot, girl. Put Samuel out of his misery."

"Well, we all have our miseries, Mary. I'm his. But I'm sure that for Gideon and Jason, the miseries of battle are much worse."

"Hell, no. Men love a good fight. If it wasn't for what all else they need, they'd never come home."

And Antonia allowed as how her future sister-in-law was probably right. She gazed out toward the river. "Still, it can't be too pleasant wherever they are at the moment."

ix
Sojourn

The *Essex* lay dead in the water, listing to port, her masts gone above the fighting tops and thin strands of smoke curling from her hatches.

The topgallant masts had been taken ashore for repair. The rigging had been stripped. This ship had been careened—purposely run onto the beach and tipped onto her side—to allow the carpenters to replace worn copper. Tons of barnacles and weeds had been scraped from her hull, and charcoal fires had been lit belowdecks to suffocate the rats, fifteen hundred of them, found dead at the gangways when the smoking was done.

If they set their mind to a task, thought Jason, Americans were a marvelous race. Just look at how they had turned this island to their will in two weeks.

The day after their arrival, they had chosen a flat piece of ground on Massachusetts Bay and raised a breastwork of old water casks to enclose it. Then Porter had turned his attention to the Happahs, who lived in the hills and were at war with the Taeehs. He tried a bit of musket diplomacy, showing them the effects of a marine volley on a water cask. But they said there would be no peace until there had been a war with the Taeehs' new friends.

So Jason Stafford, Lieutenant Downes, and the Taeeh warrior Mouina led forty Americans and hundreds of Taeehs against two thousand Happahs. On the rugged ridges and hillsides above the bay, American muskets met slings and clubs, and five Happahs died. Jason considered it a small price for peace. The awestruck Mouina said it was the most dead he had ever seen in a single battle.

Soon all of the tribes but one—the proud Typees—had made peace with the Americans. Hogs and fruit came from every valley. Women came for pleasure and *tie-ties*. And Chief Gattanewa said they would prove their friendship by building the Americans a true village. In a single day, four thousand Nuku Hivans constructed seven thatch-roofed longhouses, a ropewalk, and a wall to surround them. Porter named it Madisonville, and Jason concluded that the Nuku Hivans were marvelous people too.

None, he was beginning to believe, was more marvelous than the young woman coming up the hill toward him now. . . .

• • •

She was Piteenee, the one who had rebuffed Porter on the first day. She had taken no *othouah*, or white man, as lover, though many in her social caste had coupled with officers. She showed no interest in any American until she saw Jason returning from battle with the Happahs, his forehead bleeding where a stone had struck him.

It may have been that she admired his bravery. Or perhaps she sensed a kindred spirit, for Jason had shown no interest in any of *her* people. But she took him into her father's dwelling that day, delicately washed the wound, and served him kava, the drink that made so many of the islanders so happy, and so many more so stupid.

The kava left him light-headed, but it was the proximity of her body and exposed breast that intoxicated him. He might have broken his promise to Miss Mary of Alexandria right then, but kava and concussion caused him to pass out instead.

When he awoke, he was aboard his ship, and there he remained for the next week. He wanted no more of Piteenee's temptation. And when he learned what kava was—a root chewed by natives, spat into cups, mixed with fresh water, fermented, and strained into fresh cups for general consumption—he wanted no more of that, either.

With Reverend Adams, he took over the education of the midshipmen. Porter had established a routine that ended all work at four o'clock, after which a quarter of the crew was allowed to remain ashore for the night. Only midshipmen were restricted aboard the *Greenwich*. Reverend Adams prevailed in the protection of *their* virtue, at least. And in helping to protect them, Jason hoped to protect his own virtue, as well.

But late in the second week, he was ordered ashore. Wilson the Englishman and an old man in a breechclout were awaiting him in Captain Porter's dwelling.

"You sent for me, sir?" Jason tugged at the corner of his waistcoat, the only officer who continued to wear full uniform when he came ashore.

Porter, in shirt and breeches, complimented Stafford on his appearance, then gestured to the old man, who was so covered in tattoos that he looked almost black, except for the scales on his face caused by too much kava. "Chief Gattanewa requested this meeting."

Jason nodded. "My compliments to him."

Wilson laughed. "Quite a sight, ain't he? But he traces his ancestors back eighty-eight generations, back to Oataia, god of daylight, what brung breadfruit and sugarcane to Nuku Hiva and settled with Anoona, his wife."

Gattanewa fixed his glassy eyes on Jason and spoke through Wilson: "He wants to know why you reject his granddaughter."

"I am . . . I am very busy," said Jason.

Wilson translated the old chief's answer: "He says his granddaughter is very picky. She even"—Wilson shot a nervous glance at Porter—"excuse me, sir, these is Gattanewa's words—she even rejected *you*."

"Finish your speech," snapped Porter.

"Aye, sir," said Wilson, who looked almost as scrofulous as Gattanewa. "If Piteenee rejects Captain Porter and chooses you, Mr. Stafford, you must go with her. Otherwise you insult Gattanewa and Captain Porter, too."

"I'm not insulted," growled Porter. "I simply want to get my ship ready for sea."

"As I do, sir," answered Jason.

"Then you understand."

"Understand, sir?"

"Dammit, Stafford!" Porter slammed his hand on the desk, which caused old Gattanewa to cover his ears with his hands and moan in agony.

"Chief got bad headache, sir," Wilson said. "Too much kava."

Porter lowered his voice. "If this girl had any sense, she'd have accepted the advances of the captain himself. We wouldn't be having this conversation."

"But you're married, sir," said Jason.

"Are you really so naïve, Lieutenant?"

No, he was not. And playing Lieutenant Discipline on an island alive with lust had exhausted him. "I simply consider my betrothal a matter of honor, sir."

Porter took Jason by the arm and led him to the door. "There are over thirty thousand natives on this island. They fear us, but if they turn against us because you insult Gattanewa's granddaughter, neither my wife nor your betrothed will ever see us again."

"Are you ordering me to make love to Piteenee, sir?"

"If I ordered you to shoot her, I'd expect you to do that. I'm ordering you to guarantee good relations with her and her whole damn family."

Jason tugged his waistcoat again and set his square jaw. If the decision was out of his hands, Lieutenant Discipline would do as he was told. "Aye, sir."

Porter put a fatherly arm around Jason. "Just remember what I told you in Tripoli. Trust your shrouds. If a mast works a bit, the shrouds will hold it up."

And Wilson stuck his scraggly beard between the two Americans. "Piteenee knows more English than cusswords. I taught 'er meself."

Porter wrinkled his nose. "Are you saying that *you've* lain with her?"

"Oh, no, sir. Not me. I'm just sayin' she's smart."

"They're all smart." Porter's tone suggested much in the way of personal knowledge. "Cunning, coquettish, totally unfaithful."

"Aye," laughed Wilson, "the best and the worst of 'em."

Porter pointed a finger at Stafford. "Cunning proves their intelligence; coquetry is as natural to females here as at home; and rules of fidelity are marked only in their transgressing. However much they love their men, they seek their own amusements. And that's what you are, Lieutenant—amusement. So be amusing."

And Jason tried. At their first meeting, he put on his best blue coat and dress saber and went to Piteenee's dwelling with all the ceremony he could muster. And the *tie-tie* he brought—a brass buckle—he wrapped in a small piece of ribbon.

She was cold and formal with him, as if to let him know that she was offended by his lack of attention.

And her clothing fit her mood. She wore a *pahhee*, a cap made of gauzelike cloth, which tightly wrapped her head and concealed the hair, and a *cahu*, a dress that could be tied many ways but was tied chastely to cover both breasts, giving her an appearance of virginal modesty heightened by the whiteness of the garment.

Her eyes brightened at the sight of the *tie-tie,* which she received with some ceremony. Then she put it aside and looked him in the eye.

"You asked to see me?" he said, testing her English.

"You different. You walk as one."

Jason took that to mean he did not try to please people without reason. She added, "Piteenee walk as one."

Jason said it was a good thing and invited her to walk with him the next day.

"We walk as two . . . ones," she said. "If good, we walk as one . . . two."

He stood and bowed formally, because he sensed that formality was pleasing to her, and it put a measure of distance between them. "I will walk with you on the hilltop above our village. Tomorrow."

"Bring *tie-tie*," she said. . . .

And now he sat there, with the *Essex* and Madisonville bustling below him and Piteenee coming toward him through the tall grass. Her coal-black hair was loose and flowing. Her dress was tied at her shoulder, so that one breast was artfully exposed. And she wore the brass buckle around her neck like a precious pendant.

Before such beauty, he did not know if he could maintain the formality of his uniform. But if he did it well and did it long enough, she might tire of him and go elsewhere for amusement. Then he could say he had obeyed orders while keeping his promise to Miss Mary of Alexandria.

He greeted Piteenee with a deep bow. "Your necklace is very pretty."

"Pretty *tie-tie,*" she said, fingering it. "You bring 'nother?"

His formality confronted her dark, bright eyes, her expectant smile, her perfect white teeth, and the parts of her that he tried to ignore. "I do not think friends need *tie-ties* each time they meet."

It seemed to be what she wanted to hear, because she smiled at him. There was an undeniable regality about her, even with her dress tied at one shoulder. "You walk as one." She sat down in the tall grass and tugged him down beside her. "Every time. That good."

"Not every time."

"Not?"

"In America, I walk as two." He hoped that if he told the truth, she might back away. And mention of Miss Mary would keep her image before his mind's eye, even when he could not open his locket and gaze at her face.

"As two?" she asked.

"With a jealous woman."

"Jealous? What 'jealous'?"

"She does not like me to be with other women."

Piteenee laughed. "That good."

"Then you understand?"

"Mellikee woman"— "Mellikee" was her pronunciation of "American"—"is like Taeeh woman. We jealous too. We no let Typees have our men." With that, she undid the knot at her left shoulder, and her dress dropped to her waist.

And thoughts of Miss Mary Maynard dropped from Jason's mind.

Piteenee slipped a leg between his and turned her body so that she was kneeling before him, her breasts close to his face. "Kiss for fun. No *tie-tie.*"

But he was unable to move before the wave rising to engulf him.

So she slid her hands around his neck and drew his face to her breasts. At the same time, she gently pressed her thigh between his legs. "Kiss for fun."

The close-shaved smoothness of his cheeks met the smoothness of her breasts. Then she turned herself, letting his mouth trail across her coconut-scented flesh. "Taste other one," she whispered.

And the wave broke over him. It took him down quickly and tumbled him over. When he tried to take off his officer's coat and sword, as if to swim against the wave, she said to leave them on. "I like blue coat. I like big knife. Make you walk as one."

Then she unbuttoned his breeches, and the undertow took him out to sea.

X
Jason's Descent

"Tits. Tits is all they is, I'm tellin' you." Reuben Marshall worked at an oar and talked, as usual, to anyone who would listen.

"Tired of tits?" Gideon steered the cutter bringing a new crew ashore.

"I'm just sayin' that seein' tits every day takes away the mystery of 'em. It's like lookin' at . . . lookin' at"—Marshall's eye fell on the man pulling the oar in front of him—"the back of Badmouth Ben's head."

"A sailor who cain't tell the difference 'tween nice titties and Hazen's thick skull got no brain to dull," said black freedman Jasper Reed.

"You lads is so numb to it all," said Marshall, "you don't see what I'm sayin'. When there's titties everywhere and black niggers—no offense, Jasper—black niggers gettin' as much fun as white men, the value of the fun goes down."

"Leastways for the white men." Jasper Reed laughed.

"You ain't numbed, are you, Lieutenant?" asked Badmouth Ben with a sly grin.

Gideon just smiled. The officers had shown more discretion than the crew, but their doings were a regular topic of talk among the sailors, especially since Jason had taken up with Piteenee. Gideon said, "There's ten thousand numbing miles between here and home, lads. I see no reason to go numb till we leave."

They had now spent three weeks in a paradise of fine weather, full bellies, and fulfilled desires. Many of the sailors, like sailors from the beginning of time, sported new tattoos—little rows of parallel lines around their necks or wrists, more elaborate designs across their chests—like badges of revelry. There even had been rumblings from sailors who said that because their enlistments were up, they should be allowed to do as they pleased, even if they chose to stay.

"Just remember, lads," Gideon cautioned, "we're seamen, first and last. So long as we do a seaman's day of work, we can live like natives at night."

"Officers, too?"

"Officers and men both."

"We haven't seen Lieutenant Stafford aboard the *Greenwich* in some time," said Badmouth.

"Lieutenant Stafford's been given a special assignment."

They had all seen Piteenee wandering the hillsides in Jason Stafford's blue coat. They had all seen Jason leave Madisonville each evening and go to the Taeeh village. They all talked about Lieutenant Discipline.

But Gideon would not add to their speculations. He only wrote about them: "November 13. Last night I met Jason on the island. He wore no coat, waistcoat, stockings, or shoes. I dined with him and the girl—plantains, taro root, hog baked on hot stones in the earth—and I left knowing that Jason had surrendered to the same temptations that have taken the rest of us. Except that afterward, he admitted he was in love. I said we were all in love with this place, to which he had no response. I must watch him closely."

The next day, Gideon was in Porter's hut, making a report. "Another three weeks, sir, and the ship will be ready."

"Another three weeks," repeated Porter, "to sustain discipline, keep the islanders pacified, and finish the job. But it will be finished."

Porter never lacked for confidence, thought Gideon, which was good, because at that moment, an angry crowd of Taeehs and Happahs was coming into the village, led by Mouina, Gattanewa, and a shirtless Jason Stafford wearing sailor's trousers and carrying a war club.

"Your shoulders are sunburned, Jason," said Gideon.

"But it's good to see that your uniform is still in use." Porter glanced toward the back of the crowd, where Piteenee stood in Jason's blue officer's coat.

"A pretty *tie-tie*, Opotee!" Piteenee called the captain by his Nuku Hivan name. "*Tie-tie* from officer who walk as one."

"I walk as an officer, sir, no matter my uniform." Jason planted his war club in the sand. It was almost as tall as he was, a fine, polished piece of wood topped by a four-faced demon's head. "Mouina has brought your demands to the Typees."

Mouina stood over six feet, which made him a giant among the Americans. A billowing red cape broadened him, a headdress of red feathers heightened him, tattoos covered him. But his features were delicate and set off by mustache and chin whiskers that made him look more like a Spanish don than a savage warrior.

It was little wonder to Gideon that Porter would send Mouina on his errand, or that he had spent hours sketching Mouina in his journal.

Mouina pounded his war club into the ground and spoke through Wilson. "He told the Typees it was time for them to make peace with the Americans, to send hogs and breadfruit like the rest of the tribes. But the Typees say Mouina and Gattanewa and their people are cowards for making peace."

The warriors shook their clubs.

"They ask why they should bring the Americans their hogs and fruit, when the Americans are not brave enough to come and take them."

Mouina huffed and panted, raising himself into a frenzy that was only part performance. Porter remained motionless, equally aware of the audience.

Mouina took a step closer to Porter, a clear physical challenge. "The Typees say Opotee and the Mellikees are—"

At Mouina's next words, the natives shouted furiously.

Gideon wished he had armed his work party. But they had scattered, and there were now a hundred and fifty natives packed into the enclosure. If they decided that the Americans were not strong enough to stand against the Typees, they might turn right here . . . right now.

"The Americans are white lizards, mere dirt, no better than Taeeh testicles."

Porter gave a disgusted laugh and looked around at the warriors screaming for the Americans to strike back.

"They believe that an insult to any ally insults them," said Jason. "If you do not answer it, the Taeehs lose face. So do we."

Porter ignored Jason and turned to Gattanewa. "What does the chief think?"

Gattanewa grunted a few words. "The chief says the Typees deserve the thunder of your guns."

And the warriors roared, for the eighty-eighth son of Oataia had spoken.

"Yes, Captain," cried Jason. "The Taeehs want war. If we don't give it to them—"

"Keep your advice, Lieutenant."

Mouina pounded his club and shouted words that sent the crowd into frenzy.

Wilson stammered the translation. "Mouina *insists* that you go to war with the Typee, or he will conclude the Americans are—"

Before the translation was out of Wilson's mouth, Porter had a marine musket in his hands and was flying at Mouina, pressing the bayonet to Mouina's chest. "Call me a coward and I'll skewer you like a pig."

The great Mouina huffed and snorted, then scurried from the village, folding up on himself as he went.

After he was out of his sight, Porter turned to Gattanewa and said, as coldly as he had ever ordered the pursuit of a British whaler, "Collect your war canoes."

In his thatched house a few moments later, Porter was as furious as a Cape Horn ice storm. "Stafford, have you lost your mind, along with your coat?"

"I've endeavored to please Piteenee, sir, as you ordered." Jason squared his shoulders, as though aware for the first time of the strange picture he cut, shirtless and clutching a war club. "It was Piteenee who warned that if the Taeehs started clamoring for war, we would have to join with them."

"Lieutenant, when we dance to their jig, our jig on this island will be up. I won't be forced to make war by savages, or by officers who have turned savage."

Gideon attempted to head off the captain's anger. "If I could speak frankly . . ."

"You usually do."

"You *ordered* Lieutenant Stafford to dance to the Taeeh jig."

"And I warned him about those he would dance with. I now order him to get his coat back and put his shirt on. And . . ." Porter's eye was drawn to something at Jason's waist, along the belt line. "Lower your breeches."

Jason did not hesitate. There would be no good time to reveal what he had done. So he untied his breeches and slipped them down to reveal two parallel lines, black and broken, tattooed all the way around his torso.

Porter said, very softly, "You *are* enjoying their jig too much, Lieutenant."

And Gideon asked, "What will Miss Mary say?"

Jason sat on the beach at sunset, watching the clouds glide toward the west, watching them change from deep purple to rose to fiery red, as though they had made a conscious decision to immolate themselves in the beauty of the last light, and impulsively, he jumped into the water. He was that rarity among seamen, a strong swimmer, and he took great comfort in the rhythm of the stroke, in the cooling of the water, in the sight of the ship that was his destination.

He had promised Piteenee that he would meet her that night, close by a breadfruit tree where he had carved their initials. He knew that his absence would pain her, but the pain would be greater when he left for good.

He found his cabin in the *Greenwich* occupied by Reverend Adams, who was reading Bible verse beneath a whale-oil lamp.

"The prodigal son returneth."

"I should expect you to say something like that." Jason pulled a clean shirt from his sea trunk and dried himself. "What are you doing in my cabin?"

"Your crew has been sent back to the *Essex*. Perhaps you didn't know." The chaplain's voice dripped sarcasm.

"You have a cabin of your own, sir."

"You have abandoned this one. But the midshipmen remain aboard, under my tutelage, safe from the sailors and their lustful bragging."

Jason grunted and pulled off his wet breeches. Then he turned his ass to the chaplain and began to rummage for a new pair.

"These boys are beside themselves," said Adams, "with curiosity . . . and lust."

"Would you like me to tell them what goes on in the native villages?" Jason turned and stood naked before the chaplain.

Adams gasped at the sight of the tattoo around Jason's waist. "Young Farragut and the others look up to you. For them to see you like this . . . it will make my job more difficult."

Jason pulled on the clean breeches and threw himself on the bunk and tried to feel the rise and fall of the ship, the familiar motion that might reset his own internal compass.

The chaplain said, "These boys do not need to see men like you losing yourself to your lust. If you intend to keep up this activity, best that you stay away from the ship."

"Reverend, I'm still in command of this ship."

"You are not even in command of yourself, sir."

• • •

At dawn, Jason rose from his bunk and put on stockings and good shoes. After a week barefoot, he found the shoes tight and uncomfortable, but comforting just the same, like all discipline.

"Good morning, Lieutenant." Young Farragut was the officer of the watch.

"Man the cutter, if you please."

"Are we going ashore?" the boy asked excitedly.

"Aye."

Life came with the sun to Massachusetts Bay. The top of the hill between the Taeeh and American villages was swarming with workers piling dirt for a fort. Smoke rose from the fires in Madisonville. Boats brought sailors ashore. On the beach before the Taeeh village, the men were assembling the war canoes. And the women were gathered at the watering place, just east of the Taeeh village.

That was where Jason pointed the cutter, and the six boys twitched with anticipation. But Jason intended to remain in command . . . of the young men and of himself.

He would retrieve his officer's coat and return quickly to his ship. But his resolve faded when he saw the coat beneath the tree where he had promised to meet Piteenee the night before. She was still standing there.

When the cutter touched the sand, the midshipmen stayed in their thwarts and looked up at Jason, like dogs before their food bowls, waiting for their master's permission to eat.

Instead, he said, "Stay here. I won't be long."

He ignored their collective groan and strode toward the grove of trees.

She clutched the coat around herself and smiled bravely.

He took only a few steps before ordering the midshipmen back to the *Greenwich*. And then, like the clouds at dusk, he was rushing toward her. . . .

That night he sent word to Captain Porter that he was fulfilling his mission and would not enjoy the jig too much. Then he retired to Piteenee's house. They ate. They drank kava and laughed hysterically. And they talked.

She told him of the islands. He told her of America. She told him of their god Oataia, who brought them breadfruit. He told her of Christ. She spoke of the missionaries who had come to teach them about Christ, and of the islanders who said that if the god Christ wished them to follow him, he could visit them himself and bring some new plant, and they would not kill him, nor would they try to eat him like bread.

On the third day, Piteenee's uncle Mouina came to her house with the tattoo needles. Jason told him to make marks that would please Piteenee, then he lay across her bare thighs and endured the steady tapping of the mallet driving the needles into the skin of his back and his wrists.

And he knew he was lost. The only discipline that remained was his ability to withstand the pain of the needles, and for that, he needed kava and the soothing touch of Piteenee's fingers. The core of his honor, his faithfulness to Miss Mary, had been cut out of him, and his faith to his officer's code had collapsed into the hole that was left. In a strange way, he thought that if there was any honor left to him, it would be his new faith to this girl.

By the end of the week, the war canoes were assembled. The Typees had refused further offers of peace. They had stoned members of other tribes. They had enjoyed plenty while other tribes suffered from supplying hungry Americans.

Mouina said war would bring peace to the whole island. Then they could plunder the Typee valley for all the food the Americans would need. So he would make peace with Opotee, because no warrior could turn away from such a just war.

Jason thought that war might bring his chance to disappear into the core that was left in the middle of his being, and he hatched his plan with Piteenee. Together, they took a canoe to the north side of the island, where Porter would attack, and they hid it in the deep thicket.

From Gideon Browne's journal, November 19:

> Today I told Jason that if he hopes to rise higher in the navy, he cannot look like a common seaman; he must stop the tattooing. Reminders of his ambition have always straightened him out before. But this time he said, "I have spent my life doing things pleasing to others. Now I walk as one."

> Lieutenant Discipline has snapped his shrouds and rolls toward the rocks. The most dangerous men—to themselves and others—are those who draw their shrouds too tight, who will not admit that men make great messes. Such men sometimes make the worst messes of all.

xi
On the Patuxent

"So they cut her?" said Rebecca. "Did they take both?"

Samuel, his aunt, and his brother Walter sat by the fire in the kitchen.

"Just one. The young doctor who did it, he said the lumps were only in one. Cut her, stitched her. They say she didn't scream once."

Rebecca sucked the juice from her tobacco and spit it into her little gravy boat. "She was always a tough one."

Samuel nodded. "Like her daughter."

Rebecca asked, "How *is* your Antonia?"

"She's not his anymore," said Walter.

"Not to put too fine a point on it, brother."

"I'm no talker . . . just a plain speaker with a nose for tobacco."

Rebecca reached out and stroked Samuel's blond hair. "I thought you were unhappy because you leave in two days."

Samuel poked at a log on the grate. "I'm glad I'm going back to the fleet."

"Antonia's a plain speaker, too," said Walter, as though stating that the nights were getting cooler. "Spoke her mind to Samuel, right in public. 'Samuel, I'm afraid I can't marry you.' Just like that, in the livin' room, with me sittin' there listenin' and her mother sick to death in the upstairs room."

Rebecca said, "Walter, if you didn't have such a good heart, I'd be tempted to thrash you for a tellin' like that."

"It's the truth," said Samuel. "He needs no thrashin'."

"Thanks, brother." Walter bade them good night and lumbered off.

"You seem as if you would like to thrash someone," said Rebecca.

"I'd like to thrash Antonia." Samuel bit his cheek and blinked his eyes.

Seeing him like this, she knew that she had done exactly what she should. She had let love take its course, and it had brought its inevitable disappointment. Now she was free to do what she had planned against a family that, for a second time, had broken a lover's promise to one of the Parrishes.

"What did you mean," he asked, "when you said my interest in Antonia was the reason you refrained from doing business with Charlton Stafford?"

"You'll see soon, dear," she said. He sat curled in front of the fire, as he had so many times when he was a little boy, her own little boy, the child she had raised from birth, and she told him, "What I do in the next few months will be for your sake, too. Walter lives here on the Patuxent. You need a roof of your own."

"Once I leave, I may never come back."

"I'll give you reason to come back. I may even give you Antonia."

xii
A Great Mess

At three o'clock one November morning, David Porter led five boats and ten enormous Taeeh war canoes northeast from Massachusetts Bay.

To keep their canoes together, the Taeehs blew their war conchs, the sound traveling from one vessel to the next in a slow and steady rhythm, perfect counterpoint to the *thump-thump-thump* of the paddles striking the sea.

An ancient sound, thought Gideon, as benighted as warfare in paradise.

A stirring sound, thought Jason, as primitive as native drums drawing him on.

Dawn was breaking when they reached the Typee beach. Two thousand Taeeh and Happah warriors had traveled overland to meet them there. Then the *Essex Jr.* arrived, carrying old Gattanewa in a style that Porter said was worthy of an ally of the United States. As the chief was ferried ashore, the warriors sent up a cheer that Jason was certain would strike fear into the Typees.

The Typee villages were a mile inland, beyond a ridge, protected by a dense thicket that was cut at oblique angles by a shallow river and a single narrow path.

Jason had decided it was the perfect terrain for a disappearance.

Marine Lieutenant Gamble declared it perfect ambush territory.

Mouina agreed. But he was out to prove his bravery, and he said that if the Americans took the path while his men advanced on a wide front through the thicket, they could drive the Typees inland and pin them with their backs to the river.

Porter, eager again for Mouina's support, pronounced it a good plan and gave the order to march.

Gattanewa gave a halfhearted wave, bringing a cheer that almost knocked him from his canoe. He gave another wave, as if to say, "Get on with it," and the first stones came whistling out of the thicket—a splattering of them, then a squall from the slings of the hidden Typees.

Gattanewa's army very quickly grew less boisterous. Many took cover, and all waited to see what the Americans would do.

Porter stood amid the hail of stones as though it were no more than a gentle rain and called his officers together, warning them in a calm voice that they must show no fear, or they would have enemies all around them, Taeehs and Happahs along with Typees. Then he ordered them inland once more.

Mouina took the lead, and about a hundred of his men followed, but they were independent-minded, and orders were obeyed only if they seemed sensible. To many, it seemed far more sensible to stay on the beach and see if the Americans could dislodge the mighty Typees on their own.

And the Typees summoned all their might.

Once the Americans were in the thicket, the stones and spears began to fly so fast that Jason could do little to carry out his plan. He saw the path that led to his hidden canoe. He saw the trunk of the fallen breadfruit tree where he would hide himself, but he was more concerned with showing no fear to the Taeehs fighting by his side.

Gideon was trying, too. But he could see fear on the faces of the

Taeehs who had entered the thicket and were now disappearing into the brush, as if they knew how dangerous a thing this was.

About a half mile in, at a place where the path swung into the clear and ran along the riverbank, a vicious barrage of stones came screaming across the river, and Lieutenant Downes was struck by one that broke his leg.

There were Typees across the river, Typees still hiding in the thicket behind them, stones flying like grapeshot, twenty-eight Americans and a handful of Taeehs now in the middle of something that looked worse by the minute.

Downes told them to press on, but they knew they could not leave him to the Typees who would swarm on him as soon as he was alone.

Gideon Browne said they should fall back, but they knew that falling back would show their weakness and would turn all of the natives against them.

So Porter ordered Browne and two men to carry Downes back to the beach. Then he sent a thunderous volley of musket fire crashing into the wall of leaves and brush on the other side of the little river, then he called for three cheers. "Huzzah! Huzzah! Huzzah!"

His marines gave out with spirit, his fourteen sailors tried, and all of the Taeehs but Mouina left these white madmen alone in the jungle. They forded the river and found that the land on the opposite side was like wet sponge underfoot. But the volley and the furious cheer had worked: the Typees had fallen back.

Porter, regaining the confidence that the Typee resistance had shaken, urged his men on toward the Typee villages.

Jason went wondering what they could do when they got there and hoping he would get his chance to disappear.

At last the path rose toward the ridge beyond which the villages lay. And they saw the wall. Looming at the top of the ridge, completely blocking the path, was a seven-foot barrier of rocks and logs, bordered on both sides by an impenetrable, thorn-choked thicket. That was where the Typees made their stand.

They filled the air with war cries and taunts. They blackened it with stones and spears. They were as brave and arrogant as the Americans trying to unseat them, and more than that, they were fighting for their homes.

Even Mouina called for Porter to retreat.

Instead, Porter ordered his men to find cover and keep up the fire.

After twenty minutes of potshots, he had lost his hat, and he seemed to be losing his head. He called Lieutenant Gamble and Jason to his command post behind the trunk of a breadfruit tree. "We can't dislodge them with musket fire. We need a volley. Or we'll have to storm them."

"Aye, sir," said Gamble, a marine who followed orders and fought like hell.

"But ammunition, sir," said Jason. "Some are low. Some are out."

"Aye," shouted Badmouth Ben from behind a bush. "I just used my last."

"Three bullets left, sir," cried Reuben Marshall. "And them Typees and their slingshots, they're makin' me feel like Goliath after—"

"Shut up," said Porter, wiping sweat from his widow's peak.

Several of the Typees leaped to the top of the wall, turned to the Americans, and began slapping their asses.

Porter took aim at one ass and blew it off the wall. That sent the rest of them scurrying for cover and brought another angry shower of stones.

Then Porter turned to Jason. "Take two men and fight your way back to the beach. Bring up more ammunition."

"Aye, sir." Jason unshouldered his club, then called to Reuben Marshall and Badmouth Ben, "Bring your muskets, lads."

And they were off, down the path to the river, sprinting the whole half mile. And all the while, Jason was planning to disappear somewhere between the other side of the river and the beach.

At the fording place, Jason was fifty paces ahead. He splattered through the water, and as he scrambled up the other bank, the Typees struck. He was not surprised. In a way, he welcomed them, because they would give him his chance.

They came at him with ferocious shouts and flying war clubs, which he met with shouts and war club of his own. He growled the same growls, scowled the same furious scowls.

Then Badmouth Ben and Reuben Marshall arrived, swinging their muskets and sending the Typees scattering.

"Keep running!" Jason told them. "I'll cover the rear." He turned and faced back up the path.

"Lieutenant," cried Badmouth Ben, "you can't cover the rear when there ain't no friggin' rear. They're all around us. Come on."

As if to prove Badmouth's point, a stone came whistling from the trees and hit Reuben Marshall square in the forehead. He went down as though he'd been shot. "My brain! My brain! My brain's been squashed!"

Now more stones came whistling around them, and Badmouth Ben kicked his mate in the flanks. "Get up, you bloody squint. Get up. You ain't hurt. You ain't—"

"My brain been squashed! I can't think no more. I can't think!" He took his hands from his face.

And for all his badmouth eloquence, all that Badmouth Ben could say was "Holy Jesus," over and over, at the sight of the dent in Reuben Marshall's forehead, right above the nose, two inches wide and two inches deep.

Jason had chosen these two because he thought they wouldn't fold in a fight. Now they were both losing their nerve, and Jason knew he would have to lead them out or they'd never get word to the beach. So, with Ben's help, he dragged Reuben Marshall down the path, past the place where the fallen breadfruit lay, past the thicket where his canoe was hidden, past his chance to disappear.

On the beach, a strange tension hung in the air.

Gideon Browne was organizing reinforcements from the *Essex Jr.* while the natives drew themselves into tribal groups. At the sight of three men staggering from the woods, Gideon's first sickening thought was that Porter had been overwhelmed.

Then he heard Jason calling, "Ammunition! More ammunition!"

"It's coming!" Gideon pointed to the cutter rowing in from the ship.

"See to Marshall!" shouted Jason. "I'm going back."

"Wait!" Gideon ran to the edge of the thicket. "Wait for the rest of us."

"I'm going back." Jason looked at the feathered Happahs and Taeehs, who were crowding around Marshall. "I'll show them we're not afraid to face the Typees."

And before Gideon could stop him, Jason was running back up the path, out of the sunlight on the beach, toward the oblivion he had convinced himself was his only refuge.

"He ain't Lieutenant Bloody Discipline no more," said Badmouth Ben as they watched Jason disappear. "He don't even fight like it. He fights like one of these tattoo-assed savages."

Under the canopy of trees, there was an unearthly quiet, made even stranger by the sound of musket fire and shouting in the distance. Jason came quickly to the hidden path, to the fallen breadfruit, to the palm fronds covering the canoe.

He moved the fronds aside to make sure that no one had found his supplies—coconuts, dried pork, plantains, a small cistern of water. He should not have been surprised that most of the food was gone, eaten by animals. Nor should he have been surprised when he turned and looked into the face of Gideon Browne.

"If Porter thinks the Typees have taken you, he won't rest until they free you. If he thinks you've deserted, he won't rest until he hangs you."

"That's fine. Now get away." Jason raised his club.

"And if the Typees find you, they may eat you."

"Fair punishment for someone who's bitten Eve's apple."

"This is no Eden, Jason. And Piteenee is no Eve."

Jason cocked the club as if he would strike. He looked as resolute, and as frightened, as he had that day when he went to the Anacostia bank to duel three men. He even felt the rats clawing at his gut. He had not felt them in any fight since, but fighting his oldest beliefs was worse than war with any enemy.

"You're supposed to be leading reinforcements, Jason. That's your duty."

"I *did* my duty. I brought word from Porter. Say I was ambushed and disappeared. Then save Porter, and we'll both be covered in glory."

In the distance, a volley echoed back from the Typee wall, and sporadic firing drew closer. It sounded as if Porter had decided on a fighting retreat with low ammunition and no reinforcements.

And Jason decided to run. Toward what, he did not know. But Gideon caught him around the legs, bringing him down into a tangle of bushes and underbrush and sending the war club flying. It was an even match, except that Gideon was closer to the club, and as they struggled, he managed to get his hands on it, stagger to his knees, wobble to his feet.

Jason kicked Gideon away, started to run, saw the club in Gideon's hands, then saw it swinging at him. . . .

In Madisonville that night, Porter doubled the guard. There would be no mixing with the natives, no spies telling the Typees where and how the Americans would come the next time.

"If we don't punish them," said Porter to the officers assembled, "our position is untenable. Even our alliance with the eighty-eighth son of Oataia won't help us."

"The Typees are proud warriors, sir," said Gideon when Porter asked for opinions.

"And?" Porter's tone said that asking for opinions was merely a formality.

"If we're only to be here another two weeks, perhaps we can let them be, especially since we trust Gattanewa and the tribes on this side of the island."

"We must humiliate them," said Porter with the calm fury of a man who had been humiliated himself, "or the last two weeks will be hell. And the men we leave behind will never be safe."

At this, Jason looked up. He had been sitting in the shadows, his chin on his chest, his skull throbbing from his own war club, his mind throbbing over all that had happened on that twisting path. Gideon had carried him to the beach, a soldier struck unconscious on his way back to the fight.

Porter glanced briefly at Jason and went on. "I can't leave prizes without a garrison guarding them. I won't leave a garrison unless we dominate the island."

"Who will command this garrison, sir?" asked Jason.

"A lieutenant."

"Given my, uh, close relationship with—"

"No begging, Stafford," snapped Porter. "Leave the decision to me."

Then he told them his plan to bring the Typees to heel.

Gideon Browne knew that they would make a terrible mess.

Jason resolved that he would do as he was ordered, mess or not, to impress Porter and improve his chances of staying on the island.

Jason did not go back to the ship, however, but to the breadfruit tree where Piteenee was waiting.

She wore her dress demurely above her breasts, a certain sign that she was unhappy. "I am ready to go to you, and you are still here?"

He put his hands on her arms. "I can stay without deserting."

"Opotee let you stay with Piteenee?" She smiled in the darkness, and he thought she was the most beautiful creature he had ever seen. "Stay forever?"

"For a long time. If I do my duty. And do it well."

"Then do it." And she began to unbutton his breeches.

From the shadows, Gideon watched it all, but not to satisfy any base desire. Men and women could be seen like this all over the island, at any time of the day or night. He watched to make certain that his suspicion was valid. And it was: no matter what Jason said, he could not be trusted until the *Essex* left.

The following night, the Americans moved.

This time, there were two hundred sailors, with only Mouina and a few scouts to lead them. This time, they marched silently so as not to alarm the friendlies or alert the Typees, and they marched hard to gain the top of the ridge in the center of the island, from which they would strike the Typee valley.

Below them, fires flickered, drums beat, and Typees chanted.

"What are they saying?" Porter asked Jason, who had learned much of the language from Piteenee.

"They're rejoicing," Jason answered. "Celebrating their victory over us."

"Premature," said Porter, looking back at his men.

"And they're asking their gods for rain, so that our muskets won't work."

"Well timed," said Gideon, looking up at the clouds.

The Americans spent a miserable night hunkered down on the ridge, keeping their weapons dry in a driving rain. But by dawn, the rain had stopped and the clouds had lifted enough that they could gaze out on the valley of the Typees.

Gideon Browne called it the heart of Eden.

From the wall where the Typees had stopped the Americans, the valley ran inland some nine verdant miles, to a ribbon of white water fluttering from the island's highest ridge. As the water reached the valley floor, sunlight and earth light turned it to blue, and the slope of the earth drew it back toward the sea. Neat villages slept on either side, coconut and breadfruit groves surrounded them, and the sense of peace was as tangible as Porter's silence.

Trancelike, he stood staring at the scene below, while above, knives of sunlight sliced through the clouds.

Finally Jason said, "The men are ready, Captain, and the Happahs and Taeehs have come up to join in the attack."

Porter whispered, "I did not want this."

"We could make another offer of peace," said Gideon.

"First, show them we can make war."

Before they attacked, Porter ordered a volley from the top of the ridge, so that the Typees might send their women and children to safety. And after he had overwhelmed the first village, he made an offer of peace, which was rejected. These would be the only two expressions of charity that day. The rest was war.

Village after village fell to the Americans, and every village was burned. And the Taeehs and Happahs plundered them all, even as the flames jumped. And what they could not plunder, they killed. Coconut palms, banana trees, breadfruits—all stripped of their bark and left to pour out their sap like blood.

In the afternoon, the Typee capital was taken. Porter led his men over the corpses of the dead defenders and into a grand square surrounded by structures of thatch and palm logs. He pronounced it the most beautiful village on the island. Then he ordered it burned.

Gideon suggested that they might spare the Typee gods, who stood in carved effigy around the square.

Porter turned, a look of self-loathing on his face. "This is survival, Mr. Browne. There's nothing noble in what we do. But it must be done."

"As you say, sir. To protect our prizes." Gideon could not keep the sarcasm from his voice, but in the rising roar of the flames, Porter did not hear.

A few hours later, Jason's party reached the waterfall and stopped to drink.

Then Gideon arrived, and without stripping off his coat or pulling off his boots, he waded straight into the pool at the base of the fall.

"It won't work," shouted Jason. "You can't cleanse yourself of this with water."

"It's a bloody damn business, killing men who are protecting their homes."

"See it as they do." Jason pointed toward Taeehs plundering a village a short distance down the trail. "The Typees called them cowards. They had to fight or be dishonored, and everyone would have preyed on them . . . even here."

Gideon looked up at the majestic waterfall. "Even here."

"You said it yesterday: this is no Eden."

xiii
Rebecca's Revenge

The cold had come down in late October.

By the first week of November, fires burned on Annapolis hearths from morning till night. People said it would be a terrible winter.

Rebecca Parrish could not remember such an early snow, but she found it appropriate on the day that she went to Stafford's Fine Folly. It had been snowing the night she went there to make her promise.

The slave who answered the door summoned her into the front sitting room, and a few moments later, Antonia appeared.

"Good afternoon," said Rebecca. "I had not expected you to be home."

"I no longer have my teaching. So I've taken over the running of the house."

"A harder job than you'd think." Rebecca was wearing a black cape and a funereal brown dress. "I've come to visit your mother."

"All the way from the Patuxent?"

"We've been friends and enemies and friends again over many years. Now we're united in our disappointment for you and Samuel."

Antonia looked into the intelligent eyes and tobacco-leaf face, dried sixty-three seasons. "You'll get over it."

"But will your mother?"

"The doctors monitor her infection. But—"

"Are there signs of laudable pus?"

"Of what?"

Rebecca held up her mangled hand. "I have had to learn much in the way of medicine. When the pus appears, it means the wound is healing. 'Laudable pus' is the correct medical term."

Antonia could not imagine those two words linked. "The wound reddened. Her fever rose. The doctor said she had developed an infection. He said nothing about . . . *laudable* pus."

"Perhaps you should find another doctor."

Antonia led Rebecca down the hallway, past the great room where the promise had been made, up the grand staircase to the second floor.

The smell of sickness, like a dog's foul breath, permeated the hallway.

In Mother Sara's room, the smell worsened, but all of the windows were closed tight and a big fire was roaring.

"We're keeping the room hot," said Antonia, "to break the fever."

Mother Sara was dozing. Her breathing was labored. Her skin was flushed from the fever.

Antonia put her hand on her mother's forehead. "Still hot."

"Don't wake her," said Rebecca gently. "I'll just sit with her for a time."

Antonia looked from one woman to the other, remembering their enmity. At least that had faded during her long and now fruitless courtship with Samuel.

"You may leave us, Antonia." Rebecca took a pinch of tobacco from the box that Big Tom had given her forty years before. "You must have much to do, and we have much to talk about . . . your mother and I."

"Remember, she's not . . . not always . . . The fever has . . ."

"She's not out of her head?" Rebecca did not want that. She wanted Sara to know who was talking to her.

"Not entirely." Antonia took the washbasin from beside the bed and placed it on the floor at the foot of a chair. "For the tobacco . . . sit here."

And Rebecca was alone, listening to Mother Sara's breathing.

She imagined what nights must have been in this bedchamber, when Sara and Black Jed were young, full of themselves. She imagined them dressing on the night of the party that she had ruined for them. She remembered fondly.

Mother Sara made a sound, a soft moan, and stirred.

Rebecca said her name.

"Jed . . . Jed . . ."

Rebecca said her name again.

Sara opened her eyes. "The other children, Jed . . . They . . . they mustn't know . . . mustn't know about Charlton's mistakes."

"He has made so many," said Rebecca, drawing closer.

"So many . . . so many . . ." Sara's eyes were rheumy and unfocused.

"His debts have grown," whispered Rebecca. "Spent too much on horses, lost too much. Giving him control of the house—that will be your *finest* folly."

Sara tried to focus on the face above her.

"I know what you did in your will." Rebecca saw the flicker of understanding and leaned closer. "Do you remember my promise, my promise to take your pillow from under your head?"

"Promise . . ."

Rebecca reached under Sara's head, sank her fingers into the down feathers, and pulled. The flesh of Sara's cheek stretched. Her hair was dragged all to one side and her head turned, so that when the pillow was finally in Rebecca's hands, Sara was looking directly at the wall, moaning incoherently.

Rebecca gently turned Sara's head back, gently smoothed her hair, gently fluffed the one pillow still beneath her head. Then she held the other pillow before Sara's face, making sure that Sara could see it. "My promise. Kept."

And a sad sound escaped from Mother Sara, a long, low moaning "Nooooo," which was all that Rebecca had hoped for.

With the pillow stuffed under her heavy overcoat, Rebecca went downstairs, thinking about Biblical quotations: "Revenge is mine, saith the Lord." She bade the servants say good-bye to Miss Antonia, and walked out into the gently falling snow.

xiv
Jason's Last Temptation

"Some in the wider world will censure us for what we did to the Typees," said Porter a week later, over dinner with his officers.

"We did no more than was necessary, sir," said Jason, showing his best face, still hoping he would be left behind.

"I took no pride in it and expect no glory from it." Porter poured Madeira all around. "Fortunately, this voyage is far from over."

"Plenty of chances for glory yet, sir"—Lieutenant Downes sat sideways so he could stretch his splinted leg—"thanks to that British squadron looking for us."

"Why not go west?" asked Gideon. "Avoid the British altogether." Then he glanced at Porter and said, less confidently, "Don't you agree, sir?"

"For someone who fought beside Decatur and Eaton and Isaac Hull," said Porter, "you have some strange notions."

Gideon felt the eyes of every officer boring into him. He took a swallow of wine and looked down at the fat-glistened pork on the plate in front of him.

"I, for one, would enjoy ship-to-ship action," said John Cowell, an eager young lieutenant.

"'Enjoy' is not the word I would use," muttered Gideon.

"Glory, Mr. Browne"—Porter slapped the tabletop—"the respect of your peers. It's not something you earn by slaughtering primitives. It comes in the kind of action that Decatur and Hull and Bainbridge have enjoyed. The kind of glory they've gained." Porter's face could never be said to glow with passion, but this talk flushed him from his collar to his widow's peak.

"Yes, sir. Glory, sir." Gideon did not think he was quite drunk enough to overstep the bounds of good sense. But he was. "Glory brings advancement. Advancement brings better pay."

Porter slowly put down his glass, and the fury rose in his voice. "Glory enhances reputation, the respect of one's peers. It's all a man has."

"Yes, sir," said Gideon, retreating.

But Reverend Adams advanced. "If reputation is a concern, Captain, you might enhance yours if you began to wean your crew from Taeeh teats."

Porter scowled at the chaplain. "If I didn't give the crew a bit of freedom on this island, we'd be facing a serious mutiny, not the silliness I suspect is brewing even now in the forecastle."

"Mutiny, sir?" asked young Cowell.

"Take away a little discipline," said the chaplain, "and you risk losing it all."

"Don't worry," said Porter. "We'll straighten them out this week."

Jason cleared his throat. "Have you determined who will remain behind with the prizes, sir?"

"Lieutenant Gamble." Porter cut into his pork, entirely oblivious to the sinking of Jason Stafford at the other end of the table.

But Gideon saw, and it was like watching the *Guerrière* go down again.

After a moment, Jason said, "Given my relationship with Piteenee—"

"Your duty to her is done," said Porter. "I want my second lieutenant with me when I face the British. Gattanewa understands."

And Jason sank a bit deeper.

"Time to think about the British," Reverend Adams said gently, "and Annapolis, and your betrothed. As the captain says, your duty to Piteenee is done."

"Yes," added Gideon, his tongue still loosened. "We need you when we go in search of a fight we could avoid."

"Be thankful that you are enjoying the hospitality of my table," warned Porter. "And take care that you are not caught up in the spirit of mutiny."

In the following week, shipboard duties replaced all others.

Jason betrayed no resentment in doing them. He saw to the loading of hogs and coconuts, to the stowage of powder and shot, to the killing of the Marquesan cockroaches, which had come aboard in place of the rats. But at night, he would take the cutter ashore and hurry through the deepening shadows to the breadfruit tree where Piteenee was waiting. And they would entwine themselves in each other's arms. And when he returned to the ship, she did not complain, for he had promised that he would stay.

She believed him. At times, he believed himself.

At other times, he remembered the snow falling on Annapolis, or he studied his miniature of Miss Mary, who seemed now to be part of another life, a life of order in which the answers were hard yet simple. But when the wind sighed in the trees, when the sun warmed his face, when he smelled the coconut oil that Piteenee spread on her body, he knew that soft answers could be simple, also.

Gideon visited the girls who had offered him favor and gave brass buttons—his last *tie-ties*—to all of them. He drove his men toward discipline. And he thought of Genesis. Like Adam, he had come to Paradise and found original sin . . . in his own lust, in the fury with which they sacked the Typee villages, in the glory-seeking that now drove Porter east, toward the British, rather than west, toward escape.

The syllogism was simple: all men were marked; for all his education, Gideon Browne was no more than a man; and that was what he would tell Antonia.

"I wonder what she'll say," he said to Jason a few nights before they left.

"She's no longer my worry." Jason tried to get comfortable, but his cabin felt like a closet after weeks of Nuku Hivan freedom.

"Then Miss Mary?" Gideon swung his hammock in the hot, motionless ship. "You'll be seeing her soon, God and the Royal Navy willing."

Jason grunted, tossed, turned again.

And for a time, the little cabin was quiet, except for the footfalls of the men pacing their watches. But even as the ship slept, there was an undercurrent of anger.

Gideon had sensed it that afternoon, in the sullen manner of sailors like Will Whitney and One-Eyed Mudge. Jason had sensed it all day, as he oversaw the loading of the last hogs and listened to the sailors' talk. All hands had been ordered aboard. The sojourn was over.

"I'll be glad to see America again," Gideon said.

"I'll miss Nuku Hiva," said Jason.

Gideon could feel the heat of uncertainty rising from the bunk below him.

Then the heat seemed to explode. Jason threw himself out of his bunk. "This cabin is too close. I need air." Once, he would never have gone on deck except in full uniform. Now he padded silently up to the midships spar deck, no more than a catwalk around the open gun-deck below.

All was quiet. Jasper Reed stood watch at the stern. The hogs were sleeping, and so, it seemed, were the men of the forward watch.

Jason wandered to a dark spot, away from the lanterns, and gazed up at the stars. If he slipped over the side now, no one would notice. He looked down into the broken reflection of the stars dancing in the black water.

It would be so easy . . . .

Then he heard a whistle from the aft companionway, and Jasper Reed whispered, "All clear, lads. Come on."

Two shadows appeared on the quarterdeck, crouched low.

"Come with us, Jasper," whispered one shadow.

"I got family, Badmouth," whispered Jasper, "back in Annapolis."

"You got a mama there, but you'll have *kids* here afore long."

"Aye, and tits everywhere," said the other shadow.

"I thought you was tired of tits, Reuben."

"It ain't the tits I'm staying for. It's love."

"Come on," said Badmouth Ben, dropping a line over the side, "and you'll miss the mutiny some of the lads is plannin'."

"Mutiny?" said Jasper.

Jason Stafford came up behind them. "Give me the names of the mutineers, then back to your hammocks."

"The mutiny is blabber," said Badmouth. "One-Eyed Mudge talkin' too much. And goin' back to our hammocks ain't somethin' we've a mind to do."

"But a man will do anything for love." Reuben Marshall grinned. The crushed sinus in his forehead matched the gap where his upper teeth once had been. It was hard to believe that anyone could fall in love with such a face.

"Come with us," said Marshall.

"Aye." Badmouth Ben looked into Jason's eyes. "We'll even find the canoe you hid, so you can sail off with your doxie, just like you planned it."

"How—"

"I followed Browne into the thicket that day, to save the life of him who saved me 'roundin' the Horn."

"Come with us, Lieutenant," urged Reuben. "This here island, it's as close to the rapture as we're like to get on this earth."

Badmouth Ben gave a glance toward the bow. "And if you stay, keep your quim kisser shut, or we'll tell 'bout that canoe and how you tried to desert in the middle of a battle."

"No one will believe you."

"They fuckin' will if we lead 'em to that canoe." Badmouth slipped over the rail.

And with a little salute, Reuben Marshall went over after him.

Jason watched them go down the side of the ship and into the water, but he could not find the strength in his voice to raise the alarm.

"This island got all a man ever need," said Jasper, "and Annapolis—"

"Is on the other side of the world," whispered Jason.

"Then you unnerstand." And Jasper Reed followed his mates.

Jason understood perfectly.

The next morning, three men were chained at the gangway—two white, one black—and ship's company, quiet and sullen, stood by to witness punishment. On the shore, the native women put up a loud lamentation.

"Desertion is a hanging offense," Porter announced. "These three have been saved by Lieutenant Stafford, who testifies that they were merely sneaking ashore for a kiss. I will now show you what a kiss will cost on our last day here."

A belaying pin was tied in each man's mouth. Then each paid with two dozen lashes.

Witnessing punishment had the usual effect. Some men retched; others cast their eyes toward deck or sky; one midshipman fainted, but the rest watched every whip stroke as though it were a test of manhood; some sailors resolved inwardly to do nothing that would put them under the lash; others openly displayed their resentment.

It was this last group that worried Gideon. All across the deck, sailors were glaring at the officers. Gideon had raised the alarm when he came on deck and saw Jason at the rail. Now he was seen as a villain who kept three sailors from their fun.

Only Jason seemed to have been spared their anger, perhaps because they sensed his yearning and because he had tried to save the three now under the lash.

After they were cut down, Porter turned to the crew. "It does not surprise me that you would rather be ashore, but you are seamen before anything else. You should know that a rumor reaches me. A rumor of mutiny. An insult to you all."

Gideon watched the faces. He thought he might be able to tell who the ringleaders were. But he was not good enough. The Crab Louse was scowling. Will Whitney kept his eyes on the women ashore. One-Eyed Mudge glared at each officer in turn. But could any of them be mutineers?

Porter looked hard at every man. "If I smell a plot to take over this ship, I'll put a match to the magazine and blow you all into the next life. Now, those of you who will obey my orders, come to the starboard side. The rest, stay where you are."

And not a man, of many big talkers, stood against Porter's will. They would all leave this savage paradise and sail with him. And many would die for his glory.

The next day, *Essex* and *Essex Jr.* sailed, leaving four prizes and a garrison of men who considered themselves very lucky.

While the *Essex* band played "The Girl I Left Behind Me," the women dipped their fingers in the water and trickled it down their faces to create tears. Some laughed as they did so, but for others, seawater mingled with real tears. And for a few, a shark's tooth driven into the scalp brought blood as a sign of mourning.

Jason settled his glass on a lone figure dressed in a blue officer's coat. He focused, saw the blood running down her face, and almost threw the glass into the sea.

"We've fouled their world enough, Jason," said Gideon.

The ship heeled a bit as she began to run.

"Think on Annapolis, Jason. Think on home."

XV
Last Will and Testament

Mother Sara died on New Year's Day. A few days after they buried her, Charlton and his wife, Hannah, Antonia, and Miss Mary Maynard gathered in the office of Anson Duganey for the reading of the will.

Mother Sara had divided the tobacco lands at Stafford Hall into three sections, with the house going to Charlton and Hannah. She said it was her desire that her three children work together in tobacco farming. And should Antonia agree to that—in writing—

Mother Sara would divide the slave holdings three ways rather than two.

Duganey squinted over his pince-nez. "Your mother showed more faith in you than people expected. This prohibits you from freeing any slave who's alive at the moment. But all their issue shall be at your discretion."

"You see," said Miss Mary, "she had a great heart."

"And a great skill for creating difficulties." Could Antonia keep slaves for a generation and promise to free their children? Or should she reject this bequest altogether? Or perhaps exchange it for a larger interest in the Fine Folly?

And that was where the surprise came.

"'As the certain Annapolis property known as Stafford's Fine Folly is the jewel of the family holdings, I propose to see that it is not broken up. I leave it in the control of my elder son, Charlton.'"

Duganey peered again over his glasses. A petty man enjoying his power, thought Antonia. No wonder she had rejected him.

Miss Mary's complexion reddened. "She's just *giving* the house to Charlton?"

"And me." Hannah raised a pudgy little hand, encased in a lace glove.

Duganey smiled now. "There *is* more. Charlton is charged with overseeing the house, determining who shall live in it, and final disposition, should there be a sale. The younger siblings must sign power of attorney over to him to participate. And here I quote: 'Placing all power in one set of hands seems wisest. Primogeniture is a tradition in our family. The son for the soil shall protect the interests of the son for the sea and of the daughter whose good sense is clouded by her idealism.'"

Antonia looked at Miss Mary. "A great heart."

"I think she's made the only choice she could make," said Hannah.

"The first child is always the most responsible," said Antonia sarcastically.

Charlton angled his head to display the Stafford jaw. But his jawline had long ago faded behind a sponge of ale-soaked tissue. "I want you to live in the house, Antonia, and Miss Mary, you're always welcome. When your men come home, we'll decide who gets to fill Stafford's Fine Folly with children."

xvi
Neutral Harbor

Gideon watched the high headlands slide past as the *Essex* entered Valparaiso Harbor, and he said, "Madness."

Jason scanned the anchorage for British masts and said, "Manhood."

And Gideon knew that Jason was once again himself, for better or worse.

But they found no British in Valparaiso.

Gideon said they should be thankful and sail on.

Porter said they would wait until the British appeared.

Gideon called it madness again.

It had been eight weeks since they left Nuku Hiva. Even the men who had suffered the most in the final week had come to accept that good things could never last and the best thing to do was lose themselves once more in the rhythms of shipboard life.

Sometimes, said Reuben Marshall, men went a little crazy.

And Jason agreed. In the first week at sea, he had mended his second-best coat and polished the buttons. In the second week, he had pulled his black stock tight to cover the tattoos around his neck. By the time the *Essex* reached the Chilean coast, he was speaking of the impending battle as a matter of honor from which no officer could turn. He was once more Lieutenant Discipline.

When the British appeared, His Majesty's thirty-six-gun frigate *Phoebe* and her consort, the twenty-eight-gun sloop-of-war *Cherub*, did not simply work their way into Valparaiso Harbor. With the supreme arrogance that only the British could muster, they kept all sails set and pointed their bows straight at the *Essex*, openly daring Porter to fire.

He ran out his guns, but *Phoebe* kept coming.

Porter later wrote that he could have annihilated her right there, but he would have dishonored his country if he'd violated Chilean neutrality. The British seemed to know it, too, because *Phoebe* did not put over her helm until the moment before she collided with the *Essex*. Then she luffed up, and her jibboom swung over the foredeck of the *Essex*, nearly plucking off Jason Stafford's hat.

Americans and British sailors glared at one another through their gunports while a gray-haired officer stood on a gun at the stern of the *Phoebe* and shouted, "Captain Hillyar sends his compliments to Captain Porter and hopes he is well."

"Very well, thank you," answered Porter. "It's good to see you again, Hillyar, but you have no business where you are. If you touch a rope yarn of this ship, I'll board you instantly."

"I beg forbearance, David," shouted Hillyar. "I'm merely bound for my anchorage."

Before the *Phoebe* was snugged down, the Americans had run a pennant up the mainmast proclaiming "Free Trade and Sailors' Rights."

The British had answered with one of their own: "God and Country: British Sailors' Best Rights. Traitors Offend Both."

Then the catcalls began. Then came the bawdy songs fired like broadsides, and the surprisingly friendly joshing when American sailors encountered British sailors ashore, and then, the meeting of the officers.

It took place at the home of a Chilean friend of Porter. The Indian servant offered coffee and fruit. The officers sat on the balcony overlooking their ships. Porter brought along Jason Stafford. Hillyar came with Captain Tucker of the *Cherub*. All wore their ceremonial swords, their epaulets, and their best manners.

To Jason it seemed as collegial as meetings before the war.

Porter and Hillyar had been friends in the Mediterranean, united in their hatred of the Barbary pirates, and they looked, in every regard, like allies. Even the uniforms were the same shade of blue, though American officers wore their cockade hats with the brims folded front-to-back to distinguish them from the British. And where Porter's face was long and lean, Hillyar had the ruddy and well-fed look of a London bishop.

"My compliments on your show of seamanship the other day," said Porter.

"I did not intend to come so close." Hillyar picked up a peach and sliced into it. "Though I *was* curious."

"About what?"

"The rumor that you sailed with a main battery of carronades."

Porter shifted his sword nervously, so that it rattled on the tile floor. The rumor was true enough to make any captain nervous.

Porter's predecessor had believed the best course in battle was to put his ship alongside the enemy and slam away with as much iron as he could throw. So he had removed all but six of the long twelve-pounders, which could send a ball a half mile, and replaced them with carronades, called "smashers," which could fire a tremendous thirty-two-pound shot, but not more than four hundred yards. Ironically, while the carronades made it necessary for the *Essex* to maneuver close in order to fight, their lighter weight reduced her from the navy's fastest light frigate to a decent but slightly topheavy sailer.

Porter had reluctantly put to sea with the carronades and the battery of six long twelves, which left the *Essex* powerful enough to intimidate British whalers. But the *Phoebe* would be another story, and Porter knew it.

So did Gideon Browne, who said that fighting a properly armed frigate on the open sea with a main battery of carronades was like a man with a shotgun fighting a man with a rifle in an open field, further evidence of Porter's blind lust for glory.

And Jason knew it, too. But he said Gideon should consider how great the damage if the man with the shotgun maneuvered close, how great the glory if he defeated the man with the rifle.

That, it seemed, was how Porter felt as well, because he asked Hillyar to challenge him to a duel between their ships.

"A duel?" Hillyar made another slice in the peach.

"I would challenge you, but as you outnumber me, it would seem improvident in the eyes of my countrymen. Issue, however, and I'll answer."

"But I'm pledged to respect the neutrality of Valparaiso Harbor."

"As are we," said Porter indignantly. "Otherwise we would have destroyed you the other day."

Then Jason, Porter's expert on the dueling arts, became the second. "Captain Porter proposes we meet four miles out, sir, beyond Chilean territorial waters, but close enough for the people of Valparaiso to observe our skills."

"Observe our skills." Hillyar turned his attention almost completely to the peach, now scored by eight neat longitudinal slices. "Don't you mean, observe the bloodshed? With nothing but carronades—"

"You have the more versatile complement of weapons, sir," said Jason. "But we've studied local conditions. Of course, *Essex Jr.* is a converted whaler, without timbers to withstand *Cherub*, so we propose to leave them out of the action."

Hillyar put the peach on a plate and, with a twist of his thumb, caused it to open around its pit like a flower. "You propose that I give up my prime advantage—the *Cherub*—in the interests of what?"

"Why, honor, sir," said Jason confidently.

"Honor . . . Young men in a young navy."

"In a young nation that needs victories," said Porter. "I propose to give them one."

"My nation needs freedom from commerce raiding." Hillyar popped a slice of the peach into his mouth. "I fear we may be at cross purposes."

"That's why we're at war."

"You misunderstand me. If I can achieve my nation's needs without fighting my ship, I'll do it."

It took a moment for Porter to realize the intent of that remark, then he sat back, as if struck. "You're not planning to blockade me?"

Hillyar held up the plate. "A bit of peach, David?"

Porter almost knocked the plate from his hands. "I've sailed a thousand miles to fight you, and you propose a blockade?"

Hillyar stood. "There are so few of you, David, and so many of us. Blockade seems the rational choice."

Porter looked Hillyar in the eye. "You disgrace the Union Jack."

The following morning, Hillyar took his ships to blockade station off the mouth of the harbor. And the game began: a feint here, a challenge there, a fortnight of flat frustration for David Porter and his crew.

Then Porter received word that three more British frigates were closing in, and he resolved at last to extricate himself from the predicament into which his thirst for glory had thrust him. He would run for the open sea, drawing off the British so the *Essex Jr.* could escape, too. Then he waited for his opportunity.

xvii
Rebecca's Proposal

Spring was coming early, as if to make amends for winter.

In Annapolis, Antonia had spent the bad weather teaching her slaves to read. She knew that as long as she stayed away from Stafford Hall, her brother would let her do as she pleased, so she accepted the bargain. She brought the dozen slaves at the Fine Folly into the library, sat them beneath the portrait of her father, and took them from the alphabet toward the Declaration of Independence. Little Iris learned so well that she was soon teaching. And by spring, Zeke was studying a botany book, sounding out Latin names for the flowers he tended so lovingly in the gardens.

On the Patuxent, Rebecca Parrish had spent the winter planning her final assault. She had made many friends on the tidewater. Some had been born after the Revolution and did not particularly care that this tobacco-chewing old woman had opposed the fight their parents had fought. Some had forgiven Loyalists their mistakes. And some had secretly agreed with her from the start.

Among these were Charles and Theodosia Duganey, and they had passed their feelings to their son, Anson. More than once, information about Charlton Stafford had passed from his office to his parents to Parrish Manor. And once the son of a Parrish had entered the ranks of rejected suitors, a sort of familial connection was forged that left professional ethics on a lower plane.

So Rebecca knew before the Stafford children that Mother Sara had rewritten her will. She knew that Charlton was considering a second mortgage on the Fine Folly to pay off three gambling debts—one to a tidewater horseman named Van der Voort, whose horses had defeated Charlton's in three races the previous autumn; one to a man in Baltimore who covered bets on local races and kept a small army of thugs to guarantee payment; and one to the notorious New York gambler Dregs McGee, who, in an epic night of whist, took Charlton Stafford for thirty-five hundred dollars. And most importantly, Rebecca knew that no Maryland bank was lending money to tidewater planters because the British blockade had destroyed the tobacco trade.

Stafford's Fine Folly was in danger, which was just how Rebecca wanted it when she traveled to Stafford Hall and proposed her race. It was simple. She would run Lady Loring, a maiden, against the best horse in the Stafford stable. If the Stafford horse won, Rebecca would pay off Charlton's debts and breed her horses to the Stafford line. If Lady Loring won, Rebecca would pay off the debts, and take Stafford's Fine Folly. Either way, Charlton would be off the hook to Dregs McGee.

"I won't let you do this," said Antonia to her brother. It was March, and the world outside the windows of the Fine Folly was tinted a delicate yellow-green. "You're gambling away my birthright, and Jason's."

"You've signed power of attorney, and the will gives me control over Jason's third of the house until he returns, when he must sign as well."

"You're going to lose the house."

"I have never lost to a Parrish horse."

"Have you ever wondered why?"

Charlton dropped into the chair behind his father's desk and folded his hands on his paunch. "I've been in this house fifteen minutes, and not one of those overeducated slaves of yours has offered me a cup of tea."

"I give them Tuesday afternoons to themselves." Antonia looked out the window so that she didn't have to look at him. "If you want tea, get it yourself."

"It's precisely that attitude that has left you unmarried all these years."

"The *house*, Charlton." She turned on him angrily. "I won't let you bet the house against a woman who once swore to take your mother's pillow."

"It's done. Duganey has drawn up the appropriate papers. The race is to be held on March 28, a match race at the Stafford Hall oval. Stafford's Patuxent Prime and Lady Loring of Parrish Manor. They'll be talking about it for years to come."

Even now, with his lack of discipline so close to ruining them, Charlton had a little boy's all-consuming enthusiasm.

"Why did you never grow up, Charlton?"

He stood, suddenly angry. "Because they made me the son for the soil and asked me to learn things I had no interest in—planting, thinning, aging, squeezing a living out of slaves not much smarter than my horses . . . all while you were teaching them to read the Declaration of Independence and Jason was playing sailor boy. Gambling is my reward. Come to the race or not. But be certain that it will be run."

xviii
The Essex *and the Angels*

On March 28, half a world away, a strong southeasterly gale blew the clouds in over Valparaiso and caused the *Essex* to part her larboard anchor cable. Then, as if the wind knew what it had done, it began to blow harder, whistling in the rigging and pushing against the hull, so that the other anchor began to drag and the ship began to ride toward the mouth of the harbor.

"We're under way, Mr. Stafford," said Porter, "whether we intend it or not."

"No sense in trying to reset the anchors now, sir?" asked Jason.

"A waste of a good zephyr." Porter studied the British ships through his glass. "Blowin' right on their bows."

"With luck, sir, we might take 'em to windward and be on our way."

Porter slammed his glass shut, and his leathered face brightened like a brown shoe taking polish. "A good commander knows when to fight and when to run. Let's run. All hands."

"All hands, Mr. Kingsbury!" called Jason.

"All hands, aye, sir."

And with a cry that echoed from the quarterdeck to the midships to the forward gangway, with the sound of two hundred pairs of bare or booted feet pounding on the decks and crunching on the ratlines, the *Essex* was under a full spread, courses to topgallants, all drum-tight and singing to the tune of the wind.

The British pointed after them, but the moment belonged to the *Essex*. If she could make a single tack at Punta del Angeles, eastern headland of Valparaiso Harbor, she would outrun them for certain.

And every man aboard understood, because every man stayed at his station like coiled line waiting to play out.

"Reef topsails!" came the order, and a single reef rose in every topsail.

"Take in t'gallants!" High up on every mast, the topgallants were pulled and furled in an instant, neater than Monday's wash.

Now Porter told Stafford, "Prepare to brace yards."

Gideon Browne was at the foremast, with Badmouth Ben beside him.

The Crab Louse and Jasper Reed held the heavy double wheel.

Little David Farragut stood at his foster father's side, as if he knew that this was a day when a boy might need the protection of a man, or when a boy might become a man himself.

High up on the mainmast, One-Eyed Mudge, Will Whitney, and the others watched and listened and waited for the sailing master's cry.

"Brace yards!"

Just as the *Essex* rounded the Point of the Angels, the cry came, and two hundred pairs of hands worked in an instant to turn the ship. And just as she turned, a squall of wind exploded around the point and struck the *Essex* right on the bow.

She all but lifted from the water. There was a tremendous groan of wood against wood. Yardarms screamed on their parrels. Miles of line wailed.

"Take in topsails!" cried Porter. Fore and mizzen tops were furled in a trice. But the maintop halyards jammed, and the great sail, reefed once but stretched to bursting, became like a hundred-ton weight tearing at the main-topmast.

One-Eyed Mudge and Will Whitney and the others struggled. But the harder they worked, the harder the rogue wind gusted. And finally, with a tremendous, skull-shattering crack, the maintop snapped and went by the boards, taking Mudge, Will Whitney, and four more with it.

"Men overboard!" cried Gideon.

But the *Essex* could not come about. She could not even maneuver back into the harbor.

With the wind whipping torn rigging like useless strands of ivy, with his ship crippled and the British coming hard, Porter chose to run downwind for a small bay three quarters of a mile down the coast, there to make repairs. He had not fired on Hillyar in Chilean waters. He told Jason that Hillyar would certainly afford him the same courtesy. He was wrong.

"God damn them, Mr. Stafford," he said when the *Phoebe* and the *Cherub* ran up their battle ensigns and started toward his makeshift anchorage. "I've known whores with more honor."

"Hillyar said only that he would respect the waters of Valparaiso Harbor," answered Jason. "He cuts his words as neat as he cuts his peaches."

"Run up the battle ensigns and beat to quarters."

Jason gave no thought to the possibility that he might die, or to their damnable luck. It was time to prove himself. "Mr. Kingsbury, beat to quarters."

The drums began to pound, and the ship began to rumble with the sound of wooden gun carriages rolling out on wooden decks.

"Mr. Barnewell," said Porter to the sailing master, "order up the springs."

"Aye, sir."

"And every lieutenant to his division."

And so, thought Gideon, their noble duel would be fought aboard an outgunned cripple, anchored in the shallows, maneuvering with nothing more than springs attached to her anchor cables. He watched Jason run the pennant up the mizzen: "Free Trade and Sailors' Rights," while Lieutenant Cowell ran another up the foremast: "God, Our Country, and Liberty: Tyrants Offend Them." Then he spat and went below to his station.

He hurried along the gundeck, past the powder monkeys fetching linen bags of gunpowder, past the loaders and spongers and rammers, past all the guns of the starboard battery to gun port number one and Crab Louse Tom.

"We're ready for 'em, lieutenant." The Crab Louse spat on his gun, one of the few long twelves, like a man spitting on his palms.

Gideon liked the calm confidence of the Crab Louse. It had rallied them off the Horn. By some miracle, it might save them now. But calm confidence would do them no good if they could not bring their guns to bear.

"Listen up, lads," cried Gideon, doing his best. "The Crab Louse sailed with John Paul Jones. He's livin' proof that Yankee seamen can beat any odds."

And the men of the gundeck cheered, the deep roar echoing so loud off the blood-red bulkheads that Gideon almost believed what he was saying himself. Then he ordered them to manhandle another long twelve from the larboard side and get ready to blow the *Cherub* to hell, and he shouted it with such spirit that the men cheered again, feeding off the spirit that fed off their own.

"Cowards!" Porter growled as the British came on, then fell off, then circled back and came on again. "Like old women around a sleepin' dog."

"A vicious dog," shouted Jason, urging his gunners to hurry as they dragged two long twelves to the stern.

"We'll bite off their hand if they get too close," said Reuben Marshall.

And all the gunners cheered.

"By God," said Porter, "with men like these, I'd fight the whole Royal Navy!"

And the men cheered again, because they sensed that he meant it.

As the afternoon sun broke through, Jason's division shackled their two long twelves at the stern ports, and two more poked out of the gallery in the captain's cabin below.

Reuben Marshall and Badmouth Ben, gun captains of the spar deck twelves, were making the final adjustments, advancing the quoins to raise the barrels, priming the guns, gauging the roll of the sea.

"Aim for their gunports, lads," said Jason. "We'll cut up her riggin' after we've knocked out a few of her eighteens and evened the odds a bit."

"Even the odds, my ass." Badmouth Ben blew on his slow match.

Jason pretended he did not hear that. But he heard Reuben Marshall say, "She sure is pretty, with all them pennants and all."

"When we're done with her," cried Jason, "she'll look like a poxed whore—"

The *Phoebe* cut him off with a thundering broadside, and the

Cherub fired one of her own. In an instant, the balls struck, bow and stern, shattering rails and wrecking the springs that had been fixed to the anchor cables.

Porter called, "Fire!"

And the *Essex* answered.

A moment later, there were loud cheers from the stern as a long twelve sent a great splash up the side of the *Phoebe* and drove an iron ball into her at the waterline.

A moment after that, cheers rose from the forward battery for a shot that struck the *Cherub* on the foremast chains and sent them flying into the air.

And another moment brought a groan of disappointment as ranging shots from the carronades splashed several hundred yards short of the *Phoebe.*

Another British broadside, almost simultaneous from the *Cherub* and *Phoebe*, echoed off the surrounding hills and came whistling at the *Essex.*

Cannonballs tore up rigging and blasted through ports on the gundeck. One deadly shot came in over the stern, killed the sponger on Badmouth Ben's gun, hit the larboard rail, and sent up an explosion of two-foot wood splinters, then ricocheted back and tore off the head of the rammer, splattering Badmouth Ben and Jason Stafford with blood and brains.

For a moment, both men were frozen by the sight.

Then Jason heard a whistling, wheezing, strangulated sound that seemed, for a moment, louder than the roar of battle.

It was Reuben Marshall, breathing his last through the splinter hole in his chest. "We should've swum faster," he said to them.

"We'll see the rapture again, Reuben," said Jason, "see it soon."

"Like hell," growled Badmouth Ben. With the slow match, he fired gun number two himself. Then he stepped around Reuben's crew and fired number one.

By the time the shots hit the *Phoebe*, four new men had hurried forward to work Ben's gun, and Reuben Marshall had seen the rapture or, at the very least, been released from his pain.

On the gundeck, the roar was deafening, and the blood-red paint could not conceal the blood covering the decks. Smoke hung like burning brimstone in the air. And the stink of mangled meatlike flesh, of excrement released as some men died and others simply surrendered to their fear, hung even thicker. But for all the death around them, the men of the forward battery did their duty so well that the *Cherub* fell off.

"She's runnin', lads!" cried one young sailor, and a cheer went up.

"She's runnin' 'cause she can't stand up to Yankee gunners," said Gideon.

"She's just runnin'," said Crab Louse Tom, "to get out of line of our guns."

And he was right. *Cherub* maneuvered until she was close by the *Phoebe*, off the starboard quarter, and opened up again.

In the next half hour, hell grew a little hotter. Great clouds of smoke boiled into the clearing sky. The rumbling of the guns caused glassware to fall from shelves in Valparaiso houses. And many an *Essex* man saw the rapture, or at the very least, was relieved of his pain.

Only the four stern guns could now be brought to bear, but they were worked the way Yankee gunners always worked their guns, and after another half hour, the British ships drew off to repair the damage. But the *Essex* had been shattered, bow and stern, hull and rigging.

Gideon carried a wounded sailor down to the berthing deck, gave him water, then went forward to find the surgeon. Halfway to the cockpit, where most of the surgeon's bloody work was going on, Gideon noticed Lieutenant John Cowell lying against a bulkhead, moaning softly. It was not until Gideon knelt beside him that he saw Cowell's leg, nothing but a piece of bone and bits of tissue, and a pool of blood expanding beneath it.

"Lucky shot, Gid," said Cowell.

"Lie still." Gideon patted him on the shoulder and called to the blood-covered Reverend Adams, who was assisting the surgeon in removing a foot-long splinter from the groin of a screaming sailor.

Adams scurried across the deck to give Cowell a look. "Lieutenant, you need help right away."

Cowell put his hand on the reverend's arm. "None of that, Reverend. I'll wait my turn. Fair play. That sailor deserves it as much as me."

• • •

"Officer's call!"

Only Jason and Lieutenant Wilmer came to Porter's station by the mizzenmast. Porter kept his eyes fixed on the British. "Damage?"

"Topsail sheets and halyards all shot away, sir," said Wilmer. "Jib and fore staysail halyards gone, too. The only line not cut is the flying jib halyard."

Porter looked up. "The gaff's been shot away, too, and our ensign with it. Fix an ensign in the mizzen rigging, and nail jacks to every mast."

"*Every* mast?" said Wilmer.

Porter turned on him. "I'm not about to strike, if that's what you're asking."

Wilmer wiped sweat and trickling blood from his forehead. "You . . . you insult me, sir. I'm prepared to fight the ship to the last."

"Then *jacks*!" said Porter, with the fury of a man facing defeat in the moment he had lived for. "Every mast. Let them know who they're fighting."

"Both ships are lining up off the starboard quarter, sir," said Jason. He could have said they were lining up for target practice, safe from the *Essex* broadside and angled away from her stern battery.

For a moment, Porter's voice faltered. "Can you bring your twelves to bear?"

Jason did not see what glory would come from fighting the ship any longer. But he said he thought they could.

"I *know* we can!" cried Badmouth Ben from his gun.

Porter lowered his head until the mask of command reappeared beneath the sweat and the black powder smoke. "Your men have a fine spirit, Mr. Stafford. It would be a sin to deny it now."

"Aye, sir."

The British guns thundered again, and the *Essex* shook with the impact. When two more men died at Badmouth Ben's gun, he barely budged, but simply called for more hands.

Now Gideon came up from the gundeck. "Captain, we're holed in eight places below the waterline and—"

"Go below, Mr. Browne, and send up boarding parties, then see to your division. Your gunners will have targets very soon."

"Boarding parties, sir? We're getting under way?"

"If we can close, we can board. Better than standing here to die."

"But sir—"

"If you're not man enough to fight this ship, then hide in your cabin."

There were, by now, many people watching this duel from the surrounding hillsides, and they were amazed when the American frigate raised its one good sail, like a cripple standing on one good leg, and turned clumsily on her oppressors. Soon she was able to get out her foretop and foresail, and for a short time she was pointing at the British ships, with her forward guns jetting smoke and thunder.

The cheer that rose from the *Essex* when the *Cherub* fell off could be heard even above the concussion of the guns.

But the *Phoebe* kept up a terrible raking fire as the *Essex* hobbled toward her. People on the hillsides blessed themselves and prayed for the men on the Yankee ship. Then the wind shifted, and the *Essex*, as if exhausted, turned toward the beach.

On the gundeck, Gideon Browne ordered Crab Louse Tom to take command of the division so that he could bring another report to the captain: this was suicide. He rushed up to the spar deck and found Porter giving orders to Lieutenant Wilmer to "bend a hawser to the sheet anchor, cut the bow anchors so that we can bring the head of the ship around and expose the broadside."

"Captain!" cried Gideon. "We have fires on two decks. There's scores dead."

The news caused Porter's mask to crack for a moment. Then it hardened again. "I thought I told you to retire, damn your eyes!"

"That was my division firing down there! Fighting for nothing. Dying for nothing but your glory!"

And Lieutenant Wilmer dragged Gideon away, telling him that he endangered them all by infuriating the captain. "Besides, I need your muscle."

With the help of a dozen sailors, Gideon and Lieutenant Wilmer got the big sheet anchor into the water amidships, then they hauled hard on the hawser to swing the *Essex* broadside.

"Well done!" cried Porter. "We'll show 'em we're not finished yet."

And what guns could fire sent their shot toward the British. And as they had done so many times that day, the British answered with four times the force.

One of the horrors of battle was that a man could often see shots coming at him. A black iron ball might seem, as its momentum faded, like a boulder hurled from a catapult, losing power but still moving too fast to be avoided.

Gideon saw an eighteen-pounder an instant before it struck the rail in front of him. He had another instant to hear the cry of John Wilmer, who was struck in the chest by a splinter and fell over the side. Then the ball smashed into Gideon's leg, shattering bones and mangling muscle, but cruelly leaving the leg attached.

In the instant that it happened, he did not believe it. In the next instant, he put weight on the ruined leg and it collapsed beneath him.

"Lieutenant Stafford, get your friend below!" cried Porter to the stern guns.

There were not enough hands to help, so Jason lifted his friend and threw him over his shoulder, as his friend had done for him in the jungle of Nuku Hiva. He had no choice but to ignore Gideon's cries of pain and go staggering down the gangway, away from the horrible sights of the spar deck to new horrors on the gundeck, where blood sloshed back and forth each time the ship rolled and new fires burned both forward and aft. Jason almost took Gideon back to the sunshine.

But there were doctors in the hell below, so he kept going, down to a berthing deck covered in bodies and agony. He found an open spot and laid Gideon beside their friend John Cowell. Then he spied Reverend Adams.

"Reverend! Gideon needs help."

"No," whispered Gideon. "Cowell's turn first."

"Cowell's dead."

The explosion that rocked the ship at that moment caused the wounded who could walk to drag themselves to their feet and make for the gangways, while those who could only cry out did that.

Gideon saw the flash at the midships gangway. Jason saw it at the forward gangway. They both knew that the ship was in its death throes.

"That was just nothin' but a few powder charges." Gideon grabbed Jason's lapel. "If the fires reach the magazine, the whole ship will go. They need you above."

"I'll be back."

Just after Jason took to the gangway, an eighteen-pound ball burst through the battered hull and tore up the berth deck, killing half a dozen of the wounded, even as the surgeons dressed them.

When the screaming had ended and the ball stopped bouncing, Gideon looked down at his feet, thinking he might be able to lift himself. His left foot pointed straight up, as it should, but the right foot had turned inward and lay on the deck, like a clock hand telling the hour of nine. He tried to straighten it, but did no more than push bone through the skin. When the pain faded, he realized how badly he was bleeding, and he felt his own blood mixing with the clotted blood of Lieutenant Cowell on the deck beneath him.

He put his head back and looked toward the shot hole in the hull. At least he would die looking at daylight.

Only Jason and Lieutenant M'Knight were left to confer with the captain when it came time to strike the colors. All the other officers had been killed or wounded.

"If all our boats hadn't all been wrecked, I'd open the sea cocks and scuttle her," said Porter.

"She has enough shot holes in her, she'll sink anyway, sir," said Jason.

Porter looked toward the gun that Badmouth Ben had captained. There were fifteen bodies around it. "Damn, but they make a man proud. Proud, Stafford."

"Aye, sir. We can all be proud." Jason said the words, looking at the blood and feeling no pride.

Now a strange sight appeared at the aft gangway. Badmouth Ben, covered in gunpowder, sweat, and the blood of fifteen men, emerged wearing a clean shirt and jerkin. He looked at the officers and saluted; then he walked toward the side.

"Ben!" called Jason when he realized what was happening.

"Stop where you are, seaman!" shouted Porter.

But Ben ignored them. He went to the transom and looked back at the officers. "I took your floggin's and your irons, but I never bent my knee. And I never will, not to you, and for certain not to fuckin' English Limeys. So I'll join my mates." And before they could stop him, Badmouth Ben threw himself over the side.

• • •

Gideon's eyes were still on the shaft of daylight slicing through the shot hole. His pain had faded, and the light in the deeper corners of the berthing deck was fading as well.

Then he was aware of people moving around him.

"The leg must come off," said the surgeon.

"No!" Gideon heard himself saying, as though he were watching this event from over there, by the fresh air now blowing through the shot hole.

"It must be done, Gid," whispered Jason.

The sound of Jason's voice brought Gideon back to himself, back to his pain, and he looked up at Dr. Hoffman, a sour-faced man with gray hair and the manner of a meatcutter. Without a word of encouragement, Hoffman took his place on the inside of the leg, and Reverend Adams took the foot.

"Hold him." The surgeon passed the screw tourniquet around Gideon's thigh.

And Gideon felt tightening all around, the arms of Jason Stafford tightening around his own arms, the hands of Reverend Adams around his ankle, and the tourniquet, tightening and tightening, stopping the flow of blood and, at least for a moment, the flow of pain into the leg.

"Have you ever done this before, Lieutenant?" asked the surgeon.

Jason shook his head.

"Then do as I say and do it quickly. The faster we work, the less likely that shock will kill him. Once I've cut through to the bone, take this"—he slapped a blood-covered leather strap into Jason's hands—"and wrap it 'round the bone. Then pull back so that we keep the meat part of the thigh out of the way and I can take a few more inches of bone . . . leave a flap to stitch over so we don't have to cauterize. And he'll end up with a better stump . . . if he lives."

"Please," moaned Gideon, "just . . . just let us wait a little bit longer."

"We can't. There's no laudanum left, nor any rum. But we can't wait." The surgeon grabbed the amputation knife from the deck and wiped it two or three times across his blood-covered leather apron.

"No," moaned Gideon.

"Hold him tight, for his own good." The amputation knife had a long, curving blade, and with it the doctor was able to make a perfect slice around the leg before Gideon had even braced himself for the struggle. But as the blade sliced down to the bone, Gideon revived to his pain.

"No!" he screamed and began to twist, like an eel on a spear.

"Hold him!"

The cut was made in an instant and an eternity. With the blade of the knife, this sour-faced man, who was very good at his job, pushed the meat and muscle of the upper thigh back as far as he could—

"Noooo!"

—to reveal the bone in Gideon's thigh.

"Nooooooo!"

"Strap, Lieutenant."

For all the bloodshed Jason had seen that day, for all that he had seen in his life, this was the most shocking moment of all: the sight of living bone laid bare. It was like looking into a vulnerable soul.

"Nooooooo!"

"Strap, Jason," said Reverend Adams. "Pull his thigh back from the bone."

"Hurry!" cried the surgeon. "He's fading."

"Noooo."

Jason looped the leather around the bone and pulled against the flesh.

"No . . ."

The surgeon dropped the amputation knife at his feet, snatched the bone saw from under his arm. The blade was dull from all the cutting he had done that day, but he sawed through in a matter of eight or nine strokes, and Reverend Adams tumbled backward with Gideon Browne's leg in his hand.

Gideon fainted. Jason thought that he might.

They tied off the arteries and wrapped the bloody stump in the only kind of linen left—a clean shirt taken from the seabag of a dead sailor.

The shirts were brought by Jasper Reed. They had belonged to Badmouth Ben.

"Damn fool Ben." Jasper helped to wrap Gideon's stump. "Jumpin' overboard like that. Why'd he do such a damn fool thing?"

"To prove his bravery . . . his"—Jason hesitated, not certain that the next word could mean much with his mangled friend beside him and the pile of amputated limbs growing by the gangway—"his honor."

"The only honor is standin' on your own two feet." Jasper looked down at Gideon's stump and added, "In a manner of speakin'."

And they heard Gideon groan. "I've made a mess of that."

"No, you haven't," said Jason. And an old line echoed back to him from another dueling field: "Value honor, but hold tight to life."

xix
A Second Proposal

Only one piece of furniture remained in the Fine Folly—Black Jed's leather chair. Everything else had been packed aboard the schooner that would take Antonia, little Iris, and old Zeke to Stafford Hall.

So Antonia sat for the final time in a room redolent of pipe smoke and memories, and she cursed her brother Charlton.

"Don't worry, Miz Antonia," said little Iris. "My pa thinks Stafford Hall's the nicest place on the tidewater. He says we'll have a nice garden there."

Then Miss Mary glided into the room. "Run along, Iris. Miz Antonia and I, we have something to talk about."

"Yes'm." Iris did as she was told.

Antonia said, "I have seen Zeke crying out in the garden, all by himself. If I could give them their freedom, I would."

"Sometimes you're not very smart, Antonia. If you gave them their freedom, where would they go? This is their home."

"We take their freedom and their ambition. And when our own foolishness costs us everything, they suffer, too."

"Well, you can punish yourself for all the sins of slavery, or you can try to make a life as best you can." She put an envelope into Antonia's hands. "This arrived in the last post, from the *President*. It's in Samuel Parrish's hand."

Antonia opened it and began to read aloud: "'Word reaches me of the fateful horse race. I say only that it was inevitable. My aunt determined that one day she would own that house, and now she does.'"

"She is a determined woman," said Miss Mary.

Antonia continued to read. "'As she yearned for possession, so do I. As she offered something in return, so do I. If you marry me, you and your heirs, who would also be mine, would live in the house after

I inherit it. I would expect no dowry, and'"—here Antonia looked up—"'you could retain any slaves you cared to keep.'"

"Is this a proposal or a contract to buy a horse?"

Antonia read on: "'Once we inherit my aunt's slaves, their fate would be yours to dispense.'"

"This is a good sign," said Miss Mary. "He's learning how to bargain. He may even learn how to compromise. Any man who marries you will have to learn how to do that."

Antonia read ahead: "'I will further tell you that the *Essex* is rumored to have been sunk by the British. In such actions, lieutenants are most vulnerable, as my own experience aboard the *Constitution* would suggest.'"

"The bastard," said Miss Mary. "He's trying to scare you into marrying him. And scare me, too."

"He wants an answer."

"Then give him one," said Miss Mary.

"But what?"

"Will you choose to live here, with a navy husband who's at sea most of the time, and your beloved slaves around you, or in a cold cottage, with a navy husband who's at sea most of the time, and nothing but New Englanders around you?"

Antonia looked out at the garden. "What would my father tell me?"

"Marry for love. I would marry Jason, no matter what. But you love this house, and the chance to do good by your darkies, more than you love Samuel *or* Gideon."

XX
Homecoming

They sailed on the *Essex Jr.*, which was stripped of guns and converted to a cartel, with safe conduct from Captain Hillyar. They arrived in New York on a hot July day. Until they were properly exchanged for British prisoners, they could not serve, so Jason, Gideon, and Jasper Reed started south.

They went by coach, because the British blockade was growing tighter, and the farther south they went, the hotter it became. At

Head of Elk, they found a packet that still sailed the upper Chesapeake. So they paid passage and sailed deeper into the quilt of humidity.

Jason worried about Gideon, who grew more pallid as the heat worsened, who sweated heavily, and seemed, in the way that the sick sometimes do, to smell stronger than the other people.

Gideon insisted there was no cause for worry. He had survived the amputation and had regained his strength quickly. But he had sailed long before he was ready to travel. And he had endured great pain, he had mastered the wooden leg and crutch that Seaman Jasper Reed made for him.

They had been gone two years from Annapolis.

But no one was waiting to greet them. No one knew they were coming.

It was a summer Sunday in a government town, a mercantile town in the midst of blockade. The quiet of the place seemed like cotton in their ears, and while all of them talked of their joy at seeing Annapolis again, they felt as uneasy as men with cotton in their ears.

Gideon worried that Antonia would be repulsed by the stump.

Jason worried because of the news: the British had chased a flotilla of American gunboats up the Patuxent and into Saint Leonard's Creek, just a few miles from Stafford Hall. These were tense times in Maryland. Who knew where they would strike next? Who knew what Miss Mary would say when she saw his tattoos?

But as they moved along deserted Prince George Street, they heard music. Then they saw the majestic brick house shimmering in the afternoon sun. And joy overcame trepidation. They began to go faster, though Jason was careful not to go faster than Gideon could clump along beside him.

When they reached the stone steps that rose from the street to the front door, four unfamiliar slaves in livery and feathered tricornes greeted them, two at the bottom of the steps, two at the top.

One of them gave the tattered uniforms a look. "You gents late. Ceremony already begun."

"Ceremony?" said Gideon weakly.

Jason was already through the front door, hurrying down the hallway. He sensed that things were different, but his eyes were drawn ahead to the garden doors and the bright sunlight beyond . . . and the blue uniforms and the colorful dresses, and, yes, the spittoon by the door.

A *spittoon?* In his mother's house?

Then he saw his brother, Charlton, standing to the left of the door, face and body turned toward the staircase to admire whoever was descending. When Charlton noticed Jason coming toward him from out of the shadows, he had to look twice, as though he did not believe his eyes, and then he saw Gideon.

At that moment, there was a little musical flourish from somewhere in the garden and the strains of "Jesu, Joy of Man's Desiring," began to filter into the house.

Charlton looked Gideon up and down. "Jason, get him out of here."

Descending one side of the double staircase were three little girls, all blond and portly, wearing leggings and tight little curls and the most beautiful powder-blue dresses they had ever put on. Jason recognized them—Walter Parrish's daughters.

On the other side of the staircase were two more glorious dresses, one a powder blue that matched the children's dresses, the other of purest white. Miss Mary Maynard was wearing the blue dress, and a lace veil covered the face of the woman in white.

"The bride is ready, Charlton." Miss Mary's voice was a singsong of false gaiety.

Charlton looked as if he might pass out from nerves.

Now Gideon reached the foot of the stairs. "Antonia . . ."

"Gideon!" came the voice from behind the veil.

"Jason?" said Miss Mary. "And Gideon?"

"So you're marrying *him*?" said Jason.

"Yes, she is," said Charlton. "Go in and take two seats at the rear."

"What's going on here?" Rebecca Parrish came through the French doors from the garden, where the groom and a hundred people awaited the ceremony.

"Where's my mother?" said Jason, and from the corner of his eye, he saw the portrait in the library, not the Peale portrait of Black Jed Stafford, but a Joshua Reynolds portrait of Duncan Parrish the Younger. "And where's my father?"

"Your mother's dead," said Miss Mary, leaping into the shot hole of shock that had opened before them all. "Black Jed now hangs at Stafford Hall."

"This is my home now," said Rebecca. "And there's a wedding about to start."

Gideon's eyes were still fixed on Antonia, who seemed frozen in place. "You are marrying Samuel, after all?"

"She's made her choice." Charlton brushed past Gideon and reached up for his sister. "We will join our two families and keep this house as part of—"

"*Keep* this house?" asked Jason.

"You're marrying Samuel to keep the house?" Gideon was so weakened in the heat that Charlton's bulk caused him to stagger. His wooden leg slid. He grabbed for Jason but missed and went crashing to the floor.

His crutch flew into the air, landed on the lip of the spittoon, and like a perfect lever, flipped it into the air.

The spittoons had been cleaned, but Rebecca Parrish had been quite nervous that day. Most of her used tobacco, along with that of several wedding guests, and the medium in which tobacco floated, came flying out of the spittoon, straight at Rebecca's beautiful yellow dress. At the same moment, Antonia was coming down to help Gideon, with Miss Mary coming after her, holding up her train to keep it clean.

They all screamed at once as the mess flew.

The music stopped in the midst of man's desiring.

In the garden, curious heads turned.

And the groom, in white breeches, blue coat, gold epaulettes and ceremonial saber, stalked up the garden steps and into the hallway, with his brother, Walter, scurrying nervously behind him, in all contravention to wedding tradition.

It was bad luck for the groom to see the bride on the morning of the wedding, even worse to see her, her bridesmaid, and the aunt who was paying for the wedding, all covered in tobacco juice.

"Samuel, get out," hissed Rebecca.

Charlton was ordering the slaves to bring wet cloths to wipe off their dresses.

Antonia was kneeling to help Gideon.

And Miss Mary had been stopped in her tracks, not by tobacco but by the strange etchings at Jason's neck, where his collar had fallen away. "Jason," she said very softly.

But he did not hear, because they were all talking at once, in voices that ranged from Rebecca's furious whisper to Samuel's growl.

"Get up, damn you, Gideon!" Samuel drew his saber and pressed it against Gideon's chest. "Get up and draw your blade."

"Samuel, we have guests," said Rebecca. "All of the best people in Annapolis."

"He's come back for her. He'll have to fight me for her."

"Not another silly duel," snapped Antonia. "I won't allow it."

One of the slaves was rushing up to Rebecca with a bucket of water and a cold cloth.

"Hurry, goddammit," said Rebecca. "The bride's dress first."

Through all of this, Miss Mary still had her eyes on Jason's neck. She said his name again, took a step toward him, and said it again. But he was too busy trying to help Gideon to his feet.

Now all of the best people in Annapolis were peering through the doorway and watching through the windows.

"Draw your saber, mister . . . or did you surrender it someplace?" growled Samuel Parrish.

"He surrendered it," said Jason, "along with his leg."

And now there were gasps, of many pitches and measures, from every side of the room. Gideon's wooden leg had slipped off, and he was trying vainly to rise.

"Let me help you," said Antonia, after a moment of shock.

"No." Gideon grabbed Jason's arm and lifted himself. "Hold me up."

As Jason held him and all of the guests watched, Gideon methodically readjusted his wooden leg, tightened it. "Cussedness, boredom, patriotism—they cost me my leg. And apparently more than that."

Then he pivoted on his good leg and his crutch and started down the hallway toward the front door.

And for a moment there was no sound in the great house but the *clump-thump-clump-thump* of Gideon's crutch and wooden leg hitting the floor.

Then Antonia looked at Jason. "Charlton betrayed you, and we lost the house. I was prepared to betray Gideon so that we could have it back, at least in union with the Parrishes."

Jason glanced at his brother, who tried to set his chin the way his father had and failed, as always. Then Jason looked once more into the library that remained so redolent of his father's memory. Then he turned to his sister and said, "Antonia, it's just a damn house."

Rebecca, regaining herself despite the spit stains all down the front of her dress, said, "Back to the garden, ladies and gentlemen. The ceremony will be starting in a moment."

And Antonia smiled for the first time that day. "No, it won't." She pulled off the veil and handed it to Samuel. "I'm sorry."

Samuel took the veil on his saber and dropped it into the mess on the floor. "This is the worst betrayal I've ever known."

"I'm . . . I'm . . ." Antonia remembered Miss Mary's advice. "Samuel, a man's honor calls him to make a stand over this old thing and that, but a woman's honor requires that she be true to her heart."

"I couldn't have said it better myself," muttered Miss Mary.

Antonia looked at Rebecca. "Whether Gideon will have me or not, I'm going. The house is yours. I'm not." Then she turned and followed him down the hallway.

"Don't worry, Samuel," said Rebecca. "They're all of them fickle and untrustworthy." She turned and looked out at the faces still peering up from the garden. "It's over. If you brought gifts, pick them up at the door. And we'll serve food, so you can get your gossiping done here, before you leave."

But most of the guests were slipping out of the garden, slinking off in embarrassment for their hostess and for themselves. The foyer emptied. The wives of Jason's brother and Samuel's brother ushered the little girls up the stairs to get them out of their dresses.

And in mid-sentence, Rebecca Parrish stopped talking, stalked into the library, and slammed the door.

Samuel looked at Jason, "Is the *Essex* gone?"

Jason nodded.

"Too bad you both didn't go with it."

"I think it's time for a drink," said Charlton. "Who'll join me?"

"I will." Walter grabbed his brother by the sleeve. "You will, too."

Jason remained in the middle of the foyer. Then he felt Miss Mary's eyes boring into his back. He turned and realized he had never seen anything as beautiful, despite the tobacco stains on her dress.

"What are those things on your neck, Jason? And on your wrists?"

"Tattoos."

She touched the ring around his neck. "It is a savage symbol, isn't it?"

"I have lived among them."

She looked into his eyes. "Lived as a savage?"

He nodded. In the sudden silence, in house he had imagined so often, he could not lie.

She took his hand. "You must tell me about it."

"I'll tell you everything, though some of the details are—"

She threw her arms around his neck and pressed her lips to his.

CHAPTER FOUR

Ghost Hunting

October 9

Jack Stafford took the credit card from his pocket and slipped it into the lock on the front door of Stafford's Fine Folly.

"I thought you had this squared with the caretaker," whispered Susan.

"I meant that I had it squared with his schedule. He wasn't too friendly. So I just scoped the place out a bit. No security system . . . caretaker's at McGarvey's."

The door clicked open.

"After you," said Jack.

"This is trespassing, B-and-E. My daughter needs her mother."

"And her mother needs a good story." Jack grinned like a tempting devil.

The long center hallway now lay before her, she had her video camera slung over her shoulder, and Susan simply could not resist. She had to walk through that hallway, had to photograph it, just to see if she could imagine all that had happened there.

The door closed behind her with a heavy clunk. And the silence enveloped them both.

Jack stared at the high ceilings and the quarterdeck staircase as though he were gazing on the Sistine Chapel.

Susan could almost see the scene by the French doors, with the flying spittoon and the little girls in their blue dresses.

The house faced south, so shafts of late day sunlight came

through the windows in the rooms on the left—what would have been the dining room and great room to the early Staffords. But there were no French doors or glorious autumnal gardens at the end of the hallway, only more shafts of sunlight, falling through the windows of the nondescript rooms beyond, an infinity of light shafts and shadows, like the repeating images in a barber's mirror—the 1907 addition.

"The light'll go fast," said Jack, lifting them both out of their reverie.

He stepped into the old dining room which, from the looks of things, had been the receiving office of the nursing home. A chest-high countertop ran through the middle of the room, tying into the wall at the place where once there had been a fine fireplace molding. The fireplace itself was blocked. An ugly fluorescent fixture hung from the handcrafted medallion in the ceiling. And a sofa that smelled like an old sock sat in the corner.

"This is— Are you rolling?"

"I'm pointing the camera at you. Of course I'm rolling."

"All right . . . This is the place where the Staffords dined. Jefferson ate here. . . . Now look at it."

Outside, a car door slammed and Susan jumped, ruining Jack's little taped speech.

Jack went to the window and looked down. "Some mom and her kids in one of the little houses across the street. Now, relax. This is supposed to be fun."

"Let's go." She backed out of the room with the camcorder still running. "Be interesting. Talk about those sorrows that every generation faces."

Jack went into the hallway. She made a nice little pivot to keep him in frame.

"We aren't talking about the sorrows right now," he said. "It might bring out the ghosts."

"We wouldn't want that."

He waved the camera to follow him. "It looks like a mess now, woodwork all dinged up, floors worn, but imagine the lives that have been lived here. Imagine a man who's just burned the *Peggy Stewart* and helped to start the American Revolution, coming down the hallway, covered with mud and worry, and finding his family clustered around a dead friend."

Now he led the camera to the staircase. "Imagine a man who has been at sea for two years, lost a leg in battle, coming home to find his beloved, standing here, in a wedding dress, about to marry another man." Jack went up to the third step and leaned on the railing. "Talk about your basic slap in the face."

And the railing collapsed under his weight. But he was deft for a big guy and quick for an old guy. He regained his balance and made it look like part of the act. "Now the stage for all that drama is falling apart."

"We'll add malicious mischief to our crimes later," said Susan.

"Just keep rolling." He came gracefully down the stair and led the camera into the great room, which was still bathed in late-afternoon light.

But the room was no longer a jewel. The windows at the back had been blocked up when the addition was grafted on, the moldings were gone, and the floor had even been covered with linoleum.

"Washington danced here," said Jack. "And a Loyalist woman insulted him here, on the night of Sara Stafford's great ball. During the Civil War wounded men lay here."

"Will I get to read about that?"

"If you do a good job with this, maybe you'll earn a look."

"So I better have some good questions. Starting with, Why do you want to restore this place?"

"Because of what happened here," he said without hesitation, "and because of the things the Staffords did when they went away from here. And because I want someplace to come back to."

"What about the new section?"

"You mean the hotel that became a rest home?" He led her back into the hallway, and he stood at the place where the French doors once had been. Now there was an archway—in need of paint—and, beyond it, that infinity of rooms. "Some restorers say you fix everything so you can see how the building evolved. But between the grace of the eighteenth century and"—he glanced down the hallway—"the institutional mess we've made of the twentieth, I'm not sure."

Then he led her toward the library door and tried to open it. "The old Staffords believed this was always the most important room in the house." Locked. Out came the credit card.

The credit card didn't work, but a penknife manipulated in the keyhole did the job. The door swung open.

And there was the reason the room had been locked: a portrait of Rebecca Parrish hanging where her brother had hung a hundred and eighty years before.

"What is this?" Jack said, more to himself than to Susan.

"You ought to know." Susan read the nameplate on the frame of the painting.

"What the hell's going on here? It seems like somebody's already fixed this room up."

Susan stepped in and looked around.

There was no longer a view toward the river. The Naval Academy blocked that. And the windows themselves had been blocked up by the addition. Otherwise, the room looked exactly as she had imagined it when she read *The Stafford Story:* the room where Nervous Duncan died, where Antonia greeted Jason after Tripoli.

From somewhere down the hallway came the sound of an opening door, a heavy male footfall.

"Who's here!" The caretaker's voice echoed through the whole place.

"Not us," whispered Jack. He pivoted Susan out of the library, and they scurried down the hallway, into the addition.

"Hello!" The voice echoed. *"Hello!"*

Susan sensed that in another instant the caretaker would come out of the dining room, look down the hallway, and see them, so she pulled Jack into the third bedroom on the left.

"Great," said Jack. He was starting to look a little gray. "Now we're stuck."

Susan looked around. The room still smelled of sadness, even though the beds and the old patients were long gone. So . . . air it out. She went to the window and pushed at it. Stuck.

"Unlock it," said Jack.

"Who's here!" The voice echoed angrily.

Unlocked. Still stuck.

The sound of heavy boots drew closer.

They heard him stop by the first bedroom, then cross the hall to the opposite room.

Jack pushed with her and the window finally popped up.

The caretaker must have heard, because the footfalls turned and came directly toward their room, directly into it.

The caretaker growled, "Son of a bitch," quickstepped to the open window, saw something, and climbed out after it.

A moment later, the closet door opened and Jack stuck his head out. "He fell for it."

"My knees are shaking."

"Better than havin' your brains shakin'. Seein' that window reminded me of a trick I've had to pull a few times. Jealous husbands, you know."

Their escape route took them out the front door, then down Prince George Street, to the east. After a few turns, they went onto the Naval Academy grounds at Maryland Avenue.

By now, Jack seemed giddy, overflowing with relief and adrenaline.

But Susan was furious and giving him an earful for getting her into trouble.

"Yes, but what did you think of the house? Is it something worth fighting for?"

"I'd just like to know who you're fighting against."

"Well, considering the Parrish face in that portrait—which looked like a reproduction, incidentally—add the name Oliver Parrish to a short list that includes the Institute for Advanced Naval Planning."

"Who's Oliver Parrish?"

"Local lawyer . . . ex-Navy SEAL . . . client list that includes everyone from the NRA to the Mid-Atlantic Gay Rights Coalition. Anyone with an ax to grind against the government calls Ollie. He's never been much for estate law, but I guess he's involved with the Shank estate. And it looks like he's moving his stuff into the library."

"What about this institute? Conservative or liberal?"

"Nonpartisan. Committed to producing research for whoever pays, which usually means defense contractors and their ancillary manufacturers and, of course, the people in the places where the next generation of weapons gets made. Mostly they make their money by thinking ahead, then lobbying Congress and the Department of Defense toward their conclusions."

"I'll rephrase the question: Good guys or bad guys?"

"No easy answers, Susan. My brother is one of their chief consultants. If they get the house, they'll keep the exterior, because they have to, and turn the interior into offices. That way, they can avoid the D.C. traffic, pick all the D.C. brains on their Annapolis sailboats, and on nice Wednesday afternoons in the fall they can show their clients that."

Marching toward them from across the yard, marching in steady two-by-two lines behind their company commanders, marching to a military cadence set by the steady beat of the drums, marching between the Faculty Club and Preble Hall and Sampson Hall came the brigade of Naval Academy midshipmen.

"Afternoon drill. It's a good show, like a parade. Impresses the hell out of people," said Jack.

The midshipmen were marching past them now. Young men and women in their almost-black navy blues—shirts, trousers, ties—and white officer's hats. Hundreds of them, looking so serious and so young.

"Where are they going?"

"Mother B.—Bancroft Hall—where all of them live. The cream of America's youth, so they say . . . such cream that the taxpayer picks up the tab for all of them. Then we send them on to flight school or surface warfare school or submarine school, or to Parris Island for the ones who decide to be marines. But look at them."

The midshipmen were now sweeping past them on two paths through the center of the campus. Jack and Susan were surrounded, to their left and right, unable to break the line, so they simply stood and watched.

"Kids," said Jack. "Marched, drilled, educated, drilled, regimented, drilled, inspired, and drilled, usually into damn good officers."

This surprised Susan. "You mean you're not going to be critical?"

"You haven't read enough of my book. They can say what they want about this place—and it's had its scandals—"

"Cheating and drugs and sexual harrassment come to mind."

"Well, for all the talk of honor that you still hear, the Naval Academy is no different from the navy, which is no different from the real world in one very obvious way—it's made up of human beings. And human beings are sometimes flawed."

He pulled a diskette from his pocket and handed it to her. "You've earned another chapter. Book Five. It's about the early alternative to the Naval Academy, and how this place got started. And, as always, it's about that old house."

Jack was a mysterious old guy. She asked him to have dinner with her that night, but he said he had people to see in Washington. He'd be in touch.

Fine, she thought. As long as I have your book, I don't need you, anyway.

Back at the bed-and-breakfast, there was a message from Steve Stafford.

She dialed the number: CHINFO at the Pentagon.

"Cousin Susan. Hi."

"*Cousin?*" She had never met him.

"That's what my grandmother calls you. Listen, how about a boat trip tomorrow? I have a writer and a photographer from the *Baltimore Sun* meeting me in Annapolis tomorrow. And if you look out there about a mile, in the deep water of the Chesapeake, you'll see a big sub tender. Anchored on the other side of it is one of the wonders of the twentieth century. It's the USS *Annapolis*, here for Homecoming Weekend. It's a fast-attack submarine."

"What's it planning to attack?"

He laughed at that, which meant he had a sense of humor or he laughed at bad jokes just to seem like a good guy. Either way, she liked him, and she hoped he looked as good as he sounded. He'd make a great talking head.

"We're touring her tomorrow, eleven hundred. Bring your video cam."

"Great. Say, listen, while I have you, what do you know about the Institute for Advanced Naval Planning?"

"Good people. Do good work—not just for the military, for the whole country. My grandfather is a consultant."

So, she thought, nothing secret about this institute. But probably doing nothing that Jack Stafford liked . . . nothing that she'd like too much either. Defense consulting wasn't high on her list of noble pursuits, despite the good impression the admiral and his wife had left on her. But then a scene from Jack's book came to her mind, and it made her think in a way that she never had before: the men who armed the *Essex* could have used a little defense consulting before they sent her into battle armed as badly as she was.

"At eleven hundred, then," said Steve. "Launch leaves from Fleet Landing, by Halsey Field House."

She made a nervous laugh. "Into the belly of the beast."

Steve laughed too. "Being an old flier, I think the same way about submarines."

She considered asking him about his father while she had him on the line. But this was the first time they had spoken, so it might seem too intrusive. Better to let him reveal a little about himself before she got nosy.

After she hung up, she went to her room and inserted Jack's latest diskette into her laptop. As long as he kept giving her sections of his book, she'd keep filming him and the old house. If he asked her, she'd even film him while he shaved.

The Stafford Story

BOOK FIVE

A Hanging Offense

December 1840

In his quarters at the Washington Navy Yard, Jason Stafford read a letter from his sister:

> Dear Stubborn Old Jace,
>
> After a quarter century, the Fine Folly still comes to mind when Christmas approaches. How precious are the memories of our Yuletides there! I can still see the grand staircase festooned with laurels. I can still smell the Christmas goose and hear the carols.
>
> How proud Mary would be of her men—her Thomas a naval lieutenant, her little Georgie one of our best students here at Round Hill. And her husband leading the navy into the era of steam. . . .

That was a grandiose misapprehension, thought Jason. He sat on the Naval Board for Steamships because he had been first lieutenant aboard the first steam-driven warship, the flat-bottomed *Seagull*, used by David Porter in the Caribbean anti-pirate campaign of 1823. From the day he maneuvered the *Seagull* in a tight estuary, with wind and tide against him, Jason had been converted to steam.

Porter had long passed from the scene. But his lieutenant had been preaching steam ever since, mostly to deaf ears.

There were some six hundred commercial steamers in America, but none of the navy's twenty-one ships was steam-driven. It was no easy task to raise money for new war machines when there had been peace for twenty-five years. It was a wonder to Jason that Congress had even bothered to authorize a steamship board.

At least his son served in a navy of exploration rather than war-making. Thomas, twenty-four, had sailed aboard the *Vincennes*, which charted the Pacific in 1838 and even put in at the Marquesas. Ten-year-old George, born after miscarriages and stillbirths, could look forward to a midshipman's warrant when he finished his studies at the school where his uncle Gideon taught.

Their mother would have been proud of them. Miss Mary Maynard, who had seemed to so many like a looking glass—a simple surface reflecting her surroundings—had in fact been a well-spring of wisdom about the big things and the small. It was an everlasting wonder to Jason that he had survived the four years since her death, and a thousand times he had cursed his orders to command the naval station at New Orleans, where yellow fever had found its victim.

At least he had his sister's letters to cheer him:

> It is hard to understand, even now, why God should take Mary in her prime and let Rebecca Parrish live into her ninety-fourth year.
>
> But every day Rebecca must think on poor Samuel's death and consider its irony—January 1815, a month after the treaty had been signed but before the news had crossed the Atlantic. There was no need for the *President* to run the British blockade of New York, no need to engage HMS *Endymion*. Samuel always said that lieu-

> tenants were the most vulnerable in sea fights. The ball that killed him fulfilled his own prophecy.
>
> It's a dangerous life, but you are wise to steer both sons to the sea. As we know, an unwilling son for the soil can do great damage to family and self.
>
> Of course, had you freed your slaves when you freed mine, you would have freed yourself entirely from the soil. Charlton might then have been forced to face the coming reality. As one who served on the Navy anti-slavery patrol and boarded slave smugglers, you know how horrible slavery is. . . .

And so on and so on and so forth.

All of Antonia's letters eventually got around to slavery, but Jason and his sister had long ago agreed that they would never agree on the matter. Though he had known his share of fine freedmen, Jason believed the tradition of slavery was as much a benefit to the slaves as to their masters. And he never intended to divest himself of his only true assets—the Patuxent lands and the slaves.

But a naval officer could not also manage a plantation. He needed his brother for that.

On the day after the aborted wedding in 1814, Jason had traveled with his brother and Hannah and Zeke back to Stafford Hall. Charlton had spent the journey sipping from a bottle of brandy and apologizing for his improvidence; Hannah had stared into space; and Zeke had told Jason the story of Charlton's horseracing obsession.

When they reached the plantation, Jason had asked his brother to take him to the stable. There he had asked him which horse was the most valuable.

Puzzled, Charlton had said that the best breed stud on the farm was Patuxent Prime, who had lost the match race to Lady Loring.

"Point him out," Jason had said.

Charlton led him to the last stall in the barn, to a beautiful big bay with three socks and a smart face. Jason had patted the horse, whispered a few soft words, swallowed a few pangs of guilt, then put a pistol to the horse's head and pulled the trigger.

Patuxent Prime had collapsed like a shroudless mast.

Charlton had dropped to his knees in the stall and put a hand over the hole in the horse's head, as if he could stop the bleeding, and into the depths of his shock had dropped Jason's hard voice: "Miss Mary says I should forgive you. Consider yourself forgiven." Then Jason had pressed his other pistol to Charlton's head. "But gamble again with our family assets, and I'll shoot *you*."

In some men, this would have inspired eternal enmity. But to Charlton, it was a lifeline. He never placed another bet of any kind, anywhere. There were times when Jason wished he could shoot a brandy bottle and as easily cure his brother of the taste for drink, but one depravity was better than two, and the childless Charlton had remained ever since a reliable steward of his brother's assets.

And Antonia had remained a reliable correspondent:

> Enough of slavery. The news here is that our Johnny, all of thirteen, has determined to follow in your Thomas's naval footsteps. He is an imaginative boy who yearns to live the adventures he reads about in Fenimore Cooper and Sir Walter Scott.
>
> He reads everything about naval life, including David Porter's *Journal of a Cruise*—the unexpurgated Bradford and Inskeep edition of 1815, which describes in slobbering detail your sojourn in the Marquesas.
>
> Gideon sees the link between a strong navy and a nation's commerce. He still prides himself on having bought depressed shares of the Massachusetts whaling fleet in 1814, knowing that his own *Essex* had swept the British whalers from the sea and that once the British blockade was lifted, our whalers would pour into the Pacific without competition. We turned a tidy profit on that one.
>
> But Gideon has also warned our Johnny of the dangers of naval thinking, which cost him his leg and have cost more than one good man his life on the dueling field. Johnny is infected, however. He sees something romantic in my headlong rush to stop your duel with Samuel so long ago, and he thinks that our friend Stephen Decatur died gloriously because he died, as you navy people say, on the field of honor in 1820.

He will not be satisfied until he tests himself, and so we ask you for help. And if, by chance, you can come to Northampton for Christmas, it would be wonderful.

Gideon sends his affections. For the first time, he complains that his wooden leg tires him.

Jason wrote back:

Tell Gideon to walk every day, missing leg or no. It is the best way for a man to sustain his health. Brisk walks and rare beef.

As for Johnny, I will inquire after a warrant for late '42.

As for the Yuletide, I am going to Stafford Hall by way of Annapolis.

Your son's interest in the navy gets me thinking once again about a naval school. That's where a boy like your Johnny—or my George—should begin his education, not aboard a man-of-war with a third-rate schoolmaster teaching him the ABC's between sail changes.

Back in '24, the Maryland Assembly suggested an Annapolis site for a naval school. No one seems to remember, but I'm going to reconnoiter there; then Thomas and I sail for Stafford Hall. In attendance will be Hannah's niece, a Charlottesville widow named Margaret Redgate Harcourt. She is thirty-five, perhaps a trifle young for the attentions of an old sea dog, but I have twice been in her company and am not ashamed to say I look forward to making it thrice.

ii
Sleeping Annapolis

Jason had not been to Annapolis for ten years. This time, he went in style.

In Christmas week of 1840, the railroad opened between Annapolis and Washington. Steam had come to the land, and the world would change quickly. The train covered forty miles in the amazing time of two and a half hours. But as he and his son Tom walked from the depot, down decrepit West Street to Church Circle, it was clear that what Jason had heard of the ancient city was true: Annapolis slept.

The Assembly still met in the State House. The oystermen still dipped their tongs in the creek mouths. The watermen filled their skipjacks with crabs. And at old Fort Severn, the soldiers drilled each day. But the families that had built the great houses—the Pacas, the Chases, the Staffords—were gone. And down at the dock, no cargo came in. And along the little rows of houses on West Street and Cornhill, the paint peeled in the salty air.

But father and son made a fine picture as they strode from State Circle down to the waterfront.

Jason was still ramrod straight, and while his black hair had grayed at the temples, his square jaw had not dropped an inch. His first son was the image of him, except two inches taller—a full five feet ten.

"A naval school? Here?" asked Thomas.

"Ten acres, half a dozen buildings to house midshipmen. A river big enough to moor a frigate, the old battery for gunnery lessons."

The battery stood on the site of the Revolutionary War earthworks, where the Severn met the harbor. It was only thirty years old but seemed almost medieval—a stone circle, a hundred feet in diameter, with gunports piercing it, and squat mortars, better suited for flowerpots than coastal defense, sitting atop it.

"I learned my seafaring at sea," said Thomas.

"So did I. But it was hard learning."

"I even went to the Marquesas." Tom grinned. "And I learned plenty. I just didn't come back with any tattoos."

And Jason stopped. When his boys were little, he used to joke about the tattoos, but not now. "No one was prepared for what we found in the Marquesas. Not the boys. Not the men. A man is never prepared when he looks his own weakness in the face. But with training and discipline, he can survive, whether it's cowardice that's tempting him . . . or the Marquesan sunset."

"Mother said you almost deserted in the Marquesas. What stopped you?"

"Uncle Gideon stopped me. My training sustained me. Your mother saved me."

While most people saw Jason in his son, Jason saw only his wife, in the gentle eyes, the ready smile, and . . . suddenly he felt a rush of emotion, so he turned quickly and began to walk.

A cold wind snapped up off the river, swirling the dust on the path and giving him a reason to wipe his eyes.

Then he felt Tom's hand on his shoulder, as comforting as his own father's had been when he was a boy. Sons, he thought, were a true gift.

"Come on. I'll show you the house they still call Stafford's Fine Folly."

A short walk brought them to Prince George Street and the red brick house that seemed to smolder in the light of a winter afternoon.

"It looks like a ship," said Thomas.

"In serious need of a refit." Jason noticed the peeling paint and crumbling mortar. "She needs new varnish on every spar and oakum in every seam."

Thomas gave his father a sidelong glance. "A task you'd like to undertake?"

"It would be nice to have the ghosts shake hands with us . . . to have you and George meet your grandfather."

"One of the ghosts is looking out at us right now."

Up in a second-floor window, an ancient face was peering at them, and the front door was opening. A heavyset man in his mid-fifties called to them and invited them to visit: Walter Parrish.

Inside, Jason watched his son drink in the beauty of the old place. The floors were now coated with wax and covered with Turkish carpets as beautiful as any ever owned by the bashaw of Tripoli. In the library, the portrait of Duncan the Younger hung in Black Jed's place. But the hallway that divided the house like a keel and the staircase that resembled a quarterdeck were just as Jason remembered them.

"My aunt saw you," said Walter, leading them up the stairs to the sickroom. "She's convinced you're my brother Samuel and his friend Midshipman Stafford, come to visit her."

"Wasn't Samuel killed on the *President*?" asked Thomas.

"Play along. She's a little senile," said Walter.

Jason was struck first by the color of the old woman's chin—as brown as the cherrywood handle of a flintlock pistol. There was a spittoon at her feet and, beneath it, a spit-covered floor.

Walter's son, Dan'l, stood as the Staffords came in. He was big-bellied like his father, but without his father's placid nature. His movements were sudden; his eyes darted between the Staffords, taking in details of faces and uniforms. Then he gestured to his ancient aunt. "Don't expect us to sell because of her."

Walter chuckled. "My son has a way of getting to the heart of things."

"A pity he doesn't know how to greet a guest," said Jason coldly.

Dan'l's sharp eyes took a little nick at Jason. "If I was you, Captain, I'd want this house back."

"I don't want the house. An apology for your insult will do."

"Don't take offense," said Walter. "Dan'l's been thinkin' hard on this house. He's taken himself a bride, so he wants me to ship up here . . . leave him to run the plantation. He's sellin' off the last of the racehorses to buy up more slaves. Folks say he's the best judge of black flesh in Saint Mary's County."

"Best judge, worst manners." Jason kept a cold captain's gaze on Dan'l, whose sharp eyes soon dulled beneath it.

"If I've offended, Captain, my apology," said Dan'l finally. "But your sister in Massachusetts writes some damnably inflammatory things about slavery, and my anger at her may flow toward you."

Then Thomas said, "I believe we were invited to meet a sick old woman."

None of this had penetrated Rebecca's film of senility. She sat in her chair, peering up at Thomas Stafford, as though puzzled. Finally, she spoke. "They said a cannonball took off your head when *Endymion* caught up to *President*."

"No, ma'am," said Thomas politely. "I'm all in one piece."

"But . . . but you're dead, still and all . . . so this must be heaven."

"No, Auntie," said Walter, offering her tobacco from a tin. "It's Annapolis."

And the old lady nodded, like someone pretending to understand a language she had never heard before. Then she dipped her hand into the tobacco.

Her life was ending, but an old enmity had once again begun.

"I abhor bad manners," said Jason, back outside in the December chill. "At least you proved yourself a gentleman, reminding us all of why we went in there."

"Bad manners are often a sign of fear, Pa. Why should Dan'l Parrish fear us?"

"Because he's right. Your aunt does write inflammatory things about slavery. And now that I've been there, I *do* want that old house back."

iii
Midshipman's Warrant

The next two years, however, brought more pressing matters.

There was the design and construction of the navy's first steam-wheel frigates, the *Mississippi* and the *Missouri*.

And as the knowledge of steam power expanded, more officers came to agree on the need for a school more formal than a few instructors aboard ships, more expansive than the cram schools where midshipmen prepared for lieutenancy exams. Jason had entered into correspondence with William Chauvenet, the new headmaster of a cram school at the Philadelphia Naval Asylum, and they agreed that a way would have to be found.

But Congress could not be convinced. Of twenty naval academy funding bills introduced since 1814, only two had passed the Senate, and they had died in the House. Jason sometimes wondered if some midshipman would have to die at sea before an academy bill would pass. He could not know it, but there would be a death, and it would come close to home.

Before that, however, there was joy: Margaret Redgate Harcourt consented to add another name to hers in September of 1842, on a golden day above the Patuxent.

It was a small ceremony. Jason's sons stood beside their father. Hannah Redgate Stafford was matron of honor for her niece. Margaret's young son, Cecil, stood close to his mother. And Antonia traveled with Gideon and their son, John, all the way from Massachusetts.

The years of hauling himself around on a crutch had been hard to Gideon. His red hair was whitening quickly; his face was a fine web of wrinkles.

But Antonia had barely aged. She remained a handsome woman whose hair was black and whose spine was straight because, as her husband was fond of saying, she was always right. And she pronounced the marriage a perfect match.

The new Mrs. Stafford wore yellow chrysanthemums in her honey-colored hair and an off-white lace dress that artfully disguised the portliness she shared with her aunt. But unlike her aunt, she could warm a room with her smile, light it with her laugh.

That night, in the bedroom where Jason's grandfather had seen the pirate torches, she saw Jason's tattoos.

He put his nightshirt over his head, then discreetly removed his breeches from underneath. "It has to be said that I've lived an exciting life."

"I look forward to sharing it with you." She threw back the covers and invited him into the bed.

The old house by the river was crowded that night.

Adult couples slept in every bedroom, and in the attic above the kitchen, the children bedded down.

Everyone slept soundly, except for Antonia's son, Johnny. He was simply too excited to sleep: his uncle Jason had handed him a midshipman's warrant that evening.

Johnny Browne was going to sea at last.

iv
The Somers

She was tiny.

That was Gideon Browne's first thought when he saw the *Somers* silhouetted against the high September sky at the Brooklyn Navy Yard, with the steeples and chimneys of Manhattan rising beyond. The little brig had been named for Richard Somers, commander of the bomb ship that exploded in Tripoli Harbor, and she had been built for a new purpose: to train midshipmen and apprentice sailors in a gentler environment than a ship of war.

Gideon calculated her size and the number of crewmen—or crew *boys*—scampering over her, and it was enough to make his phantom leg ache. There would be a hundred or more on a vessel not much longer than a hundred feet.

She was a fine-lined little brig, to be sure, one that could fly with a full spread on those raked masts and a brisk quartering breeze pushing her along. But to Gideon, she looked oversparred, with nowhere near enough draft to keep her stable, and ten heavy guns taking up deck space, making her even more wobbly.

And the longer he looked, the smaller she got.

"She's beautiful." Johnny shivered with excitement. He was as gawkish and angular as his father once had been, but he had inherited the Stafford hair, and he had a warmth of manner that was all his own.

"Aye," said Gideon. "Beautiful."

"She *is* beautiful," said Antonia, hearing the tone in Gideon's voice. "Isn't she?"

A young officer who had been watching them from the quarterdeck now sauntered down the gangplank to greet them.

Here was someone, thought Gideon, in need of the training the *Somers* would provide. He was about eighteen and the sloppiest officer Gideon had ever seen. He perched his hat on the back of his head like a jaunty boy. His blue jacket showed more stains than fabric. And he was chewing a cigar like an old tradesman.

But there was something else. Gideon had always taught his son not to judge a man on physical abnormalities, and this young man's bulbous nose and prominent upper lip were no more dramatic than the features on any other face. But he was also walleyed, so much so that when he looked at Gideon, he seemed to be looking at Johnny and Antonia, giving Gideon the sense that he could not make eye contact, even as this young man was looking right through him.

Johnny did not seem bothered by the face. He was too impressed by the uniform. He started to offer his hand, but instead he chose to salute.

The young officer smiled around his cigar. "An eager one."

Gideon said, "This is my son, John Browne. And you are . . . ?"

"Midshipman Phil Spencer." He doffed his hat.

At least he had manners, thought Gideon.

"Let's see," said Mr. Spencer, stroking his chin and pretending to study young John. "All but Stafford's nephew have come aboard . . ."

Johnny's eyes brightened at the mention of his uncle.

" . . . so you must be he."

"Yes, sir, I'm his nephew."

"Well, welcome aboard the USS *Uncle-pa*."

"*Uncle-pa*?" said Antonia. "I thought this was the *Somers*."

The young man gave out with a cackling laugh. "I call it the *Uncle-pa*. Matthew Perry, commandant of the navy yard, has two sons and a nephew aboard. His brother-in-law is in command. There's Midshipman Rodgers, and you know how filthy the navy is with that name. There's you, with your famous uncle. And then there's me. I'm the son of the secretary of war. So everybody either has an uncle or a pa who put him aboard."

"Oh," said Antonia. "A rather arcane joke, sir."

Gideon said nothing. The navy certainly had changed.

"My father's quite famous also," said Johnny.

Midshipman Spencer turned to Gideon. "How so, sir?"

Gideon did not need to answer, because Johnny was eager to brag. "He lost his leg when the *Essex* fought the British in 1814. Now he teaches and writes naval history."

And the walleyes threw new interest in the general direction of the tall man with the wooden leg. "Are you the Browne who wrote *A History of American Naval Actions against the Caribbean Pirates, 1819—1824*?"

Gideon nodded. "It's been ten years."

"Your book will live a hundred years, sir." Spencer took the cigar from his mouth. "It will live as long as your subject lives in the annals of history."

That, thought Gideon, was an exaggeration.

"I am honored to meet you, sir." Spencer offered his hand. "I'm a great aficionado of pirate lore."

"So am I, sir," said Johnny, eager to forge a bond. "An . . . an aficionado."

"Yes," said Antonia, helping her son to make a friend, like a good mother. "He's even packed a copy of Fenimore Cooper's *The Red Rover*."

"It's my favorite book," said Johnny.

"Well, Mr. Acting Midshipman Browne, you'll be surprised to know it's mine, too." Spencer clapped the boy on the shoulder. "We shall have much to talk about in the midshipmen's berth, though I'll tell you it's no more than eight by fourteen feet."

"For how many men?" asked Gideon.

"Seven midshipmen—three full, four acting. But don't you worry. I'll see that your son has a bunk near the top, with good ventilation."

Gideon thanked Spencer, but he was still uneasy, and his uneasiness only increased after he met Commander Mackenzie, a sallow man who plastered his hair to the sides of his face and combed one absurdly long pomaded triangle from the crown down over his forehead, to give himself the semblance of a hairline.

Mackenzie had been chosen to educate young men because he had written several books, including biographies of John Paul Jones, Oliver Hazard Perry, and Stephen Decatur, and considered himself a man of literary as well as seafaring merit.

Gideon was glad he had written a warm review of the Decatur biography, because Mackenzie reminded him of schoolmasters he had met—the sort who could give parents comforting smiles, followed by cold stares and whippings for their sons.

The man to administer the whippings would be Chief Boatswain's Mate Cromwell, a bearded hulk with a brutal scar on his forehead and a temper that he did not hesitate to display right there in the navy yard, in front of the Brownes, as he berated two frightened apprentice seamen.

For three months after that, Gideon worried.

But what happened was worse than anything he could have imagined.

He first heard news of it on December 17, when he and Antonia returned to New York for the Christmas arrival of the *Somers*. They were greeted by a shocking headline in the New York *Herald*: "Horrible Mutiny Aboard the US Brig *Somers*—Hanging at the Yardarm!"

Antonia almost fainted. Gideon read on, hands shaking, though it would be days before the true story was known. . . .

V
A Grand Experiment

Her assignment was simple: carry dispatches across the Atlantic to the sloop-of-war *Vandalia*, on the Africa station. Along the way, her experienced crew—Mackenzie and Lieutenant Gansevoort, her three senior warrant officers, and fourteen of the sailors—would teach four acting midshipmen to become officers and ninety-four apprentice seamen to become sailors. And if they were lucky, they might get a crack at chasing a slaver.

Commander Mackenzie called it a grand experiment.

And Johnny Browne was proud to be part of it.

That was what he told Mackenzie when he met him. That was what he told his mother when she embraced him and tried not to cry. And that was what he told himself when he went below to steerage—which housed the pumps, the tiny midshipmen's mess, and the midshipmen's berths—and tried not to cry himself.

That night, rocking in the bunk that was rocking in the ship that was rocking toward Africa, he felt the rocking sickness that all men feared when they first went to sea. To ward it off, he talked in the darkness with his mates—Captain's Clerk Oliver Hazard Perry, named for his uncle, Midshipman Rodgers, and Philip Spencer.

"So, Browne," said Rodgers, the oldest, strongest, and gruffest in the little group. "This your first ship?"

"Aye, sir."

"How's your belly?" asked Perry, a seventeen-year-old boy, every bit as handsome as his late uncle.

"Belly's fine . . . berth's fine . . . captain seems fine, too." Johnny felt terrible. "It's an honor to sail with him on a grand experiment."

"Grand experiment," grunted Spencer. "It's just a way for our fathers to keep us under their thumbs."

"You don't like the navy, Spencer?" asked Rodgers.

"I'm here because of my father."

And Johnny relaxed a bit, happy that the conversation was drifting away from him, so that he could concentrate on keeping his supper down.

"Why don't you leave?" asked Rodgers.

"I tried to on my last cruise. Got drunk, got into fights, tendered my resignation, but my father preferred a naval miscreant to a quitter . . . so I was ordered to this overcrowded little catboat."

The ship rocked. The cabin rolled. The supper sloshed in Johnny's belly. And the sound of water hissing along the hull made him feel even sicker. But even if he had not been seasick, he was homesick, and that was a worse pain.

Someone took a deep breath, and then Perry said, "She's overcrowded, and she also smells."

"To high heaven," said Spencer. "Don't you think it smells, Browne?"

Johnny tried not to inhale too deeply, because the stale-piss smell of the bilge, subtle though it was in a new vessel, was still enough to start him vomiting. And a naval officer could not give up the stew of peas, fresh pork, and ship biscuit simmering in the back of his throat. "It doesn't smell to me, sir. I think it's going to be a grand experience, sir."

For a moment, there was silence. Then the snickering started. And the snickering turned to laughter that they muffled in their mattresses for fear of awakening Lieutenant Gansevoort, who slept in the tiny wardroom, or Commander Mackenzie in his stern cabin.

Johnny wanted to bolt from steerage and empty himself over the side.

But Rodgers was giving him some advice. "One thing, Browne. Spencer is an *acting* midshipman, just like you. No need to call him 'sir.'"

Spencer swung out of his bunk. "Anyone who has the good sense to call me 'sir' deserves a cee-gar. Come on, Jack. Cee-gar'll be just the thing."

They climbed to the deck, to the sky that shimmered silver in the brilliant starlight, and while Philip Spencer chuckled, Johnny Browne took one taste of cigar, then vomited up his supper, his lunch, and, it seemed, his stomach itself.

"Best thing for it," Spencer said as Johnny retched. "Get it all up. Then get your eyes out on the horizon, and before long, you'll feel just fine."

Johnny wiped the corners of his mouth. "How did you know I was seasick?"

"You wouldn't be sayin' such stuff about the captain unless you were so sick you couldn't think of anything better."

"But—"

"Don't be soundin' like such an old granny. That's what the captain is—an old granny. If you're to sail the high seas like the Red Rover, you have to be a man. You have to swagger."

"Swagger . . . right." Johnny looked out at the place where the luminescent sky touched the sea. "I'll try to swagger."

"And join an officer in a drink once in a while." Spencer pulled a silver flask from his jacket, took a sip, and offered it to Johnny.

"But the captain told us not to—"

"We're officers. If we want a drink, we're entitled. It's that crew of wet-behind-ears swabbies that he's keepin' from the grape and the grog."

"But I've never—"

Spencer shoved the flask into Johnny's hands. "It'll clear the taste of vomit from your throat."

Put that way, Johnny could not resist, because the taste of the vomit was threatening to make him sick again. He took a swallow of the brandy, which felt like fire going down and like acid a moment later as it came up and went over the side.

Spencer chuckled. "Cauterizin' the wound, Jack my boy. That's what brandy does in the belly. Stay on deck awhile and watch the horizon. You'll feel better."

So Johnny had made himself a friend. And no one had ever called him Jack before. He liked it.

Many times, in those first weeks, as the *Somers* beat eastward, Johnny Browne tried to remember his father's advice—to keep his eyes open and his mouth shut, to remember that the captain was God, and to treat every man with the same kind of respect he wanted for himself. Gideon never added that keeping a closed mouth had been his own greatest problem.

Johnny did not lord it over the apprentice seamen, as even the most inexperienced midshipmen might. He spoke ill of no one, even when he found that speaking ill of Philip Spencer was a good way to fit in with the other midshipmen. And he never called Mackenzie an old granny.

While the apprentice seamen were learning the ropes, Johnny and the other midshipmen studied celestial navigation, history, and, on a ship commanded by such a literary man, the works of Shakespeare. And every Sunday, after ship's company gathered for the captain's Bible reading and sermon, the midshipmen were expected to turn in their journals for grading.

In the middle of the third week, Mackenzie summoned Acting Midshipman Browne to the tiny wardroom. It was a fine crisp day in the mid-Atlantic, and the sunshine poured through the skylight in the trunk house, the raised roof that provided a little headroom. In this light, Mackenzie's plastered-down hair looked as though it had been painted on, and his face looked almost cadaverous.

"I've been reading your journal, John," said Mackenzie, "or is it Jack? I hear some of your mates calling you Jack."

"I answer to either, sir, although Jack seems a bit more manly, sir."

Mackenzie nodded approvingly. "Then Jack it will be."

The little brig heeled a bit in the wind, but Jack Browne no longer felt the motion in his belly. Spencer's cauterizing had worked. Now he ate like a horse through every meal of bully beef and broken biscuit, looked forward twice a week to a ration of cheese, and took a swallow of Spencer's brandy every night, for good measure. Only his homesickness persisted, but if he worked hard enough, he was too tired to think about it.

Mackenzie held the journal to the light. "You have a fine literary style, Jack."

"Thank you, sir."

Mackenzie read aloud, "'On the second day, after I had got my stomach straight, I knew why they call ships "she." Because her motion is like a mother's hand on a cradle, gently rocking on the rolling waves.'" Mackenzie looked up, eyes brightening. "You've inherited your father's felicity of phrase, with a little twist of alliteration."

"Thank you, sir."

"But once you've set such a high standard for yourself, I'd be remiss if I did not see that you keep to it."

Jack looked at his hands. After reading the one-sentence entries in his mates' journals, he had reduced his output, so as not to seem like an old granny.

"Remember, Jack, the best naval officer is one who can communicate through word as well as deed, who can let his men know what he's about."

"Yes, sir."

Then the captain's brow furrowed. "So entries like these are not acceptable: 'September 16—Anderson, Hanson, and Travis each given six lashes for skulking. September 17—Van Velsor and Gilmore, a dozen each. September 19—exercised guns for the first time. Very loud.'"

Mackenzie looked up from the journal. "'Very loud.' A boy with your descriptive powers and that's all you can say the first time you hear a thirty-two-pound carronade go off?"

"I'm sorry, sir."

Mackenzie glanced again at the journal. "'September 20—Bosun's Mate Cromwell bellowed at Manning for leaving brass collar of anchor capstan unpolished; Cromwell bellows too much and would do better to have a kind word.'" Mackenzie looked up. "So you think you know more than a bosun's mate with fifteen years of tar on his hands?"

"Oh, no, sir. It was merely an observation. You told us to observe the way in which the sailors are trained, sir."

"On September 22, you list five men who are lashed. 'Surgeon's Mate Leecock spent much of the afternoon dressing their bloody backs.' You seem inordinately interested in the lashings."

"Isn't that something to put in a log—the number of punishments meted out?"

"This isn't a log. It's a journal, to show what you are thinking and learning. So"—Mackenzie put down the journal, made a little tent with his fingers—"what do you think the floggings accomplish?"

"Why . . . order, sir."

"Then that's what you should write. This is a grand experiment, Mr. Jack Browne. We carry a dog pack composed almost entirely of pups, yourself included, and I'm the trainer." Mackenzie smiled, causing the skin on his forehead to crinkle under the plastered-down patch of hair. "When you housebreak a pup, you rub his nose in whatever mess he leaves, then give him a good whack."

"Aye, sir." What about communicating through word as well as deed? wondered Jack.

"How slovenly and stupid did our crew look in the first week?" demanded Mackenzie.

"Very, sir."

"Morning muster was a disgrace—dirty hands, badly tied neckerchiefs, torn trousers. Sail handling was abysmal. But we've cracked the whip, Jack. And it shows. And we'll continue to do it."

"Aye, sir." Jack hoped this was finally at an end.

"One more thing." Mackenzie flipped through the pages of the journal until he came to this entry: "'September 28'—last night—'joined Spencer on the fo'c'sle for a concert with several of the sailors. Spencer played "Yankee Doodle" with his jaw.'" Mackenzie's sunken eyes bored into Jack Browne. "How did he do that?"

"He can make the bones in his jaw click different notes, depending on how wide he opens his mouth, sir. The . . . the sailors find it very amusing."

Mackenzie closed the journal. "Precisely the reason that you should not be involved. Officers give orders. Sailors obey them. Mr. Spencer treats sailors as equals and entertains them like a walleyed buffoon."

"Aye, sir."

"You would do well to consort with neither the sailors nor Spencer."

"Aye, sir."

But the *Somers* was a tiny vessel. Avoiding someone was not easy, and Jack found it even more difficult to turn his back on the first man aboard who had befriended him. He tried to keep his distance, but when Spencer approached him, he could not turn away.

And as the voyage wore on, Spencer's talk seemed to focus more on the drudgery of naval life and the romance of pirates.

Jack could not deny that it was drudgery.

The routine of watch, muster, instruction, and study; the daily snapping of the lash, the endless rocking on the endless sea, the endless bully beef and biscuit, the constant bawling of the petty officers—all of it wore on him like a bastard file taking the paint off newly finished metal. And when the patina of boyish enthusiasm was worn away, the file bit into the metal itself, to see if it was soft lead or steel.

After crossing the Atlantic, Jack did not yet know which he was made of, though sometimes the homesickness all but caused him to roll up into a ball.

Three days from the African coast, they spied a sail running down on them from the east, and the *Somers* came to life. The captain ordered a course change to bring her within hailing distance. The gun crews sprang to their stations. Recognition signals went up, identifying the *Somers* as an American brig-of-war.

In response, the American flag was run up the jackstaff of the little vessel now about to pass to port.

Mackenzie put his speaking trumpet to his lips, "What ship are you?"

"The brig *America*. Bound for Charleston with a cargo of tea and cloves."

Lieutenant Gansevoort studied the ship through his glass, looking for signs of wear in the sails or rigging, in the hull and paint, signs of a vessel that was used hard and always on the run.

Jack Browne watched from the rail, his heart pounding at the possibility of action.

And Spencer came up beside him. "She's a trim little thing."

"Aye," said Jack absently.

"A few good seamen could make their fortunes on a brig like that, smugglin' slaves and attackin' merchantmen." Spencer turned his odd eye to Jack. "We could grab the cutter and a few men and take her for ourselves. What say, Jack?"

And Jack tried to joke. "Not with the captain watching."

By now the brig was in their wake, westering fast. She was no slaver.

Spencer chomped on his cigar and went swaggering toward the bow.

Jack turned to go aft and bumped into Midshipman Rodgers, who said, "Be very careful of him, Jack, and mind what you say, even in jest."

"Aye, sir."

vi
Greek Lists and Black Hoods

They did not stay long in Africa. They left their dispatches with the American consul in Liberia. They were allowed a day of liberty in the dusty city of Monrovia. They loaded water, fresh fruit, and hogs. And then they turned toward home.

In his journal, Jack recorded that there had been some sixty floggings by then: "The younger sailors are lashed with the colt, three strands of half-inch rope frayed at the ends. The older sailors suffer the cat-o'-nine-tails, which is leather. Mr. Spencer says this is a high number of floggings, but Mr. Rodgers, who has sailed with Mackenzie before, says he is a fair man, and however many the floggings, they are the proper number on a vessel of boys learning the business of naval discipline. We all think now of home."

West by north they ran, putting the northeast trades on their starboard quarter and the Americas on their bow. The days were warm and blue, the nights silvered by starlight.

But the floggings went on—sixteen more in two weeks—because touching solid ground had turned these boy sailors back to landsmen. Some moved slowly to their tasks. Some failed to stow their hammocks properly. Others were brazenly disobedient. And though they were boys, they were flogged.

Even bellowing Cromwell was heard to mutter insubordination under his breath when the captain delivered an order.

And Philip Spencer spent more and more time with the sailors. He gave them tobacco, though the captain had said that the sailors should have none. He threw coins on the deck for them to dive after. He played his jaw for their amusement. And for his own amusement, he studied charts.

Jack found him in steerage one afternoon, poring over charts of the Caribbean.

"The best cruising waters in the world for pirates, Jack, I'll be bound."

"There are no pirates left," said Jack.

"There *should* be. A boy whose father built his reputation writing about pirates should be thankful they ever lived."

"I suppose."

"You've read Cooper, Jack. You know what backbone there is in one who won't sail aboard an *Uncle-pa*, one who goes his own way, don't you, Jack?" Those wide, weird eyes turned their full force onto him. "Don't you?"

"Well, my father did not want me to join the navy."

"Then you know what I mean . . . so feel this." Spencer drew Jack's hand to the neckerchief tied loosely around his neck.

Jack felt a paper rolled into the navy blue fabric. "What is it?"

Just then Surgeon's Mate Leecock, a quiet and slender man of twenty-eight, ducked through the companionway.

"I'll tell you later." Spencer folded up his chart and went hurrying off.

"Be careful," said Leecock after Spencer was gone. "The captain don't like Spencer. I don't like him. No one does. He's not navy."

"He simply likes to read and dream, I think."

"But he misreads your father's fine book about your uncle's brave exploits against the Caribbean pirates. He thinks it's a romance."

And Jack decided a man with such a high opinion of Staffords and Brownes deserved the friendship of a boy who was both. "Yes, sir. I see where you're right."

In the succeeding week, much went on around Philip Spencer that would later be interpreted at its worst.

He allowed himself to be tattooed. He got into a fistfight with Midshipman Thompson. He spoke ill of the captain behind his back, yet presented a fawning smile to the captain's face. And he asked men if they would sail with him when he got command of his own ship.

Jack knew enough to avoid all this. He busied himself with his studies, his journal, and a growing admiration for Surgeon's Mate Leecock.

Then, on the evening of November 24, with the *Somers* a few days from Caribbean waters, Jack found Spencer in the midshipmen's berth, sketching a picture of a brig. He told Jack it was the ship he dreamed of commanding.

"It looks like the *Somers*."

"It's not. The *Somers* is oversparred . . . carries too much in the way of cannon for the purposes I'd put her to."

"And what are those?"

Spencer's walleyes narrowed, as though he was taking some final measure of Jack Browne. "To answer your question, I have three of my own."

"Three?"

"Do you fear death?"

"I suppose."

"Do you fear a dead man?"

"I suppose not."

"Are you afraid to kill a man?"

"I—"

There was movement in the companionway. This time it was Mr. Rodgers. Spencer shoved the picture into Jack's hands. "This is for you. To fire your imagination. Maybe someday your father will write about *us*."

And Spencer squeezed past Rodgers, without so much as a salute.

Jack looked at the picture: the flag fluttering at the jackstaff of Spencer's brig was the pirate's skull and crossbones. He could not let Rodgers see this. It might bring another warning or perhaps a report to the captain. But there was nowhere to throw it before Rodgers saw it, so he slipped it into his copy of *The Red Rover*, which lay on the table, and gave Rodgers a salute.

That night the breeze sang in the rigging and the November moon, called the beaver moon back in the Massachusetts hills, played its light on the decks.

Jack noticed Spencer in conversation with Purser's Mate Wales and Seaman Elisha Small. They were standing by the booms amidships, their voices low and conspiratorial.

When Spencer saw Jack, he beckoned, but Jack begged that he had to study his navigation.

He was thankful he avoided them, because at dusk the next day, Mackenzie ordered all officers aft and all crewmen forward. The western sky glowed with the purple-and-red promise of continued good sailing, but tension seemed to pull every line taut aboard the *Somers*. Jack rubbed his sleeve across his buttons to polish them, though he knew that this was no inspection.

In his cockade hat and dress uniform, Mackenzie looked like a large bird of prey falling on Philip Spencer. In a voice that was all the more frightening for its measured tone, he said to Spencer, "I learn that you aspire to command of the *Somers*."

Spencer smiled, as though surprised in the midst of a daydream. "Me, sir? Oh, no, sir."

"Last night, did you not tell Mr. Wales that you were planning to kill me, the officers, and certain crewmen, and convert this ship to a pirate?"

So, thought Jack, all the talk had been taken seriously at last. The boy had cried pirate once too often.

Spencer reddened. "It . . . it was all a joke, sir."

"Mutiny? A joke?" said Mackenzie. "Your joke may get you hanged."

Hanged. Surely, thought Jack, it was the captain now doing the joking.

Mackenzie ordered Spencer to remove his neckerchief. Spencer obeyed and the captain examined it, finding nothing. "You told Wales of a paper that you carried in your neckerchief. Where is it?"

"I've thrown it away, sir," said Spencer. "It contained my geometry lesson."

"An unusual place to keep your lessons."

"A convenient place, sir."

Whatever was going on, thought Jack, Spencer seemed calm. Jack decided it was the calm of the innocent. But how could the captain be so certain of mutiny, if it was not true? Perhaps Spencer had the calm of a convincing liar.

Mackenzie stepped closer to him. "You told Wales you carried in your neckerchief a list of conspirators. You asked him if you could add his name. He came to me instead."

Spencer lowered his head. "It was a joke."

"A witticism for which you are under arrest."

Philip Spencer was shackled, hands and feet, and taken to a corner of the quarterdeck by the arms chest, because there was no room to keep a prisoner anywhere else.

Then they searched his locker and found a sheet of geometry lessons, on the back of which was written a list of names in Greek, which Mr. Rodgers was able to translate.

Spencer listed four men as "certain" when he took over the ship, and ten as "doubtful," though he believed that four of them would join before the "project is carried into execution," and the others would not be far behind. There were eighteen more to be kept *nolens, volens*—whether they wanted to be or not—like Surgeon's Mate Leecock. The rest, Mackenzie assumed, were to be thrown overboard.

To the senior officers who saw the list, the case seemed watertight. Mackenzie decided to leave the "certains" and "doubtfuls" at large, but closely watched. He did not think they would act with their leader in irons. Besides, there was no room to hold fourteen manacled men on deck.

But in the following days, a fever of suspicion burned as hot aboard the *Somers* as tales of piracy had burned in Spencer's imagination.

If a sailor was seen to look at an officer for too long, or with any defiance, it was perceived as evidence of mutinous intent.

And when the brig lost her main topgallant mast, it seemed to Jack an accident. But Mackenzie said it was a diversion created to free Spencer, who sat in his chains on the quarterdeck and watched intently—hopefully?—as the mast was repaired.

Though no attempt was made to free Spencer, Mackenzie arrested two of the men who were on the maintop when the mast went by the boards—Elisha Small and Bosun's Mate Cromwell. Small's name was on Spencer's list, but the only other evidence against Cromwell was that he had been seen many times in conversation with Spencer.

As burly Cromwell was led to a spot opposite Spencer, Jack heard Spencer say to Mackenzie, "Cromwell is innocent. That's the truth, sir."

Was this Spencer's admission of guilt? Jack did not know. He was more concerned with the suspicious looks that some officers were now casting in his direction.

On a ship where a hopeful gaze had become hard evidence, suspicion seemed to burn even hotter as the days went on and the three supposed mutineers sat like rejected figureheads at the stern.

The officers expected an attempt on the tiny ship with every watch change, every sail change, every movement of men on deck. Finally, on November 30, tensions grew too great for Mackenzie, and five more arrests were ordered.

It was then that Jack Browne was called to the wardroom.

Mackenzie was sitting at the little table, his head lowered, his voice strained. "I sailed with your uncle, Jack. I sailed against the Caribbean pirates."

"Yes, sir."

Mackenzie looked up. He had spent three nights on deck, watching the crew, and exhaustion was closing in. "I never thought your name would be on the list."

"My name? But—"

"I'm arresting the four I consider the most dangerous, and the only other officer named. We must make examples of officers who stray." Mackenzie held up the sheet and pointed to Jack's name. "Spencer lists you as one who will join before the thing is done. You must have given him a clear signal."

Jack swallowed back the sudden sickness boiling in his gullet. "I . . . I talked with him about pirates."

"Then you admit a conversation with him when we passed the brig *America*?"

"I—"

"Don't lie. Mr. Rodgers was there." And before Jack could answer, Mackenzie pulled out the picture of the pirate brig. "And you admit to this?"

Jack realized that his things had been searched. "Spencer drew it. I should have destroyed it, but—"

"You didn't. At least you admit to your conspiracy."

"I admit that we both like the same books."

"You read Fenimore Cooper . . . a mountebank." Mackenzie plastered a smile on his face. "Read better books, like mine. And tell the truth. It will go better for you."

"But I *have* told the truth."

Manacled and leg-ironed in the bright, hot sun.

What would his father think? And his uncle Jason?

He was seated by gun number four on the port side, some thirty feet from where Philip Spencer sat at the stern. Only Spencer could save Jack's reputation, but for the hour since Jack had been brought out, Spencer had kept his head resolutely lowered.

Suddenly Jack Browne, who kept his mouth shut and did as he was told, who read Cooper and liked to talk about pirates, was leaping to his feet and screaming at Spencer, "I agreed to nothing. Tell them, Spencer! Tell them!"

Mackenzie ordered someone to quiet the boy.

And Surgeon's Mate Leecock hurried over to him. "It does you no good, Jack," Leecock whispered, "no good to carry on."

"But I've done nothing." Jack looked into Leecock's calm and gentle face. Then the emotion came, first in his throat, a familiar tightening, then in his chin, and then he dropped onto the deck in an effort to ball himself up and stop the tears from coming. But he was still a boy, and boys sometimes cried.

Leecock crouched down next to him and kept whispering. "Get ahold of yourself, Jack. Get ahold."

"But . . . but I did nothing."

Leecock looked around. "The crew are all watching. You'll never command men who see you cry."

And Jack tried to get his breath. "Aye."

"This will all be over soon."

Jack wiped his eyes, sniffed back the strands dripping from his nose. "Aye."

Leecock gave him a gentle pat on the back. "I'll speak well for you this afternoon."

"This afternoon?"

But Leecock stood up without explaining and walked away.

The sun rose higher and burned hotter.

Jack found that Leecock's talk and his own tears had calmed him. But they could not calm the fire of worry consuming him as he watched sailors one by one descend into the wardroom and emerge some time later, their eyes always fixed straight ahead, never on the prisoners.

During this time, the only senior officer to be seen was Commander Mackenzie himself. All others were below, and it was clear to Jack that the fates of the accused were being decided. But all that night, there was official silence.

Jack awoke sometime before dawn, and for a moment it was just another day at sea. His mind was at peace. Then the fist inside his stomach punched upward, sickening him with despair.

That morning the other prisoners encouraged one another, said that this would all be over soon. And none spoke hopefully of what the captain feared most—a mutiny to save them before the ship reached Saint Thomas.

But Jack barely heard their talk. He was counting—counting the links in the chain on his manacles, the clouds that passed the sun and sent shadows racing across the deck, the hairs on his arm, the number of times that his father had spoken of the dangers of naval thinking. . . .

Sometime around eleven o'clock, he heard a commotion. Crewmen were bringing up thick rope and new sail blocks from the forward compartment. But there was no need for new sail blocks. And rope? *What was the rope for?*

Commander Mackenzie once more appeared in full-dress uniform.

The boys in the rigging stopped to watch.

The petty officers did not shout at them, because they were watching, too.

The rush of the wind in the sails seemed to soften. The waves stopped hissing on the hull. The world went strangely silent.

And Jack began to pray.

Mackenzie went over to Spencer and spoke so softly that no one else could hear.

After a moment, Philip Spencer fell to his knees and cried out, "You cannot do this, sir. You cannot hang me, please."

To which Mackenzie answered, "Do you fear death? Do you fear a dead man? Are you afraid to kill a man?"

And those questions, which Spencer had asked Jack himself, drove the knife of terror into Jack's belly.

"Get up," Mackenzie was saying to Spencer. "Show those you've corrupted that you can die like an officer."

And now the words screamed in Jack's head, screamed so loud that they deafened him: *Die like an officer*.

Mackenzie turned away from Spencer and spoke to Cromwell, who tore at his manacles and proclaimed his innocence.

Then Mackenzie came down the port side, past Seaman Wilson, who was manacled beside Cromwell, toward Seaman Small, at gun number five, and Jack at number four.

In his terror, Jack tried to understand Mackenzie's method.

Spencer was an officer, Cromwell a petty officer. Both would be hanged. Wilson was a seaman, passed over. Small was a seaman. . . .

We must make an example of officers who stray.

An hour later, three men stood on the roof of the trunk house, their hands bound, and ropes around their necks. The ropes ran through the three new sail blocks on the yardarm, then back to the deck, where the crew stood in two long lines, each man with a hand on a rope.

When the cannon fired, the colors would be run up the mast and all hands would haul forward. Any who did not would be flogged.

Mackenzie stood on the middle of the trunk house and solemnly announced that each condemned man could make a statement.

Spencer's voice quavered. A stain had spread on his breeches, because he'd wet himself when they lifted him onto the trunk house, but he managed to get out the words, "Some have called me a coward. Judge for yourselves whether I . . . I die a coward or a brave man."

And a black hood was placed over his head.

Bosun's Mate Cromwell, convicted by opinion but not by evidence, said, "Tell my wife I die an innocent man."

And a black hood was placed over his head.

The third condemned man, Seaman Elisha Small, said, "Shipmates, take warnin': I never was a pirate. I never killed a man. It's for sayin' I would I'm about to die." Then he turned to Mackenzie. "You only do your duty, sir, and I honor you for it. God bless that flag and all who sail under her."

And a black hood was placed over his head.

After a moment, during which Mackenzie let Small's generous remark sink in, he gave Spencer the option of calling the moment when the cannon would fire.

From beneath the black hood, Spencer's weak voice said, "Yes, sir." The hood shook, as though the head under it were shaking. And after a moment, his muffled voice was heard, "I . . . I cannot, sir."

"Very well," said Mackenzie coldly. "Fire!"

The cannon thundered, blasting gray smoke into the wind.

The crew ran forward with the ropes.

And the bodies shot upward like puppets, twitching and twisting toward the furled mainsail and the sky beyond.

Mackenzie stood in the shadows of the three bodies until they stopped swaying. Then, like a sanctimonious preacher, he made a lesson of them—three wasted careers, three wasted lives. He told his crew to take heed. Then he called for three cheers for the flag.

And the sound those boys made burst louder than the cannon shot.

But one boy did not shout. He was curled in a ball, his manacled hands covering his ears, his teeth gnawing on his chains.

vii
Speechless

Captain Jason Stafford heard about the mutiny on the same day as Johnny's parents, because Mackenzie had dispatched a messenger to Washington the moment he dropped anchor at the Brooklyn Navy Yard.

By December 20, Jason was in New York.

He found Gideon and Antonia where they always stayed, at Doniphon's boarding house, near the Battery.

Antonia threw herself into her brother's arms. "I knew you'd come."

Gideon threw Jason the newspapers, which were filled with approval for wise Commander Mackenzie. "They're calling my son a mutineer."

"We'll get the truth."

The day was raw and gray and cut by a sharp wind that pounded against the bow of the East River ferry. The Brooklyn countryside looked brown and December-bleak, but the bleakest sight they could see was the little brig, tied up next to the receiving ship *North Carolina*, its bare masts like spindles snatching at the clouds.

"What do you know about Mackenzie?" asked Gideon.

"He served with us against the Caribbean pirates in '24. He seemed a good officer, though a trifle full of himself."

"Aren't all officers?" asked Antonia.

"This one decided he could hang mutineers without a court-martial, when only a general court-martial can render the death penalty, and only a flag officer can authorize a general court-martial."

"Will Johnny be court-martialled?" Gideon stood close to the vent stack, which radiated heat from the steam boiler.

"It's as likely," said Jason, "that Mackenzie will."

Antonia did not care who was court-martialled. She only wanted her son back.

The accused mutineers had been imprisoned on the *North Carolina*, under the command of Captain Francis Gregory, an old friend of Jason's, with a ramrod spine and an unsmiling face, known to be officious yet fair-minded. He invited Jason and Johnny's parents to his cabin and sent for the boy. Because receiving ships did not go to sea, they were equipped with comforts not known in most naval vessels, like the coal stove breathing heat in the corner of the cabin.

"I've taken the irons off the accused men," said Gregory. "Each of them has his own small cabin on the orlop deck."

"Isn't that below the waterline?" demanded Antonia. As far as she was concerned, Gregory was one more wheel in the machine oppressing her son.

"For two weeks of North Atlantic winter, madam, your son was kept on the quarterdeck of the *Somers*, with no more than a blanket to keep him warm, and cold iron at his wrists and ankles. I'm sure he prefers his present situation."

Jason reached across the table and patted his friend's arm. "We know you're being fair, Frank."

"Yes," added Gideon, "we do."

Antonia could say nothing, because her son was appearing in the doorway.

Her first thought was that he had grown taller.

He had, but he had grown gaunt, too, and that added to his age. He wore a clean shirt and breeches, and his hair was combed straight back. But boyish pimples covered his chin and blossomed above his eyebrows, and the fear in his eyes was the fear of a boy faced with unyielding authority.

Johnny glanced first at Gregory, then at the dress-blue uniform of his uncle, then at his father.

Captain Gregory excused himself, and with a gesture of the eyes, suggested that Jason step outside as well.

"He hasn't spoken to any officer since he came aboard," Gregory explained in the little gangway outside his cabin.

"Frightened *speechless?*" Jason swallowed back his anger. How could they do that to such a wide-eyed and innocent young boy?

"They're all frightened. But none of them are mutineers, if you ask me." Gregory withdrew from his inner pocket a sheaf of papers. "Mackenzie left his log aboard. I had it copied."

"*Copied*? By-the-book Frank Gregory copies a log?"

"I think Mackenzie *wanted* us to read it. He was proud of his discipline. In less than six months aboard the *Somers*, he records over two hundred floggings."

"Does he explain the hangings?"

"He said he feared for the safety of the ship. He said the crew had grown agitated, and—this is a quote—'full of angry looks.'"

"Angry looks and a boy's ciphered list." Jason leafed through the sheets of tight script. "May I keep this for a while?"

"I take no comfort in ruining the reputation of an officer. But I'm writing my opinions to Commodore Jones. Read this; then do what you will."

Just then Gideon Browne clomped out of the captain's cabin, red-faced and furious. "Do you see what they've done to my son, Jason?"

"How is he?"

"Ruined in reputation, ruined between the ears." Gideon held his fingers to the bridge of his nose, to try to pinch back the tears of fury.

"We'll save him."

"I warned him," Gideon went on. "I told him there were officers who were more dangerous to their own men than they could ever be to an enemy. I told him—"

"Calm yourself, Gid."

"Calm myself, hell. All he can say is, 'I'm sorry, I'm sorry. I didn't do it. I'm sorry.'" Gideon banged his crutch on the deck. "I should be shot for letting him join."

"I'll go and talk with him."

Gideon grabbed Jason. "Leave him with his mother. Maybe she can reach him. She's . . . she's reached ruined men before."

The *Somers* was the sensation of the month in sensation-hungry

New York, and the court of inquiry, scheduled to begin on December 28, had reporters apoplectic with excitement.

On the night before the court was to open, Jason made his way through the Brooklyn Navy Yard to the home of Matthew Perry. The commandant was not at home, but it was his houseguest that Jason wanted to see.

Mackenzie received him at the expansive oak desk in the study, beneath a heroic painting of the frigate *President,* which had been built at the navy yard. He stood and extended his hand. "Captain Stafford. A pleasure."

Jason kept his hands folded behind his back. "You're a disgrace to the navy."

Mackenzie took a more formal tone. "If you come as my superior, I will address you with the proper respect. If you come as an old shipmate with an ax to grind, allow a subordinate the leeway to defend himself."

"A leeway you did not give Philip Spencer, or my nephew."

"Your nephew is still alive."

"And he will remain alive."

"That's up to the courts. Don't beg from me."

Jason prided himself on personal control, and he needed it now. When he grew angry, he only allowed his voice to grow a little colder. "Why did you hang Philip Spencer?"

Mackenzie laughed at the question. "Because he planned a mutiny."

"Why else?"

Mackenzie looked puzzled. "What do you mean, *Why else?*"

"Why did you hang him when you did?"

Mackenzie glared a moment into Jason's eyes, but no one could meet the Stafford glare for long. "I hanged him because we were drawing close to land. I feared that his accomplices would rise at any moment. It's all in here"—he held up the sheets on which he was writing—"and the court will hear it tomorrow."

"There was another reason."

Mackenzie's eyes narrowed.

"Between the time that you pronounced your sentence and the time that you hanged Spencer, an hour elapsed."

"Yes." Mackenzie looked at Jason warily.

"During which time you interviewed Spencer?"

"The results of that interview are all in here." He once more raised the sheets of paper. "He admitted to a conspiracy."

Jason reached across the desk, took Mackenzie by the lapels, and drew his face into the smoke rising from the whale-oil lamp on the desk. "You told him that for those who have friends or money in America, there was no punishment for crimes like his."

"My talk with Spencer was in private. Where could you have heard those words?"

"You said you would hang him at sea, before his friends could save him. It satisfied your petty resentments against a boy who did not fulfill your vision of an officer. It protected your pitiful judgment from a legal system that would ask harder questions than you asked of yourself on that brig."

"Where did you hear that?"

Jason released Mackenzie. "It's in your log. Soon it will be in the newspapers. When your words are known, don't expect that any court of rational men will condemn more boys to die."

"Tomorrow, you'll see that . . ." Mackenzie flipped through the pages until he found what he was looking for. "Here I recorded what I said to Spencer. You'll see that I'm not afraid of my own words."

"All the more evidence of your bad judgment." Jason turned to leave.

"I fear no judgment but history's, and that of the Court of Inquiry."

Jason stopped in the doorway. "Officers are expected to lead, but you followed, and you followed your most craven emotions."

And Mackenzie's words followed Jason down the hallway to the front door and out into the icy night: "History will be kind to me. And so will the naval courts."

viii
Court-Martial

The court of inquiry was inconclusive, so Mackenzie requested a court-martial. To clear his name, he said.

Jason said that by submitting to naval justice, Mackenzie could avoid the civil charges that Spencer's father was trying to press, and a naval commander was always better off being judged by his naval peers.

The charges were serious: conduct unbecoming an officer, unnecessary cruelty, oppression, illegal punishment, and murder. The first two were soon dropped, but the court-martial went forward on the remaining three counts.

All winter long, evidence was heard.

Mackenzie's 13,000-word narrative of the events was quoted, praised, and criticized in the newspapers.

Captain Francis Gregory and Jason Stafford wrote letters of opinion to the court, though neither spoke directly with reporters.

Jason did not like reporters. He did not even like to see them sitting in the cabin of the *North Carolina*, with their pencils poised above their notebooks, hanging on every word of every witness. But by mid-January, stories about Mackenzie's fondness for the lash had been leaked to reporters and splattered across New York's front pages. More people, in public and in private, were coming to question his character.

Jason could not stay in New York for the whole court-martial. He was still stationed at the Washington Navy Yard, and his own family needed him, especially as his new wife had recently announced that she was pregnant.

But Gideon took a leave of absence from Round Hill School so that he and Antonia could remain near their son.

At first, they traveled each day by ferry to the Brooklyn Yard, a grueling trip in the raw, damp wind. When Gideon developed a deep cough, they rented two small rooms in a boardinghouse on the Brooklyn side so that they could travel to court by carriage.

Each day, they took their seats among the reporters and other observers, and they provided, as Antonia told one reporter, a human face for Mackenzie's victims.

And every Tuesday and Saturday they were allowed to visit their son.

The third Saturday in January was one of those deceptively bright mornings when the warming sun made it seem that winter's back had been broken. The yard, as always, was bustling with workers and naval personnel. The marine guard at the gate, a young private, not much older than Johnny, greeted them with a smile.

But they were distracted. They were having an argument.

Antonia wanted Gideon to go home to Massachusetts and recover from his cough while she remained in Brooklyn.

He refused. "Johnny needs both of us, Antonia."

"You're coughing. Your color's bad. Maybe you should take up the pipe."

"It didn't help your father. I'm staying . . . *Sweet Jesus*."

Gideon saw them first—a dozen manacled boys under marine guard, marching from the *North Carolina* toward a big brick warehouse. He started to clump after them, but he was gripped by a sudden fit of coughing and stopped.

Antonia ran ahead, hoping to catch up to them before they disappeared around the corner of the ship house. But as she approached, one of the marine guards held his rifle in front of her.

"Sorry, ma'am." The guard did not sound at all sorry.

"Where are you taking them?" she demanded.

"To the brig . . . in the cellar of the paymaster's house."

"It's our day to visit our son." Antonia tried to get around the marine, but he was quick and blocked her way again.

"Sorry, ma'am. No more visitors for the prisoners."

"No more?" And she called, "Johnny! We're here. We'll always be here!"

He was at the corner of the big ship house. He turned and answered with the litany that had become his only greeting. "Ma! I'm sorry, I'm innocent. I—"

A marine prodded him to move along, but he was frozen in place, because he saw something his mother did not.

About ten feet behind her, Gideon had collapsed on the cobblestones.

That day, Antonia did not have time to contemplate the sight of her son in shackles, that naïve and trusting spirit chained in the naval dungeon. She had Gideon to worry about.

With the help of Surgeon's Mate Leecock, she got him back to the boardinghouse and into bed. The housekeeper, a grouchy old woman named Mrs. Dimmesdale, made tea.

Leecock listened to Gideon's chest, tapped here and there, examined his sputum, listened again.

Gideon was still the color of cold gravy, but he said the pain in his chest had subsided.

"Your lungs sound clear. It's not pneumonia. And your sputum isn't bloody, which rules out consumption."

"Thank God," said Antonia.

"But your heart sounds weak. How is your appetite?"

"Fine. I start every morning with a tureen of liver paste, and I never end a day without a slice of rare beef."

The surgeon's mate nodded approvingly. "It can't be your diet, then. But your heart is weak. I think the sight of your son in irons may have upset you."

"Wouldn't you be upset?" snapped Antonia, remembering that Leecock had been one of the officers who signed the execution order aboard the *Somers*. "Weren't *you* upset when Philip Spencer swung?"

The young man sat on the bed, as if pushed down by a sudden great weight. "I don't know if we did right, Mrs. Stafford, but you two can rest easy knowin' I'll do what I can for your son."

And Antonia warmed a bit. "Thank you, Doctor."

"Why . . . why were the prisoners moved?" asked Gideon.

"Mackenzie is furious that stories about his floggings are in the press. He blames Captain Gregory and—I must be honest—Captain Stafford. He convinced Commodore Jones to remove the prisoners from Gregory's ship, and confine them in double irons, without a sympathetic captain or weekly visitors."

"Son of a bitch," said Gideon to the ceiling. Then he said, "Don't even try to persuade me to leave. Even if we can't see Johnny, he'll know we're here, doing what we can to destroy the sanctimonious, pedantic son of a bitch who did this."

As Jason had predicted, once Mackenzie's words were known, a court of rational men would not condemn more boys to die. By February, seven of those whose names had appeared on Spencer's list had been quietly released and allowed to leave the navy.

But the five who had been held in irons aboard the *Somers* remained in irons throughout the winter.

And throughout the winter, Antonia attended the court-martial of Alexander Slidell Mackenzie. She seldom listened closely. Instead, she composed articles for the abolitionist newspaper *The Liberator,* which she found all the easier to write if she imagined her son in manacles, enslaved by the ignorance of his captain and the naval system.

Sometimes, when he felt up to it, Gideon came with her.

But on the day that their son was to testify, Gideon awoke with chest pains and knew that they would only grow worse if he went.

By then the court had moved to the navy yard chapel.

Mackenzie sat in his accustomed place, in full-dress uniform, his cockade hat placed ostentatiously on the table in front of him.

A cold sleet splattered against the window, and Antonia shivered when Johnny walked up the aisle.

He wore a neat blue midshipman's jacket, which she had mended herself. But he looked gaunt and white and insignificant before the panel of twelve stern officers in their blue uniforms and gold braid.

She was glad that Gideon had decided to stay in bed, because her own heart was pounding. She was terrified that the sight of those twelve uniforms would cause Johnny to bolt from the room. But the boy sat straight and motionless, his hands subtly gripping the seat beneath him.

"State your name," said Judge Advocate Norris, the bookish young Baltimore attorney charged with arguing the government's case.

"I . . . I'm sorry . . . I'm innocent."

Antonia held her breath. She feared that he might be able to say nothing else, especially when he glanced over his shoulder and saw Mackenzie, and like a rabbit frightened by a hunter, his gaze froze on his assailant.

Mackenzie raised his chin ever so slightly, then inclined his head again, as if he had no concern over this testimony.

"Your name, son," repeated the judge advocate.

The sound of his voice broke the boy's concentration. "John Jedediah Browne. I'm sorry . . . I'm innocent."

"Yes . . . Now, how is it that you come to be in irons?"

"I'm . . . I'm sorry . . . I'm innocent."

Norris took a few steps closer and said gently, "Your guilt or innocence is not at issue here, son. It may be later, but for the moment, just give us concise answers. How is it that you come to be in irons?"

Though her son could not see her, Antonia leaned forward, and each time he tried to stutter a sentence, she nodded—*yes*—and coaxed him in her mind.

"It . . ." *Yes.* "It was . . ." *Yes.* "It was a mis . . ." *Yes. Please, Johnny!*

She willed the boy to find the voice that Mackenzie had frightened out of him.

"It was a misunderstanding, sir."

Yes!

"Did you know anything about Spencer's so-called mutiny?"

"No, sir."

"What did you and Spencer talk about?"

"Pirates . . . my father, Gideon Browne—"

"The same Gideon Browne who marched with the marines across the Tripolitan desert?"

"Aye, sir, and lost his leg aboard the *Essex*."

Bravo! cried Antonia in her mind. Bravo Norris and bravo her son. She knew right then, from the look that she saw on the faces of the court, that her son had won them over.

"My father wrote a book about pirates that Mr. Spencer read. So we talked often about pirates, sir."

"And somehow Spencer inferred that you would join in his mutiny?"

"I can't think of any other reason why my name was on the list. I'm sorry, sir. I'm innocent."

For every question, Johnny had an answer. He told his story slowly and honestly, and when it was over, any doubt about his innocence had been erased while the doubts about Mackenzie's conduct had grown.

When the boy stood to leave, his sunken eyes searched the room until they settled on his mother.

She smiled for him and gave him a nod.

Then he turned his gaze onto Mackenzie.

"You are excused, Mr. Browne," said the president of the court.

Johnny's gaze hooked into Mackenzie. "I have a question for the commander, sir."

"Mr. Browne, you are excused."

Two marines came down the aisle.

Before they reached him, Johnny said, "You once told me the best naval officer is one who can communicate through word as much as deed. Letting men know what you're about and inspiring them to do it—*that's* the heart of leadership."

The skin beneath Mackenzie's plastered-down hair reddened.

The members of the court exchanged glances, and the president said, "You may stand down, Mr. Browne."

Now Mackenzie was saying something to the court about proof of insubordination. But Antonia did not hear any of it. She was watching her son go by, and thinking how much taller he had grown.

She wondered that day where he found his strength. She later thought that it must have flowed into him from his father. Because when Antonia returned to her boardinghouse, she found that Gideon was dead.

"One minute he was coughin'," said Mrs. Dimmesdale. "Next minute he wasn't."

ix
If God Were Secretary of the Navy

A whitewash.

Two years later, Jason Stafford still believed it. And it still embarrassed him. Whether Philip Spencer's threat had been serious, as many believed, or a joke, as Spencer had claimed, or a boyish fantasy carried to a deadly conclusion, hanging him was a failure of command.

And yet, in the navy, it seemed more important to preserve respect for the overall chain of command than to question one commander's decisions.

The verdict: not proven.

But in that verdict, Jason saw the court's true opinion. Unlike civil courts, where guilty and not guilty were the only options, a court-martial could express itself in phrases like "most honorably acquitted." This court did not.

As for the five remaining prisoners, they were released, the charges against them quietly dropped, their naval careers over.

A week after the verdict, in the wardroom of the *Somers*, Surgeon's Mate Leecock put a pistol to his forehead and blew his brains out.

A few months later, Antonia wrote to Jason that her son sometimes slipped into moods so black she feared he might do what Leecock had done.

Jason answered that some good was certain to come from it all. And for two years he had tried to find it.

Now he believed that a great good was within reach, so long as he had the help of Antonia and her son.

It was a bright spring day in 1845, a new administration had taken over the government, and Jason Stafford, acting commandant of the Washington Navy Yard, was very nervous.

Three times he kissed his two-year-old son good-bye. Three times he asked Margaret for the envelope he was to deliver to the secretary of the navy. Three times she patted his chest and told him it was in his pocket, where it ought to be.

Old Zeke drove the Stafford carriage from the navy yard, up M Street to New Jersey Avenue, then over Capitol Hill to Pennsylvania Avenue.

The heart of the government, with its pudding-bowl dome, looked exactly as it had forty years before, when Jason rode out to duel Samuel Parrish. But the interior had been completely rebuilt after the British burned it the summer of 1814. Now Jason saw it as a symbol of a nation where external traditions were preserved while inner workings were reexamined every four years.

But in the navy, it seemed that the exterior changed—new ships, better weapons, steam—while the interior never evolved. In the navy, officers still believed that dueling was a reasonable way to finish difficult business, and that hanging boys could be justified within the chain of command.

Between David Porter—a brilliant leader who would duel a whole ship for a little glory—and Alexander Slidell Mackenzie, there had to be a middle ground: the professional officer—cool-headed, analytical, honorable. And there had to be a way to teach professionalism, so that boys like Philip Spencer would be weeded out before they ever infected a wardroom or a forecastle with their fantasies.

Jason wanted to make professionals. And today he would start.

The area between the Capitol and the White House had filled up considerably. It took Jason's carriage almost twenty minutes, in traffic, mud, and strong-smelling horse shit, to reach the boardinghouse on Tenth Street where Antonia and her son were staying.

Jason tried not to show his shock when he saw them.

The boy was almost eighteen now, taller, darker, more sullen. He wore wire-rimmed glasses and a dark suit that made him look almost funereal. He had returned to the sea and sailed as a mate with Jonathan Walker, the Cape Cod captain who smuggled slaves to freedom with every shipload of southern goods he brought back to Massachusetts.

Antonia had quickly grown gray, but her spine was still straight, perhaps because her son had taken up her cause.

His first words to Jason: "Isn't it time that you gave old Zeke his freedom, instead of forcing him to drive your carriage?"

Antonia said, "My Johnny is no longer a gentle and naïve spirit."

"All those months in chains, Uncle," said John. "They opened my eyes."

"Besides," added Antonia with a little smile, "it's a fair question."

Jason let the carriage rock a moment. "Do you honestly think old Zeke is in chains? And where would he go if I gave him his freedom?"

"The insoluble question," said Antonia. "Now tell me, Jace, how are Margaret and that dear little baby I'm hoping to see today?"

Jason laughed. Her talk of slavery could slide into family chitchat as easily as that. "They're wonderful. Being a father at fifty-six has made me young again."

"Traveling to Washington has made me feel five years older," she answered. "I hope this is worth it."

"Gideon would have approved."

The carriage stopped at the State, War, and Navy Building, a Georgian brick edifice next to the White House.

Antonia commented on the beauty of the White House grounds, a far cry from the days when they used to visit Tom Jefferson there.

"A pity we have that damn Tennessee Democrat Polk sitting inside," said John, "and no hope of ending slavery."

"But Polk has appointed a Massachusetts man as secretary of the navy," said Jason, holding his sword at his side as he climbed out after them. "His ancient association with your parents is our only concern today."

Secretary of the Navy George Bancroft had founded the Round Hill School in Northampton, Massachusetts, and in 1830, he had hired a one-legged veteran of the War of 1812 for the faculty. Long after he left Round Hill, Bancroft had remained in touch with the Brownes.

He was a big man with a fine-trimmed display of white side-whiskers and a gaze that could slice like a saber through lazy students or lazy ideas. He invited them to sit facing the windows so that they could look out at the White House. "I couldn't let the Brownes come to Washington without giving them time for a visit. I trust, John, that you've found a career to make up for the . . . unpleasantness."

"Yes, sir. My father would be proud."

"His mother *is* proud," said Antonia.

"And his uncle," said Jason, "is proudly using both of them to reach you, sir."

"I suspected as much, Captain," said Bancroft.

Jason placed an envelope on the table. "This is from William Chauvenet, director of the naval school at the Philadelphia Asylum. He sent us both copies, I believe, but he asked me to see that you received it personally. It's a letter that outlines his opinions about a two-year course of naval study."

Bancroft glanced at John Browne. "I see a good reason sitting right here."

"My son has found his life's work," said Antonia, "but Gideon would have been happy to know that our misfortune may contribute to a better system of naval education."

"We can have no more *Somers* incidents." Bancroft leaned back in his chair. "Chauvenet's letter reached me the week I was sworn in. My only criticism is that it doesn't go far enough."

"It doesn't?" Jason restrained himself from smiling. Smiling lessened an officer's air of authority. But this news was better than he had hoped.

"We need this school," Bancroft went on. "We need a place to house these boys. But we have to do it in a way that leaves the Congress out."

"Is that proper in a democracy?" asked Antonia. "Keeping Congress out of it?"

"Still asking the hard questions, Antonia?" Bancroft chuckled. "The president appoints me. Not Congress. They only supply the money. If I can find a way to spend what I have and do something better with it than was done before, I'll do it."

"Have you heard of Fort Severn, Mr. Secretary?" asked Jason.

"Fort Severn, in Annapolis?"

"Yes, sir. The state of Maryland wants this naval school, and Fort Severn sits right on the spot where God would put a naval school, sir, if God were secretary of the navy."

Bancroft considered this, wrote a note to himself, then another. And right before them, a plan began to evolve. "Put Chauvenet together with the best shipboard schoolmasters. Persuade the army to give over Fort Severn before Congress can stop it . . ."

"Sir," said Jason, "you've read my mind."

That night the Staffords and Brownes drank champagne at the Washington Navy Yard, and Antonia met Jason's new son. His name was Ethan, and he was afflicted with one of the worst cases of two-year-old troublemaking she had ever encountered.

"Is this a son for the soil or for the sea?" Antonia asked as Ethan lifted up her skirt.

"For whatever he wants," said Margaret. "He's our prize boy."

Gently Antonia pushed him away. "I hope you'll let me see him regularly. It's not often that I have males so interested in my skirts."

"Whenever you visit," said Jason.

"Well, I'm moving back." Antonia sat on the settee. "I decided while I was looking out Bancroft's window at the White House. There's a great crisis rushing toward us. This city will be the pivot point."

"If Bancroft gets his way," said Jason, "I hope to move back to Annapolis."

"With Stafford's Fine Folly as your home?" Antonia sensed something moving near her leg. She kicked absentmindedly.

Jason sipped his champagne. "That would be a nice way to end up."

"Do you think that the Parrishes will—" Suddenly an excruciating pain shot up her leg, and she let out a shout. Whatever she had kicked was biting her ankle.

Margaret ran behind the settee and dragged little Ethan out from under it.

"My God," cried Antonia, "that little bugger drew blood!"

And John Browne began to laugh. It was a strange sound, because he seldom laughed. "Another rebellious spirit . . . in need of naval discipline."

CHAPTER FIVE

Submarine

October 10

Did Antonia really say the things that Jack Stafford put in her mouth? Was she really that prophetic?

It was early morning in Annapolis. Time to get a little exercise. Susan left the bed-and-breakfast and jogged down the street.

Where was this story coming from? How much was Jack's imagination and how much of it had happened? He was calling it a novel, and that was a problem, because PBS would never let her use anything that wasn't documented.

The more she read, the more she wanted to get her hands on Jack's research, and the more convinced she was that she wanted to do this film.

Antonia was her own ancestor, and that boy chained to the deck of the *Somers.* They were part of her own memory stream. They belonged in her dreams, as surely as her dead grandmother did.

Susan jogged past the marine guard at Gate One, then out along Fleet Landing, to get a look at the big gray submarine tender sitting out there. She backtracked past LeJeune Hall.

She never stretched before she ran. She knew that she should, especially on a chilly October morning. So after a few more yards, she stopped and loosened those hamstrings, stretched out the Achilles' tendons.

Midshipmen, faculty, and staff were always jogging along the perimeter of the Academy, so Susan didn't look out of place.

Neither did that guy in the navy sweatshirt, who stopped to stretch when she did. She'd seen him out on King George Street. And he was right behind her when she came through Gate One.

So . . . he was lazy, too, and didn't stretch when he should.

She stretched in front of Dahlgren Hall, the mass of granite built during the Academy expansion at the turn of the century. But she was more interested in finding Fort Severn, so she could imagine Jason and his son walking around it.

It had to be somewhere near here.

She ran down Cooper Road, which separated Mitscher Hall from Bancroft, the largest dormitory in the world. Mother B. made Cooper Road feel like a canyon cut through gray granite. And somewhere near the last wing, where supply trucks rumbled up to the back of the dormitory, she found a plaque that described the fort that had once stood there, when that spot was at the water's edge instead of several hundred yards inland.

She read the plaque, looked at the picture, and noticed that the jogger in the navy sweatshirt had stopped to massage his calves.

Either he hadn't stretched enough or he was following her.

Trying to spy on her? Or hit on her? She had been hit on before while jogging, but usually it took the hitter a few miles before he made his move.

She wouldn't get any live shots of Fort Severn. So she headed toward the river, feeling looser and better as she went.

Then she glanced over her shoulder.

Still there.

Past the Santee Basin, around Dewey Field, a left turn at the bank.

Still there.

She looked at her watch. She was ten minutes into the run. This was where she usually gave a little kick, picked up her speed, and tried to sustain it for five or ten minutes. She liked the sensation of power she felt coursing through her at this point. Now was the time to test herself.

She turned away from the river, behind Nimitz Library, the modern cube of glass and concrete at the northwest corner of the campus.

Still there. Keeping pace.

She knew he wouldn't try anything funny on the Academy

grounds. All she needed to do was whimper for help, and she'd have protection descending from every corner.

But once she left the campus, who knew what he might do?

So she jogged almost to the gate at Preble Hall, then turned and ran right toward him and then right past him, just to see what he'd do.

He didn't hesitate or disguise his intentions. He lowered his head and shoulder, like a square dancer leaning into a turn, and followed.

He looked in his late forties, blondish hair, and as fit as any midshipman stepping off to class. Then he shocked her by calling her name.

She ran about five steps and stopped, right in front of the entrance to the Naval Institute Book Store. "Who are you?"

"Historians would say I'm a Stafford's worst nightmare—a Parrish with the keys to Stafford's Fine Folly." He loped up to her and offered his hand. "Ollie Parrish."

"Why did you chase me?"

"I was jogging past your guest house, the one you listed with the business card you gave to Simpson Church, my caretaker, and there you were, fitting his description—short brown hair, pretty face, and nice legs . . . uh, those are his words."

He gave her an appraising once-over that would have made her flesh crawl, except that she realized she was looking into that other gene pool, the one that included Rebecca Parrish.

So she gave him an appraising once-over right back: broken nose, squint lines, no wedding band, a nice friendly smile, but something about him . . . something very intense. Maybe that was the reason for no wedding band.

"You and I should talk," she said, trying to sound as though she had not been intimidated.

"There's not much to say. I'm handling the ancillary probate in Maryland for the Shank estate. The Maine attorney has ordered me not to allow anyone into the house until the probate business is concluded and all the members of the estate weigh in on what they want done with the house. That means no one from any military think tanks, no PBS film crews, no dinner-hour snoops."

He knew. But Susan continued to play dumb. "Who's snooping?"

"You and old Jack Stafford." He gave her a kind of cold-steel smile. "And you could be arrested for trespassing."

She thought about admitting her guilt, just so she could ask him why that old office had been restored and hung with Rebecca's portrait. But it did not pay to pull the strings on someone who seemed so tightly wrapped. "Do you have a card?"

"Not in my sweats. I live here in Annapolis and have an office in D.C. And if you get it into your head to sneak into that house again—"

"I don't know what you're talking about." She leaned down and massaged the cramp she felt coming in her calf. "But while we're on the subject of the house, will there be a time when you'll let us in?"

"Not any time soon. But if you're making a film about the Staffords, you'll have to come to me at some point, just to get the truth, so . . . how about lunch?"

The mood change surprised her. So did the remark. Of course, surprising people was probably something this lawyer was very good at. "I'm sorry," she said, "I'm touring the *Annapolis* at lunchtime, today, but if—"

And he surprised her again by rattling off a few facts: "*Annapolis*. SSN 760. A marvel. Faster under the water than most things are on the surface. Sonar so good it can hear a fish fart. Mark forty-eight torpedoes, six hundred thousand dollars each. Tomahawk cruise missiles, a million dollars each. Not navy-certified to carry nuclear warheads, thank Christ, but don't forget"—he raised a finger, like a schoolmaster—"man hasn't made a weapon yet he hasn't used. I know. I've used a lot of them. So . . . how about breakfast tomorrow. Chick and Ruth's, on Main Street?"

Whew. All of that without ever taking a breath. She wouldn't miss breakfast with this guy for anything. She said so, a bit more subtly, and Oliver was off, jogging back across the yard, then running, then all but sprinting . . . like a man twenty years younger.

A little before eleven, with Oliver Parrish still rattling around in her head, Susan arrived at Fleet Landing and was surprised again: Jack Stafford had finagled an invitation to tour the *Annapolis*, too. He was schmoozing the *Baltimore Sun* writer and photographer. And standing off to the side, letting his uncle do the talking, was someone who could only have been a Stafford.

Dark, square-jawed, wearing short-sleeved working khakis with his lieutenant's bars on the collars and a fine spray of campaign ribbons across his chest: Steve Stafford.

She liked his smile. He seemed a little cocky, which they said about fighter jocks, but not so cocky as he might have been, which they said about *ex*–fighter jocks. For a fleeting second, she calculated his age versus her own, mid-twenties to mid-thirties. He was still a boy.

And then he said, "It's a pleasure to meet you, ma'am."

No one she could recall had ever called her "ma'am."

They headed out in a Naval Academy cabin cruiser. The two guys from the *Baltimore Sun* sat up on the bridge. Jack, Steve, and Susan sat in the cockpit at the stern, so that they could look back at Annapolis.

"I know what you're thinking," said Jack.

"No, you don't," said Susan.

"You're wondering why I'm along on this little junket. Well, this submarine is the future of the navy, so it has to be in the book somewhere, probably toward the end, after the part where Steve punches out over Iraq."

"That means ejected, ma'am," said Steve.

"Please, call me Susan. 'Ma'am' makes me feel like I'm about fifty years old."

"Yes . . . and let me correct what Jack said. The submarine is part of the navy's future. But like a good football team needs a ground game and a passing attack, the navy will always need aviators to go along with the submariners."

"But, Steve, you're on the sub warfare account," said Jack. "Your job is to make submarines sound like the only things that deserve any more funding."

"We all could use more funding," said Susan.

She was amazed at how small the *Annapolis* was: three hundred and thirty-five feet, but most of it close to the waterline, the lowest profile you could find.

"Not much to it, is there?" said Jack as they descended the gangplank from the sub tender.

"The surface ship drivers call this the sewer-pipe navy," explained Steve. "You climb in a big pipe crammed with electronics and torpedoes and bunks and food, along with a nuclear reactor, and you go looking for bad guys."

They boarded at the weapons loading hatch, the largest entrance on the sub. And Susan was struck, the moment she descended, by the almost luxurious feeling of the air—cool, dry, perfectly monitored. Then her eyes adjusted. She realized that the companionway was just wide enough for one person, and the two cabins that she peeked into—one for the captain, the other for the executive officer—were just large enough for one person. She wondered if fresh air might be the only luxury aboard.

The executive officer greeted them and led them to the control room, which was about the size of a big living room, crammed with gauges, consoles, navigation tables, and two big periscopes. "This is where everything happens, the brain of the boat, if you will."

He showed them the fire control computers, the sonar tracking systems, the control stations for the helmsman and planesman. Susan had been expecting a bridge like something from *Star Trek*. This looked more like the control room of a power plant. And not a grace note anywhere in what the XO called "the most perfect war-making machine afloat."

The first thing the Baltimore writer asked was, "How much did this perfect machine cost the taxpayers?"

"Eight hundred million," said Steve Stafford with a professional and not at all defensive snap to his voice.

"Eight hundred million!" cried Susan, surprising herself. "Jesus! For what?"

Things went downhill from there.

Jack was still laughing when he and Susan sat down with Steve in Buddy's Crabs and Ribs after the tour. "Honey, if you think those *Los Angeles*-class fast-attack submarines are expensive—"

"Which they aren't," said Steve, "considering what they can do."

"Spoken like a public affairs officer," said Jack. "Tell her how much the new *Seawolf* and her sisters are costing."

"Uh . . . two billion."

"For what? The Russians are gone, and we have war in the streets. What are we spending our money on those things for? How many do we need?" asked Susan.

"It's a big ocean," said Steve. "Sixty attack submarines don't go very far."

"'A nuclear submarine fleet is the future of the armed forces,'" said Jack.

"Do you really believe that?" asked Susan.

"No, but the Russian Minister of Defense does. He said it a couple of years ago. And the Russians are still putting their money where their mouth is. While their surface navy rusts, they're building subs even quieter than that monster you saw this morning. And countries like Iran are buying submarines. And China is building them. We need more vigilance, not less. But we need to be vigilant about the way we spend our money, too."

Steve Stafford folded his arms and listened in admiration. "You know, Uncle Jack, sometimes I think my grandfather is wrong about you."

"So tell him, Steve. Tell him I want to talk to him. Get us together."

Steve drank from his beer. "He doesn't trust you."

"There are things I need to know from him," Jack went on, "and things I want him to know."

"He fears that book," said Steve. "He thinks it can hurt the navy, considering all that you've done in the past. And he worries about bad press these days, with everyone fighting for funding."

Jack pulled several diskettes from his pocket and placed them on the table. "That's why I want you to read the first six sections, so that you can see what I'm trying to do."

Steve studied the diskettes, arms still folded, as if he did not want to touch them. "Is my father's story in here?"

"I haven't written about Vietnam yet. That's why I need to talk to the admiral."

There it was, thought Susan. This whole thing was somehow coming down to Steve's father and Vietnam.

"This takes you through the Civil War," Jack was saying.

Should she wait or push a little harder? This was delicate business, this matter of Steve's father, and she had already put her foot in her mouth once that day.

"Civil War," said Steve. "Brother against brother."

"Even back then." Jack looked out the window onto the harbor. Where slaves were once landed, where barrels of tobacco brought wealth to Maryland, where French troops embarked for Yorktown, boaters now showed off the fiberglass trappings of success and obsession. "If you think we have worries today—expensive submarines and so forth—imagine this place in 1861."

Susan watched Jack's eyes glaze over. It was as if all the boats melted away and he was seeing that sleepy harbor in 1861.

"Only one person in Annapolis voted for Lincoln. It was a southern town, with a bad war rushing fast. But the Staffords stood where God put them . . . on both sides."

"What about the Parrishes?" asked Susan.

"Oh, they were here, too."

"They were also here this morning," she said, expecting more of a reaction than she got.

All Jack said was, "Oliver Parrish?"

"How did you guess?"

"I think we'll be seeing more of him."

"Are we talking about the same Oliver Parrish who knew my father at the Academy?" asked Steve. "The Washington attorney who's always suing the government over things like Agent Orange and the disposal of nuclear waste from naval vessels?"

Knew his father. Something more to add to the mix. Still Susan decided to keep her mouth shut and listen, because these two were revealing plenty on their own.

But lunch was arriving: a burger for Steve, steamed mussels for Susan, and a big plate of crab cakes, a Maryland delicacy, for Jack.

Jack looked at those crab cakes as if a moment from his youth had just been restored to him. "Here is where I belong."

"What about Oliver Parrish?" Steve asked.

"Don't you worry about him," said Jack, a little smile cracking the corners of his lips. "Just set up a meeting with your grandfather, so I can answer the important question."

"What's that?" asked Steve, falling into one of Jack's joke traps.

"How did the seafaring Staffords go from the deck of the *Randolph* to the desk of a PR flack in just"—he counted on his fingers—"eight generations."

"We all have a story to tell," answered Steve.

"So read mine and tell me what you think."

The Stafford Story
Book Six
Brother against Brother
March 1861

Ethan Stafford stood fortieth in a class of sixty-three. As long as he was not last, he did not care. Nor did he care about his demerits, as long as he did not exceed the two hundred in a year that would disqualify him from the Academy. And on that warm March night, he did not care if he received a dozen more because Alexandra Parrish had moved to Annapolis, and he had to see her.

He had spent almost four years at the Naval Academy, against instincts that would have put him at a college where he might have had some fun. He would even have been happy to run the plantation at Stafford Hall, after childless Uncle Charlton had died. But that job had passed to his half brother Cecil because Captain Jason wanted another naval son.

It did not matter that his father's eldest son, Tom, was now assistant superintendent of the Naval Academy, or that second son George was the assistant engineer at the Gosport Navy Yard in Norfolk. The Old Cap, as Ethan called his father, wanted to look through a younger set of eyes and see all the way into the twentieth century.

A man who knew the story of Philip Spencer should have known better than that, but the Old Cap was not a force to stand against.

Neither was the allure of Alexandra Parrish.

Ethan slipped out of his bed and pulled on his uniform: blue trousers, blue waistcoat, blue jacket cut at the waist with a double row of brass buttons. He even knotted his droopy black bow tie. Being off grounds would bring five demerits. Being off grounds out of uniform would bring seven.

It was eleven o'clock. Lights out. But the duty station at the entrance of the dormitory was always manned. So Ethan dropped quietly from his second-floor window to the spring-soft mud below.

The Academy that slept before him that night resembled a garden of Greek Revival buildings, some in neat lines, like the dormitories of Stribling Row, others in dignified little groups, like the pillared chapel and recitation halls. The school had tripled in size since Bancroft brought it to Annapolis. And the number of midshipmen had expanded so quickly that the frigate *Constitution* had recently been moored in the river to house the plebes.

Ethan prided himself on his lack of interest in naval tradition, but at night, when that venerable old frigate seemed ready to take sail in the moonlight, he felt something stir. She was one of those ships that had a soul. So he gave her a little salute. Then he slipped across the yard, past the grand old mulberry tree, then by the chaplain's house, where lights seldom burned after ten and the shadows offered perfect cover for someone slipping over the old Fort Severn wall. Of all the drills, he knew frenching out the best.

He moved quickly through the streets, keeping to the shadows wherever he could. No sense encountering an instructor out for a stroll. But he could not resist stopping to peer into Aunt Antonia's front windows. The lights were still burning, which meant she was probably up late, writing another article on the evils of slavery.

After a short stay in Washington, she had moved to Annapolis and rented a small house with her freed slave, Iris Ezekiel, who used her father's first name as a surname. But that night Ethan needed no opinions about slavery, or about courting the daughter of a committed slaveholder like Dan'l Parrish. So on he went.

The Fine Folly was in darkness.

Although widowed Walter Parrish had lived there twenty years and his aunt Rebecca twenty before that, no one called it the Parrish House. *Fine Folly* was just too fine a name, except to local wags who called it *Pussy's Folly* because Walter kept cats. He and his late wife, Hattie, had started with two strays picked up from an oyster shucker on Spa Creek. Now there were dozens, which was folly in itself.

Ethan grabbed a fistful of pebbles and flung them against her window. Then he gave a low three-note whistle, like the one he and Alexandra had used in their childhood summers on the Patuxent, when they had sailed and fished together, explored the riverfront woods, and kissed for the first time.

Somewhere nearby, a cat yowled.

But the window did not open.

So Ethan began to climb the wisteria trellis. It was mostly rotten, held together by the vine itself, and in a moment, he landed in the shrubbery with a grunt.

Now the window opened. "Why, Ethan . . . I been expectin' you."

"Evenin', darlin'." He went around to the east side and tested the drainpipe.

She opened the east window, and her teasing voice was like honey flowing down. "Why, whatever are you plannin' to do?"

"Climb this drainpipe and kiss you."

She laughed, low and throaty. "My daddy'd disapprove. Granddad, too."

"They would've disapproved of what we did last summer, down by the river, and at Christmas, in your daddy's hayloft, too."

"*I* might disapprove now," she said.

He stopped, with his hands wrapped around the pipe and his toes digging into the loose mortar between the bricks. "Disapprove of what?"

"You haven't declared yourself."

"I declare myself . . . every time I kiss you."

"Don't come another inch till you declare your loyalties. My brother Robby says he'll secede, even if Maryland don't. What about you? Will you be honor-bound to follow your state?"

"I'm honor-bound to do what I want, not what this Abe Lincoln tells me."

"Then you're honor-bound to visit my boudoir."

In an instant he was leaning over the windowsill, pressing his lips to hers.

"My, my," she whispered, "you've grown chin whiskers."

"You like them?"

"I don't know. I think I must feel them again to tell."

She was the lustiest girl he had ever met. She had many beaux and had admitted a few of them to enjoy her most intimate charms, and if Ethan were a true gentleman, he would have scorned her. But he had known her forever, and despite an upbringing that had taught her how to sip tea and carry herself like a lady, she was a true child of the river, like him.

He looked into her eyes, and she gave him that lascivious grin. Her face was small and a trifle pinched, but there was something feral in those eyes, something wild about the curly red hair, and her kiss was the sweetest he had ever tasted. When he felt something rubbing just below his belt buckle, he knew that this was going to be a fine night. But it was only a cat on the sill, rubbing itself against two bodies at once.

"Oh, get away," whispered Alexandra, and she threw the cat to the floor. "Silly old pussy . . . Now you may come in, my southern sailor man."

And a voice snapped from below. "You've just earned yourself five demerits, mister." It was his half brother, Tom. "Now come down here, or it'll be ten."

Ethan glanced at Alexandra, who stepped back from the window and, with another lascivious smile, opened her nightgown. "Come back soon, now, y'hear?"

And the drainpipe gave way all at once. Ethan grabbed for the windowsill, then for the lilac bush, and then he was sprawled on the gravel walk, his half brother's face looming over him. "When you decide to french out, don't stop by your aunt's house, especially when I'm taking a late-evening stroll with her."

Ethan scrambled to his feet. "No, sir."

"Now, what's this I hear about a declaration?"

"He declares his support of those states that want to keep their rights to themselves," said Alexandra from above. "We hope you agree, whether Maryland goes out or not."

Tom Stafford was childless, widowed, forty-five. He had been decorated for the Vera Cruz landings in the Mexican War and had sailed with Commodore Perry to Japan. The navy was both his mistress and his child. "My allegiance is to the Constitution, Miss Parrish. Now close your windows—and your nightgown—before you catch your death."

"Lieutenant, you shouldn't speak of a lady's nightgown. It's not gentlemanly. G'night, boys," she singsonged and slammed down the window.

Tom shooed a mewling old cat away. "We're on the morning train to Washington, Ethan. Pa's gotten us tickets to the inauguration."

"The inauguration of the Great Ape?"

"Speak respectfully of the commander in chief."

"He's not mine."

The cats were swarming from everywhere now—marmalades and tigers, calicoes, bobtails, and toms.

"You took an oath," said Tom, "and you're a Stafford. Don't forget it."

"Aye, sir." Ethan crouched down and petted one of the cats, causing a riot among the others for attention. "I took an oath to be as independent as one of you."

ii
The Great Ape

No one in the Stafford family would ever forget the words of the Old Cap to the new president the next day.

It happened at the White House, after the inauguration.

The prairie lawyer, who had promised to stop the spread of slavery into the western territories, was standing in the East Room, under a painting of George Washington. His doughy little wife stood beside him, forcing the gaiety, as though the nation were facing nothing more than a tariff fight. But the guests—members of the new administration and their families—were appropriately solemn.

Nothing could have caused more solemnity than the secession of seven states. Nothing could have been more depressing than the sight of Capitol Hill ringed with cannon. And nothing could have been more frightening than the possibility that Washington might, in a short time, be ringed by enemies, as Virginia leaned toward secession and Maryland leaned with her.

But nothing could have been more somberly hopeful than the last words of Lincoln's inaugural address: "In your hands, my dissatisfied countrymen, and not in mine is the momentous issue of civil war. . . . We are not enemies, but friends. We must not be enemies. Though passion may have strained, it must not break our bonds of affection. The mystic chords of memory, stretching from every battlefield and patriot grave, to every living heart and hearthstone, all over this broad land, will yet swell the chorus of the Union, when again touched, as surely they will be, by the better angels of our nature."

The best angel in Jason Stafford's nature was still the angel of honor, and he would stand by it, whatever was coming. Standing by him that day were family members, gathered from Annapolis, Norfolk, and as far away as Massachusetts.

And whenever the line of guests lurched forward, Ethan stepped on Aunt Antonia's heels.

Nothing, she thought, had changed with Margaret Stafford's prize boy.

The Staffords were there because the Old Cap had served the navy into his seventy-second year, and Secretary of the Navy Gideon Welles valued Jason's experience. Now the serious, imperious, long-faced Welles, who made himself an unwitting figure of fun by wearing a wig that looked like a wave cresting on the top of his head, introduced the Staffords to the president.

Jason saw before him a big shambling beast with wiry black hair, skin that had browned and faded so many times, through so many prairie summers, that it was permanently yellowed, and new chin whiskers that did nothing to disguise those garden-spade cheekbones.

Though it was not the face of a poet, Jason had to admit there had been hard poetry in the president's speech that day. But a fighter was needed now, not a poet, and no one knew what kind of fighter this Lincoln might be.

"Captain Stafford, of Annapolis?" Lincoln spoke with a hard-*r* prairie accent, in a voice that was suprisingly high-pitched for such a big man.

"Yes, sir." Jason angled his head, displaying the Stafford jaw. His silver hair and still-perfect posture were a perfect contrast to the rumpled president.

"I hear Annapolis is a fine place," said Lincoln, as if he did not know how disliked he was there.

Antonia reminded him: "At least my nephew Tom voted for you, sir."

Lincoln complimented her on her writings and shook the hands of all the Staffords, then came back to the patriarch. "A fine-looking family, Captain."

"Thank you, sir."

"Secretary Welles speaks highly of your work. We hope you're prepared to do your duty."

And Jason bristled.

A remark like that, even off-handed—coming from someone whose only military experience had been in a massacre called the

Black Hawk War; someone who had opposed the Mexican War that gave us California, the southwest, and a long measure of military glory to boot—a remark like that, coming from this Abraham Lincoln, was an absolute insult, and more than a veiled reference to Stafford slaveholding.

Jason pulled himself up to the full extent of his height and said: "*We* are prepared to do *our* duty, sir. We expect *you* to do *yours*."

"What a thing to say to the president," grumbled Antonia as they came out into the afternoon sunlight.

"Our father traded insults with George Washington and Tom Jefferson. I won't stand in awe of that Great Ape."

"Well said, Pa." Ethan laughed. "Great Ape for certain."

"It's what they're calling him in the press," said Jason. "Imagine them saying that about a president. Imagine the kind of man he must be to *let* them say it."

"I thought his speech was a marvel," said Jack Browne, whose Boston wife and Annapolis mother each occupied an arm.

"Yes," said Antonia. "It'll make these southerners come to their senses."

"We southerners *have* our senses," said Margaret. "We know that without the slaves, we'll be bankrupt."

"We'll make do if we must," said Jason confidently.

"How?" asked Margaret's son Cecil Harcourt.

"Sharecropping . . . hiring hands. It might even be cheaper than housing and feeding forty darkies."

"*Negroes*," said Jack Browne. "Call them a name that you'd call a human being, and then you'll think of them like that."

Captain Jason Stafford stopped in the middle of the sidewalk. He was not accustomed to being corrected, especially by an abolitionist nephew. "Do not tell me what to call anyone, son, black or white. I don't care how many pieces of lawful property you've managed to steal from southern masters and sneak back to Boston aboard your ships."

Jack Browne was not a man to be talked to in such a way, either. "If you weren't my uncle—"

"Now, gents," said Ethan, "let's call them nigras and be done with it."

"Thank you, Ethan," said Jason, who built any bridge he could to his youngest boy. "Some men don't seem to know how fine a line we're trying to walk right now."

"Well, I'm tryin', sir," said Ethan. "You can be certain."

"By declaring loyalty to the South?" said Tom as the procession began again.

"Now, Tom, I only said that to . . . unh—"

"To what?" His father stopped again, took a step closer to the youngest and tallest of his sons.

"Unh . . . to get into the good graces of a young lady . . . sir."

"There's an ideal for you," said Antonia sarcastically.

"At least my boy was never accused of mutiny," said Margaret, ever the defensive mother.

"Just incorrigibility," answered Antonia.

"Incorri-*what*?"

"Quiet!" snapped Jason, who was growing more irritable with age and impending crisis. "This boy has to be made to see what matters. And it's not the cultivation of a mustache and a few scraggly hairs on his chin."

"I was waitin' for you to notice that," said Ethan.

"Beards are for men who take their oaths seriously. Men who stand where God puts them . . . not boys."

And as if sent by the grace of God, a carriage struck a puddle in the street and splattered muddy water over the whole group.

Brother George took the brunt of the puddle and shook his fist at the driver. Then he saw that the others were laughing at him, so he smoothed his mustache and struck a heroic pose, despite the muddy water dripping off the brim of his service cap. "A lieutenant needs a drink to warm his bones. And Pa's reserved a table at Willard's . . . for all of us, no matter who thinks what."

"No matter at all," said Ethan. Then he raised his voice, mimicking Lincoln's high pitch: "'We are not enemies but friends.'"

"'We must not be enemies,'" said Antonia, finishing Lincoln's line. Then she took her sister-in-law, Margaret, by the arm and together they led their family on to dinner.

As Pennsylvania Avenue made its turn, all of them were struck by the sight of the Capitol in the distance.

The wooden pudding bowl was gone.

It had been handsome enough for the nation into which they were born.

But it never could symbolize the nation they would become.

Two new wings had been added to the building, and a three-tiered white iron dome was rising above the pudding bowl. A skeletal tower pierced the center of the structure like a spindle, and steel cables descended to support the completed portions, so that the Capitol now resembled a man who had not yet put on his hat.

iii
Dissolution

In the following weeks, the Naval Academy all but came apart.

Young men trained in the code of honor were torn, as only young men could be, by the dilemma of one loyalty against another. The resignations had begun when the first states went out. After Lincoln's inauguration, more and more secession badges appeared on the chests of midshipmen who had submitted letters of resignation and were now waiting for official dismissal.

Ethan wrote one, but he did not submit it. He still hoped that Maryland would go out of the Union first and the decision would be made for him.

Then, on April 12, Commandant of Midshipmen Christopher Rodgers read the articles of war to the assembled brigade aboard the *Constitution.* Fort Sumter had been attacked.

The next day, Ethan received an invitation to the Fine Folly.

All America was waiting to see *when*—it was no longer a question of *if*—Virginia would go out of the Union, and *if* Maryland would follow her. And Ethan knew that if he left the Academy, Alexandra would be waiting with more than open arms.

That made his decision easier. So did the knowledge that bags were being packed up and down Stribling Row. More midshipmen were resigning, while loyal mates were preparing for early commissions.

So Ethan took the sheet of paper from his drawer, signed it, and dated it.

> It is with regret that I resign my position at the U.S. Naval Academy. While some of my family are committed to the Union, I believe in the rights of the new Confederacy. I cannot, in good conscience, continue as a member, knowing that the Academy is a Federal institution, and that the Federal government is prepared to rescind certain rights that should belong to the states.
>
> Repectfully submitted

Ethan crossed the yard to Blake Row, with his letter of resignation in his pocket. The spring afternoons were growing longer. It was too fine a time of year for all this to be happening, he thought. At the steps of the brick administration building, he smoothed the hairs scraggling over his upper lip and from beneath his lower.

Beards are for men who take their oaths seriously . . . not boys.

Once he handed in that resignation, he would grow whatever beard he damn well pleased. Then he heard familiar voices coming from somewhere behind him: Lieutenant Rodgers, Lieutenant Tom Stafford, and Captain Jason Stafford, walking along the path from the recitation hall.

At the sight of his father, who was about as venerable as the old ship in the river, Ethan lost his nerve. He was a boy again, with a boy's scraggly whiskers. He turned quickly in the opposite direction and hurried toward the Fine Folly.

Alexandra greeted Ethan at the door. "Did you do it?"

He looked down at his shoes. "I have the letter of resignation in my pocket."

"Oh, thank the Lord." She took him by the hand and led him down the center hallway to the library, which was filled with cats and conspirators—Alexandra's father, Dan'l, and her brother, Robby, along with several other men.

Sitting in a rocking chair, feeding branches into the fireplace, was old Walter Parrish, widowed lord of this cat-smelling manor. "Good to see you, son. Sorry you're plannin' to leave the navy school, but—"

"Later, Pa." Dan'l Parrish still seemed like a man in a hurry. He asked Ethan, "Did you resign?"

"He didn't," said Alexandra. "It was as if he knew we would need him to stay where he is."

Dan'l Parrish had grown heavier, but he still moved with sharp little hitches and twitches, and his eyes never stopped darting. "You come from Union men. Can you be trusted?"

"He comes from Patuxent planters, too," said Alexandra.

Dan'l shot a glance at his daughter. "Let him talk. Cat ain't got his tongue."

"Cat'll get it if he sticks it out around here." Robby Parrish wrinkled his nose. "Or breathes too heavy."

"You know me, don't you?" said the Saint Mary's County planter Dunstable Ripley, a big-bellied man with a black beard, a big voice, and by all odds, a big opinion of himself.

"Yes, sir," answered Ethan.

"Then you know how my family feels."

"We're *all* secessionists here." Robby Parrish was twenty-two, a self-described gentleman planter with a gentleman's wardrobe. Today it was pearl-gray waistcoat and trousers, dove-gray coat, blue polka-dot cravat. The Samuel Parrish strain showed in Robby—lean physique, smart face, yellow hair—but his quick little gestures and straight-to-the-matter talk marked him clearly as Dan'l Parrish's son. The conspiratorial little wink he offered, as a way of including Ethan, was all his own.

"I been buyin' Confederate bonds ever since they started sellin' 'em," added old Walter Parrish. "Eight percent per annum."

"Pa, you hold on to your money," said Dan'l. "Wait till we take Maryland out."

"Which we would've done by now," said Ripley, " 'cept we got a governor straddlin' the Mason-Dixon line like a man sittin' on a fence."

"When he should be ridin' a rail," added Dan'l.

"It's time to wake Maryland up," said ancient Anson Duganey, who sat in the corner, squinting over his cigar.

"Sumter was a foreign fort on the sovereign soil of South Carolina." Dan'l kicked at a cat twining itself around his legs. "Maryland's sovereign soil, too."

"And we have foreign property right here in Annapolis," said Robby.

"The Naval Academy?" offered Ethan.

"And the *Constitution*," added Dan'l. "A ship named for the sheet of paper the Great Ape's wrappin' himself in."

"Think of what they'll say if we steal that ship," said Robby.

Ethan looked out the window. Beyond the garden, across King George Street, lights were burning on Blake Row, where his father and brother would soon be dining. Neither of them would ever have taken him into their confidence like this.

"When Lincoln sees that the *people* are against him, on every side of his capital city," said Alexandra, "he'll just plain have to give up the whole idea of a war."

Ethan began to speak, but his mouth was suddenly so dry that his tongue stuck to its roof. He moistened his lips and said, "I guess I've always thought that there were better ways than war to get what we want."

"This is one of them," said Alexandra.

"What . . . what is it you want me to do?"

"Hold your resignation," said Robby.

"Let them think you're loyal," said Dan'l. "Learn what you can. . . . Are the midshipmen at the gates well armed? Will they fight? Is the *Constitution* guarded?"

"Then come and tell me." Alexandra stood a bit closer, so that he felt the hoops of her skirt against his leg. It was like taking his hand in public.

"And we'll have men comin' from Saint Mary's County, from Baltimore, and from right here in Annapolis," said Dan'l. "Well armed and plenty of them."

Anson gave a laugh. "Once we take her, we'll make you cap'n of the *Constitution*."

"Do this right, son, and you can ask for Lexie's hand any time you want. Betray us, and I'll kill you." Dan'l put a glass of whiskey into Ethan's hand and made a little toast.

Ethan glanced at Alexandra, and her smile lit the dark room.

"Yes, sir," said old Walter. "We been tryin' to get a Stafford and a Parrish together a long time."

Ethan fumbled a bit more. He had never spoken of marriage. He did not even think it mattered to Alexandra.

And Dunstable Ripley let out a big guffaw. "Dan'l *was* plannin' to take a shotgun to you, but he couldn't, 'cause you made his daughter so damn happy."

Dan'l patted him on the back. "When all this is over and there's still slaves at Stafford Hall, your pa, he'll thank us."

An hour later, Ethan was eating in the faculty dining room, just off the midshipmen's mess, with his father and his half brother Thomas. The midshipmen were muted and quiet, but the Old Cap was growling at Ethan. "I come to discuss assignments, and all I hear is how many demerits you've amassed."

Ethan tried to concentrate on his boiled beef, potatoes, and carrots.

"It's been hard on these boys," said Tom. "They've seen a lot of friends leave in the last few weeks."

"I know it's hard." The Old Cap shook his head. "I thought an Academy would protect all these boys from politics."

"At least we don't have many Philip Spencers." Tom looked at Ethan. "Now Pa's come to give you a choice. Do you want river operations or blue water?"

Jason added, "I won't put you before anyone who's done better in your class, but tell me where you want to be, and I'll see if I can find a position."

Ethan's anger roiled at his father, who would let him make a small choice and ignore the larger torment. "River operations or blue water, sir?"

Jason leaned closer and lowered his voice. "We're going to blockade the South's blue-water ports, seize the Mississippi, and strangle the beast. General Scott likes the strategy. Gideon Welles doesn't know enough to object. We don't know what Lincoln will say. But *you* have a choice in the matter."

Ethan picked at a potato, swirled it around a bit in the grease, and asked his half brother, "Which way are you going?"

"My future's not under discussion here."

Jason turned to Tom. "I've already told Welles how much you know about iron cladding."

So the Old Cap had also been considering the future for a son who could consider it perfectly well for himself.

Tom stiffened. "I'd rather have a blue-water command than sail a desk."

"Maybe you'll get *Merrimack,* then, if your brother can get her out of Gosport."

So son George was on the old man's mind, too.

The Gosport Navy Yard at Norfolk was the largest Federal property in the South, worth far more to the Confederacy than Fort Sumter. There were ships, drydocks, and an arsenal of eight hundred cannon, including three hundred modern Dahlgren guns. But the prize was the *Merrimack*.

"It would be a damn shame if the secessionists got her," said Jason.

"It's a damn shame she's been out of commission for so long."

"We've sent men down to help George get her ready. But the Great Ape hopes Virginia will stay in. So he's ordered that nothing be done to inflame the Virginians—like takin' the *Merrimack* out—until the last minute . . . . *Politicians!"*

"They make the messes," said Tom. "We clean them up."

And the Old Cap returned his attention to his third son. "So what would you say to a blue-water billet with Davy Farragut, once he gets a squadron?"

"Yes, sir. Thank you, sir." Ethan stuffed a potato into his mouth to keep from saying anything else.

"Good." And the Old Cap put a hand on Ethan's forearm, the warmest physical gesture he had shown his son in years. "I know I'll be proud of you."

Ethan felt the potato stop squarely in his throat. He looked into those blue eyes, unclouded by age or doubt, and he envied the certainty he saw, born of a lifelong commitment to discipline and honor. The old man never doubted that he was doing the right thing, even if it meant serving someone as vacillating as Lincoln.

He wanted to ask his father about everything swirling around him—the resignation in his pocket, his love for Lexie, his invitation to become a secessionist spy. But he knew that his father would offer only one answer.

So he simply excused himself, saying he had much to study for if he was to be commissioned three weeks early.

"Just one thing before you leave, Ethan."

"Sir?"

"Shave."

Shave, my ass.

Damn him and his notions of fatherhood. Damn them all.

Ethan now carried intelligence from both sides: He knew what the Annapolis secessionists were planning. He knew the Navy Department's plans for the war and the protection of the *Merrimack*. And he did not know what to do with any of it.

So he went over to the river and skipped stones and contemplated the shadow of the *Constitution,* docked where the muddy Severn met the salt water of the bay, soil meeting sea, like loyalty meeting secession.

Then he went back to his room and wrote a note with his left hand, so that the script would not be easily recognized. He also purposely misspelled words and left out all punctuation:

> Lieutenant Stafford
>
> A man with sharpe ears hears much secesh talk in Annapolis bout takin fedral propertie As you sit on the only fedral propertie in town you should pay attenshun to such talk as it might save your school and your ship

Then, he wrote another note:

> Darling Lexie:
>
> The school is lightly guarded. The midshipmen are lightly armed. Forty plebes live aboard *Constitution,* and she carries no guns. But rumors have reached the brass of your plans. Move quickly. Tonight, if possible. If not, meet me at the Tripoli Monument tomorrow and I will tell you what I know.

With those two letters, he had become a double agent.

Dan'l Parrish and his secessionists did not act on Ethan's intelligence.

But Lieutenant Tom Stafford responded quickly to the anonymous note slipped under his door. At dawn he was pounding on the door of Academy Superintendent George Blake. Before breakfast, howitzers had been wheeled to every gate. Muskets and ammunition had been issued to every midshipman. By lunchtime, the whole battalion was moving cannons from the Fort Severn practice battery onto the *Constitution*, and armed details were put aboard to repel boarders.

Shortly after lunch, Midshipman Ethan Stafford submitted his resignation.

"Resignation denied," said Tom Stafford.

The Old Cap was pacing in front of the windows of his son's office.

Aunt Antonia, invited for tea rather than a family crisis, sat in the corner. Iris Ezekiel, now grown as gray as her former mistress, sat next to Antonia.

"I've made my decision," answered Ethan. "It won't be river *or* blue water."

And the Old Cap rounded on him. "Then what? Blockade-running? Confederate privateer? Privateers are little better than pirates with licenses."

"It's been a long time since I've heard that phrase," said Antonia.

"I'm not sure," answered Ethan. "Sometimes I think there must be better ways than war to get what we want."

"Resignations must be approved by the secretary of the navy." Jason picked up a pouch from the desk. "The ones I'm carrying to Washington are here. Yours is not among them."

"I've already sent a copy to Gideon Welles by post," Ethan answered.

"Good Christ."

"At least he's thorough," said Antonia, "in his delusions."

Ethan asked her, "Have you ever questioned the things you do, Auntie?"

"I've kept to my guns, and the whole world has followed me."

"Don't be so smug," grumbled Jason.

"The boy asked me a question. I make sure I'm right; then I go ahead."

"And slavery isn't right," said Iris softly.

"Maybe it isn't . . . but a state can't surrender its rights," answered Ethan.

Now Jason came closer to him. "What will your mother say?"

"That she's like many mothers, with a family torn."

There was a knock, and a Negro steward brought in a tea tray.

Tom stood, as if to end this business. "Your resignation must be accepted by the Navy Department. I expect you to conduct yourself honorably until then."

"Aye, sir."

"Now get out," said Jason, turning from his youngest son.

Ethan pulled himself to attention and said to his father's back, "I wanted to be a son for the soil, but you made me come here. Well, it's the soil the Confederacy's fightin' for. So this time, I'm makin' my own decision."

His father did not even turn around.

There were guards at every gate, but a pretty local girl in a blue dress with matching parasol could never be seen as a secessionist threat. So Alexandra strolled into the yard and met Ethan at the Tripoli Monument, an ornately carved cube of white granite, topped with a column and an American eagle, surrounded by rows of bronze cannon, some buried upright to their trunions, others pointing in admiration at the monument, and all turning green in the weather.

It was a good place to plot, for what plotter would meet so boldly?

"They're ready for us," said Alexandra. "Who told them?"

"Annapolis is a little town with big ears. Somebody heard somebody in tavern, braggin' they were goin' to take the Academy. Could've been Ripley."

"Men . . . always braggin'."

"Nobody braggin' here," said Ethan, looking around. "Two hundred and fifty midshipmen can't hold this Academy against a mob. Some of these plebes aren't yet fifteen years old. And none of them ever killed a man."

"Will you?"

"I'm just waitin' for them to accept my resignation."

"Resign? But my pa doesn't want you to resign, Ethan."

"Neither does my own. So it's for damn sure I'm not worried about yours."

"You should be, if you worry about me."

Ethan looked around, to see if anyone was listening, then he said, "Tell your pa the *Merrimack* is bein' readied to run, but they won't take her out till the last minute. A move against Gosport could gain the ship and three hundred Dahlgren guns, too. And tell him this: the Federal Navy plans to strangle the South—blockade the blue-water ports and control the rivers."

After a moment, Alexandra gave him that smile. "My father called you a traitor this mornin'. He said you must've sounded this alarm." She moved her parasol so it blocked the sun from his eyes. "I guess he'll have to trust you again."

Ethan did not tell her how traitorous he felt.

"He proclaims his southern loyalty to get into her graces." The Old Cap stood at a window overlooking the Tripoli Monument. "He resigns his commission so she'll shield his eyes from the sun."

"Give him credit for having a conscience." Tom stood beside him. "We've all made hard decisions."

"Even Walter Parrish," offered Antonia. "It's rumored he's been withdrawing cash from the Annapolis Bank, sending it south. Maybe he'll follow it."

"He'll never leave that house," said Jason.

"Perhaps not," said Antonia. "But he's promised to tell me if he does."

"It sure would be nice to leave that house to another generation," said Tom. "All my life, I've lived in navy quarters. To leave something concrete behind, especially with everything else coming down . . . it sure would be nice."

"Worry about leavin' a country behind, first," said Jason.

iv
Save a Ship, Lose a Ship

By the following Saturday, April 20, Virginia had seceded, and all hell had broken loose across Maryland.

On Friday a Baltimore mob had rioted when the Sixth Massachusetts attempted to pass through the city. Railroad bridges to the south had been set afire so the soldiers could not reach Washington. And without any left-handed notes from Ethan, rumors of an assault against the Academy had grown so hot that the battalion was mustered three times to repel mobs that never materialized.

Around three that afternoon, Ethan was called to Tom's office. He stood at attention before the desk, musket at his side, cartridge belt cinched at his waist.

"At ease," said Tom. "You're no longer a midshipman."

Ethan's legs weakened. "I thought it would take longer."

Tom held up a telegram. "Pa expedited your papers. The loyalty of slave-owning officers is being questioned. He can't have his sons damaging his name."

Ethan had expected to feel elated, but his father had found a way to fill him with guilt once again. "Damn that old man." After a moment, in which the silence hung between them like an unlit fuse, Ethan leaned his musket against the wall. "Am I dismissed, then?"

"Technically. But you're still wearing your uniform."

Ethan unbuckled his belt. "I'll turn it in."

"We've received reliable intelligence from Baltimore—secessionists are coming down by steamer to attack the *Constitution.*"

"Well, *I'm* secesh myself now." Ethan's voice was full of petulance and self-pity. He could not believe that his father would act so quickly against him.

"If I wasn't navy, I might make the same decision myself."

"Kind words, comin' from you, Tom." If Ethan could not have the understanding of a father, he found it with a half brother old enough to be his father, and he would take comfort from the grip of Tom's hands on his shoulders, and Tom's eyes on his.

"You're one of the best gunnery students here," Tom said. "And we need all the help we can get to hold this steamer off. Will you help us save the *Constitution*?"

"You mean, before I help to tear it up?"

In his office in the State, War, and Navy Building, Jason Stafford sipped tea brought by the petty officer who served as his secretary. He found lately that he needed strong brew every afternoon, or he could not muster the energy to wage his war of paper and policy, especially in that terrible week.

The most difficult cable he ever sent had gone out a few hours earlier.

He had cut Ethan loose quickly and cleanly. His prayer now was that the boy would survive the war and his wife would survive the grief of a divided family.

That message had been attached to another from Secretary Welles to the superintendent of the Naval Academy, containing the most difficult advice Jason ever offered: "Defend the *Constitution* at all hazards. If it cannot be done, destroy her."

But overriding the trouble at Annapolis was the crisis a hundred and twenty miles south, at the Gosport Navy Yard, where a week of hard work had readied the *Merrimack* to run, but a vacillating old drunk of a commandant named Captain Charles McCauley had kept her sitting at the dock.

Jason had never understood why his son George had chosen to be an engineer—a staff officer treated like a second-class citizen—instead of a line officer—a fighting leader who could command a ship. But he pitied him his present commanding officer.

McCauley was a living argument for retirement at sixty-five, thought Jason. Men in their prime, who should have been captains and commanders, were still lieutenants because superannuated officers like McCauley, more interested in their comforts and honorifics than in the navy, lingered on. And old McCauley could drink more than anyone, more even than George Stafford.

Jason looked out his window and down the Potomac. The screw sloop *Pawnee* had steamed for Norfolk the night before, carrying a line officer with orders to relieve McCauley, take out the *Merrimack*, and destroy the yard, if necessary. Traveling with him were a hundred marines, for the defense of the yard, and for its destruction, forty barrels of gunpowder, eleven tanks of turpentine, twelve bales of cotton waste. . . .

In the warm Virginia sunshine, the second Stafford son—the quickest to laugh and the quickest to anger, rawboned and whip-smart, drunk or sober—stared up at the tall masts of the *Merrimack* and just shook his head. There were other ships in the yard, including the ancient *United States*, one of the six original frigates, but the *Merrimack* was the only one worth saving. And now it would not happen.

On Thursday, George Stafford and his superior, Robert Danby, had helped Chief Engineer Benjamin Isherwood fire the *Merrimack*'s boilers. She had belched black smoke, her engines had kicked, and the first screw-driven frigate in the world, with masts to catch the wind and engines for quick maneuvering, was ready to run.

A skeleton crew had been assembled from the USS *Cumberland*, a screw sloop that had arrived for repairs, and a pilot had been hired to guide the ship down the Elizabeth River and into Hampton Roads.

But Captain McCauley had refused to give them permission to leave his navy yard. Instead, he had reread his earlier orders from Gideon Welles: "It may not be necessary that the *Merrimack* should leave on Thursday, unless there is immediate danger pending."

"Sir," George had said gently, as if to a petulant child, "we have enough men to sail the *Merrimack* across Hampton Roads, get her to safety under the guns at Fortress Monroe, but we must leave now."

The old man had looked out the window to the place where the *Merrimack* engines heaved and thumped, heaved and thumped, heaved and thumped. And he had ordered the fires banked.

"But, sir," George had protested, "there's no time to waste."

From the sweet little cloud of rye whiskey that hung around his head, McCauley had said, "Gideon Welles does not wish us to give alarm to the Virginians."

"They've already *seceded*, sir," George had cried.

"All right, then," the old man had offered another way to justify his inaction, "we need the *Merrimack* to protect the yard from the secessionists."

"We didn't remount her guns last week, for fear of upsetting the secessionists. She can't even protect herself!"

"But . . . but . . . we must keep up appearances or we'll be attacked before help arrives, so . . . so"—and he had blurted it, as if he could think of nothing else—"order the fires banked."

And no matter how rusted it was at the top, the chain of command had held at Gosport.

George had stood beside Isherwood later, watching the smoke dissipating in the sky above the *Merrimack,* listening to the engines heaving and thumping . . . heaving and . . . thumping . . . heaving . . . and . . . thumping. . . .

"McCauley's an old fool, prostrate with fear and indecision," Isherwood had said.

"We should take her out ourselves."

"Have you been drinking, Lieutenant?"

"No, sir . . . not yet, anyway. We only have to take her eighteen miles, across to Fortress Monroe, sir."

"Across to a court-martial. Engineers do not handle ships. Period."

And the chain of command and naval tradition had held once more.

All that night and the next day, the rebels had gathered. Those officers inclined toward secession had gone over the wall. And the *Cumberland* had anchored in the river and loaded all her guns with grapeshot, to fight off an attack.

But McCauley's nerve had continued to falter with every report of rebel troops arriving by train and rebel artillery batteries digging in around the yard. The truth was that they were phantom troops, arriving in empty boxcars that kept rattling a few miles out of town, then back, and the artillery emplacements had no guns.

On that Saturday afternoon George Stafford could hear the rebels yelling. But the shipyard was silent. Of the thousand men who had been employed there—in the two huge wooden ship houses, in the foundry, in the sawmills and arsenal—only a few officers remained. Even the rats had seceded.

And Captain McCauley was shuffling toward him, kicking at pages of an old newspaper and muttering to himself. "The yard's lost . . . lost and gone . . . lost and gone."

"Washington must be sending reinforcements, sir, and with the *Cumberland* in the river—"

"The rebels could come tonight and overwhelm us. There's . . . there's only one thing to do."

"I think we should wait, sir."

"We should do what we're supposed to do in these circumstances, Stafford."

And once more, the chain of command held.

When the *Pawnee* arrived a few hours later, her officers found the *Merrimack* and all of the other ships but the *Cumberland* sinking at their moorings, scuttled by order of a panicked old man who was trying to keep them from falling into rebel hands.

They also found George Stafford, in the machine shop where he had helped repair the *Merrimack* engines, dead drunk.

• • •

A hundred miles up the Chesapeake, Ethan Stafford stood at his gun and watched the river slipping seaward.

All was silent. But it was not the noisy silence of a spring night, when a man could feel the life flowing back into the land, right beneath his feet. It was the silence of fear, of boys facing their first action, uncertain of how they would respond.

Ethan was glad he had been given command of the number one gun, which was pointed downriver. It would be much easier to fire on an approaching vessel than on friends breaching the Academy walls. Still, he had managed to get one more message out before he went aboard the *Constitution*: "Whatever Baltimores are planning, Academy brass knows and is ready. If you get past the howitzers at the gates and rush the *Constitution*, you will face Dahlgren guns, double-shotted with grape. Think hard."

And the note must have worked, because so far there had been no sign of hostile activity in Annapolis.

Ethan was glad that he had helped to save a few lives, even if the note was untrue: The midshipmen did not practice with Dahlgrens, powerful modern guns that could fire nine-inch shells almost two miles; they used rifled howitzers with a range of only a thousand yards.

But with them, Ethan would do his best to save the *Constitution,* because she was a ship with a soul. It was not in the wood beneath his feet or the gun beneath his hand. Old cannon were outmoded. Wood rotted and was replaced. This ship's soul was in the faces of his mates, in their sweaty silences and little bursts of nervous talk. It was in their fear and in their commitment to hold the old ship whose heritage reached back to the days when she had shattered the ancient walls of Tripoli.

At about four in the morning, Dan'l Parrish and his daughter knocked on the door of the Annapolis State House. As Dan'l was a man well known and trusted in the town, the toothless old watchman let them in without question and carried a lantern to light their way as they climbed to the little balcony inside the cupola.

"When you plannin' to secede, Mr. Dan'l?" asked the watchman.

"Any day, old-timer. Maybe even today."

Alexandra said, "Secede *today*? You plannin' to storm the Academy with a dozen men, half of them too old and half too young?"

"Girl, you just watch for that steamer full of Baltimore boys. If she comes down in the darkness, watch for the glow above her stacks." He blew out the lantern and handed it to her. "When you see the steamer, light this, pass your hat over it twice, then blow it out. We'll know what to do."

"But, Pa, Ethan says there's Dahlgren guns on the *Constitution*."

"It's a lie. That boy's a damn liar, and when this is done, I'll tell him so."

Toward dawn, the midshipmen on the *Constitution* were beginning to mutter about another false alarm. Then the *Rainbow*, a little sloop sent out to reconnoiter, came pounding back up the Severn.

"Steamer standin' down the bay!" shouted the lieutenant aboard.

"How far?" cried Lieutenant Tom Stafford.

"Twenty minutes, maybe less."

"Smoke on the horizon!" shouted the lookout aloft.

"Beat to quarters!" cried Tom. "Concentrate fire at channel buoy number six."

"Number six?" cried Ethan over the drums. "That lets her get damn close."

"And if she's friendly I'll know who she is before I fire on her." Tom climbed aboard the *Rainbow* and told Ethan that if he showed a red flag and veered quickly downwind, they were to open up on the steamer immediately.

"You might be hit, Lieutenant," said Superintendent Blake, who had hurried across the yard to take command.

"I have confidence in our gunnery, sir." Tom glanced at his brother.

"All right, then."

Tom gave an order, and with a few smart bits of sail-handling, the *Rainbow* came about and pointed back downstream.

"This is what we trained for, lads," whispered Ethan to his crew. Then he sighted his gun at buoy number six, some four hundred yards away.

The steamer was coming hard upstream now. The little schooner, having caught what wind there was at dawn, was running down.

Superintendent Blake stood on a small box and aimed his glass over the *Constitution*'s high bulwarks. "Signal coming, Lieutenant Rodgers. Ready the men."

"Aye, sir," said Rodgers. "Steady and ready, men."

Ethan twined his fingers into his firing lanyard and peered through the port.

On the *Rainbow*, Tom Stafford warned the crew that they would be in the line of fire unless they moved quick on his order. Then he went to the bow of the little boat with his speaking trumpet in his hand.

The big side-wheeler pushing toward them showed an American flag, but Tom knew that the Baltimore rowdies would never be stupid enough to come upstream under the new Confederate colors. Then he saw men in uniforms—blue uniforms.

The steamer loosed three long blasts that nearly blew Tom off his boat.

"Hold steady, men," he said, knowing that if they fell off now, the battery on the *Constitution* might misread the action and open up on friends. He raised the speaking trumpet and cried, "What ship is that?"

The pilot came out of his house on the top deck and tried to wave them off. The big steamer, three times the height of the *Rainbow*, was pounding so close that Tom could feel the roll of the wheel vibrating in his chest.

"I say, what ship?" demanded Tom.

"The *Maryland!*" answered the pilot.

And a big-bellied officer with shoulder-length hair and a scraggling mustache cupped his hands to his mouth. "I'm General Benjamin Butler, Eighth Massachusetts Infantry. Who in hell are you?"

"Lieutenant Tom Stafford, US Naval Academy. Will you save the *Constitution,* sir?"

"That's what I'm here for."

"Then thank God! The old ship is safe!"

The big ferry was pounding past them now, and Tom was holding tight to a line, so that the paddle wave would not throw him overboard.

"I don't mean the *ship!*" shouted Butler, walking toward the stern to keep the *Rainbow* within earshot. "I mean the *document*. But I'll save the ship, too!"

Alexandra Parrish had not lit the lantern when she saw the steamer. Now she watched the little schooner go circling around the steamer like a pup around its master, and she was glad that she had waited.

Her father's voice echoed up to her from the marble floor far below. "That damn Ethan never said a word about Yankee reinforcements, did he?"

She looked down at the furious figure below. "Maybe he didn't know."

"He knew. He's not to be trusted."

Then she heard his angry footfalls echoing out.

"Pa!" she cried. "Where are you goin'?"

"To wreck a railroad."

At Hampton Roads, a sobering George Stafford stood on the deck of the *Cumberland* and watched the sky boiling red. But it was not the eastern sky he was watching, nor was it the alcohol in his head that caused the flaring of colors.

The Gosport Navy Yard had been put to the torch.

The ship houses were collapsing onto themselves in great spark-filled clouds of smoke. Ordnance was exploding. Foundries and machine shops were burning. And the *Merrimack,* her bottom sunk in the mud, her upper works soaked in turpentine, was swallowed by fire.

V
An Occupying Army

The people of Annapolis awakened to a sight that neither Unionist nor secessionist would ever forget.

From the east-facing windows of the Fine Folly, Alexandra Parrish saw it the moment she opened her eyes.

And her grandfather must have seen it, too, because she heard him curse, slam open his door, and go scrambling down the hallway. She found him in the attic, at the window in the gable end, focusing his captain's glass on the bay.

"What is it, Grandfather?"

"It's the *Constitution* . . . my good Lord, with her gunports open."

Alexandra grabbed the telescope and looked for herself.

"My own brother was shot through the lungs right on that deck, and now . . . good Lord!" Walter pointed the glass to the Academy wharf in the Severn.

There were two steamers there, disgorging the Eighth Massachusetts and the Seventh New York, while the guns of the *Constitution* covered their landing, all as neat and military as if Annapolis were enemy soil.

The old man turned his sagging face to his granddaughter. His eyes were bloodshot and bleary. His hair stuck up in little wisps all around the bald spot on the back of his head. His breath, even from a few feet away, formed a foul morning fog. "Folks always call me easy old Walter . . . say I smile too much for a Parrish. . . . Well, it's just that I never had anything to get me mad, till now."

With his duffel bag on his shoulder, Ethan came out into the yard for the last time. Whatever his father's dreams for this Academy, they were now in dust.

The area between Stribling Row and the river was covered with white tents. Smoke from the cookfires was already curling into the sky. Bugles were trumpeting, drums beating, and over by the Fort Severn gatehouse, a Massachusetts sergeant with a voice like a howitzer was mustering a company into formation.

Scuttlebutt was that within a few days, the midshipmen would board the *Constitution* and sail for new quarters at Newport, Rhode Island, or head south.

About fifty of them had gathered at the old mulberry tree, the only high ground in the middle of the Federal flood. The class leaders had called their mates together—loyal midshipmen and resignees both—to smoke a ceremonial peace pipe under the tree, a final goodbye among friends.

Ethan watched from a distance. But when one of his mates called for him to join the ceremony, he simply waved and hurried toward the gatehouse.

He had not gone far when he heard Tom's voice. "Aren't you smokin' with the boys?"

"It's a little late for peace pipes, I'd say." Ethan put down his duffel bag and offered his hand to his brother.

Tom took it. "You did fine, facin' down that steamer."

"I had a good man to count on."

Over by the gatehouse, the Massachusetts company had formed and the sergeant shouted, "By the twos, quick march!"

Tom said, "You better not be plannin' to go anywhere in the cars. Those Massachusetts boys are headin' up to seize the railhead right now. The Baltimore bully boys burned all the bridges between Baltimore and Washington. That's why this unit came here by boat."

And with the pounding of a hundred pairs of boots, on grass that a day before was worth three demerits to anyone who stepped on it, the Massachusetts men went through the gate.

Ethan patted a pocket of the tan suit he had bought in the haberdashery. "I have money. I'll buy a horse. I should make Stafford Hall tonight."

"Warn Cecil. This'll be a long war. He might make more money plantin' in beans and corn than tobacco."

"I will."

"And, Ethan . . . next time you write with your left hand, don't add that extra little curl on the end of the capital *L*. You've done it since you were a boy."

Ethan gave his half brother a little grin and kept going, right out the gate and up the street behind the Massachusetts men.

In a far corner of the Annapolis and Elkridge railroad yard, Robby Parrish swung a nine-pound hammer as hard as he could and split the coupling on a boxcar. "There you go, Pa."

Dan'l Parrish was prying the hub from every wheel. "They'll never say we didn't do our part, son."

All around them, their friends were swinging hammers and working crowbars. They had decided not to burn the rolling stock because columns of smoke would draw too much attention. But the damage would be just as permanent.

Dan'l Parrish, a director of the Annapolis and Elkridge Railroad, had seen to the destruction of his own line. Behind him were two miles of torn-up track and ruined cars. No Federal troops would reach Washington for days. By then, Virginians would have taken the city, and Lincoln would be in jail.

Now Dunstable Ripley came running into the yard. "Those

Yankees, they're swarmin' 'round the Academy like flies on shit. They'll be here any minute."

"Brush off your clothes, then," said Dan'l to the others, "and we'll march down West Street like we own it."

"Because we do," said Robby.

Alexandra could hear the blue-coated troops pounding past.

She was sitting on her bed, struggling to pull on her riding boots, while down in the barn, one of the house slaves was saddling her horse. If she rode up King George Street, past the old Liberty Tree, and across the Saint John's campus, she might reach the yards before the Federal troops and warn her father and brother. Her second boot was half on when she heard her grandfather shouting, "Hey! Hey! Look up here! Up here, you Yankee sons of bitches!"

She went flopping down the hallway and found the old man at the window above the front door, waving a small flag—three bars of red and white on a field of blue with seven stars. "Go back to where you come from!"

Alexandra grabbed the old man and pulled him back inside.

Federal officers were already coming up the steps, but she could hear her father calling to the Yankees in a voice he normally used only in the presence of women he was trying to charm. At least he was back from the rail yard, thank the Lord.

Alexandra slammed the window and snatched the flag from her grandfather. "You can't fly that in front of Federal troops."

"Then I'll go someplace where I can." He stalked into his bedroom. "Get me my good suit. I'm goin' sellin'."

"Sellin' what?"

"This house. I won't stay a day in an occupied city, by damn. I'll turn the money into Confederate bonds and hunker down at Parrish Manor."

"Get the money in gold, Grandpa," cried Robby Parrish, coming up the stairs, "and hold on to it."

"Did you wreck the railroad?" Alexandra asked.

Robby pushed aside the drapery and looked down into the street. "Those Boston boys are hurryin' for nothin'."

"Good," said Alexandra.

"Bad," said Walter. "It means they'll be in Annapolis longer."

"Wave that flag again, Pa, and they'll be in the *house*." Dan'l pounded up the stairs, sweating heavily after his labors in the rail yard and his fast talk with the Yankees.

"That's why I'm sellin'," said the old man. "Today."

"Sellin'? What kind of foolishness is this?"

"If Maryland stays in Federal hands, it's no foolishness at all," said Robby. "We'll need all the money we can get, just to keep Parrish Manor goin'."

"And even if Maryland don't go out," added old Walter, "I'm helpin' this new Confederacy. If I can't fight, I'll put up the money to let someone else fight."

Robby took out a cigar and struck a match on the window frame, as though losing respect for the house already. "If Ethan's tellin' the truth about a Federal blockade—"

"He didn't lie," Alexandra said, angrily.

"—we can put the money to work backin' a blockade-runner or a commerce-raider. Help the cause and bring in a few prizes, too."

"Prizes?" Dan'l's eyes shifted from his son to his father.

"The men who built this house funded commerce raiders." Robby drew in the cigar smoke. "Some fine fortunes were made back then, and the men who made 'em were considered heroes."

"How much do you reckon we could get for the house?" Dan'l asked Robby.

"Premium price," answered Walter, "if we sell to the Staffords."

"This house means a lot to us," said Alexandra.

"This house doesn't mean near as much as Parrish Manor," said Robby.

"It sure don't." Walter went down the hall. "I'm goin' sellin', to the Staffords."

But one of the Staffords was standing at the front door when they all followed old Walter down the stairs.

"Mornin', Ethan," said Walter pleasantly, as though bad temper should never interfere with good manners.

"What do you want?" demanded Dan'l.

"To know if you have any messages for the overseer at Parrish Manor. I'm leavin' this mornin', and I'd be glad to pass them."

"There's no message I'd trust you with, son." Dan'l stepped in front of Alexandra. "And no daughter, either."

"But if your pa wants to buy this house," said Walter, "I trust his gold."

"I'll tell him, sir, if he ever speaks to me again." Then Ethan said, "I'd like to buy that horse you were offerin' for sale last week."

"Brandy?" Walter smiled. "She was my wife, Hattie's, second favorite. Black Jude was first. I give Black Jude to Lexie, but Brandy's a sweet mare and—"

"We'll sell you the horse," said Dan'l coldly, "if you're usin' it to ride away."

"How much?"

"A hundred dollars," said Dan'l.

"She's worth fifty," said Robby.

"If you're goin' off to fight for the Confederacy," said Walter. "I'll sell her to you for twenty-five."

"I'll show her to you." Alexandra stepped around her father and took Ethan by the hand, to lead him down the hallway.

But her father stuck his big belly in front of them.

"Excuse me, Pa," she said brightly, "but this rebel needs a horse."

"I been up all night, girl, wreckin' a railroad I built with my own money. Don't be testin' me now."

"Aw, Dan'l," said Walter, "step aside. There's rebellion in the air. We can all smell it. And rebellin's all she's doin'."

"Thank you, Grandpa. We're all rebels now, aren't we?" Alexandra kept the tone of her voice carefully bright. "Now, make up the bill of sale, Daddy, while I get Ethan his horse."

For a moment, Dan'l and his daughter stood, staring hard at each other, her face frozen in a smile, his in a frown.

Then Robby mimicked his sister's tone, like a perfect big brother. "Yes, Daddy. Do that."

And Dan'l stalked into the library.

Ethan and Alexandra both knew what would happen when they got to the barn and smelled the hay.

Alexandra, pretending to be all business in riding boots and jacket, led Ethan over to a beautiful chestnut. "Do you like her?"

"Her coat's the color of your hair."

Alexandra snapped her riding crop against her boot, a sound that brought the stable slave from one of the stalls. "Take Brandy out and saddle her."

"Yes'm."

Now she turned back to Ethan, raised both hands to the back of her head, and unpinned her hair. Then she looked at him, as if daring him to swim a fast river.

With a furtive glance back toward the house, Ethan slipped an arm around her waist. She wore no hoops in her skirt, had no corset cinching her waist. "What about your father?"

"He hates the stable." And she kissed him. "He hates it almost as much as he's beginnin' to hate you. But *he's* not goin' off to fight for the Confederacy. He don't deserve a send-off." And with a deft little movement, she pivoted him into an unused stall where the hay was piled high. . . .

When Dan'l Parrish saw Ethan's bare butt and his daughter's riding boots, he did what any father would have done: he grabbed the pitchfork hanging on the wall and gave Ethan a nasty surprise in the ass.

Ethan did what any suitor would. He jumped to his feet, pulled up his pants, and said, "I would like to ask for your daughter's hand in marriage."

And Alexandra popped out of the hay. "Yes!"

"Get out," growled Dan'l. "You betrayed us."

"I did not, sir," Ethan lied.

"And you stole my daughter's virtue."

"I'm sorry," he lied. From all he had heard, one of the Ripley brothers had taken her virtue when they were both thirteen. But he would uphold a lady's honor.

"I won't let you betray her again," said Dan'l.

"I'll make the choice, Pa!" she cried.

"Shut up, you little trollop."

As Ethan moved to her defense, Dan'l pressed the pitchfork against his chest. "Prove that you're loyal to the cause and I may change my mind. Now get on that horse and go, before Robby blasts a hole in you."

Robby had appeared in the door of the barn, behind the barrels of a shotgun. He gave Ethan one of those little winks, as if to say that he wouldn't really shoot.

Ethan was a few miles outside of town in the cornfields that stretched beyond West Street. The warm sun and greening earth did little to assuage the pain he felt in his ass or his heart or his head. He was not going to Stafford Hall. There was no prospect of winning Alexandra by spending the war on a tobacco plantation. And the prospect of joining a nonexistent Confederate navy did not appeal to him, either.

But he had to do something to prove that he was worthy of Lexie Parrish.

And there were better ways than war to get what he wanted. That was becoming clear to him.

With a few subtly written letters, he had stopped a bloodletting in Annapolis. Using one's intelligence was the thing to do. Finding ways to get the right intelligence to the right people mattered, too.

So he wheeled the horse toward Washington.

vi

A New Family for Alexandra

Maryland did not secede. She had too many Unionists, too much border to the north, and within a few weeks, too many Federal troops sent by Lincoln to ensure her loyalty.

And most of the troops, it seemed to Dan'l Parrish, were in Annapolis. So he did not stand in the way of his father's sale to the Staffords.

For the second time, the Parrishes left a house they loved, in a capital they had grown to hate, and went home to the Patuxent. But they knew little of the bitterness that Rebecca Parrish had carried with her, perhaps because they also carried $2,000 in Stafford gold.

In addition to the gold, Tom Stafford had agreed to pay an eight-thousand-dollar mortgage to Walter Parrish at an exorbitant rate of eight percent, the figure pegged to the interest rate on the

Confederate bond. But that did not matter to Tom, because he wanted the house, and in those uncertain times, no bank was going to write a mortgage for any man going into battle.

What Tom did not know was that his gold would help Robby Parrish to fund a Confederate blockade-runner, while the monthly payments would keep Parrish Manor afloat. The Fine Folly became the Parrishes' hedge against disaster and gave them capital to venture on the opportunities that disaster sometimes brought.

The first disaster befell the North.

In July, some thirty miles southwest of Washington, Confederate forces overwhelmed Federal troops at Manassas, driving them back across a stream called Bull Run and sending them stumbling in panic toward Washington. A gentle shove and the capital would have fallen. Fortunately for the North, the Confederates did not know this.

Jason Stafford did, however, and he decided it was time to move his wife, George's wife, Eve, and his little grandson, Jacob, to the relative safety of Annapolis. So it was that a few weeks later, the Staffords stood again before the Fine Folly.

The sun was high and blindingly hot; horses keeled over; dogs snapped at their tails and even the fence posts seemed to sweat in the humidity: summer on the Chesapeake. But Jason knew that there were places in that old house that kept their coolness on the hottest day, and he meant to find them again, and lose himself in memories that might make the present more palatable.

The nation he served was sundered. His youngest son had disappeared among the sunderers. His middle son, now on blockade duty, had lost his reputation at Gosport. Only the eldest, who now served in the Navy Department, had remained a Stafford rock.

Beside Jason and Tom, Margaret stared at the brick facade. She had grown more morose by the week, although Jason suspected that a letter from her Confederate son would restore her mood.

Eve, a hollow-eyed girl whose year of marriage had included a mere three weeks with her husband, did not seem much interested in her new home, perhaps because her baby was squalling and plucking at her blouse.

But Antonia, who was moving in with them, could not wait to get inside. She snatched the key from Tom and hurried up the steps, calling for the rest of them to follow her.

The echo of the women's voices in the hallway made them sound more cheerful than they were. Margaret said she should see the kitchen. Antonia wanted to sit once more in the dining room where Jefferson had sat. Eve simply asked for a place to sit herself. And in the midst of it all, the two men stood silent, old Jason feeling the cool embrace of his ancestors, Tom surveying his purchase with the pride of a man who knew that he had bought well.

Then they saw her. She was standing at the end of the hall, a shadow in the light pouring through the French doors.

"Alexandra?" said Tom.

She took a few steps toward them.

And Jason's good feelings flowed out of him. "What do you want?"

"My father says I can't live at Parrish Manor if I intend to marry Ethan."

"*Marry* Ethan?" said Margaret.

"Marry my son?" said Jason.

"I love him, even if my father thinks he's a Yankee spy."

"Yankee spy?" Margaret looked at Jason.

"Her father was a fool to let this house be sold," said Jason, "and he's a fool to think Ethan is anything but a confused boy."

"I agree." Alexandra stopped sniffling. "Though I'd prefer if you just said my father was merely *misled* . . . not a fool."

"A misled fool," grunted Jason. "Now, what makes you think we want you to live with us?"

"I love your son as much as you do."

"I'm not sure I love him at all," said Jason coldly.

"Pa . . ." Tom chided the old man.

As if it was all too much for her to comprehend, Margaret pulled off her sunbonnet and lowered herself onto the chair by the dining room door.

"Well, dearie," said Antonia, putting her hands on her hips, "if you want to live here, you'll have to work."

"Yes, ma'am."

"We'll be working with the hospital that the army's starting on the Academy grounds."

Alexandra's eyes opened wide and she looked at Margaret. "Nursin' Yankees, when your own son has gone south?"

"If we don't care for other women's sons," said Margaret sadly, "who'll care for ours?"

"I s'pose I don't know." Alexandra folded her hands in front of her and looked down at the floor. "I'm just hopin' you'll take me in."

"If my son loves you, you're welcome here." Margaret rose, wearing her weight as though it were a wet wool dress. "Isn't she, Captain?"

After a moment, Jason grumbled, "If you lured my son into going south, maybe you owe the North a bit of service."

And Margaret offered Alexandra her hand. "You must know a great deal about this house, dear. Won't you show it to us?"

Alexandra looked at the outstretched hand, at the women, and she dabbed back a tear. "Work and a place to sleep . . . they're a great kindness."

"Work *for* a place to sleep," Antonia corrected.

Margaret put her arms around Alexandra, and, as if the tears were contagious, began to cry herself. "We must not forget our kindness."

Jason hated teary women, especially those who could go teary on demand. So he went down the hall to the French doors and looked out at the overgrown garden. Beyond it, soldiers were drilling on the Academy grounds. The cadence of their drums rumbled through the muffling humidity. The dust of their marching drifted in the air.

Soon the women went off with their tears and opinions, leaving Jason and Tom alone in the cool hallway.

"So," said Jason in the sudden silence, "you now own something concrete."

"Every man wants to leave something behind," said Tom. "Even a man married to the navy."

"The navy's a fickle mistress. Find a real wife. Have a family. It's not too late."

"We're in a war, Pa." Tom fingered a crack in one of the panes of glass in the door. "Who knows who'll survive, especially if we have to use wooden ships to fight Confederate ironclads?"

The word "ironclad" struck the Staffords like a knife whenever anyone uttered it, because they felt responsible for the ironclad the South now was building. If George had been able to persuade McCauley to save the *Merrimack*, the big frigate would not have been scuttled and burned to the waterline; her salvaged hull and engines would not now sit in the Gosport drydock where Confederate workmen built an iron-plated superstructure on her cut-down hull.

Responsibility was a terrible thing to those who were willing to take it.

And taking it was part of standing where God put you.

Ever since news had arrived of the *Merrimack* refit, Jason and Tom Stafford had been trying to convince the Navy Department that a single Confederate ironclad could sink all of the wooden blockade ships in Hampton Roads, and that they should be building an ironclad to meet the threat. Many agreed. Others called the idea of iron ships a humbug. And someone actually said that since iron sank, what purpose could there be in building iron ships?

But Secretary of the Navy Gideon Welles was a methodical man, given to doing things in a methodical way, so he had finally appointed an Ironclad Board, named Lieutenant Tom Stafford as secretary, and set them to writing a report.

And all the while, the Confederates were bolting iron plates onto the *Merrimack*.

"The rebels build out of necessity," said Jason. "They can't waste time writing reports."

"Neither can we," said Tom.

"Then write quickly."

vii
Letters to Annapolis

He did, and by October, a Federal ironclad was under construction at Greenpoint just up the East River from the Brooklyn Navy Yard.

Her builder—a hard-featured man of engineering genius and execrable personality named John Ericsson—had promised that he could deliver this vessel in one hundred days for the sum of $275,000. He called it the *Monitor* because it would watch over the Confederates and correct their errant conduct, as a good monitor should.

By late November, the Navy Department was sending cables almost daily to check on progress of the *Monitor*, and in early December, they sent Lieutenant Tom Stafford to Brooklyn to make an eyewitness report.

"'An amazing thing,'" Tom wrote to his father, "'with almost no freeboard and little draft. It resembles a raft topped with a tower that will allow two guns to pivot and fire over a range of 360 degrees. This tower, or turret, is driven by steam engines and should prove a devastating weapon.'"

On a sleeting Sunday afternoon, Jason read this letter at the dinner table in the Fine Folly. Reading letters from his sons—or at least from the pair who wrote—was now part of his Sunday routine.

During the week, he stayed in monastic quarters at the Washington Navy Yard and worked long hours at the War Department. On Saturdays he rode the train to Annapolis, slept in the great house of his boyhood, worshiped with the women at Saint Anne's, and after a Sunday dinner, to which several wounded men from the U.S. Army General Hospital, Division Number One, were always invited, he returned to Washington for another week of saving the Union.

He read on. "'I asked Ericsson if he still thought he could deliver the *Monitor* in a hundred days, and he laughed in my face. I did not know if I had asked him to do the impossible or had insulted him. Clearly it was the latter, as he promised he would have the hull in the water by the end of January, and ready for action a month later.'"

Jason looked at the faces around his table, which this evening included two officers wounded at Ball's Bluff. One was bandaged about the head. The other spent much of the evening staring forlornly at the stump protruding from his sleeve. But the hovering of the women and the happy gurglings of little Jacob raised their spirits, as they did for all the wounded who came through the Stafford doors.

"This letter is good news," said the one with the bandaged head.

"It surely is," answered Jason. "With luck, we'll be able to meet whatever threat the *Merrimack* is going to present when she comes out."

"Perhaps we should tell the men in hospital," said Alexandra.

"Yes," added Antonia cheerily. "It might bring a little optimism."

"No. Soldiers talk too much." Then Jason added, in deference to the two at his table, "Only officers can be trusted with such information."

The next day, Alexandra told Antonia that she was going to Baltimore to see her aunt. Instead, she bought a ticket for Washington, and an hour and a half later she entered the city that seemed, in the continuing sleet, the most frightened place on earth. A ring of defensive earthworks and forts had tightened around the city, and the steel spindle that pierced the unfinished Capitol dome now looked like a giant rusting nail.

Alexandra made her way through the muddy streets to number 541 H Street, a narrow brick boardinghouse painted a fading Confederate gray.

The door was answered by Mary Surratt, a buxom woman in her forties, with close-together eyes and a calm expression. She did not seem surprised that Alexandra asked for a man named George Thomas. In a city as full of intrigue as this one, it was not unusual for gentlemen to receive female callers at all times of the day or night.

"I'll see if he's in," said Mrs. Surratt.

The parlor was small, papered in an ugly brown pattern, and dominated by an upright piano that swallowed whatever light seeped through the drawn drapes.

Alexandra sat on the settee and waited, hoping that he was not off eavesdropping on conversations at Willard's or masquerading as a worker in the navy yard, right under his father's nose, and making notes on the things that went on there. Then she heard his familiar tread on the staircase.

The man known now as George Thomas seemed bigger than the last time she had seen him. His beard had filled in. His black hair was shoulder length. He wore a blue suit that made him look like another Washington war contractor, come to feed at the public trough, a good costume for the lobby at Willard's. And he did not seem at all surprised to see her. Without a word of affection, he said, "What's wrong?"

Alexandra's eyes shifted to the housekeeper, who, with a deferential bow of the head, closed the French doors that separated her parlor from the foyer.

Then Alexandra went to him and threw herself into his arms. "Ethan, I've missed you."

"It's dangerous for you to come here."

"I have news of the Federal ironclad." She looked into his eyes for some sign of affection, but saw only tension.

"Where from?" he asked.

"A letter from your brother. Your father read it at dinner last night."

"He mustn't consider the information secret, then, but I'll pass it on."

"The *Monitor*—that's its name—will be launched on January 30."

Ethan went to the window and peered through the curtains, came back to her, stroked his beard.

"What's wrong, Ethan? I thought you'd be happy to see me."

"I've been ordered into uniform. Someone in Richmond saw my gunnery grades."

"You don't have to go, Ethan."

"What would your father say if I deserted while you're spyin' and your brother's runnin' the blockade to supply the South?"

"If I love you, Ethan, my father's got nothin' to say."

"What would *my* father say, if all I did in this war was spy on him?"

viii
The Day an Age Ended

It was a Sunday morning, March 9. The crisis was at hand, and Jason Stafford had remained in Washington.

Union spies in Norfolk had been feeding intelligence for days: The *Merrimack*, clad in iron and rechristened the *Virginia*, had been armed with six nine-inch Dahlgrens and four deadly Brooke rifles. She had taken on crew and coal. She had gotten up steam. And she had been placed under command of Franklin Buchanan, the first superintendent of the Naval Academy, a Marylander with a nose like the beak of a hawk and the personality to match.

"Old Buck's a good officer," said John Dahlgren, commandant of the Washington Navy Yard, as he and Jason Stafford started the day in his office.

"That's the pity of this damned war." Jason wrapped his hands around a mug of coffee and let the warmth seep into his palms. Spring was coming, but it was still winter-cold in Jason's belly. "Good officers turned away . . . sons gone over . . . sons forced to prove themselves after failure . . ."

"George is with Farragut, isn't he?" asked Dahlgren.

"Little Davy Farragut of the *Essex*, all grown up, wondering how to fight his way up the Mississippi, with my hard-drinking son as his assistant engineer."

"If I'd been with McCauley," said Dahlgren, "*I'd* have been drinking too."

Jason liked Dahlgren. It seemed that everybody in Washington did. Some liked him because he was friendly but never played the hail-fellow. Jason liked him because he was navy and because he was smart. One look at the high forehead, the hard line of brow drawn parallel to the mustache, and Dahlgren's intelligence was imprinted on a man's mind like a watermark.

But Jason had not yet forgiven his son's failure. "It was dereliction. George was drunk the day they scuttled the *Merrimack*. Dereliction."

"What of Ethan?"

"A letter to Alexandra got through." Jason stared down the Potomac. "When Old Buck went down the list of lieutenants and saw that my third son was Academy, and a Marylander to boot, and could put a howitzer shell through a porthole at half a mile, he picked him for the *Merrimack*."

"Then he and Tom will be shooting at each other."

"If the *Monitor* gets to Hampton Roads in time."

There was a timid knock and a lieutenant came into the room. "Excuse me, sir, but there's a gentleman to see you."

"Who?"

"He asked that his name not be announced, sir."

"Well, send him in."

"He's out at the gate, sir. He wishes that both of you come down. It's . . . it's the president, sir."

A black carriage stood at the gate on M Street. It looked like a hearse. The man inside looked like an undertaker, or perhaps like the corpse itself.

"Mr. President?" said Dahlgren.

"I have frightful news." Lincoln told them to get in.

"Panic" was the only word to describe the White House cabinet room.

The *Merrimack* had come out the previous day, and in one awesome display, she had rammed and sunk the *Cumberland*, blown up the *Congress*, and run her former sister ship, the mighty *Minnesota*, onto a mudflat. She had been hit dozens of times, but by all accounts, every Union shot had bounced off her shell.

Now Gideon Welles sat with his arms folded and his beard set at a pugnacious angle while the rest of Lincoln's secretaries raged around him.

The most enraged of all was Edwin Stanton, secretary of war. "Yesterday was the single worst day in the navy's history. Three ships. Two hundred and eighty officers and men—"

"I am aware of the figures," Welles answered stonily.

"And what do we have to keep this *Merrimack* from—" Stanton stopped abruptly when the president and two naval officers entered the room.

"I'd hoped Father Mars would wait until I was back before assailing Father Neptune." Lincoln used his nicknames for the secretaries of war and navy.

Welles stood. "It's the secretary's job to take what criticism comes his way, sir."

"Or let it hit someone else," cracked Lincoln. "So I've brought Captains Dahlgren and Stafford. Let them draw some of the fire."

"Ah, yes," said Stanton, "the father of the modern cannon and the father of the man who failed to save the *Merrimack.*"

Jason did not like Stanton, and now he remembered why.

Stanton, an irascible pouter pigeon of a man whose chest-length beard and shaved upper lip gave him the look of a Mennonite prophet in rimless spectacles, was known to refer to Lincoln behind his back as a fool.

Lincoln did not seem bothered. Some thought this reflected his Machiavellian knowledge of politics: keep your friends close but your enemies closer. Others thought it reflected his utter lack of pride, because whenever he heard that Stanton was calling him a fool, he would nod and say, "Then it must be true, for the secretary is generally right."

Jason would never have stood for such insubordination, but he was coming to appreciate Lincoln's manner of leadership. If a man did his job with the honesty and decisiveness that Stanton ordinarily demonstrated, Lincoln could ignore his shortcomings.

Jason was also coming to appreciate Lincoln's manner of manhood. It had only been two weeks since his eleven-year-old son Willie had died of fever, and yet the president soldiered on, despite the black band on his arm and the grief-stricken madness of his wife. He had even taken time to request that Congress appropriate money to finish the Capitol dome, for it was too strong a symbol of union to remain unfinished.

Jason would never be the folksy quipster Lincoln was, but he could control his anger and soldier on, too. So he said, with polite reserve, "I would remind the secretary that once my son had the engines turning on the *Merrimack*, his duty in saving her was done."

"Since you're such an expert on duty, then," answered Stanton, "perhaps you can tell me whose duty it is now to save Washington."

"*Save* Washington?"

"This *Merrimack* has changed the whole character of the war." Stanton pulled back a green velvet drape, revealing the river, like a ribbon of silver in the morning light. "Once she destroys the squadron at Hampton Roads, she can steam right up the Potomac. Why, we could have a cannonball from one of her guns in the White House before we leave this room. She could shell the Capitol, disperse Congress itself—"

"I like that last part," said Lincoln.

"And then," Stanton continued, oblivious to the president's joke, "she'll steam up the coast and lay waste to New York and Boston. What do we tell the people of those cities? What do we *tell* them?"

"We tell them not to worry," said John Dahlgren calmly, "because the *Merrimack* will never even make it up the Potomac."

"Thank you, Captain," said Welles, "I've been telling them that. But they do not wish to believe me."

Secretary of State Seward, small and rumpled, sat at the end of the table, sucking on his cigar. "I *wish* to believe you, Gideon. I also wish the *Cumberland* and *Congress* and *Minnesota* were still afloat. Wishing will not make it so."

"But simple science will, sir," said Dahlgren.

When Dahlgren spoke scientifically, men listened. After all, he had built the most powerful cannon yet . . . scientifically. He was a man Lincoln respected.

The president cocked an eyebrow at Dahlgren. "*Simple* science?"

"The *Merrimack* draws twenty-two feet. The depth of the Potomac near Washington is less than twenty. Simple science, sir, even simpler mathematics."

"I like things simple," said Lincoln.

"Well, I demand that we give simple science a little assistance," said Stanton, refusing to let go of his anger, like a dog with an old shoe. "I propose that we fill canal boats with rocks and sink them in the Potomac as obstacles."

"Now, before we waste a lot of good rocks," said Lincoln, "maybe we should see what happens down at Hampton Roads."

"Yes. Hampton Roads." Stanton moved away from the window so that Lincoln's height would not dwarf his emotions. "Can Secretary Welles tell us what we have to stop the *Merrimack*?"

"The *Monitor*," answered Gideon Welles.

"Ericsson's Folly, you mean," said Stanton.

"She's no folly, sir," said Jason, who stood stiffly at the head of the conference table, with his officer's hat tucked under his arm.

"How many guns does she carry?" demanded Stanton.

"Two, sir," said Jason.

"Two?" Stanton looked at the president, then at Welles, with an expression of incredulity—total, contemptuous, histrionic incredulity—pulled from his lawyer's bag of faces. "*Two* guns to meet *ten*?"

"The *Monitor*'s guns are in a turret, sir," said Jason. "A tower that turns."

"And where is this *Monitor* now?"

With a small flourish, Welles held up the telegram he had just received. "Hampton Roads. She arrived last night. And I have every confidence in her, especially as Captain Stafford's eldest son is her executive officer."

Jason did not add that his youngest son was a lieutenant aboard the *Merrimack,* but Ethan probably called it by its new name, the *Virginia*.

Ethan Stafford listened to the thump of her engines and wondered if the *Virginia* might end the war by herself.

In that he was not alone.

Before steaming out the previous day, Buchanan had read his officers a letter from Confederate Navy Secretary Stephen Mallory. It suggested that once the blockade was broken, the *Virginia* could steam to New York, set the Brooklyn Navy Yard aflame, lay Manhattan under shellfire, and set the bankers fleeing—a massive crisis created by a single ship. "Such an event," Mallory had written, "would do more to achieve our immediate independence than would the results of many campaigns."

"We're too top-heavy for the open ocean," Buchanan had told his officers. "Just remember the hope your country has pinned on us today, and do your duty."

Buchanan was wounded the first day, and command had passed to Lieutenant Catesby ap Roger Jones, a serious and efficient man with more names than a small family. But Buchanan's fighting spirit was still aboard.

If they could open Hampton Roads, they would not need to attack New York, because the war would take a new turn right in the four-mile-wide channel. Hampton Roads was the keyhole of the tidewater. There met rivers from the south and the north—the Elizabeth and Nansemond, the James, and the Chesapeake, bringing the waters of the Susquehanna, the Patuxent, the Potomac, and a thousand smaller streams. And Federal ships had locked it up tight.

Today the *Virginia* would destroy the grounded *Minnesota.* Then she would turn on the *Roanoke*, the *Saint Lawrence*, and Federal Fortress Monroe, which dominated the roads. Then Virginia's door would open and the English and French would sail in with the materials of war and sail out with southern cotton. And Ethan would be glad to have been here. So long as he did not vomit.

As captain of the seven-inch Brooke rifles mounted at the bow, he had drilled dozens of shots into the Federal ships and killed dozens of men the day before. But he was not thinking about that now, because even with the ironclad casemate protecting them, this would be no turkey shoot.

That casemate reminded Ethan of the loft of the devil's barn—a hundred seventy feet long, ten feet high, with sloping sides to deflect cannonballs, three grates in the flat roof providing the only ventilation, and a smokestack running up through the middle, radiating the heat and the noise of the engines below.

If this was the future of naval life, rather than the sunshine and wind that played across his father's memories, Ethan would gladly go back to spying. He took off his black officer's hat and mopped the sweat from the band, then straightened the uniform—gray with black piping to match the hat—that still seemed stranger than a blue jacket or the nondescript clothes of a spy.

About a mile from the grounded *Minnesota*, Ethan was given permission to open fire. He stuffed pieces of cotton lint into his ears. Then he ran out the Brooke rifle and delivered a shot that exploded in the air a hundred yards beyond the frigate. He held his breath against the stink of the gunpowder, which always made him retch, and he recalculated fusing, elevation, and the speed of his vessel, as though this were a classroom problem.

His second shot struck the water just astern of *Minnesota* and he muttered, "Better . . . better . . . Tom would give me a B-minus."

His calculations for a third shot were interrupted by an inaccurate broadside from the crippled *Minnesota*. Then one of the gunners cried, "What's that thing comin' out from behind the *Minnesota*?"

Ethan peered out the starboard gunport, and a new fear, like a shard of ice, struck through the film of sweat that covered him.

A little gray mass of metal was making steam, coming straight at them.

"It looks like a big cheese box on a raft," said Midshipman Morris, the seventeen-year-old captain of Dahlgren number one.

"It's for certain a raft," said a gunner from the Norfolk United Artillery named Doolin. "Mebbe she's takin' off one *Minnesota*'s boilers to lighten her."

"She's no raft, and that's no boiler," said Ethan. "She's the *Monitor.*"

Doolin spat a stream of tobacco out the port. "Damn, but she looks funny."

"That's what the Yankees must've said when we came out yesterday," answered Ethan. "A barn roof ridin' on the hull of a steam frigate."

"This *Monitor* weren't here yesterday," said Midshipman Morris.

"She's here now." Ethan cocked his head and listened to the engines.

The *Virginia* was not ready for this. Her stack had been shot to pieces the day before, reducing the draft on her boiler fires, so her best speed was a mere four knots. Her ram had broken off in the *Cumberland*. And she carried no solid shot to batter an ironclad, because exploding shot did more damage to wooden ships.

Above the sound of the engines, Ethan heard the report of cannon fire—two quick shots, followed by two fountains of water a few hundred yards ahead of the *Virginia*.

"Look at that turret thing," said Morris. "It's movin'. What's it doin'?"

"Turnin' away," said Ethan. "So they can reload while they steam closer."

A messenger rushed forward from the little platform where Catesby ap Roger Jones was commanding the ship. "Skipper says he plans to hold her to starboard by a hundred yards. Fire on your order, sir."

A day before, it would have been ap Jones who ordered the firing. Now it was in the hands of an Academy lieutenant who had never wished to attend the Academy and who now wished, with every second, that he were a little farther away rather than a little closer to the infernal contraption steaming toward them. But this was where Ethan had been put. So this was where he would have to stand, at least for now. "Prepare to fire. On my order!"

Within a few minutes of steaming, the two ships were abeam, but the turret of the *Monitor* remained turned, like a man who refused to fight.

"What are they waitin' for?" asked Morris.

"For us to fire first," said Ethan. "Well . . . we got more guns. *Fire!*"

And the side of the *Virginia* erupted.

The concussion of shells exploding against the *Monitor*'s turret knocked three men senseless and slammed Lieutenant Tom Stafford against the side.

But no one could fall far, because that twenty-foot cylinder of iron was cramped and dark and pumped full of compressed terror. Two Dahlgren cannons, looking like great black bulls yoked together, took up most of the space. Eight men crowded around each gun. Two officers commanded. And none of them had ever known anything like this.

Tom Stafford's head felt as if it were in a tin bucket that someone was beating with a ball peen hammer, but he kept his senses and shouted, "Damage?"

And the voices around him reported. "No sprung bolts, sir. . . . Nuts all tight, sir. . . . No cracks. . . . No dents. . . . No light leakin' in where it shouldn't be, sir!"

"Then we're a fightin' ship!" he cried, trying to restrain the elation that any man would have felt after eight layers of inch-thick iron plate had just protected him from a point-blank broadside. "Report the guns."

"Loaded and ready, sir!" shouted the seaman who commanded the gun crews on the two big eleven-inch Dahlgrens.

"We know her sides'll take a shot," shouted Tom. "Let's see if the turret still turns."

The engineer turned the handwheel attached to a rocker near the roof. The rocker connected to a valve that controlled the flow of steam into a little engine beneath the turret. Turn the wheel, and the turret turned with it, at least in theory. But the *Monitor* had been rushed through construction, rushed down the coast, rushed into battle. Under the best of circumstances, some things did not work in a new vessel, and this one contained over forty new inventions, including the turret. If it did not turn, they were defenseless.

Then, over the pounding of the engines and the ringing in his ears, Tom heard the steam hissing into the machinery below. The eight-foot traversing gear gave a jolt, the turret was moving—counter-clockwise, as ordered.

The sailors in the turret cheered. The sailors laboring in the semi-darkness below heard the cheering, and they cheered, too.

Tom Stafford put his eye to the viewing slit, and the great gray mass of the *Virginia* appeared, churning through the gunsmoke and spray like some monstrous whale that he meant to harpoon. And for just an instant, it struck him: he was where he had always hoped to find himself, at the center of the war, where his naval mistress could satisfy him at last.

"Trice up gunport number one," he shouted. "Quickly."

And a shaft of sunlight shot into the turret.

There was not room for two guns to recoil at once, so they were fired in sequence, and neither gun port was kept open an instant longer than necessary, because the snipers on the *Virginia* started shooting as soon as they had a target.

"Fire!"

The sound of the explosion inside the turret was a physical thing. It had weight. It had heat. And it felt as if it were crushing the bones inside their heads.

"Number two. Open."

One shaft of light disappeared as another cut into the thick smoke.

A handler at the number one gun, a little Irishman named Malloy, now began to scream, "Don't fire! Don't fire!"

"What is it?" asked the boatswain's mate.

"Me skull . . . Me skull . . ." Malloy raised his hands to his head and pulled the edges of his porkpie down around his ears. "It feels like it's about to bust."

"Ignore him," cried Tom Stafford. *"Fire!"*

This time Tom was not so surprised by the jolt of the gun. This time he kept his eye to the viewing slit to see the impact of the shot. And he was stunned.

The 180-pound ball smashed into the starboard quarter of the

Confederate ship and glanced upward, shooting into the air and leaving no more than a dent.

"Goddamn," he said to no one in particular. "Turn the turret one hundred eighty degrees. Gun captains, reload."

As the floor began to move, Malloy cried, "Me head. Now it's spinnin' . . . spinnin' so fast it may screw off if it don't burst."

"Boatswain!" cried Tom. "Get that man below."

The turret stopped with a jerk above the hatch, and as Malloy tumbled down, a messenger from the pilothouse shouted up: "Lieutenant Worden means to run up on her port quarter, sir. He orders that you hold fire until you have a clean shot."

"Clean shot. Aye!"

And on it went. Sometimes the vessels were far apart. Sometimes they almost touched. Sometimes they ran fast. Sometimes they ran aground on the shallows and reefs surrounding the deep channel. But for hour after hour, in bright March sunshine and swirling smoke, they slammed away at each other.

One was small and nimble, all but invisible when a cloud rolled its shadow over the scene. The other was an armor-plated elephant, lumbering in the sea. But the truth was that, on that particular day, each was facing the only vessel on earth that could stop the other.

Some men were deafened by the cannon blasts, others knocked senseless by the concussion of shells. And every face was covered with the sweat and grime of battle. But the *Virginia* was not able to get around the little *Monitor* and run at the *Minnesota*.

Now, after three hours, the *Monitor* was coming straight at the *Virginia.*

"She's gonna ram us!" cried Midshipman Morris.

"She doesn't have the angle," answered Ethan.

"What should we do, sir?" cried Doolin.

Ethan peered out the port. The *Monitor* was pushing a white bow wave before it as the turret swung into position. But it was not the turret that controlled her. It was the little pilothouse protruding five feet above the deck line, right at the bow.

"What do we do?" cried the midshipman.

"We blow her damn brains out. Ready the rifle. Depress to thirty degrees. Aim for the pilothouse and wait for my order!"

In the turret of the *Monitor*, Tom Stafford ordered another one-two blast, with the same ineffectual result as all the others. Then he dropped down the ladder. It took seven minutes to reload the big Dahlgrens. By the time he had gone forward to confer with Lieutenant Worden, the guns would be ready and he would be back at his station.

He raced through the smoke-choked semidarkness on the main deck, past the officers' staterooms, through the wardroom and the captain's living room to the ladder that led to the pilothouse: a four-by-five-foot armored box . . . a wheel . . . a helmsman . . . Lieutenant John Worden, eyes pressed against the half-inch viewing slit that was the only opening to the outside. A miraculous little vessel, thought Tom, but a miserable thing, too.

"Lieutenant!" he cried.

Worden held up his hand. He would not be interrupted on the ramming run.

But from his angle in the turret, Tom had seen things that Worden might have missed. "Her bow is unarmored, John. And she's burned so much coal that her draft's lightened. The bow is rising. Ram her there and—"

"I'm trying. But this damn steering . . ." Worden shouted at the helmsman, "Another ten degrees to port. You *must* give me ten degrees."

"I'm tryin', sir, but like you say, this damn steerin'—"

The steering was another of the new devices that worked badly, if at all.

"Christ almighty!" cried Worden. "We're going to miss."

"They're going to miss!" cried Morris.

"But we're not," answered Ethan. He checked the sighting on the big rifled gun, then stepped back with the firing lanyard firmly in his fingers.

The *Monitor* was passing directly ahead, not thirty yards from his muzzle.

He waited . . . he waited . . . and *now!* He pulled the lanyard. The trigger sent a spark into the chamber of the gun. There was a tremendous report . . .

. . . And all in a second, Tom Stafford heard the sound of a Brooke rifle, the screaming shriek of a shell, and saw the flash against the viewing slit.

The helmsman spun the wheel hard away from the *Virginia.*

And Worden staggered, then fell halfway down the hatch before one of the messengers below managed to catch him. "My eyes!" he cried. "My eyes! I'm blind. Goddamn! I'm blind."

Smoke and sulfur were forced through the viewing slit, choking the little space.

"Get the surgeon!" cried Tom to the messenger.

"Never mind the surgeon!" Worden's face was blackened and covered with blood. Smoke curled from his chest-length beard, and he held his palms to his eye sockets as though trying to keep the eyes from bursting out of his head. But he somehow kept the control in his voice. "Take command. Save the *Minnesota.*"

The turning point of the battle had come, but so had the turning of the tide.

The *Minnesota* lay exposed. The *Virginia* was steaming straight at her. And the *Monitor* was rushing back into the action. Tom Stafford was calling frantically for more steam, for more speed to save the grounded frigate, when suddenly, the *Virginia* swung away.

There was simply not enough water for the Confederate ironclad to maneuver. Like one fighter spitting at another, she delivered a final shot that exploded in the air above her opponent, then she found the channel and went steaming back toward the Elizabeth River.

And it was over, as quickly as that, the issue decided not by man's machinery but by a six-hour cycle as old as time.

The newspapers called it a draw, though Hampton Roads remained closed. One thing was certain: no one would say the Staffords did not stand where God put them that day.

ix
More Letters

The enormity of the nation's cataclysm became clear that April, when Confederates attacked Federal troops at a place called Shiloh, in Tennessee. More men fell in two days of fighting than in all of the wars America had ever fought. And it was only just beginning.

U.S.A. General Hospital, Division Number One, at Annapolis was soon receiving patients by land and water. When the hospitals of Washington overflowed, railway cars carried the wounded east on the Annapolis and Elkridge line. When General McClellan's Army of the Potomac went into action on the Virginia peninsula, steamers carried the wounded down the James and York rivers, then up the Chesapeake.

And the Stafford women did what they could.

At first, the Surgeons' Corps did not welcome the assistance of any women, particularly those who had not been approved by the Army Medical Bureau's Superintendent of Female Nurses. Worse yet, the Stafford women lived in a town that was still considered secessionist in its sympathies.

But Antonia had organized an Annapolis chapter of the United States Sanitary Commission, which Lincoln had approved the previous summer. The Sanitary, as it was called, maintained a salaried male staff to inspect the cleanliness of hospitals and camps. And they were supported by a volunteer force of women, who raised money and collected whatever the soldiers needed, from dry socks to hard candy, then distributed these and whatever care they could offer.

Antonia and Margaret willingly washed wounds, changed dressings, spread ointment on burned flesh. They looked into eyes that were sometimes frightened, sometimes vacant, sometimes filled with thanks. But no matter what, they considered their own sons and did the dirty work of nursing.

The younger women approached their service more reluctantly.

For Alexandra, there was no middle ground between the polite reserve of the parlor and the intimacy of the hayloft. And she could not grow used to what she saw and smelled in a military hospital. So she stayed at the Fine Folly and made herself a kind of quartermaster for the Sanitary.

When contributions came to Annapolis, she cataloged them and stored them in the great room of the Fine Folly: socks in one corner, shirts in another, five hundred decks of playing cards in boxes; baked goods and candies and chewing tobacco, too. And for the enrichment of the men's minds, bookcases filled with Shakespeare and Dickens, and the memoirs of a woman named Hill.

As the war worsened, more medicines came through the Sanitary chapter, purchased directly to supplement the governmental supplies—laudanum, chloroform, unguents, quinine. And Alexandra cataloged them, too.

George's wife, Eve, began visiting the hospital on afternoons when she could leave little Jacob. She would go through Stribling Row, mopping fevered brows, washing faces, shaving men who could not shave themselves. And then she would read to them, like the good schoolmistress she once had been. Sometimes they had letters from home, sometimes newspapers or novels, and if there was nothing else, Eve would read letters from her husband. The wounded men always seemed happy to hear whatever she read, or happy, more likely, to hear a female voice.

George's most dramatic letter arrived on a Thursday.

Aboard the steam sloop *Hartford*, May 1, 1862

My Darling Eve,

I have sailed through the heart of hell and come out the other side.

At 2:00 A.M. on April 24, the sixty-year-old flag officer that Pa still calls "little Davy Farragut" climbed into the mizzen rigging of the *Hartford,* gave a signal, and twenty ships steamed up the Mississippi toward New Orleans. Farragut's stepbrother, David Dixon Porter, the natural son of Pa's old cap, had softened the forts that guard the river by firing—if you can believe this—seventeen thousand mortar rounds at them in six days.

Well, those forts must have been made of rock, for when our vessels appeared in the moonlight, the forts sent forth such cannon fire as Beelzebub could not conjure. Fortunately, the thick smoke that soon settled over the river made it harder for the gunners to see us. But it also made it harder for us to see ahead, and after running the gauntlet of the forts, we ran right aground.

Thank God that Farragut had draped anchor chains over our sides, as they protected against the shots that hit us. But Lord, we were stuck.

Mark you, I was in the engine room during all this. Summoned topside, I was struck by the color of the sky—red-orange dancing amid sheets of smoky shadow—the color accompanied by a continuous roar of cannon fire, screaming, and explosions. It was enough to make a man give up the drink.

The rebs had run a fire raft in under our port quarter, and flames were leaping halfway up the mizzen. Farragut shouted orders, stamped his foot, and growled, "My God, is it to end this way?"

I said, with more bravado than I felt, "Not if I can help it, sir."

He turned steel-tipped eyes to me and demanded more steam.

I said we were stoking more coal, adding resin to the fires, and opening all valves to raise our steam pressure.

Suddenly a shell exploded about thirty feet above our heads. Farragut did not even blink. But I tell you, Evie, I almost wet myself. That is the difference between a fearless commander and an engineer, or perhaps the difference between a man of sixty and one of thirty-two whose wife and child await him.

By the grace of God, we put out that fire and got up enough steam to back the *Hartford* out of the mud. By dawn, seventeen of our ships had run the forts and were steaming up to the city itself. We've tied off the main artery of the Confederacy. Now watch it die.

And the best news: I have requested transfer to one of the Atlantic blockading squadrons, where I may be closer to home and perhaps to your heart. I think of you always, and of little Jacob. Write with news when you can.

This letter was read often in the following weeks, and the wounded men never ceased to enjoy it.

"They like it because it is so vivid," said Eve proudly.

She and the other women were in the great room, which they now called the supply depot. They were folding one-piece sets of long underwear which arrived, with perfect timing, in late May.

"They like the letter because it shows a leader losing his nerve," said Alexandra.

"That's why you like it," muttered Iris Ezekiel, holding up a pair of underwear.

Alexandra kept her eyes on her folding. "Whatever are you implyin'?"

"That you would like to see all our Union leaders lose their nerve."

"I would simply like a letter of my own, from my brother Robby . . . or Ethan."

"I'll thank you not to mention painful things," said Margaret, "like Ethan's reticence. The only thing worse is Jason's. Do you know, he refuses to say Ethan's name, even in the privacy of our bedchamber?"

"If we don't talk about painful things," said Alexandra, "we'll have nothing to talk about at all."

"But," said Antonia, "the fall of New Orleans brings us closer to the end of the pain."

Alexandra said no more. She had moved into a small room in the attic, leaving the rest of the house to the new owners. She had avoided the conflicts that could arise in a home where one woman was forced to cede power to another. She had avoided Antonia's opinionated Negro friend. And she could keep her opinions on the fall of New Orleans to herself because she was in a place where she could do much good for the Confederacy. Still, she hoped for a letter, too.

But the next one came from Tom for his father.

On a hot Sunday afternoon in the middle of June, they all gathered in the garden to hear Jason read it. Margaret served glasses of lemonade with a few carefully shaved pieces of ice chipped from the largest block in the icehouse.

Aboard the *Monitor*, May 13, 1862

Dear Pa,

The rebels have burned the *Virginia.* Conclusion foregone once their forces left Norfolk to defend Richmond. She drew too much to run up the James with them, and her seakeeping was as bad as *Monitor*'s. Blew up about 4:30 in the morning with a huge flash. Ethan will have to find a new ship.

I remain on *Monitor* until a new ironclad is ready for my command. All is as well as it can be here, and I hope it is the same with all in Annapolis.

"Jason," said Antonia, "you just spoke Ethan's name."

He took a sip of the lemonade. "Only in quotation."

Margaret shook her head. "As stubborn as rock. At least he can speak George's name again, since New Orleans."

Suddenly Antonia leaned across the table and pushed up the sleeve of Jason's blue coat, revealing an ancient tattoo. "Do you see that?"

He looked at it as though he had never seen it before.

"Youthful indiscretion," she said. "Like Ethan's."

Old Jason sputtered, stood up, and stalked away without a word.

Margaret thanked Antonia. "Perhaps that will be a beginning."

"Perhaps," answered Antonia.

"I have only one question," said Alexandra to Antonia.

"What?"

"Is every act of youthful conscience an act of youthful indiscretion?"

And Antonia considered her own youthful conscience. "No. Not always."

That summer Annapolis expanded like a festering sore.

In the farmland west of the city, the federal government opened a prison camp, but not for Confederates. It was for Union prisoners who had been turned over on their word that they would not fight until a southern prisoner had been exchanged for them. Camp Parole, it was called, and it soon grew to a population of eight thousand men—sullen, emaciated, often diseased—whose own government, by the rules of war, imprisoned them because there were so many more of them than there were of the enemy.

And all the while, the battles went on and the wounded arrived: from the Seven Days of June; from Second Bull Run; and from Antietam, a Maryland creek whose name was already synonymous with the bloodiest day in American history.

But Antietam was the victory that Lincoln had been waiting for, and five days later, he announced the Emancipation Proclamation, raising stakes that were already impossibly high, and forcing the Staffords to face a hard question that Margaret's son Cecil wrote about from Stafford Hall:

> Dear Mother,
>
> Tell Stepfather two more slaves gone this week. I talked with the one known as Zeke—white-haired old Methuselah with milky eyes, must be eighty-five if he's a day—and he says that all the talk among the young bucks is of lighting out for the territories, where Lincoln has already banned slavery. Now he bans it in the rebellious states. The time must come when he will ban it in states where his power is real. Stepfather must advise on how to handle the plantation, should Lincoln free the slaves in Maryland, or should Federal troops confiscate crops, as they have done to other plantations down here.

Iris Ezekiel was with them on the Sunday morning that Margaret read this letter. The ladies were bundling medical supplies for Camp Parole while Captain Jason sipped a cup of coffee and listened.

Iris laughed at the description of her father, Zeke. "Better to call him Moses than Methuselah."

"No, Iris," said Antonia, who was cutting long strips of cloth for bandages. "It's Mr. Lincoln who should be called Moses."

"Mr. Lincoln should be called 'hypocrite,'" said Alexandra, who was rolling the strips that Antonia cut.

"You must learn the difference between hypocrisy and conscience," said Eve.

And the Old Cap chuckled, which surprised them all, since he almost never chuckled. "This isn't about conscience. It's about politics."

In the garden beyond, two wounded men were sitting on the grass, bouncing a ball back and forth with little Jacob. The baby was laughing, running, enjoying himself immensely, and he did not seem to notice that neither of the soldiers had legs.

"What do you mean, politics?" asked Eve.

"Lincoln said that if he could save the Union by freeing none of the slaves, he'd do it. If he could save it by freeing some, he'd do it. And if he had to do it by freeing some and leaving others, he'd do that. Politics."

"Whyever he did it," said Iris fiercely, "it's the right thing, and I'm for it."

Jason's face reddened. He was not used to that tone from anyone, least of all an educated Negro. "The right thing, Iris, is for you to know your place."

Iris threw down a tight-wrapped bandage and glared at Jason. "I am a free woman. I can read. And there ain't—isn't—a better seamstress in Annapolis."

"In that case"—Alexandra handed her two pairs of uniform trousers—"sew up the legs on these. I promised those boys out in the garden."

Iris kept her eyes on Jason. "Your stepson down on the plantation, he's right. You better tell him what to do before all your slaves is gone."

"Free them," said Antonia. "Do the right thing."

Margaret slapped the table. "Do not deny my husband's conscience because it isn't in accord with yours."

"We mustn't argue so," Eve pleaded. "Those wounded boys can hear us."

"We mustn't argue at all." And Jason stalked out, muttering about how he had let all these opinionated women into his life.

A week later, Alexandra finally received a letter, postmarked from a place called Terceira, the Azores.

In the hallway, she pulled it open, and while Margaret tried to read it over her shoulder, she scanned it quickly and cried, "He's safe!"

"Thank God. But . . . the Azores?"

"He's on the *Alabama.*" And she read.

She was built in the yard of Jonathan Laird, under the contract of James Bulloch, naval agent for the

Confederacy. Bulloch has worked tirelessly, getting around international law and Union political pressure, to put Confederate raiders on the sea. I hoped to assist him, serving our interests quietly. But another Maryland Confederate, Raphael Semmes, requested me for his *Alabama*. He is an old shipmate of Tom's and I had Old Buck's highest recommendation, whether I wanted it or not.

I tell you, Lexie, London would have been a fine place to desert, but my father taught me well, because here I stand, whether I want to or not.

In August, we sailed with Bulloch for Terceira, whence the unarmed and neutral *Alabama* had already sailed. There she was met by a ship carrying coal, supplies, and cannon, which turned her into a raider. Our job is simply to sink northern merchant shipping. This is the way a small navy must fight a large one. It is what Porter did aboard the *Essex* until he got cocky: you attack their life-line—their economy—and avoid their mailed fist.

Our *Alabama* is a rakish vessel, and by the time you read this, her name will be known on the seven seas, according to Semmes. They say he is a ferocious fighter. I think he is also a windbag.

Alexandra let her future mother-in-law read the letter, while she dressed for her monthly visit to her aunt in Baltimore. She took a package of baked goods, as usual. But as usual, she did not change trains at Annapolis junction for Baltimore. She rode on to Washington, now the most fortified city on earth, and went to the house on M Street.

Mrs. Surratt's skinny son John was reading a book in the parlor.

"Good afternoon, Alexandra," he said. "Do you have anything for me?"

She put the package of baked goods on the gateleg table. "Quinine."

Surratt eyed the package. "No naval information?"

"Only that my Ethan is with Captain Semmes, aboard the *Alabama*."

Surratt gave a little snort. "You bring news of *Confederate* ships, not Yankee, and enough quinine to quiet, at best, a half dozen cases of malaria."

She did not like Surratt. He was cold and judgmental, which she expected from someone who had studied to be a Catholic priest. And the huge head on that skinny body reminded her of a skull with a mustache.

"I do what I can," she said. "And the more quinine I can smuggle to you, the more you can smuggle south."

"Quinine." A young gentleman appeared in the doorway. "As valuable as bullets, I'd say."

"Thank you, sir." Alexandra was struck by how handsome he was, how perfectly his dark mustache curled around the corners of his mouth, how finely his clothes were tailored, how strong was the smell of brandy from him.

"Booth," said Surratt, taking his hand. "It's good to see you."

"I always visit my friends when I come back to town." He held up two theater tickets. "And I bring gifts."

"Are you one of the *acting* Booths?" asked Alexandra, trying to keep the excitement from her voice.

The young man executed a theatrical bow. "John Wilkes Booth, at your service, ma'am. My friends call me Wilkes. And I'd be honored if you were to attend my performance as Mercutio in *Romeo and Juliet* this evening."

"I admire Shakespeare greatly," she said.

"John Surratt can stand in for your Ethan. Any man who sails with Semmes must be a brave one. Semmes has shown Marylanders what a man of conscience must do."

"My Ethan is a Marylander, too," she answered.

"Is he, now? Well, so am I." And a strange look came across the actor's face. The eyes that could shoot a gaze all the way to the back row seemed, for a moment, to cloud over. Booth glanced down at his boots, as though his confidence had just flowed out through the soles. But how could an actor so skilled have any kind of self-doubt?

"We are all Marylanders here, then," said Alexandra.

"Yes," answered Booth, filling up again. "And we're all working for the right side. So come to the play."

That evening, Alexandra watched Booth perform while Lincoln, his wife, and their son Tad watched from the presidential box; Tad was known to be a great fan of Booth's. And any questions about Booth's self-doubt were answered, in one of the most audacious performances she had ever seen in a Washington theater.

In the midst of a speech in which Mercutio was meant to chide Romeo, Booth turned his glare toward the president's box and, while continuing his lines, wagged his finger at Lincoln, as if to chide *him* instead. Many in the audience saw the meaning of Booth's gesture. And some, including Alexandra, approved.

The next letter to reach the Fine Folly came from Antonia's son, merchant captain Jack Browne.

> Dear Mother,
>
> Have completed three Atlantic runs in the last four months, without incident. But rebel raiders have made us all quite nervous. Insurance rates rise, small firms go out of business, preferring to sell their vessels to the Federal navy, which arms them and sets them to blockade.
>
> And now for momentous news. You are the grandmother of a son named Gideon, born November 30.

That night, it rained, but there was joy in the Fine Folly.

Margaret cooked crab stew and poured glasses of sherry all around. Iris Ezekiel baked a delicious concoction of water, raisins, flour, and ginger spice she called "war cake." Alexandra whipped cream and brought out a small bottle of vanilla extract, which normally she used to perfume herself, and splashed some into the whip. Eve brought out Jacob's receiving blankets and dressing gowns, saying she was saving them for her next child, but considering how long George had been on blockade, she did not expect a child any time soon, so she would send them north for little Gideon.

And while the rain sheeted down, turning the ruined lawns of the Naval Academy to mud, chilling the men in their meager shelters at Camp Parole, casting a pall across the Chesapeake tidewater as the second bleak winter of the war came on, the women toasted the future . . . and the hope of new life.

X
Old Zeke

Two days after Christmas, Jason and Margaret went by coach to Stafford Hall. They invited Iris Ezekiel to go with them, but she said there was too much to be done in the Fine Folly supply room, and her father would understand if she did not visit.

Jason did not like the sight of Federal troops camping in this peaceful countryside, or the sound of their horses pounding along the roads, or the arrogance of their officers, who stopped any carriage they saw on the chance that it might carry spies. And after twenty years, he still felt like an intruder between Margaret and her first son. So he planned to stay just one night at Stafford Hall before heading for Hampton Roads.

At dawn, a house slave laid in a fire and left hot water on the washstand beside the bed. Jason lay in the bed for a time, until the fire took the chill off the room. Then he shaved, dressed, carefully arranged his sleeves and collar to cover his tattoos, and threw his heavy sea cape over his shoulders.

He loved his old sea cape. It was mended here and there. The moths had gotten at it in places. But it still gave him a sense of invulnerability to the cold. Sometimes it could even make him feel young again.

In his cape, he could stand on the deck of the *Essex* and feel the winds of Cape Horn. He could stroll the Washington Navy Yard with Miss Mary's hand in his, and hear her say that they were going to have a baby. He could feel the tiny body of his son Tom, quivering excitedly as he hid under the cape, and he could hear his wife's laughter when the boy leaped out to surprise her.

So much . . . so much time . . .

He could remember the cold Christmas Day, right there on the river, when Margaret told him they were going to have a baby and made him feel young again. He could recall the miserable journey to New York after the *Somers* mutiny, and the windy day when he and Tom had walked the grounds of old Fort Severn and he had seen a place to educate naval officers properly.

So many hopes . . . so much disappointment . . .

He stood for a moment on the veranda and looked out. The fields were covered in clean white. The Patuxent looked like liquid metal flowing through the cold morning.

Then he went down the rolling road to the slave huts. Thousands of hogsheads of tobacco had been rolled past those huts since the Staffords had been on the land. Hundreds of slaves had lived and died there. And Jason had never questioned any of it, perhaps because his father had never questioned it, nor his father before him. They had cared for their slaves, kept families together, and brought ignorant people knowledge of Christ. How could this have been wrong?

He knocked on the door of Zeke's hut and pushed it open.

The old black face was covered with white lather, and he was shaving into a little broken piece of mirror. "Marse Jace?"

"Merry Christmas, Zeke." Jason took a small brown fruitcake from under his cape and put it down next to Zeke's Bible and a month-old copy of *Harper's.* "Iris sent this. She's busy at the Fine Folly, fighting the war behind the lines."

The old man wrapped his long fingers around the cake, turned it over, studied it. "Hope she put some of them dried apricots in there."

"She said she did. How are you, Zeke?"

"Old. Old as dirt."

Jason went over to the hearth and raised his hands. This hut was no different from any of the others, though the barn-board walls had recently been whitewashed and the cracks stuffed with straw. In December, the little windows rattled. And the dirt floor held the cold like a grate holding heat. "Fire sure is warm, Zeke."

"Marse Cecil, he see we have plenty wood. Don't want none of us gettin' sick." The old man scraped the razor on his cheek. "Doctors is 'spensive."

"We have a good doc in Annapolis. How would you like to come back to the Fine Folly? Fix up the garden again?"

"Too old. 'Sides, Miz Antonia, she don't like slaves."

"She likes you, Zeke."

"I likes her, too. She taught me to read. She give my daughter what's rightly hers." The old man continued to shave.

"What if you weren't a slave?"

And Zeke just laughed, a noisy, wet rale that started way down in his chest and turned into a cough before it became too mirthful.

"What's so funny?"

"You, just gittin' 'round to askin' me that now."

"But we've taken good care of you, Zeke, haven't we?"

"I reckon, but they was times I took care of *you*, too."

"I remember." Jason rubbed his hands. "Now, about those bucks who lit out—"

Zeke gave another laugh and finished his shaving. "Once this is over, I reckon I'll follow 'em. I reckon most everybody will."

"But you're old. Old as dirt."

"You old, too, but they lettin' *you* fight a war"—Zeke took a rag and dried his face—"and you don't even know what it's about. Want some fruitcake?"

"Sure. It's Christmas."

"I'll do the cuttin'. Fetch down two cups off the mantel and pour some coffee."

Jason used the rag for a pot holder and lifted the tin coffee pot from the grate in the fireplace. He filled both cups. "This war . . . what do you think it's about, Zeke?"

"'Tain't about union and honor and all them fancy words. It's about folks sayin' no when folks tries to tell 'em what to do. The South say no to the North so's the black man can't say no to the white man. As simple as that."

Jason sipped the coffee—hot and black and laced with bitter chicory—and he fell back on the one word that always gave him strength. "You can't say there's no honor in it. There's honor in it if we fight for the right reason."

The old man fixed his cloudy, bloodshot brown eyes on Jason. "There ain't no right reason for keepin' a man in a little hut till he as old as dirt. Till the North swallow that worm and free the slaves everywhere, not just down south, where it don't make no difference, there won't be no honor in this here war."

Jason warmed his hands around his mug. "If you're free, will you really head west?"

"Hell . . . I'm too old . . . too scairt . . . prob'ly stay here and work for my supper."

For a time the two old men sat, sipping coffee and eating fruitcake with dried apricots. Then Jason said, "It's true, Zeke."

"What?"

"I'm as old as dirt, too."

"Ain't older 'n me."

"Old enough that I can't make a big decision without my boys. A man has to see to his heirs. It's the last honorable thing he can do."

"I wouldn't know 'bout that," the old black man said bitterly.

xi
Standing Once More

The *Monitor* looked more like a ship now. A five-foot-high iron breastwork had been added atop the turret. An awning rose above the breastwork. And aft of the turret, a thirty-foot stack had been put up to vent the ship's fires.

But she remained a surpassing strange and ugly thing.

Before he visited her, Captain Stafford reported aboard the side-wheeler *Rhode Island,* under Commander Stephen Trenchard. "Happy to have an observer with us, sir. We take the *Monitor* under tow tomorrow, leave Hampton Roads just after dawn, reach the Beaufort blockade station on New Year's Day."

"And a glorious New Year's it'll be, Commander," said Jason. "My eldest son on the *Monitor*, my second son on blockade off North Carolina."

"A reunion?"

"The first since Lincoln's inaugural."

A stateroom awaited Jason aboard the *Rhode Island*, and as he stowed his gear, he realized he had been too long away from the excitement of a new ship, from the promise of new friends and old traditions mingling in a world that never seemed to change.

Of course, when an old man imagined shipboard, he saw the sails of the *Essex* stretched in the sun, smelled the tar that seemed the viscous lifeblood of the ship itself. Turning engines, hissing steam, the smell of lubricating oil, the film of coal dust everywhere—these surprised him, no matter how often he boarded a steamer.

So did the interior of the *Monitor,* which had only a single deck for crew and machinery. This deck was below the waterline, so ventilation came through ports in the ceiling and deck registers that circulated air from blowers. While this deck was as cramped from side to side as any vessel, she had the ten-foot ceilings of a fine riverboat. And that made an old sea dog like Jason feel rather uneasy when he visited her that evening.

The conversation at the wardroom table made him feel no better. Her officers said the *Monitor* was not built for rough seas. During her rush down the coast to meet the *Virginia,* seawater had poured through her blower intakes so that the flow of oxygen to her fires had failed and her engines had stopped, which in turn had stopped the pumps. She had almost foundered. But now, her new captain, John Bankhead, assured Jason that they understood the quirks of this quirky vessel.

And Tom toasted to their next assignment—blockading Charleston.

Later, out on the deck, Jason asked Tom about his next command.

"I get the next new ironclad, with two turrets. Until then I'll help Bankhead. He's a fine man." Tom looked up at the stars. "And we'll have a fine day tomorrow."

"We have to talk, you and me and George. . . ." The old man took a deep breath. The cold air burned his lungs. "It's time to free our slaves."

And Tom's laugh sent plumes of steam rising into the cold. "It's about time."

"Then . . . you have no objection?"

"It's the only honorable thing to do, Pa." Tom was still laughing. "We should all be flayed for not listening to Antonia twenty years ago."

"Hearing you say something like that is flaying enough."

Tom put an arm around his father's shoulders. "You did your best by your father's beliefs and your sons' needs. A man can't do more than that."

"Except to make the right decision when he sees what's right."

"If it took this long to decide, then this is the time to *do* what's right. Waiting any longer *would* be dishonorable." Tom gave his father a pat on the back. "Now, this is no place to be if the seas go rough. So get back aboard the *Rhode Island.* I'll see you and George in Charleston."

And in the starlight, on the flat iron deck of the *Monitor*, a father and his oldest boy embraced for the first time since one was young and the other was a child.

Sons, Jason knew, were a true gift.

The next day was calm and clear, December-cold, to be sure, but Jason buttoned his sea cape and gulped in the salt air. He stood on the deck of the *Rhode Island* for much of the day, watching the tow line stretch and relax and stretch again, as the *Monitor* rode the swell three hundred yards astern.

The following dawn promised another day of good sailing. But the clouds soon came scudding in from the southwest. By ten o'clock, sky and sea were the same gunmetal gray from one horizon to the other, and the wind was rising.

Toward dark, they rounded the Cape Hatteras light, and that was when the seas began to run, first to three feet, then five, then six or more—nothing to a man who had rounded the Horn in a Yankee frigate, but a hard test for an iron boat whose freeboard was no more than a few feet.

After night came down completely, Jason watched the white running light on the *Monitor*'s flagstaff, pitching down, thrusting upward, pivoting crazily above the turret, which was pivoting crazily on the waves.

"As long as she shows that white lantern, sir," said Commander Trenchard, "she's under control. So come to my cabin and join me at supper."

In the next hour the wind picked up and the seas rose higher.

Aboard the *Monitor*, the evening meal became a matter of tense conversation, and sliding plates, while water forced its way through the ventilation intakes and seeped through the packing beneath the turret.

Tom Stafford downed his coffee, then went staggering back to the midships ladders directly beneath the turret. By now the leak had turned into a torrent, a perfect circle of pouring water marking the outline of the turret itself.

"We ain't in trouble, are we, Lieutenant?" asked Seaman Malloy, who was soaked with water.

"Don't you worry, Malloy. Just get back to your station."

"I'm *at* me station, sir. Me and these other lads, we're stuffin' oakum up under the turret, but it ain't doin' no good." Bearded, bandy-legged Malloy looked down at the deck and the water sloshing around his feet.

"The pumps are working, lads," said Tom gently, remembering how quickly Malloy had panicked in battle. "We're in fine shape."

That was a lie. Tom knew that when he climbed to the top of the turret and saw the rising waves. Every time the *Monitor* rode up the side of one, she exposed the iron plates that extended like a shelf over her hull, then she dropped off, slamming her bottom with a hollow roar that caused the whole vessel to shudder.

From the stern of the *Rhode Island*, Jason could still see the white lantern, but the tow ropes at his feet reminded him of strings twined in the fingers of a drunken puppet master, pulling frantically to make the puppet dance.

By nine o'clock the wind was blowing a gale, a nasty squall was pouring down, and the waves had risen so high that sometimes the *Monitor*'s light disappeared completely, only to come wobbling back into view a moment later, before it plunged sickeningly downward into another trough.

"Hatt'ras seas," said Jason to Commander Trenchard.

"The *Monitor*'s in trouble, Captain. And we're carryin' her lifeboats."

Then a red lantern appeared on the *Monitor*'s flagstaff: *Distress*.

As the *Rhode Island* rose, Jason felt his stomach drop out of him.

For the first time in his life, Tom Stafford was seasick. The vomit was right at the back of his throat, and he was doing everything he could to keep it down. But the deck was pitching. And the lanterns were swinging. And the water was pouring down like a wind-driven rain, blown to starboard, then to port, then back again to starboard, as the hull rocked and shook and bounced on the waves.

He did not want to vomit in front of the men, because panic was descending as the water rose, and vomiting officers did not inspire confidence. But his gut made the decision for him, and he retched up everything he had eaten an hour before, hating himself as he did it.

"Get 'er all out, Lieutenant!" shouted Malloy. "Right into the wash. That's what all the lads is doin'. You don't smell it 'cause of all the water comin' in."

"Stop your jawin', Malloy." Tom wiped the dribble of puke from his chin. Frightened men needed to see their officers in command, vomit or not.

Now three cabin boys staggered toward the ladder from the forward section, followed by the big-bellied black cook, his eyes wide with fury and fright.

"Get on back here!" the cook was shouting at the cabin boys. "They's a table to clear in the wardroom."

"They's a foot of water in the wardroom," shouted one of the terrified boys.

The ship hit a swell, and another of the boys began to puke all over the place.

"You there! Cookie!" cried Tom." Have these lads fetch some bailing buckets."

"Bailin'?" cried Cookie. "We in big trouble if we's bailin'."

An hour later the clouds blew off and a feeble half-moon lit the sea.

But the wind did not die down, nor did the waves settle.

Aboard the *Monitor,* all hands were bailing, and most were seasick.

One tow line had snapped. So Bankhead had cut the other, dropped his anchor, lit flares, and stopped his engines so that he could divert all of his steam to the pumps. But the water continued to pour in—around the turret, down the air intakes, and now that the anchor had been dropped, up through the loosened packing in the hawser hole, too.

The *Rhode Island* had fouled her port paddle wheel in one of the tow lines, so that she too was adrift, bathed in the unearthly greenish light of her Coston flares.

Tom Stafford stood behind the breastwork on the turret and watched the side-wheeler riding the wind toward them.

"She's going to strike us," shouted Bankhead.

"If we start the engines," answered Tom, "we'll have to stop the pumps."

"Then we'll sink. We'll hold our position and hope she misses."

• • •

Jason Stafford rushed to the starboard side and looked down at the *Monitor*. With a tremendous screech, the *Rhode Island*'s wooden hull struck the side of the little iron plug and scraped along.

Jason tried to see his son among the officers atop the turret.

Someone was screaming, "No damage!" The ocean was roaring between the vessels. The Coston flares cast huge, flickering shadows in every direction.

And there he was, standing close by the captain and calling orders down into the turret. The old man cried his son's name.

But Tom did not hear.

He was dropping into the darkness again, to check the depth of the water: two feet and holding. The air belowdecks had turned clammy and cold, as cold as the ocean flooding in.

"Lieutenant," cried Malloy, "we ain't gettin' ahead of it no more!"

Tom felt the seasickness rising again.

"Lieutenant!" A cabin boy came sloshing forward. "The water's too high. Boiler fires just went out. No more steam. No more pumps."

"Bejesus," said Malloy.

"Stay at your posts, men," said Tom. "Keep bailin'. I'll tell the captain."

Back on top of the turret, he saw that the *Rhode Island* had now drifted several hunded yards downwind.

But two Coston flares were coming toward them through the darkness.

Lifeboats from the *Rhode Island.* Thank the Lord.

And back in the fresh air, with the horizon around him, he could fight off his seasickness. Thank the Lord again.

"The fires have gone out, Captain," he said to Bankhead, still maintaining an officer's professional calm. "We're fillin' with water. We could go down any minute."

"Take the men off."

The next fifteen minutes were the most harrowing that Tom Stafford had ever lived through.

They had to move sixty men up through the turret, down the ladder on the outside, across the pitching deck, and into the little boats banging against the side of the hull. And all the while, a handful of men remained below, passing up five-gallon buckets, as if they could buy a few more minutes, even though bailing the *Monitor* was like spitting on a house fire.

One boat made it away with a dozen men. Then another.

"Send up twelve more!" shouted Tom through the open hatch.

And a bucket came up, with Malloy right behind it. "The water's at me balls, sir, but the lads is still bailin'."

"Tell them to—"

"Holy Jesus!" Malloy's eyes almost burst from his head as a wave swept three sailors from the deck. One moment they were there, clutching a rope and waiting for the lifeboat; the next, they were gone.

"They're lost, Malloy," shouted Tom. "Get below, and get back to bailin'."

Another boat bumped against the hull.

More perilous descents down the side of the turret, across the slick deck.

More men away.

"That's it!" shouted Bankhead. "Abandon."

"Abandon ship!" shouted Tom through the open hatch. "Pass the word."

One man came up, two, then a cluster of four. After a final puking cabin boy appeared, there was no one else.

"Any more down there?" demanded Tom.

"I . . . I don't know, sir. I don't think so. But the water . . . it's waist deep."

"Hurry!" screamed Lieutenant Samuel Dana Greene, who was already in the lifeboat. "Before we're battered to pieces against the side!"

"Lieutenant," Bankhead said to Tom, "down the ladder after you."

But the ladder was gone, carried away by a wave a few moments before.

So they had to rig lines and go down hand over hand, palms tearing on the rope, hips slamming against the iron turret, whitecapped waves exploding over them in the moonlight.

First Tom, then the captain, skittering across the deck, grabbing lines, smokestack stanchions, anything to keep from falling while the men in the lifeboat called to them and held out boat hooks for them to grab.

All Tom had to do was grab a boat hook and leap across the churning three feet of water opening and closing between the lifeboat and the *Monitor*. But a sudden lurch lifted the lifeboat, causing it to pitch, pulling Bankhead aboard, and pushing Tom Stafford backward so that he fell hard on the iron deck of the *Monitor*.

A boat hook was thrust at him again. "Come on, Lieutenant!" It was Cookie, standing up in the pitching boat. "Take it and jump."

"Cookie!" shouted Tom. "Where's Malloy?"

"He done stayed below . . . said he'd take his chances on a big boat with some water in it 'fore he'd try to cross the deck."

"Come on, Tom!" shouted Lieutenant Greene over the roar of the wind.

"You've done your job, Lieutenant," cried Bankhead.

Another flare was coming toward them. Another lifeboat.

Tom grabbed the boat hook, but instead of levering himself aboard, he used it to shove the lifeboat toward the stern, where the wind caught it and pulled it away from the *Monitor*.

"Tom!" cried Bankhead, leaping to his feet, as if to jump back aboard.

"Get that boat away, Captain!"

"She's goin' down, Tom!" cried Lieutenant Greene.

"Then tell that next boat to hurry! There's still men to bring off!"

Just then one of the flares on the *Monitor*'s turret burned out.

By now the *Rhode Island* had drifted almost half a mile downwind of the *Monitor*. Jason Stafford was watching through Trenchard's glass.

Flares. Black racing shadows. Whitecaps in the moonlight.

When the turret flare went out, he thought the *Monitor* had gone down.

"Goddamn," he muttered, though he wanted to cry out to God.

In the pitching darkness at the base of the turret, Tom found a line and began to climb. He was in his mid-forties, in a woolen uniform soaked with seawater, and still seasick, but he had never let himself get fat or complacent. And he was intent on doing what an officer should—lead the men that God gave him to lead.

He climbed to the top of the turret, gave one look toward the flare showing on the next lifeboat, then dropped down into the turret, past the two black Dahlgrens and through the next hatch, clutching the ladder that led to the lower deck, clutching tight because the water was rising below him.

The lower-deck lanterns were still lit, throwing their yellow light into the oily, chest-deep murk.

He hung on the ladder and shouted. "Malloy! Malloy!"

And a full five-gallon bucket was thrust at him. "I'm right 'ere."

"Abandon ship. Didn't you get the order?"

"I'm bailin'. Me and some others. Take this up and throw it over the side."

"But we're *sinkin'*. Every man for himself!" shouted Tom.

In the half-light beyond Malloy were other frightened men, passing buckets toward the ladder, doing a duty no longer needed, because they were too frightened to do anything else.

"Come on, lads," shouted Tom. "Up the ladder with you."

And another bucket was thrust up to Tom. He kicked it away.

Malloy shouted, "I seen what happened to them boys out on the deck. They couldn't swim. Us neither. The divil you know is better than the divil you don't."

All around them came a tremendous unearthly groaning as the iron plates were wrenched by the weight of water below and waves above.

"You hear that, men? Come on." Tom reached out to the frightened Irishman. "There's no need to die here, Malloy."

The water had risen to the little man's armpits.

"Come on, Malloy," repeated Tom.

Suddenly the water inside the *Monitor*'s belly became too much.

Tom felt her bow drop. It was not the first time it had happened that night. But this time, the stern followed it. Then a torrent of water poured through the hatch. It was not the first time that had happened, either. But this time, it did not stop.

Tom knew that the sea had closed over them.

So he turned and tried to climb, pulling Malloy with him.

The water rose everywhere at once, and the lanterns went out.

Tom Stafford's last breath was like ice filling his chest.

xii
Cartes de Visite

Eve Sutter Stafford still cried over Tom five months later. But it was the only tearful indulgence that she allowed herself.

She had never considered herself a woman of strength. She had always been prone to low moods and bad headaches. And she had always worried inordinately over little things, like the cross look of a stranger or the way she appeared when she dared to wear flowers in her hair. Before she met George, she had taken refuge in the airs she could play on the piano and, at the age of twenty-eight, had reconciled herself to spinsterhood.

Then she had come to Annapolis to visit her aunt Dilly, and one Sunday, at Saint Anne's, she had met Tom and George Stafford. Tom politely tipped his hat. But George's gaze started at her feet and worked its way up to her face with a kind of interest that bordered on audacity. Had she been younger, she would have reacted indignantly. But she sorely longed for someone to listen to her music. So she met his gaze with her own.

Her aunt Dilly, a dropsical old busybody who lived on Cornhill Street, described George as an "immature, peripatetic, self-centered navy boy with a taste for popskull and a level of patter just this side of the minstrel show."

It was true that George drank too much, but he made Eve Sutter laugh, and they were married in May 1860.

Three years later, Eve still did not consider herself a woman of strength, although she was raising a son in a houseful of women, nursing wounded men three days a week, teaching reading to illiterate prisoners at Camp Parole, and in her spare time, trying to convince her future sister-in-law that it was time for her to come over to the hospital and do some serious nursing.

Alexandra still resisted, but she and Eve had become close friends. On a May day in 1863, Alexandra accompanied Eve and her little son to Henry Baumgartner's photography studio on Tabernacle Street. They dressed Jacob in a sailor suit. Eve wore her favorite blue flowered dress, the one that belted at the waist and accentuated the womanly swell of her hips. She parted her hair severely in the middle and gathered it at the back, but she added a small wreath of flowers. If they were good enough for Mrs. Lincoln, they were good enough for her.

Alexandra wore a simple blouse pinned with a cameo and let the mischief in her eyes do her talking to the camera.

Little Jacob, perhaps frightened by the huge camera and the strange window that let sunlight straight through the roof, sat so quietly that the mother-and-son sitting took a mere fifteen minutes, Alexandra's even less.

A week later Mr. Baumgartner delivered two dozen cartes de visite, pocket-sized cards on which the portraits had been printed. Cartes de visite had become very popular since the beginning of the war as a way for a soldier to carry his loved ones into battle or, in this case, through a long blockade.

Eve thought her little boy looked healthy and happy in the photograph. And she liked the way she looked, too. Her gaze was direct. Her mouth, held straight, still showed a touch of a smile, and her hand was placed firmly but lovingly on her son's shoulder. It was an image to give her husband confidence.

Alexandra liked her portrait too. She liked her own look of mischief, even if the only mischief she had gotten into was the kind that could get her hanged. She sent one carte to her father at Parrish Manor. But Ethan had no address, so he would not see her until he saw her in the flesh. Then she thought of someone else who might like a portrait of her. She wrote a brief note and mailed the carte to the actor who lived at the National Hotel in Washington, D.C.

A month later, a letter arrived at the Fine Folly, from George.

> Dear Evie,
>
> Thank you a thousand times for the cartes de visite. Every day I can see how beautiful you are, how handsome my son is. At the same time, I am subdued by all the time that this war has taken from us.
>
> How does father fare? Is he finally coming to accept Tom's death?
>
> And what of Stafford Hall, now that the slaves have been given their freedom?
>
> The blockade continues in its misery. I recently heard a description I am compelled to repeat: To understand

> blockade duty, "Go up on the roof on a hot summer day, talk to a half dozen degenerates, descend to the basement, talk to a half dozen more, drink tepid water full of iron rust, climb to the roof again and repeat the process until fagged out, then go to bed with everything shut tight."
>
> Is it any wonder I chafe at the boredom? Any wonder that my thirst has begun to grow again? It is hard, Evie. But action will be just the thing. One of Tom's old friends from the Mexican War, John Winslow, has agreed to take me aboard his *Kearsage.* Her only task is to run down the *Alabama*, commanded by his old bunkmate from the Mexican War, Raphael Semmes. Tell Lexie I will not let them hurt Ethan when we find him.

This letter disturbed Eve. But if her husband was being transferred because he drank too much, it would do no good to worry. Only weak women worried. Strong women acted. That was what Antonia had told her. And before long, there was no time to worry about anything.

In the first week of July, trains began bringing the wounded from a Pennsylvania railhead called Gettysburg, first filling the Academy buildings, then the buildings at Saint John's College, and then the tents that were raised all across the Academy grounds.

Doctors and nurses worked day and night. Carpenters made crutches and measured men for wooden legs. Embalmers set up their tents, mixed their concoctions, and put up their signs.

And Eve worked harder than she ever had. She bathed infected stumps, washed the lousy hair of a man who had no arms, cleaned up men with chronic diarrhea, who looked at her with woeful embarrassment as she worked. And whenever she found herself faltering, she watched Antonia and Margaret and took her resolve from them.

And every night, she told Alexandra how much they needed her.

"I've told you before," said Alexandra, "my sentiments are not with these men. I can help in the Sanitary, but I'm no nurse . . . and surely no nurse for men who fought the South."

"Just think of Ethan, or your own brother," said Eve, "and remember that these men will never fight again. Some will never walk. Some will not even live. This is the last I will speak of these matters with you, Lexie. But you know I am right."

• • •

In late July, Alexandra finally made her way through the back garden, across King George Street, to the hospital, and informed the directress of female nurses, Miss Maria M. C. Hall, that she would like to volunteer.

Miss Hall, who fulfilled the army's maxim that nurses should be plain-looking women, sat at her desk and ran her finger down the checklist before her. "You will have to wear brown or black, no bows, no jewelry, no hoop skirts."

Alexandra did not mention that there were women in hoop skirts working right that very minute in the wards. She had already guessed, from the clipped manner of speech and dyspeptic attitude, that Miss Hall enjoyed following her orders and reading her checklists, so she simply said, "Yes, ma'am."

"You will also have to pull your hair back into a bun."

"Yes, ma'am."

"And you cannot be doing this because you are hunting for a husband."

"My fiancé is in the navy." She did not mention *which* navy.

"Now, how old are you?"

"Twenty-five."

"Disqualified," Miss Hall said almost triumphantly. "Unmarried must be over thirty."

"But my future aunt, Antonia Stafford—"

"She is your aunt?" Miss Hall's posture and attitude changed.

"Yes. She said you needed nurses, and there are so many wounded that I am surprised you would reject a woman of any age."

Miss Hall looked out at the men sitting along the river. "No, I don't suppose that we would . . . not these days."

The next day, Alexandra appeared in the hospital, wearing a bright yellow dress—with hoops, naturally—and bright yellow ribbons in her hair.

The men smiled. Some of the nurses frowned, but the younger ones, who dared to wear hoops in their skirts, smiled too, and soon there were more ribbons to be seen, and more smiles among the soldiers.

Of course, Alexandra was less interested in the soldiers than in the officers, who might still be privy to plans that she could pass to

Surratt. But she did as she was told, and twice a week, she tended the men who were set in chairs and cots, to sit by the Severn.

She found one young man particularly intriguing. He had the familiar sad gaze beneath a thatch of black hair, and his strange accent snapped words off as though he were biting them. His name was Gabriel Shank, of the Twentieth Maine, the regiment that held the Union left on the second day at Gettysburg. A minié ball had struck him in the lower leg, shattering the bone and creating another customer for the crutch makers.

Whenever she asked him if he wanted anything, he answered that he wanted nothing more than a quiet place to still the screaming inside his head. Then, on a day in his third week at the hospital, he asked her for a sketch pad and pencil.

A few days later, Alexandra visited him with Antonia, who was teaching her how to change dressings on amputated limbs.

Without a word, Gabriel showed them the picture of Lincoln he was sketching.

"I've seen Lincoln in the flesh," said Alexandra, "at the theater."

"So have I," added Antonia, and she told Alexandra to lift Gabriel's leg. Then she showed her how to unwrap the cotton bandage, carefully cut away the lint packing on the wound, and . . . here was where Antonia said that a pleasant line of conversation with the patient was helpful.

Antonia looked up at Private Shank, whose eyes were riveted to the sketch pad. "I was very impressed by Lincoln when I met him."

"Could you describe his face?" asked Shank, sketching furiously.

"His face looked like the leather on your shoe," said Antonia.

"What about his soul? I'm interested in a man's soul."

"His soul?" Alexandra's eyes were drawn to the stitched red stump now emerging to view. She heard herself say, "His soul should look like that."

"Alexandra!" said Antonia.

"No . . . no . . ." said Shank, looking down at his stump for what may have been the first time. "That's how my soul looks, too. I will sketch that pain in his face."

And he sketched a Lincoln in torment.

It was said that in those terrible years, many men aged overnight.

Jason Stafford was one of them. He could no longer keep to his work schedule. Every afternoon he found himself thinking of Tom, who had stood where God put him. The old man usually appeared in Annapolis on Friday afternoon and stayed through to Monday. He moved slowly. He came to breakfast with white stubble on his chin and grew less decisive in the big things and the small.

When Antonia called a family meeting and asked if they could bring wounded soldiers into the house, to make room in the hospital, he left the decision to the women.

So the soldiers came.

Among them was Gabriel Shank. His leg was healing, his soul along with it. He went into the downstairs ward, the great room, which was cleared of supplies and lined with a dozen cots for the amputees who had not yet learned to balance themselves on crutches. A dozen more beds were set up in the attic for men who were either strong enough to climb stairs themselves or so weak that they would have to be carried anyway.

By day, the house was filled with the scurrying of nurses, the deep voices of the doctors, the chatter of the little black boys hired to fetch water and fan the patients in the attic. By night, it was filled with groans and curses.

In the presence of all this, old Jason found himself retreating by day to the garden that old Zeke had lovingly restored, by night to dreams of soft answers and softer places, of green islands and tattooed women.

And then came a letter from Ethan, mailed from Jamaica that spring.

> Darling Lexie,
>
> We are the scourge of the seas, or so Captain Semmes tells us. We would be rich if we could get through the Yankee blockade with our prizes, so that they could be properly condemned by a Confederate prize court. As it is, we have been able to ransom a few and were forced to burn the rest.
>
> Recently, we ran down a ship off the Bahamas, which turned out to be a Confederate blockade-runner carrying gunpowder and rifles. Your brother was in command. We

> had a fine reunion. I even requested transfer to his vessel, but it was denied. So on I sail with Captain Semmes.
>
> We are heading for parts unknown. But you are always in my thoughts and no matter what you hear—*what* you hear—wait for me.

Alexandra read this letter to the family on a Sunday afternoon in August.

"My son is a pirate," said Jason.

"He's as honorable as Tom was," answered Alexandra. "Or George."

"I hope George finds him and sinks him."

"No, you don't," said Eve.

"Yes, he does," said Margaret. "His own son."

And she would not sleep with him that night.

But the old man slept, and dreamed . . . dreamed of a wind-driven rain and the sweet smell of Nuku Hiva.

In his dream, he called to Piteenee and told her the thatch was leaking. He awoke in the dark and found that his dream continued. And the sound of the wind was in fact the moaning of a man in the room above him. And the rain . . .

He wiped the rainwater from his face. It felt warm and had a strange, sweet smell. He struck a match, lit a lantern, was relieved to find that he was in the Fine Folly. Then he saw the blood on his nightshirt. And on the sheet. And on his hands. And the old man jumped up with a cry of horror, stumbled backward, recoiling from the blood.

And then he heard footsteps in the makeshift ward above him, and muffled voices. A soldier had hemorrhaged and was bleeding to death in the cot above him.

It was raining blood, even in the Fine Folly.

xiii
Alabama, Kappal Hantu

Reputation ran far and fast ahead of the *Alabama*.

By the time she made Singapore in December, even the natives of

Malaya had heard of the almost magical way that she could sneak up on her quarry, and they had named her *kappal hantu,* ghost ship.

But bad news ran far and fast, too.

Her officers had heard of the July disasters at Gettysburg and Vicksburg.

The South had been beaten back, divided, and she would be conquered, unless her commerce raiders could shoot enough holes in the pockets of Yankee shippers that they were drained of their political will as well as their money. Carrying this burden against odds that included a dozen Federal ships—dispatched solely to run him down—was Captain Raphael Semmes.

His men called him Old Beeswax because his hard-waxed mustache stuck out from his face like a spar. They also called him son of a bitch, because he believed in discipline and looked it. His eyes were small and hard, like his frame. His demeanor was so humorless that no one could recall the last time he'd laughed. His dress remained fastidious, even as eighteen months of wear frayed his vessel. And his code was simple: for any infraction, punishment, swift and sure.

He had brought twenty-seven Confederate officers with him, but the crewmen were mostly English mercenaries who had first sailed the ship to Terceira. He had negotiated prize payments and grog rations with them, and it was commonly held that if sailors negotiated before they signed, they would try to negotiate afterward. So he strung a few of them up by their thumbs for pulling faces, and the rest were disabused of notions regarding shipboard discipline. Then he went to work.

By the time the *Alabama* reached Singapore, she had run down over fifty Yankee merchantmen. A dozen more lay rotting at this neutral anchorage because their skippers would not share the sea with a Confederate raider. Ethan knew that the glory they had gained would go far after the war, so long as they were not all hanged for pirates. But he hated the price he had been forced to pay.

He yearned to climb once more into a hayloft with Lexie Parrish . . . or any other woman. At times, his need had grown so great that he'd considered climbing in with some young sailor. But the promise of the Singapore brothels had saved him from that. And nothing in his father's Marquesas memories could have surpassed two Singapore prostitutes performing the pearl-in-the-oyster.

Ethan was remembering that particular pleasure one January day as the ship cruised under sail, conserving coal. The engines were silent, the fires banked, the weather pleasant in the Strait of Malacca. Ethan idly examined a chart he had taken from a recent prize, but his mind was on a string of pearls, delicately inserted into unfamiliar territory and withdrawn suddenly at the supreme moment.

At the stern, Semmes was examining a chronometer, one of seventy-five he kept in his cabin—some in mahogany boxes, some in velvet bags, some worth as much as two hundred dollars—along with the quadrants, sextants, and charts he had taken from the captains of his prizes.

The cruise of the *Alabama* had been like the cruise of the *Essex,* a single ship scourging the commerce of a strong nation, but Ethan could not imagine his father taking chronometers for spoil. He did not believe that Semmes could have imagined doing it, either, back in the prewar days when he called commerce raiders "little better than licensed pirates."

Now, when a sail was sighted to windward, this licensed pirate lit out after her.

The clipper captain they came upon that day must have known the silhouette of the big steam-driven bark, because he laid on all canvas, right out to the studding sails that looked like wings on either side of his razor-thin hull. And the chase was on.

A Yankee clipper might make eighteen knots to the *Alabama*'s thirteen, but Semmes would keep after her for hours, blackening the sky with coal smoke and waiting for the wind to fade, as inevitably it would.

"Chasing a sail is like pursuing a coy maiden," he had once told Ethan, "the very coyness sharpening the pursuit."

And when this suitor came within range, he could order one of Ethan Stafford's warning shots from a seven-inch Blakely rifle. But this Yankee maiden was more stubborn than coy and would not heave to until Ethan had put a shot fifty yards from her bow, another no more than twenty.

Her name was *Hero*, out of Boston.

Perhaps it was the long chase, perhaps the word *Boston* on the transom, but something about this ship put Semmes in a bad temper. When they were a quarter mile off, he struck his blue British ensign and ran up the Confederate colors; then he ordered his helmsman to make a circle.

One newspaperman, who had watched from shore as the *Alabama* took a prize, wrote that the circle was worth riding a hundred miles to see—a saucy, rakish craft, keeping a distance of no more than thirty yards between herself and her prey, while her big guns pivoted to keep her prey covered. Semmes did it whenever he wanted to show off . . . or intimidate an uppity captain.

And soon enough, the captain of this ship was riding his lifeboat across the water for the pro forma conference aboard the *Alabama*.

Ethan was standing amidships, by his big Blakely, when the captain of the *Hero* came up the side. The captain was young but carried himself with the confidence of an elder. His black mustache was as luxuriant as Semmes's, his black stovepipe and frock coat as crisp as a uniform. And his eye was drawn immediately to Ethan.

"So," he said without missing a beat, "you grew the beard after all."

Ethan brought his hand to his chin and said, "Jack? Jack Browne?"

"*Captain* Browne to you"—Jack gave the ship the once-over—"and to the rest of the officers aboard this so-called ghost ship."

Semmes offered his hand. "Welcome aboard, Captain."

Jack Browne did not accept. "My hand is my own, sir."

Semmes clapped his hands behind his back. "Are you any relation to the abolitionist John Brown, so well hanged a few years back?"

"No, sir."

"Then you must be John Browne, slave-stealer and *Somers* mutineer."

"Your terminology is wrong, sir," answered Jack.

Ethan cleared his throat, warning his cousin that this cold-eyed captain was not one to insult. But Jack Browne had looked death in the face at the age of fifteen, and nothing had ever frightened him after that.

He said, "I've *freed* slaves, sir, not stolen them. And there was no mutiny on board the *Somers*. Though I recall that a Lieutenant Raphael Semmes was in command of her when she went down off Veracruz in '46."

Semmes drew a sharp breath and turned on his heel. "Come below."

In his cabin Semmes took his position, behind the table, beneath the skylight.

Jack Browne threw his papers down without a hint of deference.

Semmes glanced at them, then noticed Ethan at the door. "What do you want?"

"To see that my cousin minds his manners, sir."

Semmes nodded, unimpressed by family sentiment, and turned his attention back to Browne. "Your papers seem to be in order, sir. Now I can burn your ship."

"She's well insured."

"What is your cargo?"

"Chinese tea. Worth five and a half million dollars in London."

"Worth nothing to me. Do you have any *real* money aboard?"

Captain Jack Browne gave a disgusted laugh. Ethan had heard stories of how well Jack had acquitted himself before a court-martial. Now he understood.

"I asked you a simple question, Captain. Do you have any money? Yes or no."

"If I were set upon by Chinese pirates, I might expect such a question."

It was getting very close beneath that skylight. The big man in the black suit and the small man in Confederate gray seemed like two pieces of smoldering coal.

The ends of Semmes's mustache twitched. "Never mind. My officers will find what money you have hidden." Then he bundled up the papers and handed them back. "You may remain aboard. You'll be put ashore within the next two weeks."

"What about my crew?"

"Your niggers?"

"I have a dozen freedmen in the lifeboat, along with Cape Verdeans and Americans."

"Your niggers stay in the boat, with the rest of the half-breeds."

"And my officers?"

"They go with your niggers."

And Jack's answer filled Ethan with pride in his blood. "If those men are set adrift, your ship is no place for me. I won't desert them."

"Suit yourself," said Semmes, "but you'll have no charts or navigational tools. They're the spoils of war. If you want to sail with your niggers, you'll have to follow your nose."

"These are strange waters, Captain." Jack was not begging. He made it sound more like a threat.

"You're twenty miles from the coast, thirty more from Penang."

"My navigational tools, sir."

Semmes stepped around the table and looked into Jack's eyes. "You sail a clipper halfway 'round the globe, but you can't pilot an open boat across thirty miles of ocean?"

Just then, Midshipman Irvine Bulloch, brother of James D., came in and put Browne's chronometer, sextant, and compass on the table. "As you ordered, Cap'n Semmes."

"Those are mine," said Jack Browne.

Semmes picked up the compass and read the inscription aloud: "'To Gideon, for finding his way, from McCauley Browne, his father, January 1, 1803.'"

"My father carried that compass in the Tripolitan War. Try to steal it from me and there'll be blood on your bulkheads."

Semmes looked hard at Jack Browne, then flipped him the compass. "Find your way with it."

"I still need my charts."

"Too valuable."

"Excuse me, sir," said Ethan. "I could give him my charts, sir."

"If I thought your cousin could not make land safely, I'd take him and his whole nigger crew aboard and drop them off when I could. Don't insult my judgment by giving him your nautical charts."

And that was that . . . for the moment.

Back on the deck of the *Alabama*, Jack Browne stopped as though someone had struck him with a belaying pin. For all his bravado, the sight of smoke curling from the hull of his *Hero* seemed too much to bear.

Semmes looked into the lifeboat tethered to the side. Two dozen frightened faces, black and white, looked up. "I see you have no water with you, sir."

"Only what leaked in," answered Jack.

Still sarcastic. Ethan could not help but admire his Boston cousin.

"We have none to spare on the *Alabama,*" said Semmes. "I'll tow you back to your ship and you can get some."

But the flames were now licking up out of the hold of the *Hero*. The magnificent green-hulled clipper would soon be ablaze from taffrail to jib.

"I won't send one of my men where I wouldn't go myself," said Jack Browne, "and that ship is now no place for any man."

"You can clear out, then. Get in your lifeboat and go." Semmes strode back toward the quarterdeck. "You're the most impertinent man I've ever brought aboard this ship."

"Good," answered Jack Browne. Then he turned to Ethan. "I . . . I have something I must tell you."

Ethan did not hear the catch in his cousin's voice because he was mustering the courage to defy Raphael Semmes. He pulled from his pocket the chart he had been studying that morning and pressed it into Jack's hands.

"This is the quick route to a flogging," whispered Jack.

"If you can go into an open boat because it's your duty as an officer, I can give you a chart, because it's my duty as your cousin."

And if a man could be felt to seethe, it was Raphael Semmes, who stood by the mizzenmast, staring back at them, almost vibrating with anger.

Ethan thought he would be banished to the lifeboat right along with his cousin. And he thought he might welcome it.

Then Jack whispered to Ethan, "I have to tell you . . . Tom went down with the *Monitor*, went down a hero, saving his men."

The emotions that pounded into Ethan at that moment made it almost impossible for him to hear Raphael Semmes ordering his arrest. All he could hear was the thumping of the engines, keeping time with the throbbing in his head.

xiv
Cables and Contracts

A message traveled by a long and circuitous route from the Island of Penang to Annapolis, arriving at the Fine Folly in early May: "Have met *Alabama* and Ethan both. *Hero* gone, thanks to Ethan's captain. I'm fine, thanks to Ethan. Uncle Jace taught him well. He is a man. Jack Browne."

It was as cryptic as it was short.

The mothers in question, Margaret and Antonia, read between the lines to imagine what had gone on when the *Alabama* stopped the *Hero*.

Alexandra said, "I could have told you that Ethan was a man."

Even Jason admitted he looked forward to hearing the story in person.

"Are you softening?" asked Margaret.

"If Ethan's accused of piracy, I'll argue for leniency."

"What a father." Alexandra excused herself to go to the hospital.

It was springtime in Annapolis in the year 1864.

The flow of wounded had abated. The bloodstain on Jason's ceiling had faded, though no one had found time to whitewash it. The cots waited, clean and white, for the next shipment. A few stray cats wandered here and there.

There was still bloodletting to be done, but the garden behind the Fine Folly was an oasis of peace and quiet.

Freedman Zeke, as he now called himself, had worked wonders with the neglected plantings. Hibiscus and star magnolias bloomed once again. Petunias and poppies grew along the carefully raked paths. And Zeke had hired two more gardeners. The sound of their clippers and rakes made gentle music in the spring air.

It was now a matter of pride to Jason that he had freed his slaves. His sister called it an example of belated foresight. Jason was calling it vision, because a constitutional convention was finally gathering at the state house to abolish slavery all across Maryland.

One of the few conventioneers elected on a pro-slavery ticket was Dan'l Parrish, and he stopped by the garden of the Fine Folly that afternoon. He had lost weight and grown grayer since the beginning of the war. But any man whose son was a blockade-runner, whose daughter was a spy, and whose father had recently died, could be expected to grow gray.

"Good afternoon, Cap'n," said Dan'l.

"I'm sorry for your father's death," said Jason, looking up from a report that put the *Alabama* most recently at Cape Town, South Africa.

"The last year was hard on him." Dan'l let his eye drift across the beautiful plantings, toward the little pond at the back, where a man with one leg sat painting a rhododendron blossom. "Who's that?"

"Gabriel Shank. Decent fellow . . . stood with the Twentieth Maine at Gettysburg. Been here nearly a year now. Guess there's nothing in Maine for a one-legged fisherman."

"Nor in the South for a blockade-runner without a ship."

"I hear that Robby was finally caught."

"Trying to come in at Cape Fear. Now he's in prison."

"Was your ship insured?"

"Not even Lloyd's insures blockade-runners. The *East Wind* is now a Yankee ship. And we face the financial ruin I feared."

"I'd say I'm sorry for you, but—"

"Robby could've made millions if he'd smuggled luxuries for southern ladies. English blockade-runners left more space for muslins and perfumes than for cannonballs. But nice-smellin' ladies won't end this. That's why he smuggled munitions and medicines. Took payment in Confederate paper, too."

A fly landed on Jason's sleeve and he brushed it away. He wondered about the real reason for Dan'l Parrish's visit. He knew that Dan'l would come to it soon. He did not like Dan'l, but he admired any man as direct.

Just then Margaret came to the garden table with a tray of lemonade. She was in a cheerful mood after the cable from Jack Browne. She poured lemonade and launched into the kind of small talk that Jason knew would keep Dan'l from his point. "Your daughter has become a fine nurse, Dan'l."

"So I'm told." He took a sip of lemonade. "I suppose there's nothing wrong with helping the wounded. It's the Christian thing."

"She's a fine girl. We'll be proud to have her for a daughter-in-law someday. Won't we, Captain?"

Almost in spite of himself, Jason had come to think of Alexandra as his daughter. And Jack Browne's cable had put him in a forgiving mood toward his youngest son. "Yes. Proud."

"That's a powerful endorsement, coming from the captain," said Margaret.

Dan'l smiled wanly and fingered the black mourning band on his arm. It seemed he was becoming more circumspect with age and the weight of defeat.

"So," said Jason after the silence had grown too heavy, "I assume that you will vote for slavery at the convention."

"Yes, but it will do no good. The new constitution will bankrupt many of us in the southern counties of Maryland."

"Just do what we did," Margaret said airily. "Let your slaves go. See what fine work a freedman can do with an old garden."

Dan'l gave the garden no more than a perfunctory glance. "A strong buck was worth near a thousand dollars before the war. Using that figure, I calculate I'll lose fifty thousand dollars."

"We lost near twenty," said Jason. "But it wasn't ours to begin with. Free them. Then hire them back."

"How can I hire them back when I have nothing to pay?"

"Nothing?"

"Robby put everything into the *East Wind*. Now it's all lost, except for this." Dan'l slipped a sheet from his pocket and set it on the table. It looked very legal, which meant it was the product of lawyers, and Jason had been around enough politicians lately—most of them lawyers with votes—to distrust the product of any lawyer.

"This is the loan agreement between your son and my father," said Dan'l.

"A gentleman's agreement."

"Born of the vicissitudes of war. Our family wanted to sell quickly. Your heroic son, perhaps seeing what was ahead, wanted something to leave behind. But he had only a small portion of the cash he needed, few assets, and a uniform, all of which made the banks more nervous."

Jason remembered the first time he had met Dan'l, in Rebecca's sick room. He had countered Dan'l's shifting eyes with his own hard gaze, and Parrish had retreated. Now his gaze was not so hard, nor his mind so certain. "I took over my son's debt and his estate. I've been paying a hundred dollars a month at eight percent, just as the agreement called for."

"A ten-year note," said Margaret.

"Not really." Dan'l snapped his eyes briefly at Margaret. "The agreement shows my father's foresight. When no one thought we would be fighting for more than a few months, he decided the war could go on forever. And who could tell where interest rates would be after that long? So he gave himself the option of calling the loan, demanding payment in full after five years."

"What are you saying?" asked Margaret.

Dan'l's gaze dug and held. "I may be forced to call it. You'll have to get another loan or sell the house."

"Sell?" said Jason.

"To make good for my losses." Dan'l stood and drained his lemonade. "I'll never repossess. You'll always get your share of proceeds from a sale."

Old Jason shook his head. It was too peaceful, too deceptively quiet in his garden for him to understand the meaning of all this.

Dan'l's eyes quickly shifted from husband to wife to hard-faced old Antonia, who was just coming out of the house. At the sight of her, he pivoted like a man in a clockwork and made for the gate beside the barn.

"I heard the word 'repossess.'" Antonia glided toward Jason and Margaret.

Old Jason pulled himself out of his slouch. "He would like to repossess this house. But he still looks forward to my son possessing his daughter."

"Speak of the devil." Antonia looked to the back of the garden, where Alexandra was coming in by the King George Street gate.

Silently they watched her sneak up behind Gabriel Shank, who was engrossed in his brush strokes. She placed her hands over his eyes, playing the old guess-who game, and they laughed together. Then she stepped back, smiling, running her hand through her hair like a nervous young girl.

"Ethan had better come soon," said Antonia, "or he won't possess anything."

XV
Aide-Toi et Dieu T'Aidera

By June, the *Alabama* had steamed fifty-eight thousand miles without a refit. She was an exhausted ship with an exhausted crew. Copper curled from her bottom. Her boilers were shot. Her powder supply had deteriorated so badly that only one shell in three could be counted on to explode. But she had done her job.

And Ethan had done his, done it so well that Semmes had forgiven him his transgression with the nautical charts.

"I can't have officers disobeying my orders," Semmes had said after holding Ethan in the cable tier for a day. "But a man who can't show loyalty to his family is not a man I want aboard my ship. You'll be confined to quarters for three days more. Consider it punishment, or a rest. Lord knows, we could all use a rest."

"Yes, sir."

"And my condolences. Your brother Tom was a good man."

"Thank you, sir."

By the time the *Alabama* limped into Cherbourg, the war had turned inexorably against the South.

Semmes admitted to Ethan that he was as worn out as his ship. He had lost his passion for the hunt, and he had lost his patience with the constant grousing of a mercenary crew. Once the French gave him permission to put his vessel in drydock, he would give his officers leave and make his way back to the Confederacy. The *Alabama* would sail again under a new commander.

But like a smudge of smoke rising beyond the horizon, word reached Cherbourg that the Federal steam frigate *Kearsage*, no larger than the *Alabama* but freshly fitted and better armed, was steaming on from the Netherlands.

This had happened two years before, when Semmes commanded the *Sumter*, and the *Kearsage* blockaded him at Gibraltar. He had simply left his ship and gone on to England. But the *Alabama* was more valuable than the *Sumter*, and a better match for the *Kearsage*. Moreover, the nervous French had informed Semmes that he would have to leave as soon as he took on coal and food.

So, when the smoke of the *Kearsage* actually appeared, Semmes sent a message to the U.S. consul: "My intention is to fight the *Kearsage* as soon as I can make the necessary arrangements. I beg she will not depart before I am ready to go out."

A few nights later, the long summer twilight glimmered in the sky and danced in the water below. It was Ethan's watch, and he was considering how wonderful it would be to disappear into those colors.

"A fine night, Stafford." Captain Semmes came up beside him.

"Aye, sir."

The silhouette of the *Kearsage* waited like a well-trained watchdog, just beyond the three-mile limit.

Semmes raised his binoculars to study her. "She's lowering her colors. Do you know that the Union flag still carries thirty-four stars? They don't even show enough respect for the Confederacy to take eleven stars off for us."

"Aye, sir."

"Well, I am tired of running from their flaunting rag."

Forward, half a dozen sailors were gathering for their nightly music. Tonight one of them was playing the plaintive "Lorena" on the squeeze-box. It was a song Ethan loved, and when he sang it, he tried to replace the name of Lorena with Alexandra, but he could never squeeze four syllables into three.

A hundred months have passed, Lorena, since last I held that hand in mine. . . .

It was a sad song about a love lost to duty.

"Forgive me, sir," he said to Semmes, "but some of the lads up forward, they've wondered why we don't just disappear."

Semmes gave Ethan a smoldering look, but the heat quickly left his face. "The *Kearsage* is a fair fight. And her captain is an old friend. You don't run from such a challenge. Your father would tell you that, or Tom. It's a matter of honor."

. . . A duty, stern and pressing, broke the tie which linked my soul to thee. . . .

"Honor. Yes, sir. And a fair fight with an old friend."

But it would not be a fair fight.

When George Stafford had first gone aboard the *Kearsage*, he had described the anchor chain that Farragut had draped over his hull before he went charging up the Mississippi.

"It saved us when the *Hartford* ran aground in front of the Confederate forts, sir," George had told Captain Winslow. "It could save us from *Alabama*'s Blakely rifle, if we ever run her down."

Winslow had agreed. He was a big, bluff man with curly side whiskers and a mustache that made him look like a jolly shopkeep, but he did his work with a professionalism that George Stafford had come to admire. Not only had he ordered the anchor chain draped over the sides. He had carefully boxed it in with oak planking, so that from a distance, the *Kearsage* looked unprotected.

"I wonder what Semmes would say if he knew we had armored our sides," said Winslow to George, while two sailors folded the flag that evening.

"He won't know until one of his shots bounces off, sir," said George. "Then it will be too late."

Winslow tugged thoughtfully at his side-whiskers. "He might consider makeshift armor dishonorable."

George could not understand his captain's concern. He was an engineer. He understood how coal fires boiled water to steam, how steam was driven through lines into engines, how engines drove propellers that drove ships. Since coming aboard, he had found his salvation in his commitment to the maintenance of these machines as they pounded across the world, hunting the *Alabama.* His thirst never quite went away, but the dirtier he got his hands, the more he exercised his brain, the easier his thirst was to ignore.

"If we can make a better machine, sir," he said, "we deserve the victory."

Winslow had laughed. "I'm not sure your father would agree. But you are a very modern man, Mr. Stafford."

"When we were younger, my father always called me the Stafford staff corps layabout. Today he calls me forward-thinking."

The next morning, as the *Alabama* steamed out, with only her jib and driver set and the rest of her sails furled for close action, the band on a nearby French warship played "Dixie."

Damn that song, thought Ethan. Damn "The Battle Hymn of the Republic," too. Damn Jeff Davis and the Great Ape. Damn all shipboard autocrats. Damn every father's wrongheaded expectations for his son and wrongheaded notions of honor.

Now Old Beeswax—uniform freshly pressed, hat blocked, mustache waxed so hard that it looked like a rapier—called his men aft and scrambled atop a gun carriage so that they could see him. "This is it, lads! Remember that you're in the English Channel, theater of so much naval glory of our race, and that the eyes of all Europe are upon you. The flag that floats over you may be one of a young republic, but she bids defiance to her enemies, wherever and whenever found!"

Ethan looked over the faces of the English crew who had sailed, not for the glory of the Confederacy, but for pay and prizes. He glanced at the haggard faces of the officers whose hope had been relief rather than battle. And he thought of how hollow the captain's words must sound to all of them.

There had to be better ways than war to get what we wanted.

Then the brass wheel ring glinted in the sun and caught his eye. It was engraved with the words, *"Aide-toi et Dieu t'aidera."*

A French-speaking sailor had translated it for him in the early days of the voyage. Now it seemed appropriate: "God helps those who help themselves."

Up on the hillsides, thousands of people were coming out to watch the fight, and Ethan remembered his father's stories of the Chileans coming out to watch the *Essex* on that long-ago day.

But who could blame them, or the pilots of the little boats that came out in the wake of the *Alabama*? It was a beautiful day for a battle.

A sailor at one of the broadside guns began to whistle "Lorena."

Ethan heard the last lines: "It matters little now, Lorena. The past is in the eternal past. Our heads will soon lie low, Lorena. Life's tide is ebbing out so fast."

So he began to whistle "Dixie." He patted his coat, where he had sewn a small and very fine chronometer into the lining, sealing its metal box with wax so that it would not be damaged if he went into the water. Then he went forward to his big pivot gun and prepared to fight a final time. . . .

Seven months later Jason Stafford saw the sternpost of the *Kearsage* and realized how near a thing it was.

A shell from the *Alabama* had driven itself into the steering mechanism but had failed to explode. Otherwise, the *Kearsage* and not the *Alabama* might now be lying at the bottom of the English Channel, and his son George, rather than his son Ethan, might be among those lost at sea.

The sternpost and rudder had been removed from the *Kearsage* and delivered to President Lincoln, like a trophy of war. Now they sat in a corner of his office: two heavy timbers, banded together, and right at the place where they joined was the shell, looking like a metal egg in the teeth of a giant clothespin.

"Captain"—Lincoln ambled into the room—"I didn't know that

you were coming, or I would have sent this thing to the Smithsonian."

"Captain Stafford insisted that he pay you a visit," said Gideon Welles. "And these days, he's very willful."

"That's because I'm old, Mr. Secretary." Jason had now slipped permanently into an old man's slouch and gone completely gray.

The president's hair was still wiry black, but he looked older, too.

Jason offered his hand. "Congratulations, sir, on your reelection. Of course, it started my sister to grousing about being unable to vote."

"If women voted, we might not have so many wars." Lincoln chuckled and sat at his desk. "Now, about Fort Fisher."

"That's a Blakely shell," said Jason, oblivious to the business at hand. "My son commanded the *Alabama*'s Blakely. This must have been his shot."

Lincoln leaned back as though he had all afternoon for a grieving old man. "I can't give him a medal. But I'll give one to George, for suggesting anchor-chain armor. They tell me that after the battle, Semmes went on and on about Winslow's dishonor for fighting with secret armor."

"Semmes has no right to speak of honor," said Welles. "He's a pirate, plain and simple. He and his crew should be tried as such when this is over and hanged."

"My boy was no pirate," said Jason.

"Gentlemen, let's win this war before we start worrying about punishment," said Lincoln. "Now, what about David Dixon Porter's attempts to reduce Fort Fisher?"

"David Dixon?" said Jason. "He's stepbrother to little Davy Farragut. And little Davy's done a fine job, too. I say he deserves to get laid good and proper, just like the rest of the crew. The native girls are always askin' me about the young boys berthed on the *Greenwich*. They . . ."

Jason noticed the look that passed between Lincoln and Welles, and he realized he was reaching back a bit too far. He had been doing that more often lately. He could see how embarrassed they were for him, so he changed the subject. "I hope that my family will be able to attend your inaugural, sir."

"We'll see that you get tickets, Captain. Now, Fort Fisher . . ."

xvi
An Actor Prepares

"A ticket to the inaugural—that is something a man would covet."

Alexandra, dressed now in black, handed over what she resolved would be her last supply of quinine for the southern cause.

John Surratt thanked her without even looking up.

But Booth, who was lounging on the sofa, with his feet up on the piano seat, was more interested in the inaugural. "How many tickets can you get?"

"Lincoln promised Captain Stafford as many tickets as he needed."

"Probably thinks no one will come otherwise," snorted Booth.

Alexandra now avoided the actor whenever possible.

He was full of brandy and Confederate opinions, but afraid to fight because he feared scarring his face. He went about with a wild look in his eye, but he let others go to war for him while he bragged about smuggling the kind of drugs that Alexandra had been quietly bringing to the Surratt house for four years.

However, Booth was still one of the world's best actors, and he now played the charmer, his famous face full of a smile. "Alexandra, have I not done you a great favor, more than once, in getting you tickets to my performances?"

"Well, yes." She looked at the floor, to avoid the dark beam he aimed at her.

"Then a ticket to the inaugural is a fair exchange."

"But you detest Lincoln."

"Wilkes would see how uneasy lies the head that would wear the crown," explained Surratt.

Booth glanced at his skinny little friend. "Do I dare tell her?"

Alexandra looked up, met Booth's gaze with her own. "Tell me what?"

But Surratt jumped in. "Tell you how much he admires your family's commitment to honor and sacrifice."

Booth nodded, as though some understanding had passed between him and Surratt. Then he took Alexandra's hand. "If you can bring me close to Lincoln, I will bring you closer to ecstasy in my next performance. I will play my lines only to you."

"Won't Juliet be jealous?" she cracked.

"Perhaps it will be Desdemona, if I am Othello."

"I can't see you playing a darkie."

"Nor can I." Booth raised the back of her hand to his mouth. Then his dark eyes were once more on hers. "I carry your picture in my pocket, dear. You are an intoxication, even when you wear black for a dead fiancé."

"And you are a windbag, Mr. Wilkes Booth, especially when you woo a lady to get something you want."

Booth's smile widened to show his teeth, like a dog offering a small warning. "I woo a woman for her beauty and her loyalty to the South."

"The South is dead . . . as dead as my southern sailor."

Booth let go of her hand. "You seem most cavalier with the memory of your martyred Ethan."

"I cherish his memory. He knew there had to be smarter ways than war to get what we wanted."

"So do I," Booth said seriously.

Alexandra thought for a moment. "On that basis, I will try to get you a ticket." And perhaps he would leave her alone after that.

"You know where I can be found. At the National Hotel."

Washington had always been a muddy place, even on the hillsides, and the heavy rain on the morning of the inauguration had created a great, sucking quagmire, as if the swamp that the city had risen from were trying to reclaim it. But the great white dome was now complete. It defied the mud and shone through the miserable gray mist, final proof, as Lincoln had hoped, that the Union would go on.

It would be a much different Union, however, just as the family Captain Jason met at the train station was different, inside and out. They went with a unity of purpose that none of the Staffords could have felt four years before. There was no arguing over slavery or Lincoln now. No happily inebriated chatter from George, no sniping between Margaret and Antonia, no lecture from Jack Browne.

As they reached the crowded square at the East Front, Iris Ezekiel looked up and said, "It sure is fine."

"Fine that it's finally finished," said Antonia.

"It's just fine to be goin' the same way as everybody else for once."

The Old Captain looked over his family and realized that Alexandra was not with them.

"She had to visit a friend at the National Hotel," said Margaret, shaking the mud from the hem of her black dress.

"Visit a friend?" said Jason. "But Lincoln will be speaking in half an hour."

"She said she had promised him a ticket," George explained, "before she found out that you would only get four."

"She and her friend will just have to watch from down here, with all the younger generation." Antonia took Eve by the arm. "Except for this mother-to-be. She sits beside me, so long as she promises to name the next boy Abraham."

"National Hotel!" cried the hack, pulling his horses to a stop.

Alexandra stepped out into the Pennsylvania Avenue mud. All around her umbrellas were glistening and bobbing in the streets, blossoming like black flowers as they emerged from the hotel, rising to be ready as ladies and gentlemen hurried across the lobby and out into the street.

Alexandra slipped unnoticed past the desk clerk and up the stairs to room 228. She took a deep breath. She feared Booth's reaction to the news that she had not been able to get him a ticket.

She knocked. *No answer.*

A second time.

"Can I help you?" The voice came from behind her in the hallway. He had a beefy face and whisk-broom mustache, derby firmly in place, cravat nicely knotted and perfectly stained, right where the stickpin should have been: the house detective.

"I've come to speak with Mr. Booth," she said.

"Now ain't that nice. The second dolly today. Don't you know it ain't ladylike to be visitin' a man in his hotel, miss?"

"I have business with him."

He grinned, as though he knew what kind of business.

So she pulled a calling card from her purse, then a pencil, and on the back of the card she wrote, "Inaugural ticket not available."

The detective read it over her shoulder before she shoved it under the door. "He already got himself a ticket, dearie."

"He did?"

"Miss Clay, senator's daughter, from New Hampshire. Guess she's sweeter on Romeo than you."

"Good," announced Alexandra, and she hurried off to hear what Lincoln would say, now that Grant had Lee pinned at Petersburg.

It was taken as a sign of God's favor that the sun burst from the clouds at exactly the moment that Lincoln stepped to the podium.

Jason Stafford shivered at the glory of it, and perhaps at the damp wool sea cape, soaked by the morning rain.

"Both parties deprecated war," Lincoln was saying, "but one would *make* war rather than let the nation survive; and the other would *accept* war rather than let it perish. And the war came."

Jason and Margaret, Antonia and Eve, sat several rows behind Lincoln, on the rough plank stands constructed for members of Congress and other important ticket holders. The rest of Jason's entourage stood below, to Lincoln's right, about halfway up the Capitol steps, except for Gabriel Shank. He sat on a camp stool at the back of the crowd, probably well out of earshot. And beside him was Alexandra.

Jason could tell by the black coat and bonnet and the red hair.

"Fondly do we hope, fervently do we pray, that this mighty scourge of war may speedily pass away. Yet if God wills that it continue until all the wealth piled by the bondsman's two hundred and fifty years of unrequited toil shall be sunk, and until every drop of blood drawn with the lash shall be paid by another drawn with the sword, as was said three thousand years ago, so still it must be said, 'The judgments of the Lord are true and righteous altogether.'"

Alexandra strained to hear Lincoln's words, but the low murmur of the crowd made it nearly impossible. While Gabriel sketched, she scanned the crowd.

And there he was, in the crush of ticket holders on the pediment above Lincoln's left shoulder. She first noticed him because of a familiar little boy, the son of theater owner John Ford, pressed up against the wrought-iron railing. Behind the boy was the rotund bearded figure of Ford himself. And behind Ford, in a fine top hat, fit for an inaugeral—as Lincoln pronounced the word—was Booth.

Lincoln was reaching the climax of his speech. His voice was rising. He was looking out over the crowd.

And Booth seemed to be pushing the little Ford boy aside so that he could get closer, peer more intently, almost read the speech over Lincoln's shoulder. And now Booth's hand went to his pocket. What was he doing?

Jason was shivering. He could not help it. Wet wool and mighty words would make any man shiver.

"With malice toward none, with charity for all . . ."

Jason thought of Ethan, of Alexandra and Dan'l Parrish.

" . . . with firmness in the right as God gives us to see the right . . ."

He thought of Tom.

" . . . let us strive to finish the work we are in . . ."

He thought now of George, standing out there, resolute and sober, a staff officer with all the respect that any line officer commanded.

" . . . to bind up the nation's wounds, to care for him who shall have borne the battle . . ."

He thought of Gabriel and the women of the Fine Folly.

". . . and for his widow and his orphan, to do all which may achieve and cherish a just and lasting peace among ourselves and with all nations."

After a moment of silence in the clear spring air, the cheer burst forth.

Jason began to cry. He could not control it. He cried that he no longer had his son Tom to comfort him. He cried that he did not have his son Ethan to comfort. He cried, he supposed, because he was old. He sensed a shuddering beside him. His wife was sobbing, too. So he quickly blew his nose and wiped his eyes, for her.

As he took the handkerchief from his eyes, an envelope appeared on his lap, and the face of Antonia, the face he had known longer than any other, was smiling through her own tears. "Jack said to give it to you now."

"What is it?" he asked above the sound of the cheering.

"From the *Hero*'s insurance payment. Money to pay off Dan'l Parrish. It's Jack's gift to you, in Ethan's honor. He says you taught your sons well."

Jason looked at Lincoln as he placed his hand on the Bible. "I tried."

• • •

Now Booth was moving away, and Alexandra was feeling better, because she never knew what to expect from the crazy actor, who had grown so much crazier as the South slipped closer toward defeat.

xvii
Mourning

Five weeks later the Fine Folly was draped in black.

All America was in mourning, and Alexandra Parrish wore a blanket of guilt that would have smothered her except for the fear poking holes in it.

Secretary of War Stanton, who had tearfully consigned Lincoln to the ages on the morning that he died, was now intent on consigning anyone who had been involved in his murder to one of the lower rungs of hell.

Booth was dead. But detectives and soldiers had swept through Washington and the surrounding counties, arresting dozens of people who had known him or allegedly had known of his conspiracy. The prime suspects—a collection of ne'er-do-wells, half-wits, and stagehands—were imprisoned on the monitors *Montauk* and *Saugus*. People on the periphery, like John Ford and Mary Surratt, had been thrown into Old Capitol Prison. Mary's son, John, on Confederate business in Canada at the time of the assassination, had disappeared.

As Lincoln's funeral train made its way across New York, the train of evidence led at last to the Fine Folly.

A burly captain named Lonergan and a skinny civilian detective named Swett appeared one May morning in the company of eight soldiers. Captain and detective were admitted to the front parlor, offered tea, which they declined, and invited to sit on the settee under an engraving of the *Constitution*. This was the only downstairs room that had not housed wounded soldiers, but the sun pouring through the front window still found plenty of cracks on the ceiling and walls. After all its hard use, the Fine Folly was falling apart.

"What can we do for you, gentlemen?" Antonia wore a black dress, very plain, that emphasized her white hair and alabaster skin.

"We would like to speak with Miss Alexandra Parrish," said the captain. "We were told she resides with you."

"She has volunteered loyal help here at the division since—"

"We have no interest in her nursing history," said Mr. Swett testily.

"I am at your service, gentlemen." Alexandra glided into the room, nothing more than a red-haired shadow in a black dress. She held her hands clasped carefully in front of her so that no one would see how much they were shaking.

The captain asked Antonia if she would excuse them.

"I'd like her to stay," said Alexandra. "Miz Antonia has been a mother to me, and considerin' how . . . official you gents look, I think I'd like to have my mother sittin' here, helpin' me answer your questions."

"Why would you think you need help?" asked Swett, leaning forward, bouncing on the balls of his feet, as though he could barely control himself.

The burly captain said, "You have nothing to fear from us, dear."

Alexandra knew that was untrue.

"What do you know of John Surratt?" asked Mr. Swett.

"That . . . that he's wanted as one of the conspirators against the president."

"A boarder at his house puts you there many times, bringing packages."

Alexandra glanced down at her hands, then shot a glance at Antonia, who sat serenely, as though she were not in the least surprised at this revelation.

"Well . . . I've been there, but—"

Swett pulled a notebook out and began to write. "Yes, go on."

"Miss Alexandra is a fine seamstress, gentlemen," said Antonia calmly. "And she has been doing work in Washington for many years."

"Are you saying that her visits to the Surratt house were completely innocent?" asked Swett.

"What else would they be?"

Swett pulled out a carte de visite. "Are you familiar with this person?"

Antonia glanced at the image, as though she were Pandora peeking into the box. "It's Alexandra."

"Well, this carte was found in Booth's pocket."

Alexandra felt the collar of her dress suddenly tighten around her throat. But old Antonia barely blinked. "I read in the papers that he was carrying pictures of several women, along with a compass, a whistle, and a map. Are you investigating *all* of the women? What about the mapmakers?"

That gave Alexandra time to fashion an excuse. "I was a great admirer of his acting. I'm not the only woman who ever offered him a carte de visite."

"No. Certainly not," said Antonia brusquely. "Now, as you gentlemen have declined a cup of tea . . ." She began to stand.

Swett pulled a calling card from his pocket and held it before them. On one side was printed "Miss Alexandra Parrish." On the other was written, "Inauguration ticket not available."

Antonia gave Alexandra the slightest of sidelong glances.

And Alexandra felt her stomach drop like a gallows door. "I . . . I had to tell him. I expected him to be angry, but I did not give him the ticket."

"Yet he was *there*," said Captain Lonergan with an ingratiating smile. "At the inauguration, probably planning to do his deed that very day, before the whole nation. Surely you must have some idea as to how he got there."

"Did you question the house detective at the National Hotel?" asked Alexandra, her voice quavering. "He said a senator's daughter had come earlier that day and had given Booth a ticket."

"A *senator's* daughter?" asked Antonia.

"Yes," said Alexandra. "A senator from New Hampshire. Booth once showed me a carte de visite from her."

And Antonia, who never backed away from a fight, charged ahead. "Was that carte in Booth's pocket, too, gentlemen?"

"Never mind about Miss Clay," said Swett. "We're here to interrogate—"

"You do not suspect the daughter of a New England senator, but the daughter of a Patuxent River planter is fair game?" said Antonia in her highest dudgeon. "Well, do you know whose house this is?"

Captain Lonergan withdrew a slip of paper from his pocket and read it. "The home of a Captain Stafford?"

"Come with me," commanded Antonia haughtily.

And Alexandra felt a little better. Antonia was a force against which slavery had not prevailed. How could these two?

Almost meekly, the men stood and followed her down the hallway.

Through the French doors at the back, old Zeke could be seen tending his rhododendron, but Antonia turned sharply to the right and into the library. "Here, gentlemen, is Captain Jason Stafford."

The library, as always, was dark, leather-brown, embracing. Held in its caress was a simple pine coffin, in which lay an old man wearing a gold-trimmed blue uniform. His widow sat beside him. His only surviving son stood by the window.

"Captain Jason Stafford, of the *Philadelphia*, the *Essex*, the anti-pirate patrols, the Steamship Board, the Navy Department, and father of two navy men who gave their lives in the recent conflict."

"What is this?" asked George, looking up.

"These gentlemen," said Antonia, "do not seem to believe that Captain Stafford is quite as important as some pissant senator from New Hampshire."

Swett began to turn crimson. Lonergan simply stood at parade rest.

"They believe Alexandra was part of the conspiracy to kill the president. They have not, however, accused the daughter of this senator, who got Booth a goddamn ticket to the inauguration."

"Killing the president was like killing the captain. He collapsed an hour after he heard the news," said Margaret. "This girl has been treated like a daughter in this home. She would never have done what you are suggesting."

Swett answered, "Her own brother was a blockade-runner. She—"

Eve Stafford appeared in the doorway. Her hair was down, a silk dressing robe wrapped around her, and an infant wailed in her arms. "George, what—"

"Allow me," said Antonia, "to introduce Abraham Jason Stafford."

The government men looked at each other, then at Alexandra, who was looking at the baby, because she could barely make eye contact with any of the good people who, at this moment, trusted her more than she deserved.

"Miss Parrish? What do you have to say?" demanded Lonergan coldly.

He was the dangerous one, she knew. The civilian was just a jobber, reading names and hunting for connections. This big captain had led men in battle. He had seen fear in men's eyes and knew what it looked like.

"Captain," said George angrily, "I am going to protest this disrespect."

"My apologies, sir, but—"

Just then, a familiar clump-thump-clump was heard in the hallway.

Antonia had not been able to get used to the sound of a crutch and a wooden leg echoing through the old house. It was the sound that had always preceded Gideon. But it was Gabriel Shank who appeared.

Antonia ushered him to Captain Lonergan. "This is Miss Parrish's fiancé. Gabriel Shank, Twentieth Maine. Lost his leg on July 2, 1863. You know the place?"

The captain looked into the eyes of this confused former private, now the engraver for the *Maryland Gazette*, and to the shock of everyone in the room, Lonergan's own eyes filled with tears. "Twentieth Maine . . . Little Round Top. If the rebs had ever flanked you boys that day, I don't know but what Bobby Lee would've beaten us."

"It was a near thing, as it was, sir." Gabriel balanced himself on his crutch and took the captain's hand. "And damned awful while it was goin' on."

Then the captain apologized to the assembled family and said to Mr. Swett, "There's nothing here. Come on."

"Nothing? But—" Swett looked around the room.

"Nothing." The captain grabbed him by the sleeve. "I can see that this, this is a household of patriots. Past and future."

Little Abraham squalled and stuffed his fat fist into his mouth.

Late that night, Antonia appeared at Alexandra's bedroom door. Her white hair, unpinned, straggled to her shoulders. Her lamp bathed one side of her face in brilliant light, the other in deep shadow. "I will ask only once, Alexandra. Did you know what Booth was planning?"

"No." Alexandra wanted to say more but she could not.

"Good," said Antonia. "I was prepared to overlook the quinine."

"You knew?"

"Of course. I even followed you to Baltimore, to see where your *aunt* lived. I wasn't surprised that she lived in Washington and wasn't your aunt at all."

"I'm . . . I'm sorry, Antonia."

"If you hadn't been tryin' to help your fiancé, I would have thought less of you. I only hope you didn't try to pass naval information along with quinine."

"Mostly it was quinine."

"Mostly?"

"You said you would have thought less of me if I hadn't been trying to help Ethan . . . or my brother."

"Now that I've saved you, I'll think less of you if you do not help me get women the vote"—Antonia blew out her lamp—"so that a war like this never happens again."

xviii
Farewell

A month later, a Negro boy delivered an envelope to the Fine Folly, addressed to Alexandra. Antonia accepted it and took it across town to the little house on Spa Creek that Alexandra now shared with her new husband.

The salutation caused Alexandra's heart to jump: "Darling Lexie." Only one man had ever called her that. "I have two hours. Meet at State Circle, eight-thirty tonight. By the Old Treasury Building." There was no signature.

Antonia saw the color leave Alexandra's face. "What is it?"

Alexandra looked toward the little kitchen, where Gabriel sat sketching, then she said, "Go and get Margaret. Take her to State Circle. I'll meet you there. And tell her that she should . . . she should not be surprised by anything that she sees."

Although Annapolis was still full of soldiers, the grounds around the State House remained sacred Maryland turf. A lantern glowed in the cupola, where Alexandra had long ago watched for a Baltimore steamer. Lanterns illuminated the quiet streets that led into the circle. But the sycamore maples had leafed out, and the shadows were almost complete at ground level.

Near the Old Treasury Building, a single story of brick on the edge of the circle, the shadow of a man leaned against a tree.

Alexandra knew immediately that this was no ghost from *kappal hantu*. She stopped about five feet from the tree.

His beard was full now and covered most of his face. A sailor's slouch hat was pulled low over his forehead. And though it was a mild May night, a pea coat was buttoned tight around his neck.

"Hello, Lexie," the shadow said.

"You're dead."

He stepped toward her. "I had to do it."

She held up her hand. "You're dead, Ethan. Don't come any closer to me."

And he blurted out an explanation he had rehearsed a dozen times: "A French fisherman picked me up. I bribed him with a chronometer to hide me. I was afraid they'd put us on another raider, and I couldn't watch another man die, or kill anyone else. I had to disappear."

"Your disappearance helped to kill your own father."

His shadow seemed to crumple at the knees. He leaned against the tree. Took off his hat, ran his hands through his hair. "I figured it'd kill him if I deserted from the Confederate Navy so soon after deserting from his."

Her shock was beginning to evaporate. She did not know if sympathy was replacing it, or anger, or a kind of contemptuous mixture of both. "He was proud of what you did for Cousin Jack."

"It made no sense anymore, burnin' fine ships and settin' their crews adrift."

"Showing up in the dark at State Circle makes no sense, either."

Somewhere down on Cornhill Street a dog barked.

"We're considered pirates, the men of the commerce raiders. If we're captured, we'll be tried and hanged. I sailed as a common seaman to get here, and my ship leaves Baltimore at dawn. But I had to come back . . . to see if you'd come to England."

Now it was her turn to shock him. "Ethan, I'm married."

But he talked over her. "Some of the others, like Bulloch, they're settling in England, and . . . you're *married*?"

"Yes."

He stepped closer to her, so close that she could feel the heat of his body, smell the faint aroma of rye whiskey, see the moisture glistening in his eyes. "But I told you to wait. I told you to wait, no matter what you heard."

"Even if I heard you were lost at sea?"

"No matter *what*," he said fiercely.

"You son of a bitch, Ethan. I cried for a month when we heard. Two months. I still cry. Damn, but I'm crying now." She pulled a handkerchief from her sleeve and blew her nose.

Then she felt his arms close around her, and her body stiffened. Beneath the shock, the sympathy, the anger and contempt, was a core of fury that now ignited. "Dammit, get your hands off me, Ethan Stafford. Don't be comin' back here thinkin' you can— *Dammit*." She slapped his face. She clenched her fists and pounded them against his chest. She threw her arms around him and felt his arms close around her, his beard scratching against the side of her face.

And that was how Alexandra and Antonia found them a few minutes later, still embracing deep in the shadows, with the aroma of lilacs heavy in the air.

A mother's joy at her son's resurrection was beyond anything that Alexandra had experienced that night.

As for Antonia, she had almost expected that Ethan would do something like this.

They stood in the shadows, embracing, talking, their conversation punctuated by the sound of sniffles from all except Antonia, and then, in the distance, they heard a whistle: the night train to Baltimore.

"I have to go."

"Oh, Ethan!" His mother threw her arms around his neck.

"If they allow amnesty for the commerce raiders, I'll come back. But I'll always write. Watch for letters from a man named George Thomas." He gently unpeeled his mother's arms from his neck. Then he looked into Alexandra's eyes.

"I'm sorry, Ethan," she murmured.

He turned and hurried across the circle toward West Street, thinking as he went that it was all for the best.

Then he heard his mother's voice.

"Ethan! Ethan! Where will you go? What will you do?"

He gave her that ingratiating grin that had gotten him out of trouble so many times when he was a boy. "I'm a citizen of the world, Ma. I'll go where I please, and do what I please. God helps those who help themselves."

CHAPTER SIX

At Chick and Ruth's

October 11

Before dawn, Susan jogged up to State Circle and stopped at the Old Treasury Building, now a little tourist information center.

Ethan and Alexandra.

In the gray light, it was easy to imagine them embracing there more than a hundred and thirty years before. She could almost hear the train whistle. But the train was long gone. What she heard was the hum of the morning traffic out on Rowe Boulevard—all those Washington commuters hoping to get a jump on the Beltway traffic, oblivious to anything but the red taillights ahead of them and the voice of the weatherman on the radio.

But standing there, beneath those trees, surrounded by those ancient buildings, Susan could block out the modern world, block it out so well that she could even feel the emotions that filled Ethan and Alexandra on that long ago night.

After reading a section of Jack's book, she found herself wandering the town, looking for the places she had read about. And each morning, she ended her run in front of that old house on Prince George Street, so that she could see it in a different light and imagine another generation climbing the front steps, carrying with them hopes and dreams that were new but somehow always familiar.

That morning, as she stopped to stretch before the old house, she finally realized why so many people wanted it. The Fine Folly was one of those places where time and space had met and made a pact: time would not destroy the house so long as the house kept its window open on the past.

Of course, she was beginning to think the whole city was like that. Wherever she looked in that cozy red-brick world, she had the sense of earlier lives lived, earlier crises endured, crises that were no less daunting to those who faced them than the troubles of today.

And that kind of knowledge could comfort an old man who wrote about the past; or an old man who spent his time writing about the future, at least as it related to naval weapons systems; or someone as unpredictable as Oliver Parrish. And that reminded her it was time for breakfast at Chick and Ruth's.

She had plenty of questions for Oliver Parrish.

Despite the bad eye, Steve Stafford had read everything Jack had given him in a single night.

It was something of a secret—to civilians, anyway—that navy men were a well-read lot. Those who weren't born with the habit usually acquired it on their first six-month deployment, after the supply of videos had run out. Before long, they were reading everything from Tom Clancy to *A Confederacy of Dunces*, from David McCullough to *The Celestine Prophecy.*

So a journey from Queen Anne's War to the Civil War was all in a night's work for Steve Stafford.

The following morning he was wondering what Ethan Stafford would have thought of the modern submarine, especially if he found the *Merrimack* claustrophobic.

So far, the book seemed to be nothing but honest.

Of course, the hardest part of that history might still be ahead—the parts about his own father. He thought he knew the truth. Or he had accepted as truth the things that had been told to him. His father had died bravely in Vietnam. That was what his mother always told him. And his grandfather, too.

And that was all he wanted to know. Or was it? He looked again at the picture: Jimmy Stafford, riding the river.

Steve decided he'd make the call . . . bring the old men together, and maybe he'd learn something, too.

Betty Stafford answered, listened, hesitated. She said the admiral was feeling more bad-tempered than usual the last few days. He was stumped on his article about the new class of submarines. Disagreed with some analysts on the use of HY40 steel in the hulls and . . . then there was a long pause, and Steve could hear his grandmother thinking it over.

"Oh, hell," she said. "It's about time we got those two old birds together."

"What about today?" he asked.

"Business in D.C. Institute stuff. Tomorrow. Lunch. Whether he likes it or not."

Chick and Ruth's Delly was an Annapolis institution: a long, narrow lunch counter with stools on one side, a row of tables along the other, walls painted fresh-squeezed orange and scrambled-egg yellow. Open around the clock. Daily specials, and the best two-dollar breakfast you could buy, day or night.

Chick and Ruth's had been on Main Street since the days when there had been a grocery market and a downtown cobbler and neighborhood bars like Sam Luray's. But those places were all gone. Restaurants and chandleries and souvenir shops now did the big business downtown. The markets had moved to the malls out on West Street.

That was the way things had to be if the old town was to survive. The pact between time and space had a Faustian side, thought Susan.

And Oliver Parrish had a Faustian look. Handsome, intriguing, dangerous. He was seated at one of the tables opposite the counter, dressed in a windbreaker with a country club insignia on the pocket—a pair of golf clubs crossed like swords. As she approached him she wondered how much of her soul she'd have to give up to get him on camera.

He greeted her like a man completely relaxed with his surroundings, or maybe it was the big plate of ham and eggs that was relaxing him.

"I'm sorry to order early," he explained. "I forgot a tee time with a client."

Susan ordered coffee, raisin bran, and low-fat milk.

He looked at her as if she'd just ordered a glass of hot water and a packet of Metamucil. "I bet you have yogurt and an apple for lunch, too."

"If I'm really feeling wild, I even have a diet Coke."

He sipped his coffee and asked, "So, what did you think of the *Annapolis?*"

"Pretty amazing. It ought to be for all that money."

"I don't want to be around if they ever start shooting those six-hundred-thousand-dollar torpedoes." He squirted ketchup onto his eggs. "Because it probably means the balloon's gone up."

"The what?"

"The big one's begun. Those subs were designed to sink Russian boomers, the subs that carry the big nuclear missiles. But the Russians have eighteen or twenty boomers. So do we. And we have sixty of those *Annapolis*-type subs. Not the best odds in a big ocean. You miss one of those boomers when war starts, he launches a strike that ends American civilization as we know it."

And Susan surprised even herself with her next remark. "I guess that's reason enough to build the best submarines we can."

Oliver grinned. "You've been hanging around Admiral Stafford too much."

The sudden clanging of a ship's bell by the cash register woke anyone who was falling asleep in his eggs and it scared the hell out of anyone who hadn't been to Chick and Ruth's before.

Then the voice of Chick's son boomed out on a P.A. system behind the counter, "Ladies and gentlemen, please join in the pledge of allegiance."

Oliver winked at Susan as they stood and turned toward the flag above the cash register. "Every morning at eight o'clock."

This was going straight into the film.

Maybe she'd introduce Oliver Parrish at Chick and Ruth's—a good American in a good American institution, saluting the flag before going off to fight his legal battles.

"I pledge allegiance to the flag . . ." Susan hoped she could remember it.

". . . of the United States of America . . ." There were twenty or thirty people around her—a few scraggly Saint John's students, a couple of uniformed Academy instructors, business people, old alums back for the nostalgia, regulars, newcomers—everyone stood and joined in. She hadn't seen anything like it since grade school.

". . . and to the Republic for which it stands . . ." She remembered every word. " . . . one nation, under God . . ." She leaned forward a bit, so that she could catch Oliver's eye, let him see that she really did know the pledge.

But Oliver's eye was on something else, and it wasn't the flag. His lips were moving, but the words were barely leaving his lips.

". . . indivisible, with liberty and justice for all."

Susan followed his gaze through the crowd to the end of the lunch counter and the old newsman who seemed to have a great nose for wherever the story was that day: Jack Stafford.

The mood in Chick and Ruth's was swinging upward—as it often did after a group of strangers participated in a little ritual that made them feel like friends.

And Jack Stafford was pushing toward them, smiling, offering his hand the way he would to a strange dog. "So, Ollie, it's been a long time."

"Not long enough."

"Smile, Ollie, or I'll tell Susan here how long you let that crew cut grow after you came back from Vietnam."

Oliver picked at his eggs, as though he had suddenly lost his appetite. "I could tell people how you screwed up yourself. If you'd done your job, I wouldn't have had to *go* to Vietnam."

"That's a pretty wild punch to throw. You're usually more surgical than that."

And Oliver Parrish dropped his fork into his eggs, so that orange yolk splashed on his windbreaker. Susan saw the sudden fury come into his eyes, as if Jack had touched the wrong wire in Ollie's head. Ollie blinked once, the way some people blinked away a tear, then he said to Jack, very calmly, "Forget the Fine Folly."

"I want that house." Jack sat down beside Susan.

"You're an old bastard with three ex-wives and no kids," said Ollie. "What the hell do you care about that place for?"

"I guess"—Jack scratched at the table cloth—"I just want a place to finally settle. Something to leave behind."

And Susan heard a faint echo of Tom Stafford.

In some places, this little conversation might have attracted a lot of attention, but Chick and Ruth's at eight in the morning was simply too busy for that. Besides, Jack and Ollie just sounded like a couple of businessmen talking over a deal.

"I plan to move my firm into that house," said Ollie.

"Well, you better be careful, or somebody might let the Shank family know that the Maryland lawyer is going to try to lock up the purchase of the house for himself as soon as the estate clears probate."

"Perfectly legal," snapped Oliver, "if I can scrape up the money. Where are you going to get two or three million dollars? What bank is going to give you that kind of a mortgage, at your age?"

"The book I'm writing may blow the roof off some important American history."

"Yeah. Thirty years too late," said Oliver, as though he knew exactly what Jack was talking about. Then he stood, as though he couldn't stand Jack's presence any longer. "I have a tee time. Miss Browne, we'll be in touch. And sleep well tonight. As the admiral will tell you, the Russians have stopped targeting our cities from those submarines . . . for now."

After he was gone, Susan said to Jack, "Thanks for nothing. I was just starting to get somewhere with him."

"You don't want to get anywhere with him. Believe me." Jack picked a piece of ham from Oliver's plate. "But I'll make it up to you. I know PBS won't let you do anything without documentation, so I'll let you see my research."

A treasure trove: that was all that Susan could think when Jack opened the old suitcase in his room at the Maryland Inn.

"This is my nineteenth-century bag. Most of the twentieth I carry in my head."

And he pulled out an old packet of photos.

Susan had dreamed of Antonia's eyes, and now she saw them—sad eyes, graying hair—and that hard-faced son. The picture was taken in late 1872, just a few months before Antonia died. John Browne, said Jack, went down in a mid-Atlantic storm just five years later.

And there was a picture that Susan had seen in history books—a handful of officers, standing on the deck of the *Monitor*, inspecting the dents in the turret. None were identified, but it wasn't hard to pick out the Stafford jaw.

There were women, children, large groups, small portraits—nineteenth-century faces, direct and unadorned, stiff and unsmiling, because the early cameras and film required subjects that were stiff and uncomfortable. And, good Lord, there were cartes de visite of Eve and Jacob, and Alexandra.

"Is this like the one that Booth was carrying?"

Jack nodded. "You can almost feel it vibrate."

As the century came to an end, cameras improved. And the Staffords could smile, especially in an extraordinary photo taken on a wharf in New York: a great white ship filled the background, and before it stood three Staffords, one old, one a boy, one a man in the prime of life.

"Taken in 1897." Jack tapped his finger on it.

The old man: "George Stafford, on the wagon for thirty-three years when this picture was taken. Also dying of stomach cancer."

The young man: square face, full mustache, naval uniform. "Abraham Stafford. Thirty-two, son of George, direct heir to the naval tradition, patriarch of the twentieth-century Staffords."

The boy, about twelve: dark-haired, like his ancestors, dressed in a suit so that he looked like a little man, squinting in the bright sun. "And that's our father. Will Stafford. He made me and the admiral the crazy sons of bitches we are today. Three generations, tottering right on the edge," said Jack.

"What do you mean?" asked Susan.

"Those three sets of eyes saw the navy, from the burning of the *Merrimack* to the bombing at Pearl Harbor. But that guy right there"—Jack tapped the smiling face of Abraham Stafford—"straddled the centuries. And he was a lot like the stubborn old bastard we'll meet tomorrow."

"How?"

"He had his hands on knowledge that might have changed the way the future went. But he didn't use it because he loved the navy too much."

That was a mystifying remark, but it echoed something still rattling in her head from breakfast. "What did Oliver Parrish mean about you doing your job and him going to Vietnam, all that stuff about 'thirty years too late'?"

"Ollie's a tough nut." Jack sat back on his bed. "After Vietnam, it took him a long time to put himself back together. Then he was ready to fight everybody, because he believed that everybody betrayed those boys in Vietnam—from loudmouth journalists like me to bureaucrats who decided how the war would be fought. That's why he looks like a right-winger one minute, Larry Liberal the next, and always pissed off. The kind of guy you'd want on your side in a fight, but not the guy you'd want driving the bus."

Maybe not, but Susan was certain she wanted to know more about him.

Jack, on the other hand, was moving on to the next topic, his shoebox full of primary sources: letters, newspaper clippings, fitness reports, copies of ships' logs, three editions of *Lucky Bag*, the Academy yearbook, a copy of the thirteen-thousand-word apologia written by Alexander Slidell Mackenzie, and David Porter's *Journal of a Cruise*, published by the Naval Institute.

"Forget Oliver and follow the story of the house." He slipped something out of the sheaf. "This paper was written at the Naval War College in 1897. It put my grandfather in the orbit of Theodore Roosevelt."

"What does this have to do with the house?"

"There's a connection. You'll see."

"Is it worth reading?" she asked.

"No," said Jack, "but this is." And he gave her another diskette.

The Stafford Story
Book Seven
Two Generations and a Big Stick
May 1897

Here was a problem to challenge any officer at the Naval War College:

Japan makes demands on the Hawaiian Islands.

This country intervenes.

What force will be necessary to uphold the intervention, and how should it be employed?

Keeping in mind possible complications with another power on the Atlantic Coast (Cuba).

Most officers groused when they were assigned to the War College in Newport, Rhode Island. A year of postgraduate theorizing instead of sea duty? It was the men who drove ships who rose in rank. But so did men who went where they were sent, did as they were told, and still showed a bit of forward thinking. That, at least, was what Lieutenant Abraham Stafford told himself.

The problem had been submitted by the new assistant secretary of the navy, marked "Special Confidential." It marked this new assistant secretary—former police commissioner of New York, former cowboy, pugnacious young Republican with a fine mustache and a mouthful of teeth to make a horse envious—it marked this Theodore Roosevelt as a forward thinker of the first order.

And it was about time, thought Abraham Stafford, for some forward thinking.

By 1883, the four-hundred-ship navy of the Civil War had shriveled to twelfth in the world. Most Americans had come to see it as no more than a government-funded social club where officers prepared at their own Academy, toasted wives and sweethearts on Saturday nights, and trained in ships that still had sails, because engines were unreliable and coal was hard to come by far from home.

But a new generation had arrived, and its voice was an Academy-bred captain named Alfred Thayer Mahan. In 1890, he published his War College lectures as *The Influence of Sea Power Upon History, 1660–1783*. It was the best book Abraham had ever read and one of the most influential books of the age.

Mahan's point was simple: much of history had been determined by the clash of great battle fleets, and it would always be so. He minimized commerce raiding, coastal defense, and blockade—despite their importance in American history—because without a battle fleet, no nation could defeat an enemy that had learned the big naval lessons: Build more ships. Build bigger ships. Acquire overseas coaling stations. And when war began, watch for the main chance, the big fight to win it all, the next Trafalgar.

The British saw in his book a vindication of their three-hundred-ship fleet. The kaiser put a copy aboard every vessel in the German navy. And the Japanese, who had journeyed from feudalism to world power in just forty years, found in it another Western idea to make their own. Building warships became a proclamation of national will.

And a new equation for imperialism was formed: national strength equaled a world-girdling fleet multiplied by the far-flung possessions that supported it.

By 1897, three 10,000-ton battleships had gone into U.S. Navy service, and more were on the way. America had joined the race. A little late, perhaps, but Americans had long legs.

Abraham had served on the new battleship *Maine.* A photograph taken on her foredeck with his father and son now hung on the wall of his library carrel, and he used it for inspiration as he wrote. He treated Roosevelt's problem as he would an exercise at sea. No halfway measures. No shirking of details. No going home for supper with the family. Work as though your survival depended upon it. And state yourself as firmly as if you were giving orders to an ensign.

The War College brass were so pleased with Abraham's paper that they forwarded it to Roosevelt. It quickly came back covered in marginalia, all complimentary. Abraham had served near a decade aboard navy ships and had received hundreds of enthusiastic duty reports, but this was different, and worth every hour he had spent at it.

"The first move," Abraham had written, "is to annex Hawaii and aid the new white government in stopping unrestricted Japanese immigation, which is tantamount to colonization; not in our best interests." *Well said, Lieutenant.*

"Hawaii is an invaluable strategic resource. That is why Japan has sought unlimited immigration. But we colonized Hawaii. We brought Christianity. We provided a whaling and agricultural economy. It is time to legitimize our relationship, like a man making an honest woman of a paramour." *Honest woman, indeed.*

"Two battleships should reach Honolulu simultaneous to our announcement. Back up our words with steel, and Japan will not challenge us." *Fine phrasing.*

"Hold the rest of the fleet in the Atlantic to watch Spain. It is in our interest to have all European colonial powers out of this hemisphere, and if Cuban revolutionaries need help to oust Spanish overlords, we must stand ready to give it." *Hear, hear.*

"Once the crisis is over, build more battleships and dig the canal through Nicaragua, as the most efficient way to move our ships between oceans." *Lieutenant, you have read my mind, and at least one of my recent letters to Captain Mahan. I look forward to meeting you at my War*

College lecture on June 2. My Uncle Irvine Bulloch sailed on the Alabama *with a Stafford; could you be related?*

Explosive. That was the only word Abraham could think of to describe Roosevelt at the podium. He was no more than five feet seven. But height would have lessened the effect of the powerful chest and huge head, the sense that here was energy, plain and simple.

Outside the lecture hall, fishermen's boats and rich men's yachts peacefully plowed through Narragansett Bay. But inside, the man from New York was all bellicosity and blue-water dreams.

He would speak, he told the assembled officers, of George Washington's maxim: "To prepare for war is the most effectual means to promote peace."

Several times in the next hour, Abraham restrained himself from cheering. He preferred to play the professional officer: Stafford jawline displayed just so, mustache carefully trimmed, hair parted sternly in the middle—a face that meant business, at attention or at ease.

"All the great masterful races have been fighting races," Roosevelt proclaimed. "The minute a race loses the hard fighting virtues . . . it has lost its proud right to stand as an equal of the best."

He praised those who "dared greatly in war or the work akin to war," and he characterized the diplomat as "the servant, not the master of the soldier."

His voice was high-pitched but hard, in the way that a polished gemstone was hard but highly reflective. And when he spoke, he pounded his right fist into his left hand, like a fighter. Abraham was mesmerized.

"It is through strife, or the readiness for strife," Roosevelt concluded, "that a nation must win greatness. We ask for a great navy, because we believe that no national life is worth having if the nation is not willing to stake everything on the supreme arbitrariment of war, and to pour out its blood, its treasure, and its tears like water, rather than submit to the loss of honor and renown."

The men of the Naval War College cheered, and the next day, the press reported the arrival of a new and altogether arresting figure on the national scene.

When Abraham's year at the War College was completed, Roosevelt requested this nephew of an *Alabama* man for his staff.

And he invited the Staffords for a weekend at Oyster Bay, Long Island.

By then a treaty for the annexation of Hawaii had been approved by President McKinley and passed on to the Senate.

Japan was furious. Roosevelt was gleeful.

And Roosevelt's high spirits invigorated his five children, who infected their eleven cousins, who swarmed through the barns, over the grounds, and along the shore. After a few minutes at their mother's side, Abraham's children, Will and Katherine, joined joyfully into the riot of kids and their ringleader, Theodore Roosevelt himself.

Abraham and his wife, Julia, a Main Line Philadelphia daughter, were not unfamiliar with opulence. Certainly not at her parents' home in Chestnut Hill. And the Fine Folly was a home for the history books, even if it had seen better days. But the casual grandeur at Oyster Bay overwhelmed them. So did the energy Roosevelt radiated.

"You don't even need sea duty to be part of this," Julia whispered, as they lay in the guest bed that night.

"Do you remember the night we met?" he whispered.

"All those midshipmen, all those giddy girls eager to snatch the next Farragut . . . I told you I would only dance with future admirals."

"I said that after four generations, it was time we had an admiral in my family. Then I had to go and marry you, as soon as I became an ensign."

"Marrying me was the best thing you ever did. Who cares about some silly old unwritten law that says an officer isn't supposed to marry until he's over thirty?"

"I do, if it means I won't make admiral."

From the moment he met her, he loved her. When she threw her head back to laugh, the curve of her neck was long and graceful. The last kiss she had given him was as sweet as the first. And she was as ambitious for his career as he was.

She whispered, "Just stay on Roosevelt's good side."

"I'm a lieutenant. Most men don't make admiral till sixty. By then Roosevelt—"

"He's a high-mettled horse, Abe. Now that he's taken you on his back, don't do anything to make him want to throw you."

• • •

A few weeks later, Roosevelt took it upon himself to answer Japanese protests over Hawaii. "The United States is not in a position which requires her to ask Japan, or any other foreign power, what territory it shall or shall not acquire."

The serious press condemned his imperialist outburst. The yellow press, named for the cheap paper on which the words were printed and the cheap emotions to which they appealed, was delirious with excitement.

But Japan sent no battleships toward Hawaii.

"We were right, Abe," exulted Roosevelt. "Annex the damn island. Possession is nine-tenths of the law. Even the Japanese know that."

As always, Abraham agreed.

Then, perhaps realizing that no thirty-eight-year-old undersecretary had ever enjoyed more leeway in a presidential cabinet, Roosevelt tempered his public words. But there were still maneuvers to make.

He maneuvered a personal favorite, George Dewey, into command of the Asiatic squadron, over several officers on the sacred seniority list, a bit of legerdemain that was not lost on Abraham or his ambitious wife.

And he did his damnedest to maneuver America into a war with Spain.

"If we could get the seven Spanish battleships on this coast," he told Abraham one afternoon in the Executive Office Building, "we'd have a very pretty fight, Lieutenant. I see a war from two standpoints."

"Two, sir?" Abraham cocked his head and angled his jaw.

"First, you have the grounds of humanity and self-interest for interfering on behalf of the rebels." Roosevelt leaned across the desk once used by Gideon Welles, on which hand-carved monitors steamed over mahogany waves. His eyes did not twinkle. But there was a light in them just the same, a hard gray glint of excitement. "Second, consider the benefit of testing the navy in actual practice."

The Cuban rebellion had been a bloody and brutal affair. The Spanish had tried repression, concentration camps, mass executions. But the rebel junta had continued to fight, to sabotage, to assassinate their way to self-determination.

Finally, in December, the government in Spain sought a way out, offering autonomy to the people of Cuba, though a hundred and fifty thousand peasants remained in *reconcentrado* camps.

Americans were pleased, despite the fulminations of publishing barons William Randolph Hearst and Joseph Pulitzer, who saw war as a way to sell their yellow papers. There would be no war. And, as President McKinley promised, there would be no annexation of Cuba.

Then loyalists in Havana rioted against autonomy.

The U.S. consul general said that he feared for American citizens and American investments. It was time to show the flag.

The glint in Roosevelt's eye grew grayer but somehow brighter.

ii
George Thomas

He sat in a café on the Empredrado, in the sweet breeze that warmed the Cuban night. With a discreet pair of Zeiss binoculars, powerful 7x50s that looked like no more than opera glasses, he studied the American ship riding buoy number five.

His white suit had been cut by the same London tailor who dressed Prince Edward, though it bulged slightly under the left armpit, where he carried a new Luger semiautomatic. His beard, no longer a young man's vandyke or sea raider's bush of black, was as carefully cut as his suit, and almost as white, and he combed it with a neat part, right beneath his chin.

His pocket watch carried an engraved motto: *"Aide-toi, et Dieu t'aidera."*

He had never learned to believe in lost causes, but if there was money to be made, the man known as George Thomas would make anyone's cause his own. That was why he could afford Prince Edward's tailor.

The American ship was called the *Maine*. She was not the mightiest in the fleet. Ten-inch guns and partial armor had been enough when she was launched. Now there were ships with eleven-inch guns. Next year there would be twelve-inch guns. And after that . . .

Some considered the naval arms race one of the wonders of an age overwhelming itself in mechanized wonder. George Thomas thought it was lunacy.

The hull of the *Maine* was painted white, the color of peace, quite the opposite of her purpose, and the ship reflected the lights of the waterfront like an iceberg in the tropical moonlight.

George Thomas took a sip of Jameson's, served neat. He wanted no part of the strange new concoction of rum and American Coca-Cola that people were drinking at the tables around him. He preferred old things.

And the oldest things around were the shoes that now appeared in the bottom of his field of vision. Above them were shiny serge trousers, a blue suit jacket, a collar that looked more like a yoke, then dark eyes, fierce young face, and absurd straw boater. "Our moment is here, *señor*."

"Sit down," said George Thomas, sipping his whiskey, "before someone shoots you."

The young man sat, pulled a handbill from his pocket, placed it on the table.

Spaniards!

Long Live Spain With Honor!

> Yankee pigs meddle in our affairs, humiliating us to the last degree, and for a greater taunt, send a man-of-war. . . . Spaniards! Let us teach these vile traitors that we have not yet lost our pride. Death to the Americans! Long live Spain!

"These loyalists give us the fuel. We need only to touch the match."

"Calm yourself, *amigo*." George Thomas patted the young man's arm.

"Do not patronize me, *señor*. We have—"

George Thomas made a small pursing of his lips, as if to say that there were many eyes and ears at the tables around them.

The young man lowered his voice. "The junta pays for your services. We—"

"You speak to me very impolitely, Manuel Baerga."

"We have no time for games of grace. We are fighting for a country."

"And I am fighting with you." George Thomas had seen this kind of passion before. He knew how brightly it burned and how quickly it could consume itself. "But first, my advance. Is this evening's payment arranged?"

"*Sí.*" The young man spat the word. "She will be at the Inglaterra at ten o'clock. She will wait in the bar. Now what will you do to earn her?"

"In good time, my friend."

"The guns you bring could be brought by others. Dynamite, too. Others who are *simpático.*"

"One who is *simpático* may make mistakes. I am a professional."

"One who is *simpático* does not demand a woman every other night."

"That is part of my pay. Besides, I have forgotten more about dynamite than most *simpáticos* will ever know."

"If your reputation was not good, *señor*, you might be dead by now."

By now. A phrase George Thomas had heard before in his line of work and always found a little too open-ended. "My reputation is my shield, *amigo.*"

"We have hired you for your sword."

George Thomas took a cigar from his pocket, cut off the tip with a little silver guillotine, and lit it from the candle on the table. "Dynamite is my sword."

"*Sí.* The dynamite. Where?"

"Somewhere in Havana. To be used against an American symbol. What I do will be blamed on the loyalists, the same ones who write these handbills. Then America will enter the rebellion on the side of the rebels. It will be demanded by Yankee newspaper editors and jingoists both."

"Jingoists?"

"Patriots . . . with no self-control."

"Patriots do not need self-control," said the young man.

"What is the girl's name?"

Before Manuel answered, George Thomas heard a dull thump.

It sounded like a distant artillery piece.

But it was not distant . . . only muffled.

Before that thought was fully formed in his head, a concussion of air knocked the breath out of him and mashed his eardrums into his skull.

A plate-glass window shattered. Doorways were blown open or broken by the blast. Palm trees all along the Empredrado were bent, as if by a violent wind.

George Thomas dived beneath the table, and Manuel Baerga was knocked from his chair an instant after.

The *Maine* was exploding. A yellow-orange flame appeared just forward of the bridge. Then the whole bow section lifted into the air, and Havana was lit as if by a photographer's giant flashpan.

The flame rose with the bow, jetting a hundred . . . two hundred . . . three hundred feet upward in an instant.

Then it was gone, and the waterfront lights with it.

The sound of the blast echoed off the *catedral* where the bones of Columbus lay. It bounced off the walls of Morro Castle. It rolled north toward America.

At the same time, a cloud of smoke billowed up from the place where the flash had been, billowed up in a great column above the broken ship, billowed out toward the waterfront cafés and bodegas, billowed down with a rain of iron and steel and mangled flesh that seemed to go on and on. . . .

And then came the silence, the sound of a whole city sent suddenly into shock, punctuated only by the sound of coughing in the acrid black cloud.

Then whistles and horns and alarms were going off everywhere.

And Manuel Baerga was laughing, right there, under the table, his face not twelve inches from George Thomas's, his breath a strong steam of garlic in the smoke.

"What's so funny?"

"That I ever doubted you, *señor*."

"You think that—" Then George Thomas stopped himself. The job was done. He had not done it. But he would be paid all the same.

With no more than a glance at the wreckage of the great white ship, the man known as George Thomas took Manuel Baerga by the elbow and together they hurried toward the Inglaterra. All the while, Manuel Baerga went on about the brilliance of Thomas's plan and the even more brilliant execution.

"A mine, *señor*? Was it a mine? It had been talked of."

"Who talked of it?"

"The junta, the *simpáticos*—a barrel of black powder, a dark night, two wires running to a battery on the shore. Was that how you did it? Or did you—"

"I cannot say."

"The code of the profession." Manuel Baerga seemed overcome with excitement. He made a bad revolutionary and would make an even worse saboteur.

"The code of honor," answered George Thomas, though he saw no honor in taking pay for something he did not do, especially the murder of American sailors.

"Well, you shall have your advance. And soon . . . payment in full."

They had reached the Parque Central in front of the hotel.

Candles glimmered in windows where the electricity had gone out. The usual crowd was about, but the smoke had drifted inland and settled like liquid tension, dampening the sounds of the street.

"You have two hours with the girl. Her name is Maria," said Baerga. "I will bring the gold to your room at midnight. By dawn you will be halfway to Florida."

Cigar smoke, stale rum, and sweat vaporized in the heated atmosphere of the Inglaterra bar. It smelled as acrid here as outside. Men talked intensely in the semidarkness, and they talked of only one thing.

The bartender put a glass of Jameson's in front of George Thomas. "A man was looking for you, *señor*."

"A man?"

"A man. Of good clothing and good manners."

George Thomas did not like it when someone he was not expecting came looking for him. "Was this man alone?"

"*Sí*. He said he would be back."

Just then the lights flickered on, and there was the girl, coming toward him through the cigar smoke. It was time to clear out, thought George Thomas. But since he had to wait until midnight, he might as well enjoy himself.

She was in her twenties, which was good. He hated it when they sent him young ones. This Maria—they were almost always named

Maria—wore a red camellia in her hair and fiery red lipstick of the sort that no American or English woman would ever allow on her lips.

"I am not a whore," she announced in his room. "I do this for the revolution."

"You do not have to do it at all," he said. "If you want to leave, go ahead."

She stared at him, as if she might take him up on his offer. Then she flipped off the ceiling light. "Our contract must be fulfilled."

With her back turned, she dropped her shawl, then her dress. Then she turned frankly toward him.

In the half-light from a hotel window, all women looked alike. And when they were in his arms, they all felt alike, too. This had been his curse, and his blessing, since that long-ago night at State Circle.

Had this one not seemed so uncomfortable, he would have been more suspicious. This was the moment—after the job was done but before he had been paid—when he was most vulnerable.

He touched her gently, the backs of his fingers on the soft flesh of her breast.

"The contract does not say that you wear your gun and open your fly."

Whatever stirring he felt began to flag. "I always wear my gun."

She pressed her body against him. She wore no perfume, but the smell of her was deep and musky—fresh sweat, harsh soap, coffee—and he let it work its way through his system.

"I have heard that for all the gray in your beard"—she brought her hand to his face—"you are still very much a man, whether you carry your gun or not."

And slowly, she slipped her hand to the pistol under his arm.

He clamped his hand over hers. "The man who was looking for me in the bar. Is he with you?"

"I do not know what you speak of, *señor*." Her eyes shifted to the door.

"Yes, you do." And, as if on cue, there was a knock.

He snapped the pistol from his holster, put it to her head. She was no longer a naked woman. She was danger made flesh. "Who's there?" he hissed at her.

"I do not know."

He knotted his hand into her hair and said calmly to the door, "Who's there?"

"Señor Thomas?" came a weak voice from the other side. "Or is it Ethan Stafford? I am an old friend. My name is Martin Padilla."

"Padilla?" the girl spat. "The loyalist pig? You know Martin Padilla?"

"What do you want?" said George Thomas to the door.

"I must talk with you, *señor*. Here in your room or down in the bar."

In his room or in the bar or down in the street, there was no getting out of this. Best to do it in a dark space that he knew well.

He told the girl, "Wrap yourself in a blanket. If you move, I'll shoot you."

From under his mattress, he took a sawed-off double-barrel shotgun; then he positioned himself at the side of the door and unlocked it. "*Buenas noches,* Señor Padilla."

The man entered the darkened room as one would go into church.

George Thomas kicked the door shut and pressed the gun against the back of the gray head. There was no sound outside. No one tried to force the door open.

"I am sorry to interrupt you," said Padilla.

George Thomas flipped on the light, and cockroaches drawn out by the darkness went scuttling away again. "What do you want?"

Padilla was small, neatly dressed, with the light complexion and European features of Cuba's ruling class. "Do you not remember, *señor*? The *Virginius*?"

The *Virginius*—an old Confederate blockade-runner, commanded by a former Confederate naval officer, running guns to Cuban rebels in 1873. She had been captured. There had been a mock-trial, then executions. Forty ex-Confederates had fallen to a firing squad. There would have been more, but for the efforts of a young Cuban diplomat named Martin Padilla, and the appearance of a British warship, dispatched from Jamaica at the request of the American government. Ethan Stafford had been tying his blindfold when Martin Padilla arrived to stop the executions.

The man also known as George Thomas remembered very well. He lowered the shotgun. "Señor Padilla. It has been many years."

"*Sí,*" said Padilla, taking in the girl, the cockroaches, the rest of the room.

"A quarter-century, and still you represent a bloodthirsty regime."

Padilla shrugged, as if to say they would not solve that issue in a night. "I came looking for you because it is good to know men who know men in the American navy."

"I know none."

"George Thomas knows none. But you are known by many names." Padilla glanced at the girl.

"She knows nothing."

"Only that I hate loyalists," she hissed, "and their *reconcentrado* camps."

"Then you are working for the junta, *señor?*" said Martin Padilla.

"I work for whoever pays," said George Thomas.

"That is why you are trustworthy, *señor*. Your head is in it. But not your heart"—Padilla glanced at the girl—"I do not think."

The girl spat on the floor.

Whatever the cultured little man thought of that, he did not say. He simply took a step closer to George Thomas. "You will hear much in the days ahead. Messages will be passed in many ways between your government and mine."

"I have no government."

"But the men you know in the American navy, you must pass a message to them: the Spanish government had no part in the explosion of that battleship."

"What's in this for me?"

"Your life, *señor*. You will leave Cuba alive. And if you do not deliver the word, I will tell certain people your real name, and they will come to find you."

George Thomas was faintly aware of music coming from the park, trumpets, brassy and loud, suddenly blaring right beneath his window.

He wondered what cause there could be for celebration on such a night. And had he noticed it, he would have wondered why the hallway light had just gone out.

He stepped to the window, careful not to put himself in front of it. If he had learned anything in thirty years, it was never to stand before an open window.

That was a good lesson. Because the moment his eyes shifted

toward the street, the girl leaped for the door. In a single motion, as if she had practiced it a dozen times, she hit the light switch and pulled back the dead bolt.

The door slammed open.

Out of the hallway darkness came the flash of a pistol, then a second, a pair of flashes advancing quickly, firing indiscriminately, in little firecracker pops that could barely be heard over the blaring of the trumpets below.

The shadow of Martin Padilla collapsed.

From behind the door, the girl shouted, "Manuel! There are two!"

Immediately the pistols turned toward the bed.

The gunmen did not see George Thomas, because he never stood in front of an open window. But their muzzle flashes bracketed them perfectly. And in the little room, the report of Thomas's shotgun was like a Dahlgren thumping out a fistful of buckshot.

Above the blaring of the trumpets, George Thomas could hear the sound of bodies falling. He lowered his aim and blasted a second load. Then he dropped the shotgun and pulled the Luger from his holster.

But it was over. There was no movement on the floor, none in the hallway, and the music was receding into the park.

He went to the door, looked up the hallway and down. Nothing. The sound of the shotgun should have been heard, but the music and buzz of conversation below had deadened it, like a pillow placed over a screaming face.

So he closed the door, flipped on the light.

A setup. He had seen it coming in, and still he had come, like a horny midshipman. If not for Martin Padilla and his desperate message, George Thomas would have been right where they wanted him, in the bed, played out after fucking the girl. And they would have killed him.

He was getting too old for this.

Manuel Baerga and his accomplice, another young man with dark face and threadbare suit, looked like pieces of ground beef.

The girl had been struck by buckshot that blew through the door. She sat against the wall with the blanket around her waist and her eyes open, staring at nothing.

George Thomas, also known as Ethan Stafford, closed her eyes and pulled the blanket over her so that she did not look quite so indecent.

He stepped across the body of Martin Padilla, grabbed his carpetbag, and shoved the shotgun into it. Then he put on his white jacket and panama hat. Then he heard Padilla groan.

He knelt by the old man and said, "You took something intended for me, *señor*."

What Padilla had taken was five bullets. He would be dead in minutes.

"I have saved you a second time."

"Sí," said Ethan Stafford.

"You must promise that you will tell what I asked, *señor*. Tell them in America that my government had nothing to do with the destruction of your . . ."

"Have you told anyone my real name?"

"No . . . no . . . but if you do not do this for me, I will."

"I must do it, then."

iii
War Fever

The next morning, the *New York Journal* headline covered the front page: "*Maine* Blown Up in Havana Harbor." The evening edition, with little to go on, upped the ante: "Growing Belief in Spanish Treachery."

The following morning, Hearst's headline writers screamed: "Destruction of the Warship *Maine* Was the Work of an Enemy."

Damn all restraint.

A veteran engraver named Gabriel Shank was given a sketch to elaborate for the front page of the *New York World*. It was a view of the *Maine* tethered to buoy number five. Beneath her was an evil-looking mine tethered to a float; and tethered to the float, by means of a long wire, were two evil-looking Spaniards in a stone bunker, ready to blow the *Maine* sky high.

"I can't do it," Gabriel Shank said to the city editor.

"What do you mean, you *can't*?"

"I won't draw pictures that drag us into a war."

"What's the matter, Shank?" said a reporter who had just joined the paper. "You don't like a good war now and then?"

"There's no such thing as a good war. And no such thing as a bad peace. Ben Franklin said that." Gabriel pivoted on his cane and went thumping across the city room.

By the time the evening edition appeared, he was out of a job.

As his wife Alexandra said, it wasn't the first time.

The evening headline read: "War! *Maine* Destroyed by Spanish; This Proved Absolutely by Discovery of Torpedo Hole." It was all rumor.

In his office, Abraham Stafford reread the latest cable from Captain Sigsbee of the *Maine*: PROBABLY THE *MAINE* DESTROYED BY MINE, PERHAPS BY ACCIDENT. I SURMISE THAT HER BERTH WAS PLANTED PREVIOUS TO HER ARRIVAL, PERHAPS LONG AGO.

But why? And who could have known in advance that the American battleship would be moored to buoy number five?

The Spanish government had promised to soften its stance. The rebel junta was getting what it wanted. It did not make sense.

Abraham Stafford brooded all the way back to the navy yard.

His wife would have preferred to be living at the Portland or at Dupont Circle, but her family was not so well off as she allowed people to believe. Besides, in naval society, families who set themselves apart were asking to be ignored. And Abraham was like most naval officers—happiest in the society of other officers.

In the Academy, midshipmen were trained to believe that they were a breed apart. There were never more than a hundred in a class. They were held to high standards of academic and physical rigor. They wore uniforms with collars that looked almost clerical, except for the rank insignia. They attended regular Episcopal services, whether they were Episcopalian or not. They were bound by a code of honor that was forged in the classroom, deepened on training cruises, and sharpened by rituals, from color parades to midnight hazings. And after they graduated, all of them were united in their ambition for rank. Ambition, Abraham always told his son, Will, was the thing that would make a better navy and a better country.

Little Katherine greeted her father at the door, but when he bent to kiss her, she went racing off, shouting, "No kisses for the navy!"

With a great gust of laughter, he chased her down the hallway, through the living room, then the dining room, into the—

His mother. He stopped and turned back to the living room.

"Is it Pa?"

"No. He's only vomited a little blood this week." Eve Stafford had grown in stature as she aged. Straight skirts, high-necked blouses with puffed sleeves, hair piled in a swirl atop her head—these flattered her far more than the fashions of her youth.

"Your father doesn't think that the *Maine* was destroyed by a mine," said Julia with a frozen smile. "He would deny his son the chance for glory."

"He's trying to stop a war, dear." Eve handed her son an envelope.

It contained a cross-section sketch of the *Maine,* showing all of the frames—the vertical structural members that formed walls and compartments. At frame 32, Engineer George Stafford had sketched coal bunker A-16. From frames 30 to 18 were three magazines: A-6-M, A-9-M, and A-14-M.

"I said it when we toured her," George Stafford had written. "She was badly designed. A low-smoldering fire in the coal bunker heats the ammunition in A-14-M, the ship blows up, and we're at war."

"Your father still follows the world from his bedroom in the Fine Folly," said Eve. "He thinks we should stop the rush toward war."

"But these Spanish are butchers," said Julia. "They have it coming."

Eve looked at her son. "Don't you know this Roosevelt?"

"He sure does," said Will, who was sitting in the corner, reading the latest reports in the newspaper. He was now twelve, a splatter of pimples on his chin and a serious brow just forming. "Pa rides horses with Roosevelt in Rock Creek Park. He shoots grouse with him, too. He even uses the word 'bully' sometimes."

"From what I read," said Eve, "Roosevelt thinks this war will be a *bully* thing."

"It will be . . . won't it?" asked the boy. "A chance to show what we're made of, so that the Japanese and Germans and British will—"

"Remind me, sometime, to tell you about my days as a nurse in the Civil War. Have you ever seen a man with burns from a ruptured steam valve, dear?"

"Grandmother Stafford," said Julia, "I don't think that's an appropriate thing to be telling a boy about . . . especially just before dinner."

"But our sons for the sea must know the truth, mustn't they?"

• • •

That night, after they had taken his mother back to Union Station to catch the Annapolis train, Julia asked Abraham what he would do with his father's letter.

"Give it to Roosevelt."

"He's the path to advancement, Abraham—a sea command in wartime. Think before you dampen his enthusiasm with something like this."

Abraham thought hard and decided that Roosevelt would want to hear every opinion. So the next morning he put his father's sketch on Roosevelt's desk.

"The coal-fire theory." Roosevelt studied the plan. "We've been hearing this for three days. It's what Secretary Long believes. It's what McKinley hopes."

"My father argues the facts, sir. As you know, he was a respected engineer."

"No one respects engineers more than I do. But the last thing we want to learn is that this was the result of incompetence aboard one of our ships."

"Yes, sir . . . er, no, sir."

"We may never know for certain, but I believe the *Maine* was sunk by an act of dirty Spanish treachery. I'd give anything if President McKinley would order the fleet to Havana tomorrow."

Abraham gathered up the papers.

Roosevelt came around the desk and looked into Abraham's eyes. "We're also jingoes, you and I. We want a war. We want to prove that what we've been trying to do here is the best thing for this country."

"Aye, sir." Abraham put his father's theories away and hoped for war.

But over the next week, others tried to avert war while the assistant secretary and his young naval assistant champed at the bit.

Diplomatic notes were exchanged. A naval board of inquiry went to Havana to determine the cause of the explosion. Navy Secretary John Long—a cautious, slow-moving old man—moved slowly and acted cautiously. President McKinley, a Civil War veteran, said, "I have been through one war. I have seen the dead pile up, and I do not want to see another."

Roosevelt muttered to Abraham Stafford, "The president has no more backbone than a chocolate éclair."

And then Secretary Long took a Friday afternoon off.

For a few hours the high-mettled horse was given his head. So he kicked in the stall, jumped the fence, and all but galloped into war in a single day.

To a naval officer, raised from childhood in the belief that the chain of command was sacrosanct, what Roosevelt did seemed, at best, an act of high-principled arrogance. At worst, it was mutiny. But Abraham Stafford went along with it because Roosevelt was his superior . . . and the horse that was carrying him higher.

Roosevelt meant to remedy, in one afternoon, all the foot-dragging he had seen in the ten days since the *Maine* had exploded. He fired messages around the globe: coaling instructions to American ships on station; requisitions for ammunition; orders to move personnel; orders to purchase auxiliary vessels for the war; requests for congressional appropriations. And this to Commodore Dewey of the Asiatic squadron:

> ORDER THE SQUADRON TO HONG KONG. KEEP FULL OF COAL. IN THE EVENT OF DECLARATION OF WAR WITH SPAIN, YOUR DUTY WILL BE TO SEE THAT SPANISH SQUADRON WILL NOT LEAVE THE ASIATIC COAST. THEN COMMENCE OFFENSIVE OPERATIONS IN THE PHILIPPINE ISLANDS.

Abraham Stafford had never seen a performance like it.

The truth was, no one had.

The next day, Secretary Long hurried back to work, even though it was a Saturday, and he was heard to confide to his personal secretary, "Roosevelt came near causing more of an explosion than happened to the *Maine*. The very devil seemed to possess him yesterday afternoon."

When these remarks found their way back to Roosevelt, he told Abraham only this: "Someday they'll understand."

"I think Secretary Long understands already," said Abraham. "He hasn't countermanded any of your orders, yet."

Roosevelt looked out the window at the White House. "War has to come. When it does, the navy will be ready."

iv
Ethan Stafford

Once he was out of Cuba, it took him a week to clear up affairs in London. Then the man known as George Thomas disappeared.

He could have done it sooner, of course. In late 1865, charges of piracy had been dismissed against Semmes, and the Confederate raiders were free to come home. But by then he had become George Thomas, weapons expert for hire, and he was riding through the Mexican rebellion against Maximilian. In 1872, he was once more Ethan Stafford, sailing on the *Virginius*. In 1889, George Thomas ran guns to the Fenian rebels of Ireland. In between, he was here, he was there, working for this side or that, or living large in London.

But someday, someone who knew that George Thomas was to have died in the Inglaterra might come to London to finish the job. And he was too old for that.

Besides, he had made a promise to a dying man who believed that private diplomacy could stand against the storm that was about to smash a crumbling empire.

Stopping the war was a lost cause, and Ethan Stafford did not believe in lost causes. But he had never lost his belief that there were smarter ways than war to get what we wanted. In a strange way, that was why he had spent his life doing what he did.

For his return to America, he wore a four-button gray suit and a black derby. He also shaved off his beard, and beneath the white whiskers, he looked surprisingly youthful. Appropriate, he thought, when going back to the scenes of his youth.

But any thoughts of settling in Annapolis were dispelled in his walk from the depot to the Fine Folly. Crabtown was what they called it now, a sleepy little place on the banks of the Naval Academy, with March mud squirting up between the cobblestones and nothing much happening, beyond the oyster shucking at the waterfront and the debates at State Circle.

In the protected gardens before the Fine Folly, the crocuses were already blossoming and the magnolia buds were fat. Ethan hardly noticed the weeds, the peeling paint, and the crumbling mortar between the bricks, perhaps because he had not seen his brother in ten years.

Then he saw the black crepe hung around the doorframe.

His father, his mother, his half-brother Cecil, his aunt Antonia had all passed through the portals of Saint Anne's without him. Cousin Jack Browne had been lost at sea. Now his half brother George had joined those other links to the past, mourned that morning at Saint Anne's, bound for burial that afternoon at Stafford Hall. So Ethan rented a small steamer that got him down to the Patuxent a half hour after the funeral flotilla.

There was no hint of spring here, not in the brown fields or bare trees, not in the cold rising off the river, not in the crowd of people huddled by the family plot or the priest reading over the coffin.

Ethan did not cut straight across the field to the plot. He had long ago learned to come into things quietly. So he went up the rolling road, past the slave huts that now housed sharecroppers, then along the veranda at the back of the house.

Several officers and midshipmen stood in their greatcoats like a navy-blue wall around the civilian mourners. Ethan chose a broad navy back to stand behind so that he would not attract the attention of those seated at the grave—Eve and her bachelor son, Jacob; Abraham and his wife, Julia; and Abraham's two children, whom George had written about so proudly.

But Ethan could not avoid being noticed.

Robby Parrish, whom he had not seen since the *Alabama* stopped the *East Wind*, shot him a wink, but Robby had been so worn by growing tobacco in the exhausted Patuxent soil that the wink was the only thing about him Ethan recognized.

And then Alexandra caught his eye. Her gaze reached across the open grave and across all the years, and filled him with more regret than his brother's death.

It was a strange evening.

But Ethan was no stranger to strange evenings, and he sailed through this one, smoothly riding the conversational breezes from the dining room buffet through the study to the great hall.

He offered condolences to Eve and her sons. He showed a bit of avuncular pride to Abraham's two children. He chatted like an old shipmate with Robby Parrish. But he stayed well to windward of

Alexandra and Gabriel Shank. He talked of the weather as they sailed by. But more talk would be uncomfortable, even now.

What he wanted was to get Abraham alone, which he accomplished for a few moments in the study.

"I'm surprised to see you, Ethan," said Abraham with the wariness he had shown his shadowy uncle on the rare occasions when they had met. "Someone who brokers arms should be selling French eighty-eights to Spain right now."

"I'm out of that line of work. I always believed that strong neighbors made good neighbors. Give everybody guns and everybody gets along. But nations are like people. When they have weapons, they use them."

"So what brings you home?"

Ethan looked around the study, still painted the color of blood soaking into a wooden deck. "Stopping this war."

"That puts us at cross purposes. *I'm* trying to get it started."

"If you tell that damn cowboy Roosevelt that the explosion of the *Maine* was an accident, you might stop it."

"The coal-fire theory? We've been hearing that for two weeks."

"It's not just a theory. A trusted functionary in the Spanish government told me two hours after it happened: his government didn't do it. And I know for a fact that the rebels didn't get the chance."

"For a fact?" Abraham set his coffee cup on the mantel.

"*I* was supposed to do it *for* them."

"*You* were supposed to kill over two hundred American sailors?"

"I planned something much smaller."

"You're an arms expert who doesn't like war, yet you schemed to bring America into a war that you now hope to stop."

Ethan shrugged. "I'm a man of contradictions."

"If this story is the truth, Uncle, why don't you tell it yourself?"

"Would anyone listen to an arms expert who doesn't like war?"

Just then a towheaded boy scuttled into the room—Robby Parrish's youngest son, Charlie. "Did you see any kids come through here, Cap'n?"

"Are you playing hide-and-seek on this solemn occasion?" asked Abraham.

The boy looked down at the floor. "Yes, sir. But—"

And Ethan tousled the boy's hair. "You kids've been good for about as long as kids can be. Uncle George wouldn't mind if you played a little game."

The boy took that as permission to skedaddle, and quick.

Abraham turned his gaze to Ethan again. "Did Uncle George know you were some sort of agent provocateur?"

"I'm a man with vital information. I give it to you."

"What am I to do with it?"

"The right thing. It might help you to climb a few rungs on the ladder of rank."

"I can fend for myself on that score," said Abraham stiffly. "I don't need the help of a long-lost uncle."

"I'll remember that." Ethan took out a cigar. "But you remember that there's no honor in fighting if you can talk, son."

"You can't know much about what happened in this room, then."

"The man who died in this room did the right thing. Sometimes that means defending your family. Now it means stopping a war. So there"—Ethan lit his cigar and gave Abraham a grin—"I've fulfilled my pledge to a dying man. Now excuse me while I go and sit with your mother."

Abraham weighed Ethan's words, reconsidered his father's last letter, considered the responsibility that this old Confederate had dropped on him with a grin, as though he did not care in the least what Abraham did with it. Then he weighed Roosevelt's words—"Someday they'll understand"—and decided that Roosevelt's words weighed more than Ethan's. Then he went off to cut himself a piece of cake.

The old study was now empty . . . but for two kids hidden inside the wall. The closet door swung open and Will Stafford stepped out. He was a little old for hide-and-seek, but it had been a long day, and even a disciplined boy needed some fun.

His sister dropped down right after him. "What were they talking about?"

"War . . . or honor . . . I think," said Will.

"Oh . . . okay. C'mon, before Charlie Parrish finds us."

The wind kicked up in the middle of the night.

The old house creaked. The branches of a big oak scratched at the windows of the room where Ethan lay awake, the same room where he had lain awake as a boy, imagining his great-grandfather and the pirates.

Legends and ghosts . . . and a noisy old house.

He slipped out of bed, tiptoed downstairs, and stepped outside.

High nights, he called these, when the wind was a living presence and the clouds raced across the moon, sending splashes of silver and dark shadow skittering over the landscape.

He felt like a ghost himself—a little boy, sneaking out to fish before the sun was up, a young man galloping home from Lexie Parrish's hayloft, a midshipman sharing a flask with the brother they had buried that day.

He wandered back to the grave plots, where the fresh earth was rounded up over George Stafford and the old headstones looked like jagged teeth around it.

Legends and ghosts . . . and all their high-flown notions.

Then a voice came out of the darkness. "You look good, for an old man."

He almost expected to find that other houseguest wandering outside in the middle of the night, shawl around her shoulders and wind blowing her hair across her face. The hair remained mostly red, but for a single streak of gray at the front. People who liked her said it made her look like a woman warrior. Those who didn't said it made her look like a red-haired skunk.

"Hello, Lexie," he said. "I couldn't sleep. What are you doing up?"

"Visiting an old friend." She gestured to the headstone of Antonia Stafford Browne, 1787–1873. "She said, 'Always ask.' I always have."

A shaft of moonlight fell on them, and they were both young again. Just as quickly, a shadow swept across the little graveyard.

And he asked her something that had always puzzled him. "Why didn't you have kids, Lexie?"

"Gabriel's wounds were worse than most people knew."

"I never had kids either."

"Children would have been a gift, Ethan."

"Just be glad a man loved you."

"Two men loved me." She pulled her shawl tighter. "And I had a cause. As Antonia always said, if women had been given the vote, we might not have had a Civil War."

"Antonia always thought too much of her own opinions."

"So . . . what are you going to do, now that you're back?"

"I don't know. I have money. I have ideas."

"Any dreams?"

"I dream of a place to settle."

"So do I. But Gabriel's never stayed in one place for long. Baltimore, Boston, New York . . . now Washington. And always he digs in his heels over something or other and loses his job."

"Sounds more like a rebel than a Yankee."

"That's why I love him. But a place to settle would be nice."

Ethan looked up at the clouds, like souls rushing toward their fate in the moonlight. "Sometimes we just don't get what we want."

V
A Splendid Little War

At the end of March, the navy board of inquiry delivered its verdict.

After taking testimony from survivors, after analyzing the way in which the *Maine* had buckled, the way the water had geysered when she exploded, even the number of fish killed in the harbor, their conclusion was unanimous: a mine. They could not fix blame, but as one newspaper wrote, if the Spanish could not stop this from happening, it was time for a new government in Cuba. And if the Spanish would not close the brutal *reconcentrado* camps, it was time for them to go.

Abraham felt vindicated in his silence.

But there was no silence in America. "Remember the *Maine*, to hell with Spain": The slogan was heard in saloons and sitting rooms. It danced on the telegraph wires. It screamed, with some editing, across the front pages of America.

And Ethan Stafford wrote Abraham another letter: "Not surprised you kept your mouth shut. Might not have changed the course of things, anyway. But you'll never know. Do not get killed. Your kids need you. I am bound for Oklahoma. They say they've discovered oil."

The declaration of war came toward the end of the month.

So did Abraham's orders. He was assigned to the *Iowa,* the most modern ship in the fleet, with Roosevelt's promise of command when an auxiliary cruiser came into service. It worked out the way he and Julia had always hoped.

The weekend before Abraham reported to Hampton Roads, he took his Will to Annapolis to witness a color parade, always a stirring sight, especially so as the first classmen prepared to graduate early and join the fleet. There was purpose in the march, confidence in the faces, purity in the white drill order. Never had a John Philip Sousa tune resounded more powerfully.

But young Will Stafford seemed solemn. Neither the music nor the snapping of the colors nor the cadence of the march could improve his mood.

"You've been very quiet lately," said Abraham, as they walked around the Fort Severn battery, which had been roofed over and turned into a gymnasium.

"It's the war, Papa."

"The approach of war can be a frightening thing, son. But if you mean to come to the Academy—"

"I do, sir."

"Well, this is where you study war. How to fight it, how to prepare for it, how to avoid it if you can. When I see the way the Germans and Japanese and British are arming themselves, I see serious challenges ahead."

"They say nations are like people. If they have weapons, they'll use them."

Abraham stopped. "Has Uncle Ethan been bothering you somehow?"

"No, sir. I . . . it's just that I . . . I was in the secret passage at—"

"Eavesdropping?" said Abraham sternly.

The boy looked down, kicked at stones on the path.

Abraham had made his peace with this. He had not expected he would have to help his son to do it. He put his arm around the boy's shoulders and drew him along. "What is it you want to know?"

"Did you ever tell Theodore Roosevelt what Uncle Ethan told you?"

"No."

"But . . . you said that we should study how to avoid war."

"And how to *prepare*. By fighting this war, we may prepare for the next one, and if we're prepared, we may be able to avoid it altogether."

The boy furrowed his brow and considered this logic.

Abraham knew it was not simple. "Sometimes, son, there are larger issues than our own consciences. Sometimes our duty is to ask first what's best for the navy, because what's best for the navy is what's best for the country."

"Yes, sir." The boy looked out at the harbor and decided that his father must be right. His father was always right.

Thanks to Roosevelt's act of high-principled arrogance, which now looked like fine-tuned foresight, the Asiatic squadron and the Atlantic Fleet were ready for war. And the Spanish navy was no match. The Spanish had iron, the Americans had steel. The Spanish had cruisers, the Americans had battleships.

In the first week, Admiral Dewey barged into Manila Bay, told the captain of the *Olympia*, "You may fire when ready, Gridley," and destroyed the Spanish fleet. A few weeks later, Spain's Atlantic squadron was shattered by the *Iowa,* the *Oregon*, and the rest of the Atlantic Fleet at Santiago, Cuba.

Theodore Roosevelt called it a "splendid little war."

vi
Plebes

Five years later, on a brutally hot day in July 1903, Will Stafford stood with his mates in the new Class of 1907 and took the oath of a midshipman "to support and defend the Constitution of the United States." The words resounded in his ears and filled him with pride in himself and his heritage. They also filled him with some trepidation, because they meant that plebe summer had begun.

By the end of the first week, most of the boys suffering through it were prepared to believe that the heat, like the rest of their torment, was the doing of their instructors—a hand-selected group of grim-faced lieutenants, first classmen, and ensigns charged with the job of whipping them into shape.

As a navy junior, Will had known about this hell before stepping into it. He was not surprised by the haircut that looked as if it had been done by a red Indian, or by the regimentation of the eighteen-hour days and seven-day weeks, the constant drilling with a heavy Springfield rifle that grew heavier by the hour, the memorization of the laws of basic seamanship, or the regulations.

There were regulations for everything.

Plebes were not to turn corners; they were to square them: come to a stop, make a forty-five-degree pivot, and go, quickly. In the presence of superiors, they were not to make eye contact unless it was invited; instead, they were to keep their eyes front, or "in the boat," at all times. At meals, they were to sit with their butts perched on the front two inches of their chairs. And when they secured their rooms, there was even a rule for the placement of books in bookcases—one and a half inches from the edge of the shelf.

Will knew it all had a purpose.

There were ways of doing things, time honored and tested. If the boys who came to the Academy hoped to become gears in the machinery of President Theodore Roosevelt's navy, they had to mesh smoothly. So it was best if they looked alike, acted alike, and thought alike, too. Then they could begin the process of learning to be leaders.

Whenever Will faltered during plebe summer, he reminded himself that what was best for the navy might not always be pleasant for a seventeen-year-old plebe, but what was best for the navy was sure to be good for the country, too.

Few of his friends, however, could fall back on such truths when they were rousted from bed at six in the morning and ordered to drill before breakfast, or when they were told to drop and do fifty while reciting the Gettysburg Address—backward—in hundred-degree heat. They had come from very different worlds.

Jimmy Branch, Will's roommate, was a New York City boy who said that nothing in New York had ever been like this.

Hiroaki Tanaka, the fourteenth Japanese national to attend the Academy, met Will at the first meeting of the plebe boxing team. He said, in surprisingly fluent English, that he had come to demonstrate the strengthening bonds of friendship between America and Japan, then offered his hand to Will.

Raymond Spruance, who was always lined up somewhere near

Will Stafford by simple virtue of the alphabet, admitted no great love of military tradition, but his family had fallen on hard times, and the best way for him to get an education was at a place where the government footed the bill. Long-faced, skinny, soft-spoken, he endured plebe summer with a stoicism that impressed Will Stafford far more than all the cursing and complaining and lights-out bellyaching echoing up and down the halls of the New Quarters, the brick dormitory built after the Civil War and already entering its last year of life.

Roosevelt's expanding navy would have a modern academy to serve it. The center of the yard, where the trees had been growing for six decades, remained a haven of cool shade. But new land was being created from the Severn mudflats, an imposing granite chapel was rising, and a fence ringed a massive construction site that within a year would be Bancroft Hall, home for all the midshipmen.

Will and his mates agreed, when they weren't grousing, that there could be no better time to have come to Annapolis.

They also agreed that the best thing about plebe summer was that they survived. The second best thing was that there were no upperclassmen, especially the youngsters, or third classmen—known as sophomores in the civilian world—who had only recently completed plebe year and wanted others to know its misery.

All that changed in September.

One evening, Will told Jimmy Branch that it was time for a closer look at the navy's first submersible, the *Holland*, a fifty-four-foot, sunfish-shaped contraption moored in the Severn River.

Jimmy was reluctant. No one was supposed to go aboard any vessel, even a skiff, without permission.

"C'mon, there's a big moon out," said Will. "I just want to see her."

"Not much to see. Why do you think they call it a submersible?"

"One of us may command a submersible someday."

Jimmy just laughed at that crazy proposition.

"I guess you haven't read your Jules Verne."

"The navy'll go to war in one of Langley's flying machines before it fights twenty thousand leagues under the sea."

"So," said Will, "you're yellow?"

That did it. Will and Jimmy Branch were standing in the Severn moonlight ten minutes later.

"There it is," cracked Jimmy. "The future of naval warfare."

It was no more than a two-foot-high hatch sticking out of a metal grating that formed the deck. The grating was only about a foot above the surface. River water sloshed gently against the sides, the smell distinctly muddy.

"Yes, sir," said Jimmy, "I'd take on one of Roosevelt's new battleships in that."

"My father talks about forward thinking," said Will. "You have to imagine things that haven't happened yet."

"I do. She has a different name every night."

"Come on. Stop clowning. Let's go aboard."

Then a voice came out of the darkness behind them. "Midshipmen." Standing on the dock were two third classmen.

Immediately the plebes came to attention, eyes in the boat all the way.

"What are you doing?" asked the taller one. His name was Dennis Dawson, and he already had a reputation among the plebes.

"We were looking, sir," said Will. "Looking at the submersible."

Dawson smiled. "Curious little plebes?"

"Yes, sir."

"Did you know that curiosity killed the plebe?"

"No, sir," said Jimmy. "But we've seen it kill a few cats."

Dawson's smile broadened, as if he liked nervous little plebe jokes as much as he liked tormenting nervous little plebes. "Well said. Get out of here . . . both of you."

As Will stepped from the dock onto the path, he sensed that he was being watched for any infraction.

"Midshipman!" cried Dawson. He said the word like someone sliding a shell into a shotgun.

"Aye, sir," said Will.

"Your mate made a nice turn just then, but yours was like sloppy diarrhea. Back up and square the corner."

"Aye, sir." Will Stafford backed up, went forward, stopped, turned forty-five degrees, and did it quickly. That, he hoped, would be enough.

It wasn't. Dawson ordered him to drop and deliver twenty.

Without a word of protest, Will did as he was told, right there by the river, while that lock-and-load voice counted the push-ups.

"One . . . two . . . three . . ."

Bear it manfully. Make no faces. It's all part of the process.

"Eight . . . nine . . . ten . . ."

Don't even think about the fact that Congress passed an anti-hazing bill years ago, or that hazing is supposed to be a court-martial offense.

"Fifteen . . . sixteen . . . seventeen . . ."

Some things are part of the tradition, and the only ones who should be upset are the ones who aren't hazed, because no one cares about them.

"Twenty. Stay right there, mister." Dawson's voice slipped another shell into the chamber. He knelt so that his face was close to Will's. "Now kiss the ground where you learned to square a corner. Kiss the dear old Academy."

Still perched on fingertips and toes, Will put his face to the walk.

"*French* kiss," said Dawson. "Give the Academy some tongue."

And once more, closing his eyes, Will Stafford obeyed. He put his lips on the gravel walk, opened his mouth, and licked the stones as if they were the lips of a beautiful woman. At least now, he thought, he could say that he had French-kissed *something*.

"Hey, Denny," said the other third classman, "why don't you take your pencil and make a little hole in the sidewalk, then tell him to fuck it?"

"What about that?" whispered Dawson in Will's ear.

Will tried to smell alcohol, but Dawson was cold sober, which made this even worse.

"Would you like to fuck the Naval Academy earth?"

"I don't think he would, sir," said Jimmy Branch.

"No one asked you," growled Dawson. "Be quiet or you'll do the fucking." Then he turned his face back to Will Stafford. "What about it?"

Will's fingers were beginning to cramp. He dipped a little bit, to relieve the pressure of his weight.

"No one told you to move," said Dawson. "Now, what about it? Would you like to fuck the Academy?"

Whatever fear he had, whatever restraints held him in check, this was not something Will Stafford would bear. He took his eyes out of the boat and glared at Dawson. "No, sir, I would not, sir. And fuck you, sir, if you try to make me, sir."

To Will's astonishment, instead of ordering fifty more push-ups, Dawson stood quickly, gave Will a kick in the ribs, and cried, "Attenshun."

"He was damn lucky that Lieutenant Hart happened along when he did," Jimmy Branch said when he and Will were back in their room.

"He should have punished them," said Spruance. "They're not supposed to be hazing people. Not by law, at least."

"Still, you were very brave," said Hiroaki.

"Or very stupid," said Spruance. "Dawson'll be watching for you now."

"Maybe not," said Jimmy Branch. "When Hart asked us what we were doing, Will said we were just asking directions."

"Smart," said Hiroaki. "Very smart."

"Unlike this hazing business," said Spruance.

"Hazing makes us toe the line," said Jimmy. "The third classmen haze us, and we'll haze the plebes next year."

"It's childish," answered Spruance. "Designed to make us think like everyone else, when we should be learning to think for ourselves."

"But," said Hiroaki, "a good soldier must think like those around him."

"He must also think like his enemies," said Spruance.

"Yes, yes," said Hiroaki. "That is important, too."

For weeks, Will Stafford waited to see what Dawson would do, but Dawson ignored him. He seemed more interested in the quantity of his hazings than the quality. And since this was the largest fourth class in the history of the academy—some 280 men—Dawson had a long way to go.

Besides, Will Stafford had done the right thing that night. His reputation was good among the upperclassmen.

As Christmas approached, he was beginning to feel more relaxed.

His natural homesickness had abated somewhat. Like all plebes, he was restricted to the yard, but he had no impulse to french out.

He also had a staunch first classman, or senior, watching over him—square-headed Bill Halsey, fullback on the football team. Halsey was not the brightest light among the men of 1904, but he was smart enough to know that if he was going to take a plebe under his wing, as most first classmen did, the son of a prominent commander was a good choice.

And Will's friendships among his mates were growing stronger, too.

Jimmy Branch was high-spirited and funny, an average student and an above-average athlete. So long as he didn't eat beans in the mess hall, he was a fine roommate.

Hiroaki Tanaka revealed something new about himself at almost every meal. He was, like all of the Japanese who had attended the Academy, descended from a noble samurai family, but his skill was not only with an ancestral sword; gloved fists were his best weapons.

Ray Spruance kept mostly to himself, was seldom hazed, and did little to stand out, but it was already clear that he would be in the top ten percent of his class. Of course, it would not do him much good, because he thought for himself, demonstrating a quiet kind of rebellion that did not always sit well.

As in geometry class. Everyone had already manned the boards—drawn problems from the instructor and regurgitated memorized solutions in chalk. Memories, rather than analyses, had been evaluated. Now, they were moving ahead.

Lieutenant Flanders called for the four ways to prove that a quadrilateral was a parallelogram.

No one, of course, raised a hand. It was much better to make the instructor call upon you. That way, you didn't look like a *drag*—an all-purpose term used to describe anything from an overeager student to a girl on an Academy date.

So Flanders picked men out. "Stafford. Give me the easiest way."

"The easiest way, sir, is if the opposite sides are parallel, sir."

"Very good."

In quick succession, three more plebes were pointed out, and three more answers arrived at: opposite sides are congruent; opposite angles are congruent; any pair of consecutive angles is supplementary.

"Very good. Next problem."

Spruance raised his hand. "Excuse me, sir. But there's another way."

"Not according to the book."

"I know, sir, but I figured out another way."

"Oh, you did, did you?" Lieutenant Flanders had a pinched face and hard rimless spectacles, and he never gave the impression that he was happy about where he was. He held up the book and said, "The men whose names are on this spine have written a whole *book* on geometry, mister, and you're telling me that you know more than they do?"

"It may have been an oversight on their part, sir."

"Men who write books are thorough people."

"Yes, sir," said Spruance, "but I gave this some thought."

Will cleared his throat, to warn Spruance there was no future on this tack.

Flanders picked up a piece of chalk. "Suppose you show us the product of your thought."

So Spruance went to the board and drew a parallelogram. Then he drew diagonals through it from the corners. "A quadrilateral is a parallelogram when the diagonals bisect each other, sir."

Flanders studied it for a moment, stroked his chin, reddened a bit. "Yes, well, you're right, Spruance. But the procedure was to memorize the answers in the book and move to the next problem. Follow the procedure next time. That's how we do things around here. Now, sit down."

There was a moment of silence; then Jimmy Branch raised his hand. "Sir?"

"What?"

"Sir, will the Spruance proof be on the test, sir?"

"That's a demerit, mister. Disrespect."

Will left opinions about the Academy's method of brute memorization to Spruance. He had too much brute memorization to do.

And he had too much practicing: under the eye of Hiroaki Tanaka, he was becoming a proficient boxer.

And at night he fell into too many long talks, during which young men educated each other about things not found in books.

There was only one topic of talk when war broke out between Russia and Japan: the Russians had brought their Asiatic fleet to Port Arthur, on the Chinese coast, to assert their rights over Manchuria. But what the Russians considered a show of force, the Japanese saw as opportunity. On a February night, a Japanese squadron sneaked into Port Arthur and launched a devastating torpedo attack on the sleeping Russian battleships. For many nights afterward, the plebes analyzed the surprise attack and tried to outdo each other in the number of textbook references they could be heard to use. Nothing could make a plebe feel more like an officer than wrapping his mouth around a term like "torpedo spread" and actually knowing what it meant.

And no matter what was happening, they talked about girls. Once a month, there was a hop, and girls came from Baltimore and Washington and Annapolis. And once a month, Will Stafford fell in love.

The dances were held at Dahlgren Hall, one of the massive new granite buildings that would flank the future Bancroft Hall. Outside, Dahlgren presented its grand arched facade to Annapolis Harbor. Inside, the hops transformed it into a plebe's fantasy of glittering lights and lilting waltzes and crinoline petticoats whooshing gently over the floor.

A superintendent of the Naval Academy had said that an officer who did not know how to dance was deficient in the most important of social graces. This, of course, led to regulations, carefully laid out by the Department of Discipline: no modern dances would be performed; the midshipman was to keep his left arm straight during all dances; a space of three inches was to be kept between dancing partners; a midshipman was not to take a young woman by the arm or hand after the dance; and he was not to leave the floor until the dance ended.

And there was at least one unwritten regulation: plebes should not attempt to dance with young women who had drawn the attention of upperclassmen.

It was not until April, at the Spring Hop, that Will Stafford broke the unwritten regulation. There were two reasons.

His sixteen-year-old sister had appeared with several friends. She had wrapped a satin ribbon around her waist and put on her mother's cameo, and she was busy captivating—of all people—Hiroaki Tanaka. And if this was not reason enough for Will to make an error in judgment, the young woman walking past him was.

She was not as tall as the girls around her, though she moved easily beneath a green satin dress. And her brown hair was piled luxuriantly on the top of her head. Of course, women seldom wore their hair in any other way. It would have been positively immodest for a girl to let her hair down in public, but even the most modest female fashion had its attractions, and Will's eye was drawn to the place where her upswept hair revealed the delicate skin at the back of her neck.

Almost instinctively, he followed her. "Excuse me."

She turned—a broad smile, a simple nose, eyes set wide, without pretense, open to just about anything coming her way, including a dance with Will Stafford.

"And the Band Played On" was the song.

But from somewhere behind him, Will Stafford heard a shotgun shell slip into a chamber. It was Dawson. "This young lady danced the last dance with me."

"Yes," said Will, coming to attention, eyes, as always, in the boat.

"And I would like to dance with her again."

Will knew that the girl was studying him, and no doubt judging him by what he was about to do. "The young lady has accepted my invitation for this dance, and it would be impolite of me to withdraw it now."

Dawson smiled. "But I would like to dance with her again."

And the girl spoke up. "Excuse me, Midshipman Dawson, but I would—"

"Excuse *me*, Miss Jane Lord," said Dawson, his smile gone, his neck reddening above his high collar, "but I am speaking to this mid . . . this *plebe*—"

"—whose invitation I have accepted." Miss Jane Lord was not one to back down. "It would be as impolite of me not to dance with him as it would be of him to withdraw his invitation."

Will took his eyes from the boat. "You'll excuse us, Mr. Dawson."

And the band played on.

Will Stafford put his left hand on the small of her back, kept three inches between them, and extended his left arm, every inch the gentleman.

She looked into his eyes. "Thank you for being so resolute, Midshipman . . ."

"Stafford. Will Stafford."

"Dawson is an ass—pardon my French—but to preserve us from further embarrassment, I'm afraid this will have to be my last dance for the evening." She squeezed his left hand with her right. "So let's enjoy it."

And they swirled among the other dancers, the perspiration from their hands mingling delicately.

When it was over, Miss Jane Lord thanked Will Stafford and told him he was very polite. Then she headed toward the cloakroom, sweeping right past Dawson.

Will tried to follow her, but his way was blocked by the double row of brass buttons on Dennis Dawson's chest. Behind him were three of his friends, and none of them was smiling. The band stepped into a Strauss waltz, and Dawson very deliberately stepped on Will Stafford's foot.

Will did not flinch. He knew that if he reacted, it would look as if he were striking a superior without provocation, and that was how Dawson's friends would report it.

So Dawson pressed harder and growled, "Look at me, Stafford."

Will simply shifted his eyes.

"How does it feel, *plebe*?"

Will clenched his teeth. "Take your foot—"

Another voice growled, "Dawson!"

Bill Halsey was shorter than Dawson and the other third classmen who had closed around Will, but when he entered their tight little circle, he looked as if he might butt them all through the arched front doors and right into the river. "This is *my* plebe you're bothering, mister."

Will felt the pressure on his foot released. Even in the Academy, the chain of command held.

"Now, my drag and I want to enjoy the rest of the hop," said Halsey. "My plebe does, too. Spoil it for us, and I'll spoil it for you."

And Dawson offered Halsey a wide smile.

Around midnight, Will lay awake, thinking alternately about Jane Lord smiling at him and about his own sister dancing with a samurai.

Suddenly the door burst open, and a metallic voice shouted, "Sandwich!"

Will rolled over. "What the—"

"Sandwich time! Plebes out of bed!"

It was dark in the room, but the door was open to the silhouettes of three men reeling drunkenly.

"Plebes out of bed."

Thump!

"Jesus!" Will jumped up, realizing that they had just pulled Jimmy Branch, mattress and all, out of his bunk.

The door was slammed and locked, and the lights flashed on.

And there was Dawson, smiling one of his smiles. "Sandwich time. The class of '06 is hungry. What plebe are we going to eat?"

"Get out of here," said Jimmy Branch sleepily.

"Be quiet," one of them warned, "or we'll eat you."

"No," said Dawson. "We want a Stafford sandwich."

One of the others ordered Will to lie down on the mattress that they had dragged onto the floor.

"Go to hell," said Will.

"What did you say?" demanded Dawson. "Are you rejecting a direct order? Do you know what this means?"

"That you'll haze me for another month. I can take it."

"Get on the mattress," growled Dawson. "Now."

"No."

And Dawson stepped over the boundary. He grabbed Will by the collar of his pajamas, stuck out a foot, and pulled Will over onto the mattress.

Before he could get up, Will's own mattress was slapped over him, pinning him face down.

"Sandwich!" screamed one of the third classmen, and they piled on.

The plebe sandwich was a third-class favorite, a paralyzing torture that put three big men on a plebe's back. The harder Will struggled, the more fun they seemed to take in trying to find his head under the mattress and stomp on it.

And then Will felt a foot plant itself on either side of his head, pinning his face to the bottom mattress. This was a new trick. When he tried to move, another set of feet planted itself around his hips. And a third set was planted on either side of his feet.

He struggled and kicked. He screamed against the horsehair in the mattress. Were they hazing him or trying to kill him?

And suddenly all the bodies were lifted off of him.

Jimmy Branch had thrown a cross-body block that was as good as anything he had ever thrown on the football field. At the same moment, Hiroaki burst into the room, swinging a broomstick like a samurai sword. He brought it down on one head while Jimmy delivered another hard body block that slammed one of the upperclassmen against a door.

In an instant, Dawson was the only third classman left standing.

"You're in trouble now," warned Dawson as Will Stafford crawled to his feet, gasping and cursing. "I'll put out the word. You can't take a hazing."

"You put a hand on me. That changes things." Will pointed a finger at Dawson. "I have the right to fight back. Tomorrow night, in Halsey's room. Be there, and bring your fists, *sir*."

The next day, Abraham Stafford came to visit his son the plebe.

He was serving another tour in Washington, at the Bureau of Ships. He missed sea duty and sea pay, and at thirty-nine years old, he still stood eighteen years away from captaincy. But as Julia always told him, good things happened when he came into the orbit of Theodore Roosevelt. And in Washington, Theodore Roosevelt was the sun.

It was a warm spring Sunday, and Will would have loved the chance to go to his grandmother's house for dinner. But his father was a stickler for regulations, and plebes only had liberty on Saturdays.

So father and son strolled around the Academy while Will tried to find ways to bring up two uncomfortable topics.

They studied the construction site where Bancroft Hall was rising into something altogether impressive. They wandered toward the river and looked at the *Holland.* Abraham pronounced the submersible an interesting experiment, but never a threat to a fine battleship.

In the yard, the trees were leafing out. Beneath them, young ladies were strolling with the upperclassmen, and every midshipman snapped a salute at the commander. Will liked to be seen in the yard with his father. It was one of the wonders of the working blue uniform that it could make a plebe and a commander look very much the same, except for the rank insignia on the high collar. Now that he wore a uniform, he felt closer to his father, almost his equal. The fact that he had grown two inches in the last year helped, too.

"What do you think of these Japanese, Father?" he asked.

"Admirable people. Hardworking, industrious, doing a good job on the Russians . . . I hear that Hiroaki danced with Katherine last night."

Two midshipmen came past. *Salute, salute.*

"You don't mind?" Will was surprised, and relieved, too.

"Dancing is a perfect form of social communication, to be encouraged between nations as much as between men and women. Just so long as no one falls in love after a single dance."

Will did not like to tell tales on his sister, and Hiroaki was his good friend, but there were some things that his father had to know. Now that the truth about his sister was out, Will clapped his hands behind his back and tried to find a casual way to bring up his other problem.

By the time they reached the Tripoli Monument, he had thought of nothing, so he decided to be direct. "Were you ever hazed?"

"Oh, sure." Abraham nodded, smiled benignly. "Everyone gets hazed."

"But isn't it against regulations?"

"When regulations meet traditions, regulations sometimes lose. A good hazing lets you know where you stand in the chain of command. And it helps you to think straight when someone forces you to recite a page from *Jane's Fighting Ships* while you're standing on your head."

"Did . . . did an upperclassman ever put his hands on you in a hazing?"

Abraham stopped and looked at his son. "Did someone—"

Will looked down at the gravel path.

"Have you done anything about this?" asked Abraham.

"Not yet, sir. There are regulations. There are also traditions."

"You have two choices, then." Abraham put his hand on Will's shoulder. "Follow regulations and put the boy on report. Or follow tradition and beat the shit out of him."

And Will felt better. "If I end up on report for fighting, you'll understand?"

"I'll even have Mother send you a cake."

They met in Halsey's room, just after supper.

Desks and chairs had been put up on the beds, creating a kind of boxing ring.

The weapons: three-ounce gloves.

The length: three-minute rounds until someone quit or was knocked out, or until the seconds decided the fight should be stopped.

Will Stafford's second was Jimmy Branch.

Dawson brought one of the usual faces seen with him on his hazing hunts.

It had been agreed that if Will won this fight, there would be no further hazing on him or his friends. If he lost, the last month of plebe year would be hell.

"Steam right in at him," said Bill Halsey in the corridor before the fight. "You're skinnier but just as tall. Hit him one in the belly, and he should fold up."

A few moments later, Ray Spruance whispered in his other ear, "If I was fighting him, I'd size him up, reserve my strength, and save my best punch for the moment when it might do the most damage."

Will did not do either.

When the bell rang for the first round, Dawson danced to the middle of the room, gloves high in perfect Marquis of Queensberry style.

But Will Stafford came slowly into the center of the room, with his hands low, and stuck out his chin.

A look of puzzlement came over Dawson's face. Why wasn't he ready to fight? Why was he offering his chin? For a split second Dawson lowered his hands.

That was all Will Stafford needed. From nowhere, he sent his right hand hurtling toward Dawson's nose. And the lights went out for the third classman from Ohio.

"A single punch, well placed." That was how the story would be told.

When Dawson came to and tried to claim that he had been suckered, Bill Halsey told him there was a difference between "suckered" and "outsmarted." "Do you want everyone to say that Will Stafford's fists were a little quicker than yours, or did he just have a better plan? Now shake hands and agree that all troubles are settled."

It may have been that Dawson realized how tough an opponent Will Stafford would be no matter how long the fight lasted. Better to lose quickly than over fifteen or twenty rounds of pounding. Will wanted to believe that Dawson realized he had been beaten fair and square and accepted the verdict honorably. Whatever the reason, after a moment of hesitation, Dawson extended his hand.

"Where did you come up with that idea?" Jimmy Branch asked Will later.

"Hiroaki. He told me what the Chinese philosopher Sun-Tzu said: 'In war, opportunity is all. If the enemy leaves a door open, you must rush in.' I lowered my hands, Dawson opened his door, and I rushed in."

vii
Will and Hiroaki

Will and his mates took their first summer cruise aboard the *Hartford,* the ancient steam sloop that Farragut had run up the Mississippi forty-two years before.

Will liked sea duty. The salt air and sense of mastery over the elements were the tonic he had hoped they would be.

Some evenings, he sat in the foremast crosstrees, out of the flow of the stack exhaust, away from the thump of the ancient reciprocating engines, and he studied the battleship *Texas,* squadron flagship, steaming out ahead of them, a white-hulled giant with yellow topsides and black guns that had thundered at the Spanish just six years before. Now she was as outmoded as the *Hartford* herself.

This twentieth century was going to move fast, he knew. Someone would figure out how to fix bombs to those flying machines that they were testing. Submersibles would carry the kind of long-range torpedoes the Japanese had used on the Russians at Port Arthur. And who knew how much more would be learned from the war between Japan and Russia?

And who could have guessed that one of their own—Hiroaki Tanaka—would be recalled to fight in that war when the summer cruise ended at Hampton Roads?

Will realized, as he bade his Japanese friend good-bye, that he envied him the chance to see war firsthand. He was also glad to be getting his Japanese friend away from his sister.

"Home is the sailor," cried Granny Eve when Will came into the

Fine Folly garden two days later, "home from a summer cruise aboard his grandfather's ship!"

Eve was sitting in the shade of the grape arbor, flanked by Alexandra Parrish and his own sister, Katherine, who seemed to grow more beautiful by the month. She had inherited their mother's blond hair, their father's strong jaw, and a rebellious streak that must have come from shadowy Uncle Ethan.

Before Will could tell a single story of his summer cruise, Katherine announced that she had just joined Alexandra's Washington chapter of the National Woman Suffrage Association.

"Mother won't be happy about that," said Will.

"She can't stop me from thinking for myself." Katherine raised her chin.

"That's right." Eve laughed. "Why shouldn't your sister enter the grown-up world, like you, Willie?"

"Eve, I swear," said Alexandra, "the older you get, the more willful you get."

"I call it wisdom," Eve answered. "Wisdom to go with the strength we both learned from Antonia. I just wish my bones weren't so brittle."

Katherine took her hand. "You've given us your strength, Grandmother."

"To say nothing of a check for the Suffrage Association. Now, Will, go inside so we ladies can talk about spending my money. Gabe Shank bought a bucket of beer at Middleton's. He's in the study. Have some man talk with him."

Will had always found the cartoonist to be a great antidote to the other people in his life. Gabriel had been on Little Round Top. He knew war on an intimate basis. Will's father had seen it from the bridge of the *Iowa* while sending shells at fleeing Spanish ships. Most of the classroom warriors who taught him about concentration of force and projection of power had not seen it at all. And Gabriel hated it more than any of them.

Gabriel was snoring in one of the big leather chairs, beside an empty beer bucket. On the table in front of him were several new cartoons.

In one, Theodore Roosevelt sat in a rocker on the Pacific Coast, a shotgun across his lap. He was watching the Russians and Japanese circle each other on the other side of the Pacific. The caption read, "Trouble ahead, no matter who wins."

In another, a steam shovel bit into Central America and Theodore Roosevelt shouted to the operator, "Dig it fast. I may have to use it soon."

Now Katherine came into the study. She seemed less full of herself than she had in the garden. She glanced at the sleeping Gabriel, then said, "I was expecting Hiroaki to be with you."

"He was recalled." Will gave her a note that Hiroaki had asked him to deliver.

After she read it to herself, she went over to the windowsill, to a houseplant that resembled nothing so much as a giant spruce in miniature. She picked up a pair of shears and made a few tiny cosmetic cuts on one of the branches.

Will asked who gave her the plant.

"Hiroaki. It's a bonsai."

He thought he saw her blink back a tear. "Katherine, he's a Jap. You shouldn't be acting like this."

"I'll act however I want." She made a few more cuts, and it seemed to calm her. Then she wiped her eyes and slipped a letter from her pocket. "Since we're exchanging envelopes, this one is for you."

It was from Miss Jane Lord of Baltimore, who said that she would look for him at the Academy's first fall hop. And Will knew that his second year was going to be better than the first. . . .

It was. He pulled a solid 3.4 average. He drilled well. He boxed well. He danced well with Miss Jane Lord. Dennis Dawson never bothered him once. And every Thursday, when youngsters had liberty, he visited his grandmother. Early in the year she kept up her habit of cooking crab cakes and gossiping. But around Christmas, she fell and fractured her hip. By June, she was dead.

Her service would be smaller than the one for their grandfather. But it would follow the rituals established when Jedediah Stafford had died: a service at Saint Anne's, a voyage to Stafford Hall, burial in the family plot.

On the morning of the funeral, Katherine, Will, and their father stood at the French doors, looking out at the rhododendrons just bursting into flower. Father and son, in their dress blues, were speaking in low tones about Japan's most recent victory.

"The Russians didn't learn the big lesson at Port Arthur," said Abraham. "Know your enemy and respect him."

"So Admiral Togo made them pay," said Will with a note of authority. "Sitting at Tsushima Strait, just waiting for them to sail by, coming out with guns blazing—"

Katherine's cup rattled on her saucer. "Was the cruiser *Nisshin* one of the ships at Tsushima Straight?"

"Yes. According to the reports, she took several hits. Why?" asked her father.

"*Nisshin* is Hiroaki's ship," said Will. "Gone a year, and she can't get him out of her mind."

Abraham frowned. "But at the last hop, she danced three dances with that first classman—what was his name?"

"Chet Nimitz."

"Yes. Nimitz." Abraham looked at Katherine. "Isn't he a fine fellow?"

"Perhaps, but he didn't invite me to the Ring Dance."

"Perhaps he fears opinionated women." Abraham always spoke gently to his daughter, and with several mourners already gathered around the corpse in the front parlor, and several more at the coffee urn in the dining room, gentle voices were in order. "Or perhaps it's woman suffragists that he fears."

"*Girl* suffragists is a better term." Julia Stafford came down the stairs, looking more regal than ever, with a few fine strands of silver in her blond hair and a delicate strand of pearls against a black silk blouse. "If she thinks *American* men dislike opinionated women, the term 'geisha' should be explained to her. That would end her infatuation with some Jap."

Abraham looked at his wife. "Did you know that this was going on?"

"It isn't easy to miss a Japanese postmark on your mail."

"Mother," Katherine hissed, "I'm seventeen years old. I'm—"

Abraham's brother, Jacob, lurched in from the study, smelling of bay rum and bourbon. He was turned out in starched shirt, gray cravat, striped trousers, dove-colored vest, and toilet paper covering the shaving cut on his chin. "Could we have a little quiet, out of res . . . res . . . respect for my mother, please?"

"Sure," said Abraham. "Sure, Jake."

"Now, Jacob," said Julia, smiling through her teeth, "wouldn't you like a nice cup of black coffee?"

"My mother is dead. I want another drink."

"Get him upstairs, Abe," she said. "He can't go to the church like this."

Just then the doorbell rang. It was Alexandra and Gabriel Shanks.

"Ah, the leading suffragist troublemaker," said Jacob, "and her troublemaking husband, too."

"They've been constant friends," said Abraham.

"Are they constant enough to buy this house?" And Jacob shouted down the hallway. "Do the Parrishes want this house back? I'll sell my half, and I don't think my brother can buy it, considering his fancy uniform and lousy navy pay."

"Get him upstairs," Julia hissed once again. Then she pasted a smile on her face and glided down the hallway. "Alexandra and Gabriel! How go your little battles?"

"They go larger and larger." Alexandra gave a smile just as broad and just as phony. "Is it true that you are planning to sell this house?"

"Oh, good Lord, no."

That summer, President Roosevelt brokered a peace treaty between Japan and Russia. The treaty of Portsmouth was a carefully crafted piece of diplomacy designed to protect the balance of power in East Asia, and American commercial access along with it. The Japanese, who were winning, were given a free hand in Manchuria, while the Russians were released from the payment of reparations. This last part angered the Japanese, who believed that the victor should pay for nothing, and anti-American riots erupted in Tokyo.

Nevertheless, Hiroaki returned to Annapolis in September, and on his second afternoon back, he and Will went to the old Fort Severn gym, put on five-ounce gloves and headgear, and talked around their mouthpieces while they sparred.

Hiroaki admitted that after commanding a gun at the battle of

Tsushima Strait, he was finding it hard to rejoin life at an American naval academy.

"Then why did you come back?"

Jab. Jab. Duck. Jab. "I promised your sister."

"Hiroaki," *Jab. Feint. Jab. Jab.* "I tell you as a friend, it can't work."

Hiroaki took out his mouthpiece. "You forbid me to see her?"

Will dropped his hands. "My sister has a mind of her own. So do you."

"If you forbid me to see her"—Hiroaki bowed—"I am honor-bound to obey."

"My sister has a mind of her own. So do you." *Put 'em up.*

That fall, the class of 1907 march was heard for the first time. It was called "Anchors Aweigh." As winter came on, everyone was whistling it.

Will Stafford was whistling it one night, writing a letter to Jane Lord, when Jimmy Branch burst into the room.

"Son of a bitch," he said.

"What?"

"That Minor Meriweather. I just caught him hazing a plebe."

"I've caught *you* hazing plebes. I've hazed plebes. The only person who doesn't is Ray Spruance."

"You or I might make a plebe recite the line of battle at Santiago. And if he can't do it, we make him go and study it, and come back with the line of battle for Manila Bay, too. But this Meriweather is another one like his pal Dawson."

"Our old friend." Will leaned back in his chair. "So what did Meriweather do?"

"He had a plebe over a crapper, making him recite Japanese fleet stats from *Jane's Fighting Ships*. Every time he got a wrong answer, he had to drink a teaspoon of toilet water."

"With or without?"

"What?"

"Piss."

"Without. Otherwise I would have fought him right there."

"You're going to fight him because of what he was doing to a plebe?"

"Tomorrow night. Room three-oh-three. Will you second me?"

"Of course." Though he thought it was foolishness.

Three-ounce gloves.

Three-minute rounds until somebody quit.

Will's fight with Dawson, a year and a half before, seemed like ancient history. But there was Dawson, a first classman, seconding Minor Meriweather.

Will reminded Jimmy Branch that he did not have to fight to protect some plebe. "I've asked around. This Meriweather is tough."

"You can't back away from a fight. It's like a challenge to a duel."

Will could not argue with that. This was now a matter of honor.

They started fighting at eight o'clock. By nine-thirty, they had gone twenty rounds. There was blood everywhere—on the fighters, on their gloves, on the walls—and both of them were looking through eyes swollen like eggplants. But they refused to stop.

Twenty-one. Neither man could even begin to avoid the other's blows.

Twenty-two. Neither man could raise his arms.

Twenty-three. Neither man could move.

Now Will and Dennis Dawson agreed, as the responsible seconds, to stop the fight. Jimmy and Meriweather shook hands and staggered back to their rooms.

"Good work, Jimmy." Will cleaned up his friend, massaged his back, and pressed hot cloths to his face. "You upheld your honor. You did fine."

"Yeah. Honor." Jimmy winced. "Now, if I can just see tomorrow."

"If it's any consolation, Meriweather looks as bad as you."

"Good. Good. Don't tell the brigade commander why my eyes are black." Jimmy rolled over and slipped into a deep sleep.

In the morning, Will Stafford could not wake him nor could anyone else. Despite the best efforts of Theodore Roosevelt's personal physician, Jimmy Branch died the next day.

"Naval Cadet Killed in Academy Fight!" screamed the *New York World*. In the *Washington Post* a Gabriel Shank cartoon showed duelists on the steps of Bancroft Hall—James Barron shooting Stephen

Decatur in 1820, and two midshipmen, stripped to the waist.

At the court-martial, Will Stafford and Dennis Dawson testified that it was a fair fight, ended fairly. On this, at least, they agreed. Meriweather was acquitted of manslaughter charges, but convicted of conduct prejudicial to good order, and confined to the yard for a year.

The seconds in the bout were not charged.

Many people, including several congressmen, believed that all concerned were let off too lightly. So the navy, ever sensitive to the feelings of those who controlled naval appropriations, cracked down. Discipline tightened, and for the first time in decades, the Academy enforced its anti-hazing laws.

Will Stafford wondered why they had not done it all sooner.

Then he began to question why he was even at the Academy, and he made the mistake of doing it over a family dinner in Washington. His mother's eyes filled with tears and she left the table. His father reminded him of his heritage, of tradition and regulation.

Will was soon spending more time in the gym than in the classroom, and his grades began to slip. He became the best fist on the Academy team. In every fight, he barreled in, took his opponent's blows, waited him out, wore him out, then battered him viciously. In every fight, he saw Meriweather's face, and sometimes he heard his father, blandly reminding him of tradition and regulation.

Then one night Hiroaki challenged him to a fight.

"Why?"

"Because you need a lesson."

Will reminded Hiroaki it would be a lightweight against a heavyweight. But Hiroaki insisted. They would wear headgear and five-ounce gloves for protection. Ray Spruance would be the only judge. They would fight for seven rounds.

"Why only seven?" asked Will.

"That will be enough," said Hiroaki, "to teach your lesson."

They fought in the Fort Severn gymnasium, with no light but moonlight streaming through the windows. No one knew of this meeting, and it took place well after taps, because if they were caught, they would be disciplined.

When Spruance pressed the stopwatch and said "Time!" Will came straight to the middle of the room and raised his gloves. But he should have known that Hiroaki would not be like other opponents.

Hiroaki was small and quick and full of feints. For three rounds, he danced and dodged, flicking little jabs that stung on the sides of Will's head, then retreating fast before Will could counterpunch. Each jab was a point for Hiroaki, and he took the first three rounds.

Then Will began to make progress. He took the fourth and fifth, but he had to chase Hiroaki all over the ring to score. Finally, in the sixth, he cornered Hiroaki and caught him hard with a flurry that put him down and left him woozy.

Three rounds apiece.

Starting the seventh, Hiroaki seemed tired, ready to go down. His hands were low. His feet were slow.

Now was the time for Will to finish him. Hiroaki ducked Will's first left, but took a right off the side of the headgear. Now Will's arms were open and Hiroaki was close. With a sudden and almost invisible flurry, he drilled his fists into Will's gut—five, six, seven times, knocking the wind out of him.

Suckered, thought Will as he landed on his ass. *Outsmarted.*

In a moment, Spruance was beside them, whispering, "Round seven goes to Hiroaki. You lose."

"He suckered me," said Will.

"You forget everything I teach you," said Hiroaki, untying his headgear. "You forget what Sun-Tzu teaches: 'Victorious warriors win first and then go to war; defeated warriors go to war first and then seek to win.' No matter how many matches you win, you are defeated because you have lost your way. You have no plan for your fights . . . and none for what you do each day."

"And remember this," said Spruance, putting it more bluntly, "the men in the top third of the class graduate early. At the rate you're going, if you don't make it out then, you may bilge out altogether. So do what Jimmy would want. Get back to the books."

Tradition and regulation. Conscience and loyalty. Will had hoped that as he grew older, these terms would become simpler, that the standards he was taught at the Academy would make everything clear. But no one could make things simpler, not the navy, not a father who once had it in his hands to stop a war and didn't try. Only friends made things simpler. He knew that now.

viii
Hiroaki and Katherine and John Paul Jones

They found him buried beneath the floor of a house that had been built over his Parisian grave. His body had been preserved in a cask of brandy, so there was no doubting who it was. Others could have laid claim to the paternity of the U.S. Navy and a place of honor in the crypt beneath the new Academy chapel. But Washington was already interred at Mount Vernon, and Nicholas Biddle had been scattered to the elements when the *Randolph* exploded.

John Paul Jones had raised the flag for the first time over an American warship. He had won the most famous ship-to-ship battle of the Revolution. And he had been the first victim of postwar cost-cutting in American history. Who better to symbolize the navy?

Jones spent a year in a makeshift mausoleum in the middle of the yard. Then, in April of 1906, Theodore Roosevelt came to the Academy for an official commemoration ceremony. It took place in Dahlgren Hall, which was draped for the occasion with American and French flags and filled with more brass than Will had ever seen, including the guest of honor, in a flag-covered casket before the speaker's platform.

Will would remember little of Roosevelt's speech. From where he was sitting in the balcony, he couldn't see more than the back of Roosevelt's head. Besides, he was far more interested in looking at Miss Jane Lord, who had accepted his invitation to the event and to the Stafford family reception afterward.

"She's rather pretty, in a girlish sort of way," whispered his mother at the reception in the garden of the Fine Folly. "What about her family?"

"Mother, you know the rules against midshipmen marrying."

Julia patted her son's hand. "Of course, dear, but you know that a mother likes to see her son well married. And her daughter, too, so perhaps you can tell me why that little Jap made it onto the guest list?"

From where they were standing, beneath one of the flowering cherry trees, they could see Katherine, Hiroaki, and Jane Lord in animated conversation. Ray Spruance was listening with a polite expression on his face.

"Why couldn't she be spending time writing to that Spruance boy? He's a trifle shy, but he's no Jap."

"Don't call Hiroaki a Jap. He's my friend. He stood by me when Jimmy died. And he has no more plan to marry Katherine than I have to marry Jane."

She pursed her lips. "You should come to Washington more often, Willie, so that we can argue without the phony smiles."

Abraham, in his dress uniform with the gold epaulets, joined them. His smile looked as uncomfortable as the epaulets. "Where's Jacob?"

"He's in the dining room, beside the punch bowl," said Julia.

"Is Irene with him?"

"You mean the middle-aged divorcée who sank her hooks into him a month after Eve died, just so that she could inherit half of all this?" asked Julia.

"Save the sarcasm," snapped Abraham. "I want to make sure he's sober. Irene, too. The president has decided to accept our invitation after he visits the superintendent's house."

And Julia lit up like a flare. "The president is coming here?"

"Yes . . . yes . . . Now, all the guests will want to meet him. We'll have to arrange a receiving line in the house."

Julia smoothed her hair. "No one's lived in this ark for almost a year, Abe. It's barely clean. Let's receive him out here."

Members of the Navy Band had been hired for the day to play light airs and marches in the garden. The trees and flowers were in full bloom. And the scaffold-shrouded dome of the Academy chapel dominated the scene, a perfect symbol for the navy that Theodore Roosevelt had brought into existence.

"All right," said Abraham. "Out here. I'll see that my brother is under control."

"And see that Alexandra keeps her mouth shut," added Julia. "I won't have that damn suffragist doing anything to upset the president."

By the punch bowl, Jacob Stafford and his new wife, Irene, were in loud conversation with Alexandra, Gabriel Shank, and a man in a Prince Edward beard and blue suit.

Irene's voice had a crack that sounded like nails being pulled out of a board, and she was laughing at something that the bearded man had just said.

"Abraham." The bearded man extended his hand. "I'm sorry I didn't RSVP, but I'm a traveling man and—"

"Ethan?" said Abraham. "I didn't recognize you with the beard."

Ethan stroked his chin. "My common state for forty years or more."

"It's been what—"

"Eight years. Since the *Maine* exploded." Ethan said that with a significance that no one but Abraham himself noticed.

"Have you struck oil?" asked Abraham.

"A few times. Here and there. Oklahoma . . . Texas . . . California."

"We've been talking about places to settle," said Jacob. "I asked Ethan if he thought he had any settling rights to the Fine Folly."

"I said I gave up my rights when the *Alabama* went down." Ethan's eyes shifted to Irene. "The new Mrs. Stafford found my words more hilarious than I had intended."

"That's because she thinks we should sell the house," said Jacob.

"Really?" This piqued Ethan's interest.

"Selling is not planned," snapped Abraham. "Now, the president's coming. And I want all of you on your best behavior. Jacob, that means no more punch. And, Alexandra, none of your women's suffrage talk."

"But it may be my only chance to—"

"Please," begged Abraham.

Julia came fluttering into the house. "He's here. He's coming through the back gate from the Academy."

Out in the garden, the band was playing "Hail to the Chief."

Abraham looked around at this deck load of loose cannon. "Please . . . all of you . . . This is very important to me."

"The ladder of rank," said Ethan. "We understand."

"Of course I'll greet your guests," said the president to Julia Stafford. "But you must promise to give me a tour of this house afterward. Imagine—Washington, Lafayette, Jefferson, Preble. Not to mention all the Staffords."

Julia dipped a perfect curtsy. She made sure that her husband was ensconced next to the president, under a pink-blossomed cherry tree, and she put herself next to her husband. "We'll introduce everyone as they come through the receiving line, sir."

From close range, husband and wife could shoot down any embarrassments, the first of which approached with Alexandra.

But Roosevelt cut it off with a grin. "Alexandra and Gabriel Shank. By Godfrey, it's good to meet you both. That cartoon, Shank—the one with me holding the shotgun, watching the Pacific—that was smashing. Captured my thinking exactly."

"Thank you, sir," said Gabriel. It was hard to impress Gabriel, but Roosevelt worked his magic.

"It's a great honor to meet a member of the Twentieth Maine." Then Roosevelt turned his energy onto Alexandra. "It's also an honor to meet a woman who steps into the arena. We respect those who try greatly, no matter their position."

Alexandra was plainly shocked. "You've heard of me?"

Abraham admired how well Roosevelt could wrap someone with his own philosophy and make anyone feel like an ally. He had done it with the Japanese and the Russians. He did it now. For all his youthful bellicosity, he had become a diplomat and, in the best sense of the word, a politician.

"You're quite a couple," said Roosevelt.

"Why, thank you." And Alexandra slipped her hand into Gabriel's arm.

Quite a couple. Those words hurt Ethan Stafford more than he would have expected. But Roosevelt cheered him up in an instant by recalling his own Bulloch uncles—one who built the *Alabama*, the other who served as a midshipman beneath Lieutenant Ethan Stafford. He was good, thought Ethan, whether he was maneuvering a nation toward war or winning friends in a receiving line.

And now Roosevelt was receiving the midshipmen and their young ladies.

Abraham introduced Jane Lord, who was too level-headed to be impressed by a handshake from anyone, even the president. She gave Roosevelt a straightforward eye and her own firm hand, and his grin broadened a bit more.

Now Roosevelt turned his gaze onto Midshipmen Stafford and Spruance and he pretended to think hard, remembering the navy list that he had probably studied that morning. "Both in the top third of your class . . . both scheduled to graduate early and take billets in the new fleet next fall."

"Aye, sir," said Will and Ray Spruance. Neither added that he would be glad to find out if the old saying was true: Don't judge the navy by the Academy; wait until you get to the fleet.

"Well, good luck, boys." Roosevelt was extending his hand to the next midshipman as Abraham introduced Hiroaki Tanaka.

Hiroaki executed a deep bow.

Roosevelt stared into the young Japanese eyes. "You were at Tsushima Strait?"

"*Hai.*" Hiroaki reddened at slipping into Japanese.

"I was so excited when I heard about your victory, I became almost like a Japanese myself. I spent the whole day talking about the battle. Admiral Togo is a man of great brilliance."

"*Hai.*" He did it again. He was as badly tongue-tied as he might have been in front of the emperor.

"What do your friends from Eta Jima think about your coming to our Academy instead of theirs?"

"They . . . they envy me, Majesty."

"Not 'Majesty,' Hiroaki. 'Sir' or 'Mr. President' will be fine. You're a welcome guest in this country."

"Thank you."

Roosevelt held on to Hiroaki's hand longer than anyone else's. It was as if he were trying to see America through eyes that had seen Japan's naval might in action. "Now, Hiroaki, how long are you planning to stay?"

Hiroaki tried not to meet Roosevelt's gaze, or Will's, or Abraham's. A look of mortification etched itself into his face, as though he could not lie but did not wish to tell the truth.

Katherine whispered in his ear, "Go ahead, Hiroaki. Tell him."

Hiroaki looked down at the ground.

So Katherine spoke for him. "Hiroaki is hoping to become an American citizen, Mr. President."

"This is my daughter, sir," Abraham said to Roosevelt.

"A pleasure to meet you, Miss Stafford." Roosevelt took her hand.

"The pleasure is ours, sir," she said. "Hiroaki and I are hoping you'll see your way toward helping him to become a citizen."

Roosevelt inclined his huge head in an attitude of polite attention.

The grin, with big horse teeth that showed yellow stains and cracked brown fissures, did not change. But the neck, which was as wide as the head, seemed to redden.

Abraham was attempting to usher his daughter away while Julia was already ushering two more guests forward.

But Katherine kept talking. "You see, Mr. President, Hiroaki and I are in love."

Roosevelt's grin froze before it fell off. He shot a glance at Abraham, then at Hiroaki. "You come from a noble family. What do they say?"

"I . . . I haven't told them. I—"

"Mr. President"—Julia was pressing forward while pushing her daughter along—"allow me to introduce . . ."

Most of the guests were unaware of what had happened.

A few minutes later, while Katherine was talking about the scene with Jane Lord, Hiroaki left the Fine Folly.

The president replaced his grin, restored his charm, and received all the guests, then he cheerfully demanded his tour of the house—downstairs, upstairs, all the way to the attic—with Abraham on one side and Will on the other.

In the attic, he took in the rotting hand-pulled fans that hung from the rafters, the dozen cots collecting dust and junk, and for a moment, he removed his glasses and pinched the bridge of his nose. When he regained himself, he said, "This room is a monument to your family and what they did for so many."

"Mr. President," said Abraham, "I must apologize for the scene that a certain member of my family created in the garden. Katherine is a headstrong girl."

"My daughter Alice is as headstrong as they come," said Roosevelt. "That's good in a young person. But—"

"I've been hoping that this relationship would die of its own, sir," said Abraham.

"They seem like two fine people. But right now, California is trying to stop Japanese immigration while I try to maintain good relations with Japan. Your daughter should know that this is not a good time to be putting the president on the spot."

"I'm very sorry, sir." Abraham could see his career and his son's dissolving to dust right there in the dusty attic. "We should never put the president on the spot."

"Excuse me, sir," said Will, "but I believe I can take care of this affair."

"You would be doing a great favor," said Roosevelt, "to both your father and yourself."

Will did not have to say a thing. That night Hiroaki admitted that he could not love Katherine the way she loved him. He had come to that decision even before she had humiliated him that afternoon.

"A Japanese girl would never have made excusements for me before the emperor. I have decided to return to Japan to finish my schooling at Eta Jima."

"Have you told her?" asked Will, restraining a smile.

"I will tell her tomorrow. She will be very sad."

"She will be very mad . . . at all of us."

A few weeks later, the academic year came to an end. Will accompanied Hiroaki to Union Station in Washington, where he would board a California-bound train—an American midshipman in service blue and a young Japanese once more wearing the uniform he had worn in the battle of Tsushima Strait.

"Thank you for teaching me to box," said Will.

"I taught you how to outsmart your enemies and value your friends."

"One thing we know," said Will, "navy men can meet almost any place."

"*Hai.*" Hiroaki no longer seemed embarrassed to speak his native tongue. "And we will always meet as friends."

Will gave a quick nod. "*Hai.*"

"Hiroaki!" A girl came running through the steam. She wore jodhpurs and a riding jacket and boots, and her hair was flying loose as she came.

Ladies scowled. Men seemed shocked. Women seldom ran in public or shouted in public, and unless they were on the back of a horse, they never wore breeches of any kind. But Katherine did not seem to care. "Hiroaki!" she cried again, and the clouds of engine steam lifted for a moment.

"Katherine!" said Will. "How did you know we were leaving?"

"I asked Father."

"You're speaking to him again?"

"Yes. I'm even speaking to *you*." Then she turned to Hiroaki and handed him a tiny crabapple tree, carefully trained and trimmed to resemble a much larger one. "I started this the spring I met you. It was cut in the garden at the Fine Folly."

"A bonsai." He took it with a deep and formal bow. "*Hai*."

"*Hai* yourself."

Hiroaki did not sit on their side of the train when it pulled out of the station. He chose the other side, perhaps so that he would not have to wave good-bye.

"So," Will said to his sister after the train had left. "Am I forgiven?"

"I met someone from Harvard last week. Very rich, very enlightened."

"Hiroaki was very rich, too, but I don't think he was too enlightened."

"He wanted a geisha for a wife, not a suffragist," she said.

"Have you ever thought of what you will do once you get the vote?"

"Stop wars."

Will fought the impulse to laugh at that. Men had been dreaming of stopping wars for centuries, but their dreams always led to bigger weapons and bigger wars. Maybe this twentieth century would be different.

They walked in silence for a time; then she said, "He was not the same after he came back from Tsushima Strait. Do you know what he said to me the night he told me it was over?"

"What?"

"That he had come back because of an old Japanese saying: 'Know your enemy.'"

"He didn't mean you, Katherine. He meant Roosevelt."

ix
The Big Stick

The following spring, Abraham and Julia agreed that if they did not sell the Annapolis house, they would be forced to sell the Patuxent house, too.

Jacob and his hard-drinking spendthrift of a wife had announced that they planned to see the world, so they wanted their half of everything. Abraham tried to reason with his brother, but Jacob was adamant.

Julia's parents could not help, despite their Philadelphia airs. And navy pay was not enough to maintain a house like the Fine Folly. So they decided to sell it outright, use their half of the proceeds to buy Jacob and his wife out of Stafford Hall, then strike them from the family register forever.

A short time later, a letter arrived from Ethan, now living in Los Angeles.

> Dear Abraham,
>
> Alexandra writes that you have put the Fine Folly up for sale. The enclosed draft meets your price, whatever it is. Simply fill in a fair amount. I trust your honor in the matter.
>
> It is not my intention to live there. But I would like a place to stay when I come east, and I know that Alexandra and Gabriel would like a permanent home. We are all old now. We do not need much space. A room for me. A small apartment for them. My plan for the house can embrace such dreams.
>
> You see, Annapolis is becoming a town of visitors—Maryland legislators and navy parents—and Annapolis could use a hotel. So I have retained an architect to create plans for two hundred rooms to be built over the garden, with the main house providing reception and public rooms. We save the house and make our money work for us, too.
>
> I hope you will not be angered that I profit from the family legacy. But then, you did nothing to enhance the legacy in 1898, so it may not matter to you. We might have stopped a war, Abraham, but there was a ladder of rank to be climbed.
>
> Unless I hear otherwise, I shall consider this deal consummated.

Abraham accepted immediately.

The truth was that he did not care particularly for the house. And he did not have time to negotiate because he was now the navy representative on the Joint Board advising the president on military matters, and a crisis had arisen.

San Francisco had segregated "Mongolian" schoolchildren as a first step in controlling Japanese immigration, which had so many West Coast whites worried about the yellow peril. The Japanese were outraged. A Tokyo newspaper cried, "It will be easy work to awake the United States from her dreams of obstinacy when one of our great admirals appears on the other side of the Pacific. Why do we not insist on sending ships?"

And once again, Roosevelt brokered a compromise, a gentleman's agreement between the sovereign government of Japan and, of all things, the San Francisco School Board. The Japanese agreed to limit emigration to the United States, so long as the children of Japanese in America were not segregated in American schools.

But Roosevelt told Abraham that he did not want the Japanese thinking they could snatch the Philippines or Hawaii because they negotiated over San Francisco. "I have nothing but the friendliest possible intentions toward them. But I'm not afraid of them, and the United States will no more submit to bullying than it will bully."

"As you say, sir, 'Speak softly and carry a big stick.'"

When Abraham and the rest of the Joint Board were invited to Oyster Bay on June 27, Abraham brought the navy's recommendation for waving its big stick—a Pacific Ocean exercise by the combined American battle fleet.

What evolved was something more: a grand world-circling cruise of America's white warships. The Japanese would be comforted by America's friendliness, yet reminded that her navy had grown under Roosevelt to the second largest in the world, and American ships would cruise wherever and whenever they wished. The rest of the world would hear the message, too.

In December, in waters where the *Merrimack* and *Monitor* had dueled half a century before, the Great White Fleet assembled—sixteen battleships, with pennants fluttering, guns polished, crews at attention, and spotless white hulls reflecting the afternoon light.

When the president's yacht, *Mayflower*, hove in sight, the ships delivered a twenty-one-gun salute that must have been heard in Washington.

Most of the midshipmen and ensigns whom Will Stafford knew were somewhere in the fleet—Spruance, Halsey, even Dawson. Will was assigned to the new battleship, *Missouri.*

His father was sailing as a member of Rear Admiral Robley D. Evans's staff. It was clear that he would make admiral before anyone else in his Academy class, except for William Sims, now Roosevelt's right-hand naval man.

Will had never seen his mother so happy as at Thanksgiving, when they had all gathered at Stafford Hall: the house was newly painted and papered and furnished with all the best from the Fine Folly; the family was newly expanded—Will with his fiancée Jane Lord, Katherine with her Harvard boy, Harold Blake; and their father had been newly promoted, so that their mother could refer to herself as Mrs. *Captain* Julia Stafford.

Will knew, as he looked out from his ship on that December day, that his mother and sister were somewhere on the shore, amid the thronging crowds, watching Evans's flagship, the *Connecticut*, lead the parade out through the Virginia capes while her band played "Auld Lang Syne."

"Have you ever seen such a fleet on such a day?" Roosevelt exulted to reporters aboard his yacht, the *Mayflower.* He stood in the bow, doffing his top hat again and again to the ships and the waving sailors. Then, like a little boy trailing after his father, he ordered her to follow the armada through the Virginia capes and tag along for a few miles more. It was reported in the papers that Roosevelt cried with emotion when his white ships disappeared at last.

He had built a new navy after the vision of Alfred Thayer Mahan. Of course, in Europe they were already building even newer navies, and *Dreadnought*-type battleships, with more armor and bigger guns; and somewhere, someone was figuring out how to fix guns and bombs to those flying machines. . . .

On that same bright December day, Ethan Stafford watched a bulldozer dig into the garden behind the Fine Folly. It was good that it was winter, he thought. That made it easier to uproot the old cherry trees and rhododendrons. He had rewritten his will to include the hotel he would build here. Half would go to Alexandra and Gabriel, half to the young Spanish woman who shared his California bed.

He intended to leave nothing to Commander Abraham Stafford or his descendants except a pair of powerful Zeiss binoculars, "to help you find your way." Beyond that, he would recall what Abraham Stafford once said: that he could fend for himself and did not need his uncle's help.

X
Samurai

Will Stafford filled reams of paper with his observations on the voyage and mailed them at every opportunity to Jane.

When the white ships passed through the Strait of Magellan at the tip of South America, Will thought of his ancestor in the lonely *Essex*, fighting for weeks in these treacherous waters. He even read passages of David Porter's journal to his messmates, emphasizing the name Jason Stafford wherever Porter mentioned it.

Under steam, the hellish passage of eighty years before was reduced to two twelve-hour days.

At Valparaiso Harbor, a quarter-million people greeted the American ships, and Will picked out the little inlet where the *Essex* had made her last stand. Then it was on to San Diego, Los Angeles, San Francisco, Puget Sound. In every port, there were balls, parties, receptions, fireworks, ship illuminations, rounds of drinking, and entertainment such as a midshipman could never have imagined.

By July, they had reached the fabled Sandwich Islands. *Hawaii.*

Will wrote to Jane that when they paraded through Honolulu, he needed only to raise his ceremonial sword and he could catch the flowered leis being tossed through the air.

> The next day, I met my father, whom I had not seen in six weeks. He took me on a tour of a magnificent harbor. Its name does it justice. They call it Pearl Harbor. Fine heights surround it. The anchorage is deep and extensive.

> And a large island sits in the middle. Were there facilities here—docking, coaling, repair, and the like—we could tie up the whole fleet and still have room to entertain the Japanese navy, too.
>
> Father is writing a report on Pearl Harbor, because Congress has put up a million dollars to make it a Pacific Fleet base. As Father said, Congress makes its share of mistakes, but not in this case.
>
> We leave tomorrow for the South Pacific, New Zealand, Australia, the Philippines, Japan. I do miss you. It is said that we will be gone another seven months. I hope you can stand it. I'm not sure I can.

The Great White Fleet arrived in Yokohama in October. Any fears of Japanese unfriendliness were dispelled before the anchors were dropped. Houses were hung with Japanese and American flags. Receptions and parades took them from Yokohama to Tokyo and back. And during a visit aboard HIJMS *Mikasa*, American admirals were hoisted onto the shoulders of Japanese junior officers and paraded around the deck like conquerors . . . or comrades.

Ensign Hiroaki Tanaka, of HIJMS *Nisshin,* was part of a group invited aboard the USS *Missouri.* After a tour of the ship and a fine luncheon, American and Japanese officers posed for a photograph under the battleship's turret, their arms linked in friendship. Hiroaki and Will Stafford sat cross-legged in the front row.

"So," whispered Will as the photographer set up the shot, "tell me about the old Japanese proverb, 'Know your enemy.'"

Hiroaki smiled. "It is a universal proverb. Why else would you be here?"

That night, in a Yokohama geisha house, Hiroaki introduced Will to Japanese culture, and once Will had gotten over his modesty in the presence of women, he enjoyed himself completely.

After separate baths, in which the geishas washed the men as gently as if they were children, Will and Hiroaki slipped together into a large steaming tub of water, where they soaked and talked and recalled their plebe summer.

Then, wearing luxurious silk kimonos, they ate sushi. Will had expected to be repulsed by a plate of raw fish. But he should have known that the Japanese would offer only delicacy in the flavors and beauty in the presentation. Each taste of fish, wasabi, and rice was like a little explosion of energy in his mouth. The warm sake reminded him of mild turpentine, but it did its job, and soon he and Hiroaki entered into a round of toasting.

"To Theodore Roosevelt," said Hiroaki.

"To the Emperor," answered Will.

"To the *Missouri*."

"To the *Nisshin*."

"To your beautiful sister and her lifelong happiness."

"To your beautiful geishas and our night-long happiness."

"To our glorious Admiral Togo."

"To meeting him tomorrow."

"To knowing one's enemy."

"To the friendship such knowledge will bring."

"To the gift that a friend can bring." Hiroaki clapped his hands.

And two new girls emerged. Their hair was arranged even more elaborately than that of the others. Their faces were covered in white powder, which made their skin look like delicate porcelain; their red lips were like small blossoms. They sat before the men and sang songs that Will knew were a prelude to something more.

Then they knelt and unfastened the men's kimonos. Will told himself that this was part of the culture they had traveled so far to understand. He could not insult his old friend, and there was no graceful way for him to stand up and leave. And he had never seen anything more enticing than a red kimono drawn back to reveal the dark hair between a young geisha's legs.

The great Admiral Togo appeared before American midshipmen and ensigns the next day, in a Yokohama garden. It may have been that he wished to show them the implacable face of the samurai warrior. Or perhaps he wished to gaze upon the young faces of the American navy that he might someday be forced to fight.

Whatever the reason, Will found it the most memorable scene of the journey.

Togo, through an interpreter, delivered a few words on the glories of naval life and the battle of Tsushima Strait. Then the Americans crowded in around him.

Three cheers were called, to which Togo responded with three formal bows.

Then the Americans, growing more exuberant and bolder in the presence of a man who was a bona fide naval god, raised Admiral Togo onto their shoulders, as the Japanese junior officers had done to the American admirals aboard the *Mikasa.*

Will was at the edge of the crowd, cheering with the rest. In the middle of it all, Bill Halsey was whispering something to the interpreter, who smiled a bit, then whispered to Togo's aide, who looked shocked, but passed Halsey's words to Togo nevertheless.

The admiral looked down at the sea of American faces, his own face as cold and controlled as a kabuki mask, and he gave one brief nod.

There was a great cheer and Togo was carefully lowered to the ground.

A blanket appeared from somewhere and was spread before him. At the urging of the Americans, Togo took his place in the middle of the blanket, sitting with arms folded and legs crossed. Once he was in place he looked at the young Americans and nodded again.

And with a roar, they lifted the blanket, and with a rising and falling chant—*one . . . two . . . three*—they flung him skyward.

He rose into the air in the same position in which he sat—arms folded, legs crossed, expression frozen.

"One!" cried the young Americans.

Then, with another joyous roar, the admiral was thrown into the air again.

"Two."

And then again, the highest yet. Admiral Togo flew upward, as tightly wrapped as a human cannonball. And for a split second, he looked straight at Will Stafford. Will felt the eyes dig into him, take the measure, challenge him.

Then Togo dropped from view, but Will was still looking up at the sky . . .

. . . and he heard another thunderous roar . . .

. . . another explosion, but not of voices . . . of ordnance . . .

. . . and the roar grew louder. . . .

• • •

It was the roar of time racing ahead and shooting backward simultaneously.

Will Stafford was twenty-four, and in a flash . . . he was fifty-five.

And the eyes of the samurai were still looking right at him, taking the measure of him.

Was Will young, or was he fifty-five? Was he awake, or was he asleep?

The plane, an Aichi Type 99 carrier-based dive bomber, went roaring away over the heights to the north.

Jane came running out of the house. "Will! What's—"

"Get inside!"

"Oh, my God!"

Two miles to the south, Pearl Harbor was disappearing.

Huge columns of black smoke were billowing into the air. The swarming planes looked like bees attacking a string of wallowing water buffalo. And the concussion of the blasts, felt up there on the Aiea Heights, was like the gasping of the air itself.

Even from where Will and Jane were standing, they could see the explosions against the sides of the battleships, and the huge geysers of water that seemed to rise in slow motion until they towered five times higher than the basket masts that gave the American ships their distinctive silhouettes.

"Captain! What's happening?" Maureen, their daughter-in-law, rushed out of the house with a pair of binoculars in her hand. "Is this some kind of drill?"

"This is no drill," said her father-in-law, snatching the binoculars.

"Just thank God the *Enterprise* isn't here," said Jane. "Otherwise we'd be losing a carrier, too."

"And maybe Billy?" asked Maureen.

Jane put her arm around the young woman. "Don't you worry about our Billy. He's smarter than all of us put together."

"He's smarter than I am, that's for certain," said Will, peering through the binoculars. "The *West Virginia*'s hit. The *Oklahoma* . . . Jesus!"

Now Juan, their Filipino houseboy, came running out, "Captain Will . . . Captain Will, they call you from Admiral Kimmel office. They say fuckin' Jap planes everywhere—Hickham, Kaneohe—"

"Juan," said Jane coolly.

"Wheeler, Bellows, Ewa . . .they say this is no fuckin' drill—"

"Juan," she repeated.

"They bombin' the shit out of everything—"

"Juan."

"Huh?"

"I've told you not to swear."

Two more planes were rising up from the harbor toward them. Nakajima 97s, known as Kates—torpedo bombers.

"Get down!" cried Will.

As the Kates went over, the lead plane loosed a burst of machine-gun fire that tore up the lawn, ripped up the veranda, and blasted through the house.

"Sons of bitches!" cried Jane Lord Stafford.

"Missus, no be swearin'," said Juan.

"It's this," said Will, gesturing to his crisp white dress uniform. "They're shooting at this. They should be . . . Jesus, we were stupid!"

"They're shooting at all of us," said Jane. "There's nothing special about you."

"*I* read the war warning two weeks ago," said Will. "I helped to write Plan Orange at the War College. 'Japs open Pacific War with Sunday morning attack on Pearl Harbor.' I've seen the war warnings for forty years."

Just then a tremendous column of smoke shot straight up from one of the ships. At the same moment, a long, furious jet of fire shot out over the bow. A moment later, the windows of the Staffords' little hillside house rattled, and they felt the concussion of the blast, then they heard it echoing.

By the time it roared past, the whole forward section of the *Arizona* had disappeared behind a hundred-foot curtain of flame. The main magazine had erupted—a million pounds of explosives. No one could have survived the blast.

"Oh, God!" cried Maureen.

Jane pressed her hand to her mouth and thought of her sons.

Will Stafford thought, briefly, of suicide.

"Oh, good Lord, Will, how could this happen?" cried Jane.

"Opportunity is all," said Will. "If the enemy leaves a door open, you rush in."

"So now what?" asked Maureen.

“Now that he’s rushed in, we slam the door shut and beat the shit out of him.”

“That good,” said Juan. “But I think they just blow the fuckin’ door off its hinges.”

CHAPTER SEVEN

Meeting the Admiral

October 12

Susan had not forgotten her 1992 trip to Pearl Harbor. . . .

She had resisted the idea of visiting the hull of an old battleship on her second honeymoon. Just another guy thing. She wanted to go straight to the Big Island. She had heard that Honolulu was just a mid-Pacific Miami, with so many Japanese tourists that you couldn't tell who had won the war.

But the marriage counselor had told Susan and her husband, Rob, that they should solve their problems through compromise, so a few days of history at Pearl Harbor would be followed by a few days of volcano hiking on Hawaii. Then they'd get the divorce they both sensed was inevitable.

At the National Park Service Visitor Center, they saw a film that told the story of the attack—16mm news footage enlarged for the wide screen, booming stereo sound track, authoritative narrator. Susan was no student of history, maybe because Rob was a frustrated assistant professor of history, and he had taken out his frustrations on a few willing female history students. But she was glad he had given her a summary of the events on the drive from Honolulu. It was good background for the film.

During the Great Depression, Japan, like so many other nations, had given herself to her militarists. To preserve Japan's sovereignty, and their own ascendancy, the militarists had decided to drive white colonialism out of Asia, replacing it with something they called the

Greater East Asia Co-Prosperity Sphere. This was a fancy name for the yellow colonialism of Japan, and the millions of Chinese who were slaughtered in the decade before Pearl Harbor could distinguish it only by its savagery.

Finally, in the summer of 1941, the Japanese occupied the capital of French Indochina, with the approval of their German allies, and President Franklin Roosevelt decided that enough was enough. It was the first time that many Americans had ever heard the name of the capital—Saigon—or the other name for French Indochina—Vietnam—and already they heard trouble.

Roosevelt froze Japanese assets, banned the sale of raw materials, and stopped the flow of American oil, which had been fueling the Japanese war machine.

"Now," intoned the narrator of the film, "Japan's back was to the wall."

"Oh, really?" Susan's husband said out loud. He was the kind of guy who liked to show how smart he was by talking back to movie screens and television anchors, and that alone made him divorceable, but in this case, he was right.

"All they had to do," he whispered, "was stop their aggression and get out of Indochina, and the oil would have flowed."

So, she wondered, who was telling this story, the winners or the losers, or someone trying to placate both?

And then the *Arizona* exploded on screen—an astonishing piece of color footage taken at the moment when a five-hundred-pound bomb detonated in the forward magazine, lifting the ship from the water and in a single flash killing over a thousand sailors—more U.S. Navy men than were killed in the Spanish-American War and World War I combined.

Susan found herself getting angrier—at the film and, almost irrationally, at the Japanese tourists in the audience around her. What was wrong with her? She was not supposed to be so susceptible to this kind of emotion. She had studied haiku in college. She loved sushi, for God's sake.

Then the audience was ushered out into the blinding sunshine to board the launch that would take them to Battleship Row.

Little was left of the ships that had been sitting there on the morning that America changed forever. The *Arizona*'s crumpled foremast had long ago been removed, along with three of her four gun turrets. Now the only things that could be seen above the water were the moorings to which the *Arizona* had been tied, the rusting barbette from her C turret, and the white marble memorial that looked like a gentle wave rolling over the wreck.

Susan read the list of men who had died on the ship and were still entombed within her. She thought briefly of her own uncle Eddie, who had been on one of the battleships and had never spoken about it until the day he died.

From the deck of the memorial, she looked down at the rusted hull. She watched the tide rushing out, making little riffles above the barbettes and the hull fittings, and a Japanese tourist threw flowers onto the water.

Then Susan saw the oil, rising near the rusted remnants of a ventilation shaft, rising and spreading in an iridescent minor-key rainbow of colors, rising every few seconds from a ship that had been dead for half a century and was still bleeding.

This was no guy thing. This was about the families those men had left behind and the future they'd never had. It was about the concussions of a blast that had traveled through time. And most of all, it was about the decisions people made to make history. It did not have to happen like this. It never did.

And the oil had mingled with the flowers, and the tide had carried them both away.

And she had thanked her husband for bringing her. . . .

Jogging down Prince George Street to the harbor, she thanked him again for getting out of her life six months later, leaving her with their daughter and her films.

And this film would have to include that: the USS *Annapolis*, still sitting out there, because Pearl Harbor had led to that, too. Americans had resolved that they would never let something like Pearl Harbor happen again. Submarines like the *Annapolis* all but guaranteed it. And groups like the Institute for Advanced Naval Planning tried to make sure that the guarantees were backed up in green American cash.

In a submarine, four men in black wet suits synchronize watches. Then, one by one, they climb into the forward escape trunk. The hatch closes beneath them.

"Now, the water floods the trunk . . . while on the surface, all is quiet."

The ocean is gray-black. The lights of the enemy target can be seen in the distance. And now, rising like spirits from the sea, two small motorized contraptions that look like a cross between a jet ski and a torpedo, begin to speed silently across the water toward the enemy target, each carrying two of the SEALs.

Now the music, which sounds like the music for all of these films—dull, obvious, generic—begins to pound.

"The new Sea Sprite ultra-silent jet ski insertion vehicle, from Danson-Crafting, the leaders in swimmer-delivery vehicles."

Blank screen.

Steve Stafford flipped on the lights in a little video viewing room at CHINFO. There were televisions tuned to CNN everywhere in the place. The whole Pentagon was wired into CNN. But there were also rooms for the private examination of film footage like this.

The reporter from the *Baltimore Sun* had asked to speak with someone who had commanded a sub in World War II but still had a modern perspective. Steve had called on the best broad-range expert he could think of.

And the admiral did not disappoint. He even came all the way to Washington, bringing that little film and plenty of charm for someone who would help get the story out. "That piece of film is the kind of thing we're being asked to consult on at the institute these days, at least those of us who were Op 02."

"That's Navy Department talk for the Submarine Warfare Division," explained Steve Stafford.

The reporter, a young guy on his first big feature piece, jotted down a few notes, and the admiral suggested they continue their talk in the park at the center of the building. "That way, I can watch for my next appointment."

Once they were settled on a bench in the shade, the admiral went to war, taking the reporter through World War II, the Cold War, the moment in the Cuban Missile Crisis when he joined the picket line of submarines and destroyers stopping the Russian ships, right through the 1980s, "when the money flowed like water."

"How would you categorize the present?" asked the reporter.

The admiral said, "You know, there's an old joke: after John Paul

Jones, who were the two greatest heroes in U.S. Navy history? Admiral Yamamoto and Admiral Gorshkov."

The reporter chuckled politely at that.

"It was true," said the admiral. "They gave us something to build against. Now, it's us against the chaos theory."

Steve chuckled at that because it was one of the admiral's favorite phrases. It was also true.

"Chaos demands a versatile response. Now, my World War Two boat, the *Nautilus,* sank enemy shipping, conducted periscope intel missions, and put marines on beaches at night. The current SSNs take that same versatility and enhance it a thousandfold."

Just then Steve noticed an old man in a shiny brown suit and skinny brown tie appearing at the south entrance corridor: Lloyd Shank.

Lloyd Shank was a retired Defense Department lifer. He and the admiral had met at a seminar of Civil War enthusiasts in 1963, familiar Pentagon faces recognizing each other off-campus. They had talked, Lloyd had mentioned that his great-uncle, Gabriel Shank, had been with the Twentieth Maine. Tom had recalled the name from his own family's past, and they had been friends ever since.

Steve Stafford liked old Lloyd, who wore black-framed eyeglasses that had gone out of style in the sixties, smoked three packs a day, punctuated his talk with a cynical seen-everything insider's chuckle, and, according to scuttlebutt, knew the location of more buried bodies than there were in Arlington National Cemetery.

The admiral saw Shank, too, and with the polished grace of a smooth-talker, he quickly summed up for the reporter: "The point is that we're less worried about the Russians in deep water today and more concerned with projecting our power through the littoral zone. So we need a new generation of submarines to meet the new challenges. And all those exotic swimmer-delivery vehicles are part of the program. It's called forward thinking."

Then he shook hands and excused himself.

"Don't forget lunch," Steve reminded him.

"Absolutely. Your grandmother is thrilled that you're bringing that PBS gal down to the Patuxent . . . She's hoping you're sweet on her."

"She's ten years older, Grandpa."

• • •

By noon, when Steve Stafford's car ran in under the sycamores, the admiral was galloping Wildair across the Patuxent fields.

"He sees us," said Susan, who was sitting in Steve's back seat.

"Looks like he's been waiting," said Jack. "I think it's going to be all right."

Steve did not tell them that the admiral was not expecting Jack.

Betty was talking before she even opened the door. "You're early, Steve. And Cousin Susan, so good to see you again."

"It's good to see you, Betty," said Jack.

"Oh, Jack . . ." She gave him a quick hug. "It's been too long."

Susan glanced into the dining room, where the old Filipino houseboy was hurriedly setting another place at a luncheon table set for four. Susan did not know Betty Stafford well enough to read the nervousness in her gestures. The extra place was the first inkling Susan had that the admiral was going to be surprised by Jack.

"So," Betty was saying to Jack, "where do you plan to live in Annapolis?"

"At the Fine Folly, if all goes well."

Betty's plastered-on smile crumbled, and she looked at Steve. "I guess he doesn't know?"

"Know what?"

"The institute is moving very quickly to buy the house."

"The Institute for Advanced Naval Planning?" said Jack.

"*I* didn't know," said Steve. Then he realized why the admiral had been at the Pentagon that morning.

Jack's whole body seemed to sag. "It wasn't supposed to happen this fast."

"I called Lloyd Shank as soon as I heard you were in town." The admiral now appeared in the doorway from the dining room. He was wearing a brown turtleneck and a brown tweed jacket. His face was flushed after his long gallop. "I told Lloyd to bypass the damn lawyer who's handling the ancillary probate in Maryland. Go straight to the Maine lawyer who's the administrator of the estate, make a preemptive bid. Four million."

"My typical brother." Jack glanced at Susan. "Instead of calling me to say hello when I come to town, he gets about the business of screwing me. Has the offer been accepted?"

"Lloyd Shank is contacting the other blood relatives. We can't get a purchase-and-sale agreement until the estate clears probate, but we'll have something on paper by tomorrow."

"Do you know who the Maryland lawyer is?" asked Jack.

"Why should I? I'm just an overseer of the institute. The day-to-day running—"

"His name is Oliver Parrish, " said Jack.

Betty brought her hand to her face. "Oh, my. Our Jimmy's friend."

The admiral's flush deepened.

Susan was trying to make sense of it all, and not doing a very good job of it. But before she tried very hard, it was over.

"I'm sorry, Steve, and Cousin Susan, but I've lost my appetite," said the admiral. "The minute he comes here, he starts bringing up things that we don't want to talk about. And it takes my appetite right away."

"I came here to try to talk with you, Tom. To try to make you understand what I'm doing in this book."

"I've read it, Grandpa," said Steve. "Or at least part of it."

"Tell me about it sometime. I have a new horse I want to exercise."

"You're a stubborn bastard," Betty said to her husband. "And I hope Cousin Susan puts that in her film."

"I don't care." And he stalked out.

"Miz Stafford, I got a nice lunch ready," said Juan from the doorway. "Nice crab cakes for everybody. I don't want 'em to go to waste just 'cause the admiral a stubborn bastard."

"I've told you before, Juan . . . you're not supposed to swear."

Jack calmed down over the crab cakes.

He wouldn't talk about the book any more. He told Betty that he would give her the first seven chapters before he said another word about it. And maybe she could talk some sense to her husband. "I can't get the story right until I've interviewed him."

And Betty promised to see what she could do.

What amazed Susan through the rest of the meal was the way all of them could avoid the big problems sitting right there on the table looking at them—just chitchat their way around everything. Maybe it was a learned skill.

By the time they were leaving, Betty was going on about this and that, and Jack was chuckling at all her jokes.

Steve, however, had run out of things to say.

And his silence took on weight as they went past the front room on the way out. He stopped in the doorway, then stepped into the room, as if he could not resist. In a moment, he was standing in front of the picture of his father and the framed Purple Heart beneath it, studying them as if he had never seen them before.

"Steve visits his father's medal whenever he comes," explained Betty. "I think it comforts him to see his father here among all the other Staffords. Makes him feel rooted."

Susan could see why. She had sensed it before but not really taken it all in: the room was a shrine to all the characters in Jack's book. Black Jed, painted by Charles Willson Peale, hung over the fireplace. On the opposite wall, painted by some long-forgotten Chesapeake artist, was Captain Jason Stafford. There was a portrait of Abraham Stafford in one of those front-to-back cocked hats that admirals had worn in full dress until the thirties. And familiar photographs filled in every space between doorframes and windows.

She was drawn to a photograph of three brothers in the bright sunshine on Waikiki, with Diamond Head behind them. It looked like it had been taken sometime before the Second World War. She recognized Jack and the admiral, both young and powerful, but—

"That's their brother Billy," said Betty, anticipating Susan's question.

"Is Billy in the book?" It was the admiral. He had appeared at the screen door, as though he could not stay away from an argument.

"Of course he is," said Jack.

So the admiral opened the door and came inside. "Tell me one thing, Jack. This book of yours, do you tell the truth about what you did in 1942, when you were tramping around Honolulu with Eddie Browne?"

"Uncle Eddie?" said Susan. "My uncle?"

"Your family drops in and out of our story a lot," Jack explained. Then he said to his brother, "I want to write the truth about everything. That's why I write about myself in the third person. And that's why I'm here."

"All right, then," said the admiral. "Let me read what you have. If you tell the truth about 1942, I'll sit down and talk with you."

And Susan saw what might be her only chance. "I'd love to get that on tape."

The admiral said, "If I agree to talk, you can film us under a tree right on the Academy grounds."

"If you agree to talk," said Jack, "will you agree to stop the purchase of the Fine Folly?"

To that, the admiral shook his head.

"If I can't get the house, then at least I'll get the truth out of you, you old son of a bitch."

"I'll see what truth I get out of your book, first, you older son of a bitch."

The Stafford Story
BOOK EIGHT
Dispatches from Armageddon
December 7, 1941

"Yes, Mr. and Mrs. America, the lights have gone out all over Europe." Jack Stafford brought his mouth closer to the microphone. "But our peacetime cities still illuminate the Atlantic night and silhouette Britain-bound freighters."

The microphone wiggled its toes.

"While somewhere out there, the U-boats lurk." Jack kissed the microphone, right on the pad of the big toe. From the other end of the bed came a giggle.

"Hey," he said, "you wouldn't laugh at Edward R. Murrow."

"Edward R. Murrow wouldn't kiss my big toe."

"He's not trying to get a job at CBS."

Lois Hoyt leaned on her elbows and looked down at him. She was no beauty. All the makeup in the world couldn't do a thing about the bent nose or the army of crows that had gone stomping over her face. Maybe that was why he was working down here, where the view was better.

What a bastard. But what a life—suite at the Plaza . . . lunch from room service . . . pink panties and boxer shorts rumpled in the sheets.

She gave his ass a squeeze. "Come up here, lover boy."

He was only twenty-three, but he wasn't quite ready. He'd done it twice the night before, once already today, and it wasn't even quarter of two.

"Let me finish my audition," he said.

"Honey, you've been auditioning since last night. An executive secretary can do a lot for a guy with good pipes. And I don't just mean the voice."

He brought his mouth to the sole of her foot and scratched his stubbled cheek along the smooth skin, making her twitch. . . .

At about the same time, Lieutenant Bill Stafford was coming home at fifteen thousand feet, piloting a Douglas Dauntless SBD, with the beauty of Oahu unfolding before him and a beautiful wife waiting at home.

His plane was one of eighteen dispatched by Admiral Halsey from the *Enterprise* shortly after 0600. They had flown to scout sectors a hundred and fifty miles ahead of the task force. Now they were pushing on to the Ford Island Naval Air Station. *Enterprise* had been due back at Pearl the night before, but bad weather had delayed her in transit from Wake Island.

Now the weather was magnificent—a few high clouds, intense blue sky, unlimited visibility. He was flying toward the morning sun, so the surface of the sea flashed like liquid silver, and the mountains of Oahu appeared to him as they must have to the first Polynesians, looming up in jagged silhouette from the sea.

What a great way to make a living.

"Hey, Lieutenant," asked his rear-seat gunner, Jake Stimpson of Barstow, California, "do you see smoke comin' up on the south side of the island?"

"Roger," Bill said into the intercom. "Must be burnin' an awful big cane field."

"I didn't know they burned . . . Jesus!"

"What?"

"Japs!"

"Come on, Jake. It's too early to be jokin'—"

Then Bill heard the distinct *bup-bup-bup* of a fifty-caliber machine gun and felt the plane bounce once . . . twice . . . a third time, as if someone were hitting it with a sledgehammer.

"Jesus!" cried Bill.

Bup-bup-bup.

"Jesus!" screamed Jake. "I'm hit!"

"What? What? Where are you hit?"

"Oh, Christ . . . Oh, Christ, Lieutenant, I'm hit in the balls. Ohhhh—"

Bup-bup-bup. There were three of them.

"They're Japs," screamed Jake. "What the fuck is goin' on?"

Bill didn't know, and he didn't have time to think about it. He swallowed hard and told himself to stay calm . . . be professional.

Japs. Zeros. You couldn't mistake the big red meatball insignia and the silver flash of the wings. And they were shooting at him!

The Dauntless was good, but it was a dive-bomber, not a fighter, and the Zeros were the best fighters ever built. If he hadn't believed that two minutes ago, he believed it now. Because no matter how he banked or dived, they were on him, peppering him with their fifty calibers.

Jake Stimpson moaned, "There's blood pourin' out of my boot."

"Hang on."

He was over the island now. In a few minutes, he'd be over Ewa Field, within range of American antiaircraft batteries. And whatever was happening, the antiaircraft was working. He could see bursts of it, opening like black flowers in the sky ahead.

Then one of the Zeros peeled off and went after another Dauntless.

With a quick little bank and a dive, Bill Stafford had one of the others in his sights, for just an instant, and he fired his fifty calibers. But it was only an instant. That Zero shot out of his field while the other one jumped on him from behind. *Bup-bup-bup.*

A shot whizzed past his ear and blew out the front windscreen. Jake made a gurgling sound, like the last quart of water going down the drain. Then the plane shook as if it had flown over a pothole in the sky. Big black AA bursts were coming up all around him, and the Zeros were pulling away.

Jesus! His own people were shooting at him now, from Ewa, and the needle on his fuel gauge was dropping. His beautiful blue plane was hit in the tanks. He'd never make Ford Island. If he didn't jump now, he might never make it out of the plane.

"Jake! We have to bail out." But he knew that Jake could no longer hear.

So he banked south, out over the water. Then he pushed back the canopy. At a hundred and forty mph, it was like jumping from the back of a galloping horse, except that he didn't fall. He blew backward and upward, into the blue Hawaiian sky, while the Dauntless shot away and then down toward the blue sea below.

On that crisp, clear Sunday afternoon, Betty Merritt sat in the dining room of the Stafford House Hotel, and decided she was the luckiest girl in the world. The diamond on her finger was small, but every way that she turned it, it caught the firelight and made little sparkles that could be seen in all of the mirrors covering two walls of the room.

The mirrors made the old great room feel spacious, even though the windows that once looked out on the garden had long ago been plastered over and covered with blue-and-gold draperies, because the hotel had been grafted to the back of the house. The dining room was half full, mostly with midshipmen and their drags, a term Betty had decided no one would ever use on her again.

At a nearby table, an older woman sat alone. She had silver blond hair and wore a blue pinstripe suit with huge shoulders, like Rosalind Russell's in *His Girl Friday*. She noticed Betty beaming at her engagement ring and lifted her wineglass. "Congratulations. I hope your marriage is as happy as mine was."

Was. Betty simply said thank you and dropped her eyes to the menu. This was not a weekend for any kind of unhappiness. This was a weekend for Tom.

She had met him when his father was commandant of the Boston Navy Yard and her father was a judge raising funds for the restoration of the *Constitution*, which was moored there. They had been children then. Now they were grown up, and in love.

She would graduate from Wellesley in the spring. Her Tom—it felt good to think of him as *her* Tom—was graduating from the Academy that month and moving to submarine school at New London. With war in the wind, the navy was expanding rapidly. But that, too, was an unhappiness, so she put it out of her mind.

She had come down on the Friday train from Boston. On Saturday, they had gone into Washington to see Cary Grant and Joan Fontaine in *Suspicion.* Their dinner at Willard's must have used up all his pay for the month, but from now on, it would be their restaurant, and "Moonglow" would be their song, because it was playing in the background when Tom slipped the ring onto her finger.

On the train back to Annapolis, they had found themselves alone in one of the cars. And he had kissed her . . . and kissed her again . . . and she had let him get all the way to third base under her overcoat. It was not something that nice girls were supposed to do. But she wasn't a girl anymore. She was an engaged woman.

"May I sit down, miss?"

"Good afternoon, Mr. Midshipman." She patted the back of her hair. She had spent the whole morning doing it up in that jelly-roll style he liked, and the approving once-over he gave her made all the nuisance worthwhile.

In single-breasted jacket, brass buttons, and black tie, Tom Stafford looked self-assured, if a bit too stiff. But that made him all the warmer when the granite jaw cracked and he smiled. He was not as handsome as his brother Billy or as much fun as smart-ass Jack. But he was the most solid man she had ever met.

"You know," he said, "Washington danced in this room, Jefferson, Lafayette, and Theodore Roosevelt all walked these halls . . . and my Aunt Katherine is sitting in the corner."

"I was wondering if you'd see me," said the lady in the Rosalind Russell suit.

"What are you doing here?" asked Tom.

"My annual sentimental journey. We were here for the last time—your grandparents, your father, my Harry, and me—in December of 1907."

Tom stepped over to Katherine's table and smoothly guided her back to his, amid protests that she shouldn't break up what was obviously an intimate little dinner.

Tom looked around at the other midshipmen and their drags and said, "How could anything here be intimate?"

"Well, in that case"—Katherine plunked herself down—"I'll assume you're both twenty-one and order Veuve Cliquot to celebrate . . . if they have any here."

They drank to the engagement, to each other, and to the Shank sisters of Maine, who had inherited half of the hotel from their uncle Gabriel, and who had just bought out the fragmented estate of Ethan Stafford's late-in-life California lover.

"What does this mean?" asked Betty.

"The Stafford House stays in the hands of friends," said Katherine.

"I love this old place," said Betty.

Katherine patted her hand. "I love it, too. I love it as the Stafford House, I loved it as the Fine Folly, and I love knowing that the Shanks love it too, because without women like Alexandra Parrish Shank, whose portrait hangs in the front parlor, you and I and all the other women sitting here letting the boys call us drags—"

"Now, Aunt Katherine," said Tom, "that's tradition. It's almost regulation."

"Quiet, young man," Katherine said imperiously. "Without *women* like Alexandra, we would never have gotten the vote."

"I haven't voted yet," said Betty.

"When you do," said Katherine, growing more garrulous with a third glass of champagne, "ask the hard questions. And after you do, you'll vote for America Firsters and stay out of Europe's troubles."

"Oh, Katherine, that's just what Hitler wants, and his Jap allies, too."

"Don't call them Japs." Katherine looked at Betty again. "I've been a widow for twenty-three years, dear, because we couldn't keep out of a European war."

"Uncle Harry was a brave man." Tom offered a toast to Katherine's husband, who had been killed on a destroyer doing convoy duty in the North Sea in 1918.

After a few moments more, Betty offered a toast to Alexandra.

Katherine said, "And to Alexandra's inspiration, Antonia Stafford Browne."

At that moment, Antonia's great-great-grandson, Lieutenant Edward Browne, OOD of the *West Virginia,* had been in hell for twenty minutes, and already it felt like an eternity. Maybe that was the point of hell.

The small horrors were happening as quickly as a man could see them: A sailor in flames staggered to the side and struck the water with a steaming hiss. A human hand lay on the deck, blown from God knew where. Men at an antiaircraft gun were literally sliced in half by bullets from a diving Zero.

And overarching the small horrors was the great canopy of hell, of boiling black smoke and flames that closed and opened like fluttering curtains, one moment shutting out the light completely, the next moment revealing a deceptively blue sky and deceptively tiny planes streaking through it.

There were seven battleships moored in two rows. *West Virginia* was outboard of the *Tennessee* and had already taken three torpedo hits. To the stern and inboard, the *Arizona* resembled a burning oil well, one derrick twisted forward, the other still standing amid the flames.

And if there could be a more horrendous sight than the *Arizona*, it lay forward of the *West Virginia*, in the form of the red hull and giant screws of the *Oklahoma*, which had taken four torpedoes and capsized in less than ten minutes. Now her great basket masts were buried in the mud and hundreds of sailors were trapped in upside-down darkness, with the water rising around them.

The *West Virginia* was listing. But Browne saw no panic. The men had drilled for air attacks, and after the initial shock, his training had taken over. A crew was below, counterflooding to bring the ship back onto an even keel, so that when she sank, she would settle upright in forty-five feet of water. And the executive officer, Commander Hillenkoetter, was shouting orders to the antiaircraft crews on the deck below. And out on the starboard side of the bridge, Captain Bennion was conferring with his navigator.

Suddenly a tremendous blast rocked the *Tennessee*, moored inboard of the *West Virginia*. The concussion knocked Browne off his feet, and shrapnel tore through the bridge like a fistful of marbles fired into a bucket.

The captain went down, and he didn't get up. He lay in the bright sunlight beyond the starboard hatch, with a six-inch piece of metal protruding from his belly.

Browne could not believe how quickly the red stain spread across the midsection of the captain's uniform. There could be no hope for him. Still, Browne rounded up the pharmacist's mate and a Negro messman named Dory Miller, and told them to get the captain off the bridge.

"Don't touch me, dammit!" cried Bennion when Miller bent to lift him.

And Miller did as he was told. No messman challenged a captain, or any other officer. Negroes were allowed on the bridge only to serve meals or swab decks.

"I'm in command," said Hillenkoetter, "Get the captain below."

"Fight the ship!" cried Bennion.

Another explosion knocked everybody to the deck. Then, without another word, Dory Miller lifted the captain and carried him to whatever safety there might be off the bridge.

And hell burned hotter. Another torpedo slammed into the port side, sending a tremendous geyser of water shooting into the air above the ship.

"Jesus!" cried Hillenkoetter. "We have to put up more AA."

Another explosion rocked her. Flames jumped on the number three turret. And a Zero was diving, wings spitting fire as it came.

But somebody on the deck below them was answering with fifty-caliber AA fire that took off the right wing of the plane and sent it pinwheeling over the bridge.

"It's Miller!"shouted the exec. "Who taught a messman to handle AA?"

Dory Miller now swung the gun onto a torpedo plane and poured a stream of fire right at its nose. There was smoke pouring from the plane's engine cowling, but still she was boring in . . . boring in . . . aiming straight for Dory Miller. But Dory didn't budge. He drilled three bullets into the windshield, bringing an explosion of red inside the cockpit, and the plane pancaked into the water.

"Damn," said Hillenkoetter. "He's good."

Captain Will Stafford, assistant operations officer, Pacific Fleet, reached CINCPAC headquarters by 0817. Admiral Husband E. Kimmel was standing at the window, staring out at the devastation.

Kimmel glanced at Will, then turned his eyes back, as if punishing himself by watching. He had always moved with a sense of the importance of his position. But take away the white uniform and the four-star shoulder boards, and Kimmel would have resembled nothing so much as a middle-aged salesman with gray hair and bags under his eyes.

Will tried to think of something positive. "Thank God the carriers aren't here."

Just then something flew through the open window and struck Kimmel in the chest, then clattered to the floor. He looked down at the black splotch it left on his jacket, then stooped and picked it up:

a spent fifty-caliber bullet, fired from somewhere out over Battleship Row.

"It would have been merciful if it killed me," Kimmel said.

After Sunday dinners at Stafford Hall, Abe and Julia settled in with *The Wrigley Chewing Gum Hour* at two o'clock, followed at three by the New York Philharmonic on CBS.

Abe wasn't much for classical music. He preferred Sousa marches or that big-band music the kids were so crazy about. But Julia loved the longhairs, and she loved to be *seen* loving the longhairs. In every city where they had been stationed, she had managed to get herself onto the board of the local orchestra because, as she said, it was a good way to meet the best people.

She had once told Abe that by fulfilling his ambition, he had fulfilled hers. She had gotten to call herself Mrs. *Captain* Stafford, naval attaché in London, and Mrs. *Rear Admiral* Stafford, president of the Naval War College.

Abe now spent his mornings riding across the fields and his afternoons writing articles on naval subjects that interested him. Julia planned monthly trips to cities with naval bases, where they visited old friends and basked in the camaraderie of naval society. That afternoon, by the fireplace in the red-painted study, she did a crossword puzzle while he read a letter from Ernest J. King, commander in chief of the Atlantic Fleet: "'Dear Admiral: Just read your article in *Naval Institute Proceedings* on Royal Navy takedown of *Bismarck*. Excellent.'"

"Oh, Abe," said Julia, her mind drifting, "I do hope that Katherine's not drinking as much."

"She's a grown woman who works for a U.S. senator—even if Burton K. Wheeler's a head-in-the-sand America First moron. Golf, champagne, and isolationist politics suit our merry widow well."

"A seven-letter word for 'feed,' beginning with an *s*—"

"Sorghum," he said and went back to his reading. "'It was dumb luck that the British planes had caught up to *Bismarck*, considering how badly they were deployed, but raw bravery on the part of the fliers who bored in and put a torpedo into her rudder.'"

"What do you think of young Tom going to submarine school?" she asked.

"A wise idea. In fact, this letter is from Ernest King—"

"That arrogant, adulterous Anglophobe son of a—"

"Now, Julia, there aren't many men who've commanded the New London Submarine Base *and* the Hampton Roads Naval Air Station. King knows that the next war will be fought in three dimensions. There'll be plenty of room for advancement in submarines and aviation, too."

"It's not 'One son for the soil and one son for the sea' anymore," mused Julia.

"One grandson above the sea, one below, and one good son on it."

"And then there's Jack."

"Proof of the *real* family saying: 'Some offspring for the sea, some for trouble.'"

"Trouble?"

"Jack's headed in that direction. Like our Katherine. And my brother Jacob. And wandering Ethan, God rest him."

"What about Will? Do you think he'll ever make admiral?"

"You know how it works, dear. Every year an Academy class comes up. Fifty-eight made flag rank in Will's class, out of two hundred and nine. At least Ray Spruance made it."

Abraham finished reading King's letter: "'I like your last line—"The most modern battleship on earth, brought low by an old biplane, is a lesson to all of us." You're a real forward thinker.'"

And the radio crackled: "We interrupt this program to bring you a special CBS bulletin. This is John Daly. The Japanese have attacked Pearl Harbor by air, President Roosevelt has just announced. The attack was also made on naval and military activities on the principal island of Oahu."

That was all. Back to the music. Abraham and Julia looked at each other.

"Does this mean what I think it means?" she asked.

"It means war . . . six months before we're ready for it."

"Well, yes, war . . . but if Will gets blamed for letting Pearl Harbor get bombed, he'll have absolutely *no* chance for flag rank."

"Now, go on, you two." Katherine picked up the check. "Have a nice dance."

Most of the young diners had already gone off to the Sunday afternoon hop at Smoke Hall. The Stafford House had quieted down, but there was a sudden commotion in the hallway, the sound of female voices, of scurrying feet, of high-pitched nervous chatter. Then several of the girls came into the dining room, followed by two armed marines who had escorted them back.

Tom was ordered to return immediately to the Academy. And no time for any lingering good-byes. Because the United States was at war.

The shock of it all overwhelmed Tom and Betty.

But Katherine had been shocked before. "This is the stupidest thing the Japanese could have done," she said after Tom had gone off.

"Are you still an America Firster?" asked Betty.

"We're *all* America Firsters now." Katherine squeezed her hand. "We're all on the same side, and I'm on yours when I tell you this: now that we're at war, you better love that boy as hard as you can for as long as you can."

Four times in fifteen hours—a new record.

"Now"—Jack slid down to Lois's foot again—"let's talk about the Pacific."

There was a knock. "Room service."

She pushed her foot against his cheek. "Answer that, beautiful. You could use a little energy."

Jack put on a white terry cloth robe with a gold *P* embossed on the breast pocket and told the bellhop to put the tray by the window overlooking Fifth Avenue.

"Beautiful afternoon, sir. Hard to believe what all's happened."

"Yeah?" Jack flipped him a half-dollar and lit a cigarette. "What all's that?"

"Japs. They gone and bombed Hawaii. Just come over on the radio."

For a moment, Jack stood there, cigarette lighter flaring beneath his nose.

"What did he say?" Lois came into the room in a matching robe.

Jack snapped his lighter shut. "We're at war."

"Yes'm," said the bellhop, inflating with that sense of self-importance that comes to people delivering bad news. "Word is, Japs are plannin' to invade Hawaii."

"Jesus." She slipped the cigarette from Jack's lips and took a long drag.

Jack looked at his watch: three o'clock, Eastern Standard Time, which made it nine-thirty in Hawaii. His first instinct was to call his brother at the Naval Academy. But he was a reporter now. A reporter called the city room.

"Goddammit, Jack," shouted the voice in his ear, "where are you?"

"I'm . . . I'm with a"—Jack glanced at Lois—"a friend."

She shoved his cigarette back into his mouth and began to pace back and forth in front of the windows.

"A friend," grunted Jack's editor, bilious old Harry Dowd, who always smelled of hot dogs and had mustard on the corners of his mouth. "Aren't you a navy brat?"

"My brother's a lieutenant on the *Enterprise*. Do you know if they got her?"

"We don't know much." Harry burped into the phone. "And there'll probably be censorship, but American Press Service wants to get some bread in the gravy out there while it's still hot. 'Course, if a lieutenant's the best you can do—"

"My father's on Admiral Kimmel's staff. Kimmel's the CINC-PAC."

Lois stopped pacing and puffing.

Harry Dowd burped again . . . probably drinking a Moxie with his hot dog. "What the hell is a sink-pack?"

"Commander in Chief, Pacific Fleet," said Jack. "But if I know the navy, heads'll roll tomorrow. My father's might be one of them."

"Well, we'll gamble. Pack your bags."

After Jack hung up, Lois said, "Honey, CBS may be able to use you after all. How would you like to be our stringer out there?"

"You mean, send you stuff that somebody else will read on the radio?" Jack grabbed a bottle of beer from the room-service ice bucket.

"Sounds swell, doesn't it?"

"No, thanks." He stuffed half a sandwich into his mouth. "No lines on CBS, or a byline on wire service stories picked up by half the papers in this country?"

She took another drag on her cigarette. "You're a hard one, honey."

"When you're ready to put me on the air, call me."

Lunch went down fast. He dressed fast. He had the feeling that from now on, everything would happen fast.

• • •

Aboard the battleship *Nagato*, on the Inland Sea, Captain Hiroaki Tanaka studied a chessboard and made a move. When Admiral Yamamoto had a moment, he would make a move of his own. But there was a grander game being played, with airplanes and warships as the pawns and knights, and the great map on the wardroom table as the chessboard.

At fifty-seven, Hiroaki was the oldest member of Yamamoto's staff, older than the admiral himself. They had been shipmates aboard the *Nisshin* at Tsushima Strait, and Yamamoto—father of Japanese naval aviation, architect of Japanese naval strategy—still respected Hiroaki's knowledge and good counsel.

Like Hiroaki, Yamamoto had lived for a time in the United States, had felt the energy that lay fallow in the American earth, and did not want war with her. But when the Japanese leadership insisted that war was inevitable, Yamamoto had decided to neutralize the American fleet so that he would not have to face an attack on his left flank while he was sweeping into the oil fields of the East Indies.

"In the first six to twelve months of a war with the United States," he had told the cabinet, "I will run wild . . . But if the war continues after that, I have no expectation of success."

Now the rampage had begun. At 0300, the radios—silent for days while *Kido Butai,* the carrier striking force, slipped across the Pacific—had begun to sing.

"Tora! Tora! Tora!" Complete surprise has been achieved. Then the litany of destruction from the pilots; then the messages of shock from the Americans: "Air Raid Pearl Harbor X This is no drill."

The officers in the *Nagato* wardroom had taken their example from their leader, showing little emotion. A few handshakes, glasses of sake, and plates of dried squid were the only show of celebration.

By 0500, two attack waves had sunk or damaged eighteen American ships and left most land-based aircraft at Hawaii in smoking piles. The First Air Fleet had been so well trained that they had even delivered torpedoes into a mine layer at the 1010 dock, where they had expected to find the aircraft carrier *Enterprise.* But she wasn't there. Neither was the *Lexington.*

What Americans would later call a sneak attack had actually been a brilliant *surprise* attack delivered on an enemy whose enormity had guaranteed its complacency, whose bureaucracy had assured that no controlling intelligence would see what was about to happen, and whose bickering diversity had guaranteed its refusal to confront the reality of war. But by dumb luck, or the grace of God, the carriers had escaped.

A third attack wave had been planned, to destroy oil tanks, submarine pens, and drydocks. But Admiral Nagumo, in command of *Kido Butai*, feared those missing American carriers, even though he had six of his own. When he was told that the damage he had done would keep the Americans reeling for six months, he decided to withdraw.

And no one aboard the *Nagato* could persuade Yamamoto to overrule him.

So Hiroaki went out on the bridge to drink in the cold December air and compose a haiku for his wife and son: "The birds fly eastward/ To bring freedom from the west. / The cold gray sea smiles."

Then Yamamoto appeared in a winter coat with a collar of rabbit fur.

"Had we destroyed the oil tanks and drydocks, we would have forced them all the way back to San Diego," said Hiroaki. "But we have our six months."

"And yet"—Yamamoto tugged at the glove on his left hand, which covered the stumps of the fingers lost at Tsushima Strait—"I fear that we have awakened a sleeping giant and filled him with a terrible resolve."

"At least you know your enemy."

ii
Christmas in Hawaii

Jack Stafford was shocked, not by the devastation at Pearl Harbor but by the sight of his father.

Will Stafford had suddenly gone gray, and the color draining from his head seemed to be pooling under his eyes. He looked as wrecked as the ships still smoldering in the distance.

The new commander in the Pacific, Chester Nimitz, had called his first meeting for 2000 on Christmas night. No one complained. This was war, and the Japanese did not celebrate Christmas. But Will

Stafford expected that he and several other good men would be sent packing that night.

It was a bleak Christmas, just about everywhere.

On one side of the globe, Japan's German allies were reaching ever farther east and west. The German army was within sight of Moscow, and U-boats were feasting on Allied ships.

On the other side, the Japanese were fulfilling Yamamoto's prophecy. Ten hours after Pearl Harbor, Japanese planes struck Philippine airfields. Two days later, they caught Britain's new battleship, *Prince of Wales,* and her consort, *Repulse.* If there had been any doubt that the battleship was no longer the queen of the seas or that Japanese pilots were now the princes of the air, both sank with the ships. The American-held island of Guam fell the same day. The mid-Pacific airstrip at Wake Island fell on December 23, and Hong Kong on Christmas Day.

Season's greetings.

One of Jack's fondest memories was of his mother, keeping Christmas in a very simple way for her three little boys, no matter where they were stationed.

Each Christmas Eve, they strung popcorn, lit candles, and hung just five ornaments, one for each member of the family—a star at the top of the tree for Dad, a small woodcut of a manger for Mom, a brass trumpet for Billy, a three-dimensional silver snowflake with points going in every direction for Jack, and a simple red ball for Tom. And it always looked right—in family housing at Norfolk, in the commandant's house at Boston, or on a potted palm in Hawaii.

Traditions were good, thought Jack, especially in bad times and strange places. And what could be stranger than wearing a flowered aloha shirt to celebrate Christmas on a tropical hillside, in a light tropical rain, in a bungalow that looked as if it belonged on Cape Cod? Unless, of course, it was the sound of "Silent Night" played on the upright in the living room.

"That song takes me back," said Will Stafford.

"I see snowflakes," said Eddie Browne, who was doing the playing.

The great-grandson of John Browne had gone to college in the NROTC program as a way of paying for his education at Dartmouth. He was slender, soft-spoken, and the Staffords were glad that he had looked them up in Hawaii.

"So, Eddie," said Jack after the song was finished. "How did you go from a lieutenant on the *West Virginia* to naval intelligence in two weeks?"

"Classified." Will Stafford handed his son a bottle of Primo Hawaiian beer.

"It seems that everything on this damn island is classified, Dad."

"This is a war," said Will.

"When they heard I was a musician," said Eddie, "they put me with Station Hypo, in that sweaty bunker at CINCPAC."

"Classified," said Will, taking another swallow of bourbon.

"All the boys from the *California* band are there, too. We're cryptanalysts."

"Classified," said Will.

"Why musicians?" asked Jack.

"They figure we know one alternate language already—sharps, flats, notes. Maybe we can figure out a lot of meaningless symbols and read the Jap code."

"Any luck?" asked Jack.

"Classified," said Will.

"Dad," said Jack, "do you know how stupid you look, wearing dress white shoes and trousers, and a shirt with giant red camellias on it?"

Will Stafford's face seemed to stagger, as if it could not decide to frown or smile. Then he laughed for the first time in nearly three weeks.

The sound was so alien that Jane and their daughter-in-law, Maureen, and Juan, the Filipino houseboy, came running into the living room.

"Did someone crack a joke?" asked Jane. "We could all use a laugh."

"The joke is these shirts," said Jack. "At least Eddie had the good sense to wear his officer's jacket."

"Well, it's good to hear a little laughter again," said Jane.

But dinner was still served on a bed of tension.

Will worked his way through a third bourbon, then a fourth.

Jane kept reminding him that he had an important meeting with Admiral Nimitz that night, a not very subtle code for "Shut yourself off."

Billy was on patrol with the *Enterprise,* which was worrisome enough.

Billy's wife, Maureen, a dark-haired, dark-eyed New York girl, picked at her ham and said how much she hoped she could get a military job so she would not have to return to the States with the rest of the military dependents.

And Jack, whose decision to become a reporter had been disappointing enough, kept annoying his father with questions about the attack.

Finally Will growled, "Read the damn press releases."

"Dad, I need an angle. They wouldn't have sent me out here unless they thought I had an inside track at CINCPAC."

"You mean me? I pulled the strings to get your press credentials, but after tonight the only inside track I'll be able to give you is how to find the head on the minesweeper I'm banished to. My career's finished."

"Dad, you shouldn't have to take the rap. I'd be willing to bet the navy had warnings popping off all over the place and they just didn't see them."

"So you want me to tell you everything, and you'll blow the lid off the navy's incompetence at Pearl Harbor, and somehow it'll save my career?"

"Now you're talking." Jack leaned back, beaming. "I might even tell the truth about how many ships were sunk."

"Don't forget, Mr. Reporter"—Will pushed back from the table and stalked toward the bedroom—"what's good for the U.S. Navy may not be good for someone sniffing through the droppings of the worst day in American history, but what's good for the U.S. Navy is good for the U.S.A."

Jack furrowed his brow, repeated that to himself, shook his head.

"It's something your grandfather used to say, dear," said Jane.

"But the newspapers said we only lost one battleship. I expected a little censorship, but . . . the whole damn fleet is sunk. Isn't the truth good for the U.S.A.?"

"Remember, dear, we can't always tell the story exactly the way every little reporter would want." Jane's voice began soft and sugar-sweet. Then, it grew a little harder, then a little louder, just as Jack remembered. "We're expecting a Japanese invasion, dear, at any moment. We're fighting for . . . our . . . goddamn . . . *survival!* If your father tells you not to blow the lid off a pot that was blown to smithereens three weeks ago, you should pay attention . . . dear."

And so ended Christmas dinner.

For dessert, they had pineapple upside-down cake, Kona coffee, and brandy. Juan served on the veranda, with the gentle rain falling beyond.

"Your mother right," said Juan. "No goddamn reason to be botherin' you father like he some kind of fuckin' Tojo Jap or somethin'."

"Juan," said Maureen, "Mrs. Stafford keeps telling you about your swearing."

"Ladies like Maureen don't like that kind of language," Jack said sternly.

Maureen laughed, a good throaty sound, the first sign of animation Jack had seen from her in two days. "Don't worry about me. But someday, Juan, somebody might not realize you were raised by a bunch of American sailors at Cavite, and they won't understand why you swear so much."

"Yeah," said Juan. "Little goddamn Filipino orphan. No mammy, no pappy, just Uncle Sam . . . and the Staffords."

Just then a flight of planes came in low from the north, roaring over the house, rattling plates, and scaring the hell out of Maureen.

"Don't worry," said Eddie. "They're not Japs. They're Dauntlesses."

"Dauntlesses?" She jumped up and ran out on the lawn.

Jack and Eddie followed her, and for a time, the three of them stood there squinting up into the rain as the big blue planes roared down to Ford Island.

"I can't see the insignia," said Maureen.

"It's not VS-Six, so they're not from the *Enterprise*."

"Christ . . . you never know if it's Japs or Billy or . . . *Christ*." She ran back into the house, once more the worried little rag she had been during most of the two days that Jack had been there.

"For a minute, I thought they were Japs, too," Eddie said to Jack. "After what they did to the *West Virginia*, I'm happy to be in a bunker lookin' at ciphers all day."

"What about those ciphers?"

"Sorry, Jack." Then Eddie thought a minute. "But if you want a good story, talk to a colored messman by the name of Dory Miller."

There was an old navy saying: "One 'awshit' wiped out a thousand 'attaboys' in an instant." And they had just been through the worst "awshit" in American history.

Most of the men who gathered for the night meeting at CINCPAC—Vice Admiral Wilson Brown, Captain bald-as-an-egg "Poco" Smith, Captain Walt Delaney, Will Stafford with his hangover—expected no "attaboys" from the new commander in chief.

Chester Nimitz's hair, once Aryan blond, had turned white without any help from the Japanese. His complexion was red even before the Hawaiian sun got to it. And his eyes were blue, as Prussian as his name. But for all the German in his background and all the stars on his collar, he was soft-spoken, gentlemanly, almost unassuming. He wished them a Merry Christmas and gave them an "At ease."

Will sat and shielded his eyes from the overhead lights that glared off the white uniforms like searchlight beams boring right into his hungover head.

But Nimitz made him feel better fast. "We were lucky they got us where they did. If they'd caught those battleships at sea, they would have sunk them all. We'd never be able to raise one of them. And they would have killed a lot more men."

Then Nimitz said he would accept no letters of resignation. Period.

"I need you all, and I want to hear no more stories of men going gray over what's happened. Let's make the Japs go gray instead."

iii
An Annapolis Wedding

It did not happen on a bright Sunday afternoon, in the presence of proud family and friends. There was no Episcopal priest, no ring, no marriage license, no blood test. Truth was, there was no real wedding.

The navy did not want its young submarine officers marrying. And of the three brothers, Tom Stafford was the most respectful of naval authority.

Their commissioning ceremony took place on a gloomy December afternoon. Tom's grandparents came up from the Patuxent. Katherine came out from Washington. And Betty's parents, who had embraced their daughter's fiancé as their own, came down from Boston. It was an understatement to say that the atmosphere was subdued. These young men were going straight to war. Few classes in the history of the Academy had graduated knowing that.

Still, the dinner that Abraham and Julia hosted at the Stafford House generated a few cheerful toasts, especially after a few bottles of Veuve Cliquot had been offered up to the serious toasts.

And that evening, Tom and Betty went for a final walk through the yard.

The snow was falling gently, softening the sounds of a quiet town and a quiet campus, so that nothing could be heard but the whisper of the flakes.

In the shadows before the chapel, Tom wrapped his arms around Betty and kissed her. A dusting of snow piled up on his hat and on the shoulders of her coat, and a dozen midshipmen hurried past them on their way back to Bancroft from the library, all eyes in the boat and not a smart remark from any of them. . . . Then he whispered, "Till death do us part."

She looked up into his solemn face. "Oh, Tom, don't be talking like that."

"*Say it.*"

"All right. Till death do us part."

"If we say it, we can face it." And then he pulled her against him and held her tight, squashing her face against his overcoat.

"Tom," she whispered into the wool, "I've been taking my temperature, Tom."

He looked down at her. He had been holding her so tight that a button of his coat had left the imprint of an anchor on her cheek.

She smiled and took him by the hand. "Come on."

At the Stafford House, Katherine was sitting in the hotel lounge, the room where Union men had interrogated Alexandra after Lincoln's death. A fire roared in the fireplace, above which hung a Gabriel Shank portrait of Alexandra. A glass of sherry was in front of Katherine, and she was flipping through a golf magazine.

"Wait here," said Betty in the hallway. "I'll handle this."

From the hallway, Tom watched Betty sit with his aunt, say a few words, make a few gestures. And Katherine beamed. It was as if she had just been asked to be someone's godmother. Without another word, she reached into her purse and took out a key.

With the night manager looking the other way, Betty led Tom through the French doors at the back to a room on the first floor.

"What did you say to her?" asked Tom.

"Something she said to me a few weeks ago . . . about love."

iv
A Deal

On a fine Hawaiian morning just after New Year's, Jack Stafford was called to his father's office at CINCPAC. He went with his notebook and a sharp eye for everything in the big old building overlooking the submarine pens. "A Peek Inside CINCPAC" might make a good title for an article, if he could get it past the censors.

Jack found his father at his desk, once more in charge as assistant operations officer of the Pacific Fleet. The graying of his hair had slowed, and the bruised look was gone from beneath his eyes. He was all business in the wash khakis that Nimitz favored for his working uniform. "A nice article you wrote about that messman Dory Miller."

"Thanks, Dad. How did you happen to see it?"

"The censors passed it on to me before they pass it back to you."

Jack felt his jaw muscles tighten. "Pass it back?"

"The navy doesn't think America's quite ready to make a colored messman the hero of Pearl Harbor."

"But, Dad, he *was* a hero. I talked to him. A high school dropout from Detroit, and he stood out there firing a gun he'd never even been trained on."

"That gun could've blown up in his face."

"C'mon, Dad."

Will fidgeted with the papers on his desk. "I know he's a hero, Jack. But we just don't think he's the best example of a hero we can find right now. After all, the army has that Colin Kelly, flying a B-17 into the *Haruna* in Lingayen Gulf."

"That didn't happen. The *Haruna* was nowhere near there."

"Well, maybe not, but the marines have that Devereaux on Wake Island. Imagine a guy radioing a message, 'Send us more Japs.' It's the best damn line of the war."

"'Send us more Japs,' my ass." Jack was no respecter of rank. He didn't have one, didn't want one, and wouldn't get one, thanks to a heart murmur. Still, he was intent on doing his part for the war effort. And his part was telling the truth to the American people, because the truth made people free, and freedom gave people real strength. "I bet that marine major said, 'Send reinforcements, and fast.'"

Will pushed his papers from one side of the desk to the other. "Jack, a lot of rabble-rousers at home are agitating for us to open all ratings to Negroes."

Jack leaned forward in his chair. "Rabble-rousers?"

"We'd be playing right into their hands if we gave them a colored hero before we have a white one."

Outside, heavy hammers and pile drivers and drills kept up their incessant racket. Planes roared overhead. Ships pushed in and out of the harbor. And Jack filled his voice with the sound of disappointment. "Is this what you believe?"

"The navy's not ready for mixed-race berthings, Jack."

"You mean, what's good for the U.S. Navy may not be good for Dory Miller, but what's good for the U.S. Navy—"

"Is good for the U.S.A." Will plastered a condescending smile on his face, as he would have done with any reporter. "You bring a bunch of colored boys into berthings where white men are sleeping, put them in a mess where white men are eating . . . it's a recipe for trouble."

"I thought the Japs were giving us all the trouble we needed."

"Dammit, Jack, you don't know anything about the fleet. It's a world of tradition and regulation . . . no place for social experiments."

"What if I disagree? What if I try to file my story anyway?"

"You might as well go back to New York and try to get on the radio."

Jack thought about the sole of Lois Hoyt's foot. He thought about Dory Miller's big heavyweight fists and all the energy in them, just waiting to be released. And he knew his father was still holding some kind of an ace. "If I bury the story . . . ?"

Will pointed out the window. "Do you see the ten-ten dock?"

"The *Enterprise*. She got in this morning. Billy locked himself in his bedroom with Maureen two hours ago. Juan says we should send for an oxygen tank. Ma's pretending she doesn't know what he means."

Will chuckled at that. "Bill Halsey's in command of the *Enterprise*. He's steaming out on the tenth. I won't tell you where, but I will tell you that he's one of the few naval officers I know who actually *likes* reporters looking over his shoulder."

"And?"

"He says you can bunk in with Billy and his bunkmate, get some real combat stuff. But you'll put on wash khakis like the rest of us—no insignia—and do as you're told. We can't have any troublemakers out there."

"Troublemakers are against tradition and regulation, right?"

"Do you want the chance or not?" snapped his father.

"Halsey *is* good copy." Jack threw his head back and did a Halsey croak. "'Before we're through with 'em, the Jap language will be spoken only in hell.'"

"Does that mean you see my point?"

Jack asked himself what good it would do if he filed the Dory Miller story and got himself banished from Hawaii in the process. On the other hand, after he'd established a byline, he could get the Dory Miller story published anywhere.

And he could rationalize anything. *What a bastard.* "I'll do it."

"Good. And when the time comes, I'll submit this." Will reached into his desk and took out a paper recommending Dory Miller for a Navy Cross. It was undated.

V
Aircraft Carrier

They called her the Big E, but her name had descended from the dawn of American naval history. An earlier *Enterprise* had been a twelve-gun sloop that sailed against the Barbary pirates.

"This *Enterprise*," wrote Jack Stafford, "sails against modern pirates."

> She is one of four operational aircraft carriers now in the Pacific, and to her has fallen the honor of delivering

> Nimitz's first counterpunch in the Great Pacific War—a raid on the Marshall Islands.
>
> She is near nine hundred feet long, covered from one end to the other with a gray wooden deck that looks like nothing so much as the boardwalk at Atlantic City. But no peaches and cream here. It's more like Yankee Stadium, with a Murderers' Row of Douglas Dauntless dive-bombers, Devastator torpedo planes, and Grumman F4F Wildcat fighters circling above, ready to take the field. And all around the warning track are five-inch guns, 1.1-inch antiaircraft pom-poms, and fifty-caliber machine guns.
>
> Instead of a dugout, a slender gray island rises out of the deck on the starboard side, four stories high, carrying the stack, the big basket mast, and the bridge that is the brain center for our manager, Admiral William F. Halsey, who looks like a craggy old mountain man, come down to the sea. . . .

Jack leaned back from the little desk in his brother's little stateroom and read what he'd written. Maybe he had a few too many metaphors working at the moment—baseball, mountain men. . . . He hadn't even laid eyes on Halsey.

"Now hear this! Now hear this! Flight crews and LSOs to the flight deck. Stand by to receive aircraft."

Jack jumped up from his typewriter. This he had to see.

When a carrier was in port, the squadrons flew off to Ford Island. Now it was time to bring the air wing aboard. Jack had been told that he could go anywhere from the 01 deck to the island bridge, so he hurried to the gangway. He followed it up one flight, then two, three. And . . . did that lieutenant tell him he could step out on the 02 deck or the 03? What the hell, he'd go to the 03. The view would be better.

And was it ever. What a sense of power to stand up there, with the ship gliding over the waves and the ballet beginning on the flight deck below. Maybe dance would make a better metaphor than the ball game.

The arrester cables were tightened across the deck, a dozen of them, a dozen chances for the plane to catch and stop. The flight crews, wearing soft helmets of different colors for identification, moved to their positions. The landing signal officer began his gyrations with the signal paddles—too high, too low, just right. And the first Dauntless approached in perfect cut position—flaps down, landing gear down, tailhook extended like a stinger.

Jack fumbled with the windblown pages of his notebook and wrote, "Squadron leader Wade McClusky comes in first. Clear to see why he's boss. Puts that plane down like a saucer of milk for the cat."

The palm of a hand appeared in front of Jack's face, holding rubber earplugs.

Jack took them. "Thanks."

Another plane was coming in now, and Jack was trying to watch it.

"Put these things in, or you'll be sorry." The old man's face was creased and sunburned. Gray hair scraggled out from under a khaki baseball cap.

"That's Billy Stafford coming in," Jack said.

"You don't know where you are, do you?"

Halsey. Jack felt his stomach drop. "The flag bridge?"

"Reserved for the admiral. Today, consider yourself the admiral's guest."

"Thank you, sir."

"In exchange, I expect stories that'll make 'em stand up and spit bullets back home. We're here to kill Japs, but America needs a shot in the arm, too. I'm countin' on you."

Jack thought he was immune to speeches like that. But it was hard to be cynical on the Big E, with Halsey looking you right in the eye. Jack muttered something about doing his best, and then, instinctively, he saluted.

"You're not wearin' a cover, son. Correspondents get overseas caps, just like the fliers. Wear it and I'll return your salute. Now, here comes your brother . . . right in the groove."

Jack had spent little time with Billy since he went off to the Naval Academy in 1931, and he had spent most of his childhood doing the opposite of what Billy did. If Billy liked baseball, Jack turned to tennis. If Billy was a math whiz, Jack would read Shakespeare. If Billy chose to be the Annapolis golden boy, Jack would head off to some Ivy League egghead factory. But today, Jack was very proud of Billy.

"He's a helluva flier," said Halsey. "Now get the hell off my bridge."

Jack and Billy looked a lot alike, both near six feet, dark-haired, strong-featured in the Stafford way. But Billy was harder, almost stringy, and presented a face to the world that suggested no complication whatsoever. One look at him told you what he was thinking. Cynicism was not in his flight bag.

"Melon!" he cried when Jack came into the pilots' ready room.

"Melon?" Wade McClusky was at the coffee urn, filling a big white cup.

Jack gave his brother a "Thanks, pal." He had one of those heads that could be called leonine if someone wanted to compliment him but had looked a size too big for the rest of his body when he was a skinny kid. So the nickname was natural.

He extended his hand to McClusky. "Call me Jack."

"Jack the journalist," said McClusky. "We call your brother 'Balls.'"

"Because I fly my plane like it was gliding on ballbearings."

"So," said Charlie Osterhausser, Billy's bunkmate. "We got the whole Stafford anatomy. Melon Head and Balls."

And Jack was welcomed aboard.

Billy said that once you'd gotten over the majesty of it, you realized that the carrier was a seagoing factory: below the hangar deck—a giant service station packed with planes—the ship was a honeycomb of passageways and compartments unique only in their ugliness, nothing but gray paint and steam pipes. And it was all getting uglier, because everywhere Jack looked, sweaty sailors were on their hands and knees, swinging hammers and chisels against bulkheads and floors. *Chip, chip, chip . . .*

Jack thought it was some kind of punishment duty.

"Not this time," said Billy. "We have to get all the paint and linoleum off the ship. We found out on December 7 that they burn like a son of a bitch."

And yet there was majesty to the Big E.

To feel it, Jack stood on the island at night, when the ship was darkened down, and the wondrous wind blew, and the luminosity enveloped her in a sky so full of stars that it was more silver than black, in a sea that showed great phosphorescent wakes streaming out behind all the vessels in the task force.

"I've always wanted Maureen to see this," said Billy. "Then maybe she'd understand."

"I didn't understand until I saw it." Jack felt the motion of the great ship rushing through the sea, saw the darkened silhouettes of the other ships all around them. "It makes you feel like part of something a lot bigger than yourself."

"And the best part"—Billy grinned—"is that I'm part of it on the ship, but up in the air, I'm all of it. I'm the reason they built the damn ship in the first place. The god of the flight deck, that's me."

"You never were one for humility."

Billy gave a little shrug. "You neither."

Jack looked up at the stars.

For a month, they delivered hit-and-run strikes against lightly defended targets—73,000 tons of enemy shipping sunk, thirty-five Japanese planes shot down.

The unblooded American pilots gained the confidence they would need when the real fights began, because even though no one had more inbred cockiness than American flyboys, no one knew better how much more experienced the Japanese fliers were . . . and how much better was their equipment.

However, the raids did nothing to stop Yamamoto's rampage, and Jack said so in his first article.

But Billy read it before Jack filed it. "Is this what the folks back home want to hear, on top of all the other bad news?"

"Don't you think they want the truth?"

"You have to make these raids sound good, Jack. We're doing more than just swatting flies out here."

Jack was surprised at how easy he found it to write the story the way his brother and Admiral Halsey wanted him to. It was part of the war effort. And it paid off. To reward him for his fine dispatches, Halsey invited him out for another raid in March.

vi
BuOrd

While the Big E was at sea, the orders came through for the wives of military personnel to leave the island. Will had tried to get Maureen a job, but he wasn't the only one without any pull. Even admirals would sleep alone. If Hawaii was invaded, it would be defended by professional soldiers, not by men fighting for their wives and families.

At least Will had some pull with friends at the Bureau of Ordnance in Washington, and a week after she arrived home, Maureen went to work as a secretary in the old State, War, and Navy Building, and stayed in Katherine's apartment at Dupont Circle.

The navy wasn't simply a lot of ships. It was, like most government organizations, an interlocking and overlapping system of production, management, and waste that expanded to spend whatever money was allotted to it plus ten percent more.

The Bureau of Ordnance oversaw the design and production of naval weapons systems. Some were simple, like the five-inch gun. Others were more complex, like the torpedo that, in the latest Mark XIV design, included a steam engine for propulsion, a gyro mechanism for direction, a 750-pound warhead, and a Mark VI exploder.

When the war began, there were only a hundred torpedoes at Pearl Harbor. Now, four months into the war, complaints were echoing back from submarine captains about their poor performance. The Bureau of Ordnance was bringing a captain down from the Navy Torpedo Factory in Newport, Rhode Island, to handle the criticism, and this captain had requested Maureen Stafford to do his typing.

She couldn't figure out why.

But one of the other girls thought she knew what the scoop was. "He probably saw your picture. He's been through here before. Name's Dawson. Dark hair going silver on the sides, killer smile, better looking at fifty-seven than most men are at thirty. Never married, and a real swordsman. Must have seen your picture."

"I'll show him the picture of my husband, too—in his flight suit, with his forty-five and his bowie knife."

"It's been a long time since I had a Stafford working under me."

Before she even looked up from her typing, she decided that here was a good one for BuOrd, because his voice sounded like a shotgun shell being slipped into a chamber.

"Good morning, sir."

He extended his hand. "Any relation to Will Stafford, Academy class of '07?"

"My father-in-law."

"A lucky man." He gave her that killer smile.

She kept her eyes on her typing, and the other dozen girls in the typing pool kept their eyes on her.

"Of course, old Will wasn't too lucky on December 7, was he?"

"None of us were, sir."

He leaned a little closer to her, so that she could smell his Old Spice after-shave. "We'll straighten things out."

vii
On the War Beat

In March the navy finally released the name of Dory Miller, and the *Pittsburgh Courier* became the first newspaper to report that Dory Miller had been recommended for a Navy Cross. Jack missed his scoop, and he heard about it in a telegram from Harry Dowd: NICE WORK SO FAR. BEST COVERAGE IN US OF MARSHALL RAID. BUT APS COUNTS ON YOU FOR HUMAN INTEREST LIKE MILLER STORY.

Shit, thought Jack. You just can't win.

On their second night back from the Marshalls raid, Jack and Billy and their father had dinner at the house on Aiea Heights.

A cool breeze blew up from Pearl Harbor, and the wind chimes rang. But the sound was hollow and sad, because the women were gone.

After dinner and a few brandies, Jack showed his father the telegram from New York: "I got burned for burying my first big scoop."

"But you were doing some real reporting," said Will. "And Halsey likes you."

"I didn't tell the truth." Jack looked at his brother.

"You did your job," said Billy. "And I did mine. The harder we work, the sooner we get the girls back."

"That's right," said Will. "Hard work . . . not boat-rocking, which is all they're doing back in Washington, forcing the General Board to let Negroes in as gunners, clerks, signalmen—"

"From what I saw," said Jack, "this navy can use all the help it can get."

"Now that we've run a few raids"—Will lit a cigarette—"write the Dory Miller story. You can even say we're preparing to bring blacks into general service. It might stimulate enlistments. But add that all training and service will be done in *segregated* units. We don't want to scare away any whites."

"Why do I get the feeling you're using me, Dad?"

"Because I am," said Will. "And Nimitz is using me. And Roosevelt is using Nimitz. And the country is using all of us, whites and Negroes both. And the clearer you can make that, the sooner we'll get this job done."

"And that's patriotism," said Billy, "getting the job done."

Jack filed a Dory Miller piece the way that his father wanted it, but this one was not so easy, and Jack was not so proud of himself.

A few days later, Jack was back on the *Enterprise,* sailing for a rendezvous with her sister ship, the *Hornet*, and the biggest morale-boosting raid of them all. Strapped to the deck of the *Hornet* were sixteen B-25s, twin-engine long-range bombers, never before launched from a carrier.

On a miserable gray day some seven hundred miles east of the Japanese home islands, the B-25 flown by squadron commander Jimmy Doolittle went rolling down the flight deck. Would there be enough room for the plane to make her run? Would she lift off? Or would she drop into the sea and sink beneath the ship?

Jack compared it to watching an eagle try to take off from a sparrow's nest. But with a thirty-knot wind blowing, and the carrier making twenty knots of her own, the big army bomber rode up into the air just like a kite.

On both ships, men cheered, and the lumbering planes made for Tokyo.

Franklin Roosevelt would tell the world that they had taken off from Shangri-la.

It wasn't much of a raid. The B-25s only carried four bombs each, and most Japanese people did not even know about it.

But Yamamoto was so mortified that he took to his cabin and brooded for a full day. When he emerged, he told Hiroaki Tanaka that there could be no further dispute over his next objectives: strike close to American territory, establish a defensive perimeter, so that Tokyo could not be menaced again, and draw the American fleet into the battle that would be Japan's Trafalgar.

On a sailing ship, the scuttlebutt had been the water cask where sailors stopped to drink and exchange gossip, like the modern office water cooler. Now shipboard rumor was called scuttlebutt.

When the *Enterprise* turned back to Pearl Harbor, scuttlebutt had it that something big was up. She had missed the battle of Coral Sea, where Japan's New Guinea landings were stopped, but where the carrier *Lexington* had been sunk and the *Yorktown* had been hit. Now the *Enterprise* was one of only two undamaged American carriers in the Pacific, and she was racing home. Something big, for certain.

A few days before she docked, Jack saw the the strangest sight he would see in the whole Pacific War. But he resolved he would not put it in his articles, because he thought that the admiral had gone plain crazy, and that was not something that Americans needed to know.

Halsey was spending hours perched on the flag bridge, in nothing but his underwear, with his hands and arms extended, like a bird drying its wings in the wind.

The crusty, unflappable old admiral had paid for his unflappability and now was literally crusty. Nervous exhaustion and heat had given him a miserable burning rash, and his only relief was that cooling breeze.

If Jack had known that Halsey's rash would cause him to miss the most pivotal naval battle of the twentieth century, and one of the most decisive battles of history, he might have filed a story about it just for spite.

viii
Preparing for Battle

Morning intelligence briefing at CINCPAC: Nimitz and staff, the biggest bunch of gold collar pins in the Pacific, sat on their hands, waiting for a Lieutenant Commander. Joe Rochefort, senior cryptanalyst in charge of Station Hypo, Pearl Harbor Signal Intelligence, wanted to deliver this report in person. And right now, he was the most important man in Hawaii.

For weeks, Rochefort had been shuffling around the CINCPAC bunker, dressed in carpet slippers and smoking jacket, sleeping on a couch, while he and his staff of cryptanalysts, linguists, and a few displaced bandmembers tried to make sense of a message from Yamamoto's headquarters, intercepted on May 5.

Just as the Japanese had come to believe they were unbeatable, they believed their code, JN25, was unbreakable. They were wrong. After two weeks of decryption and guesswork, Rochefort was sure that a Japanese naval offensive was coming. But to where? Oahu? Midway Island? The West Coast?

Rochefort arrived with two assistants, Lieutenant Commander Wilfred Holmes and Lieutenant Ed Browne, both looking as if they'd slept eight hours and shaved with hot water. But Rochefort—hangdog face all stubbled, hair hastily wetted and combed—reminded Will Stafford of dirty dishes soaking in a sink.

"Morning, gentlemen." Rochefort did not bother to come to attention. It was not that he was insubordinate. His mind was simply too full of other things.

"What do you have for us?" asked Nimitz, without any irritation.

"Not much more than we had yesterday, Admiral, but I'm guessing Midway." Rochefort pointed to the map laid out on the table, to the little pile of sand and coral eleven hundred miles northwest of Oahu. A 300-degree course line could be drawn from the Big Island of Hawaii northeast through Oahu, Kauai, and the French Frigate Shoals, right to Midway and its airstrip, the last geographic outpost in the Hawaiian Archipelago, the last American outpost in the Central Pacific.

"What do you base your guesses on?" said Nimitz.

"The Jap transmissions refer to this as Operation MI."

Will Stafford said, "Isn't this a little obvious?"

"The Japs have gotten lax," said Rochefort.

Nimitz looked at the map, on which three aircraft carriers with American flags were spread over the Pacific and seven carriers with Japanese naval ensigns were clustered around the Japanese home islands. "We can't commit what little we have on the basis of guesswork."

Now Rochefort introduced the other two officers. "They have an idea."

Holmes and Browne explained that in all of the transmissions, the objective of Operation MI was called AF. Since Midway was connected to Hawaii by an underwater cable, they could secretly instruct the commander of the island to transmit a false radio message: "Midway's water evaporators have broken down and the island is short of water."

"If we hear the Japs talking about AF's water supply," said Rochefort, "we'll know they're going to Midway."

"I like it," said Nimitz.

A new George. That was what they said when Tom Stafford reported aboard the USS *Nautilus* at Pearl Harbor. On a submarine, the lowest ranking officer was George, as in, "Sir, there's shit overflowing in the head." *Let George do it.* "Sir, there's a hole in the pressure hull." *Let George do it.*

This George had completed his three-month course at New London, Connecticut. He had spent a few days at Stafford Hall. Then he and Betty Merritt had boarded a train for San Francisco.

A few months earlier, such a trip would have been scandalous for an unmarried couple, but the war had changed all of that. Betty's parents, being parents, had warned her about a honeymoon before the wedding, but they hadn't tried to stop her.

So Tom and Betty had made love as their sleeper car rolled past the mines of West Virginia and the factories of Ohio. They had made love with the spring sunshine glinting off the cornfields of Iowa. In the Rocky Mountain moonlight, they had made love, too, and in the Fairmont Hotel, by the window, looking out at the fabled fog. They had danced to "Moonglow" at the Top of the Mark. And Tom had promised her, when he boarded the transport to Pearl, that he would come home.

"Just do the job this time," she had said, "so that our sons never have to leave their wives like this."

Now Tom was ready to begin training that would lead to the words "qualified for submarines" on his record and a dolphin pin on his chest. But to qualify, he had to be able to do every job on the boat, from firing a torpedo to patching a leak.

Commander Bill Brockman—dark-haired, about thirty—read Tom's orders, made a few noncommittal remarks, then showed him the tiny stateroom where he would be bunking with Lieutenant Larry Steinberg, the diving officer.

"He's our resident Jew," said Brockman. "Reservist out of Yale. Good guy. Now, I'm sure your father wants to see you. So you're off duty till 0800."

"Thank you, sir. And, sir, if you don't mind, sir, I'd appreciate it if the crew didn't know who my father was, sir."

Brockman smiled. "You want to make it all on your own?"

"Yes, sir."

"I'll see that you do. Or drown trying. . . . And one more thing."

"Sir?"

"Boat rule: one 'sir' to a sentence. You're not in the Academy anymore."

"Yes, sir." Tom liked his new CO already.

On the dock, he gave the *Nautilus* another look. He had been told that a navy man always remembered his first ship. What Tom would never forget was this view, with the sullen gray submarine sleeping peacefully in its pen while acetylene torches sparked and jackhammers rang across the harbor, around the carcasses of the great battleships.

Will Stafford always told his sons it was good to be interested in the things that interested their commanding officers. It made for a smooth command and, sometimes, a friendly one. After the confidence that he had brought back to CINCPAC, Nimitz could have announced that his favorite hobby was lighting fires in the fuel dump, and Will would have brought the matches.

Nimitz preferred pitching horseshoes or going to the target range to squeeze off his frustrations with a 1911 pattern forty-five-caliber automatic.

That afternoon, Will and his newly commissioned third son took their forty-fives up the Makalapa Heights to the target range. Nimitz wasn't there, nor were any of the other staff members, so father and son had the cardboard cutouts all to themselves.

Will fired six shots that made a perfect box around the heart of the target, which some sailor had drawn as a rising sun. "So how's mother?"

"A little restless at Stafford Hall, but she knows Grandma and Grandpa are happy to have her. And on weekends, Aunt Katherine and Maureen come down."

"Is Maureen happy at BuOrd?"

"Typing forms for the distribution of torpedoes isn't her idea of aiding the war effort."

Will squeezed off half a dozen more shots, putting all of them into the target's head. The shell casings jingled on the ground. "Tell me about this girl Betty."

"Mom and Maureen and Aunt Katherine think she's swell."

"Good." Will changed clips. "I wish they were in San Diego so that I could get to see them sometime. But it's best that they're near home. If something should go wrong, home'll be the place to be."

"Nothing'll go wrong, Dad."

"That's what I believed when I was a young officer . . . on convoy duty in the Atlantic in 1917. Then I saw the torpedo track and felt the concussion when it hit the freighter off our port quarter. That was when I realized that this wasn't a lot of theory anymore. Someone was trying to kill me."

"I'm not worried." Tom raised his pistol. "I have to live to make admiral."

"You've been around your grandmother too long. She still thinks *I'm* going to make admiral."

"Maybe you will." Tom sighted the target.

"Something big's coming, Tommy. You may have people trying to kill you damn soon."

In response, Tom squeezed off a single shot that pierced the red rising sun at the heart of the target. He didn't do it with a cocky flourish the way Billy would have. He didn't announce what a good shot it was, like Jack. He just did it, calm and efficient.

"Good eye," said Will, trying not to sound too impressed.

Two days later, Ed Browne was given the first half of a short Japanese message to decrypt. Several others in Station Hypo also had it, and several more were working on the second half.

He took a drag of his cigarette and a sip of coffee. Sometimes he thought that it was nicotine and caffeine that gave Station Hypo its name. They were like carbohydrates and protein. But they kept you working, and that was what mattered.

Within fifteen minutes, he had the first two letters, and his hands began to shake, but not from the caffeine. The first two letters were *AF*.

When someone else said that he had the word "water" in the second half of the message, Rochefort said, "I think Yamamoto just swallowed the worm."

On May 26, the *Enterprise* and her crust-covered admiral reached Pearl Harbor. Halsey's diagnosis: acute dermatitis. The fightingest admiral in the U.S. Navy, as one writer billed him, was out of the fight before it began. All he could contribute was his recommendation for a replacement: Rear Admiral Raymond Spruance, commander of the cruiser squadron that protected his *Enterprise*.

Except for gray hair and deepening lines, Spruance had not changed at all since the Academy days, forty years before. He was still slender, studious, seldom seen to smile, as economical of gesture as of word, just about the most un-Halsey-like character Halsey could have recommended. Worse, he was no flier. He was a ship driver. How could he understand the use of naval aviation in warfare?

But he and Halsey had been friends for years, and Halsey trusted his judgment completely, which was good enough for Nimitz.

Will sat in on the briefing that afternoon at CINCPAC. Spruance was told that he would take command of *Enterprise* and *Hornet* and head for Midway, to be joined by Admiral Fletcher in the *Yorktown*, if she could be repaired. They would take a position some two hundred fifty miles northeast of Midway and set the trap.

Spruance would have two or three carriers, six cruisers, twelve destroyers, a screen of three submarines, and eleven more submarines on patrol west of Midway. Rochefort guessed that the Japanese would bring four carriers, four battleships, nine cruisers, as many as twenty-four destroyers, and a dozen submarines. He guessed the carriers would strike first to take out the marine air force at Midway. Then Yamamoto's main body would arrive to support the landing of the Japanese troops.

No one needed to point out the odds. If Rochefort was right,

Spruance was facing the most powerful, battle-hardened naval force that had ever sailed. Yet he listened as though learning of a color change for the paint on the flight deck.

Afterward, Will walked with Spruance back to the dock, where a launch waited to take him out to his cruiser.

"It's in your hands now, Ray," said Will. "If you don't stop them, they'll sail right into Pearl Harbor three days after you're beaten."

"I know," said Spruance, ever the man of few words. "How's Jane?"

"Back on the Patuxent." Will glanced at the sub pen where the *Nautilus* had been the day before. "I'd like to have her here. It's hard, sending sons off to fight."

"It is hard. My Edward's out on patrol," said Spruance. "But Margaret and young Margaret are back in San Diego."

"At least you get to fight. That takes your mind off the worry."

"Don't worry about Billy or Tom. But your other son, Jack, he's a reporter, isn't he?"

Will nodded, as if ashamed to admit the black sheep.

Spruance looked down at the dock. "That could be a problem."

The next afternoon, Jack got the bad news, right on the Big E.

Morale mattered, and even though the *Enterprise* was preparing for battle, Nimitz had come to the ship to bestow decorations in an honor ceremony. Jack had climbed the island for the best view of the crew assembled on the flight deck, of the band playing "Ruffles and Flourishes," of the guests of honor, front and center—eleven officers and one very proud Negro messman.

Jack was describing Dory Miller's fullback shoulders and big hands, which looked even bigger in contrast to his dress whites, when his father appeared on the island. "Did you ever see anyone happier than that Dory Miller, Dad?"

"He deserves what he's getting," said Will. "He always did."

"So . . . what's up? We've got Spruance bringing his flag aboard. A forty-eight-hour turnaround. They've topped off every tank on the ship."

"A lot of gas."

Jack flipped through his notebook and reported the exact amounts: 19,080 barrels of fuel oil and 82,485 gallons of aviation gasoline.

"And they've had sailors packing ammunition belts with shells, balls, and tracers around the clock," he added. "What's happening?"

"I can't tell you exactly, Jack, but—"

"All right, all right." Jack laughed. "I'll let the Japs surprise me."

"I'm afraid that's not going to happen, son. Ray Spruance doesn't want reporters on his ship."

If someone had told Jack Stafford, five months before, that he would feel as angry as he did at that moment, he would have laughed. "I've been with this team since the beginning, and now I'm cut before the big game?"

"You've got a new manager. He doesn't like publicity and thinks journalists are a distraction to a fighting ship."

"Goddammit!" Jack slammed his hand so hard on the rail that several sailors on the deck below looked up.

"Get off the bridge," whispered his father through clenched teeth.

"I'd like to tell that sour-faced Spruance—"

"Say anything out of line and you'll be back in New York, covering Harlem tenement fires. Just go get your gear and get the hell off the ship, or Halsey won't ever take you back."

Jack shoved his notebook into his back pocket and smoothed his overseas cap. This fight was lost, but there would be others. So he decided to make a graceful exit. And he resolved that he'd find a scoop of his own right there at Pearl Harbor.

On that same day, Hiroaki Tanaka stood on the sunny bridge of the *Akagi* as she steamed through the Bungo Strait. For the forthcoming invasion, Hiroaki had been advanced to the staff of his old friend, Chuichi Nagumo, commander of *Kido Butai,* which now comprised four Pearl Harbor carriers—*Akagi, Kaga*, *Hiryu*, and *Soryu*—along with destroyers, cruisers, and battleships.

Some on Nagumo's staff resented having one of Yamamoto's men on the bridge. Perhaps Captain Tanaka was a spy rather than a liaison between *Kido Butai* and Yamamoto's main body of battleships, following several hundred miles behind.

But Admiral Nagumo welcomed one whose son had just joined the First Air Fleet. That, of course, was the real reason Hiroaki had requested this assignment. He wanted to be close to his son, Minoru, now aboard *Akagi*.

Nagumo wore a little gray mustache and set his jaw like a pugnacious bulldog, but there was a trace of diffidence in his eye that Hiroaki had always liked. It made him careful. Even if Nagumo had made too quick a withdrawal from Pearl Harbor, his carriers were still afloat and ready to do more damage.

It was Navy Day, anniversary of Tsushima Strait, a good omen for the fleet. And the "victory" at Coral Sea, in which fliers reported sinking both the *Lexington* and the *Yorktown*, had raised morale to new heights.

Still, Hiroaki was bothered.

High morale had become overconfidence, which led to a complex plan calling for *Kido Butai* to attack Midway ahead of the troop transports and Yamamoto's main body, while submarines set up pickets at Oahu, aerial reconnaissance monitored Pearl Harbor, and a secondary force struck the Aleutians. Complexity caused lack of focus: Was their goal the extension of a defensive perimeter or a decisive battle with the Americans? And what if the American fleet appeared *before* they took Midway's airstrip?

Hiroaki could not know that the plan was already spinning out of control: Their code had been broken. The *Yorktown* was under repair in one of the Pearl Harbor drydocks that Nagumo had failed to destroy. An American seaplane tender had anchored at French Frigate Shoals, where the Japanese had planned to refuel their reconnaissance planes, meaning there would be no overflights of Pearl Harbor. And the submarines would reach their stations too late to catch the American carriers.

Had Hiroaki seen how these ironies were accumulating like snowflakes on the roof of the Imperial Palace, he might even have composed a haiku.

But the day was too brilliant, the headlands of the Bungo Strait too beautiful for bad thoughts. Even careful Nagumo displayed his confidence, telling Hiroaki that he believed the enemy lacked the will to fight.

It was then that Hiroaki remembered boxing in the moonlight with Will Stafford, and he remembered how relentless the American had been, even in defeat.

In Washington, summer had arrived and, with it, a letter from the new commander of the Asiatic Submarine Fleet, Charles Lockwood.

He had read patrol reports describing torpedoes that ran too deep or failed to explode. He was convinced that something was wrong and wanted the Bureau of Ordnance to conduct tests.

It fell to Captain Dennis Dawson to respond.

He called Maureen Stafford to his office. She had moved quickly up the secretarial ladder at BuOrd, her shorthand skills as admired as her long legs.

Dawson was standing by a window that looked out onto somebody else's window across the street. He gave her that smooth smile. "Take a seat, Miss Stafford."

"*Mrs.* Stafford."

"I forgot. In wartime, in this city, we all seem to forget sometimes. . . . Tell me, *Mrs.* Stafford, do you like your job?"

"Yes, sir."

"Good. I want you to be comfortable. Ample break time and so forth."

She had stopped crossing her legs when she went into his office. She couldn't stand his eyes, probing toward her nylon covered thighs like a hand. Now she kept both feet planted firmly on the floor. "I don't need breaks, Captain. The harder we all work, the sooner I'll get my husband back."

"Then let's get to work." And whatever anger he felt at her went into his letter:

> The answer to your query, Admiral Lockwood, is simple. The torpedoes do not run too deep. And the Mark VI exploders are as good as anything the Nazis are using. I should know. I helped to develop them. When your skippers learn to attack a ship and fire a torpedo properly, they will have the kind of success that their weapons systems guarantee.
>
> As for the tests you propose, sir, they are highly unscientific. Torpedoes cost $10,000 apiece. Shoot them into enemy ships, not into nets to check how deep they run.

"That should shut him up," said Dawson. "We're here doing our damnedest, and they think all we do is play golf and chase skirts."

"Whatever would give them that idea?"

• • •

The next day, Task Force 16—*Enterprise*, *Hornet*, their destroyers and cruisers—streamed past the shattered battleships, past the *Yorktown* in her drydock, and out into the Pacific.

Will Stafford and Jack stood by the submarine pens and watched them go.

"I wish I was going with them," said Will.

Jack laughed a bit and said, "So do I."

"After this fight," said Will, "I'm putting in for a cruiser command."

"What will your policy be about reporters?"

"What's good for the U.S. Navy is good for the U.S.A."

Jack pulled out his notebook. "Let me write that down."

Just then, a flight of Dauntlesses came roaring over. One of the planes dipped low and tilted its wings as it went past.

The number on its fuselage was 6S2. Billy's plane.

ix
War in Three Dimensions

As the eastern sky silvered toward dawn on the morning of June 4, 1942, the carrier *Akagi* turned into the wind and prepared to launch planes. *Kido Butai* was some two hundred miles northeast of Midway.

Hiroaki Tanaka was filled with pride and apprehension both. Nine Zeros and eighteen dive-bombers were revving up for the launch, and his son Minoru was the fourth Zero in line.

At 0230 he had sat with Minoru in the flight mess and eaten the traditional meal served to a Japanese warrior on the morning of a battle—rice, soybean soup, dry chestnuts, and sake.

Talk in the flight mess had been high-spirited, for all the fliers believed this would be an easy run. Minoru had tried to keep up the conversation with his father, a sure sign that the boy was more nervous than he wished to appear. But Hiroaki had remained calm and, in fatherly fashion, acted more stern than he felt.

After the meal, Hiroaki had gone back to his cabin, and there he had tied around his son's waist the ceremonial belt of a thousand stitches, embroidered by his mother with a Rising Sun and the image of a tiger—a thousand stitches, so the custom went, made by a thousand passersby in the street, who sent a thousand prayers and a thousand wishes for good luck.

Minoru, taller than his father, had bowed solemnly. Hiroaki had bowed in return and remained bowed much longer than a father should bow to his son, so that his son would not see the tears that filled his eyes.

And now the air officer was waving his green lantern and the first Zero was shooting down the deck, past the Rising Sun painted on the forward elevator.

And from the deck crews below came the roar, *"Banzai! Banzai!"*

Hiroaki watched the Zeros streak toward Midway, their taillights like a long string of gleaming garnets, and he prayed that all would return.

ENTERPRISE, 250 MILES NORTHEAST OF MIDWAY, 0445

"Did you hear the one about the guy who brings his dog into a bar and says, 'Hey, who wants to bet my dog can talk?'" asked Charlie Osterhausser.

"That joke stinks," said Bill Stafford.

Twice they had gone to their planes. Twice they had come back. Now they churned about the ready room in lightweight khaki flight suits and yellow Mae Wests, riding their own currents of caffeine and adrenaline.

Bill poured his fifth cup, black and hot.

Wade McClusky said he'd be pissing down the pipe as soon as they got into the air.

"Whenever that is," answered Bill.

"Spruance can't launch till he knows where they are," said McClusky. "Then we all go together."

Coordination was all in an aerial attack: torpedo planes came in at two hundred feet while dive-bombers struck from twenty thousand, and enemy defenses were split. But torpedo planes had to reduce their speed and fly a straight course across the water. Without fighter protection, they were the biggest clay pigeons in the air.

Lieutenant Gray commanded VF-6, the fighter squadron. He

said, "We'll fly at fifteen thousand feet, just below the bombers. If the torpeckers call for help, we'll drop in a flash. So nobody needs to worry."

"Right. Right." Bill had been over it all a hundred times, but a hundred and one didn't hurt. "We all go together, or they can take us on one at a time."

"Right," said McClusky.

"So, anyway," said Charlie, "the bartender tells him, 'Dogs can't talk . . .'"

AKAGI, STEAMING SOUTHEAST, 0500

The sun was up now, as big and red as the imperial symbol itself.

A sailor handed Hiroaki Tanaka a message that had been flashed by beacon from the cruiser *Tone:* "Scout Plane Four is now airborne."

Nagumo glanced at the message but showed no emotion.

"That plane was ordered to launch at 0430," said Hiroaki.

"The *Tone*'s catapult is sometimes unreliable," said another officer.

Hiroaki looked at a chart that showed the vectors the cruiser scout planes were supposed to fly. If he were Halsey, and if he had come to Midway, he would put himself *there*—northeast of the island, two hundred miles out, at a bearing of about 95 degrees—just five degrees from the course to be flown by Scout Plane Four.

"What worries you?" asked Nagumo softly.

"We have had no reconnaissance of Hawaii, sir. And now Scout Plane Four launches late. If American ships—"

Nagumo nodded. "I have kept forty planes armed with torpedoes. If we sight American ships, we will strike immediately."

Hiroaki wished they had that new radar. He wondered if the Americans had it.

ENTERPRISE, STEAMING SOUTHWEST, 0600

They did. It was not good enough, however, to show distant surface activity, and as yet it showed no Japanese planes.

Wade McClusky went up to flag shelter and took Bill Stafford with him to relay any news to the other fliers, who were growing more nervous by the minute.

The sun was coming in the windows in flat new early-morning rays.

Spruance was sitting in a padded seat on a small pedestal. He was hatless and tieless, too. He had stopped wearing a tie on the day that Nimitz took his off. The officers around him had taken their ties off soon after Spruance did.

Miles Browning, Halsey's bad-tempered chief of staff, started to berate the fliers for entering unsummoned, but Spruance stopped him. "It's all right. They should know what's happening."

Browning scowled and turned his attention once more to the loudspeaker above him, which was tuned to Midway's scout-plane frequency.

"One of the Midway PBYs reported a sighting about thirty minutes ago. Enemy carriers," said Spruance. "Now we're waiting for a positive location."

And there it was. The speaker crackled and spit: "Two carriers and battleships, bearing 320 degrees, distance 180, course 135, speed 25."

The officers leaped for charts and spreaders. The PBY scout had given the navigation figures for Midway. The figures now had to be calculated for the American carriers which were part of a giant triangle, with Midway on the bottom, the Americans on the upper right, the Japanese on the upper left.

It was done, then done again, then given to Spruance.

He wrote the figures on his maneuvering board and calculated the distance between his task force and the Japanese. "One hundred and seventy-five miles."

"Yes, sir," said Browning.

Then without so much as a deep breath, Spruance said, "Launch the attack."

Launch? Billy Stafford wanted to shout. But he kept his mouth shut. Fighting spirit was one thing, but launching at maximum combat range for the Dauntless or Devastator torpedo plane? If they made it back, they'd be flying on fumes.

Spruance's face was impassive. As if he knew what Billy was thinking, he said, "We all have jobs this morning, gentlemen. Get to yours."

And Billy realized he was not one of the gods of the flight deck, just a cog in a machine, a machine oiled by commitment and by the kind of cool professionalism displayed by Spruance . . . and by blood.

"I know what you're thinking," said McClusky, back in the gangway. "But he's right, and he's a bigger gambler than Halsey. He's throwing everything at them and hoping they don't find us in the meantime. We deliver maximum damage or we get our asses kicked."

"At least he's decisive."

A HONOLULU BROTHEL, 0645

Eddie Browne woke next to . . . no one. The bed was empty. His head was pounding. His mouth felt as if someone had stuffed it with a chamois cloth.

He grabbed his pants and checked his wallet: empty.

He jumped up and stuffed a foot into one of his trouser legs. Then he felt that strange sensation at the base of his skull, half pain and half wooze, that told him he wasn't hung over yet: he was still drunk. So the natural thing to do when he stumbled was fall.

In the next room, Queen Loretta was swinging a leg over Jack Stafford. "This one's on the house, baby."

"What the hell was that?" said Jack, hearing something against the wall.

"Don't worry about it. Big spender like you don't need to worry 'bout nothin'." Queen Loretta was a beautiful coffee-colored woman from Baton Rouge, who, with a high-demand wartime skill, was quickly becoming one of the richest women in Honolulu. She pressed her breasts to his face, and . . . the door slammed open.

There was Eddie, pulling on his pants. "I'm on the duty roster at 0900, and all my money's gone. One of these bitches robbed me."

"Say, now!" Loretta jumped up and wrapped herself in a robe. "I don't run no clip joint. You upped for a whole night. Two hundred bucks." She jerked a thumb at Jack. "Him, too."

Jack grinned. "That's the truth."

Eddie ran a hand through his hair. "Oh, yeah . . . Well . . . we have to go. I have to get back to Station Hypo."

"Station Hypo," muttered Loretta, "sounds like where y'all belong."

Eddie looked at her with dull drunk's eyes. "You never *heard* of Station Hypo."

Jack pulled on his pants, then stuffed a ten into her hand. "Go get your hair straightened, honey. On me. And forget what Eddie just said."

"Hell, sugar. I can't even remember that boy's name."

"So," said Jack when he and Eddie went squinting out onto North Hotel Street. "You were awful touchy about Station Hypo."

"Of coursh I'm . . . Jesus!" He wobbled a bit, then lurched ahead. "Of course I'm touchy. She may run the best house in Honolulu, but she could be a Jap spy."

Jack grabbed him by the elbow and steered him up the street, past noisy bars and the storefronts where sailors were lining up with five dollar bills in their fists, even at seven in the morning.

"Can't be late today," said Eddie. "Today's the day."

"For what?"

"To kick the shit out of the Japs. Or get our butts invaded."

"Tell me somethin'—"

"Say, you got any aspirins?"

"No. Tell me this. I keep hearin' we broke the Jap code. Is that—"

Eddie brought his finger to his lips. "Sssh! Don't say that so loud."

It was true, thought Jack. *What a story.*

NAUTILUS, AT PERISCOPE DEPTH, 0650

Tom Stafford sat in the wardroom and studied a book of ship silhouettes.

They had been submerged for two and a half hours, and the air was starting to thicken with the smells Tom had forced himself to ignore since the cruise began—strong male sweat, stale cigarette smoke, diesel oil that got into your clothes, then your pores. And today the smell of nervous tension was as real as the sweat. They had intercepted the PBY scout-plane report locating the Japanese ships. Now they were hunting.

Lieutenant Larry Steinberg sat down opposite Tom for a moment and spooned three teaspoons of sugar into his coffee.

"Why is it that some of these Jap carriers have their islands on the port side instead of the starboard?" asked Tom.

Steinberg shrugged. He was big and swarthy, with curly hair that seemed to get thinner on top every day, while his beard grew thick and fast. "Beats the hell out of me. They read their books backwards too. All I know is, if we sink a carrier we'll all be heroes, no matter where the island is. But don't worry about it. Our torpedoes don't work."

"That's a lot of baloney."

"The Mark XIV is a giant turd—runs too deep, magnetic exploder doesn't work, and if you rig it to detonate with a contact exploder and you hit the target head on . . . forget about it. The exploder breaks off and nothing blows up."

"The navy wouldn't send us out with faulty equipment," said Tom.

"The navy, my friend, is like any other corporation. When someone at the top makes a mistake, his people cover for him, because their heads roll if his does. BuOrd blames our skippers for lousy shots but they're making lousy torpedoes."

Tom just shook his head. "I don't believe you."

"Just wait."

AKAGI, HEADING SOUTHEAST, 0705

Klaxons sounding, spine-snapping electric alarms going off throughout the ship: *general quarters*. The first American planes from Midway were appearing—six Avenger torpedo planes and four army B-26 bombers fixed with torpedoes.

The carriers were steaming in a large box formation. *Akagi* was trailed by *Kaga*, with *Hiryu* and *Soryu* several miles to starboard, four flat yellow decks steaming resolutely through the sea, four huge targets. But for some reason, all of the Americans picked on *Akagi*, and over the next few minutes, every officer competed in a contest of keeping a calm face, while *Akagi* swerved and dodged like a motorboat beneath a cloud of antiaircraft bursts.

Three American planes managed to slip through the Zeros and come at the ship from starboard and port at the same time, a perfect pincer. But one torpedo exploded when it hit the water; another bubbled by at the stern, the third simply disappeared.

Someone on the bridge scoffed at the terrible American weapons and tactics, and the terrible pilots, too. Hiroaki was not so certain. Those planes had come in without fighter cover, committing hara-kiri in order to strike a blow.

Now Nagumo turned his attention back to the problems developing over Midway. Squadron Leader Tomonaga had radioed that there was need for another attack to neutralize the airfield. Since none of the scout planes had found American ships, Nagumo authorized the rearming of his reserve torpedo squadron with fragmentation bombs.

Hiroaki glanced again at the 100-degree line that Scout Plane Four had followed, and he wondered what was out there.

NAUTILUS, HEADING NORTHWEST, 0710

"Mr. Stafford," said Commander Brockman. "Take a look."

Tom Stafford stepped to the periscope. He was always surprised by the intensity of the colors and the steadiness of the image when he looked at the ocean from sixty feet below.

This time he was surprised to see war, or at least the black smoke of war, hanging on the horizon.

"We've found the fight," said Brockman. "Mr. Steinberg, course 340 degrees true. And sound battle stations."

AKAGI, STEAMING SOUTHEAST, 0740

The next message made Hiroaki's balls tighten. It came from Scout Plane Four: "Sight what appears to be ten enemy surface ships."

Right there, right where he had expected them, found by the plane he had expected would find them—the plane that was launched thirty minutes too late.

On the hangar deck, half of the reserve planes had been rearmed with bombs. The rest still carried torpedoes to use on surface ships.

So Nagumo invited opinions from his officers.

"Until we know what kind of ships the Americans have," said Hiroaki, "we should not remove any more torpedoes."

"Scout Plane Four identifies no carriers," said Commander Genda, the slim and almost girlishly handsome flier whose beauty was matched only by his arrogance. He had led the Pearl Harbor raid and should have been flying today, but pneumonia kept him down. "The planes from Midway are the danger. We must strike Midway again."

After a moment's thought, Nagumo agreed with Hiroaki: Stop the rearming. Hold the remaining torpedo planes until further news arrives from Scout Plane Four.

VS-6 AT 15,000 FEET ABOVE TASK FORCE 16, 0745

"What a mess." Bill Stafford circled above the carriers. "What a fuckin' mess."

Spruance had just signaled the dive-bombers to head out alone. The launch had been going on for nearly an hour, and the lumbering torpedo bombers were still on the deck, while the other planes waited in the air, wasting fuel.

It was bad enough that the wind was blowing from the southeast, forcing *Enterprise* and *Hornet* to steam *away* from the enemy in order to launch. And worse, a Japanese scout plane had just been sighted in the distance.

"I guess we're on our own, Lieutenant," said his gunner, Airman First Class Omer Royal of Lubbock, Texas.

With McClusky leading them, they headed on the course that had been so carefully calculated and recalculated in the flag shelter an hour before.

On a clear day, at 15,000 feet, they could see over twenty-five miles, but this was the largest battlefield on earth—the Pacific Ocean and all the air above it. A mistake of one degree could send them into blue infinity, and a sighting made an hour ago might be meaningless now.

Bill flew on McClusky's starboard wing. Their Dauntlesses, the scout squadron, carried 500-pound bombs on their centerline racks and 100-pound bombs under their wings. Earl Gallaher's bombing squadron carried 1,000-pounders. And every plane carried two fixed fifty-caliber machine guns in its engine cowling and two swiveling thirty-calibers yoked together at the rear seat. Thirty-two Dauntlesses, flying to stop the mightiest fleet in history.

Billy glanced at the picture of Maureen that he had taped in the corner of his instrument panel. Then he peeled it off and stuck it into his pocket.

"Lieutenant, did you ever hear the one about the guy who brings his dog into the bar and says, 'Who wants to bet my dog can talk?'"

"Have you been listenin' to Osterhausser?"

NAUTILUS, HEADING NORTHWEST, 0755

"Up scope," said Brockman.

The greased shaft rose and Brockman pressed his forehead to the eyepiece. "Radio masts over the horizon, bearing 333 degrees true. I think the whole Jap fleet is steaming this way and . . . enemy aircraft. Down scope."

"Down scope, aye."

"And take her down to a hundred feet. That plane is strafing."

Like a living creature, the submarine tilted forward, seemed to breathe in water, and began its descent.

Ping. Ping.

At first, the sound was faint, barely heard by anyone on the boat.

Ping. Ping.

The Japanese had begun echo ranging. The strafing planes had radioed a location. The destroyers and cruisers were coming over the horizon. And the *Nautilus* was suddenly going from hunter to hunted.

AKAGI, STEAMING SOUTHWEST, 140 MILES FROM MIDWAY, 0815

Kido Butai was under attack by more Midway-based planes—Vindicator bombers that flew so badly the American pilots called them Wind Indicators; Dauntless dive-bombers; and nine B-17 Flying Fortresses, dropping bombs from 20,000 feet.

The Vindicators and Dauntlesses hurled themselves as bravely as the first group. They came in low, they came in high, but they came in without fighter cover, and the Zeros swarmed like bees protecting their hives from great lumbering bears.

Meanwhile, the B-17s proved that high-altitude level bombing of fast-moving ships was like trying to drop pebbles on ants running around the sidewalk.

Bomb geysers rose everywhere, creating strange and beautiful seascapes, sparkling white fountains of water that glittered for a moment in the bright sunshine and then were gone. Every explosion produced a thump or thunder of different pitch or volume. But not one American plane scored a hit.

The real jolt came with the next message from Scout Plane Four: "The enemy is accompanied by what appears to be a carrier in a position to the rear of the others."

A *carrier.* Hiroaki saw the expressions of shock forming around him. But they lasted only a moment, because the Midway attack force had just appeared on the horizon, in need of refueling and rearming, like children calling for food.

From the *Hiryu*, Vice Admiral Yamaguchi signaled that they should attack at once, with half of their torpedo planes carrying bombs and the rest carrying torpedoes. But Genda insisted that the first wave be landed on. Otherwise they would be launching a half strike while valuable planes and pilots were splashing all around them.

Now Nagumo agreed with Genda. The first strike would be brought in, while the reserve planes, which had been armed with torpedoes and rearmed with bombs, were taken below and *re*-rearmed with torpedoes.

In the next hour, the complexity of the plan would cause chaos on the hangar deck. But after that, they could strike like fury at whatever was out there.

Even if his son had not been among the fliers in the first strike, Hiroaki would have approved. And a haiku came to mind: "In the fog of war / The hard decisions demand / Minds of silk and steel."

But the snowfall of ironies was growing heavier.

NAUTILUS, UNDER ATTACK AT 150 FEET, 0819

Crump! The boat shook with the shock wave of the explosion.

A moment later, a smaller sound struck the hull. *Ping. Ping.*

Crump! Ping. Crump! Crump! Ping.

Two Japanese ships were echo-ranging, and two others were depth-charging.

"Sonar. Give a range on those charges," called Brockman.

"One thousand yards, sir," said the sailor at the headset.

"Mr. Stafford, stand by the TDC. I want a shot at one of these guys."

"Aye, sir." Tom got the words out, even though his tongue had spent the last twenty minutes stuck to the roof of his dry mouth.

At 0800 they had sighted four ships steaming toward them on a course of 135 degrees. Brockman had decided to attack the big one, the *Ise*-class battleship. But they had been sighted by a scout plane, strafed again, bombed, then depth-charged—a pattern of five, followed seven minutes later by six. Now this.

A depth charge did not have to make a direct hit to kill a submarine. It just had to explode close enough to crack the right fittings or crush the pressure hull. Then . . . Tom put these thoughts out of his mind and counted four more explosions. Then nothing for a minute . . . two minutes . . . three minutes . . .

"All right, Mr. Steinberg," said Brockman. "Plane us up to periscope depth."

Tom Stafford took a deep breath of stagnant, sweat-soaked air in the little control room. Periscope depth? Even though this was Brockman's first command, he was shrinking from nothing.

Brockman put his eye to the scope and whistled softly. "I have ships, ranges all above three thousand yards, on all sides, moving across the field at high speed, circling away to avoid us. You'll never see this in any exercise."

Then they heard a new rumble. It was not a depth charge but something else, something huge.

"Jesus!" cried Brockman. "That battleship's firing her broadside at the scope."

Now a call came from the aft torpedo room. Tom answered the phone.

"Lieutenant, sir, deck torpedo number nine is running hot in the tube."

"Hot in the tube?"

"Depth-charging sheared off the torpedo retaining pin, sir."

"That's what they're shooting at," said Steinberg. "They see the bubbles."

"So let's show them some more bubbles," said Brockman. "Ready tubes one and two."

Tom felt an electric charge go through the whole boat. They were fighting back, and his tongue wasn't sticking to the roof of his mouth anymore.

Brockman calmly called out his periscope estimates: range, 4,500 yards; course, 130; speed, 25 knots.

Tom punched the figures into the TDC—the torpedo data computer—which looked like a fancy adding machine. Then he entered the sub's course and speed. And the TDC rang up a firing solution for the gyro angles in the torpedo.

"Set track angle eighty degrees starboard on tube one, sir, with a one-degree right offset on tube two. Depth, twenty feet."

Steinberg repeated the solution. And Brockman gave the okay.

"Pray the magnet works," muttered Steinberg.

A contact exploder striking the battleship's anti-torpedo armor belt was a bad bet. Better to use a magnetic exploder that would go off below the hull.

"Fire one," said Brockman. Seconds later: "Fire two."

And the boat shuddered from one end to the other—the strong, almost reassuring *thump* of torpedoes away.

Then another call came from the torpedo room: number one did not fire.

"Shit," said Steinberg, giving Tom a look. "A new wrinkle for the Mark XIV."

"Number two running hot, straight, and normal, sir," said the sonar operator. "But I have screw sounds coming fast."

At the scope, Brockman cursed. "Target changed course. And more coming. Take her down to a hundred and fifty feet, Mr. Steinberg."

"One hundred fifty, aye, sir."

"And get ready for a pasting."

Crump! Ping. Ping. Crump! Ping. Ping. Crump!

AIEA HEIGHTS, 0830

Jack filled the mug in front of Eddie. "Three black coffees, a cold shower, and your head's *still* spinning?"

Eddie Browne looked up at the ceiling and immediately looked down. "What the fuck is a Singapore sling, anyway?"

Juan put plates of scrambled eggs in front of both of them. "Somethin' comin' today. Cap'n, he gone at five o'clock. What is it? Big battle or somethin'?"

"Classified," snapped Jack.

"Oh, yeah. Everything classified around here lately." And Juan went scurrying back to the kitchen. "Classified this, classified that. I thinkin' of classifyin' my ass."

Jack told Eddie to eat if he wanted his hangover to go away.

"I told you, I'm not hung over. I'm still drunk."

"Well, eat something anyway."

"You know what stinks about this thing? Another guy and me, we figured out where the Japs were going, and we won't get any credit till the war's over."

"How did you do that?"

"AF and fresh water."

"AF? That sounds like a code."

"I'll tell you if you keep your mouth shut."

"Sure." What a scoop. *What a bastard.*

VS-6, AT 20,000 FEET, HEADING SOUTHEAST, 0900

"Where, oh, where can those little Japs be? Where, oh, where can they be?"

"I thought you Texans were supposed to be strong and silent," said Bill Stafford into the intercom.

"Ain't many Texas boys can sing like me."

"I'd rather hear those stupid dog jokes."

They were forty minutes from the point at which Spruance had predicted that they would find the Japanese, and they were alone, with not a trace of the other squadrons. At least the VS-6 and VB-6 groups had held together. If they found the Japs, they would have to attack with or without fighter cover and take their chances.

God of the flight deck *and* cog in a machine. Billy decided he could be both. Only gods could ever feel the intensity of the powerful pacific blue that enveloped those blue planes. But the sound of the engine vibrating in his ass and the sight of the fuel gauge dropping toward empty reminded him that he was just another interchangeable part.

"So . . . the bartender slaps down five bucks and says, 'Let's hear him talk.' So the guy says, 'Rover, who's the president?' Dog just looks straight ahead. 'Ah, Rover, name the Andrews Sisters.'"

"Maxine, LaVerne—"

"C'mon, Lieutenant . . . the dog don't say nothin', and they lose five bucks. Once they're outside, the guy says to the dog, 'So why didn't you say nothin'?' And the dog says, 'Well, think of how much more we can make *tomorrow* night.'"

NAUTILUS, AT PERISCOPE DEPTH, 0900

Persistence. That was a word Tom Stafford would not forget.

Brockman had been depth-charged twice, but the sonar contacts had moved away again, and *Nautilus* was back in the hunt.

Brockman put his face to the eyepiece. "Aircraft carrier. Range: sixteen thousand yards; bearing: 013 degrees relative. AA bursts all around her. And a destroyer coming on. Ready tube two. We have a shot right down his throat."

Once more Tom Stafford fed the calculations into the TDC. At 2,500 yards, Brockman gave the order, and the torpedo thumped out of the boat.

"Running hot, straight, and normal, sir," said the sonar operator.

Forty-five seconds . . . fifty . . . a minute . . . Another miss.

"Propeller coming closer," said sonar.

"Take her down. One hundred feet."

And Tom Stafford heard a noise that he would hear in nightmares for the rest of his life—a clanking sound, like an anchor chain scraping over the hull, or the chains of some Dickensian ghost calling him to his own grave. Someone said it was a drag wire that the Jap destroyers trailed in the water to find submarines.

Click-click.

"Shit," said Steinberg.

"What?"

"That's a depth-charge detonator. It just armed. Very close. Hold on."

KA-BOOM!

"Mr. Steinberg, two hundred feet!" said Brockman calmly.

Click-click. KA-BOOM!

The sub sighed and sucked more water into its tanks, then tipped forward.

AKAGI, TURNING NORTHWEST, 0918

Hiroaki Tanaka thanked the gods of war.

His son's Zero had just grabbed an arrester cable. Minoru was pushing back the canopy, running to deliver his report to the air officer in the ready room.

The defensive box formation had broken down. *Akagi, Kaga*, and *Soryu* were cruising in a wide triangle, with *Kaga* slightly astern of the other two. *Hiryu* had run ahead by several miles. But the birds were back in their nests. In another half hour, every one would be refueled and rearmed. So Nagumo ordered a turn to 70 degrees, straight at the American ships beyond the horizon.

And then they saw them. The first American carrier planes.

Somehow, a torpedo squadron, VT-8 from the *Hornet,* had found the Japanese fleet before anyone else, and they were beginning their own slow charge, without fighter cover, without hope.

After two attacks, it was all becoming as ritualized as a Kabuki play. The cruisers made smoke screens. Then the rhythmic one-two, one-two beat of the pom-pom batteries began. Then came the *bup-bup-bup* of the fifty-caliber machine guns, their tracers rising like delicate birds. Then the demonic scream of the Zeros roaring from 15,000 feet. And one by one, the Americans were sent spinning, tumbling, and spiraling into the sea.

How could they allow those planes to come in alone? Where were their fighters? Where were the dive-bombers?

"To starboard!" cried Genda.

One of the Americans, trailing fire and smoke, was diving straight at the island of *Akagi*, straight at Hiroaki Tanaka's head.

"Hard aport!" cried the captain, and the huge *Akagi* swung so fast that Hiroaki fell against the admiral, who grabbed the binnacle to stay on his feet.

Bup-bup-bup. The American rear-seat gunner swung his machine guns at the bridge in a final, furious gesture of defiance. The slugs struck the island, shattered the glass in the bridge windows, buried themselves in the bomb-fragment padding.

But the big plane screamed past, missing the island, missing the deck, hitting the sea and disintegrating like all the others.

Fate was a matter of feet, thought Hiroaki, sometimes a matter of inches, sometimes of minutes.

He righted himself and offered a hand to Nagumo, who looked at him for a moment with that glimmer of diffidence in his eyes. Then the admiral stood on his own and wiped the sweat from his upper lip with a gloved hand.

A sailor delivered a message to Hiroaki. "From destroyer *Arashi:* Have depth-charged an American submarine trailing to the south of the fleet. Results unknown."

VS-6, AT 20,000 FEET, 142 MILES SOUTHEAST OF THE *ENTERPRISE*, 0930

The TBS—the voice radio telephone that enabled American fliers to talk to each other and to their ship—was crackling in Bill's ear. As far as they knew, the Japanese could not monitor the channel, but they still kept its use to a minimum.

McClusky said to the rest of his squadron, "Here's where we're supposed to find them. See anything?"

"I see the Midway shoals off to port," said Charlie Osterhausser, who was flying the last plane on the left. "Big columns of smoke risin' from the Jap strikes."

"Jap ships? Anybody?" said McClusky from the lead plane.

All Bill heard above the roar of his engine was silence.

"Any friendlies?" asked McClusky.

More silence.

What a disaster. The thirty-two Dauntlesses were still together. But where were the fighters? Where were the torpeckers? Where were the Japs?

Defeat in detail. That was what the Japs had done for the last six months. Hold a powerful force together and catch pieces of the enemy before they could organize. Now it was happening to the individual air squadrons of the *Enterprise*, *Hornet*, and *Yorktown.*

Bill peered ahead, into the lead plane. McClusky had his head down, looking at something—fuel gauge? maneuvering board? Or was he just trying to make up his mind? Had they arrived ahead of the Japs? Had the Japs made a turn?

"This is Stafford. I've got about twenty minutes of fuel, sir, then I'll have to turn back or splash."

"Right."

And several other pilots came on with the same information.

"Okay," said McClusky, his voice snapping with authority. "I think the Japs have turned. We'll stay on a 240-degree heading for another thirty-five miles. Then we swing northwest. Everyone stay in tight."

Bill Stafford gave McClusky a thumbs-up. And on they flew.

CINCPAC, 0930

Jack Stafford had less difficulty than most newsmen getting past the marine guard, perhaps because his father was assistant operations officer.

Will was in the head, so, with a wink at Lieutenant Commander Walter Sullivan, his father's assistant, Jack said he'd have a seat in his father's office.

"Don't open any desk drawers, don't read anything, don't touch anything," said Sullivan, a big-jowled Irishman from Boston, with a quick temper and a sharp tongue, the perfect executive officer.

"Sometimes, Walter, I don't think you like me."

"I don't like anyone who's always askin' questions."

As soon as Jack sat down, he saw some papers on his father's desk and tried to read them, though they were upside down.

Through the office door, Sullivan was giving him the eye.

Jack gave him a wink. *Just doin' my job.*

Then Jack's father stalked in trailing a Lucky Strike smoke screen. "What brings you to CINCPAC, with your notebook and your tongue hangin' out?"

"I need a little background."

His father dropped into his chair, snuffed out one cigarette, lit another. "First of all, what do you know?"

As Harry Dowd had once told Jack, play dumb whenever possible. Harry said he knew that couldn't be easy for a Harvard man, but real reporters had to do it every day.

It didn't work with his father. "No games, Jack. What do you know?"

"Not much more than I knew when they threw me off the *Enterprise*. But my guess is there's a big battle under way somewhere. Midway, maybe? And judging from the pile of butts in your ashtray, it's touch-and-go."

"We're not getting direct reports . . . radio silence. We're just picking up transmissions between ships and planes."

"How did we figure out that the Japs were coming to Midway?"

"Classified."

The buzzer rang. "That's Nimitz. Now, the last thing we need is reporters. Go play golf. Tee times are easy these days. When I can fill you in, I'll call."

The bum's rush. Jack had gotten it before, but never from his own father. Of course, he had his prime source already.

VS-6, AT 20,000 FEET, 0952

"So, Lieutenant," drawled Omer, "what you think's a dog's philosophy of life?"

"I don't know. What?"

"If you can't eat it or screw it, piss on it. And speakin' of pissin', I'll be busy for a few minutes back here, so don't let no Japs get on your—"

"Quiet."

The TBS was crackling. Somebody from one of the fighter squadrons was radioing a Japanese position, but it was garbled, hard to read.

So Bill turned up the gain on his radio just as Miles Browning shot back on the powerful *Enterprise* transmitter, "Attack! Attack at once!"

And Wade McClusky cut in: "Wilco. As soon as we can find the bastards!"

Bill chuckled. The tension had long ago dissipated. His high-intensity adrenaline had run out. Now he expected that they would be back aboard the *Enterprise* before long, drinking coffee, complaining, and—

What was that? To the north. It looked like a scratch on the polished blue finish of the sea.

"Commander. It's Stafford. I see a wake, bearing 350 degrees, about twenty miles."

McClusky grabbed his binoculars and peered to the north. "It's a Jap destroyer. Goin' like hell. Must've been left behind. This could be it."

McClusky swung his plane north, and the VS-6 formation, like a flock of geese, swung with him. Gallaher and Best's VB squadron swung a moment later.

And Bill felt his stomach clench. He hadn't run out of adrenaline after all.

As they flew over the destroyer, he wondered why it was straggling so far behind. He could not have known that it was the *Arashi*, which had stopped to attack his brother's submarine.

AKAGI, STEAMING NORTHEAST, 0958

Hiroaki Tanaka stood in the doorway of the ready room and glanced in at the pilots having their meal of rice, tea, and sweet crackers. It was a roomful of loud voices, quick gestures, the excitement of samurai after battle and the anger of warriors who had seen friends die. And there was Minoru, explaining his tactics to the flight leader.

He would let the boy have his moment. They could talk later.

He went instead to the hangar deck, to check on the rearming. Never had he seen men work with such frantic efficiency. The crews in their short-sleeved white shirts and short white pants madly did the business of refueling planes, removing bombs, replacing torpedoes, refilling machine-gun belts, rolling the loaded planes to the elevators, lifting them back to the flight deck. Ordnance lay everywhere—bombs on open racks, torpedoes, belts—and gasoline lines formed a snakepit across the deck. But there was no time to stow anything. Just get the planes back in the air.

Then the Klaxon sounded: *general quarters*.

And another act of the drama began.

The Americans once more were unprotected. But this group was tactically the best. They executed a perfect split, with seven planes peeling off after the *Kaga*, and seven making their run at the *Hiryu*.

Hiroaki grabbed his binoculars and watched them. One after another they splashed gallantly. But he was not admiring them. He wanted to see their markings: carrier planes. A second division of torpedo bombers. That meant . . .

"Admiral, I think there is a second American carrier."

VS-6, AT 15,000 FEET, 1005

"Yeah," said Omer, finishing a joke. "And if I had a dog as ugly as you—"

"Holy Christ."

"What?"

"There."

Bill Stafford knew that he would never forget that moment, or the strange godlike feeling that came over him. From three miles up and fifteen miles away, the striking force for the mightiest fleet that had ever sailed looked like a lot of slugs leaving white slicks on the surface of the sea.

"Tally-ho!" said McClusky into the TBS.

AKAGI, 1015

They were finally turning into the wind. The aft flight deck was once more crowded with torpedo bombers, which needed a long runway for takeoff, and the elevators were bringing back the last of the Zeros to lead the attack.

Engines were revving up to a roar that Genda called "the sound of victory."

And now the lookouts were screaming that more torpedo planes were coming to port, this time with five fighters covering them.

These were carrier planes too. A *third* carrier? That was impossible.

The air was once more alive with screaming engines and thundering antiaircraft, with tracer fire and exploding swirls of smoke. The water was once again laced with the wakes of fast-maneuvering carriers and churning torpedoes.

But none scored. Of the forty-one torpedo bombers that attacked that morning, only four would even make it home. *Kido Butai* was still untouched, ready to deal a death blow to American naval power in the Pacific.

Nagumo nodded, and the signal was passed to launch.

Hiroaki looked down at his son's plane. Minoru was in his cockpit, fourth on the deck. Hiroaki made a small sign to him and said a small prayer.

VS-6, AT 15,000 FEET ABOVE *KIDO BUTAI*, 1025

When the Spartans stood in the pass at Marathon, when British sailors smashed the French line at Trafalgar, when a handful of farmers and fishermen from Maine held the Union left at Gettysburg, they may have known that they were turning history like a gate on a hinge. More likely, they knew only that if they fought well, they might survive to fight again.

And that was what Bill Stafford was thinking. That, and *Don't fuck up, because you'll never get a chance like this again.*

For the first time in six months, fate was pulling for the Americans. The enemy was disorganized. His fighter cover was down at sea level chasing the last of the torpedo bombers. His decks were covered with planes . . . and bombs . . . and fuel.

Bill Stafford leaned on his stick above the *Akagi*. Others peeled off toward the *Kaga*, and by some miracle of dumb-luck coordination, or by the grace of God, the *Yorktown* dive-bombers had just found the *Soryu*.

"Hold on, Omer!"

And don't fuck up, because you'll never get a chance like this again.

Two planes dropped ahead of Bill Stafford, straight at the yellow deck and the tiny silver planes.

He felt the crushing pressure of the dive in his chest, heard the scream of his own engine in his ears. If there was AA fire, he didn't notice it. If there were Zeros coming at him, he was counting on Omer to hold them off.

The first plane dropped its bomb. And an explosion of water geysered up. A near miss.

The second plane released from 2,400 feet, and a moment later there was a tremendous blast just forward of the island.

Now came Bill Stafford, dropping out of the sun, straight at the red Rising Sun painted on the midships elevator.

5,000 . . . 4,000 . . . 3,000 . . .

The plane sounded like all the vengeful furies released in the volcanic blast of the *Arizona* six months before.

2,000 . . .

Omer was whooping like a cowboy in a rodeo.

1,500 . . . *Release.* The plane kicked up and Bill pulled back on the stick. Then, against the best advice, he glanced over his shoulder to watch. The yellow bomb was falling . . . falling . . . like a petal or a seed . . . and . . .

A tremendous ball of flame blossomed upward, followed by an even larger one that blew men and airplanes into the air and over the side.

Omer Royal shouted, "Yahooooo! Look at that bastard burn!"

Akagi, 1027

No! It did not happen!

The second bomb had blown up twenty feet from his son's plane, blown it to pieces, but the gods would not take Minoru so young, with so much to give.

He looked at Nagumo and the others—all slack-jawed, stunned, their faces blackened by the blasts. And he was gripped with a need to do what a father should. Instead of controlling his emotions and assisting the direction of damage control, he left the bridge. By the time he reached the flight deck, he knew they would never control the damage all around them.

And from some strange place in his mind, an old saying ran through his head, one that he used to recite when teaching his little boy to mind the details of whatever he did, and one that told the story of this day, from the moment that the *Tone*'s scout plane catapult malfunctioned: *"For want of a nail, the shoe was lost, for want of a shoe, the horse was lost, for want of a horse went the king, for want of a king went the kingdom."*

He ran to the middle of the deck, where his son's plane had been. Now there was nothing but a hole in the flight deck.

His son was gone. His wide-eyed little boy. His serious young man. And with him, all hope. All for what? For the empire? For the emperor? Let the snow crush the roof of the Imperial Palace.

Suddenly the ship shuddered with a tremendous belowdecks blast that sent fire and debris up through the hole like water in a fountain.

Hiroaki's uniform burst into flames, and his last rational thought was to thank the gods for taking him to his son.

STAFFORD'S DAUNTLESS, UNDER ATTACK, 1030

"We got two on our tail, Lieutenant."

Bup-bup-bup-bup.

"Keep it comin', Omer. Keep it comin'."

Like bees whose nest has been kicked over, the Zeros attacked with redoubled fury.

Bill felt the bullets hitting his armored seat and drilling into his engine cowling.

He climbed back to 5,000 feet, and two of them were still on his tail. At 10,000, he was going to dive and try to lose them, if he could make it.

Bup-bup-bup.

Omer Royal poured a tremendous fire stream as the Zeros swung in behind him one after the other, then pulled out to dodge the tracers and armor-piercing bullets from his twin thirty-calibers until finally he yelled, "Yahoo! Yahooo! One down, one to go."

Bill screamed, "Hold on, Omer!" Then he tipped the plane straight for the water . . . straight for the water . . . straight . . . for . . . the . . . water. . . .

At five hundred feet, he pulled out of the dive, then threw down the flaps, spinning the Dauntless into a skid, as if she had hit an ice patch in the air. The Zero shot past, and Bill Stafford nailed him with his own fifty-calibers, right in the gas tanks.

Yes! All he'd needed was a shot. The Zero could hunt like a hawk because it was built like a bird, light and flimsy, with no armored seats, no self-sealing gas tanks. Bill Stafford's shot had literally blown that Zero out of the sky.

Now they could go home.

But a few miles south, their oil pressure began to drop.

NAUTILUS, AT PERISCOPE DEPTH, 1145

After an hour of depth-charging, she had no more than a ruptured hydraulic line, and no injuries.

Brockman put his face to the eyepiece and whistled softly, then he said to Steinberg, "Have a look at this."

"Holy shit." After a few moments, Steinberg let Tom Stafford have a look.

The horizon to the northwest looked as if three fuel dumps had been bombed. Three columns of thick black smoke were rising straight up and leveling out at five thousand feet. Two columns were rising from over the horizon, but one was in plain view, about eight miles away.

"Here's a test, Stafford," said Brockman. "Without looking at your book, tell me the class of that carrier. I want to know, because we're going to finish her."

"Uh . . ." Tom turned the ring to bring the scope to full magnification. "The island is to starboard, sir, and, I can't quite tell, but I think she has a fold-down starboard stack . . . I'd say she's *Soryu* class, sir."

"The Academy trains you boys well."

"Thank you, sir."

"Now go see the chief engineer. Find out how much time we have on our batteries if we maintain a speed of two-thirds ahead. Then get aft and see to soldering a ruptured hydraulic line."

"Let George do it," cracked Steinberg.

Brockman grabbed the intercom and told the crew what he had just seen. From one end of the boat to the other came the strange muffled sound of men cheering in enclosed spaces, in dense air.

ADRIFT, 1345

Charlie Osterhausser had seen Bill Stafford's Dauntless hit the water. He had rocked his wings when he flew over, which meant that their position had been noted and someone would come for them. It might be a PBY; it might be a destroyer; it might be a sub.

Until then Bill and Omer would float along in their yellow rubber raft and watch the show from the cheap seats.

Two of the Japanese carriers were dead in the water. The middle one had continued to steam north, hopelessly trying to stay in the fight. Meanwhile, the undamaged *Hiryu*, on the distant horizon, had launched a strike.

Bill watched all of it through a small pair of Zeiss binoculars his grandfather had given him, powerful 7x50s that looked like nothing more than opera glasses.

Omer pulled out the emergency survival all-purpose fishing pack, which contained hooks, hand lines, feathered drails, a little net, and a booklet on the preparation of raw fish.

"What the hell are you doing now?" Bill asked.

Omer grinned. He was a career sailor, long-faced, leathered, somewhere in his thirties, and completely unfamiliar with any but navy dentists, most of whom were completely unfamiliar with anything but pulling teeth. "This here's a big damn fishin' hole. Let's see if this little booklet tells you how to catch fish."

"Omer, there's a battle going on."

"Fish don't know that. But keep that forty-five handy, Lieutenant, case I catch us a shark."

Bill thought about that for a moment and decided it wasn't a bad idea. He pulled out the heavy black pistol and laid it in his lap. Then he went back to his binoculars.

He wasn't worried about the Japanese. They had moved on to the northwest, following a battlefield that moved as inexorably as the turning earth itself. Every bomb, every explosion, and every ditched plane along the seventy-five-mile path of battle had already been swallowed by the sea, and it seemed now as if nothing had passed this way since the beginning of time.

Except for that periscope appearing about half a mile to the south.

He saw the wake first, just a little moving riffle on the surface. Then he focused and tried to remember the differences between American and Japanese periscopes. One of them had an asparagus-stick top, the other a straight finger. But damned if he could remember.

So he decided not to wave. Best wait for the PBYs.

NAUTILUS, 1350

Tom Stafford was passing a short distance from his brother, but Commander Brockman's 360-degree periscope sweep did not reveal any yellow rafts, perhaps because downed fliers were not the object of the chase. It was that carrier, still under way but still burning.

Half a dozen times, Brockman told Tom to check his silhouette book against the vessel in the periscope to make certain they were not sinking an American carrier.

At 2,700 yards, Brockman fired three torpedoes at a track angle of 125 degrees starboard and a depth of sixteen feet.

"Running hot, straight, and normal, sir!" cried the sonar operator.

Brockman watched the wakes track right toward the ship, and described their progress. Three minutes . . . four . . . the wakes had reached the ship.

"Hit!" said Brockman at three minutes and forty-five seconds. "Flames jumping, bow to midships."

After congratulations all around, he asked the other four officers in the conning tower to view and verify: fires rising, men abandoning ship, boats pulling away.

Larry Steinberg was the last to look, and Tom sensed that something was wrong as soon as he stepped away from the scope.

"We just bagged a carrier," said Brockman. "Why do you look like the Dodgers just lost the World Series?"

"Shouldn't sonar have picked up the explosions?" asked Steinberg softly.

"Sound does funny things underwater, Larry. What else but our torpedo would have made her burst into flames?"

"Induced explosions from her fires, sir. She was burning when we got to her."

"A small fire in her stern. Now look at her."

Steinberg put his eye back to the periscope. Tom knew that he wanted credit for the carrier as much as they all did. "She's burning like the *Arizona,* sir."

"All right, then." Brockman grabbed the intercom. "This is the captain speaking. Notch one Jap carrier into your belts."

ADRIFT, 1415

"Hunker down, Omer," said Bill Stafford. "Here comes a destroyer."

"Shit-all."

"Damn sub's leading her right to us."

Omer pulled out his knife. "You keep that forty-five handy, Lieutenant."

As the first depth charge was dropped, Omer said, "There goes the fishin'."

For an hour, the Japanese destroyer crisscrossed the area, depth-charging the hell out of every square inch. The surface of the sea exploded and rumbled. Geysers rose. Huge hills of white water came up like bubbles in a simmering stew and, once or twice, the raft almost capsized.

Bill and Omer wondered how deep the sub had gone to escape, and they wondered if the Japanese would forget about them in all the action. No evidence of the sub ever came up, which they took as a good sign. But when the destroyer turned toward them, they knew it was a bad sign.

They were prisoners before nightfall.

They were taken to the *Arashi*'s wardroom, not much different from an American wardroom, except for the picture of Hirohito instead of Franklin Roosevelt. A pharmacist's mate gave them ointments for the contusions they had suffered, then water and a little rice. Then they were left with a single, grim-faced guard.

Bill asked Omer, "How much do you know about Midway?"

"I been there once."

The guard growled at them: no talking.

Bill made a gesture for a cigarette.

The guard shook his head: no cigarettes.

Bill turned to Omer, still trying to be casual. "We tell them we were attached to Midway two weeks ago. We tell them all we know about the island, because *they* know it, too. We tell them nothing about the Task Force Sixteen."

The guard growled again. Moods were not good in the imperial fleet that day.

Through the porthole, Bill could see one of the reasons: American dive-bombers had found the *Hiryu* and were sweeping down at the big flat silhouette, leaving great clouds of red, orange, and black erupting after them. It was like watching those telescope films of eruptions of the sun.

And Bill knew, with a strangling sense of despair, that he was as far away from those dive-bombers, and his own carrier, and the girl whose picture was in his pocket, as he was from the sun.

CINCPAC, 1830

If there ever had been a day when Will Stafford could say "What's good for the U.S. Navy . . ." it was today.

Of course, his joy was tempered. They had no casualty lists yet, but the torpedo squadrons had been wiped out, and half of the pilots in VS-6 were missing. He told himself there was a fifty-fifty chance that Billy was safe aboard, and if he was among the missing, a fifty-fifty chance that a PBY was fishing him out of the water already.

It looked by then as if they might lose the *Yorktown*, but the *Hiryu* was definitely going to join the other three Jap carriers, and *Enterprise* and *Hornet* were untouched. So long as Spruance played it close to the vest and didn't go chasing Yamamoto's battleships in the dark—and there was no reason to expect Ray Spruance to change his character after forty years—this one would go down as a huge victory.

When Jack arrived, Will filled him in and promised that he would get Jack the Nimitz communiqué an hour ahead of everyone else. "I shouldn't, but if I can do something for one of my boys, I'll do it."

That was when Jack realized how worried his father was. It was as if he knew that two of his sons were beyond his help, so he would help the one that he could.

"Thanks, Dad. Can you tell me about something Eddie Browne said—"

"Whatever Eddie Browne said, keep a lid on it. Tell the story the way we want you to, and everyone will be all right."

ABOARD THE *ARASHI,* 2200

Bill Stafford looked at the tip of a dagger held under his nose.

"This very sharp. You like you balls? You tell truth."

"I've already told you the truth."

Young Lieutenant Kita—skinny and slight with a little mustache like Hitler's—stepped back and nodded to the marine beside him.

Slap!

The interrogation had been going on for two hours and was now being conducted under the red lightbulbs of a darkened ship.

"I told you," said Bill, "we were detached to Midway two weeks ago."

"But you *navy* flier. Why they do that?"

"We're from the *Saratoga*, and she's been torpedoed."

"We know." Kita smiled. "We have good torpedo. Not like yours."

"I wouldn't know. I drop bombs."

"Torpedoes your sub fire at carrier—two miss, one hit and break in half."

That was a bad sign, thought Bill. *They* were giving *him* intelligence. That meant they weren't worried about it going anywhere. It was also a sign that he was in the hands of amateurs. Of course, he had known that as soon as they started the interrogation with both subjects in the room.

"I tell you something. Now you tell me. How many American carriers?"

"I flew from Midway with the marine dive-bombers under Major Henderson."

"I think you lie." Then he turned to Omer, held the dagger beneath his nose for a moment, just to let him see it. "You think he lie? He officer. You sailor wearin' blue dungaree. He think he better than you. He lie, right?"

Omer looked into the Japanese officer's eyes. "You know what I think?"

Lieutenant Kita smiled. "Say what you think."

"If I had a dog as ugly as you, I'd shave his ass and make him walk backwards."

Lieutenant Kita stood up straight, looked around to make sure that neither of the others could understand what was just said. Then he nodded to the marine.

Slap!

Omer Royal barely reacted.

Lieutenant Kita turned back to Bill Stafford. He pawed through Stafford's personal effects on the table—cigarette lighter, pocketknife, standard issue bowie knife, those fine binoculars—and he picked up the photo of that beautiful Irish face.

"You want to see her again?"

"We all want to see our wives again," answered Bill.

"Well, you tell truth, you see her."

And Bill Stafford once more recited everything he knew about

Midway, based on guesswork and secondhand information. He even told them the exact length of the airstrip.

"Keep tellin' 'em that stuff, Lieutenant," said Omer, "all the way to the prison camp."

The questioning went on for another hour, until the skipper appeared and called the lieutenant outside.

At least it was a pleasant night, thought Bill, even if he still had his hands tied behind his back. A cool breeze was blowing through the open doors on both sides of the wardroom, and the moonlight was shining on the surface of the sea.

Now Lieutenant Kita returned, but he did not make any eye contact with the prisoners. He was carrying a sidearm, which he offered to the other Japanese officers, neither of whom would take it.

And Bill realized, with a sudden sense of the absolute and utter waste of it all, that there was not going to be a prison camp. These faces, in this dim red light, were the last that he was going to see.

Lieutenant Kita seemed to be pleading with the others. He even picked up the binoculars, offering them in exchange for the execution. But nothing could convince them to do what the skipper had apparently ordered.

So, in a shaking voice, Lieutenant Kita told the Americans, "Please to stand up."

Bill and Omer looked at each other.

"I don't like this," said Omer.

"No talking," said Kita.

Bill tried to say something, but his throat had closed up tight. He gestured with his chin to Omer, and they both stood.

What a waste, he thought. What a fucking waste.

With his pistol, Lieutenant Kita gestured to the door. "Go."

But Bill did not move. He looked down at the table, at the picture of Maureen, lying amid his pocket junk.

He tried to speak again, and the lieutenant realized what he wanted, so he picked up the picture and put it into Bill's breast pocket.

"Thank you."

"Orders," said the lieutenant apologetically. "War bad."

And prodded along by the guard, they were led out, down the

deck, past the torpedo tubes and the five-inch gun turret, to the depth-charge racks at the stern.

The destroyer was moving fast, leaving a long white wake gleaming in the moonlight behind it.

Bill thought of how beautiful it all looked, and he wished that he had been able to show it to Maureen, just once, that wondrous wide sea in the night.

Then Omer Royal drawled, "Hey, Lieutenant, once there was these two dogs—"

It was the last voice that Bill Stafford would hear.

A hand drove itself into his back and sent him into the churning wake.

He felt Omer falling beside him, but his senses were overwhelmed and Omer faded from his thoughts.

The foaming wake rolled over him and rolled him over in its embrace. He tried to tread water, but his hands were still bound tightly. He rolled once to the surface and saw the face of the moon. He cried Maureen's name and cursed at all the wonderful things he would never see. And he was swallowed into the phosphorescent warmth of the Pacific night.

Gods did not die and cogs did not cry . . . only men.

x
Missing in Action

At 1245 on June 6, while Spruance was still launching planes at the stragglers of the Japanese fleet, Nimitz issued his first battle communiqué.

By the time the other reporters saw it, Jack had read it, underlined it, and filed it on the wire, with a story to follow. The first sentence: "Through the skill and devotion to duty of our armed forces of all branches in the Midway area, our citizens can now rejoice that a momentous victory is in the making."

Who the hell wrote this stuff? Nimitz himself? It read like lead.

Jack punched up the prose and dug up whatever else he could. He even went over to Hickham Field, to interview the army pilots who had done the high-level bombing. Lieutenant Colonel Sweeney said his squadron had personally sunk three of the carriers, and, hell, "We never once had to look for the enemy because the navy planes had located the task force perfectly."

A lot of newspapers would swallow Sweeney's story whole.

But Jack would tell the real story: it was impossible to hit moving ships from 20,000 feet; it took navy dive-bombers. This would put Jack in tight with navy fliers, no matter what else he ever wrote.

Jack and his father stayed up late that night, in the blackout darkness, listening to the KGMB Glenn Miller broadcast. Jack sipped his Primo, Will his Jack Daniel's. They talked a lot about baseball. They tried not to mention what was sitting on the veranda in front of them like a bad-tempered dog. No sense worrying about Billy until there was something concrete. Talk about the good news, instead: the *Nautilus* was back on patrol after putting three torpedoes into a Jap carrier.

Then, out of nowhere, Will said, "I knew a Jap once."

"At the Academy?" asked Jack.

Will nodded. "He was my best friend. Now he's probably . . . Ah, hell, he's probably worried about his sons, too."

The doorbell jangled Jack awake around nine.

A moment later, Juan came into his room with a yellow Western Union envelope. "About time you get up. Your dad and me, we already been to church, and he gone to CINCPAC."

Jack snatched the telegram. It was from Harry Dowd, filed at 10:00 A.M. in New York City: READ ALL ABOUT IT IN DAILY NEWS: "NAVY HAD WORD OF JAP PLAN TO STRIKE AT SEA." GREAT STORY. WOULD HAVE BEEN NICE FOR APS. GET FOLLOW-UP FROM INSIDE, OR GET NEW JOB. TEXT TO FOLLOW.

In the shower, Jack figured it out: someone in Naval Intelligence had told a reporter all about Station Hypo and the Jap code. Now it was all over the papers in New York, and probably in Chicago and Washington, too. Scooped again.

By now some spy had mailed the article to another spy with a short-wave radio—probably a German on the Maine coast, who could transmit to a U-boat. From there it would go to Berlin. And finally the news would reach Tokyo: "America knows something you don't: your code has been broken." Then the code would be changed.

So why not build up morale by making those code breakers look like heroes?

Jack knew the whole story, right down to the little trick with AF and fresh water. He could even see the headline: "How We Trapped the Japs."

An hour later, a second telegram arrived with the *Daily News* article: THE STRENGTH OF THE JAPANESE FORCES WITH WHICH THE AMERICAN NAVY IS BATTLING SOMEWHERE WEST OF MIDWAY ISLAND . . . WAS WELL KNOWN IN AMERICAN NAVAL CIRCLES SEVERAL DAYS BEFORE THE BATTLE BEGAN, RELIABLE SOURCES IN NAVAL INTELLIGENCE REPORTED HERE TONIGHT.

All right. The whole thing: AF, Station Hypo, Pearl Harbor Signal Intelligence . . . Should he name names?

Why not?

He sat down at his neat Smith-Corona portable—gunmetal gray with green keys—put in a sheet and a carbon, and began to pound.

At CINCPAC, two messages crossed Will Stafford's desk around lunch time. One was bound for Nimitz, the other was for Will himself.

The one for Nimitz was a furious cable from Admiral Ernest J. King, Chief of Naval Operations. It quoted the *Washington Times-Herald,* which had carried the *Daily News* story: STORY UNSIGNED. WASHINGTON DATELINE BUT MAY HAVE COME FROM PEARL. SECNAV CONSIDERS IT VIOLATION OF ESPIONAGE ACT. FBI WILL INVESTIGATE. FIND LEAKS AND PLUG THEM. NOW.

Jack. That was Will's first thought. Jack and his whore-hunting pal Eddie Browne. And Jack hadn't even had the balls to put his name on the article.

This deserved more than a phone call. *Right now.* So Captain Will Stafford put on his hat and headed for the door, but Wally Sullivan blocked the way. "You better read the second message, sir."

Slowly Will stepped back to his desk and picked up the telegram. It was an operational message from Spruance. Appended to it was a sentence from an old friend who understood a father's worry. "Captain Stafford: Bill Stafford VS-6 missing in action."

The words struck Will so hard in the chest that he almost fell down.

"Are you all right, sir?" asked Sullivan.

Will took out a cigarette and lit it. "Drive me . . . Drive me up to my house, if you will, Wally. I need to see my son."

On the way, the pain subsided. It wasn't the first time Will had felt it pass through him, like a fist traveling through his chest. And the business with Jack couldn't wait. It shouldn't wait just because Billy was floating somewhere in a raft.

The house on Aiea Heights was dark and cool, even at midday. When they first arrived in Hawaii, Jane had picked it out because she knew the hipped roof and overhanging eaves would keep out the strongest of the sun's rays.

Will and his aide followed the sound of a clattering typewriter to the dining room, where Jack was sitting in his bathing trunks, head down, cigarette burning between his lips, fifth cup of coffee on the table in front of him. "Oh . . . hi, Dad."

"What are you writing?" Will's voice was strained, and his face was as gray as Jack's typewriter case.

"Uh . . . it's a news story."

"About what?"

With another Mickey-the-Dunce smile, Jack rolled the sheet and the carbon off the platen and piled them, face down, with the other pages, even though he wasn't quite done. "It's about the battle."

Sullivan was inclining his head, trying to read the yellow Western Union telegram beside Jack's typewriter.

Jack deftly folded it over, then plastered his best smart-ass grin on his face. "Don't open any drawers, don't read anything, don't touch anything."

Sullivan gave him a fifty-caliber glare of his own.

Juan came through the doors from the kitchen. "Oh, cripes. Two more for lunch. Why the hell you don't call?"

"Get back to the kitchen, Juan," said Will Stafford.

Juan did a quick pivot.

Now Jack realized how serious this was. The captain never snapped at Juan, no matter how many four-letter words he strung together.

Will put his palms on the table and brought his face close to Jack's. "Now, you son of a bitch, have you heard of the Espionage Act?"

"Uh . . ."

"What about the FBI? You heard of them?" Will took a deep breath to control his fury, but he wasn't having much success. "I told you that whatever you'd heard from Eddie Browne was not to be printed."

"Listen, Dad . . ." Jack picked up the telegram from Harry Dowd.

"Listen yourself. I just got word that Billy's missing, and you're sitting here in your bathing suit, giving up military secrets." And he felt the chest pain again, hitting harder. He angled his head and hunched his left shoulder, as if to control it, but he couldn't. He straightened, turned away, dropped onto the sofa in the living room. "Get me a drink."

Jack Daniel's. Served straight and served quickly.

"What about Billy?" said Jack.

"What are you writing?" demanded Will, trying like the pilot of a torpedo bomber to hit the target, despite the pain in his chest and the worry in his heart.

"An article. But I haven't given up military secrets, Dad."

"No," said Sullivan, who by now was waving Dowd's telegram at him. "But it looks as if you were getting ready to."

"Is it about Station Hypo and the Jap code?" asked his father.

"The world knows already. I'm just giving them the full story."

"You fool," said Sullivan.

"Quiet," said Will. Then he took a long swallow of bourbon and felt the warmth light up his chest. "Jack, if you put your name on an article, you'll be in jail tomorrow. You'll be hurting the country and yourself, too."

"That's what you told me about the Dory Miller piece, too. You people don't want a free press. You just want mouthpieces."

"For months we've had one advantage—we could read the Jap code. That cat may be out of the bag now, but don't make it any harder to catch her."

"But—"

"This isn't about your windbag notions of a free press. It's about doing the right thing in a war. . . . Now I'll trouble you two to take me to the hospital."

The next day another telegram arrived from Harry Dowd: LOUSY STORY. NO DETAIL. NO SCOOP. EXPECT TO BE RECALLED.

Jack had done it again. He had backed away from a big story. It was the least he could do to ease his father's mind and maybe help his heart, which, from everything the navy docs could tell, wasn't in very good shape.

Jack had caved in so often that he was beginning to feel like a sandhill.

But the next day, another telegram from Harry Dowd made him glad he had listened to his father: AUTHOR OF DAILY NEWS PIECE IN TROUBLE FOR DIVULGING SECRET. APS GLAD YOU SAT ON ANY INSIDE INFO.

Betty Merritt had been invited to Stafford Hall for a June weekend with her future in-laws.

While Maureen rode out with old Abraham, Betty, Jane, and Grandmother Julia spent Sunday afternoon studying the bridal magazines that Julia had been collecting since she heard that there was going to be a wedding. They sat on the veranda, looking down the row of sycamores that had been growing for over two centuries, while Katherine stood on the lawn practicing her new passion—the repeating golf swing.

"Now, darling," Julia was saying, "you must have the wedding right here."

"I think my parents would like to do it in Boston," said Betty.

"It's the bride's choice." Katherine looked up from a chip shot. "As soon as the navy says Tommy can get married, she should go to wherever he is and marry him."

Julia sipped tea and made a face. "But that's so untraditional, dear."

"We're at war." Katherine took a swing. "Priorities change."

"They sure do," said Jane, "kicking the wives out of Hawaii the way they did."

At the far end of the sycamores, something flashed—sunlight on a chrome bumper—and a big black government Oldsmobile growled down the drive.

"Oh, Lord," said Jane softly.

"Oh, Jesus," said Katherine when two uniforms stepped out of the car. One was a captain, the other a chaplain.

Betty thought, *Not Tommy. Not my Tommy.*

Maureen came galloping into the front yard, reined in her

horse, saw the two solemn faces. "Oh, Jesus. Not Billy. Not my Billy."

And for Jane Lord Stafford, it didn't matter. Someone was gone.

xi
A Scoop

From his room on Hospital Point, Will Stafford could look out on Battleship Row and the submarine pens. But he preferred looking at the faces of the two sons who had come to visit him.

He did his best to seem like the old navy boxer, ready to answer the bell. But all the fight had gone out of him. "What are you boys doing to celebrate the end of Tommy's first patrol?"

Tom and Jack looked at each other. As boys, Melon had called his serious little brother Smiley. They had been close-in-age rivals who never got along, and they had grown into cordial siblings who never hung out. The idea of hanging out together in blacked-out Honolulu struck them both as pretty funny.

"Some of the guys are getting together at the Royal Hawaiian for a celebration," said Tom.

"Good. You should celebrate with your shipmates," said Will. "And show Mr. Correspondent here how we treat our submariners. It might make a good recruiting story."

"But with Billy—"

"You can't sit here and look at me," said Will. "They're wheeling me down to Halsey's room. He'll scratch and I'll wheeze, and if Ray Spruance comes by, we'll tell him how smart he was not to go after the Jap battleships at night. He knew when to hit and when to run, like a good boxer."

"Can I quote you, Dad?" asked Jack.

"Forget about quoting me. Go have some fun, the both of you."

"You're right," said Jack, keeping up the appearance of hope. "When they find Billy, he'll be mad if he thinks we weren't drinkin' all we could on his behalf."

As soon as his two handsome sons went past the nurses' station, Will Stafford let go again. It was the third time that day that he cried. He'd stopped trying to control it. Neither tradition nor regulation said anything about a father's grief.

Barbed wire on Waikiki Beach.

That was a sight that was hard to forget.

If the Japs decided to take the Royal Hawaiian Hotel, they'd have to fight their way past beachcombers at the waterline and sailors smooching nurses on the sand. Then they'd face barbed wire strung on fence posts ten feet high and, behind it—defending their turf from Adirondack chairs, throwing Primo bottles, and fighting like maniacs—a lot of submariners who'd finally gotten a few days of liberty.

Of all the dirty, dangerous, high-pressure jobs in the navy, submarine service was the worst. Men who were willing to endure cramped quarters, long sunless patrols, and almost certain death if their vessels were sunk deserved the best R&R they could get.

That meant the Royal Hawaiian Hotel.

There were no more tourists, so the navy had taken over the grandiose pink edifice that looked more like a bashaw's castle than a Polynesian vision of paradise. It was now the R&R annex to the submarine base at Pearl Harbor. Suites that had once cost fifty dollars a night rented for twenty-five cents. And the magnificent dining room, where black tie had been de rigueur for dinner, was now a good place for a hamburger and a beer with an ocean view. It was such a good spot that officers were seen to mingle there with their men, maintaining the democratic tradition of the submarine fleet.

Twilight still glowed, so the blackout curtains were open and a nice breeze fluttered through the potted palms.

Tom found Larry Steinberg and six other officers sitting together. Some were from the *Nautilus,* some not, but it was a fine, friendly group, and before long, Tom and his reporter brother were downing bottles of Primo with the rest of them.

Women, of course, were in short supply, so the table in the middle of the room, where five nurses from the naval hospital sat with three officers, was drawing plenty of sidelong glances. And sitting among the women was Lieutenant Commander Walter Sullivan.

Jack gave him one of those smart-ass winks and got back to his new friends. He raised his beer, "To the men of the *Nautilus*, who sank an aircraft carrier."

Larry Steinberg raised his, "To the Mark XIV torpedo, which leaves the issue in doubt."

"What?" Jack's antenna turned quickly toward a new signal.

"Are you having trouble with the Mark XIV, too?" asked a lieutenant named Chase, just back from a war patrol.

"Isn't everyone?" said Steinberg.

"You saw the fires jump on that carrier," said Tom. "So did I."

"She'd been burning for over three hours," said Steinberg. "And what about the fish that wouldn't fire out of tube one? And the number nine, running hot in the tube?"

Tom took a swallow of beer. "The fish we fired at *Soryu* went off."

"Then why didn't the sonar operator report it?"

"Captain's visual sighting supersedes it," snapped Tom. "They're recommending the captain for a Navy Cross, and I say he deserves it."

"It was a balls-out attack, no question about it, but the torpedo was a fuckin' dud, I'm telling you."

It was dark enough that they needed lights now, so the waiters were closing the blackout curtains, and the room was getting as hot as the talk.

"This argument sounds familiar, guys," said Chase. "We had to put six torpedoes into one freighter to put her down. A fuckin' old rust bucket."

"Wait a minute here." Jack took a long swallow of beer and hoped that no one saw the wheels turning. "Are you guys saying the navy's sending you out on patrol with torpedoes that don't work?"

"That's what I'm saying," said Chase. "I've seen it with my own two eyes."

"Why are you saying *anything* to this guy?" Lieutenant Commander Walter Sullivan, his face redder than usual, stood over their table.

Jack did not look up. "Sully, if I was sitting at one of the only tables in Hawaii where there were ladies, I wouldn't be wasting my time with . . . me."

Sullivan ignored Jack. "Whatever you guys say to this snoop will end up in the newspapers."

"That might not be a bad idea," said Steinberg.

"He almost blew the cover on major intelligence," said Sullivan, "just to get a story."

"You what?" said Tom.

"I'll tell you later."

"Naw," said Sullivan. "Why don't you tell us now?" His voice was growing louder and the room was growing quieter. "Why don't you tell all the men in here how you'd be happy to take away the best advantage we have—knowledge of the Jap code—just so you can get your story in the newspapers."

"Why don't you shout it a little louder," said Jack. "I think there were two or three Japs back in Tokyo who didn't hear you."

Jack was not surprised that Sullivan was a mean drunk. What was worse, he was a mean drunk who kept himself in shape: twenty minutes a day on the heavy bag, twenty on the speed bag, and the rest of the day just being a nasty asshole.

No one gave Jack a chance when Sullivan grabbed him by the collar and pulled him to his feet.

Jack had been a mediocre football player at Harvard, a terror on the tackling dummy, but with feet like lead. And he'd never hit anyone except his brothers with his fists.

Tommy had been an Academy boxer, like his father. But he had no intention of striking a lieutenant commander. "Excuse me, sir—"

"Fuck you," said Sullivan.

"That's a helluva way to talk your CO's son," said Jack with a smile.

"My CO's bein' shipped home with a bum ticker, so fuck the both of you."

Tommy now realized why Jack was so calm: he had a hand behind his back, and it was wrapped around the neck of an empty beer bottle.

That was no good, thought Tom, so he made a grab for his brother, and Sullivan whacked him with a backhander that bounced him off a banquette and onto the floor. Then Sullivan made a fist and nailed Jack right in the nose.

A little voice told Tommy he would never make admiral if he struck a superior officer. But another little voice said to hell with tradition and regulation; no one pushed a Stafford around.

So he delivered a shot into Sullivan's jaw that didn't even stagger the big Irishman. At the same moment, one of Sullivan's friends came flying over the next table, only to be met by Jack Stafford's fist in the belly.

And then war broke out, right there in the Royal Hawaiian Hotel.

A clump of submariners plowed into each other like rugby players. In one giant scrum this mass of khakis and whites went lurching through the dining room, upending tables, breaking glasses, spilling hamburgers and beers, and with a great tearing sound, fell through the blackout curtains and into the gardens.

Like a beacon, a huge shaft of light shot into the Waikiki darkness. And from up and down the beach, the whistles of the Civil Defense workers, the blackout police, joined the screeching whistles of the Shore Patrol.

"Cheese it," shouted someone. "Shore Patrol."

And the scrum broke up, just as the lights went out in the dining room and everything was plunged into darkness again.

Tommy made it home to the Aiea Heights before curfew.

Jack stayed in Honolulu and introduced Lieutenants Steinberg and Chase to the joys of Queen Loretta's.

Around eight the next morning, Tom was awakened by the clatter of a typewriter. He staggered out to the dining room, where Jack sat, in nothing but boxer shorts and black eyes, pounding out a story.

"Bad enough you get me into a brawl with a superior officer. Now you wake me up on my one day of liberty?"

Jack pulled the last sheet of paper out of the typewriter. "Read it."

Over the years, Jack had never invited Tom to read anything he'd written. After a few lines, Tom was wishing he hadn't been trusted with this: fifteen hundred words on the Mark XIV torpedo: ". . . waste of taxpayers' money . . . throwing away the lives of brave men . . . torpedo may not have exploded against the Japanese carrier . . . if the Bureau of Ordnance buries its head in the sand . . ." and so on.

"Jack, this'll never get past the censor."

"I have a friend in the censorship office. I introduced him to Queen Loretta last week. He thinks I'm a swell guy."

"But the Staffords have a name in the navy, Jack. This article—"

"You were out there. What do you *really* think?"

"I don't think we should be airing our dirty laundry."

Jack lit a cigarette. "I've hidden a lot of it in the last six months. With some of it, I was glad. Sometimes you stay on the inside. But sometimes you don't. This story goes public."

But the story came back: "Rejected for transmission." No military censor was about to let Jack Stafford tell the Japs that American subs were shooting blanks.

A week later, Jack said good-bye to his father in the bright sunshine by the submarine pens. The *Nautilus* was already gone, and Will was going home. Jack put an envelope in his father's hands. "Read this, will you? And see what you can do with it."

"Can't stop boat rockin', can you?"

"Will you just read the damn thing, Dad?"

"I don't need to. Tommy told me what's in it."

"Hey, Captain," said Juan. "Launch is ready. We got to go."

Jack shook his head. "I'm just trying to make a difference, Dad."

"I don't need to read it, Jack, because I think you're right. But give it to me anyway, and I'll see what I can do."

Jack had not expected those words to hit him the way that they did. He fought the impulse to throw his arms around his father. There were a lot of other men watching and embraces were . . . What the hell. He did it, and he was glad, but saddened to feel how much weight the old man had lost. "You put up with a lot from me, Dad. Thanks."

"Just remember—"

"What's good for the U.S. Navy is good for the U.S.A.?"

"Sometimes . . . and what's good for the U.S.A. is good for the U.S. Navy."

A few weeks later Maureen Stafford was taking dictation, with both feet planted firmly on the floor.

Katherine, who had lived through such grief herself, had said that the best way to fight it was to get back to work, get out with people as soon as she could. But why, wondered Maureen, did "people" have to mean Captain Dennis Dawson?

Suddenly the permanent leer on Dawson's face turned a kind of pukish yellow. He came to attention and saluted.

"You son of a bitch." A tall man with four gold stripes on his arm stalked into the office. He had a widow's peak, a cleft chin, and a scowl that could stop a bullet: Admiral Ernest J. King, once called the most even-tempered man in the navy—*always* in a rage.

He flung a pile of papers at Dawson. "This almost made it into the newspapers."

Dawson glanced at it, his hands shaking. "Why, those damn sub jockeys—"

"No," said King. "It's you piss-poor bureaucrats. Do you know that after that stupid letter you sent, they started test-firing their own torpedoes in the Pacific?"

"No, sir."

"Well, they run ten feet too goddamn deep! Just like Lockwood said in his letters . . . just like it says here."

Dawson couldn't have looked any worse, so Maureen stopped looking at him and just enjoyed the sound of his stammer.

"Wh-what would you like me to do, sir?" asked Dawson.

"Pack. You have a new command. Minesweeper. Reykjavik, Iceland."

And Maureen smiled for the first time since she'd heard the terrible news. She thought her father-in-law might smile, too, because he had set this up, with the help of his own father's connection to King . . . and his son's good writing.

"I . . . I believe in that torpedo, sir," Dawson said, "and so do a lot of people in BuOrd."

"Spoken like the ass-coverer you are. Well, tell the other ass-coverers I want more tests. By July first, I want instructions, corrections, and anything else we can radio to those subs out there. Or I might print this fuckin' article myself."

Dawson's body almost melted under the heat of King's anger and profanity.

Now the admiral turned to Maureen. "I'm sorry for the bad language, Miss—"

"Mrs. Maureen Stafford."

King picked up the article and pointed to the byline on the top sheet.

"My brother-in-law. Wiseacre Jack."

"Is the submariner your husband . . . or the missing flier?"

"The flier."

"Well, they're all fine men, and if you ever need a shoulder to cry on . . ."

xii
Grand Horrors and Private Passings

Tommy and Jack did not see each other again during the war.

Jack sailed again aboard the *Enterprise* to a place called Guadalcanal and some of the most ferocious land and sea fighting in history. In 1944 he published a book called *Dauntless*, about the VS-6 squadron, halved at Midway and halved again at Guadalcanal. Warner Bros. made it into a movie and Jack was on his way.

Tom was finally able to get married just before he took command of his own boat. And he was on his way, too.

The submarine service would prove the most dangerous branch of the navy, to both the enemy and the submariners themselves. With improved torpedoes, submarines would sink more enemy shipping than surface ships and naval aviation combined, but almost a quarter of the submariners who sailed out would never come home. Tom would be one of the lucky ones, and his combat bravery would win him the Navy Cross.

Will Stafford took a Navy Department desk job in the new five-sided building which had risen beside the Potomac.

But not even grandsons could heal the heart broken in June of 1942. It jumped an extra beat every time a car pulled up at Stafford Hall, because more bad news could come at any time. He died about three months after his father, which was merciful to his father, at least.

Jane found him in the red study at Stafford Hall. He had been looking at old photographs—of their courtship, of his boys, of Academy moments and the cruise of the Great White Fleet. On the floor was a photograph of American and Japanese officers posed under a battleship's gun. Ensign Will Stafford sat cross-legged in the front row, his arms linked with those of a Japanese ensign.

The inscription on the photograph read, "Know your enemy . . . and make him your friend. Your friend, Hiroaki."

CHAPTER EIGHT

Melon and Smiley, Sitting on a Bench

October 13

The call came to Susan at seven o'clock. She was just getting ready for her morning run.

It was Steve Stafford, sounding as excited as a kid who'd just gotten tickets to a big rock concert. "Get your video camera. We've got nice weather and an old man who's ready to talk to his brother."

"The admiral liked Jack's book?"

"He said Jack was honest. He didn't like what Jack wrote about his private life, but—"

"Where do you suppose Jack got all that?"

"The admiral thinks it came from their aunt Katherine, the stories about the cross-country train ride and all that."

"I can imagine. He's pretty straight," said Susan.

"What the admiral liked was what he read between the lines."

"What was that?"

"How much Jack loved their brother Billy."

Susan said, "I think he loves his brother Tom, too."

There was silence at the other end of the line, and Steve's voice came back, filled with emotion. "This morning, I called Jack . . . told him what the admiral said. And he told me he loved my father, too, and he was dedicating the book to him."

He had opened the door, so she stepped in. "How much do you know about your father?"

"Enough that I came to the Academy, like him. Enough to know he died bravely."

"Is that all?"

"For now, it's enough. I have to make some phone calls so that you can set up your camera on the Academy grounds. I'll see you this afternoon." He paused, and she could hear him thinking something over on the other end of the line. "Maybe we'll both get some answers."

About forty minutes later, Susan made her daily jogging stop at Stafford's Fine Folly.

It didn't take much of an act of imagination to see it as a hotel. It took a little bit more to see Tom and Betty Stafford sneaking in for some premarital passion.

"The Shank sisters divided the house among fifteen cousins." Oliver Parrish materialized beside her. Where he'd come from, she couldn't tell, although she suspected the silent approach came from his SEAL training. "And somehow, that admiral bastard has one talk with some old Defense Department hack and he pulls them all together."

"Good morning to you, too," she said. "Have you been waiting for me to run by?"

"I hoped you might." Oliver looked up at the house. "We can't match a preemptive bid of four million. Neither can old Jack, no matter how much he gets for his book."

Oliver was dressed in his windbreaker and pleated khaki trousers.

"More golf?" she asked. "Don't you ever work?"

"Golf relaxes me. And today, that's what I need . . . But first, want to see Rebecca? See her without worrying about being discovered?"

"Sure."

In a few minutes, they were inside the Fine Folly, in the library.

"This was going to be my office." Oliver took a seven iron from the golf bag in the corner. "I even started setting it up, which I shouldn't have. Now Rebecca goes back to my office in Washington, and the admiral gets to use this house to write his articles about the next fancy weapons system. Just what the world needs."

Susan studied the face of the portrait. Rebecca wore a green dress, and her mangled right hand was hidden in one of its folds, but her look was hard and defiant. It was a look she had passed on to this distant nephew, and Susan suspected that there was a mangled part of him, too, also hidden somewhere.

"The admiral and Jack are going to talk today," said Susan, "on camera, in the yard. Why don't you come? You might learn something."

"There's nothing I can learn from those two."

"Well, maybe you can teach me something."

Oliver offered her the golf club. "How about letting me teach you how to swing a seven iron?"

She had to laugh. "You mean, where you put your arms around mine to show me how it's done? I don't think I'm quite ready for that."

"Oh, well"—Oliver shrugged—"it's been a bad week. Even my best come-on isn't working."

"Not with me, anyway. But what did you mean the other day, about Jack not doing his job and you ending up in Vietnam, and all that stuff about 'thirty years too late'?"

"I told you, it's been a bad week. I shouldn't have said any of that."

"Why not?"

"I just shouldn't have. That's all." And that angry look came into his eyes again. He blinked once and the anger disappeared so quickly that Susan wondered if she had imagined it.

It would have been better if she had seen it clearly. Then she might not have kept at it. "You sounded really bitter about Jack and the admiral both."

"I *am* bitter." The anger snapped back in his eyes and his voice. "I'm bitter that I'm not going to get this house. I'm bitter that I've failed in three marriages." Oliver picked up his golf bag. "But every man's his own master, and any mistakes I made were my own. The one place I never make a mistake is on the golf course. If my round ends in time, I might come by and see those two old hypocrites."

Susan couldn't believe how quickly this interview came about.

But the admiral was a man of his word. So now here they were, Jack and his brother—Melon and Smiley—sitting on a bench in the middle of the Academy yard.

She hooked each of them with a lavalier lapel-pin mike and angled the tripod so that she could pan back and forth.

The admiral straightened his sport coat and chatted with Steve and the Academy's public affairs officer. Jack just sat with his legs crossed and watched the midshipmen go by.

That meant both of them were nervous, because the admiral didn't go in for much small talk, and Jack was always making with the jokes.

Susan framed a nice two-shot of the brothers sitting in the cool shade, with Bancroft Hall in the background. "I'm ready whenever you are."

And it began.

Jack approached his brother cautiously, with easy questions about Tom's days at the Academy and in World War II, about his command of a submarine during the Cuban Missile Crisis, about his candidate-screening interview with Hyman Rickover, when he joined the nuclear submarine navy.

Betty stood near Susan and listened with all the attention of someone who had never heard the story before. Juan sat on a nearby bench and read a newspaper. After a time, Jack stopped to study his notes. The admiral looked at his watch.

Then Jack said, "What I'm really interested in is Vietnam."

"We all had a role in Vietnam."

It felt to Susan as if a cold wind had just kicked up off the river. But she knew that the chill was coming from those two old men, each looking ten years younger than he was, each highly accomplished, each completely convinced that he had done the right thing in the war that never went away.

Jack uncrossed and recrossed his legs.

The admiral squared his jaw.

Jack put down his notebook. He didn't need notes now.

Susan locked down the camera and stepped out from behind it, so that she could watch without the viewfinder in the way.

This was it. But for several seconds neither of them spoke.

Surprisingly, the admiral cracked first. "You know, I really didn't have much to do with Vietnam. In the summer of 1964, I went to work for the assistant CNO for submarine warfare, Op 02. But that summer, Op 03—that's surface warfare—was developing new ASW strategies."

"Come on, Tom, you're blinding us with these abbreviations. ASW—antisubmarine warfare. Make that the last one."

The admiral reddened a bit, but the anger passed, as if he knew he was on camera and couldn't stalk off just because his brother was belittling him. "All right. The surface warfare boys wanted an Op 02 liaison, so I was shifted for eight weeks in 1964."

"Eight pretty hot weeks," Jack said. "Can you tell me about Operation DeSoto?"

There was a long pause, as if the admiral was thinking this over, preparing a defense, perhaps. Then he said condescendingly, "You need a little background, first."

"All right. But don't go back too far. Let's pick up the story after Vietnam's been ruled by the French, seized by the Japanese, and restored to the French, who are finally chased out by Ho Chi Minh and his—"

"—Communists," said the admiral. "As soon as they set themselves up in the north, people started fleeing south to freedom. That's how it always worked with Communists. There was never any compromising with Communist sons of bitches. That's why we finally got smart and spent them into oblivion under Reagan."

Susan sensed movement behind her. Steve was stepping a little closer. Betty was making a small gesture with her hand: calm down, Tom.

The admiral nodded and lowered his voice. "Kennedy understood Communists, too. There were still only seven hundred advisers in Vietnam in his first year as president. There were fifteen thousand when he was killed."

"Some people say he was getting ready to bring them all home."

"He was a cold warrior. And so were the guys around him. They're the guys Johnson inherited, along with a very sticky situation."

"Which we proceeded to make stickier."

The admiral aimed a finger at Jack. "I warned you, Jack. If you're going to pull your wise-ass crap in front of this camera—"

"Sorry." Jack leaned back. "Were you ever in Vietnam?"

"No. My job was tracking Russian submarines. That was our big worry then. Now it's just one of many. But you're right when you say that I was in Op 03 during a very hot time."

"The time of the Tonkin Gulf," said Jack, leading him.

The admiral simply nodded.

Jack waited a moment for more of a response, and when none came, he led a bit more. "The time of Operation DeSoto and Op Plan 34A?"

But the admiral would not follow where Jack was trying to take him. He simply leaned back and stroked his chin, like a professor. "The historical facts of that whole incident are well known today, Jack."

Maybe it was the irritating condescension in the admiral's tone, or the frustration of waiting so long for this moment, but Jack could not restrain his sarcasm. "You may be a submariner, Tom, but you can blow up a smoke screen as well as any destroyer captain who ever drew breath. What's known is that the whole incident was a giant lie, a lie that got us so deep into that war that we thought we'd never get out."

"I warned you, Jack. If you want me to walk off, keep talking like this." The admiral drummed his fingers on his knees for a few moments. "What the evidence indicated then does not correspond to what we know now."

And the pause between them was like winter.

Finally Jack said, "Sorry . . . tell me about Operation DeSoto. How did it relate to all this?"

The admiral chewed on his cheek, as if to control his anger. "Why are you driving so hard at this, Jack?"

"Because I can't decide what to tell about this story, and"—Jack glanced now at Steve—"about the things that came after it."

"Our Jimmy's death? That had nothing to do with the Gulf of Tonkin."

"You know," said Jack, "I covered up the truth myself back then, but now I'm close to revealing it."

"The truth is simple. We thought we were hit, and we hit back."

"We were misled—misled at Tonkin and a thousand times before and after. And all the lies led to Jimmy's death."

The admiral shot a glance at his grandson. "What is Steve supposed to think of that?"

"He may want to know."

The admiral grabbed his little microphone and ripped it off his lapel. "That does it. I taught my son the same thing our father taught us: you do your job, and you do it with honor."

"What's good for the U.S. Navy is good for the U.S.A.?"

"Damn right." And the admiral stalked off camera. He grabbed his wife by the arm and told Juan to follow.

"Wait a minute, Juan," said Jack.

"Huh?"

"I'd like to talk to you."

"Me . . . but I—"

And Betty took Juan by the arm. "Come on, Juan. I'll help you."

"This I have to see," said the admiral.

"Me, too," muttered Oliver Parrish, who had once again materialized beside Susan.

The story that Juan told and Betty embellished was much the way Jack had already written it.

The Stafford Story

BOOK NINE

The Limits of Power

August 1964

Captain Tom Stafford wanted air conditioning. Betty said it would be a sacrilege in the old house on the Patuxent. Their ancestors had survived without buzzing window units spoiling the dense, liquid silence of their summer afternoons. As long as the sycamores shaded the house and the evening breeze fluttered up from the river, Betty and Tom and the Stafford boys could survive, too.

Of course, the August heat didn't bother the three boys out on the back lawn: Her son Jimmy and his friend Ollie Parrish were two wiry nineteen-year-olds with crew cuts and good grades, good athletes going into their second year at the Naval Academy. Her son Willie was no slouch either, even if he *had* been listening to too much of that English rock and roll. He had just finished his second year at Columbia, and had come home, as the captain said, with more than his share of notions.

The boys were having a fine time on the new putting green—laid out and hand-built by the Staffords, father and sons—because no matter what notions any of them had, they all loved golf.

And Betty loved the simplicity of playing Mom with lemonade and cookies, because little else was simple with college-age sons.

"Miz Betty! Miz Betty!" cried Juan from inside the house. "Telephone call. That damn Jack. He callin' from New York."

Betty cursed under her breath, because with Jack, nothing was simple.

Juan put his hand over the mouthpiece. "He a nosy bastard. He start askin' me all damn question."

She took the receiver. "Jack?"

"Is this darling Betty?"

"When you call me darling Betty, I know you're looking for something."

"I'm looking for your darling husband, Pentagon source extraordinaire."

"If he knew you called him that, he'd never take your calls."

"Well, ask him if he'll take this one."

"He's not here. He was called in to Washington."

"But it's a Sunday."

"What's this about, Jack?"

"The Pentagon just issued a vague press release about an American destroyer in the South China Sea being attacked by enemy patrol craft."

"Tom works for the assistant CNO for submarine warfare. That's Op 02. Destroyers are Op 03, surface warfare."

"Come on, Betty. I was born at night, but it wasn't last night. Tom's the Op 02 liaison officer attached to Op 03, for God's sake. He's helping their antisubmarine warfare techniques, and with his nose for what's going on—"

"Jack . . . I do not divulge my husband's secrets."

There was a long pause and then Jack said, "You know, Betty, sometimes I wish I saw you first."

"I would have run the other way, darling Jack."

That night Betty did not ask her husband anything specific, only mentioned that Jack had called.

"Snooping?"

"He was asking about a press release."

Tom sipped his bourbon on the rocks and looked out at the river.

"Tom, what happened?" She would not have asked that much, except the boys had gone upstairs.

"Three North Vietnamese PT boats attacked a destroyer, the *Maddox*, in the Tonkin Gulf," he said. "Fired machine guns, torpedoes. I guess we have photographic evidence . . . bullets, too. The captain called in an air strike from the carrier *Ticonderoga*."

"What was the destroyer doing there?"

Tom looked into his coffee cup and said, "Minding its own business."

This, of course, was a lie. The *Maddox* had been on something called a DeSoto patrol.

DeSoto was a naval intelligence gathering mission. A van loaded with sophisticated electronic surveillance equipment had been put aboard the *Maddox*, which was then ordered to steam close to the coast. Her mission: to play radar tag with the North Vietnamese, duping them into turning on their newly installed radar, so that she could plot the installation sites for future reference.

This, thought Tom Stafford, was simply prudent. American planes were already flying covert air strikes into Laos. It was only a matter of time before they struck North Vietnam. And under something called Op Plan 34A, the CIA was training South Vietnamese commandos who raided northern coastal installations by sea. Things were heating up.

According to Tom's friend Lloyd Shank, Defense Department staffer, the administration had been working up a resolution to permit the president to introduce ground troops into any Southeast Asian country where he deemed there was a Communist threat; and planners for the Joint Chiefs of Staff had been ordered to select targets for bombing.

But President Johnson had surprised a lot of people that day by not responding militarily to the attack on the destroyer. As Lloyd Shank explained, Johnson did not think there was sufficient provocation for an air strike. So he ordered a second destroyer, the *Turner Joy*, to enter the same waters with *Maddox,* "just to stir things up a little more."

And that was when all hell broke loose . . . or seemed to.

ii
A Phone Call

It was about 0950 the next morning when a "Flash Precedence" message arrived in the Navy Command Center, on the fourth deck of the Pentagon: the destroyers *Maddox* and *Turner Joy* were under attack and calling in air cover from the *Ticonderoga*.

At 1100, Defense Secretary McNamara called the Joint Chiefs together, along with National Security Adviser McGeorge Bundy and Secretary of State Dean Rusk.

Tom, of course, was not in this particular loop. But his brother Jack was right. He had a nose for what was going on, along with an unimpeachable source in Lloyd Shank.

And what was going on sounded frantic: Thunderstorms were swirling through the Tonkin Gulf that night, making visibility difficult and stirring the seas so high that the little destroyers rolled like the tin cans they were nicknamed for. The North Vietnamese PT boats were firing torpedoes. The American destroyers were firing back. The sonar men were tracking enemy torpedoes from every direction. But there was not a single hit on the madly maneuvering destroyers, or on the squadron of A-4 Skyhawks and Crusaders that provided air support, firing rockets at anything that looked even remotely like a North Vietnamese PT boat.

Meanwhile, McNamara, Bundy, and Rusk, all more grim-faced than usual, left the Pentagon and headed for a National Security Council meeting at the White House. And orders rippled through the Joint Chiefs' command staff: "Select North Vietnamese targets for air reprisals."

Tom saw these orders channeled through to Op 03 and felt his stomach turn over. It was nothing like the experience of taking a submarine to a blockade station off Cuba in October of 1962. But it seemed like they were moving closer to war. And to a man with sons—even a military man, *especially* a military man—the approach of war was something to make a stomach turn over, at least once.

Then Tom reminded himself that he was a professional, and his stomach was just empty. It had been a long morning. Time for lunch.

In the five-acre park in the center of the five-sided building, officers of every stripe and every service were hurrying back and forth, civilians, too. No one ambled, meandered, or simply strolled at the Pentagon. The taxpayers' time clock was ticking every second of the day and night, and a crisp step was the order of march, even between the water cooler and the men's room.

Tom took a little table in the shade and opened his brown bag. It was cheaper than eating in the mess, and after so many years when he was at sea, Betty liked sending him off every morning with a little bag and an extra snack for the long drive home. This afternoon's menu: tuna salad on white, two peaches, and coffee from the vending machine. And ten minutes to himself, just to try to make sense of what was happening.

This might be a bloody nose for Ho Chi Minh. Or it might be something more. No one believed that, of course, but why had they prepared that resolution, with its talk of ground troops? And why, in June, had they decided to postpone a vote on it?

About a month earlier, over a bottle of bourbon, two Civil War enthusiasts had spent an hour talking about Lloyd Shank's great-uncle Gabriel at Gettysburg. Then the talk had moved to another civil war, and Lloyd had shown Tom the list of talking points that had been prepared for the unlucky Defense Department official who would defend the resolution before Congress.

A potential question: *Does this resolution imply a blank check for the president to go to war over Southeast Asia?*

A good answer: *{It} will indeed permit selective use of force, but hostilities on a larger scale are not envisaged and, in any case, any large escalation would require a call-up of reserves and thus a further appeal to the Congress. . . .*

That kind of assurance should have made Tom feel better.

But he remembered Korea. The president had called it a police action. That police action had turned into a full-scale three-year bloodletting.

He had lost good friends in that war, some in the air over Korea, some in the accidental fire aboard the carrier USS *Essex,* that burned so fiercely it bubbled the paint on the cruisers that came in close to help. Damn but he hated half-assed wars.

He also hated the kind of second-guessing that he saw on the cables coming in that afternoon. The latest message from Captain Herrick of the *Maddox:* "Review of action makes many reported contacts and torpedoes fired appear very doubtful. Freak weather effects and overeager sonarmen may have accounted for many reports. No actual sightings by *Maddox*. Suggest complete evaluation before any further action."

Before long, the Joint Chiefs were demanding more information from Herrick. And McNamara was on the phone to CINCPAC. And Lloyd Shank was on the phone to Tom, telling him they really needed something solid from the navy on Tonkin, because the president was not waiting for confirmation. He was calling congressional leaders to the White House to give them the word: he was striking back against what he called unprovoked aggression.

Despite frantic messages—"Who are your witnesses? What is witness reliability? Most important that positive evidence substantiating type and number of attacking forces be gathered and disseminated"—Herrick could come up with nothing. And the word from the *Ticonderoga* debriefings was that the fliers had seen nothing, either.

By the time he left the office at ten o'clock that night, Tom Stafford no longer believed the second attack had happened.

It was already tomorrow morning on the other side of the world, and the retaliatory strike was just launching from the *Ticonderoga* and the *Constellation*. Tom probably had friends in some of those planes. But they were two hours from their target, another hour from preliminary reports, two hours more before they were debriefed aboard their ships.

So he decided to go home.

In the hallway, he bumped into Lloyd Shank, wearing one of his shiny brown suits and skinny brown ties. The tie was splattered with cigarette ashes and his black-framed glasses had slipped halfway down his nose, but Lloyd gave no more notice to them than he did to the saucer of baldness widening on the back of his own head. He always left the impression that he had more important things to worry about.

"So, Captain," he said, "what would Lincoln think?"

"About what?"

"Meddling in someone else's civil war? Lincoln's biggest fear was that England would meddle in ours."

"This is just a single attack."

Shank gave that cynical chuckle. "After the strike, there'll be a day for the dust to settle. Then McNamara will appear before the Foreign Relations Committee to propose the resolution."

"The one that was shelved last month?"

"Eh-yeh."

"Why?"

"Ours not to reason why, though nobody said we can't wonder a little bit. G'night, Tom."

Tom Stafford wanted sleep. This was a sure sign that he was getting old. Navy men never slept in a crisis. They kept going. That was as much a tradition in the military as it was in medicine. But he believed that a wide-awake officer was better than someone who was punch-drunk from too many four-hour sleep shifts.

He kept a room in Alexandria and often stayed there when things heated up, but he loved that long drive back to the house on the Patuxent, especially when he needed to decompress.

As he crossed the Potomac, he looked out at the Capitol dome and the monuments swimming in pools of white light. They comforted him somehow, even if Washington's advice against entangling alliances had not been heeded.

And the turn south comforted him, too, for the farther toward the Tobacco Coast he traveled, the deeper grew the embrace of the night and the calming sensation of entering the past. But the car radio kept him wired to the present. The eleven o'clock news announced that the president would be addressing the nation thirty minutes later. And cantankerous Senator Wayne Morse was complaining once more about the president's Vietnam policies, and . . .

Click. He turned off the radio.

Feel the past.

It was so much simpler. Even the past of twenty years before had been simpler. Japan had bombed American ships; the nation had mobilized.

This was different.

If we had been hit, we should hit back, or this pissant Ho Chi Minh and his Communist allies would think they could push us around.

But what about that resolution? Why had they prepared it, and prepared to present it, then changed their plans? And why were they presenting it now?

The answer, along those dark roads, was clear: *Politics.*

Requesting a war resolution was like waving a red flag. In election years, presidents wanted to promise that American boys would not spill their blood on foreign soil. So the administration had decided to wait until after the election.

Then came this business in the Tonkin Gulf.

The same cynicism that had led them to shelve the resolution now led them to revive it. A president should not wave a red flag. Bloody shirts were a different matter. Johnson would tell the country that this attack was a blight on our national honor, and national honor was the bloodiest shirt of them all. And he would prove that he was as tough on communism as Barry Goldwater, his Republican opponent.

As he drove under the sycamores and pulled the car up to the front of the house, Tom Stafford was beginning to think that the real blight on our honor was the manipulation of this event for . . . *politics*.

Betty's light was out, but Juan was awake and waiting for him. He was more than a houseboy. He was an old friend who knew exactly what Tom needed—a tall bourbon and water. "Your brother call. Askin' more damn questions. What's goin' on?"

"Let's find out." It was eleven-thirty. Tom went into the front room and turned on the television.

And there was the great basset-hound face of Lyndon Johnson—long snout, drooping jowls, ears that seemed to flap when he moved his head. Then that honey-slow Texas drawl. . . .

"My fella Americans . . . Aggression by terror against the peaceful villages of South Vietnam has now been joined by open aggression on the high seas against the United States of America."

Tom took a long swallow of bourbon.

"Hi, Dad." It was Jimmy, wearing pajama bottoms and a T-shirt.

"What's goin' on?" Ollie Parrish staggered in after him, an overnight guest with an early tee time.

Tom gestured at the television screen.

Johnson was saying, "Repeated acts of violence against the armed forces of the United States must be met not only with an alert defense but with a positive reply. That reply is being given as I speak to you tonight."

"Wow." Jimmy slipped onto the floor in front of the television set.

"Holy shit," said Juan.

"Holy shit, indeed," said Willie, coming into the room.

"Don't swear just because Juan does." Tom drained his glass.

"We're probably hitting oil facilities in the city of Vinh . . . PT boat bases on the Vietnamese coast."

"Holy shit again," said Ollie.

"A real air strike?" said Jimmy. The surprise in his voice was fading behind the excitement that rose in too many young men when a war was starting.

"Real bombs. Real planes. Real pilots," said Tom.

All Juan could say was, "Oh, shit. Oh, shit. Shit. Shit."

"Pour yourself a drink, Juan, and shut up," said Tom. "While you're at it, give me a refill."

Bourbon sloshed into two glasses now.

Johnson was saying that our response was limited and fitting: "We Americans know, although others seem to forget, the risks of spreading conflict. We seek no wider war."

"War?" Betty had come sleepily downstairs in her robe.

"Not a war, Mom," said Jimmy. "Just a little retaliation." And he filled her in on everything in half a minute.

She squinted at him, sitting there on the floor with his legs crossed, looking like a ten-year-old. "This has you all excited, doesn't it? Our little navy boy just finished with his first summer cruise aboard a carrier, and now he thinks he knows it all."

"I've seen our air power, Mom."

"That's right, Mrs. Stafford," said Ollie. "There's no reason for us to be frightened by these North Vietnamese."

"Of course not," said Tom, and he drained his second drink.

On the screen, David Brinkley was recapping the president's speech.

"My only regret," said Jimmy, "is that it'll all be over before I'm out of the Academy." Then he got up and kissed his mother. "Good night."

"*My* only regret," said Willie, "is that Dad won't be able to play golf with us tomorrow. I always win when Dad's my partner."

After all the boys had gone back to bed, Betty looked at her husband. "Will it? Will it be over before Jimmy's out of the Academy?"

"This is a one-time thing." He said it, and he hoped it, despite what he'd heard.

"From New York! It's *The Tonight Show Starring Johnny Carson.* Johnny's guests tonight are Orson Bean, Hermione Gingold, Steve

Lawrence and Eydie Gormé, with Skitch Henderson and the NBC Orchestra, and me, I'm Ed McMahon. And now, heeeeere's Johnny!"

Betty turned down the television. "Can you guarantee it?"

"I can't guarantee anything, Betty. But this is nothing compared to the Cuban Missile Crisis."

Betty knelt beside her husband in his big easy chair. "Remember what I said to you in San Francisco, before you headed for Pearl Harbor?"

He gave her a little smile. "You mean, 'Let's do it by the window, so we can look out at the city?'"

"Afterward . . . I asked you to do the job, so that when we had sons, they'd never have to leave their wives, or their mothers, like that."

He reached out and ran a hand through her hair, through the gray streaks working their way into the strawberry blond. "Don't worry."

"Are you coming upstairs?"

"In a bit."

She went to bed, and a moment later Juan came back with the bottle of bourbon and an ice bucket.

"You want another one, Juan?"

"Why the hell not? I stay up and watch that Johnny Carson with you. He funny damn bastard."

When Tom awoke, the national anthem was playing over an American flag.

Then sign-off. High-pitched electric noise. Snow on the screen.

The bourbon bottle was on the coffee table, half empty. That meant they'd be finding Juan's head in the toilet by dawn.

Tom trickled a little more bourbon into his glass and looked at his watch: 0110. Early afternoon in the Tonkin Gulf. He went into the old, red-painted study, opened the closet with the secret panel, fumbled about for the phone book that contained the number of the Navy Command Center at the Pentagon, and placed a call.

It was about then that Juan decided to get up, because his little room off the kitchen was spinning. He hoped it might settle down if he went for a walk. But the kitchen was spinning, too, and the dining room was going around so fast, he had to sit down before he fell down. So he pulled out a chair and put his head on the table. Then he cursed to himself because the captain was dialing the phone in the study.

Tom's call was taken by the duty officer, an old friend named Dutton. "Tom! You should be in the rack."

"Can't . . . can't sleep."

"You don't sound too good. You, uh, you been into the barleycorn?"

"When did you ever see me drunk?" Tom snapped.

"Sorry, Captain. What can I do for you?"

"Is the raid over?"

"Latest word is that we took out ninety percent of the oil facilities at Vinh and most of the PT boat bases."

"Casualties?"

"Right now we're showing four planes down. Two pilots unaccounted for."

"Shit."

"No . . . War."

Now Tom was wide awake. And he wanted to talk. Talk to someone who understood. So he poured a bit more bourbon and called Lloyd Shank.

In the dining room, Juan wasn't really listening to the captain's conversation, but he heard every word between moans.

"You awake, Lloyd?"

"Who the hell is—"

"It's Tom. I just thought you'd want to know. Mission accomplished."

"What . . . oh, good. Good." The sleep quickly cleared from the voice on the other end of the line. "McNamara'll be in a good mood tomorrow."

"About this Foreign Relations Committee, Lloyd, will they be trouble?"

"Did you call me up to ask me that?"

"Isn't that Wayne Morse, from Oregon, on the committee?"

"Eh-yeh. And from what I've heard, he's going to fight whatever kind of resolution we go for. He's a hard case. Nobody much listens to him, though."

"Will . . . uh . . . will McNamara tell the country about DeSoto or 34A?"

"Of course not," said Shank, "especially since it looks like that first North Vietnamese attack was responding to a 34A commando raid.

They thought they were hitting back at South Vietnamese support ships. A giant case of mistaken identity."

"Will McNamara reveal how little evidence we have on the second attack?"

"McNamara told the president we'll know exactly what happened in the morning." Shank gave that little chuckle. "I shouldn't be telling you any of this, but there's no stopping it now."

"What do you mean?"

"McNamara said that in addition to air strikes, he plans to send—I think it went like this—'major U.S. reinforcements into the area. These include ships, men, and planes.' Sounds like that land war in Asia that a lot of generals have been warning us against. 'Course . . . LBJ didn't bat an eye."

"Jesus."

"This is classified, Captain. Whole conversation is classified. Like I started to say earlier tonight, 'Ours not to reason why, ours but to do and die.' Now go to bed so you can serve your country tomorrow."

Tom Stafford had just been told that he had lied to his wife. This was *not* a one-time thing. It was part of a master plan. And the American people were being kept out.

He supposed that might not be such a bad idea in a country where the president led us into war, and a few minutes later we were watching Johnny Carson play a question-answering genie called Karnak. The public didn't need to know everything. It didn't *want* to know everything. In order for nations to advance their interests, some things had to be kept secret. He'd believed that for as long as he had been in the navy.

But he had lied to his wife. He hated lying to his wife. When he couldn't tell her something, he stonewalled instead. Stonewalling she understood. Lying infuriated her. But this hadn't really been lying. He had told her what he wanted to believe himself.

For some reason, Tom's mind drifted back to a long-ago morning in Hawaii, when he had read his brother's story about Mark XIV torpedoes, and Jack had said, "Sometimes you stay on the inside. But sometimes you don't."

But Tom had taken an oath. And a Pentagon officer had just said that everything he was telling him was classified. To break his oath, or the bond of friendship with Lloyd Shank, would be against everything Tom had ever been taught, against every military instinct he possessed. You don't fuck your buddy . . . or the service. What's good for the U.S. Navy is good for the U.S.A.

But at the Academy, they taught you a code of honor. You stood for something. You didn't cheat. You didn't lie. And you didn't keep your mouth shut when you knew somebody else was lying. Well, somebody else was getting ready to tell a whopper to the Senate Foreign Relations Committee and the American people, too.

Sometimes you stay on the inside. But sometimes you don't.

If he passed information to his brother, it would be like showing a little gold dust to a prospector. Before long, there'd be holes all over the landscape.

So he picked up the phone, called the Pentagon again, got the home telephone number of Senator Wayne Morse.

He did not hear Juan moaning in the next room. The argument in his head was too loud: This is wrong. It's right. Make the call. Go to bed. Stay up and brood. Call your brother. Call the senator. Wake your wife and tell her the truth. . . . And still he twirled that Academy ring on his finger.

Make the call.

He had a picture of Wayne Morse in his mind's eye—Brylcreemed hair, all gray at the temples, little Clark Gable mustache, out of style when Gable was still alive, blue suit, perpetual scowl. Once a Republican, now a Democrat, and not particularly liked on either side of the aisle.

"Senator Morse?"

"Who is this?"

"I'm sorry to wake you, Senator. This is . . ." Tom took a swallow of bourbon. "Never mind. I'm a friend."

The senator coughed. "*Friends* don't call me at two in the morning."

"I'm sorry, sir." Tom's ice cubes rattled close to the receiver again.

"You can't say who you are, but you can drink."

"Dutch courage, sir."

"Dutch courage . . . You in the navy, son?"

Tom almost hung up. "How would you know that?"

"Dutch courage. An old navy term. Dutch sailors got drunk before they sailed into battle against the English."

"Let's just say that I know something about destroyers, sir."

"In that case, I'm wide awake."

Tom Stafford swallowed. "Is it true that you're opposing the resolution over this Tonkin Gulf incident?"

"Depends on the resolution."

Tom could not reveal what Lloyd Shank had just said, but he could lead Morse in the right direction. Then it would be up to this representative of the people to speak out, or not, and Tom's conscience would be clear. "If you want the truth about the Tonkin Gulf, sir, ask the secretary of defense to produce the log of the *Maddox*."

"Why?"

Tom twirled the big class of '42 ring on his finger. "You'll be surprised to learn that she was much closer to the North Vietnamese coast when she was attacked . . . if she was attacked."

"That's interesting . . . what else?"

"Ask McNamara what the true mission of the *Maddox* was."

"Can't you tell me?"

"I'm not at liberty, sir."

"By rights, you're not at liberty to be making this call. But you're making it, Captain—what is your name?"

"How do you know I'm a captain?"

"Lucky guess. You have to be a captain or better to be hearing all of this. Now, I'll never reveal your name to anyone."

"I'll make it easy for you, sir. I won't reveal it to you."

"You're not doing me much good here, son. Any code names I can spring on the secretary?"

Code names. He wants code names. Tom realized that he had gone too far. He should have done what he was sworn to do and kept his mouth shut. "I'm not at liberty, sir."

"Why have you done this?"

"I . . . I don't know. Just ask what I've told you. Find out the truth." And he hung up.

Never mind *why* I've done this. What is it that I've done?

He brought his hand to his mouth. He thought he might be sick. He looked at the glass on the desk and decided that the bourbon was to blame. He grabbed it and threw it into the empty fireplace, so that it shattered on the bricks.

He looked around the ancient red room. He imagined an earlier

Thomas Stafford, fighting pirates right there at the threshold. For over two centuries the Staffords had been extending the threshold, extending their defensive perimeter, so they would never have to fight in this room again. And . . .

There was Juan, standing in the doorway. "I think I gonna be sick, Captain. You lookin' pretty fuckin' sick, too."

"Did you just hear—"

"You talk too fuckin' much. Keep me from passin' out."

"Don't ever tell anyone what you just heard."

Jimmy Stafford lay wide awake, listening. His father's voice had traveled up through the open closet, up through the secret passageway where he had hidden as a boy, and right into his gut.

He looked over to make sure that Ollie was asleep, that he had not heard what his father had just done. The crew-cut blond head hadn't moved once during the talk below, and the deep measured breathing had not changed, even when the glass shattered.

That was good, because Jimmy would not want anyone to know what his father had just done.

In the morning, Tom Stafford showered and shaved and studied his face in the mirror. One thing miserable navy sleep schedules had taught him was the way to look like polished brass on four hours of rack time, even with a big head.

He took two aspirin, slapped on the Old Spice, checked for gray hairs at the temples. Finding none on a forty-four-year-old head, he tightened his tie and told himself that last night had never happened. Once more he was Captain Tom Stafford, rigorous and incorruptible, intent on coffee, grapefruit, and raisin bran.

"Where's Juan?" he asked Betty.

"Victim of the bourbon bottle. I told him to sleep in. . . . Why is there a broken glass in the fireplace?"

"I stayed up to make sure that we hit our targets. I was at the news—"

"The radio says we lost four planes."

"North Vietnamese Triple A is very good. But we hit our objectives."

Once the house was empty—Tom off to the Pentagon and the boys to the golf course—Betty took a cool shower, the only kind worth taking in August. It made her feel better. But while she was toweling off, she heard Juan talking on the telephone down in the foyer.

"No, the Captain gone to work. . . . Yeah, yeah. The Pentagon. Where the hell else he go? . . . I don't know nothin', Mr. Jack. Why you keep callin' and asking me questions? I don't know fuckin' thing about no fuckin' bombing, and I gettin' goddamn sick and tired of you callin' up and tryin' to trick me into tellin' fuckin' secrets so you can put 'em in the newspaper. . . . What you mean? What secrets? I just got one word for you, Jack: fuck you."

Slam!

Now Betty heard him walking around, all but whimpering, "Fuck . . . fuck . . . oh, fuck."

"Juan," she said softly from the second floor. "What's this secret?"

"The one I not supposed to tell."

"Which one is that?"

"You tryin' to trick me now, too!" he cried. "And I . . . I got a very bad fuckin' headache!"

She could hear him stalking away, so she came halfway down the stairs, even though she was wrapped in nothing but a towel. "Juan. If this secret involves the captain, you can tell me, and maybe I can take it off your shoulders."

He came to the bottom of the stairs and looked up, craning his neck until his eyes met hers. "You think so?"

"I help the captain with all his secrets."

iii
The Camel's Nose

They had built a shopping mall just outside Annapolis, out in the section they still called Parole, after the Civil War camp. They had spread their squat buildings and tarmac across the green racetrack where Annapolitans had run their horses for a century or more. And they called it progress.

Betty Stafford was not so certain.

Route 50 was now open all the way to Washington. But the trains had stopped running in 1950, making Annapolis the only state capital without either air or rail transportation. And Main Street merchants were losing business to the mall. But yachtsmen had discovered the town, which would bring new money. But new money would drive the hardworking watermen, who wanted nothing more than low-priced moorings and thirty-cent drafts, up into the back creeks.

And all the while, the midshipmen came and the midshipmen went, four thousand of them now, filling Mother B, learning their long-standing lessons of honor and discipline while immersing themselves in new studies designed to meet the needs of a nuclear navy.

It might all be progress. It was certainly change.

Driving into Annapolis that morning, Betty Stafford was painfully aware of change everywhere, starting with her husband, who was now making midnight phone calls to politicians. And the Stafford House Hotel, where they first made love, had become a nursing home.

That hotel had survived wedding receptions, fires, and a guest list that had been shrinking ever since the auto turned overnighters into daytrippers. And those guests who did stay overnight wanted modern conveniences, like a bath in every room. So in 1956, the ever-practical Shank sisters had called upon their cousin Lloyd to find a new use for the property. He came up with the idea of a nursing home: old people in an aging building in an ancient town.

On Tuesdays, Betty volunteered at the Stafford House.

It was good for the soul, and it was a good way to visit Aunt Katherine, who spent her days in a wheelchair, in what was still called the Alexandra Room, watching television and reading golf magazines. Latent diabetes had caught up to Katherine, taking the sight in her left eye and her left leg below the knee. But she still had her hair done once a week, and she relished her reputation as a hard case among the nursing home staff.

It was hot in the old house. All the windows were open and a big ceiling fan pushed the heat around. Outside, the bright sunlight beat on the awnings.

"Hello, Katherine." Betty gave her a kiss and the latest issue of *Time* magazine.

"I was just dreaming of the night you asked me for the key to my room," said Katherine. "I was sitting right over there in the corner, having a nice glass of sherry. . . . I'd love one now, but of course the dia-damn-betes makes such small pleasures impossible."

"Did you hear about the bombing last night?"

"Of course. I may have just one eye, but I stay in touch. Tell your Tom not to let it go too far."

"He says it's not going to go any further than it already has."

Katherine turned her head so that her good eye was fixed on Betty. "It always goes too far, dear. You know that. It's like the dia-damn-betes. A little ingrown toenail, a little infection, a little bombing, and, oh, it isn't going to go any further than that, but the next thing you know, they're taking off your leg or taking you to war. Don't trust them. Always ask the hard questions."

Always ask.

As always, Katherine was right. But Betty couldn't do it.

If she asked her husband what he had said on the telephone, it would do no more than get him mad at Juan. But she knew someone in the business of always asking. And he was professional enough that he would protect sources. So, with a pile of dimes, she headed for the pay phone and called New York.

Sworn to secrecy by someone who had pumped someone else for information.

But a source is a source.

Jack Stafford flew to Washington that afternoon. But the Senate Foreign Relations Committee hearing was closed, so he couldn't do what Betty had suggested: watch Wayne Morse and pay close attention to what he asked.

Instead, he called his brother and asked if he could come down to the Pentagon.

Tom sounded shocked to hear his brother's voice so close, but he recovered smoothly enough and told Jack to come ahead. An hour later, they were sitting in the five-acre park that smart-ass Jack always called ground zero.

Tom bought Jack a cup of coffee and offered to share his sandwich.

"No," said Jack. "You need all your strength for keeping America free."

"You are a sarcastic bastard."

And the next fifteen minutes were straight party line. Whatever the president had said was what Tom said to Jack. Jack knew that Betty's little tips had somehow been gleaned from her husband. But whatever had gone on the night before was not going on now.

Tom was . . . well, Tom. Melon's kid brother, Smiley. The captain on his way to admiral.

So Jack decided to name names without betraying Betty. "Isn't Wayne Morse on the Senate Foreign Relations Committee?"

Jack noticed just a flicker of surprise cross his brother's face.

"I think so."

"He's been pretty tough on the president. What will his stance be?"

"I don't know. But he's in a clear minority, I'd say. Everyone in the country is lining up behind the president."

"I guess we all should. Even if this bombing run is just the camel's nose."

"I think it's the camel's tail," said Tom. "The camel is running away from us."

Two days later, a column was syndicated to fifteen daily newspapers in America. It had Jack's usual mix of hyperbole, irreverence, sarcasm, and solid reporting:

The Camel's Nose by Jack Stafford

> They say that if a camel gets his nose under your tent flap, you better watch out, because the whole two-humped beast will be in your lap before you know it.
>
> Why is it that nobody in the Senate but Wayne Morse of Oregon and Ernest Gruening of Alaska seems to think that this Tonkin Gulf Resolution has a pair of big snorting nostrils on it?
>
> Everybody else is just rolling right over, in Congress and the press.
>
> Now, I'm all for hitting back if someone hits us. In a world that moves much faster than most deliberative bodies can deliberate, the president needs to be able to strike fast if we're struck. And we've done that. Whatever those North Vietnamese PT boats may have done, we've

more than compensated with our strike on the Vinh oil facilities and PT boat bases. If that's where it stops, President Johnson deserves a pat on the back.

But now everyone is saying that we should remember Munich in 1939, when the European powers tried to appease Hitler. So let me get this straight: Ho Chi Minh is Hitler, and a country with no industrial base is a threat to the most powerful industrial democracy in history?

Sure, they're Communists, and make no mistake, these Communists are sworn enemies of the kind of personal freedom that allows me to write this column three times a week and that allows you to read it. But Senator Morse is just asking us to remember the Constitution.

No one seems to be listening.

I watched ninety-eight lawmakers roll over today, because we *may* have been attacked on the high seas by a few torpedo boats. I wasn't surprised that Barry Goldwater voted for this resolution. But George McGovern? Gene McCarthy? These men are accustomed to looking before they leap. And if they look closely at this Tonkin Gulf Resolution, they may see before them the gaping maw of a land war in Asia—unwinnable and unworthy of our blood.

Wayne Morse has been critical of presidents Johnson and Kennedy in their Vietnam policy before. But he was especially furious about this event. Why? Does he know something we don't? Did someone in the know get to him, turn up the gas under him, so that his simmering anger was brought to a rolling boil?

Listen to what the senator from Oregon said in the Senate chamber last night: "I believe that history will record that we have made a great mistake in subverting and circumventing the Constitution of the United States by means of this resolution. . . . We are in effect giving the president war-making powers in the absence of a declaration of war."

He's right. Too bad no one bothered to listen. The legislators were all out in the lobbies or in their offices, just waiting to come back and vote. Maybe, if someone got to Wayne Morse, he should come forward with what he knows. That might get the Senate's attention.

Of course, it might be too late. The vote was 98–2 in favor of giving the president a free hand in Southeast Asia.

I think—yes—the camel's head is under the tent, and the son of a gun is looking right at me. Hey, do camels bite?

CHAPTER NINE

The Last Story

October 13

The shadows in the yard were longer now.

Most of the curious midshipmen who had been listening had gone off when the little Filipino began to speak. What could he have to say?

Little did they know.

Watergate had the anonymous Deep Throat. The Vietnam War had the anonymous Pentagon staff member who called Wayne Morse on that August night in 1964. One of them brought down a presidency, but the other could not stop a war.

The person who made that phone call had disappeared from history as completely as Deep Throat.

And now Susan had him. The question was, would he let her tell the story? Could she use the footage?

Susan wished that she had two cameras so that she could film the admiral's reactions while Juan and Betty told the story of that August night.

The admiral sat to one side, folded his arms, set that famous old Stafford jaw, and never said a word. He never even moved. By the time Juan and Betty had finished talking, Susan could have mistaken Tom for the statue of Tecumseh, the Indian immortalized in bronze before Bancroft Hall.

And if a woman could be said to look frightened and relieved at the same time, it was Betty Stafford.

"Smile, Betty. You've just told the truth," said Jack. "You too, Juan."

"If I didn't have a big damn prostate, I'd be pissin' in my pants for tellin' it," said Juan.

"Don't worry," said the admiral. "You won't be court-martialed."

"Neither will you," said Jack. "If you're still afraid of this, I won't tell it."

"I'm not afraid of anything. Have you written it?"

"I roughed it out last night. Now Betty and Juan have given me some detail."

"Did you know it was me when you wrote that Camel's Nose article?" the admiral said.

Susan zoomed in slowly.

"I guessed. Where else would Betty have gotten that information?" said Jack. "But I promised her I wouldn't say so, and she promised Juan. And I always protect my sources."

"Professional honor?"

"Personal honor," said Jack. "That matters more. That's why I've sat on it all these years. That's why I'm here now."

The admiral looked at his grandson. "What about Steve's father? Have you written his story, yet?"

Jack shook his head. "I had to get past *yours* first."

"Would you like me to turn off the camera?" asked Susan.

"No. Let's tell this now." The admiral looked at the camera. "This is a hard profession. You need men of courage and conscience and foresight, too."

Instinctively, Betty put her arm around him.

"Since that night, I've never known which was worse—that I made that call to Wayne Morse, or that I didn't have the courage to shout it from the rooftops."

"I don't think shouting it would have changed anything," said Jack. "And Wayne Morse only had one vote."

"That isn't what you said in print back then."

"Those were different times."

"I envied you, Jack," said the admiral. "And I hated you. You didn't have to worry about loyalty to the navy. You could just take a scattergun and start blasting. And the more you wrote, the more I hated you. When we lost our Jimmy, I dumped that on you too, because you weren't backing our boys."

"I just wanted them to come home." Jack looked at Steve, who had been listening, dead silent, through all of this. "I wanted that boy to have a father."

"I had a father," said Steve. "I just didn't know him."

"He was a brave man," said the admiral. "I've told you that. All the reports say so. Even Oliver Parrish, and he knew, better than anyone."

Susan had been so mesmerized by what she was filming, she had forgotten about Ollie. Now she turned to him, but he had vanished.

"I didn't notice him leave," said Steve. "I thought we might put him in front of the camera next."

"Did he agree to an interview when I wasn't looking?" asked Susan.

"No. But Jack told us he had to interview his brother before he could write about my father. Well, from everything I know, I'd think the only way to write about my father is to interview Oliver Parrish."

"You let me be the reporter," said Jack, pumping the good cheer into his voice, as though he knew that things had been heavy enough for one afternoon. "And one thing reporters like to do is eat and drink. Now that the admiral's given me his scoop, I'm buying."

They went to Cantler's Crab Shack for dinner. The tables were covered with brown paper. Everyone was given a lot of napkins and a wooden mallet to crack the crab shells. And they ordered a big pitcher of beer to go with dinner.

Then Melon and Smiley went at it as though they were kids.

The admiral, baited often that day, started out with a little baiting of his own. "You know what I've never been able to figure out? How could that Jimmy Carter, an Academy man, and a nuclear submarine man to boot, let everything go to hell the way he did?"

"Vietnam taught him not to trust the defense wonks. He didn't believe in blank checks for the military." That was Jack's standard answer.

And on it went, the brother-against-brother debate: The Reagan defense buildup and the six-hundred-ship navy? Yeah, but what about the deficit they helped to build along with those ships? But they brought the pride back to military service, and they let the Russians know we weren't going to roll over. . . . But now look at our cities. . . . "Here we go with guns and butter," said Betty.

"I'm just glad," cracked Steve, "that there's enough money for the institute to buy that Fine Folly. Give them someplace quiet, so they can think up ways to keep me in business." It was the first time that day that Susan had seen Steve relax.

But she was still wondering—and worrying—about Oliver Parrish. As Jack started complaining about the sale of the Fine Folly, she went out and called Oliver's house. No answer. So she called his Washington office and left a message on the voice mail: "For a guy who makes a living out of confrontation, why did you walk away from a confrontation just begging to happen?"

Back at the table, Jack was still at it. "What do you think Lloyd Shank would say about selling you the Fine Folly if I told him about that leak to Wayne Morse? You know, a lot of people used to speculate that was him."

"I don't think he'd give a damn," said the admiral. "He wants some of the institute's money, and I want that house. I want it more than you do, Jack."

"And I want the sense of freedom I had in an A-6 again," said Steve, pouring his third beer and growing a little wistful. "A complicated piece of machinery, but the idea behind it's real simple. Know what you're doing and live. Push the wrong button and die. I'm getting tired of funding debates and fielding reporter's phone calls and—"

"You don't like the gray areas?" Jack asked. "Young guys don't believe in them . . . at first."

"I've seen a few today," said Steve, glancing at his grandfather.

"Sometimes you think you're standing on firm ground, son," said the admiral, "and it shifts, right beneath your feet."

"You know," said Steve, "I read the reports of my father's last action, and I've always wondered about one of the guys who survived, an engineer named Little, he never made a report . . . always a gray area to me."

The admiral glanced, briefly, at his wife. Then his voice was smooth and soothing. "Things get jumbled in wartime, Steve. And sometimes, things get lost."

"Just remember," said Betty, "your father stood for something."

A long drive didn't appeal to anyone that night, so the Staffords from the Patuxent and Washington checked into the bed-and-breakfast where Susan was staying.

After an hour of editing, Jack gave them all something to read and went back to his room at the Maryland Inn to keep writing. He had confronted the first half of the Stafford Vietnam conundrum, the long-hidden secret. Now he had to face the harder part, the murky events on a little stream on the Mekong delta.

About one o'clock that morning, Susan Browne was awakened by the sound of fire engines.

It was the first time she had heard a middle-of-the-night noise in Annapolis.

Those fire engines sounded nearby.

Then she smelled smoke.

She rolled over and glanced out the window. Flames. *Jesus.*

In an instant she was out of bed and grabbing instinctively for her video camera.

Within minutes the whole house was awake and all seven guests—the Staffords, Susan, and two grandmothers from Philadelphia—were running for the door.

The Stafford House Nursing Home was burning.

From a block away, they could hear the flames crackling and see that eerie red-orange smoke boiling up into the sky.

The fire station was right on East Street, a block and a half away from the Fine Folly, so the fire engines were there as soon as the alarm was called, but the fire had moved fast.

The street in front of the house looked like a battlefield. Powerful lights were pointed at the house, powerful streams of water were already hitting the front roof. Firemen were rushing up the stairs, smashing through the front door with their axes.

And above it all was the sound of a tremendous roar, as if a century of dried wood and more than two centuries of hopes and dreams and pretensions were going up.

"You son of a bitch!" cried the admiral, racing up to Jack. "You did this, didn't you?"

"Go to hell, you old fool." Jack's attention was on the fire chief in the white helmet. "Chief! Chief! Try to save the old part of the house."

"We'll be lucky to save any of it, mister!"

"So make a line of defense by the staircases at the back of the old—"

"Ask him," the admiral shouted to the chief. "Ask him where the hot spots are, because he set it."

The chief turned away from them.

"You did this, Jack," the admiral said again, "just so we couldn't get this house."

A fireman appeared in the Palladian window just above the door, the window from which old Walter Parrish had once waved a Confederate flag. With a swing of the ax, the glass in the window shattered.

"Jesus!" cried Jack.

And then the windows flew out of the front room on the east corner, the Alexandra Room, and Betty Stafford cried out as though the ax had struck her.

Ventilating the fire, they called it.

The front windows on the west side went next, an explosion of glass from two corners at once. Susan thought of all the famous men who had eaten in that room, and she could not bear to watch, but she had her video camera with her, so she raised it and rolled tape.

Steve Stafford ran up to the fire chief. "Is there anything we can do?"

"Just keep those two old men away from me."

"A defensive line, Chief!" Jack was crying. "The back of the house doesn't mean anything, but—"

The chief snapped at Steve Stafford, "Get them away, or I'll have them arrested."

Steve grabbed Jack and pulled him to the other side of the street. "Come on, Jack, let them do their job."

Two firemen appeared in the doorway and called for reinforcements.

Suddenly Jack broke out of Steve's grasp.

Susan caught him in her camera and followed him as he went. She felt like a news photographer, filming a terrible moment rather than intervening.

Jack flew across the street, raced up the steps to the landing in front of the Fine Folly and was struck from the side by a body that sent him sprawling then pinned him down.

"I have to get in there. I have to tell them—"

"I told them!" It was Oliver Parrish, covered in soot and sweat. "I told them to save the old house and forget the rest."

Jack wrestled himself into a standing position. "We have to save your caretaker, that Simpson Church."

Oliver grabbed Jack and pulled him away from the house as another group of firemen rushed up, pulling a heavy hose behind them. Then he said, "Simpson's dead. The firemen found him in his room. They think the fire started there."

"He set it?"

"I don't know," said Ollie. "Jesus. I hope he didn't think I was serious when I said I wished somebody would burn the damn place down."

Later, while streams of water were still pouring onto the house, Susan noticed Jack and Oliver disappearing around a corner.

She followed and caught up to them at the waterfront, just as they sat down on a bench.

Oliver took a swallow from a flask.

Jack took out a little tape recorder and began fiddling with it.

"The admiral's story is out," said Oliver. "I guess there are things I can talk about. Things I should talk about. And that woman standing behind me can sit down and listen too."

So, she thought, this ex-SEAL still had eyes in the back of his head. And now it was time for his story.

The Stafford Story
Book Nine (Part Two)
The Limits of Power
June 1967

Jimmy Stafford's wedding was at 9:30 A.M. on the second Tuesday in June.

It was an odd time to be getting married, especially if you were doing it for the first time and both families approved. But midshipmen were not allowed to marry, so right after commissioning, they lined up, and every hour on the hour, the weddings went through the magnificent Academy chapel. It was like a military version of a Las Vegas marriage mill.

Jimmy chose his brother as best man, and Oliver Parrish hid his disappointment well.

Ollie had no brothers. His mother had died when he was a baby. And his father had been more interested in building a subdivision at Parrish Manor than in raising a little boy. So the great-grandson of Robby Parrish had spent a lonely childhood along the river, dreaming of Civil War blockade runnings and Chesapeake pirates, nurturing a wild streak that got him into trouble more times than his disinterested father ever cared to know about.

But the Staffords liked Jimmy's friend. Whenever they were staying at Stafford Hall, they treated him like a member of the family. And after Aunt Katherine introduced both boys to the game of golf, Ollie's wildness faded before the fanatical focus the game required. When the time came to apply to the Academy, Captain Tom Stafford spoke for Oliver Parrish.

Still, hints of wildness remained beneath a fresh layer of Naval Academy discipline: his hair was shorn in a forbidding square-head crew cut, his features were interrupted by a dramatically broken nose; and he was built like a chain-link fence.

On that bright June day, Ollie was just one of two dozen dress-white classmates who arched their swords over Jimmy and his bride, Rebecca Blair of Baltimore, then paraded to the reception at Ogle Hall, the eighteenth-century mansion that housed the Naval Academy Alumni Association.

Old friends and family filled the house. Jack was there, just divorced for the second time. Brother Billy's widow, Maureen, came with her second husband, a tool-and-die salesman named Smith. Lloyd Shank was chain-smoking in a corner. And old Aunt Katherine was wheeled down the street from the Stafford House by a black orderly named Simpson Church.

Both of Katherine's legs were now gone at the knee. But the vision in her left eye was good enough that she could still read and tend the bonsai she kept on her windowsill. And, as she was fond of saying, she could still dream of hitting a five iron a hundred and twenty yards.

With two champagne glasses, Oliver found his way to where she sat.

"Now, you know I'm not supposed to drink, Ollie," she announced haughtily. "Go find some pretty girl."

"Later. Have some champagne. A little won't hurt you."

"Excuse me, sir," said Simpson Church. "But she ain't supposed to drink."

"C'mon, Simpson." All the midshipmen who visited the nursing home knew Simpson, because he told all of them about his brother, Chief Petty Officer Horace Church. Ollie was one of the few midshipmen who promised to look Horace up when he got out in the fleet, even though there were thousands of CPOs in the navy.

"Well," said Simpson, "I s'pose I could look the other way."

"A favor I won't forget." Oliver winked. "This lady taught me how to make a chip shot from the edge of the green with a choked-down seven iron. She should be the first to toast the good news: I'm off to San Diego, to the school for SEALs."

"SEALs?" Katherine almost dropped the glass.

"Sea, air, and land special forces." Ollie raised his glass. "In the littoral zone and along the rivers, we're the guys for intelligence gathering, hostage rescue—"

"You couldn't choose something safe?"

"I thought you'd be pleased." Oliver lowered the glass. "I'm going where my concentration and training can make a difference."

Jimmy slipped up behind Ollie, beaming and gleaming as only a bridegroom wearing navy whites could. "Aunt Katherine, we want you to be in the receiving line with us."

"Did you hear what your friend has gone and done?" asked Katherine.

"I'm proud of him." Jimmy threw his arm around Ollie and they gleamed together, like two young knights.

"If we don't stop them where they are," said Ollie, "they'll just keep coming."

Katherine looked down at the remains of her legs, perhaps hearing echoes of things she had heard before. "I suppose you'll end up in Vietnam, too, Jimmy."

"You wouldn't want me to go anywhere else, would you?" Jimmy laughed at a question not worth asking. "After Surface Warfare School, I'm requesting a destroyer on WestPac deployment."

There was something Katherine could toast. "To the safety of a destroyer."

"To the bravery of two young men"—Captain Tom appeared, wielding a champagne glass of his own—"fighting for their country."

"In a stupid war," grunted Katherine.

"You've been reading too many of Jack's articles," said Tom.

Now Jack swaggered over, a typical sixties incongruity—the middle-aged man trying to look young, the glen-plaid gray suit clashing with the Beatles mop top haircut. "Is somebody taking my name in vain?"

"From what you've been writing lately," said Tom, "somebody should be taking you out in a back alley."

"You know this war's a mistake, Tom." Jack sipped his champagne. "It's just that I have the courage to say so."

The string quartet reached the crescendo of Vivaldi's *Spring*, and Tom's neck reddened against his dress-white collar like blood on snow. "These boys are the ones with the courage, Jack. And you should be celebrating it."

"I celebrate the courage it takes to go to Vietnam, and the courage it takes to ask why we should." Jack glanced out the window at the bride, who was in the garden with her mother-in-law, Betty Stafford. "But today, I celebrate true love. You've got yourself a beautiful girl, Jimmy." Then Jack glided out through the garden doors to introduce himself to the newest member of their happy family.

After a moment, Tom said, "No matter what you read in the papers, boys, the thing to celebrate is your Academy training. It's given you everything you'll need out there—discipline, professionalism, a sense of honor. They make courage easy."

Both boys mumbled *yes, sirs*.

"But you be careful, Ollie. SEAL work is dangerous. And damn few see any advancement from it. I want you to climb the ladder, just like Jimmy."

"Advancement, sir?" That remark made Ollie Parrish bristle. He considered his decision the purest he had ever made, driven by the simple, Academy-bred desire to go where the job was and do it. "I thought we just wanted to get this war over with, sir, no matter how any of us thought when it began."

"Enough," cried Katherine. "This war talk is sinful when we have that beautiful girl waiting for us in the garden. Just look at her."

Jimmy's bride had taken off her veil so that her golden hair, styled and sprayed into a neat flip, shimmered in the sunshine. She called herself Beck, because it made her sound strong. But she looked, to the men gazing at her, like a soft angel, and none of them could imagine leaving her to fight a war on the other side of the world.

ii
Destroyer Duty

They named destroyers for navy men and marines who died heroically. So it was not surprising that a *Gearing*-class destroyer launched in 1948 was named for Lieutenant William Stafford, or that his nephew was the first Stafford to serve aboard her. She displaced twenty-four hundred tons, could make thirty-four knots with her twin-screwed steam turbines engines, and drew nineteen feet, which let her go places that cruisers and battleships could never approach.

Jimmy wrote to Beck that he knew she was a good ship the first day out of San Diego—a Monday in October 1967—when he and two other lieutenants were called to the CO's cabin. Commander Charles Copake had three folders in front of him.

One belonged to Lieutenant Johnny Wilson. "Academy, '66," said Copake. "Good fitness reports. Good."

The next belonged to Jimmy Stafford. "Academy '67, good academic standing, good reports from Newport. Good."

The third report belonged to Peter Terwilliger, a tall, skinny guy with heavy black-rimmed glasses. "A graduate of an NROTC program at the University of Western Illinois, '67. Good grades, good basketball record for a small Division II school. Good."

Then Copake picked up the folders, piled them, and ceremoniously dropped them into the wastebasket. "Welcome to the real navy. I will form my opinions based on performance, not on who went to the Academy and who didn't, nor on whose father is on staff for the CNO, or whose uncle writes a nationally syndicated column that appeared in today's *San Diego Union*, questioning why we are in Vietnam, which he does every week."

Jimmy looked down at the tops of his shiny black shoes. "My uncle's a broken record, sir."

"Your father is, too. But he makes music I like."

Green.

It was the color of peace and fertility. Jimmy had never seen anything greener than the jungle coast he surveyed from the *Stafford* bridge three weeks later.

And every green day died in a spectacle of reds and purples that filled him with awe. He would lean against the rail, feel the comforting roll of the ship, and wonder at the hell burning beneath the beauty. Then he would get about the business of doing what a junior grade lieutenant could to put out hell's fires.

He would take his position in the Combat Information Center, in the eerie red light of a darkened ship. The radio would be tuned to a preset high-frequency band, the two turrets would be turned toward the coast, and they would wait.

And while they waited, Jimmy considered the irony of what they waited to do.

At birth, the American navy had attacked British supply lines because it could do nothing else against the most powerful navy in the world. Now the most powerful navy in the world was the American navy, and its main role, in the biggest war of the generation, was attacking enemy supply lines.

Eighty-five percent of North Vietnam's war matériel came through Haiphong Harbor from the Soviet Union. In a logical war, the navy's first task would have been the mining and blockading of Haiphong. But nothing about Vietnam was logical, because the politicians were fighting it, and President Johnson feared a direct challenge to the Russians. So the navy wasted its awesome power stopping supplies after they'd been put on trucks and sampans and sent south. It was like trying to stop droplets of water after they had been poured into a sieve.

Intelligence might pick up word of six trucks, sitting in six different jungle patches, somewhere in the demilitarized zone, and none worthy of an air strike. But once night fell, and the six trucks came together, their convoy could be a fine target for the guns of a destroyer cruising in close. But the roads were buried beneath the jungle canopy, sometimes two or three miles in back of the beach, so the destroyer needed eyes.

For that, there would be a young marine, given a radio and some training in enemy evasion, then told to watch this crossroad or that bend or that jungle clearing. Coordinates on the point of the attack would already be established. But gunnery was not an exact science, and that young marine on the ground would be on the radio after the first shot.

"Right thirty." Come right thirty yards.

The communications officer would pass the word to the commanding officer, and Stafford would plot the next shot, and the communications officer would send the word to the weapons officer, all in a matter of seconds. Then they would hear turrets turning right thirty on their barbettes, and the whole ship would heel with the recoil of four guns firing at once.

If it went well, the next transmission might go like this: "Hit lead truck. Road blocked. Trucks stopped. Right ten for turkey shoot. Out."

The spotter might be heard once or twice more in the course of the barrage. Then he would disappear into the jungle to find his way back to his platoon.

And when his four-hour watch ended, Jimmy Stafford would go to the wardroom for coffee and maybe a piece of cake. Then he would go to the cabin he shared with Terwilliger, leave the hatch open so that he could look out at the sea, read a book for a while, think about his wife, then try to sleep.

And sometime before he drifted off between his clean sheets, Jimmy would see that grunt, with his face blackened, the radio pressed to his ear, and the sweat trickling from under his helmet. And he would feel a twinge of guilt.

Eventually, Jimmy had a tour as communications officer, so he was working the radio one night off Quang Tri Province when they got word of a Communist convoy moving down the coast just south of the Viet estuary. North Vietnamese sampans had loaded above the demilitarized zone and sneaked into the estuary with a shipment of Soviet-made rockets, grenades, and AK47s. Now the convoy would take the weapons south to supply elements of the regular North Vietnamese Army operating in the area and would then disperse like seeds into the general population.

The sunset was particularly beautiful that evening. But Jimmy had stopped noticing, because the guilt that he felt grew worse each night. All his study of naval history told him that he was doing one of the things the navy did best—providing close artillery support from a secure gun platform.

But who were those marines he heard, operating alone in the jungles, acting as the eyes of the *Stafford*, night after night? And how many of them survived?

They sat that night in the Combat Information Center and waited. The place for the attack had been plotted. The time of convoy arrival, based on intelligence reports, was 2200. The air, even out there on the destroyer, was so thick with humidity that you could drink it.

At 2205, Jimmy heard the transmitter on the other end click on. That was all. Communications were short and sharp and as sparse as trees in an ocean.

Jimmy glanced up at the orange hands of the clock. "Charlie's late."

"Maybe Charlie knows we're waiting for him," said Copake.

Terwilliger lit a cigarette.

Jimmy sipped coffee.

At 2300, *click.* "Contact. Convoy in target zone, speed—uh . . . Oh, oh . . . Jesus . . ."

Jimmy looked up, "Target in zone, sir."

"Inform the weapons officer."

Blam!

The guns spit fire and five-inch explosive shells.

Click. The voice sounded strained, high-pitched. "You got some, but there's hundreds. Bicycles. They're using bicycles. There's women and little kids. They're scattering. Over."

Jimmy heard rising fear in the marine's voice. Be professional, he reminded himself. "Spot us. Over."

The voice came back, breathing hard. "Ten right."

"Roger." Jimmy repeated the message through the communications link to the weapons officer.

The guns were adjusted.

Blam!

"They're using bicycles, sir," Jimmy said to the skipper.

"Shit." Copake jammed his pipe into his mouth, and bit down.

Click. The radio was on again. "Good shot. Repeat."

"Roger that. Good shot. Repeat," said Jimmy.

Copake cursed again and nodded.

Blam! The *Stafford* shuddered.

"They're retreating. Twenty, twenty-five yards right . . . uh . . . "

Jimmy heard the rat-tat-tat of automatic weapons fire in his headset.

"Spotted. I'm moving," said that anonymous marine.

Jimmy looked up, working hard to keep the control in his voice. "They're on to him. He called for twenty-five right."

"Then give it to him."

Jimmy wiped the sweat from his forehead and passed the word. The World War II guns blasted again. He could not imagine the carnage as those five-inch shells tore into people on bicycles. But bicycles were a favorite way for the VC to move supplies. A single bicycle could carry 175 pounds of matériel at a time—more if the rider was a woman or child.

Click.

The marine was back. They hadn't got him yet.

"Dead dinks everywhere. Women, kids, and VC—"

Blam! The sound of an explosion almost blew Jimmy's headset off. It was so loud that he thought he saw the flash in front of him, even though it had happened across three or four miles of water.

"I'm . . . I'm—" *Blam!*—"I'm bracketed. That was a grenade. Give me twenty left."

Jimmy looked up at the captain. "Covering fire, twenty left."

Copake nodded. The order went out.

Blam!

"Good shot. Uh . . . I'm hit. Out." And that was the last they heard from him.

That night Jimmy Stafford slipped between cool sheets and hoped that the roll of the ship would lull him to sleep. But he kept seeing that marine, bracketed and frightened, hoping to fight his way out of a VC pincer. And he felt like a coward.

Ollie Parrish hadn't chosen the easy route. He was out there somewhere, like that marine, looking the war in the face.

Jimmy could not imagine the fear that marine must have felt when the VC closed in. And yet he could not imagine going home and telling folks that his contribution in the great war of his generation was to deliver artillery onto people riding bicycles. What would his wife think of him? Or his father, who had overcome one night of doubts to stand firm on his oldest beliefs?

"Hey, Terwig," he whispered to the lower bunk.

"Mmmm?"

"You awake?"

"What?"

"Do you think the gooks got that grunt?"

"Who knows? Just be thankful you're where you are. Best thing I ever did was get into the NROTC. Clean sheets. A full belly . . ."

Spoken, thought Jimmy, like a civilian. There had to be something more honorable for a twenty-two-year-old Academy-trained lieutenant.

iii
A Game Warden

"You what?" said Betty Stafford.

"I volunteered for Operation Game Warden. I thought you'd be proud."

They were sitting on the veranda at Stafford Hall on the last Sunday of March, 1968. The six-month deployment of the *Stafford* had ended in San Diego with two weeks' leave for a young lieutenant bound for the PBR (Patrol Boat, River) school on the Sacramento River delta in California.

It was a warm day, with spring more than a promise along the Patuxent and civil unrest more than a threat in American cities.

As the call-up of reserves and the draft reached deeper into American homes, the resistance to this faraway adventure grew greater. And then came the Tet offensive. Americans and South Vietnamese had beaten back every attack, but the world had seen enemy infiltration into every corner of South Vietnam. A lot of Americans thought that they smelled a rat, and one of them seemed to be Beck Stafford, now a student at George Washington Law School.

She had greeted her husband at Dulles International wearing some kind of flowered peasant shirt, bell-bottoms cut just above the crack in her ass, and a ratty fatigue jacket that looked like something some GI had thrown away.

Jimmy had tried to hide his shock. But a lot had changed in six months. When they got to their Plymouth Duster, on the third level of the parking structure, he had even noticed a blue bumper sticker with a yellow daisy on it: "McCarthy for President."

But before he could say anything she had slipped in behind the wheel and pushed the Beatles' *Magical Mystery Tour* into the eight-track.

And he had said, "Your hair . . . it's different."

It was parted in the middle, long and straight, with an almost ethereal sheen.

"You like it?"

"Uh . . . yeah."

"It's magic." Her fingers had slipped into the luxuriance of it and returned a moment later holding a badly rolled cigarette. His golden angel had fallen.

"Is that what I think it is?"

"Come on, Admiral. Don't be so straight. Take a toke."

He might have been able to fight the marijuana, but if it was the path to what he had been dreaming of since he left San Diego . . . well . . . the parking level was deserted, and the Beatles sounded stoned in their Strawberry Fields, and what the hell . . .

He noticed no effect from the grass, except that it burned. But it sure loosened her up. Right there on the front seat of the car, with the jets roaring overhead, she had managed to twitch a leg out of those silly pants and straddle her husband in his dress khakis, then press her lips to his in the longest kiss of his life. There was no thought of protection. No thought of discovery. No thought of anything but their two hungry bodies fitting together as perfectly as a plug and a socket.

And when it was over, her lips still on his, he had begun to giggle.

"Pretty cool, isn't it? Sex, drugs, and rock and roll."

"Yeah. Cool. But what I want to know is . . . is . . ."

She had pressed herself against him and he had started to respond again. "What is it you want to know?"

"Is Paul the Walrus . . . or the Eggman?"

"Coo-coo-coo-choo." And she had slipped onto him again.

By the time they got back to the Patuxent, the excitement had worn off. It was clear that Beck was a very confused and frustrated young navy wife, not entirely certain that she wanted to *be* a navy wife. "So, what's Operation Game Warden?" she asked.

"It's my own command."

His father nodded. "It's the fastest track to promotion that a junior grade lieutenant can hope for."

"Don't be so worried about moving fast," said Betty. "The navy's a long career, just so long as you're around to enjoy it."

"But what the fu . . . What the heck *is* Operation Game Warden?" demanded Beck.

"It's the navy's program of supply interdiction in the Mekong delta," said Jimmy.

"Four thousand square miles of mangrove swamps, mud flats, canals, and rice paddies. Few roads, fewer bridges. Home to five million of South Vietnam's fifteen million people." The captain rattled off the figures like a machine gun. "An absolute logistical nightmare."

"Oh, I have those," Beck said sarcastically. "Really far out, when I can remember them in the morning."

That brought a glare from her father-in-law.

She turned to her husband. "So what kind of command do you get?"

"A PBR—fiberglass, thirty-one feet long, with a GM engine running two Jacuzzi water jets for propulsion, two fifty-cals forward, one at the stern, and a grenade launcher in the cockpit."

"And you shoot all those things?" she asked.

"Of course."

"At Vietnamese?"

And six months of pent-up fury and frustration exploded from

Jimmy Stafford, all of it directed at the girl he had married. "*Of course* we shoot them. We shoot them at gooks, at dinks, at VC Communists who want to kill anybody in the country who doesn't think like them. We shoot them at Charlie, because Charlie is shooting at us."

And she just shook her head, as though the worlds that they inhabited had grown so far apart she could not imagine them ever coming together again.

"Uh . . . perhaps we should have dinner," said Betty.

That night, in a televised speech, Lyndon Johnson shocked the nation by declining to run for a second term. The war had taken its most famous casualty. This happened about three hours after Jimmy Stafford realized that his marriage had been a mistake. Or perhaps the mistake was his choice of career.

Before he headed for California, Jimmy visited his great-aunt Katherine for the last time, but she had begun to fail and barely knew him. He said good-bye to his parents. Then he and Beck drove to New York to visit his brother Willie, who was studying at N.Y.U. Law School.

Willie wore a flowered shirt, hair down to his collar, a drooping mustache, and bell-bottoms that made him look like some kind of new sailor. He said "man" a lot and told his brother he was planning to practice public interest law. "You know, defending tenants against greedy landlords, class action suits against greedy polluters, stuff like that."

"Just thank God for that heart murmur," said Jimmy, "or you'd be defending your ass."

"I do, man. Every day."

Within a few months, Jimmy Stafford was back in that green, green land where, strangely, things were beginning to make more sense than they did at home. Martin Luther King shot dead with a high-powered rifle. Robert Kennedy taken out in a hotel passageway. Riots every night. College takeovers . . .

Beck had met him in San Francisco to say good-bye. They had stayed at the Fairmont, courtesy of his parents. A bouquet of flowers had been waiting for them in their room, with a note from Betty and Captain Tom: "The Fairmont has joyous memories for us. We hope it will have the same for you."

At the Fairmont, they had smoked marijuana and screwed for three days straight. Sometimes Beck put in her diaphragm, sometimes she didn't. Then she had flown east for the demonstrations at the Chicago convention. Jimmy had boarded a commercial flight in California, routed through Honolulu, to Saigon, with the *San Francisco Chronicle* on his lap.

A Dispatch from Chicago by Jack Stafford

"The whole world's watching."

That's what the demonstrators were chanting in the streets last night, as the Chicago police, who wear those funny checkers on their service caps, like they were glorified taxi drivers, acted the way no self-respecting cabbie ever would.

Last night those cops rioted, plain and simple, shooting tear gas like fireworks, beating kids who did no more than run away from them. They demonstrated an unprofessional rage that was frightening to behold, especially in a city with such big shoulders and so much muscle to put behind those nightsticks.

And tonight, inside the convention hall, Hubert Humpty Humphrey Dumpty, the saddest happy warrior of them all, will take the podium. While the nightstick-crazed horses and men of Mayor Richard Daley are doing their damnedest to push him off the wall, while they stamp on a few of the fundamental principles of democracy, like the right of free assembly, and while the dark cloud of LBJ hovers above, Humpty will accept the nomination of the Democratic Party for president.

This has to be some kind of booby prize in 1968. The victory cigar that blows up in your face. The blue ribbon pin that sticks into your chest and gives you blood poisoning.

I saw this country live through a depression. I covered the first six months of World War II in the Pacific. But I'll say this straight out. The last four months have filled me with more fear for my country's future. . . .

That was where Jimmy Stafford stopped reading. He believed in the future.

And it was good that he did, because two months after his arrival in the Mekong delta, a letter came from Beck. It was not the Dear John letter he expected. It was joyous news instead. He was going to be a father.

He was ready, because by then he had earned himself the black beret of the riverine forces.

Rung Sat Special Zone was an area fourteen miles south of Saigon that belonged hook, line, and sinker to the navy. The reason was simple. There were no roads for anybody else to do any fighting. Things here traveled by water. And it was the job of the river patrol boats to see that only friendly things did the traveling.

Each PBR team comprised two boats. A lieutenant commanded the lead boat and the unit; a chief petty officer commanded the second boat.

When Jimmy was introduced to his CPO, the name Horace Church did not register. Jimmy was more impressed by the size of the big black chief, the crisp salute, the steady gaze.

"I been on the river six months, Lieutenant. I know it good," said Horace.

"I'll count on you, Chief," said Jimmy.

Horace Church smiled. "Thank you, Lieutenant. Six months down, six months to go, and not dead yet, sir. I hope to keep it that way."

"Where you from, Church?"

"Annapolis, sir. Born and bred."

"Annapolis. Are you any relation to . . . Hey, I know your brother."

"Simpson. Yeah. Hardworkin' man. Works in the nursin' home by day, works in a transmission shop at night. Hopin' to have a family."

"What about you?"

"Sir?"

"Any family."

"The navy, sir."

"Me too. From way back."

"My grandma tell me I got an ancestor sailed on the *Essex* a long time ago, 'fore they decided we weren't good enough for anything but messmen."

"Well, mister, it was my grandfather who recommended Dory Miller for the Navy Cross after Pearl Harbor," Jimmy said proudly.

"That's good, sir." And a smile crossed the chief's face. "Now who in the hell is Dory Miller?"

At the Academy, leadership seminars taught that the man to count on in a pinch was the chief petty officer, the navy's equivalent of the top sergeant—tough, smart, practical, experienced. And Horace Church was the best, even if he didn't know who Dory Miller was.

Privately, Horace offered advice and experience, always with a deferential *sir* at the end; publicly, he was the bridge between a green lieutenant and a veteran crew including two tough black guys from New York, both with the last name Washington (the big one called George, the little one Martha); a beefy black kid from Mississippi named Lester Thurlow, who always had his nose in a book; a pair of career navy engineers, Ben Bennett and Jack Little; a smart-ass from the North End of Boston, Frankie Donatello; and two farm boys named Johnson and Trager, who said they joined the navy to see the world.

In the first week, the TOC—Tactical Operations Center—gave the newcomer easy duty—two twelve-hour night shifts on the widest part of the Mekong, where the chance of VC ambush or river contact was small; then two day shifts stopping sampans heading for Saigon. In that week, Jimmy developed his operating patterns, got to know his crew, and looked forward to those cold beers awaiting him back at their base, a hamlet at the spot where the Long Tau River emptied into the Mekong.

Then he was expected to pull his weight.

Across the delta, PBRs under Game Warden were searching up to 100,000 small craft a month, and since there were only 120 PBRs, that came to over eight hundred stops per boat, per month, or twenty-seven a day.

In addition to the PBRs, the delta was covered by a hundred larger and more heavily armored PBFs, for Patrol Boat, Fast, and monitors, which looked like old Civil War vessels and were nicknamed Zippos, after the cigarette lighters, because they carried flamethrowers that could shoot a jet of gasoline a hundred yards.

And the logistical support for all these vessels was typically American.

In some places, five-hundred-foot tenders were anchored in the middle of the Mekong to become floating docks and secure barracks. Some units were based on barges protected by patrol rings on the bank. And some, like Jimmy's unit, were based in hamlets that were considered secure. But nothing was truly secure in-country.

To improve security along the waterways, American planes had been spraying a chemical defoliant called Agent Orange, and that astonishingly green land looked, from the PBR, like a land in retreat. Now, along many of those rivers of living brown water, there was a dead strip of lighter brown vegetation, and in the distance, the green. Sometimes the middle band was not light brown but a charred black, after the Zippos came through and burned off the dead growth.

But Agent Orange had not denuded the landscape, not by a long shot. Most of the waterways were still lined with elephant grass, and mighty mangrove swamps still could be found in the Mekong delta. And the best security was still that PBR.

It had a covering called a T-top over the cockpit, to keep the skipper out of the sun, and it could turn, at full speed, in a thirty-foot circle, one second heading upstream, the next going down. This feature came in handy when an ambush erupted on two sides of a river at once, although sometimes nothing helped in a firefight but firepower, as an event in the third month proved.

They had followed an oversized sampan into a canal that was only about thirty yards, with nothing but tall elephant grass on either bank.

Jimmy thought it was running pretty low in the water to be carrying nothing but baskets of fish, so he came up alongside and told the oarsmen at the stern to stop. Horace Church stayed fifty yards behind in the covering boat.

A family was running the sampan—an old grandfather, his wife, his son, and two rather pretty granddaughters.

The grandfather smiled at them and gestured Jimmy aboard.

On the radio, Horace told Jimmy, "Bum setup, lieutenant. Be careful."

And Horace was right. As soon as Jimmy Stafford had one leg

aboard the sampan, both banks erupted with machine-gun and rocket fire.

An explosion on the sampan blew a little girl off the stern and knocked Jimmy back onto the PBR. The sampan was protecting his boat from the right bank, so he shouted, "Left bank!"

And his men knew exactly what to do.

Lester Thurlow swung the fifty-caliber machine guns and started mowing down the tall grass. Frankie Donatello launched a belt of thirty-six grenades. Johnson drilled fifty-caliber fire from the rear of the boat. Ben Bennett took the M60, while Horace Church and his men sprayed the right bank.

And in the midst of it all, Jimmy saw the old man pull the pin on a grenade.

Yes. Now throw it at those VC sons of bitches! Fight back, old man!

But . . . the old son of a bitch was turning to drop the grenade onto the PBR.

Jesus!

Jimmy hesitated an instant, but that was all. He turned his M16 on the old man and blasted him backward, into his own boat.

There was the muffled *crump* of a grenade exploding in the sampan, and then it was over: VC driven off; one family of weapons smugglers wiped out; engineer Jack Little nicked in the buttocks and furious at Jimmy Stafford for leading them into an ambush.

The encounter left Jimmy shaken for days, because in a land of death, these were the first people he had killed.

But Horace Church led him on the first step toward the six-month river religion, so called because it never took more than six months to get it, and then you had to practice it for just six months more.

"You did good in that firefight, sir," said Horace the night after it happened, "but there's times when it's best to just let 'em go."

"We're supposed to interdict. And I was right. That boat was carrying AK47s."

"There's a lot of right guys out here who's dead. We supposed to get home alive, sir. And you got more to live for than most, with that little baby on the way and all. You see a sampan headin' up a narrow canal like that, let the motherfucker go. Nobody won't know any different."

iv
Meeting Bob Hope

Horace Church gave good advice; but after three months of interdiction, all Jimmy could see when he drifted off to sleep was that old man pulling the pin on his grenade. It seemed now that every little boat looked suspicious; every Vietnamese smile seemed false; and the green, green land looked browner every day.

So why not interdict their supplies at the source? Stop the infection before it spread. Mine Haiphong and dare the Russians to do something.

Damn all spineless politicians.

Jimmy's father had always said, "When all else fails, serve with honor." Horace Church now said, "When all else fails, get home alive."

And the picture Jimmy now carried inside his helmet, of Beck with her expanding belly, caused him to hear Horace's advice more clearly than his father's.

Why die for some spineless politician when that little child was waiting at home, along with a wife who liked having sex with him and might love him after all?

Then one afternoon they received orders to report to a base some twenty miles south of their usual patrol area. Lieutenant Jimmy Stafford's unit had been requested as an insertion force by a team of navy SEALs.

"Sheeyut," said Horace Church when he saw the order.

"What?"

"This SEAL commander. He got a bad rep. One crazy motherfucker. They call him Bob Hope."

"Bob Hope? Why?"

"You'll see."

Then Jimmy looked at the name and laughed. He knew Bob Hope.

They went south, cutting through canals in Vinh Long province, and came into the Hau Giang near Can Tho.

The SEAL barge looked like a big slab of rust baking in the sun. PBFs and little STABs (SEAL Team Assault Boats) were moored all around the edges. Two Sea Wolves, modified Huey helicopter gunships, sat on the deck, and right in the middle were four Quonset huts. From one of them, someone was piping some very serious rock and roll onto the PA. It sounded like something from *Wheels of Fire*. Eric Clapton going crazy on "Crossroads."

And there he was: Bob Hope, also known as Oliver Parrish.

He was wearing olive drab skivvies, shower shoes, dog tags, and shades. And, of course, he had a golf glove on his left hand, a six iron in his right. Three buckets of golf balls were lined up beside him, and a small army of Vietnamese kids paddled in the river and ran along the bank, waiting for him to swing.

"Hey!" shouted Jimmy. "Is that Bob Hope?"

At the sight of Jimmy, Ollie loped over to the edge of the barge, swinging the club like a walking stick, the way Bob Hope did it when he came out to tell jokes to the troops. "Hey, Jimmy! I keep tryin' to get these motherfuckers to call me Jack Nicklaus, but Bob Hope's the best they'll do."

Ollie still wore his hair in that crew cut, but he had been in the sun so long that he was almost brown. He threw an arm around Jimmy and welcomed him aboard, then he shouted to the rest of the crew, "The beer cooler's in Hut Four. There's a pool table in Hut Three. But stay the fuck out of Hut One. That's the Spook Bin. Bunch of CIA guys in there. Get yourselves hurt."

Then he looked at the little Vietnamese kids and waved them away. They all waved back and shouted and shook their fists and cried, "Bob Hope! Bob Hope!"

"Tomorrow," he shouted, then he repeated it in Vietnamese.

One of the Vietnamese kids gave him the finger, and two or three of the SEALs sitting around laughed like hell.

It was clear to Jimmy that no matter who the CO was on this island of rust, Lieutenant Oliver Parrish was in charge.

"I give the little dinks a penny for every twenty-five golf balls they bring back," said Ollie. "You should see 'em fight over it. Free enterprise in action."

"That's one way of lookin' at it."

Ollie's office in the Quonset hut was air conditioned, which was a true luxury. He played the host like a river baron. He told Jimmy to sit in the big rocking desk chair, asked him if he wanted the Rolling Stones instead of Cream, then put "Satisfaction" on the PA. Then he pulled two beers out of a refrigerator in the corner.

"Beer?" Jimmy grinned. "On a navy vessel?"

"This is a SEAL vessel, babe. The spooks in Hut One run the show. But they drink more than we do." Ollie popped the tab on his can and toasted.

Jimmy toasted back. "It's good to see you."

"Wait until I'm done before you say that."

"What's this job you need me for?"

Ollie leaned back and put his feet up on the desk. "We do a lot of bad shit in this unit. Assassinations, kidnappings, throat cuttings. There aren't many rules."

"And?"

"I wouldn't have asked for you on any of that shit. But this is different." Ollie picked up a little sawed-off nine-iron that he kept on his desk. It had a full-sized head and a perfect grip, but the shaft was only half the length of an ordinary club.

"You have to bend a long way to swing that," said Jimmy.

"I swing it at skulls." Ollie grinned.

Jimmy was chilled, because the words came out as though they were part of a golf score. "Uh, the job, Ollie. What's the job?"

"POW rescue, up near the Cambodian border. Gook stronghold back in there. You've got VC pouring across the border from Cambodia day and night. They have three full divisions and eleven main force battalions in the area. But the CIA spooks are saying there's two navy fliers, about three kilometers in from a little stream called the Tien Doc. If we can get to them quick, we can save them from a stay in the Hanoi Hilton."

"It sounds dangerous."

"What's your point?"

Jimmy shrugged.

Ollie got up. "Stopping sampans loaded with dead fish and AK47s can be dangerous, man. Shootin' up the riverbanks can be dangerous. Cuttin' the throats of VC tax collectors in their hooches can be dangerous, too. And none of it's worth doin'. But this—*this* is what your father would call servin' with honor."

Jimmy didn't like the way Ollie's voice rose and fell, like he was fighting demons inside every sentence, and he must have hesitated to answer a little longer than Ollie wanted, because suddenly that broken nose and crew-cut beer breath were right in his face.

"What are you waitin' for, Jim-babe? Isn't this why you left destroyers? To look Charlie in the eye? To smell a little blood? Or did you just do it to get a promotion? Your dad might be worried about that. Your dad is always worried about how things look. He proved that back in '64. An August night. I don't know if you were awake, but I was. Mr. Captain Honor, makin' sneak phone calls because he didn't have the balls to say the truth out loud."

That felt to Jimmy like a slap in the face. There were times he had convinced himself he had dreamed that whole thing. There were times when he believed it was his own little secret, his father's one aberration in a life of loyal service. But now he remembered something Ollie had said at the wedding: "I thought we just wanted to get this war over with, no matter how *any* of us thought when it began."

After a moment Jimmy's calm quiet had an effect on Ollie, who stepped back and said softly, "Come with me and you'll look the enemy in the eye tonight. Stay here and I'll take your fuckin' boats and go myself."

Jimmy swallowed his shock and tried to sound professional. "Why PBRs?"

"PBFs are too big. You can hear them five miles away. Zippos are too slow. And STABs are too small."

"Will we have air support?"

"The Sea Wolves are going up to a little clearing near Chau Doc. If we call 'em, they'll be over us quick. But the main thing is, we need quiet. If Charlie can't hear us, he won't see us. We'll be in and out before he knows it."

And Jimmy offered his hand. "Here's my deal: never tell anyone what you heard comin' up through the closet that night on the Patuxent, and you're on."

Ollie grinned, like a crew-cut skull. "Let's go kick some ass . . . honorably, of course."

By 1700, they were on their way.

There were four SEALs in each boat, including two Vietnamese who had been trained by the SEALs. The November afternoon sun, not much different from the July sun in these latitudes, was dipping toward the horizon. And Chief Petty Officer Horace Church was looking very unhappy, although Ollie said that meeting Simpson Church's brother was one goddamn good omen.

Ollie rode with Jimmy in the lead boat, and for the first hour or so, the river was wide and brown and safe on both sides.

"I'm glad you came along," said Ollie. He was now wearing camouflage pants with a black VC pajama top, a green bandanna, and sandals made from old rubber tires, like the ones the VC wore. In his ammo belt, which was filled with number four shotgun shells, he carried a navy K-bar knife and that lethal sawed-off golf club.

"You know why else I wanted you, Jimmy?"

"Why?"

"If a PBF takes a rocket, the shot explodes against the aluminum and sends shrapnel everywhere. But these PBRs, they're fiberglass. It gives up easy, and a lot of times, a rocket just comes in one side and goes out the other."

"I've seen it happen."

"Sometimes the rocket doesn't explode until it hits a gook on the other bank. Charlie kills Charlie. It's almost Oriental."

"What is?"

"Turning your weakness into a strength. Turning fiberglass into armor."

It was near sunset when they approached a bend in the river and Lester Thurlow saw something in the water up ahead.

"What does it look like?" Jimmy asked.

"Shit, it looks like sea monsters."

Half a dozen gray-and-brown masses were floating on the current, each with four legs sticking out and jaws open.

"Don't slow down," said Ollie. "It could be a trap."

"What are they?"

"Dog carcasses." Ollie picked up an M16 and fired at one, then at two more.

"What are you doin'?" demanded Jimmy.

"They could conceal mines. It wouldn't be the first time."

But none of the dogs' bodies blew up, and Ollie said it was all right to proceed.

As they came around the bend, they saw the source of the dead dogs.

Two PBRs were stopped beside a fifty-foot junk which had been shot to pieces. One entire crew was aboard the sampan while the other boat covered.

Jimmy stopped, and the CPO in command of the second boat told them what had happened.

The PBRs had tried to stop the junk, but it kept running upstream, refusing to stop even when they fired across the bow. Then the captain had come out with an ancient rifle, and that was when both PBRs opened up. They killed all three crewmen and riddled the hulk with fifty-cal fire, and all the while that the bullets were going through the hull, they could hear—strangest damn thing—they could hear dogs howling. When they approached, they found that the whole junk was loaded with mutts stolen from downstream.

"Why stolen?" asked Jimmy.

"Pets downstream. Lunch upstream. The dink thought we was comin' to take the dogs back. Now the lieutenant's so torn up about killin' them all that he won't believe there's no VC contraband aboard. He's takin' her apart board by board."

Jimmy glanced at the junk, which towered over the American vessels, an ancient and strangely graceful thing. "Does he need any—"

"He needs shit," said Ollie. "Keep goin'."

"I'm still in command here, Lieutenant." Jimmy glared at Ollie.

Ollie brought his hands together in an Oriental gesture of appeasement. "So sorry. But we have a fuckin' mission."

And on they went.

A short time later, over the thrumming of the engine, Ollie apologized. "I get a little jumpy when the mission approaches. I've been through some bad shit out here, Jim."

Jimmy wrapped his hands around the wheel so that the comforting power of the boat vibrated into his hands. "Yeah," said Jimmy. "Me too."

The sky to the west was blood-red now. Night would drop like a curtain in ten or fifteen minutes.

"It was those damn floating dogs," said Ollie. "Do you know what I saw in those floating dogs?" said Ollie.

"What?"

"Defeat . . . The people we're supposed to help think we're the bad guys. They run when we come after them. They float mines in animal carcasses, drop grenades in our boats. And we keep takin' land, hearin' the locals swear loyalty, and as soon as we leave, the land goes back to the VC."

"It makes you want to go home."

"It does." Ollie looked hard at Jimmy. "But you won't. And neither will I."

And on they went, toward that blood-red sky.

Around 1900 hours, they turned off the main river and ran in under a deep canopy of mangroves.

It smelled like places in Florida where Jimmy and his father and brother had gone to fish for snook over the years. There was a kind of mulch-pile funk in the air, a smell of water and earth, of decay and rebirth, all happening around the giant roots of those ancient trees.

At midnight Ollie took out his map and studied it with a little penlight. He looked out at the way the river turned and said, "Here."

Jimmy ran the boat over to the south bank, cut his engines, and zipped his flak jacket up to his chin.

Following the procedure, Horace Church pulled his boat in on the north bank, about forty meters behind Jimmy's.

In the sudden and total silence that followed, the sounds of a mangrove swamp came to life—the cry of the night birds, the million different chirps and squeals and clicks of the insects, the rustling of the SEALs opening their packs and hunkering down in the cockpit to prepare themselves.

When Ollie stood, his face was entirely green. He wore a hypodermic syringe loaded with morphine on a chain around his neck and a sawed-off shotgun in a homemade holster on his left leg.

"It's show time." Then he popped two tablets into his mouth.

"What are those?" asked Jimmy.

"Dexedrine. Make you hear like a dog and see like a hawk. And the fuckin' mosquitoes won't bother you at all. You want a couple?"

"I just want to get the fuck out of here as fast as I can."

Ollie snapped his fingers, and his Vietnamese SEAL squawked just like one of those night birds.

"If it's all clear," Ollie whispered to Jimmy, "you'll hear that, three times, fast. Then we'll be coming out in that clearing about forty meters ahead. You stay right here. We'll come to you, and we'll slip away like we were never here."

"Right." Jimmy swallowed hard and tried to sound confident.

"If you hear any kind of explosion, or more than three or four shots, call in the Sea Wolves and get your ass up there to that clearing with the lead boat. But don't fire until you're certain you're not going to hit any friendlies."

"How the fuck do I know who's friendly?"

"We're the ones with the green faces." Ollie glanced at the phosphorescent numbers on his watch. "Let's synchronize at 2400 right now. If you don't hear any squawking birds by 0200, listen for gunfire. There's a bottle of Skin-So-Soft in my bag. It keeps mosquitoes away like Raid."

And without another word, the SEALs were gone.

The noise of the jungle grew louder.

And the smells of funk were mixed now with the smell of an American hand lotion that someone had found was the best mosquito repellent known to man.

By 0100 the hum of the insects was like a giant electric current, plugged in and running all around them. On the boat, nobody said much, and downstream, the covering boat had disappeared into the darkness.

Jimmy Stafford said the Lord's Prayer to himself and thanked God for night.

At 0115, something splashed in the water nearby. Frankie Donatello whirled with his M16, and Jimmy screamed "No!" Then he whispered it, and Frankie settled back.

At 0132, Lester Thurlow, sitting in the open fifty-cal turret in the bow of the boat, farted.

From the stern, Jimmy said, "Maintain silence, sailor."

The other three chuckled just a little bit.

At 0149, Jimmy checked his watch and checked the other boat. He wondered what Horace Church was thinking of all this just about now.

At 0156, a rocket screamed out of the jungle on the south side, barely missed the T-top of Horace Church's PBR, and exploded in the trees on the opposite bank.

"Oh, shit!" cried Lester Thurlow.

Jimmy grabbed the radio and called in the helicopters.

And the firefight erupted. Two more rockets streaked past Horace's PBR, leaving their trails of light and smoke and exploding in the woods beyond. Horace pulled the boat out, and his men answered with a tremendous barrage of gunfire into the south bank, followed by the *crump-crump-crump* of a whole belt of grenades going off among the trees.

And that was the moment when Jimmy heard automatic weapons fire coming from the insertion point—that clearing some forty meters upstream.

Everything was blowing up at once, including the plan. Jimmy didn't know what to do, but he knew he had to act. So he gunned his engine, sending the PBR out into the middle of the stream. But instead of going forward, he swung back downstream and ordered his men to pour fire into the trees on the south bank, in support of Horace.

At the same moment, the north bank erupted—another VC patrol, maybe connected with the ones on the south bank, maybe not—and they were firing at Jimmy's boat.

Bullets were slamming off the T-top and sparking everywhere. A rocket went clean through the bow of Jimmy's boat, right past Lester Thurlow's ass.

And Frankie Donatello of the North End of Boston lost the back of his head when an AK47 round hit him in the face.

"Oh, shit. Oh, Jesus!" cried the farm boy named Johnson.

"Don't panic!" screamed Jimmy, and he clamped his hands around the wheel, trying to keep his cool in the midst of the sudden chaos.

Blam! Blam! That was Ollie's shotgun. The sound was unmistakable over all the other racket. The SEALs were coming out.

And Jimmy knew he had to get to them. That was the plan. Follow the plan. Always follow the plan. So he swung his boat again, back upstream, and gunned it right up to the clearing where he should have gone in the first place.

In an instant he counted two SEALs and one guy running in leg irons.

"Hold your fire!" cried the first SEAL to reach the boat. "You've got three more back in the woods."

"I can't hold for long."

Now machine-gun fire was stitching holes in the side of the boat.

"Request permission to return fire," cried Thurlow from the forward guns.

"Hold your fire."

The POW got to the boat and they pulled him in. He didn't say anything, just collapsed on the deck and began vomiting blood. Then the two SEALs clambered aboard.

Blam! That shotgun again. And Ollie was shouting from the trees, "Open fire! Open fire!"

At the same moment, a star shell burst over the river, bathing the scene in an eerie flickering glow as it rode a little parachute back toward earth. . . .

And Jack Stafford stopped writing. He had been working all night. Now the sun was coming up, pure and simple, as if to illuminate that dark scene so long ago. He flipped on his little tape recorder and replayed Oliver Parrish's description of the fight, which had been investigated, but never fully understood from that day to this.

"I was calling for covering fire because I knew that no one else was coming out of that jungle that I cared about. It was time to blanket the place with grenades and fifty-cals. But for some reason, Jimmy's boat pulled away from the clearing with two SEALs and one POW, and he left the rest of us in there on some very hot ground.

"It could have been the flare that frightened him, or sitting there holding his fire while rockets were flying all around his head. . . . I know I should never have told him to hold his fire like that. But in all my ops, I never lost a man to friendly fire. It was a thing I had.

"So anyway, Jimmy's headed downstream, right into the mess Horace Church had gotten himself into, and my guys on the boat were screaming at Jimmy to turn around, but he had a death grip on the wheel and he was screaming at his men to fire into the south bank."

Jack's voice: "Was this a setup?"

"I never knew, and neither did the intel people. It sure felt like a setup, but there was enough VC activity in the area that two patrols might have found us at once. We'll never know."

"Sounds like there's a lot we'll never know."

"Well, it was plain to my guys that Jimmy had lost it, because he was taking his boat right into the space between Church's boat and the bank, right into a crossfire. I'll never know what got into him, but at that point, one of my men pulled out a Makarov 9mm automatic that he'd taken off a dead dink—a very cool weapon to be walking around with—and . . . shit . . ."

Jack heard Ollie's voice waver. He stopped the tape. He sat for a moment, thought for a moment more, and asked himself if it was time for the truth, or time for something more. Then he began to write again. . . .

Jimmy Stafford never hesitated from that point on.

He knew that Horace was in trouble, and as long as he couldn't pour the kind of fire he wanted onto the bank beyond the clearing, he was damn sure going to do what he could to help Horace Church and the covering boat.

He shouted at Thurlow to open up, and the fifty-cals tore into the south bank of that stinking little trench, beneath those stinking big trees, and sent wood splinters and tracers flying amid brutal steel-jacketed slugs.

This act of bravery—and that's what it was—allowed CPO Horace Church to turn the full force of his fire onto the north bank, which lit up like Tracer Land at the amusement park.

Then Church came to the side of his boat, made eye contact with Jimmy as he went downstream, and . . .

Jack took a long drag on his cigarette and started the tape again.

"Only two of the guys on Church's boat survived. One of them, the navy engineer, Jack Little, said that Church screamed at Jimmy, something like, 'What the fuck are you doin'? Get out the way and get back upstream. I'll cover you.' But Jimmy just kept going."

Naw, Jack decided. That wasn't the way the world would read it.

Church made eye contact with Jimmy as he went downstream and gestured that he would go up to the clearing and pick up the last of the SEALs. It made perfect sense, because Jimmy's boat was already full and a gut-shot POW, who would miraculously survive, was still puking blood all over the deck.

So Jimmy waved back to Church and said they would provide support, because now they were out of position and would have to turn around in that narrow stinking stream before they could return to the aid of the men in the clearing.

Horace Church shot forward, and at that moment, Jimmy's boat was exposed to fire from both banks, but he said they'd provide support, and they did.

Gunner's mate Lester Thurlow delivered withering fire onto the north bank, even though one of his fifty-cals jammed. Seaman Johnson operated a single fifty at the stern until three bullets and a tracer hit him in the back. Engineer Bennett raised the M60 light machine gun to the crook of his arm and sprayed lead up and down the south bank.

Meanwhile, one of the green-faced SEALs was operating the hand-cranked grenade launcher, sending belt after belt of grenades into the woods on both sides.

And Lieutenant James Stafford kept his hand on the helm, guiding that boat despite heavy fire that had already torn through one arm and a leg. . . .

Click.

"I saw Church's boat kick in the water and come shooting toward us. He was going to save us, not Jimmy. So we hunkered down among the roots of those big mangroves, trying to return fire, but it was pretty heavy. There were two of us SEALs—we'd lost two in the village—and the second POW, who was using my forty-five to do what he could.

"The VC had fired two more of those fuckin' star shells over our heads, so the whole place was lit up like a roadside rest station for long-haul truckers, and I could see way downstream.

"Jimmy's boat was not turning around, and I tell you, I cursed that son of a bitch. Really cursed him for running out on us in a firefight.

"Thurlow told me later that one of my SEALs was screaming at Jimmy to turn the boat around, but Jimmy just seemed frozen."

Jack's voice: "So he was running?"

"Who knows? Running. Panicked. Courageously trying to draw fire . . . From where I sat, it looked as if Jimmy'd reached the end of the gauntlet when his boat turned quickly to the left, as if he was going to make the turn and come back up. But it wasn't a smooth turn at all.

"He could have been trying to turn. Or that could have been the moment when my SEAL with the Makarov squeezed off a shot into Jimmy's neck, right at the C-1 vertebra, right under his helmet. A shot like that cuts off all your motor reflexes, but you have to fall somewhere, and if the wheel spun to the left when Jimmy went down, that's how the boat would have gone.

"We'll never know, because a rocket took that SEAL's head off about three seconds later, and the boat slammed into the opposite bank.

"Church came whooshing up to us at that moment and . . ."

Click. Let's see what we can do to dress that up a little. But be careful of the prose. You're starting to sound as if you're writing a battle citation.

Two more star shells flickered to life, casting their deathly light down across the scene.

And Horace Church reached the clearing with guns blazing.

At the same moment Jimmy Stafford turned his helm a little to the right, to pick up some extra room, then spun to the left, so that he could swing about and shoot back upstream. This was not over by a long shot, for any of them.

Thurlow was still firing from his forward machine gun, pouring it onto the north bank. Bennett was dead, and one of the SEALs had taken over the single fifty, while the other fired a sidearm into the trees, providing covering fire for Jimmy Stafford.

But just as Jimmy went into his turn, a Vietcong rocket exploded near the stern, killing both SEALs and badly wounding Jimmy Stafford.

He tried to keep to his feet and complete the turn upstream. But a shot from an AK47 struck him in the neck, killing him instantly.

With a tremendous crunch, his boat slammed into the huge roots of the mangroves on the north bank, and VC came swarming. But they had not reckoned with Lester Thurlow of Biloxi, Mississippi, the only survivor of Jimmy's crew. He fought off twenty-five Vietcong who tried to get at him, firing his forward fifty until he ran out of ammunition, then falling back to the bloody cockpit, where he grabbed the M60 and kept up a furious stream of hot lead, while Horace saved the men still on the ground . . .

The rest of it could flow the way Ollie had told it, so Jack just let the recorder run and basically typed the story up as third person action.

"Church was one brave black bastard, and I loved the sight of that big face, screamin' down at me to get into the boat.

"The helos were coming now. You could just hear them. And you could feel that chop they make in the dense, humid air. We were almost out. And that was always when I was the most scared. We dumped the second POW into the boat, then Church started pulling me and the other SEAL aboard. And all the while, we were putting up a wall of lead in two directions.

"And then, the dinks broke into the clearing. They must've heard the helos, and decided they'd rather put on a suicide charge than let us get away. About fifty of them came flying at us. We cut down half of them, but . . . but . . . Jesus, you don't know what this stuff was like, Jack."

"I can imagine."

"My K-bar was gone, and I was out of ammo, but they"—Ollie's voice grew stronger—"they didn't call me Bob Hope for nothing. I took out that golf club and brained two or three of them. Stove their fuckin' skulls right in. And then—a big blinding flash and, Boom! the Sea Wolves were over us, blasting rockets all over the fuckin' place and sweeping the ground with this line of tracers that was the most beautiful thing I ever saw.

"Church spun that boat out of there like it was a Boston Whaler and shot right downstream to Jimmy's boat, where Thurlow was blasting and screaming and blasting away.

"When he saw us, he picked up the wounded POW, threw him over his shoulder, and jumped from one boat to the other . . . Man he was strong . . . and as brave as any man I ever met . . . he said everyone else on the boat was dead, and—"

"Was it over?"

"Remember the fuckin' fat lady, Jack. There was one final motherfucker, sitting out there with a rocket. Just as Horace leaned on the throttle, I saw it coming out of the trees. It wobbled a little bit, the way they always did before their fins deployed, then it came right at the cockpit . . . took Horace's

head clean off, killed another guy, Trager, too. Then machine gun fire from the other bank took out those two black guys they called George and Martha . . . they can be real assholes in the navy when it comes to nicknames. Anyway, that engineer, Little, he took the wheel and got us the fuck out of there. But . . . I don't guess I've ever left."

Click.

Let's give a good last graph.

They had gone into hell. They had faced the demons of war and their own demons, too. They may not have wanted to be there, any of them. Call it honor, call it courage, call it the simple commitment of men in combat to look out for each other. But when the time came, they all stood where God put them. Then they went another step. And the baby that Beck Stafford was carrying could be proud of the father he would never see.

And that was that. Jack wouldn't use anything else on the tape, but he played it through to the end.

"When it was over, plenty of medals were doled out. Purple Hearts everywhere. A Navy Cross for Lester Thurlow and a posthumous one for Horace Church. I gave that medal to Simpson myself. And we tried to get one for Jimmy, no matter what he'd done. I guess I felt guilty about draggin' him in. But that engineer on Church's boat, that Little, he didn't like Jimmy for some reason, so, from his angle, it seemed like Jimmy had lost it under fire, which was probably the truth.

"And it was enough of a shadow that Jimmy didn't get the Navy Cross. The admiral pushed for it, and he saw to it that Little's report sort of disappeared, along with a few other things. Lester Thurlow was the only one who saw anything up close, and he stuck to his story that Jimmy was trying to do two things at once and just got stuck in the middle, a brave man doing his best under fire."

"Why do you think Thurlow did that?"

"Well, maybe it was true. And Thurlow was a very astute guy, into black history and all that. When I told him that Jimmy's grandfather had recommended Dory Miller for the Navy Cross back in 1942, Lester said he'd always stick up for a Stafford memory. And Lester was a man of his word."

"Funny how those things work," said Jack.

CHAPTER TEN

Telling the Story

October 14

Jack was satisfied.

He had done Jimmy Stafford justice . . . and Horace Church . . . and Ollie Parrish too. He felt that he had been fair to his brother. And as he wrote the final lines, he remembered what his father had said to him on the dock at Pearl Harbor, the last time they had been together: "What's good for the U.S.A. is good for the U.S. Navy."

Now he made several copies of the chapter, took the diskettes and the laptop, and went out.

The morning was cool, the sky clear and shimmering silver. Smoke hung in the air, and the smell of it was strong and pungent all over Annapolis. Jack was glad he'd had Ollie's interview to occupy him through the night, because he surely would not have been able to sleep.

He dropped a diskette with an explanatory note into the mail slot at Oliver Parrish's house on Duke of Gloucester Street.

Then he went to the bed-and-breakfast.

The admiral was in the shower when he arrived, so he left the diskette and laptop with Betty.

Then he went to Susan's room.

She was drying her hair. Her eyes were owlish from lack of sleep. "What are you so chipper about?"

"I finished the Vietnam chapter." And he gave her a diskette.

"So fast?"

"I'm used to deadlines. But Ollie did all the work. I just put it into words."

"You wrote what Ollie told you, and you're still smiling?"

"Just read it."

"What about Steve? Are you going to give it to him?"

"Just read it." Then he went to Steve's room.

Steve was already showered, and the dress blues that he'd been wearing the previous day still looked crisp and pressed.

"You're headed back?" asked Jack.

"Due at the desk at 0900."

Jack offered him the diskette.

Steve looked at it as though it might bite him. "Is this about my father?"

"I think you'll want to read it."

Then he went down to the dining room and waited.

Juan came down first, bright and rested, perhaps because he had slept through all the commotion the night before. "Mornin', Jack."

"I hope you're not mad at me for putting you on the spot yesterday."

"Hell, no. I like bein' the center of attention. It don't happen often enough." Then Juan noticed the sideboard, laden with fruit salads, pastries, and covered dishes. "I like somebody else cookin' breakfast once in a while, too."

As Juan headed for the food, Susan came into the little dining room, a heated sunporch on the side of the old house. She gave Jack a kiss on the cheek, but she had no time for questions because Steve Stafford was coming into the room right after her.

"I thought I knew everything that was certain about that night," he said. "I didn't know my father made a deal with Oliver Parrish before they went up the river."

"Why do you think Oliver never revealed what he knew about the phone call to Wayne Morse? Your father wanted to protect *his* father's honor. And Ollie kept his word to your father."

Steve slipped into a chair. "Did you ever wonder why there are only two reports—Oliver's and Lester Thurlow's—even though that engineer named Little survived, along with another SEAL?"

Jack shrugged. "I don't worry about things that don't exist. Lester Thurlow was in your father's boat. He was the best eyewitness."

Steve brushed at a piece of lint on his blue jacket, took a deep breath, and said, "Do you think my father lost it under fire?"

"It was a very messy action. But you've read the book. What do you think?"

Steve looked into Jack's eyes, as if to find proof of what he had read. "I've always thought it was a very messy action, too. But you've given it some perspective."

Jack grinned. "That's my job, Steve."

"Of course," whispered Susan, after Steve had stepped to the sideboard, "nobody ever called you a reliable narrator."

Just then, Betty and the admiral came down, and Susan headed for the sideboard, so that they could have a little privacy with Jack.

Betty said nothing. Her eyes were red. She just gave Jack a kiss and followed Susan.

Admiral Tom Stafford sat down next to his brother. "Thanks, Jack."

"No thanks necessary."

"Did you talk to Ollie Parrish?"

Jack just nodded.

"Did he say anything about the medical reports? That Jimmy died from a 9mm slug in the neck?"

"He said enough, and I read the reports"—here Jack gave his brother the old reporter's hard eye—"I never found a medical report of any kind . . . anywhere. And I never found the report by that engineer, the one named Little."

The admiral, who always prided himself on outlasting anyone's gaze, looked down at the tablecloth. "If you know how to do it, it's very easy to make an unhappy truth disappear in a pile of papers."

"That's why I wrote this as a novel. It's much easier to make up the official record if you don't have it. Then you get to fill in the blanks the way you want. Of course, I wanted to write it so that Jimmy came home."

"The part about Jimmy going up the river to protect my secret . . . is that true?"

"It's true according to Ollie. But Jimmy would have gone anyway. He was a hero for going. They all were, and that's how it should be written. You deserve to hear that just as loudly as you deserve to hear about your own doubts. One story is the truth. Let the other one become a legend."

After breakfast, they all went down Prince George Street to the source of the smoke still hanging over Annapolis.

The fire engines still surrounded the Fine Folly. Gawkers, too—local folks, a few midshipmen, a few reporters, and a D.C. television crew. A snakepit of hoses covered the street.

The 1907 addition to the Folly was a pile of smoking rubble. But that big burly fire chief had been listening to Jack. He had set his line at the old house and had fought like hell to save it.

The old house still stood, windows shattered, walls scorched, but its structure still sound.

While the others went toward the house for a closer look, Jack and Susan ambled over to Oliver Parrish, who was leaning against a lamp-post, his hands shoved into his pockets.

He gave them a glance, then looked back at the house. "Now, nobody gets it."

"Any thoughts on why Simpson did this?" asked Jack.

Oliver shook his head. "Who the hell knows if he did it at all? He heard me last night, after I'd had a few, saying how mad I was that this place would end up in the hands of men who spend their time looking toward the next war, and—"

"I think they're trying to stop the next war," said Jack.

Oliver turned his big square head, his gray-blond crew cut, and his broken nose in Jack's direction. "I would have been mad if it had gone to you, too, Jack, because you knew about the admiral's phone call, and you covered his ass."

"Don't make it so simple," said Jack. "Besides, the rest of the world knew the truth about Tonkin six months later. Lyndon Johnson told a couple of senators that our navy could've been shootin' at whales, for all he knew."

Ollie shook his head again. "Tonkin was the place where the politicians started lying to us."

Jack patted him on the shoulder. "Ollie, politicians have always lied to us. Military men, too. Sometimes they don't even *know* they're lying."

"Sometimes," said Susan, "men make terrible messes."

"Sometimes," said Jack, "it helps to know this."

Oliver nodded. "You cleaned up that mess on the Tien Doc."

"Oliver," asked Susan, "after all these years, why did you decide to tell it at all now?"

Oliver thought for a moment, as though the question had not occurred to him. "There's a lot of truth-telling going on around here. So I gave Jack one more chance to write the truth about the Staffords. I'd say he did a fine job."

A short time later, the fire chief let them into the Fine Folly.

Strangely, the house seemed once more to be part of the eighteenth century. It was smoky and cold. Water dripped through the ceiling and covered the floors. But there was light flooding in at the back, filling the foyer and the great room and the library in a way that they had not been filled in nearly a hundred years.

Once more the grand staircase rose around a door that led to the outside, and beyond it rose the green copper dome of the Naval Academy chapel.

"Oh, Lord," said Betty, looking into the room where Washington had danced, where Civil War soldiers had suffered and died, where Betty herself had met Aunt Katherine on the day the Japanese bombed Pearl Harbor. "Everything is ruined."

"The plans for the institute are, at least," said the admiral. "Without the addition, there's not enough room for us. But it would seem like a sin not to fix this place up."

"A terrible sin," said Betty.

"I think we should restore it," said Steve Stafford, who knew the Fine Folly only from what he had read in Jack's book.

"Who's we?" asked Oliver Parrish.

"All of us," said Jack.

"We don't really agree on much of anything," said Oliver.

Jack looked around. "I think this place can stand up to a few petty disagreements."

Just then the fire chief and one of his men climbed up through the opening that led to the back of the house. "You folks might be glad to know that Simpson Church didn't set the fire. It started back at the electrical box in the basement of the hotel section. Another job the owners put off for too long."

"So," said Betty, "it was just an act of God."

Susan looked out at the bright sky beyond the ancient doorway. "Maybe you should say it was by the grace of God."

That afternoon, the *Annapolis* pulled away from the sub tender in the harbor and headed back down the bay.

People who watched her from the dock of the ancient city were struck by how insignificant she seemed beside the big sub tender, at how graceless she seemed when surrounded by the sailboats and the nimble power boats skimming close for a look.

She was bound for deployment with the Sixth Fleet, operating in the Indian Ocean, near the Strait of Hormuz.

Intelligence reports and satellite photos indicated that two Kilo submarines, bought from the Russians by Iran, had been practicing mine-laying techniques in their own territorial waters. A well-laid series of mines across the Strait of Hormuz would throw the world into the same kind of turmoil that had drawn Steve Stafford to the gulf a few years before.

Americans knew nothing of this and might never know. If the time came, Steve Stafford would tell them. If not, he would continue to tell them that the fast-attack submarine and the carrier battle group were America's first line of defense.

Retired Admiral Thomas Stafford would agree with his grandson. He would call for another *Seawolf* submarine, and a new generation of SSNs after that, a multibillion-dollar investment in our children's future. The chaos theory among nations, he would write, demanded that we defend ourselves as staunchly as we could.

Susan Browne would make her film.

Oliver Parrish would continue to insist that we spend too much on submarines and airplanes, and on missiles designed to fly through windows, down hallways, and into beds.

Jack Stafford would just try to finish writing the story of his family, their follies, and all their fine achievements.

In the last scene, the *Annapolis* would reach the hundred-fathom curve. The officers would scramble down from the bridge. The hatches would be secured. The big submarine would begin its dive to classified depths at classified speeds, already listening for pirates.

And after everything, that ancient house in that ancient city would still be sturdy enough to hold it all.

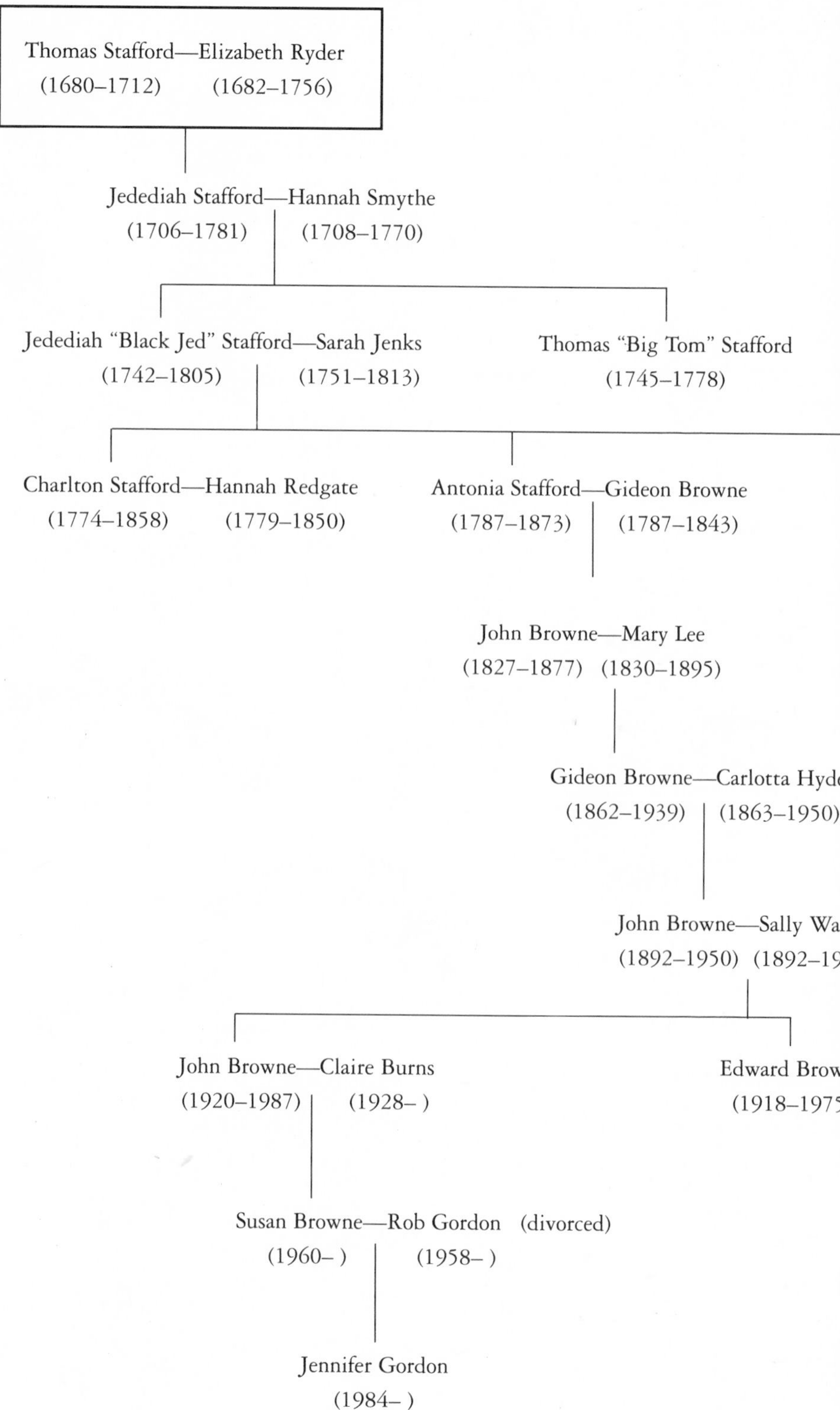

Thomas Stafford—Elizabeth Ryder
(1680–1712) (1682–1756)
Jedediah Stafford—Hannah Smythe
(1706–1781) (1708–1770)
Jedediah "Black Jed" Stafford—Sarah Jenks
(1742–1805) (1751–1813)
Thomas "Big Tom" Stafford
(1745–1778)
Charlton Stafford—Hannah Redgate
(1774–1858) (1779–1850)
Antonia Stafford—Gideon Browne
(1787–1873) (1787–1843)
John Browne—Mary Lee
(1827–1877) (1830–1895)
Gideon Browne—Carlotta Hyde
(1862–1939) (1863–1950)
John Browne—Sally Wal
(1892–1950) (1892–19
John Browne—Claire Burns
(1920–1987) (1928–)
Edward Brow
(1918–1975
Susan Browne—Rob Gordon (divorced)
(1960–) (1958–)
Jennifer Gordon
(1984–)